LAMENT
OF
LIGHT

LAMENT OF LIGHT

THE XYRI NEXUS

BOOK ONE

BRIANNA YOUNG

The Xyri Nexus: Lament of Light

Copyright © 2025 by Brianna Young

All rights reserved.

Cover Art by Sandra Winther

Illustrations by
Nikkotari
Wintermaiden11
Shuravf
Luy Co
Brianna Young

To the little girl who liked to play pretend,
who had more imaginary friends than real ones,
who found a story in everything...
Look at us now, kid.
We finally set one free.

CONTENT WARNINGS

Violence

Death

Mentions of SA

Mentions of DV

Car crash

PART ONE

THE APEX PREDATOR

*The capabilities possessed by the Xyri have always been too
big for us to handle. They turn men into gods,
wielding power over life and
death, and everything in between.
Humanity is better off without them.*

- A World Without Xyri

1
Kaida Fights Death

Kaida landed on the roof beside Lycan and scanned for dead bodies on the street below. Times Square was bustling with people, and those bright lights burned against her eyes.

"He's back?"

Lycan nodded. "There's way more this time, see." He pointed. "They're just standing there, waiting for us."

She sucked in a breath, assessing their options. Last time they fought Vendetta's band of dead people, it hadn't gone well. She'd been dreading his return. And now he was in the most crowded place in all of New York, ready to unleash them on civilians.

The zombies stood stiffly on the sidewalks, easy to spot, as they were some of the only unmoving bodies in the area.

"Do we have a plan?" Lycan asked, breath visible as he exhaled, his yellow eyes shining at her.

Kaida always got lost looking at him, with those little flecks of silver, like stars, scattered across the black mask around his eyes. She forced herself to look up at the black wolf ears sticking out of his blue hair instead.

"I don't have a plan," she admitted, feeling small.

"Then we should make one, fast," Lycan replied. "The second the zombies move, it's over. When they attacked Morningside it was just a handful, and people still got hurt."

"I know." Her hands shook as she looked at the people below.

"It's your call."

He always assumed she was smarter, that she could find the answers. She *hated* that.

"Hey," Lycan whispered. "Us against the world."

She took a deep breath, meeting his eyes. "Us against the world."

After a moment, she had a plan of sorts ready to go.

"Okay. You go left, I go right. We try and herd them in the middle of the street over there. Keep them contained, away from the civilians. Once we're down there, they'll come for us. And everyone else will get the hell out of the way."

Will they though? her Xyri, Zig, asked in her head.

She ignored him.

"Then what?"

She exhaled. "You know what."

He nodded, looking grim.

Kaida took a deep breath then leaped off the roof. Her bat-like wings stretched out as she soared through the air, before arcing low and landing in front of a group of the dead.

They came alert, their empty eyes following her. She took a step back and they moved with her as her wings retracted back into her suit.

"Alright, come on..." she urged as she moved faster, walking backwards into the street.

Ren, please be careful, Zig muttered.

I'm always careful.

Most people hadn't noticed the zombies, but they *did* notice Kaida. They couldn't miss her, with her dazzling red-scaled suit and that golden glow. She urged Zig to make it shine brighter. That got everyone's attention, and people knew where Kaida went, bad things followed. Cars came to a dead stop as she took over the road.

A middle-aged man who barely looked dead lunged at her, a knife gripped in his white knuckles. She dodged it easily as light poured out of her hand, forming into a long rope at her side. She whipped it toward the zombie, wrapping it around him. It changed from pure white light into shiny solid matter, containing him. More light spiraled out of her hands as three more zombies came at her. Finally, the civilians began running away.

She had no fear for herself. They couldn't hurt her, not unless enough of them overwhelmed her. Even then, her suit should protect her. But they could hurt other people. And... they *had* been people. People recently kidnapped. People whose loved ones didn't even know they were dead yet. And now they'd see New York's heroes killing those loved ones all over again.

She refrained from hurting them for this reason, trying only to contain them as she danced through the bodies with her ropes of light. But for every one she tied up, five more arrived. She tried catching sight of Lycan, but he'd been pulled farther away. Dread filled her as an entire crowd of the dead appeared, headed straight for her.

"I thought you said he couldn't make this many!" she yelled, jumping back, landing in another pile of zombies.

He should not be able to.

A hand wrapped around her neck. She gasped as she was pulled to the ground. They started piling on top of her and she recoiled at the stench. Light streamed out of Kaida, shapeless but strong, forcing them back until it turned into a crystal-like dome that solidified around her, keeping them at bay.

He is doing too much too fast. You remember what happened to Lycan, the night of the fire?

How could I forget? she thought back as she tried to catch her breath.

Lycan almost killed himself that night. Rewinding time over and over, trying to save everyone. She'd held him in her arms for hours, waiting for him to wake up or stop breathing. It had been a close call.

"There's no way Vendetta is that stupid." She got to her knees, preparing herself.

Dorixi is an interesting Xyri. He might not have warned him, Zig replied.

Can you sense him anywhere? Is Vendetta close?

He must be, but I can not say where.

She grunted as her light fell away. Zombies were crowded around her. She jumped up, wings popping out as they crashed into each other. She didn't go far, landing back on the street behind them to get a better look at what was happening. Silver constructs glowed in the distance. Lycan was somehow even farther away.

Her section of Times Square was eerily empty of civilians now, so she didn't have to worry about them as she took to the air again. Weird, how easy that was, after months of being terrified to fly.

Told you you'd get used to it.

She didn't respond as she dove for Lycan. He had at least ten of the zombies in cages of solid silver, their glow like beacons in the night.

"You good?" he yelled as she landed beside him.

"He's trying to separate us."

She took in his side of the battle as one of his cages puffed to mist and the zombie ran at them. She sighed, light forming a rope again as she weaved it around the zombie. Even more were coming from behind Lycan.

"How does he have this many?"

"I don't know!"

One of them lunged for Lycan, a glint of silver in its hand. An iridescent sword formed in her fist and she rammed it through their chest. The zombie—*the person*—stilled. Her sword vanished, shock registering as they dropped.

"Kaida?"

"He was... gonna stab you," she mumbled, taking a step back, hands shaking. She damn well knew a little knife wouldn't do *anything* to Lycan. But seeing it go for him had ignited something inside of her. She was so afraid of losing him.

They were already dead, Zig whispered. *You did not kill anyone.*

Her heart raced, no words coming to her. More dead people poured into the street, and she realized they were coming from the sewers.

"That's gotta be at least a hundred people..." Lycan said, eyes wide with horror.

Panic threatened to overwhelm her. "What do we *do*?"

He put his hands on her shoulders, forcing her to look at him. "We end it. We *have* to end it. If we don't, he'll keep killing, making more..."

She took a deep breath and nodded. Ending it didn't just mean stopping the zombies, it meant finding Vendetta and ending *him*.

"Go up," she said. "You've got better eyes. He has to be close to be controlling so many. *Find him.*"

"You got this by yourself?"

She rolled her shoulders, crystalline sword forming in her hands. "I've got this."

He nodded as silver poured out of his foot, shaping into a small surfboard. Then he took off, board carrying him up into the sky. Kaida sucked in a breath and readied herself as they came at her in a wave.

Deep breaths, Ren. They are already dead.

She swallowed as she swung her blade, slicing through two zombies at once. The smell of them was starting to overwhelm her and she tried not to gag as she continued moving, sword in hand. It didn't seem to matter how many she cut down, as more took their place. Kaida held her ground and they dropped like flies around her. But then she saw the face of someone she knew among them. Jan. She'd been a regular at the bakery since Ren was just a little girl, coming in at least once a week for the coffee cake muffins. Her once joyous face was now pale, sickly. Dead. Ren hesitated as she got closer, hands shaking as her sword misted away.

Ren!

She blinked through her tears. The sword formed again and she rammed it through Jan's chest. Now twice dead. *Don't think about it don't think—*

Something grabbed her leg from behind and she stumbled, losing the sword. She spun to find two small children no taller than her waist trying to stab her legs with little rusty knives. She stared in shock. *He killed children?* She couldn't comprehend it as tears burned in her eyes.

I'm sorry, Ren. But they are already dead. The only thing you can do now is end it, and give them peace.

Ren closed her eyes as her sword reformed. She couldn't look, couldn't see. Her blade made contact and bile rose in her throat.

Lycan scanned the surrounding buildings, trying to keep his focus on finding Vendetta, and not on Kaida in the street below. But his worry won and he glanced down, watching Kaida fight death. She swung her blade and spun through the bodies with grace. They dropped, one after another, never standing a chance against her. Her bright suit kept his attention. The red scales, outlined in glowing gold, covered her torso and legs. It contrasted nicely with the black sleeves that went from her hands to her biceps, matched with the black from her feet to her calves, like boots. With golden glowing flames twirled around her arms and legs, she was absolutely stunning. Beautiful and destructive.

Bellamy, you need to focus, Zeli growled in his head.

Right, sorry.

He forced himself to look away. Vendetta had to be close. He'd wanna see it all. They knew his goal was to kill the two of them, though they still didn't know *why.* But in trying to make that happen, he'd killed what looked like hundreds of people, turning them into his army of the dead.

Why is that even a thing a Xyri can do? he asked.

Dorixi is one of the first, like Kirzigith and I, Zeli answered. *Creation, destruction... these powers have always existed.*

Absolutely insane!

He soared to a different roof, looking for movement, but he caught himself glancing at Kaida again, his heart racing. She was completely surrounded.

Focus.

He shook his head and looked away. He *had* to trust her to handle it. So he continued scanning the area till something caught his eye. There was movement on a roof across the street. *Gotcha.*

He had Zeli extinguish the glow in his suit so Vendetta wouldn't see him coming. Icy wind rushed past as he flew across the sky on his board. Vendetta's eyes were glued on Kaida as Lycan crashed into him, knocking them both back onto the roof. Vendetta grunted as he rolled away from him.

Lycan pushed himself up, glaring at the guy. He hated his suit. Black with red, like blood, dripping down it. Instead of a mask around the eyes, his entire face was covered in white and black, like a skull. Silvery white eyes stared out of it, sizing Lycan up.

"You're finished," Lycan hissed.

"Not finished till you and your girlfriend are dead," Vendetta growled back as he lunged for him.

Lycan tried to dodge but something sharp grazed his side. He spun, silver streaming out of his hand into the shape of a sword. Before it could solidify, Vendetta was on him and Lycan grunted as something pierced his chest. He stumbled back in surprise.

Bellamy!

He ignored her and the pain as he launched at Vendetta, throwing them both off the roof. They spun in the air before slamming into the cold pavement. Air rushed out of his lungs.

You're okay, you're okay, Zeli mumbled, as if trying to convince herself instead of him.

Yeah, he thought, breathless. *I'm fine.*

He pushed himself up to face Vendetta, who was on his back a few feet away.

"It's over."

Vendetta smiled as he rolled and pushed himself to his knees. "They're gonna kill your girlfriend. Then they're gonna kill—" He coughed, blood spraying out of his mouth as he got to his feet and stumbled toward Lycan.

He sidestepped him easily, then a silver sword appeared in his hand. As Vendetta turned to face him Lycan rammed the sword through his stomach.

Vendetta gasped, white eyes turning red, like blood was leaking into them. Lycan's sword puffed away and the guy fell to his knees, coughing up more blood.

He's dying.

Lycan nodded. *Will he heal from that?*

No. He has stretched himself too thin. Once it begins... it can not be stopped unless Dorixi fuses with him.

Will he?

She seemed to consider. *No.*

Lycan let out a slow breath. "So much for your vendetta."

He finally looked afraid.

"Your zombies die when you die, yeah? *Don't* hold on." Bellamy was surprised to hear the venom in his voice, but he couldn't hide his anger. The pain. He kicked Vendetta in the chest and he fell back to the ground, gasping for a moment before his body stilled, eyes unblinking.

After a moment the suit vanished, revealing a pale face with dark hair and green eyes, still bleeding red. He looked so *normal.* Perhaps just a few years older than Lycan. He stepped back as a strange creature appeared beside the body. About the size of a golden retriever, similar to Zeli. It had shaggy black fur that looked like it had been dipped in bright red paint around the neck. The face was more like that of a bear, with a red diamond-shaped crystal in its forehead. Glowing red eyes stared up at Lycan, seeming sad, regretful even.

The Xyri didn't speak to him, slowly turning away.

Should I...

There is no cage that can hold him. Let him go.

He nodded, then went looking for Kaida. His heart pounded a panicked beat as he took off running. There were countless bodies on the ground. He was frantic till he spotted the red of her suit. She was hunched over on her knees, head hanging low. Still.

Lycan slid to the ground beside her and pulled her into his arms. She was crying but seemed uninjured. He held her against his chest. "It's over," he whispered.

She nodded, but didn't respond. The zombies would have lost their control once Vendetta died, turning into normal corpses again. But how many had she brought down before they stopped?

"I... I killed them," she muttered, hoarse.

"*We* did. You and me, Kaida. You and me..." He didn't loosen his hold on her as snow began to fall around them.

2
They Will Come

Ren sat cross-legged in her bed, laptop open in front of her. Every word spoken in the podcast made her heart jump and drop, over and over.

"I'm telling you, the violence that young woman displayed—"

"No, no! You *can't* convince me Kaida did anything wrong. People were being taken, murdered, then their dead bodies were *puppeteered* around the city causing more harm and damage. She put an end to it."

"I'm not saying that wasn't good, Penny. But the footage... she ran through those bodies like they were nothing!"

"Cause she's a *superhero*. With superpowers. Doing her job! You're not convincing me she was in the wrong, Max. And what about Lycan?"

"Didn't see Lycan kill anyone but the actual villain."

"Kaida didn't kill anyone. They were already dead."

"All I'm saying is Lycan took care of the real problem."

"Fuck that. Kaida was out there doing the hard work, he had the easy job if you ask me."

Ren fell back on her pillows and groaned.

This is the second time you've watched this.

"I'm aware."

Are you going to keep doing it when you know it's upsetting you?

"Maybe."

Will you stop doing it when I remind you that our Bond means we're so strongly tied together that your messy emotions are rubbing all over mine and I don't particularly want to be upset right—

"Ughhhhh," she groaned again, cutting him off. "Fine." She sat up and paused the podcast. "Sorry."

Ren, you saved lives. You did not take a single one.

"It feels like I did."

You're stupid, though.

She snorted. "Thanks."

Anytime, kid.

She glanced at Zig, curled up on the end of her bed. He looked like a small dragon. Red glittering scales, black wings, pure golden eyes. But every time she looked at him she just saw a cat, with the way he curled in on himself, head lying on his feet... Not to mention the lack of scales on his chest and tail, where he was covered in soft black fur. He was *just* like a cat. One who gave her magical powers and spoke in her mind. And one who didn't usually sleep in her bed, but he was always closer when she was sad. Though she'd only been focusing on the podcast to forget about Vendetta.

It had been a few days since the battle in Times Square, and the identity of Vendetta had finally been released. The day after Christmas no less. *Happy holidays, here's the name of the murderer!* He was a boy named Carter Sharp, and Ren had known his sister, Clea. She died a few months ago. Ren never knew why Vendetta had been so hellbent on killing her and Lycan, but now she understood.

Kaida failed to save Clea that day. Watched her die right in front of her. She *should* have saved her. This entire time she blamed herself for Clea's death, and Carter killed all of those people *because* of her failure. He'd been Clea's legal guardian, loved his little sister more than anything. But Ren had no idea how far off the deep end he'd gone after her death. She closed her laptop and shoved it aside.

"Zig?"

She always thought she'd never get used to his eyes. No iris or pupils, they were entirely golden. After a year of being Bonded to him it seemed normal now.

"Why are Lycan and I the only heroes? You told me when we Bonded that others would come. And others have come but they've been terrible. Why aren't there any who wanna do good with their powers?"

Zig was quiet as he stood up and stretched. Light reflected off the golden diamond-shaped crystal in his forehead as he moved.

Nearly two hundred years without a Bond, Ren. Too much bad blood after the war. We made an agreement, not to Bond for a very long time. And two hundred years seems long to you, but not for beings who live forever. I broke the agreement. Azazelith broke it. Way too soon. We knew that meant those who—

"Were maybe more evil?" she suggested.

I suppose, yes. They would come first. They'd be more willing to break the contract once they knew we had. I promise you others will follow. Others like you and Lycan. After what we went through... it's just going to take time.

"The body count of Vendetta was two hundred and sixteen people, Zig. If there was a time for new heroes to Bond, it was last week."

I know patience is a hard concept for you, Ren Rivers, but they will come.

She sighed.

It's so easy to die, he continued. *A new Bond is very fragile. The Xyri know this, but the humans don't grasp it. You feel so strong. You're so ready to go to ten, and skip one through nine. With things calming down now after Vendetta, it'll be a good time for them to Bond.*

"What about your Xyri friend? It's been like two months since he said he was watching someone to Bond. Where the hell is he?"

Likely waiting for a dramatic moment. But I imagine it won't be long now. He has made his choice.

Her thoughts circled back to Vendetta and Clea, that loss burning fresh like a band-aid ripped off a wound too soon.

"So," she said with a sigh. "Do you think the world hates me more or less now?"

Is that not why you were watching that video? Those people seemed to be the opinion on the matter.

"They don't matter. But they give me an idea of what people are saying."

Do they?

She glared at him. "I don't want sass from my lil dragon cat, okay?"

Not a cat, Ren. Xyri. He shook himself, wings flapping for a moment before he tucked them back in at his sides.

With a smile she grabbed her phone. She'd been ignoring several texts all afternoon. Jasper appeared to be losing it.

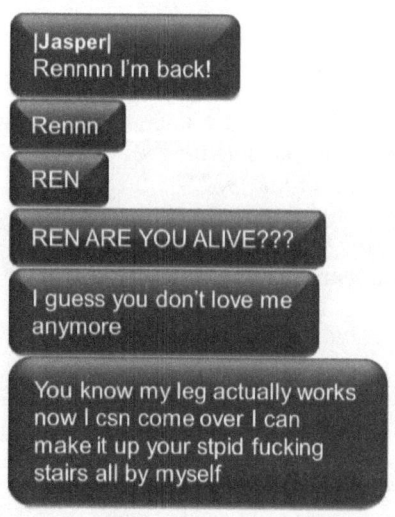

|Jasper|
Rennnn I'm back!

Rennn

REN

REN ARE YOU ALIVE???

I guess you don't love me anymore

You know my leg actually works now I csn come over I can make it up your stpid fucking stairs all by myself

RENNNN

She giggled.

|Ren|
Sorry lost track of time
making Bellamy's present

Uhh how about tomorrow?
Can stay over after
Bellamy's party!!

|Jasper|
Ohh what did you make
him??

And perfect I'll come over
before partyy

|Ren|
Haha it's not finished yet I
been struggling

Also can't wait to see you I
miss you so muchhh

ALSO we have Christmas
presents still under the tree
for you!!!

That done, she checked her texts from Ocean.

|Ocean|
Did you see the footage of
Kaida in times square? Can't
believe you get to live near
all the action!!

Ren grew nauseous. She ignored the text and opened her chat with
Lycan instead.

|Starface|
Feeling any better today?

She smiled as she leaned into her pillows.

|Bunhead|
Define better?

|Starface|
You've slept and eaten and maybe not cried?

|Bunhead|
2 out of 3 but I'm not saying which.

|Starface|
Acceptable.

Wanna hang out later?

Ren sighed. She hadn't been out as Kaida at all since the night they stopped Vendetta. She'd been busy, what with doing Christmas and missing Jasper and sulking... but she couldn't put it off any longer.

|Bunhead|
I suppose. When and where?

|Starface|
Spruce street

Around 7?

|Bunhead|
See ya then, wolf boy

She crawled out of bed with a sigh and went down the stairs into the main room. She had the entire floor to herself, so much space. Her bed was lofted, with her closet built in underneath it. Behind the loft was Breadcrumb's area, with multiple cat beds and towers by the big back windows, plus a litter box. Though the fluffy orange Maine Coon was nowhere in sight.

She grabbed some clean clothes from one of the dressers in her closet before heading into the bathroom across from the loft. She hadn't been practicing enough self-care and did *not* want Lycan noticing.

Once ready she went downstairs to check in with her dads before leaving.

She found Dad in the kitchen breaking down Valkyrie boxes for recycling. His smile went all the way to his eyes, lighting up his whole face.

"Hey, little dragon."

"You're in a good mood," she said as she grabbed a water from the fridge. She liked that she looked like him. Same dark brown hair, though his curled more than hers. Same copper skin and deep brown eyes. Everything about Dad felt warm, safe.

"I just feel like I can finally breathe."

She frowned. "What do you mean?"

He met her eyes, staring down at her. "You have no idea how terrified I've been every time you walk out the door. With people going missing these last few months, all the murders... I'm just glad it's over. I can be a *little* less worried."

Ren's heart swelled. "Dad..."

He pulled her into his arms, hugging her tightly. "You hungry? Can whip up something special for dinner. Arrow should be home soon."

"Not yet. Was thinking of going to see Jasper for a bit. He got back today."

"How's he doing?"

"Better. The cast is finally off and he can walk now. Gonna kidnap him tomorrow. He's staying over, unless his dad's being a dick."

Dad's eyes darkened at the mention of Jasper's father. They all knew what kind of man he was.

"I'll make something special tomorrow then."

She grinned.

"Before you go, there's a package from Ocean there."

"Oh!" Ren spun around and grabbed the box from the counter, excited.

Ocean had been Ren's best friend since she was little, but she moved to France when they were eleven. After five years living there, the girl still couldn't get a package to them on time.

"Only a day late, that's impressive," Ren said as she ripped the box open. Then she laughed. "It's cookies."

Dad grinned. "Of course it is."

They'd also sent Ocean's family cookies for Christmas.

"Okay, I'll be back in a bit."

"Make sure you text her a thank you," Dad said as he pulled the cookies out of the box.

"Will do."

Breadcrumb rubbed against her legs as she turned around. She scooped the fluffy cat into her arms and gave him a big kiss before setting him on the kitchen table. Dad let out a heavy sigh, and she giggled as he picked Bready up and put him on the floor.

Then she made her long trek down the stairs. The sun had already set on Grove Street by the time she made it outside.

Why not portal?

Wanted to let Dad know I was leaving, she replied.

Ren had spent the first fifteen years of her life being the perfect daughter. She never lied. She was never late. She told her dads everything. Their relationship was so open and trusting, but then a little over a year ago a weird little Xyri showed up and gave her powers.

Things had been stressful since then. Ren was constantly late, disappearing at odd times. Telling lies that weren't even believable. She'd disappointed her dads more in that time than in her entire life combined. Not to mention she almost lost Jasper over a bad lie. She was working hard to make up for those disappointments, being honest when she could.

You just lied about going to see Jasper, though.

Ren sighed. *I can't be perfect, Zig. Not anymore.*

I'd say you're more perfect now.

She smiled as she walked, her boots crunching on the snow. *Thanks.*

Once she was far enough away from home she dipped into a dark corner and transformed into Kaida, the suit coming over her in a flash. Power poured through her, making her more awake, alert, energized, and blessedly warm against the cold.

Now we fly.

Kaida's wings weren't always out. She defaulted to having them off when suited up, but with a single thought they'd pull out of her back like a flower blooming in the sun. With a grin she started running down the street. People gasped and pointed as she passed. It was a strange thing, to be famous. Everywhere she went they'd know who she was. And yet, they would never know her, not at all.

She leaped into the air, wings working to carry her up. She soared higher and higher, trying to ignore the flips and flops in her stomach as she watched the ground get farther away.

You'd probably survive that fall, Zig said.

How high would I have to be to for sure die? Wait no! Do not answer that!

Never tested it. He sounded amused.

She rolled her eyes as she flew toward the tall building in Lower Manhattan that was her meeting spot with Lycan. She landed delicately on her feet, wings shaking a little.

Rolling her shoulders, she approached Lycan slowly. His suit was mostly black, but it bled into a dark blue in his arms and lower legs, which shined with little stars. The glow of the silver belt around his waist drew her eye as he turned to look at her, a smile on his face.

The eight point star in the center of his chest also glowed silver. But his mask was her favorite part. Black, shaped like a normal eye mask except for where it dripped down into the shape of stars on his cheeks, with silver specks, like glitter, scattered across it. His eyes were outlined in a soft blue, like eyeliner, which made his yellow eyes pop. She glanced up to the black wolf-like ears sticking out of his cobalt blue hair and grinned at him.

Lycan smiled as Kaida walked over. So gorgeous, with her bright pink space buns on top of her head, and little bits of purple hair, bleeding into pink, framing her face. She stared up at him out of a red and black mask, her blue eyes outlined in gold. She was brighter than the city lights below, with the glowing flames that twirled up her arms, shining in the dimming light. Her bat-like wings matched her suit well. Thin red membranes, with gold lines, like lightning inside them, separated by black joints. She slowly folded them in as she stopped in front of him.

He knew she was putting in an effort to make it seem like she was back to normal with that smile. But she couldn't hide the truth from him. She wasn't okay, but neither was he.

He wished he could tell her about Vendetta. But to Kaida he was just a normal guy who went on a murderous rampage. To Bellamy, he was Clea Sharp's brother. And he fully understood why the guy called himself Vendetta now. *Don't think about that.*

Nerves ran through his entire body as Kaida stepped closer, looking out at the view. It was an intoxicating sight, but she put it to shame.

"So..." He wasn't sure how to begin.

She met his eyes. "You alright?"

He let out a breath and looked away. "Fine."

"Sorry I haven't been around since..."

"No, it's fine. Really."

"Did you wanna do something tonight? Or just patrol?"

"Uh..." He swallowed. How did he tell her?

You don't, Zeli growled in his head.

He sighed. His Xyri didn't approve of him confessing to Kaida. But he never expected her to, considering the rules set by the Xyri during their first week with the powers. He remembered her words so clearly.

You are not under any circumstances allowed to fall in love with that girl. Do you understand?

He thought he had.

You will not have anything but a platonic relationship with her.

He followed that rule fairly well so far.

Do you want to hurt her? Kill her? Her whole family? Want her to hurt you? Your mother? Things go bad when you intermingle like that. It is too complicated and no longer allowed. Are we clear?

He thought they'd been clear. But it was one thing to say, 'sure, I won't fall in love with this girl I just met whose identity I don't even know. Not a problem!' and then another to spend over a year by her side, fighting criminals and villains and for each other and... he hadn't *meant* to fall in love with Kaida.

But every time he looked at her he felt like he was going to explode. It was a heart racing, blood pumping, all-consuming feeling. No one knew him like she did. No one understood him. He knew the rules. They weren't allowed to be together. But that didn't mean he couldn't be honest with her. Lycan *had* to tell her. He'd go insane if he didn't.

"Patrol?" Kaida asked, frowning.

"No patrol. I just... wanted to talk," he finally mumbled.

"About what?"

Bellamy, don't do this.

He ignored Zeli, looking into Kaida's eyes. Then he gently grabbed her hands in his, stepping closer. She didn't seem put off by it, watching him curiously.

"After a year of doing this with you I've..."

"What is it?"

"I've realized I'm..." *Just say it. Spit it out.* "I... Kaida, I'm in love with you."

Her blue eyes widened, lips parting in surprise. But she didn't pull away. She didn't do anything. Lycan waited, heart pounding like a drum.

"I know it's against the rules and you might not feel the same and that's... it's fine!" he blurted. "I just... I had to tell you. It was eating me alive. I need you to know, even if it doesn't—I mean I'm not expecting you to, I... Kaida... I love you. I needed you to know." He swallowed. "Please say something?"

He felt a tremor in her hands as she pulled them out of his and took a step back.

"I'm sorry. I... I can't." For a moment she held his eyes, then she turned away from him, taking three steps.

Then Kaida jumped off the roof.

3
Wouldn't Risk It

Kaida flew in circles, afraid to land. Afraid to go anywhere. Something was *wrong*. She thought maybe she wasn't breathing. Zig was speaking but she couldn't understand. Her hands shook and there was a ringing in her ears. She finally forced herself to stop on a random roof.

Breathe, Ren. Please breathe.

"What's happening?" She hunched over on her knees, head spinning, throat tight as her heart pounded in her chest.

I believe you are panicking, kid. Portal, now.

I can't.

Yes, you can.

She lifted her head, one hand on her chest, the other out in front of her. Then she grabbed the air and *pulled*, groaning as she did so. The air split and tore, building into an electric portal rimmed in a burning pink lightning, the center dark as night. She crawled on her hands and knees through it, settling down inside.

Breathe.

She closed her eyes, leaning forward till her forehead touched the cool crystalline floor of her portal.

You're okay, Zig whispered.

Am I?

Her stomach twisted with nausea as her heart raced. *Lycan...* "We're not supposed to," she whispered.

No, you are not.

She sat up slowly, chest aching as she pulled her legs up and put her forehead on her knees. Here she thought they'd been doing a good job following the rules their Xyri gave them. So why did Lycan have to break the biggest one?

The memory was strong in her mind, sitting on that bench in Prospect Park. Only the second time she'd met Lycan, as their Xyri explained the rules to them. She listened. She remembered.

Trust me, given enough time, you and that boy will

develop feelings for each other. But it is best if you keep those feelings locked away tight, never to be acknowledged, Zig had said. *No love, sex, reproduction. Nothing but friendship.*

Ren had been sure...

"I just met Lycan. We don't even know each other and according to you, we're not allowed to know each other, so... I don't think we gotta worry about us ever..."

"Falling in love?" Lycan had finished.

"Yeah, it's not gonna happen."

But she'd been wrong about how they wouldn't know each other. Zig tried to tell her, there was a lot more to a person than their name, their real face. She didn't know a lot about Lycan's normal life, yet she *knew* him. Knew him better than most of her friends at school. *But I am not in love with him...*

Sure about that?

"Yes!" She balled her hands into fists to stop the shaking. "I have feelings for someone else... which..."

Is probably the only reason you think you are not in love with Lycan yet?

"Why would you say *yet*? Like it's inevitable? Just cause your past Bonds almost always fell in love and some of them went a *little* insane doesn't mean Lycan and I will!"

I would prefer you didn't.

She let out another breath and slowly leaned back till she was stretched out, staring up into the sky of her portal. She never got tired of the sight, like looking out from the heart of a galaxy. It felt like being in an aquarium tunnel, only instead of fish surrounding her, she had stars. Beautiful, burning stars. Time moved slower inside the portal. She didn't have to rush, the five minutes till detransformation wouldn't kick in till she walked back out. Air slowly filled her lungs as she tried to calm down, watching the slow swirl of golden stars above.

"It would hurt you..."

What would?

"If something bad happened. If I... died or..."

Yes, Ren. It would hurt me.

"Why do you keep Bonding, if it hurts when you lose us?"

Zig was quiet and she wondered if he'd answer.

Because I love it. I love humans, despite your flaws. The way the Bond feels. We can not use the powers without a human Bond. That rush you feel when you use your power, we feel it too. But when it breaks, it... it's traumatic. Breaks something inside of us. He paused. *I told you about the man, Xenos. How he'd help us when we lost a Bond.*

"Yes. The mysterious man who's lived forever. Friend of the Xyri. You said he's been missing."

For seventeen years. I worry... we should be able to find him, yet we can not. And now we're Bonding again. And Bonds are breaking. There is no one to...

"Help the Xyri?"

Zig sighed.

"I wouldn't do anything to hurt you, Zig," she whispered. "You told me from the start that being with Lycan could end horribly. I wouldn't risk it." *But Lycan would...* she chewed on that thought. He didn't actually say anything about... he just said—

She sat up, horrified. "Oh *god*."

What?

"I didn't say anything! He poured his heart out to me and I just. Oh my *god*. Zig, I jumped off the roof and just left him there!"

You said sorry before you jumped, he offered.

"I am the worst person *ever*. Oh my god." She closed her eyes.

It took a few minutes to force herself to stand and exit the portal. She came out into her rooftop garden back home and relaxed a little as the portal closed behind her and the suit came off. The familiar sight of the high brick walls and fake green grass were comforting. She passed the lounge chairs and lifted the skylight hatch that led down to her room. She dropped in beside her bed and pulled the hatch closed before flopping onto her pink blankets. Zig appeared at the foot of her bed, doing his little cat stretch.

Her phone buzzed in her pocket. She was terrified to see a text from Lycan, but it was just Jasper. She smiled as she opened a picture of a small black poodle mid-trot on the sidewalk. He sent her a picture of every dog he saw.

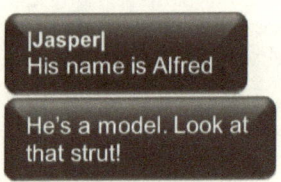

|Jasper|
His name is Alfred

He's a model. Look at that strut!

|Ren|
So dignified!

She hated that she couldn't tell Jasper about any of this. Maybe he'd have good advice for what to do when one of your best friends says they're in love with you. *His advice probably wouldn't be to jump off a roof.* With a sigh she grabbed the basket of half-finished crochet projects from the corner and sent a picture to Jasper.

|Jasper|
Oh no. how many is that??

|Ren|
Seven

|Jasper|
you should combine them into little frankenanimals. Then give them to meeee

|Ren|
Crochet chimeras! I could, but not today.

Gotta finish the one I'm actually giving him

|Jasper|
Which one is that?

|Ren|
A good question! Gonna work on it more before bed.

You'll be here before party?

|Jasper|
How early you want me? An hour or two

|Ren|
Or twelve?
JK. An hour at least?

I don't know what to wear.

|Jasper|
I got you boo. Be there at 1

She considered texting Lycan while the phone was in her hand but decided she couldn't handle it yet. The thought made her nauseous. Kaida would fix things, but later. She didn't even know *how* to fix something like this. In her hesitation she texted Ocean instead.

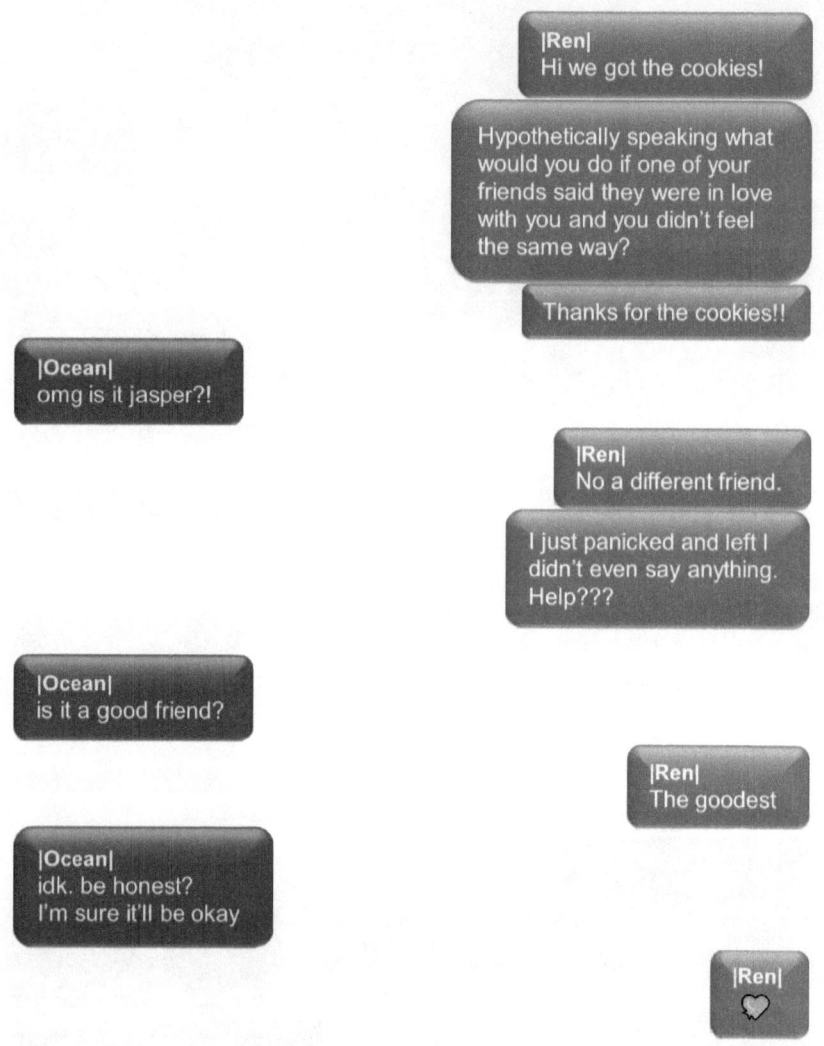

|Ren|
Hi we got the cookies!

Hypothetically speaking what would you do if one of your friends said they were in love with you and you didn't feel the same way?

Thanks for the cookies!!

|Ocean|
omg is it jasper?!

|Ren|
No a different friend.

I just panicked and left I didn't even say anything. Help???

|Ocean|
is it a good friend?

|Ren|
The goodest

|Ocean|
idk. be honest?
I'm sure it'll be okay

|Ren|
♡

Ren sighed. She couldn't worry about Lycan now. She had to finish Bellamy's present. She pulled out her crochet hooks and a new skein of yarn, working late into the night.

The next morning Ren was jittery. She couldn't shake Lycan's confession, the look in his eyes, the *words*. They played on a loop in her mind. *Kaida... I love you. I needed you to know. Kaida... I love you. I needed you to know. Kaida... I love you. I needed you to know.*

She tried to get it out of her mind, focusing instead on her nerves about going to Bellamy's party. She hadn't seen him recently, since they were on winter break.

When Jasper arrived, she had to actively force herself to keep from telling him what happened with Lycan. Jasper was her best friend in the whole world, but she wasn't allowed to tell him about that part of her life. No one could know.

"You okay?" he asked, his bright blue eyes narrowed.

"Fine. Just missed you." She hugged him again, relaxing in the warmth of him.

"It's only been a few days," Jasper replied, arms tight around her, his chin pressed against her cheek.

She pulled back, offended. "You saying you didn't miss me?"

"Course I did. I've been going *insane.*" He smiled wide, making his dimples pop as he ran a hand back through his short brown hair. "Okay, let's find your outfit then you can show me what you made him."

She nodded and followed Jasper upstairs into her bedroom.

He stopped in his tracks once he passed her bathroom and loft, looking into her living room.

"What?"

"Your room is a *mess*. What the hell," he said with a laugh.

Ren blushed as she glanced around. Piles of yarn were all across the purple couch in front of them, baskets with crochet stuff were dumped out by her desk to the right. And dirty clothes were on the floor to the left by the closet.

"This is what happens," she said, grabbing his arm and steering him into the closet, "when my best friend leaves. I go insane."

Jasper let her push him, a grin on his face.

"Alright, what are we feeling?" he asked as he ran a hand over one of her dressers.

"I don't know. Who else is gonna be there?" She'd been invited by Nico, so she only knew he'd be there.

"Nico, Kevin obviously. Ashley. Nari was invited but..."

Ren nodded. Nari didn't really hang out much since Clea died. She forced the thought away as Jasper continued.

"Lola maybe. Does it matter?"

"If I know who else is going I can guess what they'd wear so I'll know if I should dress up or down."

"Oh, Renegade, you couldn't dress more down if you tried."

She opened her mouth in offense.

"I mean it in the most *loving* way possible. But you always got super casual vibes, which is great!"

"Well, we're just watching movies, right? It'll be weird if I dress up for that."

Jasper nodded. "And it's cold."

"Okay. Pick something, just keep it normal."

Jasper's smile widened as he rummaged through her drawers.

An hour later Ren was dressed in an oversized dark blue sweater with red patterns woven through it, and cuffed straight blue jeans. She preferred baggy jeans, though. It was a strange thing, being Ren and being set in the ways she liked to dress in clothes she could hide in, then to go out as Kaida where her every curve was shaped for the world to see. And they did see and they did have opinions. She'd stopped wearing tighter clothes the week she Bonded. What would Jasper think, if he knew the truth?

With a sigh she sat down at her desk, where Zig was currently splayed out. She gave him a flat stare.

I need to do my makeup, can you move?

You never do your makeup.

That's not true. I do it like... three times a year. And this is one of those times.

He grumbled, eyes closed. She glanced at Jasper, who was scrolling through his phone on her couch, his back to her. He couldn't see Zig of course, but seeing her interact with something invisible might cause suspicion. She scooped Zig up and dropped him on the floor. He huffed, flapping his wings at her.

That was uncalled for.

You're uncalled for!

"Knock knock!" Dare called from the trap door in her floor as he lifted it up and came into the room.

"Daddy Arrow!" Jasper said with a grin as he turned around.

Dare groaned as he came to stand beside Ren's desk. "Can't you just call me Dare, like Ren does?"

"But you're *so* daddy," Jasper replied with a pout.

Dare sighed. "Do you need a ride to the party?"

"No, we're walking!" Jasper stood and walked over. "My leg works now."

"Very proud of you," Dare said.

He was a tall man, even taller than Dad. With pale skin, black hair, bright blue eyes, and a strong five o'clock shadow. He was also covered in tattoos, but they were hidden under his black sweater.

"Do we have any gift bags?" Ren asked.

"Yeah, I'll dig them out of the closet downstairs for you."

"Thanks!"

She finished her makeup then grabbed her gift for Bellamy before they made their way downstairs. Dare had brought the box of gift wrappings to the kitchen, and she sifted through it frantically.

"You look nervous," Dare said as he watched her.

"Nervous? To give a handmade gift to the guy I like on his birthday? *Nooo*, why would you think that?"

"I think you should tell him," Jasper said. "Tonight."

Ren's head snapped up. "Huh?"

"Tell Bell you like him. Like, how bad could it go?"

Ren's stomach turned. She knew exactly how bad it could go. Bellamy could do to her what she'd just done to Lycan. *I'm the worst person ever.*

4
The Bear Is Not Better Than a Car

Bellamy couldn't force a smile for his mom when he walked out of his room on the morning of his seventeenth birthday. He felt like he'd never left that rooftop on Spruce Street. All the ways he imagined Kaida reacting... that had *not* been one of them.

Rejection, he expected. Even upset, because admitting he'd fallen in love with her was admitting he'd broken the rules. But her just leaving? Flying away...

"Belly!" His mom looked so excited when he walked into the kitchen. "Happy birthday, baby!" She pulled him into her arms, hugging him and swaying excitedly.

"Thanks, Mom."

She stepped back, looking up at him, then her smile fell. It surprised him sometimes, how similar they were. He had her same dark blonde hair and green eyes. Even the same smile.

"What's wrong?" she asked.

"Nothing. Didn't sleep well."

Her eyes narrowed. "What happened?"

"Nothing."

"Bellamy Owen Grey, you tell me what's wrong right now."

He sighed. "Just... a thing with a girl."

Her eyes widened. "Oh! Is this the girl you're always talking about? The one you wanted to take to the dance last year?"

He blinked. "Ren? No it's..." He paused. "*Yes*. Yeah, Ren." He couldn't exactly tell her he was madly in love with a superhero, and he knew that superhero personally because he was *also* a superhero. Pretending it was a friend from school was easier.

"Is she coming to your party?"

His eyes widened. "I think so."

"You should tell her how you feel," she said with a soft smile.

Bellamy almost laughed. *Yeah, that'll go great. Ren would jump right off the damn balcony.* No. *Ren* wouldn't. But Ren wasn't who he was in love with. He tried to force a smile.

28

"Uh, I think I'll wait a bit. Yeah."

Mom nodded, her green eyes shining up at him. "You're seventeen now. I was seventeen when I fell in love." Her eyes grew sad again and she reached up to brush a thumb against his cheek.

He almost asked who that was with, but held his tongue. Mom never talked about stuff from before he was born.

"Do you want your present?" Her demeanor changed from soft nostalgia to burning excitement as she bounced on her toes.

"Sure."

"Get dressed."

He frowned. "We're leaving to get it?"

"You'll see."

He went to his room and got ready. Every few seconds he'd get distracted, checking his phone to see if Kaida texted. She hadn't.

Should I text her?

No, Zeli answered.

He glanced across the room at the black and silver Xyri curled up in the blue armchair by the window. She was striking, with silver specks all over her black fur, like little stars. Her face was pointed the other way, determinedly not looking at him.

You're still mad at me?

She sighed before slowly lifting her wolfish head, turning her silver eyes on him. The wisps of silvery mist curling up from the tips of her ears seemed to make her look even angrier.

Yes. Not only did you go against my wishes, but you went and got your heart broken. I do not like seeing you hurt, Bellamy.

He nodded. *I had to tell her though. It was killing me.*

She turned away again, silver-tipped tail twitching.

"And now I've ruined it," he mumbled. "What if she hates me? Doesn't wanna be partners anymore?" His heart ached at the thought. He couldn't be Lycan without her.

That is unlikely to happen.

But it could happen? You and Zig are always partners, right. So maybe you guys can convince her to stay with me?

Zeli looked back at him, light refracting off the silver crystal in her forehead. *I don't think we'll need to. The girl probably just needs some time. Everything will work out.*

He nodded.

Mom was waiting in the living room, a small black box in her hands. She grabbed his arm and pulled him to the front door. He went silently, unsure what she was up to. Once they were in the elevator she handed him the box.

"Open it."

A silver key was nestled on blue tissue paper inside. The elevator doors opened on the parking garage under their building.

"Is this…"

She stepped out and he followed her down a row of cars till she stopped beside a shiny dark blue car with a giant red bow on top of it.

"Ta da!"

Bellamy stared in shock. "This is for me?"

"Yes!" She looked so happy, and her joy seeped into him a little. "You're a good driver, responsible. You're seventeen now. It seemed like the right time."

"Wow. Can we go somewhere?"

"Anywhere you want, Belly Bear."

He grinned. For a single moment as he drove, with his mom giddy in the passenger seat, he didn't feel like he was gonna die from the pain of losing Kaida. He felt like a normal kid who just turned seventeen.

By the time they'd driven around, picked up breakfast, and driven back, his joy started wearing off. But he pretended to be excited when the catering his mom ordered for the party arrived that afternoon. A line of people brought in food trays as Mom directed them to the kitchen island. There was so much that she had to put some on the dining table as well.

"This seems like a lot," he said as the people left and Mom started rearranging things.

"I wanted to make sure there was enough. It's fine if it's too much." She started lining cups and sodas on the back counter.

He shook his head, smiling. "Thanks, Mom."

While he waited for his friends to arrive he sat on the couch and considered texting Kaida. She'd given him a little wolf keychain two weeks back for his birthday. He never expected a gift from her, but of course she gave him one anyways, guessing awfully close to the right day. He imagined putting it with his car key and sending her a picture of it.

Kaida was his best friend. Sure, he couldn't tell her who he really was. But he told her so much beyond that. The little things. Things that *mattered*. He should be thrilled about the car. He should be able to text his best friend and tell her about it. But he couldn't bring himself to do it. If she didn't wanna talk…

Eventually there was a knock at the door. Bellamy forced a smile as he found Nico on the other side.

"I am *so* ready," Nico said, his dark brown curls bouncing as Bellamy shut the door behind him. His brown skin contrasted with his bright amber eyes, and his face was filled with a stark white gap-toothed smile. "I got music for downtime before the marathon. Made three playlists, just in case."

"Thanks."

Nico frowned as they entered the living room. "I promise it'll be chill, don't look so bummed already."

I'm bad at pretending to be happy, huh?

You're not usually pretending, Zeli replied.

"Not bummed. Also remind me to show you what my mom got me later."

Nico raised an eyebrow. "Intrigued. I told everyone to be here by three. We start movies by four, should be done by eleven. Which is when Kevin and Ashley have to leave, but everyone else is good to stay till midnight if we're running late."

Bellamy nodded. "How many people are coming?" He hadn't planned on having a party at all, but Nico convinced him a few days back. Since it was so last minute he'd put Nico in charge of everything, including who to invite beyond Ren, Jasper, and Kevin.

"Enough people to fill up your oversized couch," Nico replied as they looked at said couch.

It *was* big. Dark blue and shaped like a horseshoe, across from a big TV mounted on the wall. He glanced at Nico.

"So, how many?"

"I don't know. A few I invited couldn't come. Probably ten total? Including us. I think. I was reasonable, I *swear.*"

Bellamy smiled.

"We should pull the curtains shut before we movie," Nico added. "You have more windows than walls."

"Right." The entire back wall of the apartment was just floor to ceiling windows, with two different doors leading out to the balcony. Sunlight poured through them. "Also my mom ordered too much food, so hope you're hungry."

"Always hungry," Nico replied as they moved through the room, closing the curtains.

After a few minutes Jules, Lola, and Harper all arrived together. Though all three were blonde, they couldn't have looked more different. Jules was the tallest, though still a little shorter than Bellamy. Her hair was up in a messy bun, her golden skin glowing. Harper's hair hung loose around her pale face. She gave him a fleeting smile as her blue eyes darted around the room curiously. Lola was the smallest, with fair skin covered in freckles, and her hair cropped short.

"Damn, Bellamy," she said as they entered the living room. "This place is huge."

"Right?" Nico said.

Bellamy blushed. Someone knocked and he moved to answer, ignoring the embarrassment at his privilege. Kevin was waiting in the hall, a wide smile on his face. The shorter boy looked like a mischievous elf, with his bright brown eyes, and ears that were a bit big for his face.

Before Bellamy could close the door, Ashley arrived. Her long red hair hung down to her waist. She grinned as he let her in.

"Is that a suit of armor?" she asked.

"Uh, yeah. My mom likes weird stuff like that," he replied with a shrug.

"So cool."

"Is Jasper coming?" Harper asked as she settled on the couch beside Jules.

"Should be," Nico answered.

Bellamy checked the time. Ren and Jasper should have been there already. Ren lived just down the street from him.

"You guys can help yourselves to food while we wait."

He was anxious with so many people in his house, and he had to remind himself that they were his *friends* and it was *okay*. Bellamy wasn't used to having friends, even still. Before freshman year he didn't have a single one, aside from his mom. He'd been homeschooled and they moved around so much, never staying in one place long enough for him to make a real connection. That was until they came here, and he met Ren. She'd been his guiding light at school.

Finally the bell rang, and relief filled him when he opened it to see Ren and Jasper standing outside.

"Happy birthday!" Ren said excitedly as he held the door open for them. Her long dark brown hair was half down, half up, and her bright brown eyes were framed with subtle makeup. She held a blue gift bag in her hand, twirling it anxiously as they walked inside. "This is for you."

"Oh, thanks." He took it from her, curious.

Jasper looked like he was trying not to laugh, his dimples prominent as he pursed his lips. His brown hair was combed back, brushing against his ears. His electric blue eyes were so bright against his fair skin. Bellamy used to think they were contacts, with how unreal they looked.

"Uh, there's food in here, if you're hungry."

The girls were all piled onto the couch, chatting quietly while the boys were circling the food.

"Ren, did you get him a present?" Nico asked. "He said no presents!"

Ren blushed.

"It's fine," Bellamy said.

"¿Estás tratando de que todos se vean bien mal, o que tú te veas increíble?" Nico said with a raised eyebrow.

Ren stuck her tongue out at him and Nico laughed.

Bellamy met Ren's eyes then nodded toward the hall. "Come here for a sec?"

She followed him down the long hallway to his room. He shut the door then sat on the edge of his bed. Ren stood by the door awkwardly, arms folded around herself like she was cold, even though she wore a big sweater.

"You can sit."

"Right." She slowly sat beside him as he opened the gift bag. "I know Nico said no presents but... well I wanted to get you *something*. But I didn't know what and so... I made this. It's kinda silly but..." She trailed off.

Bellamy pulled out the softest stuffed animal he's ever touched. A brown bear made of light and dark brown yarn. The eyes were green, and there was a little stuffed book hanging from the bear's teeth.

"I spent all night making it," Ren whispered.

He looked up, meeting her eyes. Her cheeks were red, making the freckles scattered across her nose and cheeks stand out even more.

"Ren this is so—" He stopped. "Wait, you *made* this?"

"Yeah. It's crochet."

"This is so sweet. I love it."

"Yeah?" Her entire face lit up, brown eyes shining. "I didn't... I didn't know what your favorite animal was, so... I made you mine."

He stared at her, heart swelling. That's what he'd said when he gave her a gift on her birthday last year. *I don't know what your favorite book is, so... I got you mine.* He blinked as he looked at the book in the bear's mouth. The Little Prince. That was the book he gave her. His favorite. He felt oddly emotional as he looked back up at her, and for a moment he could almost see her in that princess dress again, sparkling tiara in her hair.

"I'm obsessed. Does it have a name?"

"Not yet. You can name it."

"But you made it. So, we should name it together."

She bit her lip. "Uh huh. Okay. Here's what we do... I pick a name, and you pick a name. We say them at the same time. Then we combine them into one weird name."

He grinned. "Perfect. One, two, three—"

"Rufus."

"Richard."

Bellamy laughed. "Rufus?"

"Yeah! Uh, okay. So... Rufard?"

"Rufard. My beloved bear. It's *perfect*, Ren. I love him."

Ren's smile was infectious. "I'm glad you like it."

"Literally the best gift I've ever gotten. And my mom gave me a *car* today. So, that's saying something."

"The bear is *not* better than a car," Ren said flatly.

"It is to me. Thank you, Ren."

Aside from his mom the only other person to ever give him a gift was Kaida. He forced that thought aside and put the bear on his desk next to his laptop. The feet were heavier, so it sat up perfectly without tipping over. It added a lot of personality to his room, considering he hadn't done much with it after all this time. The room was small compared to the rest of the apartment, but he managed to fit a full bookshelf in by the door, a smaller one in against the window, and some single shelves on the wall by his bed. They were all overflowing.

He still couldn't believe Ren made the bear. "You're a great friend, you know that?" he said as he opened his door.

Ren looked sad and shook her head. "I'm really not."

"Shut up. You're amazing."

She smiled but it seemed forced.

They came back out to everyone making plates of food. Jasper's blue eyes lit up and he grabbed Ren, pulling her to the other side of the room. Bellamy sat on the couch and got the first Star Wars movie ready as the rest of them slowly filed in with their food and drinks. Their plan was to watch all three movies in the original trilogy.

"Bellamy, why are you so much older than us?" Kevin asked through a mouthful of chips. "I'm not even sixteen yet, and you're seventeen."

"Uh."

"You know why," Ren said as she sat down beside Bellamy. "Cause of the homeschooling? He started as a freshman instead of a sophomore so he wouldn't feel behind... he told us that the first week we met him."

Everyone stared at her and Ren blushed.

"Yeah, *Okay, Ren,*" Jasper said. "You're not special cause you know things about Bellamy. Okay *I* know things about him too. Like how he's never seen Star Wars, like a fucking *psychopath.*"

Bellamy laughed.

"I've never seen it either," Harper said, eyeing Jasper.

Jasper shook his head. "We got some educating to do..."

They started the movie, and Bellamy leaned back then glanced at Ren. "Thanks," he whispered.

"For what?"

"Being you."

Her blush deepened, but she smiled before turning back to the TV.

Bellamy found he was enjoying himself as the night went on. The movie was good and he liked being around his friends, despite his anxiety. It was easy to remember all the years without any friends. Now his couch was crowded with people who wanted to spend his birthday with him. He was grateful, but something was missing.

He checked his phone again. Kaida couldn't ignore him forever. Eventually something would come up, and they'd handle it together like they always did. Surely.

By the time they got onto the third movie, both Kevin and Ashley had fallen asleep. Bellamy's mom came out of her office and walked down to the front door. A moment later she came back with a strange man in tow. He was tall, with long dark hair, wearing a black trench coat.

Bellamy got up without even thinking and slowly walked over to the office door, then leaned against it, listening.

"I can't do this today," his mom whispered. She sounded angry. "It's my son's birthday."

"I'm aware. But I also recall you asking for my *help* with the other one," the man replied in a British accent.

"Don't. Not today," she continued.

A pause. "As you wish."

He heard movement and rushed back to the couch. He hopped into his spot between Ren and Nico, breathless, just as his mom and the man walked out and back to the front door.

Ren raised an eyebrow at him.

Bellamy put his finger against his lips and she nodded.

A second later Mom came and stood behind the couch.

"How is everything? Everyone good?" she asked, scanning the group as Nico paused the movie.

"We're good, thanks," he replied, heart still pounding in his chest. He realized Mom was trying to sus out which of the girls was Ren. He did *not* need her saying something to make Ren think he liked her like that. He'd had enough rejection this week and couldn't handle anymore.

"When's the movie over?" she asked as she brushed his hair back on his head.

He glanced at Nico.

"About twenty minutes left, Miss Grey!"

"Does anyone need a ride home?"

"Oh!" Bellamy felt a jolt of excitement. "Can I drive them?"

Mom frowned then let out a breath. "Sure, but you come straight home after, got it?"

"Yes, love you!"

"Love you, too." She kissed the top of his head and retreated into her office.

"Your mom is *so* cute," Jules whispered.

When the movie was over Ashley and Kevin left immediately, their rides already waiting outside. Jules had driven Harper and Lola, so they went together. That left Nico, Ren, and Jasper.

"You guys want a ride?" he asked as he grabbed his shoes.

"Sure, I'll text my mom," Nico said.

"My dad can pick us—"

Jasper put his hand over Ren's mouth. "No, her dads don't love her that much we for sure need a ride."

Ren's cheeks turned bright red and Jasper laughed.

"It's fine," he continued. "I'll text your dads right now, you know they'll say yes!"

"If you're sure," Bellamy said as they went down to the garage.

Ren's cheeks remained red while Jasper insisted she ride shotgun as he and Nico climbed in the back.

Bellamy grinned at her and she smiled. "Jasper, I don't actually know your address," he said as they pulled out.

"Don't need to, I'm staying at Ren's tonight."

"Gotcha."

He dropped Nico off first, then went to the bakery.

"Happy birthday," Ren said again as she got out of the car.

"Thanks! I love my bear!"

She giggled and closed the door.

He went straight home after like Mom wanted, feeling exhausted. Socializing with people was more tiresome than fighting criminals. Though, he did prefer this.

The moment he climbed into bed he heard sirens in the distance.

Could be nothing, Zeli offered as he got out of bed with a sigh and went to his balcony. *Sirens go off every twenty seconds. It's your birthday, you don't have to.*

I do have to, he replied. He checked his phone one last time before the suit came over him and he jumped into the air.

5
Winged and Green and Glowing

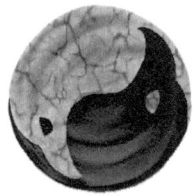

Dread settled in Jasper's stomach as he entered the apartment. A shout. A bang. Tremors in his skin. His mom appeared around the corner, tears streaming down her pale face. She stopped when she saw him and quickly wiped her eyes.

"Hey, baby. How was your night?"

Jasper didn't respond, staring over her shoulder as his dad came down the hall, a storm in his eyes.

"Where the hell have you been?" he growled.

"At Ren's," he muttered, heart racing. "You guys said I could stay last—"

"You're grounded."

Jasper sucked in a breath as he stared back at the taller man, continuously thankful he didn't look a thing like him. Dad had thick black hair, amber eyes, and a strong jaw. But all Jasper saw when he looked at him was the storm.

He didn't need to ask why Dad forgot he'd given him permission, nor why he was a raging mess right now. He could smell the liquor.

"You said I could go," he replied, trying to stay calm and sound confident.

Mom sniffed as she stared at them. "We did, Bobby. We told him he could stay."

Dad just grunted. "There's a mess in there. Clean it up." With that he stumbled into the kitchen and disappeared into the bathroom.

Jasper turned to his mom. "Are you alright?"

"Yes. He broke a vase. I'll get it before I go," she said as she blinked her blue-gray eyes, trying to disperse the rest of her tears. He saw himself in her all the time. Same eyes, same dark brown hair. Same defeat in her face, same tension in her shoulders.

He sighed. "You're going to work now?"

She nodded.

His stomach turned. She worked a double yesterday and was already going back? She looked like she hadn't slept at all, with those bags under her eyes. And Dad was home, drunk in the middle of the afternoon. He balled his hands into fists.

"It's fine, Mom. I'll clean it. Love you." He kissed her cheek then moved past her to deal with the mess.

"You're not grounded," she said softly. "He'll forget he even said that."

Jasper nodded, hands shaking as he swept up the glass. He wanted it clean before Dad came back out. He didn't wanna give him any reason to do more than yell and break things and make Mom cry.

Dad returned just as he dumped it into the trash. "Stay in your room," he mumbled as he brushed past him into the living room.

Will do, Jasper thought as he went to his room and gently closed the door behind him.

Then he froze.

A small black and green dog with wings was staring up at him from the middle of his room. In the back of his brain he knew this could only be a Xyri, but the front of his brain hadn't caught up yet. So he stood very still, holding his breath.

It tilted its weird head to the side, looking like some bizarre mix between a dog and a zebra, with those neon green stripes across the black fur. There were weird feathered tufts coming out of its head instead of ears. And it had eyes of green that glowed, along with a shimmering green diamond-shaped crystal in its forehead. Black and green wings were tucked against its back.

Jasper's brain finally got a hold of itself. The only reason a Xyri would show itself to a human is if they were Bonding that human. Which meant Jasper's life was about to change. All his dreams were coming true. This ancient wise creature wanted to bestow him with abilities beyond belief. It was *actually* happening.

He waited, not entirely sure how the process went. The Xyri just stared at him with those glowing eyes.

"Well?" he finally said.

A smile formed on its fox-like face, revealing silver fangs. It was ridiculously unnerving. Jasper swallowed as it stepped closer and something hit the ground. A glittering black circle. The Xyri pushed it toward him with its nose. Jasper went to his knees, trembling as he picked up the bracelet and slid it on his wrist. Warmth spread through him as it tightened, forming to him.

Become, a raspy voice said in his head.

"Uh. Yes?"

You gotta be more confident than that, kid. Get it together.

Jasper smiled nervously. He didn't want the Xyri changing its mind on him.

"I accept?"

It started laughing at him. *You're so not ready for this. Can't wait to see what Bonding a child is like. But Kirzigith did it, so it can't be that hard. Still. Three billion years, never Bonded a baby before.* Jasper didn't know what to say. "I'm not that young. I'm sixteen." More laughter. *Yes. A child. Xyri don't Bond children. Should be interesting. You know the drill? Powers and responsibility, yada yada.*

"Yeah of course." He thought he might be sick. "But... is there more I should know?"

Eh, you'll figure it out. I been watching you for a while. Seemed right to pick you, considering.

"Considering what?" he asked as he stared at the bracelet. It was textured and so black it seemed to suck in the light around it. "How do I actually like, suit up?"

You can do it with just a thought, but you gotta be more intentional with it at first.

"Meaning?"

Really focus on wanting it, and picture the suit coming over you. He took a deep breath, trying to imagine it. A rush of power swept over him and he watched in awe as his clothes and skin were covered in black. It was so smooth and happened so fast. It didn't even feel like he was wearing anything. There were thin glowing green lines running down the suit. He turned to the mirror on the back of his door to get a better look.

"What are my powers?" he asked as he spun around. The Xyri was nowhere to be seen now.

You got a whole pocket full of powers, kid. You can fly, but that's just a bonus. Power set is strength, speed, sound, scent, and sight.

"What... does that mean?"

You can tap into strength. Get very strong. Tap into speed. Get very fast. Do you need a handbook, kid? It's not that complicated. Wanna see something far away, tap sight. Need to smell better? Tap scent.

"Okay. I think I get it. Can I only do one at a time?"

You can do it all at once, but I wouldn't recommend it. Might explode your brains, so don't try it unless you're feeling really frisky.

"And I can fly? How do we do that?"

Just gotta pull your wings out.

"What?" Jasper was so confused.

The Xyri groaned in his head and then Jasper saw it in his mind. Wings extending out from his back. He concentrated, envisioning it. He expected it to feel weird but it felt like... stretching. The wings unfolded, spreading out till they touched both sides of his small bedroom. The black feathers were shiny, with little lines of green and silver in them.

"That's fucking cool."

Yeah! Now jump out the window!

Jasper considered that for a moment, then shrugged and lifted his window up, climbing out onto the fire escape. It was difficult to do with giant wings.

He wasn't exactly afraid of heights, but he was five floors up. Yet he'd climbed out there so many times since they moved into the building. Those intrusive thoughts that always told him to jump seemed to be laughing at him now. *I have wings...*

Jump, kid. You probably won't die.

"Probably?"

He felt a sensation like shrugging come from the Xyri.

"Where did you go?"

Is that a serious question?

"...yes?"

The Xyri sighed. *When you're in the suit I am in you. Kind of. It's complicated, but basically we are one. I don't have a physical form when you suit up.*

"Weird. You said something before... picking me was right? Why?"

He felt a moment of hesitation from the Xyri and thought he might not answer.

Well, you're friends with the best hero this generation has. Easy choice.

Jasper frowned. "Huh?"

Kaida. Lady of Light. Dragonheart. Ren Rivers. Did you hit your head? We haven't even jumped yet! I been watching you for months, you're with that girl nearly every day.

Jasper was very still. There was *no* way. He would know. There was no fucking way she... he closed his eyes, stomach turning. The night of his basketball game. She disappeared all day and lied about it. It was *so* unlike her. He never figured out why, she refused to tell him. But Ren *never* lied and *never* missed important things before... before the Xyri returned.

We jumping or not?

Jasper opened his eyes and threw himself over the railing without thinking. Cool wind rushed past and his stomach dropped. There was no time to panic, his wings spread out, like they knew what to do all on their own, and he glided in a smooth arc before he could hit the pavement. Then he soared upward. Everything moved so fast as he flew. It didn't take long to get used to the sensation. By the time he landed on Ren's roof he thought he had a handle on it.

What are we doing?

Jasper didn't answer. He wasn't in control of himself as he pulled open the skylight door that led into Ren's bedroom. He slipped inside and spotted Ren sitting in the middle of her floor with her cat. He jumped off the loft platform, landing in front of her.

Ren screamed and scooped Breadcrumb up. She held him tucked under one arm protectively while her other arm was out toward him, defensive. Her brown eyes were hard as steel as she stared him down.

"Who are you?"

"I know you're Kaida." He was surprised to hear the venom in his voice.

"I don't know what you're talking about," she hissed back. Her eyes were filled with fear, but she remained steady.

"How do I take the suit off?"

Needs intention. See it and make it happen.

He sighed, trying to force it off with a thought. The suit vanished. "I know you're Kaida," he repeated, tone a little softer now.

Ren dropped her cat. "No." She shook her head, eyes wide and horrified. Then she fell to her knees, head hanging low. When she looked up at him tears were pouring down her face.

"I'm sorry sorry I'm s-so sorry." She was practically choking on the words.

His anger evaporated and he rushed to her. "It's okay. It's okay." Jasper pulled her into his arms, holding her tight as she continued to cry, mumbling apologies.

Shit shit shit. He rocked her back and forth, unsure what else to do. He'd only ever seen Ren cry once. She didn't even cry when Clea died. She shut down, went numb, unresponsive. But she never *cried*. The strongest girl in the whole world and she was sobbing in his arms.

"Renegade, it's okay. It's okay."

"I'm s-so sorry," she mumbled into his shirt, now soaked with her tears. Her hands clung to him. "I wanted to t-tell you. I want to. I am. I c-couldn't. I. Oh *no*." She was gasping for air.

"Shh, Ren. Shh. It's okay, just breathe." He wiped the tears from her cheeks and brushed her hair back. "It's okay."

She didn't seem to think so, continuing to cry. Several minutes passed before she stopped. He sat there, with her head in his lap, her red-rimmed eyes staring up at him.

"How did you find out?" she asked with a sniff.

"My Xyri told me."

"Your..." She closed her eyes. "How long have you been Bonded?"

"Like, five minutes."

Her eyes snapped open and she sat up, turning to look at him. "How the hell did your Xyri find out?"

"Uh, I don't know."

He looked to the side where his Xyri was lying down, head on its paws like a normal dog. Only winged and green and glowing.

"Poziarne?" Ren hissed. "Show yourself!" Anger seemed to be replacing her guilt.

Her eyes widened as she stared at Poziarne. Jasper was pretty sure Xyri could choose who saw them or not, but he really didn't know enough about them.

"You *told him* I'm Kaida?" she demanded.

The little Xyri lifted his head. *Yes.*

"You broke the main rule! You weren't even supposed to know I was Ren. And you went and told my best friend!"

I don't know why you're so mad. I heard you telling Kirzigith you wished you could tell him. Seemed like I was doing you a favor.

Ren rolled her eyes. "No. This isn't my fault, Zig. I... I was *so* careful." A fresh tear slipped down her cheek.

"Zig?" Jasper asked softly.

She let out a breath and wiped her eyes. "Zig, let him see you."

An animal appeared beside Ren. It looked like a goddamn dragon. Small, like a cat, but with scales such a bright red they belonged in a movie. It didn't look real. And yet it looked *so* real. The little creature stretched out its wings. Black, with small veins of gold running through the membranes.

Nice to properly meet you, Jasper Nightingale, the dragon Xyri spoke in his mind.

"Uh... likewise?"

Ren put her face in her hands. "This wasn't supposed to happen. But Poziarne came to Zig one day and said he wanted to meet me, and Zig trusted him cause he's *stupid* and then *I* was stupid and accidentally detransformed in front of Poziarne and that was like two months ago and now..." She uncovered her face. "What kind of Xyri gives away someone's identity? It's against the *rules!*"

Kirzigith said things needed to be different this time, Poziarne replied.

Ren gave him a flat stare. "Different for *him* and *Zeli*." She let out a breath and looked at Jasper.

"Ren, it's *okay.*"

"No one is supposed to know." She looked sick. "The Xyri don't even know."

He understood. It was a rule. Ren was a good kid, a good student. She followed any rule that made sense to her and did it perfectly. And somehow, by Jasper finding out, she was breaking a big one. He'd done this to her. He hurt her. And he didn't know how to fix it.

This isn't the end of the world, Ren. It'll be alright, her Xyri said in a soft reassuring voice. He sounded *old.* Jasper could hear the weight of the years lived in that voice.

Ren smiled sadly as she met his eyes. "I'm so glad you know."

"You are? You seemed pretty... upset a second ago."

"I've wanted to tell you every single day since I Bonded. Every five minutes. It *killed* me, not telling you. Lying and hurting you and not being honest..." Her eyes welled up again. "You're not supposed to know and that might be very bad but I... god I am *so* relieved."

She leaned over and hugged him, resting her head on his shoulder as she held onto him. "If you're mad I understand and I'll do whatever it takes to make it up to—"

"Not mad, Renny. I *swear*." He was still shocked. Processing. But seeing Ren break down like that... he couldn't be angry with her. He just felt guilty that he ever made her feel bad about those times she was lying to protect herself.

"The night of my last game..." he whispered. "You were Kaida? And Kaida was saving people, wasn't she?"

Ren pulled back and wiped her eyes.

"The fire in Brooklyn. A Bonded, Pompeii... she accidentally started the fire. Lost control. Lycan and I tried to get everyone out. But... people died that night. Lycan went back in time, over and over and over. But he wasn't supposed to. He almost died trying to bring them all back. I was with him, alone in the dark on a random rooftop. He was unconscious for hours and I didn't know if he'd make it." She swallowed. "I couldn't leave him. By the time I came home, your game was long over and there was no lie I could tell you that... you'd believe."

He remembered. He'd spent that entire night being worried sick about her. Because of *course* Ren wouldn't miss his game. But she never showed. His dad had been watching, judging him. Jasper did not play well. He disappointed Dad and Ren wasn't there to make it better. She wasn't there at all. He'd been sure something bad happened. Then when she finally texted him in the middle of the night, it was all lies. He hadn't spoken to her for two weeks after that, he'd been so upset. So petty.

"Ren..." He thought he might cry, eyes burning with guilt and shame.

"It's okay," she whispered, shaking her head.

"Oh god." His throat got tight. "That day at the Met? When Clea died? Oh my *god*."

Ren closed her eyes, more tears slipping out.

"I tried to save her," she whispered, voice cracking. "I tried so hard. I thought... I thought once I got the beam off her I could portal her out but... she died so fast once it was free. She trusted me and I let her die. I wasn't... wasn't strong enough. I couldn't stop it I..."

Jasper shivered as he pulled Ren into his arms again. He'd never been more afraid in his entire life than that day. When everything went to hell he couldn't find Ren. The whole building shaking, breaking, collapsing. People screaming. Their whole class had been there on a school trip. But they hadn't been together when it started, cause Jasper was being a little bitch and not talking to her. When everything stopped he'd panicked, searching through the rubble. When he finally found her she was dirty and bleeding and unable to speak.

They all knew Ren saw Clea die that day. But he didn't know, couldn't know... Kaida had been there, trying to stop it. To save them. No wonder Ren had been so numb after.

He continued to hold her as this went on. Hugging, crying. All the realizations of what Ren had been through this last year, and how he hadn't been there for her. Not really. Not enough.

That's not your fault, kid.

He glanced over at his Xyri. He'd been quiet for the most part.

"I have powers now," he whispered with a grin. "You're not alone anymore, Ren. You got me. And Kaida has me, too."

Ren sniffed, a small smile forming. "I wasn't alone. I had Lycan. If not for him I probably would have lost my mind, though. But, you knowing now, that's—"

Jasper gasped. "Lycan! Holy fuck. Lycan!"

Ren blinked. "What?"

"You *know* Lycan! Oh my god. You're Kaida. Have you had a secret boyfriend this *whole time* and I didn't know? I can't believe this."

Ren laughed but there was no humor in it. "Oh boy. So, *no*. I have not had a boyfriend. Lycan is in fact just my partner. My friend. We're extremely close. And we're never *ever* allowed to be more, our Xyri said so. But but just two days ago Lycan told me he was in love with me and. Um. *Yeah*."

Jasper stared at her, trying to process. "Lycan is in love with you? Fuck. He's so hot. What did you say when he told you?"

Ren laughed nervously. "Hah. *Well*. Um. I sorta jumped off the roof."

6
Magic Broken By Truth

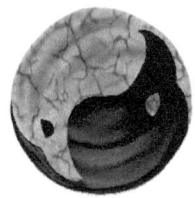

Jasper was face down on Ren's kitchen table, eyes closed. He stayed over again, and they'd been up most of the night talking about all the various things Ren had done as Kaida. He missed so much. A whole secret life. He knew it wasn't his fault he hadn't been there for her, because he didn't *know*. And he wasn't supposed to know. But he still felt bad. Ren was his best friend, the most important person in his world, and he didn't even notice how much she was going through.

"Head off the table," Cas said.

Jasper groaned, sitting up as Ren's dad placed a plate of bacon and eggs in front of him.

"Why are you so tired?" he asked. "It's noon."

"We definitely went to bed on time," Ren whispered. "Definitely didn't just get up before you came back."

Jasper yawned.

"¿A qué hora se fueron a dormir?" her dad asked as he put a plate in front of Ren.

"Tarde," Ren said with a smile.

Jasper stared between them, not understanding a word.

"¿Haciendo que?"

"Hablando." Ren's eyes widened. "Teníamos *mucho* de qué hablar."

Cas sighed. "En la cama a las once, pequeña dragón, ¿entiendes?"

"Si señor." Ren grinned up at him.

Jasper scratched his head then picked up his fork, trying not to be annoyed. He sucked at Spanish and Ren was the only reason he wasn't failing that class. But he still couldn't follow a conversation when her and her dad switched to it.

"He says we have to go to bed on time tonight," Ren whispered.

"For sure," Jasper replied around a mouthful of food.

"You need anything else?" Cas asked. The tall man looked exhausted, bags under his eyes, reminding Jasper of his mom. He didn't understand how he kept the schedule of getting up at two in the morning some days to bake all night.

"No, we're good. Go nap!" Ren insisted.

Cas frowned. "You going out or staying in?"

"Gonna play games after food. Super productive."

"Do you have any laundry upstairs?"

Ren nodded slowly.

Cas smiled. "Bring it down *before* you get distracted. And wake me if you need anything." With that he went downstairs, leaving them alone.

Ren watched Jasper while she chewed on her bacon.

"What?"

She shrugged, looking anxious. "It's your second day Bonded. How do you feel?"

"I feel fine. Should I not?"

"Zig says it can be weird sometimes."

"Was it weird for you?"

She pushed her eggs around her plate. "A bit? But I think it's different for everyone. Lycan adjusted without an issue."

"When do I get to meet him?" Jasper asked.

Her cheeks turned red.

"Oh right. Still haven't talked to him?"

She shook her head. "I don't know what to say."

"Right, but once you sort things out, I get to meet him?"

Ren's eyes darkened. "No. I mean, *yes*. But not yet. You have so much to learn."

"I do?"

Pozi started laughing in his head. Jasper glanced around but didn't see the Xyri. He didn't see Ren's, either. Just her cat, Breadcrumb, walking across the back of the sofa.

"Yes," Ren mumbled through a bite of food.

He sighed and stared across the room. One floor of Ren's house was bigger than his entire apartment. And she had five floors. Though the first one was the bakery, so maybe that didn't count.

Ren finished her food and took her plate to the sink. He always liked her kitchen, with the white counters, black cabinets and the big island across from the round table where he sat. He envied the *space*. It opened to the living room, with three small couches across from the fireplace, and a huge flat-screen above that. They had so much *stuff*, but it never felt crowded. Breadcrumb jumped off the couch then sprinted over to the cat tree by the window and started tearing at one of the pillars on it.

"Earth to Jasper?"

He turned. Ren was staring at him.

"Finish your food," she said before she dashed up the stairs.

He sighed and shoved his last bite in his mouth, then put his plate in the sink. He crossed Ren on the stairs, bringing a basket of her laundry down and plopping it beside the washer. He couldn't even *imagine* having a washer and dryer in his apartment.

Once in her room they sat on her purple couch and Ren turned to face him.

"So. Rule number one. I am Ren."

He smiled. "What?"

She tilted her head to the side and then she was in the suit. Ren no longer stared back at him, with her long brown hair, brown eyes, and freckled face. Instead, a girl in a mask with blue eyes and purple-pink hair watched him intently. Her suit was so intricate, with those red scales, outlined in glowing gold, and the orange flames twirling up her arms. It was so *cool.*

"You don't have to do your hair?" he asked. It had gone from hanging loose, to up in two neat buns in an instant.

"Nope." She grinned. "I'm Kaida. See the difference?"

"Well, yeah but—"

"No *but.* I am Kaida. You never *ever* call me by any other name, understand?"

"*Oh*, right. Okay."

Her suit came off. "I'm Ren. You never ever call me by any other name."

He grinned. "What about Renegade?"

She grabbed a throw pillow and hit him in the face with it.

He laughed. "Sorry!"

"You have to take this seriously!"

"I am! I am!"

Are you though? Pozi asked.

Jasper sighed. *I'm trying to.*

"I am so serious, Jasper. You can *not* fuck this up! You have to get it in your head that I am two different people. And so are you, now. You can't meet Lycan or even go out in your suit till you get this down."

He nodded. "Okay, I'll work on it."

She leaned back and closed her eyes. "Rule number two is I'm *tired.*"

"Come *on.*" He smiled. "I gotta learn stuff. What else should I know?"

She sighed. "So much. You have any questions? We can start there."

"Where are our Xyri? Like, where do they go? I can hear Pozi but he isn't here and it's weird."

Ren grinned as she tucked her legs up underneath her. "Well, my

Xyri and Lycan's Xyri are together a lot when neither of us are suited up. Pozi might be with them?"

"What do they even do on their own?"

She giggled. "Well, last week Zig and Zeli went to a *show*."

He snorted. "You're kidding."

"Nope. No one can see them, if they don't want them to. They can go anywhere. He doesn't always tell me what they do though."

"So there's no limit on our connection to them? Distance wise?"

"Nope. Zig could be on the other side of the world, and I'd still hear him. Feel him. You can transform any time, without them being near, so long as you're wearing your Xyrial."

"What's a Xyrial?"

Ren gave him a flat stare. "Yours is presumably the black bracelet you got on? Be careful with that. People might get suspicious of you suddenly wearing jewelry when you weren't before."

He looked down at the bracelet, only half an inch wide. It did kinda stick out against his fair skin. "I'll just tell people it was a gift from you."

Ren smiled. "That works."

"Wait, what's your Xyrial?"

She slid her hand under the neck of her shirt and pulled out a necklace. The gold chain was long, with a golden pendant on the end, about an inch and a half tall, and shaped almost like a claw.

Jasper stared at her. "You told me that was your dead aunt's necklace!"

Her smile widened. "Yes, and it was the perfect lie cause no one questions why I always wear it."

"Wouldn't your dad know if it wasn't hers?"

"I just told him I found it in a box of her stuff and that I wanted to wear it. They were close, but he wasn't gonna have every piece of jewelry she owned from eighteen years ago memorized. He thought it was sweet I wanted to wear something of hers. Didn't question it once."

"Devious."

Ren nodded as she tucked it back under her shirt. "You have to keep your Xyrial on you at all times. But you can ask Pozi to alter how it looks, if you want."

Jasper nodded. "Another question."

Ren sat up straighter.

"You didn't recognize me when I showed up in the suit yesterday. And before knowing you were Kaida I literally never would have guessed that was you. How the hell does that work? Like, I know *your* face better than my own. How could I not know?"

"Magic," Ren answered. "No, seriously! Zig says I could be standing in front of my dads as Kaida and they'd have *no* idea. No one can see through the mask, it confuses them. I didn't even need to change my eyes and hair. I could have looked exactly like me in the suit and *still* no one who knows Ren would ever guess Ren was Kaida based on looks alone. You can't even recognize the voice. It's all magically masked by the Xyri."

"That's wild."

She nodded. "But, now you know it's me you can *see* me behind the mask. Magic broken by truth."

He smiled. "Why did you change your hair then?"

Ren sat back, hugging the pillow against her stomach. "Separation, mostly. It's *very* important to see yourself as two people. I am Ren *and* I am Kaida, but never at the same time. Looking very different, acting different, it helps with that."

Jasper frowned.

"Oh!" She untucked her legs excitedly. "Another thing you should know, kinda awkward but... you're gonna live longer now."

"Huh?"

If you don't die first, Pozi muttered in his head.

"Bonding extends your natural lifespan. It kinda weirds me out a bit. Thinking if I'm not like, murdered or sickly I'll just... live longer than everyone I know by a small margin? But now you will too and this makes me feel *so* much better."

Jasper didn't know how to process that. "How much longer?"

"About fifty years longer than average? Give or take. Zig wasn't super clear, it's different for everyone but... it's definitely longer."

"Huh." That was daunting. "We're gonna grow old together."

"Very cute of us," Ren replied with a grin.

I like this, Pozi said softly.

Like what?

You and Ren. We really do never reveal the identities. Humans never know who's behind the masks. The Xyri never know who the other Bonded are. It's always secret. It's safer that way. But this is more fun. More interesting.

You weren't supposed to tell me she was Kaida, though, he replied as he stared at Ren. She seemed happier now than she had yesterday.

Yes, but... I think it's better. In this one instance, maybe. Just don't out her, kid. Or we'll have a huge mess to deal with.

Right.

I'm serious. Anyone finds out Ren is Kaida and she becomes a target. Her life depends on your ability to keep this secret. And yours depends on the same. The world is so different now. The way information travels. You have to be careful.

Jasper swallowed. *Right.*

He leaned back and closed his eyes. Ren hit him with the pillow again and he laughed.

After that they actually did play games for a bit, till Arrow came home with dinner and they went down to eat with her dads. Jasper had more questions, and concerns. But Ren didn't seem in a rush to teach him, so he tried not to overthink things.

They went back to Ren's room after dinner, sitting on the floor behind the couch with Breadcrumb, Ren waving a wand around for him to chase. He used to be annoyed by how nice her room was, with the soft gray carpet and the even softer blue cloud rug on top of that. Her room was so light and colorful, like a candy store. Light blue walls, pink shelves, purple couch, and her rainbow curtains on those big windows. She had so much storage for her crochet stuff by her desk, and a whole TV on the wall across from the couch. The back area that was just for her cat was bigger than his *entire* bedroom.

Jasper sighed and looked back at Ren, that soft smile on her face, and remembered the footage he'd seen of Kaida in Times Square.

"Ren?"

"Hm?"

"Now that I know everything... I just wanna make sure you know you *can* tell me everything."

Her face softened. "I know."

He nodded.

Ren's phone started beeping and she dropped the cat toy, eyes widening as she scanned the screen. "Shit."

"What?"

"Big fire in the Bronx. I should go."

"Can I come?" Jasper sat up, excited.

Ren blinked. "Uh. I think we should wait. You need more time, you know?"

"Oh, okay."

She frowned. "Sorry. I swear I won't be long."

"What about Lycan?"

She hesitated, looking down at her phone. "I could text him..."

"Wait, you have his number? I thought everything was secret. You said even Zig doesn't know who he is under the mask."

She shook her head, shoving her phone in her pocket. "It is secret. We use an app that generated fake numbers for us. Comes through in our normal texts, but we don't have each other's real numbers."

He nodded. "Makes sense. Go, save the world. I'll be here."

She smiled as she transformed and climbed up the steps to her loft bed, then out through the skylight.

We should go with her! Pozi said, appearing beside him.

Jasper smiled at the fox-sized Xyri. "Nah, I'll only get in her way. I don't actually know what I'm doing yet."

Boo.

Jasper pet Breadcrumb while he searched his phone, trying to find news about the fire. It took only a minute to find live coverage.

Lycan was already there, flying in and out of the building on his silver board. Jasper smiled. How could Ren not be in love with him? He watched anxiously, waiting for Kaida to show up, but she didn't. Lycan was getting everyone out while firefighters tamed the flames.

"Kaida has been spotted nearby. We don't yet know why she hasn't come down to assist her partner," the reporter said as the footage shifted. Kaida stood on a rooftop in her bright red suit, snow drifting lazily around her. "But Lycan appears to have gotten everyone out safely."

Jasper was sure he'd never seen both heroes in one place without them working to fix the problem together. *Is she that afraid to talk to him after he said he loved her?* The answer was likely yes. Ren did *not* handle embarrassment well.

Jasper sighed then frowned. Breadcrumb was staring directly at Pozi, his fluffy tail swishing back and forth. *The cat can see him? Huh.*

7
A Very Merry Coming Out

Ren sat across from Jasper on her bedroom floor. Two weeks now, since he learned her secret. Two weeks of trying to teach him everything she knew about being Bonded.

"Pozi still hasn't told you what your second power is?" she asked as Breadcrumb rubbed against her side.

"Nope. I still don't get why it's such a big deal."

She sighed. "Lycan almost killed himself overdoing his second power. They're... different from the main one. I think it's smart to wait till you're used to everything else first." She was *not* about to go through that with Jasper.

"How long did Zig wait to tell you about your portals?"

She bit her lip.

"Well?"

"Uh... about a week? But that was different! He knew I'd listen to his rule of not using it right away!"

Jasper rolled his eyes and scooped Breadcrumb into his lap.

"Also it can be hard getting used to the five minute thing," she added.

"The what?"

Ren stared at him. "Once you trigger the second power you have around five minutes till you'll detransform. Every time. It takes a *lot* of energy to use it, from both human and Xyri. So you have to be *smart* about when and where you use the second power."

"Being smart is hard."

Ren smiled as she picked up her phone. Then she groaned. "I gotta go."

"Can I come this time?"

"Absolutely not." She stood and slipped her phone in her pocket. Then the suit came over her in a surge of power. She stretched as she climbed the stairs of her loft bed.

"Oh, come *on*, Ren. I've been Bonded for two weeks now! You haven't let me go out at all!"

She glared down at him. "If you're looking at me in the suit and calling me Ren, you're not allowed to go. I'm Kaida in the suit. *Only* Kaida. Not in the suit I'm Ren. You *have* to get this right! And you still haven't picked your name. Trust me, you don't pick one, the media will pick it for you." That's what happened to Fable.

Jasper sighed, shoulders slumping. "I'll get it down, promise."

"I'll be back after I fix whatever's happening in the park."

He grinned. "Look at you, going out and fixing the world. Your confidence as Kaida is mind blowing."

She snorted. "Thanks. Don't go anywhere!"

After lifting the skylight she climbed out, crossed the roof, then hopped onto one of the chairs against the brick wall. Her wings erupted from her back and she glided steadily, wondering if Lycan would be there.

They still hadn't talked and it was killing her. They'd technically seen each other twice these last two weeks. Once, where she got to the scene too late and he was already handling it, so... she let him handle it. Then another where she arrived first and he watched from a distance, waiting to see if she'd need help. When she didn't, he left without talking to her.

It wasn't that she didn't wanna talk about it. But she had no idea *what* to say after rejecting him. She was afraid maybe he didn't wanna talk to her. Like, ever again. The way they'd handled the last two problems made her worry they just... weren't partners anymore. She'd somehow ruined one of the best relationships she'd ever had. One she *needed.* One she was sure she couldn't live without.

Maybe we should focus on the task at hand? Zig offered.

Don't actually know what the task at hand is, she replied. *Reports just said people were acting strange in a certain area. Any ideas?*

Not yet.

She glimpsed Lycan in the air and her heart raced in a panic. He watched her, then slowed when they met each other's eyes. *Oh god.* He didn't smile at her like he normally would. She descended, landing on the street, and a moment later he landed beside her.

"Hi." The word came out as a squeak.

He frowned. "Do you know what that's about?"

"Not yet."

"Wanna handle it yourself?"

Her heart twisted. "No. We don't know what it is. We should go in together."

"Oh, yeah? You weren't feeling very *together* last time we talked, so I wasn't sure." The hurt in his voice was like a knife to her chest.

Her hands shook and she balled them into fists. "We should talk—"

"Oh, *now* you wanna talk?"

"— after we deal with this!" she finished with a hiss.

"Yeah. Fine." He turned away, kicking his board up and flying toward the park.

Kaida growled under her breath as she followed him, annoyed. He wasn't even gonna give her a chance to explain?

You could have explained two weeks ago, Zig said.

You're not helping!

Confusion hit her like a ton of bricks and her wings gave out. She yelped as she fell, hitting the ground hard. Lycan was in the grass beside her when she sat up. She was pleased to see it had affected him too.

"What the hell was that?" He blinked a few times, as if that would fix it.

"An illusion?" she suggested, looking for signs of Fable. But this didn't feel like Fable. This was... a whole party.

There were at least forty people caught up in the chaos, some of which were whistling while dancing in a circle, one hand on a hip, one in the air like... teapots. Some were singing while crawling on the ground. And then there was the giant golden throne in the middle of the park, with a giant person sitting on it, watching them from above.

"What is this? Glitter?" Lycan held a hand out as flecks of what she'd mistaken as snow drifted down around them. It was in fact glitter, shimmering in every color.

"Okay. I'm guessing the person on the throne is making this happen."

"Yes, *very* clever. Whatever would we do without you," Lycan mumbled.

Kaida glared at him. "Oh, you wanna deal with the giant hallucination maker all by yourself? Fine by *me!*"

She spun around then stopped. There was a giant cat the size of Godzilla stomping around the park. The people who weren't caught up in the singing, dancing, or crawling, had started screaming and running in a panic.

"This isn't real," she muttered.

"Neither is your dress, but I wasn't gonna question it."

Kaida blinked, looking down. "Uh. Huh. Zig, what is this?" She was wearing a dress now, but it still looked like her suit. Red and gold scales, poofing out around her waist.

It's not real, you're still you. Promise.

She sighed and looked back at Lycan. He had a top hat on now, and a giant bow tie around his neck. She couldn't hide her grin.

"This is Alice in Wonderland. The dress, your hat... giant cat behind us. It's an Alice in Wonderland illusion."

"Never seen that movie," Lycan muttered as he looked around. "Should I be worried?"

Her smile widened. "You know it's a *book*, too?"

He met her eyes, lips curving slightly. "I'll add it to my list."

The glitter was piling up around them on the ground.

"This doesn't seem harmful? And it doesn't feel like a distraction, not like Fable's illusions."

"So, what are we dealing with here?"

"Hold on, what are they singing?" Kaida took a careful step toward the teapot people, who now looked like *actual* teapots to her. Lycan followed.

"A very merry coming out! A very merry coming out!"

She smiled and looked back up at the giant throne person, who was watching them with a wicked grin.

"It's a coming out party... interesting."

"What's not interesting is that." Lycan nodded to the giant cat, still circling the park. People were still screaming over there.

"The cat is the radius?"

"Probably."

"Wanna herd the people beyond that point?"

"And you handle the real problem without me?"

She spun to face him. "That's not what I meant!"

"Course not. Cause you can't handle a problem. You'd rather *run away* from it."

She swallowed, eyes burning. It hurt because it was true. "Can we *please* focus on this problem, and talk about our problems after?"

"I don't know, can we?" His eyes were pleading.

"Herd the people out, Wolf Boy. Then meet me at the throne. We deal with this *together*."

She didn't wait for his response as she stalked off toward the throne. Her stupid Alice dress swished at her sides. *It's not real.* Neither was the throne. But the person sitting in it was very real. She just needed them to come back to her level...

Light danced on her fingertips as she considered their options. After a moment Lycan returned, the park now mostly clear of civilians.

"What now?"

Music started playing.

"Is that August Rain?"

"My name is Wonderland, actually." The person from the throne appeared in front of them, now normal human sized. "But I can see the confusion," they continued with a grin.

Kaida blinked as she took in their appearance. They were a little taller than Lycan, with short wild pink hair that curled at the top, but was shaved on the sides. Their mask looked like an infinity symbol around their eyes, pink on one side, gold on the other, stark against their deep tan skin. They wore a long pink coat over the suit, which looked like black pants and a white shirt, covered in splashes of color. And golden yellow gloves up to their forearms that matched the golden yellow boots they wore.

The most interesting part was the pageant sash across their chest that read **WONDERLAND** in all caps, with a small *they/them* beside it.

"Turn it off," Kaida said sternly.

"You can't turn this off," they said with a smirk. "But you're welcome to try."

She raised an eyebrow. "I'm not in the mood to deal with this right now, so if you could—"

"She's not in the mood for much," Lycan mumbled under his breath.

Wonderland grinned, stepping back. "Trouble in paradise?"

Kaida glared at Lycan before turning back to Wonderland. "If I have to fight you to get you to stop whatever this is, I'll do it."

"I'm sure you will. That might be fun," Wonderland replied.

Kaida held her hand to the side and a sword of light formed in her fist. As it solidified, rainbow glitter started sticking to it, making it even prettier in the light of the setting sun.

A silver sword appeared in Lycan's hand a moment later. Wonderland grinned wickedly as something formed in their hand.

What are they doing? she asked Zig as she stepped back.

She could make a weapon since her power was creating constructs out of light. But she couldn't *summon* one yet. Zig said at a certain point she'd be able to, every Bonded could, but only once the Bond was strong enough. It bothered her that after sixteen months she still couldn't do it.

Their Bond is strong.

Do you know who they're Bonded to?

I'd have to guess it's Tailsi.

This person is brand new, Zig. How are they summoning a weapon already?

Their weapon appeared to be a flail. The stick gripped in their hand was a shiny gold, while the chain and spiky ball were hot pink.

This is the first time you've seen them. It does not mean it's their first day Bonded. I'd guess they've been Bonded for at least a few months now.

She growled in annoyance as Wonderland swung the flail.

"Cute," Lycan said flatly. Then he raised his sword.

Both weapons clashed in the air, and it was clear Wonderland had little to no training even if they could summon their weapon already.

Lycan forced them back, one step, two, four. Wonderland's cocky smile vanished, replaced with worry as Lycan continued his assault. Kaida spun her blade, waiting, but Lycan was relentless.

"Got a lot of pent-up rage, huh?" Wonderland spat. "Is it cause you're fighting with the missus?"

Lycan growled.

"I'm not his missus," Kaida said with a sigh.

"Oh, *there's* the problem!" Wonderland laughed as they jumped back. "Maybe you guys need therapy. I will charge for it, though. Nothing is free!"

Kaida rolled her eyes as her sword melted into a rope and she whipped it toward Wonderland. They looked surprised as it circled around them. A wave of nausea hit her and she stumbled. Her ropes puffed away and Wonderland disappeared. In their place was another her and Lycan, their arms wrapped around each other, their mouths wrestling for dominance. She turned to Lycan, *her* Lycan, still beside her, wide eyed and blushing.

"That's not real... where did..." She had to force herself to stop staring at the fake Kaida and Lycan, who were making very intimate noises now. Wonderland was gone. With a sigh she looked at Lycan. He was staring at the ground, head hanging low, eyes hollow.

Kaida growled as she formed her sword again and slashed it through the illusion. The fake them disappeared into a puff of pink smoke.

The world came alive around them, music replaced with voices. The entire park had been taped off and police were on standby, holding back the crowds. They'd wanna know what happened. Lycan hadn't moved.

She sucked in a breath and walked toward a group of officers. They noticeably stiffened as she approached.

"Was anyone hurt?" she asked.

"None that we know of but—"

"It was all fake. An illusion or hallucination," she interrupted. "There's a new Bonded, called Wonderland and—"

"Did you deal with it?" one of them asked, his bright blue eyes boring into her.

"They're gone. Disappeared. If they return I will handle it." She didn't wait for a response as she went back to Lycan. He usually dealt with the cops for her. He was still as stone, staring at nothing.

"Ly, can we talk now?" she whispered.

He slowly looked up and nodded. "Where you wanna go?" he asked, lifting his foot, silver board appearing under it.

"Anywhere."

She stepped on and loosely wrapped her arms around his waist as they took off. There was no real reason for Kaida to ride on his board when she could fly herself. But they did that early on in their partnership, back when she'd been too afraid to use her wings, and even after, they kept doing it. She liked not having to be in control when flying. Maybe she shouldn't have done it this time, but she was desperate to fix things between them. Doing this normal thing they always did made her relax a *teeny* bit before they landed on a roof somewhere in Midtown.

She stepped off the board then grabbed his arm, pulling him around to face her. "I know you're mad at me and you have *every* right to be after how I—"

"Not mad, Kai." He met her eyes, sighing softly. "I expected you to reject me. I just... I didn't think telling you how I felt would cause me to lose you."

Kaida blinked. "Lose me? You didn't lose me. You'll never lose me."

Lycan frowned. "It feels like I did, considering..."

She blushed, shame taking over her. "I panicked, okay?" Her hands started shaking as she tried to explain. "We *can't* be together. You *know* that. So when you told me you love me... I just—" She closed her eyes. "My intrusive thoughts won. I was on the edge and my brain said jump! So lo hice y luego no supe qué decir después de eso porque pues ¿que se dice después de eso?"

"So, you didn't say anything?"

She opened her eyes with a sigh. "I was so afraid. That you'd wanna stop being friends. Stop being partners. And I think it was easier to not reach out, so you couldn't tell me that. I wanted to live in denial a little longer."

He tilted his head to the side and she smiled. Every time he did that he seemed more like a lost dog than a boy. The wolf ears in his hair didn't help.

"Kai, you're my best friend. I literally never wanna stop working with you."

Relief. Heart-pounding, blood-rushing, relief. "Really?"

"Yes, really." He smiled. "So, we're still friends?"

She let out a high-pitched sound and threw her arms around him. As he wrapped his arms around her she was reminded of the weird hallucination Wonderland had shown them. She was thankful Lycan couldn't see her blush as she pressed her face into his chest.

"I missed you," he whispered, chin resting on top of her head.

"Missed you too," she mumbled as she pulled back, trying to be calm. "I'm so sorry for how I reacted."

"It's okay. You don't owe me anything. I was being a jerk before. I'm sorry."

"No." She shook her head. "You're *not* just some guy on the street who hit on me, okay? You're one of my best friends. My partner. I *did* owe you more than that. You deserved way better and I'm so so sorry."

He pulled her back into his arms. "Fine, you're forgiven."

She smiled, trying to relax, but her heart continued racing as he held her. When she pulled back he stared down at her.

"Can I ask you a question?"

She nodded.

"If..." He licked his lips. "If those rules didn't exist, do you think, maybe..."

Ren swallowed, heart beating even faster somehow. "Um. I..." She took a deep breath. "I actually... sort of have feelings for someone else."

"Oh." He blinked, then nodded slowly. "Okay. Uh, how about if the rules didn't exist and this... other person didn't exist?"

She took a step back, her panic rising again. *Don't jump don't jump don't jump.* "Honestly? If there were no rules and no... other person..." She paused. *Okay maybe jump.*

Breathe, Ren.

She steadied herself, unable to lie to him. "Yes. I... I could see a situation in which we would..."

Lycan's yellow eyes widened.

"Does it make you feel better to know that? When we never ever can?"

"No. No I feel much worse actually." He smiled bitterly, shaking his head. "It's fine. I'm fine."

"I'm so sorry. I wish..." She couldn't finish that thought.

"Don't be. I just want you. As a friend I mean! I just want things to go back to normal."

"We can do that," she replied, ignoring the traitorous beat in her chest.

He seemed to hesitate. "Does it bother you? Knowing how I feel? Is it like, awkward?"

She shook her head. "No, I'm glad you told me actually. I want us to be able to tell each other things, to be honest. Especially when we can't about a lot of stuff. I feel..." She smiled. "Flattered. Like, actually extremely very *very* flattered. Cause you're perfect and I'd be the luckiest girl in the world if we were... if we *could*. But I *hate* hurting you. Like, I feel physical pain inside me knowing I hurt you. So if... if I do anything to make it worse, you know, if I—"

Lycan smiled and pulled her right back into his arms, gently hugging her. "You can't make it worse, promise."

She grinned up at him. "You and me?"

His smile brightened. "You and me."

8
Forty Percent

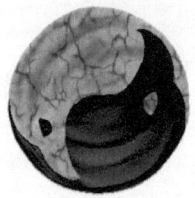

Jasper sat across from Ren on the fake grass in her rooftop garden, as the sun set in the distance. The fairy lights hanging on the brick walls got brighter as the sky darkened.

"Again," she muttered.

Jasper tried not to sigh from boredom.

The suit came over him in a blink. Ren was having him put it on and take it off over and over. The transformation needed to be intentional, which was the point of practicing. He needed to train his brain to make it an intentional action so he didn't accidentally panic transform in the middle of class or something. It made sense, but it wasn't exciting stuff.

"Can we do something else?" he asked sullenly as the suit disappeared again. Ren frowned at him over her bag of pretzels. He shivered.

"I know you wanna go out and do stuff, and I promise we will soon. But I really want you to get the small things down first. It'll make everything loads easier for you in the long run, okay. Learn from my mistakes."

He rolled his eyes. "Fine."

I agree this is boring, Pozi said as he tucked his wings into his side.

The Xyri looked annoyed. Probably didn't like the constant on and off of suiting up either. Jasper had learned a lot about the Xyri since Bonding. Like how they could phase through anything. But somehow Jasper couldn't phase through things in the suit, which was unfair. Some things from the Xyri did transfer to their human, though, like how in the suit he could understand and even speak in any language. Apparently the Xyri knew them all. He wondered if he could somehow use it to cheat in Spanish. But it only worked when he was *in* the suit.

"We should practice your smaller powers," Ren said after a moment.

"Small powers?"

"The sight and scent stuff?"

Jasper shrugged. "Those seem kinda useless for a fight."

You're useless, Pozi grumbled, offended.

He smiled. "How do we test them?"

Ren set her bag aside, pushed herself up then walked over to the two chairs against the brick wall. She climbed up on one and looked out over the edge. Jasper put the suit back on and followed, climbing on the second chair.

"Do your sight thing, tell me stuff you see that's far away."

"Uh, okay."

He blinked, then tapped sight. It was more mental, than physical, tapping into the specific powers. He just had to want it, and then his eyesight changed. Everything zoomed in, getting crisper. Even the colors seemed richer.

"Alright, I see a cat in an apartment window."

"Which apartment?"

He pointed. "That way, it's a light brick building. Looks about twenty floors maybe."

"Uh, Jasper?"

"Hm?"

"I don't see a building that tall."

He grinned. "Fucking cool."

"What's the cat look like?"

"Little black and white one. Very cute."

Ren giggled. "Okay, do the hearing one."

He blinked his vision back into focus then hopped off the chair. Ren sat beside him as he closed his eyes and tuned hearing.

"I can hear your dads."

"Yeah?" She sounded excited.

"They're trying to figure out what to make for dinner. Cas is humming. Arrow's complaining about a client." He smiled. "Breadcrumb is purring. Uh, I can hear music from the bar next door. People are singing. Sounds fun."

"This is cool!"

"Yeah, okay. It's cool." He could hear so much. One of Cas's tenants in the other side of the building just broke something. A bowl? They were cursing a lot. A dog was barking in another apartment.

See how useful this can be?

Yes, he admitted. *Very cool, Pozi.*

Pozi seemed pleased.

They continued practicing those two, but refrained from tapping into scent. Jasper had no desire to smell New York better than he already did. He wanted to practice speed and strength, but there wasn't much he could do with those on Ren's roof. She promised he could practice once she let him meet Lycan.

"Ren?"

She looked up. "Yeah?"

"Why exactly aren't you and Lycan allowed to be together? You never really explained that."

She sighed and laid on her back, staring up at the sky.

"Not gonna tell me?"

"It's cause when Zig and Zeli's Bonded humans get together it doesn't always end well."

"End well how?"

"On the low end, they stop being partners. On the high end... they've killed each other and stuff."

"No fucking way. Seriously?"

She closed her eyes.

"How many of them? Like, what's the percentage?"

"Forty percent."

"Forty percent of their Bonded killed each other?"

She released a breath and looked up at him. "Forty percent ended badly, one way or another."

"Okay, wait. How many of them fell in love though? That can't be all of them."

"Seventy percent."

He scratched his head. "I'm bad at math, but only seventy fell in love and only forty ended badly? There's clearly some not bad ones in there."

She sat up slowly. "Losing Lycan is not worth the risk."

Because you do love him, don't you? Jasper kept the thought to himself. "So, you're scared to lose him and that's why you're so set on the never ever rule?"

"Zig and Zeli made it very clear they didn't want us getting romantically involved. It's not a hard rule to follow." She made a face that made him think maybe it was very hard and she just couldn't admit it. "Especially when you know how bad it could go."

"There's literally no universe in which you or Lycan would go insane and kill each other. Even if you dated and it didn't work out. Like, look at us!"

"Doesn't matter."

"Ren—"

"Their last Bonded were *married*," Ren interrupted. "For like years. And they killed each other in the war."

That shut him up. He sat back, thinking on it.

That's not the whole story, Pozi said.

So what is the whole story?

Pozi didn't answer. Jasper sighed.

"Why do they always make their humans work together then, if it can end so badly?"

Ren smiled slightly. "They're codependent."

"Like us?"

"If I had forever, I'd spend it with you."

Jasper smiled. "Same."

He wanted to press her further about Lycan, but decided to drop it and laid down on his back beside her. It was freezing now that he wasn't in the suit anymore, but Ren seemed fine, so he didn't complain.

They didn't have the rule before, Pozi mumbled.

What do you mean?

This rule about them not being allowed to be together romantically. This is new. When last we Bonded, Kirzigith and Azazelith did not put such limitations on their humans.

Jasper cracked his knuckles. *So what changed?*

Everything. You ever wonder why they've Bonded literal children?

No.

Pozi laughed. *You don't question things enough, kid. No Xyri has ever Bonded a human under the age of twenty-four. Until Kirzigith chose her.*

Really? He glanced at Ren. She was back to munching on her pretzels.

Kirzigith didn't just break the contract. He broke every rule and routine he has ever followed. He and Azazelith went into this looking for different, new. They not only chose children, but children who were very different than someone they'd normally choose.

Jasper thought on that for a moment. *What about me? Am I different for you?*

Only in age.

Why'd you Bond me, if I'm so young?

I'm unoriginal.

Jasper smiled. "I have a question."

Ren turned to look at him.

"Why aren't there any heroes, or even villains anywhere else? Like, why are we only in New York? Xyri used to be all over the world in the old days. At least, I think they did? I'll admit I don't pay enough attention in history, but that's how it's portrayed in the comics."

"Does Pozi tell you nothing?" Ren asked as she sat up again.

"Not really. He's more a learn as you go type."

Ren rolled her eyes. "They're all here cause of Zig and me."

"What do you mean?"

"They weren't supposed to Bond, right? But Zig Bonded me. And Zeli Bonded Lycan. So a *lot* of Xyri came here to watch, to see what we'd do, how things would play out. Zig says there just happens to be a high concentration of Xyri here now, and so a lot of the new Bonded are here. But, theoretically there should be more everywhere, one day."

Jasper nodded. "Why weren't they supposed to Bond? I still don't understand why they stopped in the first place."

Ren sighed. "They won't tell us. Something *very bad* happened at the end of the war, which caused them to leave the humans. Zig says they broke contract because of a missing immortal man. I don't know much."

"Immortal?"

"Yeah."

"Huh." He sat up with a sigh.

He'd have to go home soon. Sometimes he was allowed to stay at Ren's on school nights, but not always. If Dad was in a mood he wouldn't even bother asking.

"Now what?" Ren mumbled.

"I should go."

She frowned. "You could stay."

"Nah, not tonight. But I'm down to stay over the weekend."

"Okay. We can do more stuff after school?"

"Sounds good." He stood, stretching.

"Do not jump off the roof," Ren said as she got up.

"Why not?"

She laughed. "My dads know you're here? If they don't see you leave that'll be weird."

"Could say I went down the fire escape?" Ren gave him a flat stare and he laughed. "Right. Never mind."

They made their way down to the kitchen where her dads were laughing as they made dinner.

"What are you kids up to?" Cas asked, his smile bright.

"Heading out," Jasper muttered.

Arrow frowned. "Not staying for dinner?"

He sighed, wishing he could. Ren's dad wasn't just a magician in the bakery, everything he made was awesome. But Jasper's mom was a fine cook, too. She just worked a lot, so he liked staying here for dinner, so she wouldn't feel like she had to cook for him after feeding people at the diner all day.

"Nope."

Ren made a pouty face at him. "Saddest dinner."

"See you tomorrow," he said with a wave.

"You'll be here before school?" Ren asked, as if he wasn't always there to walk her to school every single morning. He was never late, not after...

"Always," he said.

When do you think you're actually gonna do fun hero things? Cause I didn't Bond you so we could sit on our asses every day, Pozi said as Jasper made his way down Ren's annoying stairs.

If it wasn't Ren I would have already started. And probably gotten myself killed. She's right to hold me back, even if it's super annoying.

The Xyri groaned and Jasper smiled.

You know she's right, too. I'm impulsive and I think maybe you are too? We should listen to her for now.

She reminds me of Azazelith.

Ren does?

Yes, Pozi answered. *And that's not a compliment!*

Jasper shook his head.

Ren sent a text to Lycan during dinner asking if he wanted to patrol later. They'd seen each other a few times since they made up, but not once had he initiated it. He used to text all the time, but now he seemed to be leaving it up to her, which was annoying. She knew he was still worried about things between them and that was *also* annoying, since she told him it was fine. He texted back a bit later.

|Starface|
I'm down. When you wanna meet?

|Bunhead|
Later I'm busyy

|Starface|
Doing what?

|Bunhead|
Dishes.

Give me like an
hour.

|Starface|
That's a lot of dishes.

See you in an hour.

She finished the dishes and collected her basket of clean laundry
Dad left on the dryer. She was tempted to just leave it, but she had the
time, so she sat on her closet floor and started putting the clothes
away. Her phone buzzed with a text from Ocean, distracting her.

|Ocean|
Did you ever work things
out with your friend?

|Ren|
I did!

|Ocean|
Are you still friends? It
didn't get weird??

|Ren|
It didn't.

|Ocean|
And how do you feel
about it? Knowing they
love you?

|Ren|
I don't know. I like that he was
honest. And I think we're good
after talking it out. It feels
good.

Why?

|Ocean|
No reason! Glad it
worked out!!

Once she was done with laundry she suited up and left through the skylight. Lycan was already waiting for her when she landed on their roof on Spruce Street. He grinned as she walked over.

"So," he began. "I was thinking we could start with—"

"You being weird?" she interrupted.

"What... did I do?"

"You haven't texted me since we made up."

His head tilted in confusion. "I literally texted you an hour ago."

Kaida rolled her eyes. "I meant texting me *first*." Hearing herself say it made her feel silly, but she couldn't back down. "You never text to ask about patrolling or just hanging out, or just to talk! Not since..."

He swallowed. "Right. I guess I'm just afraid, if I do you'll think—"

"That you're my best friend and my partner and you're *allowed* to talk to me? Whenever. *Always*. We agreed nothing changes after your confession. So don't change this. *Please.*"

He nodded. "I'm sorry." A smile came over his face. "Didn't realize it would bother you so much."

She blushed, annoyed by his grin. "Come on, let's patrol. What did you wanna start with?"

"Oh, right. So." He paused, his suit splitting at his hip as he slid his hand in to pull his phone out.

She smiled at the big silver star on the back of the phone. It was still so neat that their Xyri could camouflage their phone cases to match their suits. It wasn't something they knew they could do before Bonding them.

Everything is new with you, Ren, Zig said.

Good new?

So far.

Lycan leaned closer to show her his phone. "So, this happened like an hour ago. People are *saying* it's a new Bonded. No footage, but multiple people say they saw a girl in a suit destroy the statue in Columbus Circle. Figured we should take a look."

"Sounds good."

His board appeared and he gestured for her to get on. She hesitated, then wrapped her arms around him with a sigh.

When they arrived she noted the tall statue that usually resided there was in fact gone.

"Be alert," she whispered as she hopped off his board and stalked toward the pile of rubble in the center.

"What kind of Bonded could destroy a statue so easily?" Lycan asked. "They say she just touched it and it crumbled."

Crumbled how? Zig asked.

Dunno. Only a few people saw it. They aren't here anymore, Kaida replied. The surrounding area was eerily empty now.

"Zig is worried," she said as Lycan knelt by the rubble.

"Zeli is too." He sighed and stood up. "Says it could be a handful of Xyri, but she doesn't seem excited by any of the prospects."

Rightfully so.

Kaida groaned. "Can't we have a single moment of peace?"

Lycan gave her a sad smile. "It was just a statue. Not a person, so... we can call that a win? No need to worry yet, right?"

She nodded, but her worry remained. It always did.

9
Not-Boyfriend Boy Friend

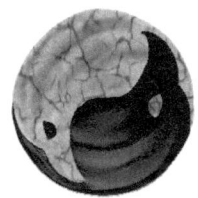

Jasper leaned against the wall inside the bakery. He always loved the loud colors inside the small space. The cabinets and counters made a rainbow across the shop, and there were tiny pride flags of different varieties hung on the walls. Even the door leading into the back was painted with a rainbow. And the whole place smelled *divine*.

He grinned as Marigold eyed him suspiciously from behind the counter. Jasper never could tell if Ren's cousin actually disliked him or not. She definitely disliked his constant theft from the bakery, but Ren's dad had given him permission to take stuff, so he did. Mari didn't like it. She was on track to become assistant manager to her uncle, and much like Ren, she liked following the rules. Which meant telling Jasper off for stealing every time he stepped inside. It amused him, how similar she and Ren were, when the two weren't *actually* related.

He'd had a crush on her for a while, after he and Ren broke up. Marigold had such a delicate face, pale and heart shaped, with pink hair that fell to her shoulders. But she was five years older than him, and he wasn't delusional.

"Do you have to be here?" she asked after a moment. "You'll scare away real customers."

"Waiting for Ren. She got a phone call from someone who isn't me. Super suspicious."

Mari rolled her eyes but didn't argue.

Jasper glanced out the window to where Ren was talking on the phone. His curiosity was killing him. He'd spent so long worrying about her. Every time she was late, or missed something, or lied. Now he knew the truth. She was a superhero. *And so am I.*

Are you? Pozi asked. *I have yet to see any superheroing from you. I've been bored, kid.*

Ren won't let me.

If it was anyone but Ren, he wouldn't listen. But she was his best friend, and for sure smarter than him. She kept stressing how important it was that no one find out who they really are. Even Pozi said that was important. He hated to admit they were right to worry. It wasn't that he couldn't keep a secret. Jasper wouldn't tell a soul. But he would make a mistake. Like calling Ren by the wrong name, or saying something he shouldn't. Accidents could and probably would happen.

So he gladly let her try and beat the rules into his head thoroughly before letting him loose on the world. But he was so excited to actually *do it*. He'd been tweaking his suit design the last few days, and he was working on his name. And Jasper knew exactly what he wanted to do for his entrance into the world of heroes. He promised Ren he'd wait, but if Fable showed up somewhere, Jasper *was* going for him.

The door opened and Ivy Jones walked in. She was a tall girl who worked across the street at Deviant Ink, the tattoo shop Ren's dad Arrow owned. Brown skin, black hair with a fade on the side, and those thin gold wired glasses... Ivy was stunning. Her honey eyes lit up when she saw Marigold behind the counter.

"Hey, Mari!" She smiled brightly, as if surprised to find her there.

"Hey, Ives. Donut this time?"

"Sure," Ivy replied. "Did you redo your hair?"

"Yeah, did it last night."

"Looks great. The pink really suits you, makes your eyes pop."

Mari smiled. "Thanks."

Jasper leaned back into the wall, wondering how many times Ivy would have to flirt with Marigold before she understood what was happening.

"Is that a new bracelet?"

Mari looked down then held her hand out toward Ivy. "Yeah! My mom got it for me."

"So cute." Ivy reached out and touched the little flower charm on it, not so subtly brushing her fingers against Mari's wrist before pulling back.

Jasper couldn't hide his smile as Mari handed Ivy a small bag and she left.

"You know Ivy's flirting with you, right?" he said as he pushed himself off the wall.

Marigold stared at him. "What?"

He walked behind the counter to grab himself a donut. "Tell me you at least know she's very gay?"

Mari frowned. "I know she likes girls but I don't really know if—"

"*Very gay*. And she's really into you."

She looked so confused. "No she isn't."

Jasper almost choked on the donut as he laughed. He swallowed the bite then smiled. "How often does she bring you coffee in the mornings?" He witnessed this many times while waiting for Ren before school.

"Almost every day I work."

"And, the days she doesn't see you in the morning, she's here in the afternoon..."

"Cause the bakery is *good*. We're the best in the West Village!"

Jasper took another bite of his chocolate strawberry donut.

"She's not into me," Mari continued.

Before Jasper could respond the door opened again. He turned, expecting Ren, but it was Ivy, back with a blush in her cheeks. Jasper grabbed a second donut as he watched them.

"Hey, totally forgot but... you busy tomorrow? Was thinking we could go to the movies, if you're free?"

Marigold shot a glance at Jasper, her blue eyes wide, before she forced a smile back at Ivy. "Sure. Just text me."

"Cool, see ya tomorrow." Ivy bit her lip as she left again.

Jasper burst into laughter the second the door closed. "You just said yes to a date with a lesbian!"

"It's not a date. Movie isn't a date... is it?"

"Might be."

Ren finally came inside and he released a breath.

"Finally, who the hell were you—"

"You guys have to come!" Marigold interrupted.

Ren blinked, looking between her and Jasper. "Come where?"

"Ivy invited me to the movies and your stupid little friend said it's a date. But it's not a date if I bring my cousin and her stupid little friend. *Please* come?"

"Uh... to the movies? On your date?" Ren asked, confused.

"Not a date! I don't think? Not if you come!" Mari was flushed, eyes wide as she stared at Ren.

"You could just ask Ivy if it's—"

"Absolutely not."

Jasper chuckled.

"Okay, we'll go." Ren said. "Text me details, kay?"

"Thank you!"

With that Ren grabbed Jasper's arm and dragged him through the back door.

"We're not late for anything, calm down," he mumbled as she pulled him straight through her dad's office and out through the door that led to her endless staircase.

"I know, just stressed. Sooner we do our homework the sooner—"

"You get to go see Lycan?"

She turned a sharp glare on him. "You can't just say shit like that!"

He winced as they turned up the next staircase. "Sorry! Notice you didn't deny that though."

"I told you I am *not* in love with him! But we finally made up and things are normal and I'm just... happy. About that."

"Uh huh. When am I allowed to do things with you guys? Do I ever get to meet him?"

She smiled. "Soon. I have a plan."

"Course you do. How soon we talking?"

"By end of next week, maybe? Only if you can stop saying names you *shouldn't* be saying!"

"What am I meant to call your not-boyfriend boy friend?"

She tilted her head a little as they turned the corner up the next staircase. "Ly?"

Jasper laughed. "That's barely different. If you don't want me to get confused we gotta have something else." He grinned. "What about The Wolf?"

Ren shook her head. "Come on."

She didn't stop till they were in her room. He was excited that going up all those stairs didn't tire him as much as it used to.

You're welcome.

He grinned, looking around. He had no idea where Pozi was. He'd been with him that morning, but didn't follow him to school. It was still weird, hearing him but not seeing him.

Ren went straight to work, unpacking her bag at her desk.

"Ren, who the fuck called you? Was it wolf boy?"

She glared. "No, it was Ocean."

"Ah. What did little miss France want?"

Ren sighed as she opened a notebook. "Said she had a bad day, just wanted to chat. We're gonna do proper video call this weekend."

"Okay, back to wolf boy... he forgave you for the roof self-yeeting and everything's just fine now?"

Ren let out a breath. "Yes."

"Not awkward at all?"

"Nope."

"Uh huh. You realize you're literally vibrating with excitement at seeing him tonight. Like, Ren. I'm not stupid. *You're* stupid if you don't know you like him."

She laughed. "I don't, not like that. Besides, you've seen me with Bellamy."

Jasper grinned. "You really like Bell more?"

"Yes."

"Prove it."

Ren raised an eyebrow at him. "How? And don't say to tell him cause I won't!"

"Invite him to the movies. It's a group thing with your cousin, it won't be weird. Not even a date. Just friends. Going to the movies."

Her eyes hardened. "You think I won't do it?"

He shrugged, trying not to smile.

"I'll do it. Tomorrow at school. I'll invite him." She blushed as she said it.

Jasper wasn't entirely sure she would, but he didn't doubt her affection for Bellamy. He just doubted her insistence on having no feelings for Lycan, too. Putting his attractiveness aside, she spent over a year secretly fighting crime with the guy and *he* fell in love with *her*. And admitted it even though it's against their rules. Jasper was so invested in the drama of it all. Maybe when he finally got to see them together in person he'd really know if Ren was lying to herself or not.

The next day Ren felt sick every time she saw Bellamy. Her stomach twisting into knots, heart racing. She chickened out over and over until she finally cornered him at the start of their world history class.

"Hey, Bellamy?"

He turned. "Hey, Ren. What's up?"

He was so gorgeous, she forgot to breathe. With those sharp cheekbones, square jaw, and tousled blonde hair that was shorter on the sides and had a slight curl to it. His bright green eyes held her in place.

"I was... I was wondering if you maybe wanted to go to the movies with me and Jasper tonight?" She started talking faster. "My cousin invited us cause she's maybe agreed to a date with a friend and she freaked out and so she's turning it into a group thing and so I figured I'd invite more friends. Like you. Cause you're my friend and uh. Yeah. So... movies tonight?" She was gonna throw up.

"You want *me* to go to the movies with you?" he asked slowly.

"Yes." Her hands were shaking and it took all her self control not to cradle her stomach, feeling more and more nauseous as he stared at her.

Bellamy's face lit up with a smile, accentuating his perfect cupid's bow. "I'd love to."

"Really?" She was gonna *super* throw up.

"Yeah, what time?"

"Uh, movie is at eight, at Alamo Drafthouse in Manhattan. You know where that is?"

"Yeah, I can meet you there. Eight?"

Ren nodded, overly aware of the sweat gathering under her bra. "Yeah eight. See ya then." *And also right now cause class just started.*

She spun away from him and rushed to the back corner to sit beside Jasper who was watching her with wide eyes.

"You did it?" he whispered.

"Gonna vomit," she hissed, putting her face down on the desk.

Jasper rubbed her back, but didn't say anything. She did it. She actually asked Bellamy to the movies. As a group hang with her cousin and *not* a date. Not her ideal asking-Bellamy-out situation, but it was *something*.

10
Lack of Actions

Bellamy scooped up the stack of Valkyrie packages outside their door, dropped them in the hall with his bag, then went looking for Mom. He knocked on the office door before pushing it open. She clearly wasn't inside. The room was small, with bookshelves covering every wall, and her desk in the middle of the room. He glanced out the large window to be sure she wasn't on the balcony before turning to leave, but a stack of books on her desk caught his eye. His heart raced as he got closer. The one on top was called *A World Without Xyri*. He picked it up, checking the one under. *Xyri Bonds: Life and Death*. He pushed that one aside. *Secrets of War*. And under that was *The Complete Catalog of Xyri and Their Powers*.

What's wrong? Zeli asked.

Uh. He swallowed. *My mom has books about Xyri on her desk.*

Zeli didn't respond, but a moment later she walked through the wall and came to sit beside him. He held one of the books down in front of her.

Could be a coincidence? You've not done or said something stupid, have you?

"No. I don't think so? I've been careful, Zel. There's no way she knows about me. But... why would she have these?"

Maybe it's to do with her work at the museum. Or she's just curious, like everyone else these days. We stayed away for two centuries. So much information about us was lost in that time. It's surprising how little your generation knows.

He opened one of the books, flipping through it, taking in that old book smell. "Do we know about all of you? Like this catalog of powers, does it have every Xyri in it?"

Zeli laughed. *No. I say I'm surprised by how little people remember, but there was so much they never knew. And what was lost was intentional. We didn't want you remembering.*

Bellamy frowned at that.

I Bonded nearly every other century, but I guarantee I am not in that book, she continued.

"Uh. But... you're in the comics, right?"

I am not. My human was. She sounded so annoyed by that.

He smiled. "Stardust, right? She was your last..." He trailed off. She never liked talking about her. "What was that you said about... not wanting us to remember? Remember what?"

Zeli stared up at him, her silver tipped tail twitching.

"Not gonna answer me?"

She sighed. *There is a reason so much of the war didn't make it into your history books. You think I am going to undo all of that hard work to satisfy the curiosity of a seventeen year old boy?*

"I guess not." He looked back at the catalog. There were no real pictures, just drawings. He wondered if any of the currently Bonded Xyri were in it.

"Did Xyri ever show themselves to people they weren't Bonded to?"

It is extremely rare for us to do so, but it could happen.

How accurate could the drawings be? Did they just guess? Did they have the Bonded describe their Xyri? Or did some of them actually sit for the drawings? There really was so much they didn't know.

He picked up Secrets of War and started flipping through it, curious.

"We knew why we were fighting. The Bonded had too much power, too much control. We had to stand up against them. It all made sense at the time.

No one told us why we stopped fighting. The war was won, they said. The Bonded disappeared. Everyone with powers just took off. Most of them were never seen again. And neither were the Xyri.

They say we won the war. But it never felt like a victory. 90 million people died by the end. Was it worth the cost? I can't say that it was."

Bellamy knew the death toll of the war, but seeing it in a firsthand account like that still shocked him. He flipped a few more pages, realizing this entire book was made up of different perspectives of the war. He saw the name Stardust and paused to read.

"I saw Stardust fall. Our leader in the field, the one we looked to for hope, for courage. She tangled with Lifelight in the air, her former partner. They fought for only a moment. She was dead before she hit the ground.

Somehow, Lifelight was dead too. In that moment it was like the entire world held its breath. We were no longer enemies, but mourners, united in grief.

How were we to continue after that? It felt like we lost the point of what brought us to fight in the first place. Yes, the Bonded had power over those without, but there were better ways to handle it. We didn't need to fight. We didn't need to die for it."

His throat went dry as he read the words. He knew Lifelight and Stardust killed each other in the war, but this didn't explain *why*. And Zeli would never say. But they'd been partners before. What could have gone so wrong to cause that? He couldn't imagine *ever* turning on Kaida like that. Not even a war could come between them.

He heard the front door open then close and he panicked, tossing the book back on her desk. He tiptoed out of the office and peeked around the corner. Mom went straight to her room, so he sprinted down his hall to his room and closed the door behind him, heart racing.

You're still worried. You think she suspects?

No. No, there's no way. I just feel... panicky. Like I'll definitely say something dumb if she sees me now. Need to go calm down.

Fair enough.

Ren stood outside the theater with Marigold and Ivy, both of whom looked awkward. Ren groaned as she received a text from Jasper.

|Jasper|
Can't come. Was gonna sneak out but dads super bad tonight I can't I can't so so so so sorry

|Ren|
Should I come over??

Sometimes Jasper's dad would rein in his rage if Ren was around. He still thought she was Jasper's girlfriend, and tended to put on a good face for her. If he was already in a temper though, Jasper wouldn't let her come by. But she didn't know how else to help. Her hands shook as she waited for him to respond. *I have powers. There's a way I could help.*

Do you want to do that? Zig asked softly.

I want to protect him. That's why you chose me. To protect people.

Help them. What good am I if I can't help the person I love the most?

I won't forbid you, Zig said. But I worry what such actions might do to you.

I worry what my lack of actions will do to Jasper.

|Jasper|
It's fine Renny promise
see the movie have funn
text me when it's ovr?

|Ren|
Are you sure? I can be
there in 10!

|Jasper|
Please don't. Just see
the movie. See you
tomorrow love you.

|Ren|
Love you more

She shoved the phone in her pocket and looked up at Mari and Ivy, both of whom were staring at her.

"Jasper can't come."

"What about the other friend?" Mari asked.

Ren sighed. "I don't have his number. He said he'd come but... he probably just forgot." Or he found something better to do. She could message him online but... she was too worried about Jasper to even care. "We can just go in. It's fine."

They nodded and Ren followed them inside. She was sure Jasper was right, that Ivy liked Marigold and this was meant to be a date of sorts. It wasn't so awkward if a group showed up, but now she was just Mari's younger cousin, third wheeling. She wanted so badly to leave, fly straight to Jasper's house and... she sighed as they settled in their seats, Mari sitting between her and Ivy.

She didn't take in any of the movie, spending the time talking to Zig as she sent him to go check on Jasper. He reported nothing terrible. Jasper's dad was drunk and angry, but he wasn't currently taking it out on Jasper at least.

Ren still couldn't relax, and was surprised when the movie ended and Mari nudged her for them to leave. She had a thought as they walked out, so when their car arrived she let Mari and Ivy get in, then stepped back.

"I'm going the other way," she said, which wasn't true. "I'll get a different ride. No its fine, you guys go!" She shut the door on them before Marigold could argue. At least that way the two of them had some time together to maybe figure out if they'd been on a date or not.

She pulled her phone out and texted Jasper again as she started walking.

> |Ren|
> You okay?? Movie done. I can come over!!!

She stared at the phone as she moved, waiting for him to respond. He should still be awake, but he didn't text back. Her anxiety grew with every step and she texted again.

> |Ren|
> Jasper??? Text me back or I'm coming overrrr

Her boots splashed in a puddle as she walked, her phone gripped in an iron fist.

Ren?

She started typing another text, ignoring Zig.

Ren!

She was yanked to the side, her phone flying out of her hands as someone pulled her and shoved her against a wall. She was so shocked she didn't react as the man pushed a cold sharp knife against her throat. Her Xyrial burned against her chest.

Transform now, Zig hissed.

Can't, he'll see.

"Do it!" the man spat.

What had he told her to do? Her mind was blank, heart pounding. The Xyrial grew hotter.

"What?"

"Give me your bag, bitch." The man's breath was pungent against her cheek.

She winced as she awkwardly pulled the bag off her shoulder and handed it to him. The man threw it behind him and pressed the knife harder against her neck. She tried not to gag.

"Pretty little thing, aren't ya?"

Ren, do it now! Zig was frantic, mirroring her own terror.

It held in her place. She couldn't move. Couldn't scream. Couldn't change. The man grabbed her arm and pulled it up, pinning it above her head.

Zig was screaming. This finally forced her to find her voice. A sound burst out of her, echoing in the alley. The man's hand collided with her face and she snapped her mouth shut in surprise.

Ren? Ren please!

11
Always Both

Lycan moved fast as a scream pierced the night. He fell to the ground behind the burly man who was pinning the girl to the bricks. Lycan saw her face and his heart lurched. *Ren.* Rage erupted in his chest as he stretched out his hand. Something burned within, something new and different as a black and silver whip appeared in his hand. He didn't stop to question it as he flicked his wrist. The end of the whip wrapped around the man's arm and Lycan pulled. The man's entire body flew back, slamming into the opposite wall with a thud.

Ren stared at Lycan with terrified eyes. He turned away, forming a cage of silver around the man, who was now slumped, unconscious, on the ground.

Bellamy's rage thrummed through him as he faced the man. A cage wasn't good enough. The man didn't deserve to *breathe.*

Bellamy, Zeli whispered. *He's contained. Check on your friend.*

He growled under his breath as he turned around. Ren was still against the wall, her eyes locked on the man. Her neck was bleeding, her face red, and the top of her sweater was torn. Lycan approached her slowly, desperately shoving his rage down.

"Are you okay?"

Her eyes snapped up but she didn't speak.

"Hey." He gently placed a hand on her shoulder. "What's your name?"

She blinked a few times. "Ren Rivers."

"You're okay, Ren Rivers. Yeah? You're okay."

Her brown eyes were still scared. "I..."

"Say it. You're okay. Come on, say it back to me," he whispered.

She held his gaze. "I'm okay."

"Again."

"I'm okay."

"Again."

She inhaled sharply. "I'm okay."

"You are."

She let out a slow breath and leaned forward, pressing her face into his chest. He put his arms around her without thinking. This was Ren. *His Ren.* It was strange to realize he'd never hugged her as Bellamy. He held her tightly now as Lycan, not wanting to let go. She stayed there a moment, breathing deeply against him, before pulling away.

"Thank you. That was... excellent timing."

He grinned down at her. "I try my best."

"Your best is perfect. Thank you."

"You're welcome. Are you..." He paused, eyes lingering on her neck. "Here, let me just..." He gently rubbed his thumb against the cut, wiping off the blood.

Ren stilled, her eyes staring into his.

"Breathe, you're okay, remember?"

"Right." She laughed nervously. "I'm okay."

His eyes moved down to her torn sweater, and how much was showing under her collarbone, the tan skin red and irritated.

"Can you close your eyes for a second?"

"My..." She frowned.

"Please?"

She sighed and closed her eyes. He watched her carefully as he pulled the suit back across his torso, just enough to pull off his jacket. The suit recovered him in seconds.

"Okay, here."

Her eyes opened and her frown deepened. "What?"

"Put this on."

"Where did this come from?"

"My body." He laughed. "It's mine. Put it on, *please*?"

She seemed so confused as she slowly slid her arms into his jacket, shaking her head slightly as she zipped it up. He let out a breath as she looked up at him with a raised eyebrow. "Better?"

He smiled and slid his hands under her hair, pulling it back out. "Better. Can I take you home now?"

"Um."

"How do you feel about flying?"

Ren stared at him, looking even more confused. She shook her head. "Can we walk? I don't... like heights."

"Of course. Give me just a moment, alright?"

Ren nodded. He gently squeezed her shoulder, before turning away.

The second his eyes landed on the man the fire in his chest *burned.* *Calm, Bellamy.*

Ren stood frozen as Lycan pulled out his phone to call the cops to collect the man in the silver cage. She looked down at the blue jacket. Why on *earth* did he give it to her? *He's never done something like that before, has he?*

She sighed and forced herself to move, retrieving her bag and her phone. Her hands shook as she opened a text from Jasper, careful of the newly cracked screen.

|Jasper|
I'm fine Renegade.
How was the movie?

She let out a shaky breath, unable to respond. Lycan approached her, putting a gentle hand on her back.

"We can go now, if you're ready. Where do you live?"

"Do you know Over The Grainbow Bakery in West Village?"

Lycan grinned. "Yeah."

"Take me there."

He kept his hand on her back as they walked, seeming extra protective. Did she look that helpless? *I acted that helpless.* She tried to remember if Lycan was like this with other people they saved, and she just hadn't noticed. But she couldn't deny she felt better at his warm touch.

"I'm still shaking," she whispered, holding a hand out in front of her.

"That's a fairly normal reaction," Lycan replied.

Not for me. She felt stupid. She was a goddamn superhero, but she couldn't even stop some guy from taking her bag? Why had she been so afraid?

You were Ren, Zig said softly. *You insist on pretending Ren and Kaida are different people. But you are both. Always both.*

"How'd you get to me so fast?" Ren asked, trying to distract herself. "Was that a coincidence?"

He glanced down at her. "I was nearby. You hear a girl scream like that, you don't think, you just run."

She smiled. "What was that thing you used, to pull the guy away?"

Ren had never seen Lycan use something like that before. All his constructs were pure silver, but that thing had been black and silver.

He grinned, looking away from her as they walked. "So, all Bonded can do certain things. Summoning a special weapon is one of them, only... you can't do it right away. Takes time for the Bond to strengthen. You need to really be in sync with your Xyri. That was the first time I ever summoned it."

Ren blinked. *How's he summoning his weapon before me?*
He saved you with it, maybe focus on that part?

Right. Her heart raced as she looked back up at him. "First time you summon your fancy weapon, and it's for me."

He met her eyes. "Guess you're special."

"No, I'm not. But I'm still really glad you were there. I... thanks."

"You've now thanked me three times," Lycan noted.

"The magic number. No more."

He laughed as they turned a corner. She only now realized how far away from home she was.

"So, why were you out by yourself?"

Ren sighed. "Cause I'm stupid. I was supposed to take a car home. And I did not do that."

"Why not?"

"Got distracted."

Lycan nodded, but didn't press. She shoved her hands in her pockets... *his pockets*. Her heart raced a little as it dawned on her that she was wearing his jacket. It smelled nice. Clean. And it was soft. She never expected to meet him as herself. But she never should have been in a position to *need to*.

"How are you feeling?" he asked after a few minutes of silence.

"I'm fine."

"You're sure?"

"*Yes.*" She stared up at him, frowning.

He was being *so* weird. Lycan cared about the people he helped, but giving her his jacket? Keeping his hand on her back as they walked, asking if she was okay when she clearly was... he never went to these lengths. *He does not know I'm Kaida.* The thought terrified her. But he *couldn't* know.

"You know I could probably find my way home from here," she mumbled, watching him closely.

He looked down at her with narrowed eyes. "What kind of hero would I be if I didn't make sure you got home safe?"

She smiled without meaning to. "Are you always this thorough with people you save?"

"Of course."

Liar. But she couldn't deny she liked it.

After a while she finally saw the bakery and some relief washed over her. Jasper was okay. And she was home.

"So, you live inside a bakery. Very interesting."

Ren laughed. "I live above it. This is my dad's bakery."

"Ah."

"If it wasn't closed I'd totally give you some free cookies or something. You could come back tomorrow!"

Lycan smiled down at her, awfully close. "You don't owe me anything, Ren Rivers. Your safety is all I need, and you're safe now."

Ren couldn't stop herself from hugging him again. Her arms were already around him when she realized how awkward it might be. She was Ren, not Kaida. But she needed the comfort his embrace provided. He hugged her back all the same.

"You look like you're gonna say thanks again, and as we determined, you've done that enough already."

"Gracias."

He tilted his head a little. "Funny."

She gave him a smile then walked to the side of the building and unlocked the door, glad to see her hands stopped shaking.

One step at a time she slowly got herself under control. Her dads did *not* need to know what happened. When she made it up she turned the corner to find both her dads in the kitchen, wearing matching aprons and covered in flour. She smiled as she got closer to see they were baking cookies.

"Hey, how was your mov—" Dad stopped talking when he saw her. "What happened?"

She blinked, confused, as both of them rushed toward her. Dad gently lifted her chin to get a better look at her face. *Oh, right.* That man had hit her. What state was her face in?

"Um." She didn't know what to say.

"Ren, who did this to you?" Dare asked as he wiped his hands on his apron, anger brewing in his blue eyes.

"Uh. I got mugged on the way home," she muttered.

"What? ¿Estás bien?"

"Si, si. Estoy bien... Lycan saved me."

They both looked surprised. *"Lycan* saved you?"

"How... far into needing saving were you?" Dad asked. "¿Estás herida? Necesitas—"

"Estoy bien, enserio," she answered with a blush. "My phone screen cracked though. But it's okay." *You're okay.* "I'm okay."

"Wait, where was Marigold?" Dare asked.

"She took a car with Ivy."

Dad's eyes darkened. "Why weren't you with them?"

She blinked. "I... I told them I'd get my own. And then I... I wasn't thinking I just started walking. Jasper's dad was being a dick and he never came to the movies yo le andaba texteando y empecé a caminar sin pensar y—"

Dad pulled her into his arms, holding her tight. "You're not walking anywhere alone anymore," he said.

"Dad, I'm fine, it's not—"

"En serio, Ren," Dad continued as he pulled back to look at her. "If Jasper isn't walking with you to and from school, we'll walk you. Or drive you."

"And I'm talking to Mari about letting you go off on your own like that," Dare growled.

"No, Mari didn't do anything wrong! It was my choice!"

Dare didn't respond. She could tell he was barely containing his rage.

"I'm fine, okay? I'm gonna go shower."

Dad sighed. "Did you eat?" His tone was softer now as he brushed some hair behind her ear.

"No."

"I'll have something ready for you when you get out." He kissed the top of her head.

Ren nodded, unable to speak. Once she climbed through her trapdoor she sat on the floor and closed her eyes. Zig laid beside her, resting his head on her leg.

"Sorry," she finally mumbled.

Ren, you scared me.

She nodded. "Scared me, too."

I know I told you that no one can ever see you change. But there's a much more important rule that supersedes that one.

"What's that?"

Never ever let anything bad happen to you. You fight and you never stop fighting, no matter what.

Ren blinked.

I don't want to lose you. You understand? It's been so long since I had a Bond. Losing you... Ren, it would break me.

Her eyes watered. *Cause it always hurts to lose a Bond?*

Losing you...

She swallowed. "It wasn't a big deal, Zig. The guy just wanted my bag."

Zig hesitated. *Ren, why did Lycan give you his jacket?*

"Cause... it was cold? I guess."

Zig seemed worried as he stared up at her.

"I'm sorry I didn't protect myself," she continued, trying to appease him.

He sighed. *You think Ren and Kaida need to be separate. But you*

take it too far. If Ren is in trouble...
Right. I'm sorry. I'll try to do better.
He nuzzled his face against her hand as she sat there, trying not to cry.

12
Strawberry

The next day she tried to dodge Jasper's questions as they walked to school. Apparently her dads texted him, making it explicitly clear she wasn't allowed to walk alone. She didn't wanna tell him why. Just like he didn't wanna tell her what happened with his dad. But she knew something did. She'd bet money he wouldn't take that hoodie off all day.

"Shut up about me, okay? I literally only care about you," Jasper hissed as they entered the school. "What the hell happened to your face?"

She sighed. *Should have covered it with makeup.* The bruise on her right cheekbone wasn't *that* bad, but it was noticeable. "It's nothing."

"Ren Robin Rivers—" He pulled her to a stop. "What. Happened?"

She deflated. "Some guy tried to mug me after the movie. He... hit me, with a knife I think? I don't know. It was a blur till Lycan showed up."

Jasper's blue eyes were hard as steel. He pulled her into his arms, surprising her. She pressed her face into his chest while his arms slid under her backpack.

"I should have been there."

"It's okay. I'm fine." He didn't let go. "Are you okay?" she mumbled into him.

"No. No I wanna kill someone."

She pulled back, looking into his eyes. "I swear I'm a thousand percent fine."

The bell rang and she jumped.

"Lycan saved you?" he asked.

She nodded. "Yes. And I can tell you all about that after class. We're gonna be late."

He smiled slightly. "You don't look like you care about that."

She eyed his arms again, wondering how much he was hiding. "I don't."

88

His smile faded.

"Later, kay?" She forced a smile before moving away.

When she got to class she plopped into her seat and put her head on the table.

"Ren?"

Her head snapped up as she looked at Bellamy, sitting beside her. He looked so good in his dark green zip up jacket, and light blue jeans. She sat up and swallowed. "Yeah?"

"I heard you talking to Jasper in the hall. Something happened to you?" He looked concerned.

"Uh. Yeah." Her heart raced. "It wasn't a big deal. Lycan saved me."

Bellamy smiled. "That's good. Pretty cool, too, yeah? Being saved by him?"

Ren shrugged. Bellamy's smile fell and she realized that's not what he wanted to hear. If people knew she'd been saved by one of New York's heroes, of course they'd wanna hear all about that. She tried to force a smile as she sat up straighter.

"I was really lucky he was there," she said.

Bellamy was staring at her so intently, his green eyes searching hers. She wished she could shrink back and hide from him.

"You're upset that you needed him to save you, aren't you?"

How can he see that so easily? "I just... feel silly, I guess? I was being stupid and I wasn't supposed to walk—"

"It wasn't your fault," Bellamy interrupted. "You didn't do anything wrong. And... it's okay to need help sometimes."

She nodded slowly. "It wasn't that serious, the guy just wanted my bag," she said with a shrug.

Bellamy frowned at her.

"What?"

"Uh. Nothing. I'm glad you're okay."

"You are?"

"Of course, I'd hate if something bad happened to you."

Heart pounding. Blood rushing. "I—"

"Alright, settle down, I'm here," Mrs. Moore said as she bustled into the room and put her bag on her desk.

Bellamy smiled at her. She had to force herself to look away.

Ren was buzzing from that interaction all the way to lunch. At that point more people knew what happened to her and were excitedly discussing her wondrous rescue at the hands of Lycan Silverstar. She liked them focusing on that part, at least.

Jasper led the way through the cafeteria full of round blue tables to their usual spot in the corner, where Nico and Bellamy were already seated.

Ren started unpacking her lunch, passing things to Jasper.
"Bell, why'd you bail on Ren last night?" Jasper asked.
Ren froze.

Bellamy stilled as he looked from Jasper to Ren. She was pointedly
ignoring them.
"Oh god."
Jasper raised an eyebrow. "You told her you'd go to the movies. So
did I, but my dad wouldn't let me. So I texted her and told her that. So
she *knew* I wasn't coming."
"Jasper," Ren hissed as she grabbed his arm, her cheeks burning
red.
Jasper ignored her. "So, we both bailed on her. And then what
happened? She got hurt. That's what *fucking* happened. So where
were you?"
Guilt rushed through Bellamy, flooding his every thought. He'd
completely forgotten about the movies. He'd been so distracted after
finding those books in his mom's office. So paranoid she knew he'd
Bonded. He spiraled, completely forgetting his plans.
He glanced past Jasper at Ren, who was blushing so hard her
freckles looked like the specs on a strawberry. As he took in that bruise
on her cheek again he wanted to die.
He hopped up, moving around Jasper to sit on Ren's other side.
Then he grabbed her hands, forcing her to turn and look at him. Her
brown eyes were wide.
"I am so so sorry. I should have been there. I didn't mean to stand
you up, I swear."
"It's fine, ignore Jasper," she said, looking down.
"No, it's not fine. I should have been there. I would have taken you
home. You—" Never would have gotten hurt. *This is my fault.* "I
should have at least texted and told you I wasn't gonna make it. I'm so
shitty, I should have—"
"You don't have my number."
"Oh." That was stupid. "You should give me your number, so I can
text you next time."
Ren looked confused. "Next time?"
"Yeah. I mean, I'm not gonna bail next time. If there is a next time?

I guess you might not invite me somewhere again, but if you *do* I wanna go. I *will* go. And I'll text you to tell you that!"

Ren's blush began to fade as she smiled slightly. "Uh, okay." She glanced down at their hands.

He was still holding them, her tan skin soft and warm against his. "Sorry." He dropped them, heart racing.

"You're still wearing it," she noted, eyeing the yarn bracelet she gave him on the first day back after winter break.

"Of course. It's my most prized possession."

Ren laughed as she pulled out her phone then handed it to him. "Add your number."

He tried to still his thumping heart as he took the phone. "Why didn't I have your number?" he asked.

"You... never asked for it," she mumbled.

He looked up. "Was I supposed to?"

"If you wanted it?" Ren blinked.

"I did. I... I'm not good at things," he continued. "I guess I'm not used to people wanting to hang out after school, probably why I got sidetracked last night."

Her smile was soft. "It's okay."

For a moment he thought maybe she was actually mad. She should have been. She got hurt and so much worse could have happened, if not for Lycan. For the first time since Bonding he really wished he could tell someone he was Lycan. If Ren knew *he* saved her...

With a sigh he handed the phone back to her.

"Texting you so you have my number," she whispered.

> |Unknown|
> What happened wasn't your fault. But I'm down for a next time? :)

He couldn't hide his smile. "You're not mad?"

She shook her head.

"I..." He struggled to find the words. "I don't want to lose you. You're my favorite person here."

Ren's cheeks somehow got redder. "Your... *what?* Favorite. I... you won't lose me. My favorite. I, you are..." She groaned, closing her eyes. "Que alguien me calle por el amor de dios."

Something hit Bellamy in the head. He frowned, looking at the chip on the table as Nico threw another one at him. He somehow forgot other people were sitting with them. Nico flashed Ren a big smile and she seemed to relax.

"De nada," Nico said, bowing his head slightly. "Also, he sucks at texting, be warned."

Ren raised an eyebrow.

"I... I'll be better."

"For her?" Nico asked.

Bellamy blushed. The only people he really texted often were his mom and Kaida. He forgot to text Nico back all the time.

"I'm adding him to the group chat," Ren said softly. Then she passed him a cookie from her lunch.

He smiled, recalling her offering to give free cookies to Lycan last night.

When school was over he found Ren, wanting to make sure she was safe walking home. He was pretty sure Jasper walked with her every day anyways, but he worried. He spotted her cornered at her locker by Amy, a tall redhead, mumbling something about Jasper. Ren looked annoyed until the girl walked away and Jasper appeared. Bellamy watched them leave together before heading home.

He snuck back into Mom's office to see if the books were still there when he arrived.

Zel?

I'm out. Do you need me?

Out where?

With Kirzigith. Do you need me?

He smiled. *No.*

His Xyri had a better social life than him. How sad was that? He wondered if Ren would actually wanna hang out with him again outside of school after he let her down.

With a sigh he scanned through the office, but all the Xyri books were gone. He looked through the shelves, but he didn't see any that sparked suspicion.

Someone was moving outside. Bellamy froze. He hadn't heard the front door. He rushed into the living room, but no one was there. The front door closed. Bellamy spun, looking down the hall, heart thundering. No one was there. He opened the front door, peeking into the hall. No one was there.

You wanna come back now? he asked Zeli, heart racing.

13
No Winner Due To Bird

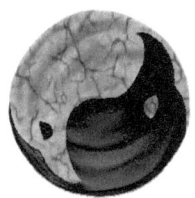

Jasper paced through Ren's room, suit on, energy buzzing. Kaida stared at him with stern blue eyes as she sat on the edge of the loft, legs dangling in front of her closet.

"Are you really ready?"

"I'm really ready."

"Hm."

He rolled his eyes. "Come *on*, you said we could do it tonight! I've been *so* patient. Didn't bug you at all last week since you got mugged, and then it was Arrow's birthday. But I'm ready to go insane if you don't let me—"

"*Fine*. But I should warn Lycan first." She pulled her phone out and started typing.

"What are you telling him?"

"That I found a stray."

"Ha ha." He walked up the steps and sat beside her. "Why blue eyes?"

"Hm?"

"As Kaida. You have blue eyes. But you've never struck me as the type of brown-eyed-girl to envy the blue-eyed ones."

"I stole them from you."

"What?"

Kaida smiled. "Can't you tell? These aren't just blue eyes. They're *your* blue eyes. The prettiest ones I've ever seen. So I stole them."

Jasper stared at her, heart swelling. "Really?"

"Yeah, look." She held her phone up and opened the camera. He leaned in, putting his head beside hers. Then he saw it. Her eyes were the exact same shade of blue as his. His throat tightened. He knew he had nice eyes but...

"You should change yours, as Apex."

Jasper nodded.

What color would you like? Pozi asked.

He had him cycle through several colors, then settled on yellow, like Lycan's.

Kaida laughed. "That completes your look. Ready to go, Apex?"

"Ready to go, Kaida."

It had taken time to get used to calling her Kaida, and not Ren. He'd seen videos of Kaida for a year without knowing she was Ren. But being with her now, she *felt* like Ren, and that had been tripping him up. But he was sure he had it down now. And she'd been pressuring him to pick his name so she could train her brain not to call him Jasper. He settled on Apex. It seemed fitting. He was the new apex predator in a world of heroes and villains, and he was ready to kick some ass.

They went out through the skylight, and he followed her across the rooftop garden where she climbed up on a chair.

"Dim your suit," she whispered as she stepped up onto the brick wall.

"Huh?"

She means the glow, Pozi answered. Just like that, his suit went dark, turning all black.

"Oh."

Kaida smiled as she faced that five story fall as her wings came out. Bright red, like her suit, with veins of gold running through them. They reminded him of bat wings, with the black joints separating the membranes. His wings were different. He relaxed as they unfurled. Extending wider than Kaida's, they were made of fine silky black feathers, like a bird. He grinned at Kaida then jumped into the sky.

Flying with his best friend over the city was something he never could have imagined, but it thrilled him like nothing else. They soared through the sky like ethereal beings. Those stars were shining for them.

He'd only flown a few times, and worried he wouldn't be able to keep up, but he thought he was actually faster than her. Only, he didn't know where they were going.

It wasn't long before Kaida descended toward a skyscraper, shining bright in the dark. He landed beside her on the roof and pulled his wings in, nervous now that they'd arrived.

"Stay back a second," she whispered.

He nodded, watching as she crossed the roof toward the tall silhouette standing on the other side, staring out at the water.

Kaida walked slowly, anxiety raging. Lycan stood still as she stepped up beside him and let out a breath.

"Where's your stray?" he asked as he turned, looking down at her, a small silver something twirling through his fingers.

"You thought that was a joke, didn't you?" she asked nervously.

He tilted his head a little, his hand stilling. "It's not?"

"No... so, um." She flexed her hands. "Here's the thing. There's a new hero. Bonded to a Xyri who knows my Xyri. Uh. So we met. And I brought him here." She smiled with all her teeth.

"O... kay." Lycan looked past her into the darkness, his fidget toy puffing into mist.

Kaida released a breath and grabbed his arm, gently pulling him back across the roof.

"Lycan, meet Apex. Apex, meet Lycan."

Apex stepped out, his suit glowing dramatically again. He'd finally finished tweaking it, settling on black as the base. Glowing green lines ran down his arms, the sides of his legs, and across his waist. There were matching marks, like claws in canvas, raked across his chest and across his knees. His mask was the same. Solid black around the eyes, but with lines of glowing green that looked like claw marks extending out of it above and below the eyes on both sides. And there was a black hood pulled up over his hair, outlined in glowing green. It was ridiculously dramatic and she loved it.

"Hi," Apex mumbled, waving awkwardly.

"Hi." Lycan didn't look very impressed.

Kaida sighed. "So, Apex has a pretty cool power set, and I think he'll be a great addition to our team and—"

"*Our team?*" Lycan interrupted. "We just met this kid and now he's on our team?"

"Not a kid," Apex argued. "Kaida is *barely* older than me."

Lycan blinked, turning to look back at Apex. "How the hell do you know that?"

"Cause her birthday is a month before mine?" Apex replied.

"I'm gonna kill you," Kaida hissed.

Apex realized his mistake, eyes widening. "Shit. *Sorry.*"

She closed her eyes, sighing heavily. "You couldn't even last one minute? *One minute* without saying something you shouldn't!"

"I'm sorry!"

"You know him," Lycan said flatly. "You know him and he knows you. Not Kaida, the *real* you. That's fucking great." He turned and stalked across the roof.

She sighed as she glared at Apex. *"Really?"*

"I said sorry!"

He looked upset so she tried to calm herself. "It's fine. Not a big deal he knows we know each other," she whispered. "Just *please* be careful. Lycan and I cannot, under any circumstances, know each other's identities. Think before you speak, okay?"

"I swear."

She nodded and walked over to where Lycan stared out at the city lights.

"Are you mad?" she asked.

"No."

"You sound mad."

"You sound like you don't need me anymore," he muttered.

Kaida blinked then grabbed his arm, forcing him to face her. "That's the *dumbest* thing you've ever said."

His yellow eyes softened a little.

"I'll always need you. In fact I'm very needy, okay? I am so *so* needy. You couldn't get rid of me if you tried."

He smiled.

"I know it's weird to bring in someone new, and even weirder that I know that person but... I really think if you give him a chance you guys could be friends."

He nodded. "I just... don't want this to change."

"Nothing's changing between us, Starface. I promise."

"Alright." He swallowed. "Why exactly are you guys allowed to know, though?"

Kaida could read the hurt in his eyes. She took a deep breath. "I met his Xyri a few months ago, as Kaida. And, I accidentally detransformed in front of him. I know I know, *don't* wanna hear it," she said, holding up her hand. "Anyways when his Xyri Bonded him he told him my identity. I swear *I* didn't tell him. I've never told anyone."

Lycan seemed to soften a little.

"It's all an accident. But, we can't take it back. He knows and I know and so... we know." She felt the unspoken 'but you don't know' hanging in the air between them. "I'm sorry."

"It's fine. What's the plan? Is he patrolling with us?"

"I was hoping we could train him. He's strong and fast and has good instincts. But he doesn't know how to apply that to the sort of things we deal with." She smiled slightly. "We didn't have anyone to train us, and getting where we are now was hard. But, it doesn't have to be for him."

"Okay. Let's see what he's got."

Kaida grinned and pulled Lycan back toward Jasper. She could see anxiety in him, the way he stood, eyes darting between her and Lycan. She needed to go easier on him.

"Ready to go?" she asked.

Apex frowned. "Home?"

She shook her head. "No, it's time to see what you can really do. Be prepared to get no sleep."

Apex raised an eyebrow.

"Try to keep up," Lycan said as he summoned his board.

Kaida stepped on it, wrapping her arms around his waist. They flew off into the sky, leaving Apex to follow.

Lycan tried to calm his racing thoughts as they flew to a park where he and Kaida liked to train. It was usually clear of people at night.

So, there was a new person on their team. That wasn't a bad thing. They needed more heroes. But he couldn't help feeling like he was losing something special. Being a team with Kaida... it was the thing that kept him going. Now they were gonna be a trio?

He landed in an open clearing of the park, board disappearing as he and Kaida stepped into the frosty grass. Apex's landing was annoyingly smooth.

Lycan sighed and turned to Kaida. "What do you wanna do?"

She considered for a moment. "Probably keep it one on one for now?"

"You or me?"

"I don't trust either of you, but I also don't trust Apex to come at me properly," she replied.

"Come at you?" the boy asked, yellow eyes moving between them.

"Yeah. We're gonna fight. But that means you have to actually fight me. Can you do that?"

Apex looked like he couldn't. "Can I fight him instead?"

Kaida sighed.

"It's fine, Kai," Lycan whispered.

"Remember this is training," she said. "You aren't *actually* trying to kill each other, okay?"

"It'll be fine." He smiled at her as she made a chair of light and sat down to watch.

"How do we determine who wins a test fight?" Apex asked.

"Whoever gets restrained first loses. Can do best of three," Lycan replied.

Should warn you, Poziarne's powers are pretty intense, Zeli whispered.

You literally give me power over time, Zel. I'm not worried.

Zeli laughed.

He counted down to three and Apex crashed into him, faster than Lycan expected. He landed with a roll in the grass and blinked in surprise. Silver poured out of his hands, shaping into ropes as he stood.

Apex jumped up, wings flapping to carry him out of reach. He gained some height but didn't get far before Lycan sped through the air after him. He was faster and caught Apex midair, grabbing his wings. Apex gasped, then he changed, size and shape shifting as he and Lycan tumbled through the air. Apex turned into a large bird and slipped through Lycan's fingers. Lycan was so surprised he didn't reorient himself before crashing to the ground.

He groaned as he sat up and watched the bird flying in confused circles. It looked like an eagle, only the feathers were sleek black and it had glowing green eyes. Kaida stood up, her light chair puffing away as she stared at Apex the bird.

"Did you know he could do that?" Lycan asked as he pushed himself up and walked toward her.

"No. I don't think he knew either." She bit her lip.

After a moment of flying in circles there was a loud *crack* and the bird was a boy again as Apex crashed back down.

"What the fuck what the fuck what the fuck," Apex hissed under his breath.

"You were a whole ass bird," Kaida said as she knelt beside him.

"Pozi told me to do it without telling me what it would do. That was *so* weird." His eyes were wide. "Wait, are we still fighting? Did I win?"

Lycan smiled. "No winner, due to bird. We can go again once you've recovered."

"Oh yeah, five minutes," Kaida muttered. "Uh..." She looked around the giant field.

"Box him up."

Kaida nodded, forming a box of light around Apex.

Lycan felt stupid. He hadn't really figured out what Apex's powers were before their fight, and that was a disadvantage.

"Am I in timeout?" Apex's muffled voice said from the box.

"Yep," Kaida answered with a smile.

That is a disadvantage you have in every fight with a new Bonded, Zeli said.

True.

Everyone knows what you can do, but you don't always know what they can do. This was a good test.

"Your box is pretty," Apex mumbled.

Did you know he could turn into a bird?

Yes, Poziarne is powerful, as I said. Augmentation of the body. And you trust this Poziarne?

"Did you change back yet?" Kaida asked.

"Oh. That's what we're doing," Apex replied.

Kaida met Lycan's eyes and smiled.

Poziarne is like a child among the Xyri. Third generation. He's impulsive and chaotic. But, good. He has never once made a mistake in his Bonds, despite his nature. Not even I can claim that feat.

Lycan pondered that. If Zeli trusted him, and his choices for whom he Bonded, Lycan couldn't complain. He trusted Zeli wholeheartedly.

He's not better than me, though. Right?

He felt Zeli's amusement. *No one is better than you, Bellamy Grey.*

Kaida flew after the boys, watching as they tangled in the air once more. Apex had a problem with trying too hard to overpower Lycan without really thinking about the approach. On the other hand, Lycan was patient and calculating, evading each tackle, making his moves at the exact right time. She hoped Apex could learn faster than they did, since he had two people to show him the way.

They fell to the ground again in a smaller clearing. She followed, landing a few feet away. Apex was laughing. A good sign.

Is this good? Zig asked as she walked, staying out of their way.

Is what good?

Having Jasper here, in this part of your life? Does it make things easier for you?

She considered that as she watched the boys get up and ready themselves for a new fight. *Yes. Not hiding things from him anymore...* She smiled. *Seeing them together. My boys.*

Good.

She walked the perimeter of the little clearing while the boys wrestled in the center. She'd been worried about them meeting, but they seemed to be getting along alright. Lycan wasn't holding back, but neither was he being aggressive. He was simply training Apex to the best of his ability.

This is definitely better.

Zig seemed happy to hear that.

Something caught her eyes and she diverted her path, curious. As she got closer she saw a lamp post, though it seemed... off. She touched it, surprised to find it wasn't metal, but wood. Next to it was a bench, also made of wood. She frowned as she sat on it, running her hand over the smooth grooves in the bark. Looking closer she noticed it had grown straight out of the ground. Beside the bench was something small and green. She got on her knees, running a hand over it, while her other hand lit up with a ball of light. It was a bush in the shape of a dog.

Zig, you see this?

He grew tense.

Zig?

He sighed. *That's the work of a Bonded.*

Kaida released a breath and threw her ball of light in the air. A moment later the boys came running over.

"What's wrong?" Lycan asked.

"Is that a dog?"

"It's a bush," Kaida answered as she turned to look at them. "A Bonded made these."

"Bad Bonded or good?" Lycan knelt beside her, looking closer.

"This, so soon after that statue," Kaida said. "More *are* coming."

They might be one and the same, Zig said softly.

"Zeli says they could be the same person."

"Zig just told me."

Apex stared between them. "It's a bench and a dog. And a post. Why are we worried about this?"

It could be one of two Xyri, Zig said. *Nagalix or Voltius.*

You don't seem excited by either prospect?

Nagalix rarely Bonds, but if she's back I... do not know how that would go. If it's Voltius... He fell silent.

That bad?

Yes.

She met Lycan's eyes, knowing Zeli was probably telling him the same thing. He gave her a reassuring smile.

"Us against the world," he whispered.

Kaida nodded. "Us against the world."

14
Who's Driving The Tricycle

Kaida felt better about things now that they were a few days into training Apex. She sensed some tension between the boys at first, but they were getting along perfectly now. And Apex was getting a better hold on his powers, with no accidental animal transformations, and only one intentional one.

Jasper confided that it was super overwhelming to shift like that, and he didn't think it would be useful in a fight. She had to remind him he'd literally flown from Lycan's clutches when he did it. She could see its uses, he just needed more practice.

Today Lycan set up an obstacle course for them across several rooftops in Midtown with things to run through, jump over, and fly around. The path was indicated by solid silver arrows, and of course Apex turned it into a race.

"You know that's not fair," she growled through gritted teeth as they leaped off one roof and landed on the next one over. "You're faster than me, you literally have speed on steroids!"

"I'm not using it right now!" Apex yelled back.

Is he lying?

I could not say, Zig replied.

The silver arrow in front of them pointed down. She barely noticed in time and formed a slide as she angled her jump. Her slide took her to the street, and she ran across the pavement. Apex wasn't behind her. She grinned as a flash caught her eyes. Someone was taking pictures, but that couldn't be helped.

Kaida and Lycan gave up on being private long ago. It was either only go out to fight crime or let themselves be seen doing things in the suits. She'd never forget the first time they got pancakes together. Two in the morning and they just sauntered in, surprising the night crew of that diner. They still went to that same place all the time.

She caught sight of an arrow pointing up and her wings popped out as she jumped up, taking flight. Apex flew past, laughing. Kaida rolled her eyes. Did it count if he skipped the dip to the ground?

The arrows pointed down again, back to the rooftops. She pulled her wings in as her feet connected, and Apex landed in front of her. Lycan waited ahead, two roofs over.

Light poured out of her, shaping into a bridge just as Apex jumped across the gaps. She didn't slow her pace as the light stretched out across the roof and covered the next gap. Apex landed, then he moved with a blur across her second bridge, closing the distance between them and Lycan only seconds before her.

She growled as she came to a stop. "Cheater!"

"Lycan didn't say we couldn't cheat." The grin Apex gave her was the same one she saw every time he beat her in a game. It was infuriating. She smiled back.

"Is he disqualified for cheating?" she asked, turning to Lycan, who was fidgeting with a new silver toy.

"Uh, I did say whoever got back to me first wins."

"Wow. And here I thought you loved me. One week with Apex and you're already choosing him over me."

Lycan smiled. "I didn't choose him at all."

"You can though, if you want." Apex grinned. "I'm very down."

His toy puffed away.

"Besides," Apex continued, "you're the one who wanted us to get along. This counts, doesn't it?"

"If it makes you feel better," Lycan mumbled, "I still feel like the third wheel here."

Kaida stilled. "You do?"

"Little bit."

"Was my innuendo not clear?" Apex asked.

"You hush," Kaida hissed at him before turning back to Lycan. "You are *not* a third wheel."

"There are three of us though," Apex said, smiling. "That's like a tricycle, and those have three wheels."

Kaida took a deep breath. "Not helping."

Lycan was grinning though. "Who's driving the tricycle?"

"Kaida, obviously," Apex replied.

Lycan's grin widened. "Yeah, we're not in control."

Kaida relaxed a little. "Funny. But seriously, I want—" Something exploded in the distance. She stood still for a moment, heart racing. "Shit. We should go."

"I'm so ready!" Apex said.

"No, not you." She shook her head. "I know you think you're ready but... let us just see what's happening first? If we need help I'll call."

"But..." He looked sad, his smile gone, a little pout in its place. "Tricycle?"

"Not today."

Lycan gave him an apologetic smile as he kicked his silver board up. Kaida hopped on without hesitation.

"I'm serious, stay here! We'll be back!" she yelled as Lycan zipped them into the sky.

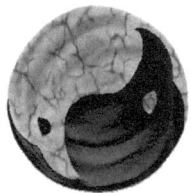

Jasper tried not to be annoyed with Kaida. But it was like she put him in timeout. What was the point of having powers if he wasn't really allowed to use them?

You can use them, Pozi said.

Ren will be very mad if I do.

What if they need help?

Jasper hesitated. She said she'd call if she needed him but... what if it was so bad she couldn't?

We could take a little looksy! If they have it handled we come back and no one has to know.

Jasper smiled. "You're a bad influence."

Nonsense. Don't be boring, Jasper.

He frowned as he went to the edge of the roof, looking into the distance.

"Why do you call me Jasper? Shouldn't you call me Apex now that I chose a name?"

Absolutely not.

"Why not? Ren makes such a big deal about the names. Keeping identities separate and stuff."

You could lose yourself in it. It's happened before and it's not pretty. Some separation is good, perfect even. But you don't wanna go too far in either direction. We do our best to keep you grounded in who you really are. And you are Jasper Nightingale. I won't let ya forget.

"I guess that makes sense. She seems so stressed about it, though."

Ren... Pozi paused.

"What? What is it?"

I told you on purpose.

Jasper frowned as he leaned against the railing. "What do you mean?"

I didn't actually mean to tell Kirzigith I was Bonding you, but... I gave him a hint and he's smarter than I like to admit.

"What kind of hint?"

Said I was Bonding someone Ren knew. Thought it was funny. But he knows me too well, and he knows who she knows, he put it together. So... he asked me to tell you, after we Bonded.

"Tell me... that she was Kaida?"

Yep. He's been worried about her. Thought it would help her.

"Is she okay? Like, should *I* be worried?"

I think she'll be fine. She's a strong kid. But keep this between us, ya? Kirzigith doesn't want her to know.

Jasper smiled. "That he did something nice for her?"

We aren't supposed to. You don't understand how deep this rule goes. It would be so easy, to just send one of us to follow a Bonded, to wait till they detransform to see who they really are. No Xyri will cross that line. Sometimes identities get leaked, but never by the Xyri, Pozi replied. *Now I have Azazelith out here thinking I've messed up after three billion years of perfection. It's annoying.*

"So, Zeli doesn't know Kaida is Ren?"

No. I've always believed in the rule. It's better in the end, keeps everyone safer. But... He felt joy from the Xyri. *I really like this.*

Jasper grinned. He liked it too. He couldn't imagine Bonding Pozi and *not* telling Ren. It had to be so hard for her. He was extremely lucky he didn't have to go through that.

He leaned out over the railing. Kaida hadn't called. They were probably fine. They didn't need him.

Oh, wow. There she is.

Jasper straightened. "Who?"

Look down, to the left. Ears.

His heart stopped as someone in a skintight black bodysuit walked by on the street below. Tall black ears, like a rabbit, were sticking up out of their light brown hair. A soft purple glow shone from parts of the suit. *Fable.*

"Did you say she? Fable's a guy... *isn't he*?" Jasper asked as he moved along the edge of the roof, watching, heart racing in his chest.

I mean his Xyri. Nellithi. She's never Bonded a human before. He sounded impressed.

Jasper's hands shook as he stared at Fable. One of the worst villains to Bond a Xyri. Evil. Heartless. A monster. His stupid fucking suit made people underestimate him. A guy with bunny ears couldn't be that intimidating, could he? But Jasper knew the truth. Fable was *ruthless.*

Are you... going to kill him?

We're gonna take him down, he replied, climbing up over the railing.

By killing him?

Jasper frowned. *You're down for murder?*

The Xyri hesitated. *It's her first Bond. I... I don't want to take her human from her so soon. You can't understand that kind of pain.*

Jasper hesitated. *Not gonna kill him. Just stop him.*

Fable walked along like he hadn't a care in the world. Jasper wondered if maybe he was responsible for the explosion the others went after. Fable had done that before, putting up illusions in one place to distract, while he went off to do something else. And Kaida didn't know.

Smart. Pretend we're doing what she'd want.

Not pretending, Poz. She knows what Fable did to me. To that little girl...

Jasper jumped, dropping down behind Fable. He turned at the sound, surprised to see Apex there.

Jasper swallowed his panic, being so close to this guy again, those purple eyes piercing into him. His mask looked like soot smeared around his eyes, as if they'd been on fire. It made him sick.

The suit was mostly black, with a high collar around his neck. The purple glow at the center of his chest reminded him of a black hole, sucking in all the light. Glowing purple lines ran down the sides of his suit, wrapping around at his knees. Then there were the damn ears. A purple glow emanated from inside them.

Fable moved his hand a little. It set Jasper off and he lunged, crashing into him as he tapped strength. They hit the ground hard. Fable grunted, confused, as he stared up at him. Jasper smiled through his terror and punched Fable in the face with all his strength.

Everything changed. Fable disappeared and Jasper was floating on a raft in the middle of a dark ocean, wind ripping at him as water sprayed in his face.

It's not real!

I know that! Jasper panicked regardless, unsure what to do. It *felt* so real, he couldn't see beyond the illusion.

Stand up, you're on solid ground.

Can you see through it?

No, but I can sense it. You're not calm enough to catch it.

Jasper nodded and forced himself up, expecting his body to topple off the tiny raft and get swallowed by the angry currents below. He didn't fall but the illusion remained. He clenched his hands into fists and stepped off the raft into the water. Only it wasn't water. He hit solid ground and took another step, eyes shut tight.

You're out!

Jasper opened his eyes and the sun shone in them. He was back on the street, alone. He tapped sight, enhancing his vision as he looked down both ends of the street. Finally he spotted Fable, casually walking away.

Jasper's wings burst out of his back and he took to the air, flying with the speed of a falcon. He rammed into Fable with the force of a tiger. Fable groaned as they rolled on the ground.

"What's your problem?" he yelled.

"You're my problem!"

I can't believe she finally Bonded, and Xenos is missing it.

Fable forced himself up and backed away, a snarl on his face. "Who the fuck are you?"

Not sure what I think of her choice, though.

"I'm Apex. And I'm here to ruin your life like you ruined mine."

Fable's purple eyes narrowed. *"Fine."*

Apex tapped speed and strength then rushed him. They collided before hitting the ground. Fable struggled beneath him just as Apex's eyes stopped working. He couldn't see anything. He couldn't...

Debris rained down around him while his ears rang from the explosion. He blinked as ash fell into his eyes. Pain. He couldn't move. Something enormous pinned him down. Someone was crying. He craned his head to the side in time to see Fable walk out of what remained of the building, not a scratch on him. He walked right past the little girl. Jasper forced his arm up to wipe his eyes, smearing dirt across his cheeks.

"Please," the girl muttered, watching Fable leave her there. "Please?"

Jasper tried to move. Nothing happened. The girl continued to cry.

"Can you move?" he asked her.

She met his eyes and shook her head the tiniest fraction. "I can't see daddy. Is daddy okay?"

Jasper looked past her. The body was in pieces. His eyes burned as he forced himself to look back at the little girl. She was bleeding from cuts across her arms and face, her body pinned under a shelf.

"He's just asleep," Jasper whispered, throat raw. "It's gonna be okay."

The girl nodded as tears leaked out of her eyes. "It hurts."

"I know. But it'll be okay. Help will come. I promise."

She nodded again, lips trembling.

Jasper screamed as he slammed into something. His hands shook. For a moment he was back in that shop. Trapped. Helpless, as a child died beside him. He screamed again as he tried to get up.

"Pozi I can't see!"

Calm, Jasper. It's not real. Your eyes are fine. Your body is... mostly fine. Breathe. Steady. Get up and step to the left.

Jasper moved and heard a grunt of frustration. Fable was still there. Jasper could still end this.

"I don't know what your problem is," Fable hissed from somewhere in front of him. "And I don't care. Find someone else to fight."

"You should have killed me the first time," Jasper growled, anger fueling him.

Something moved around him, wrapping him tightly, cutting off his circulation. He groaned, heart pounding as he struggled against it until it stilled and he couldn't move. He couldn't move. He couldn't...

Flashing lights. Red. Blue. Red. Blue. A girl's limp body, eyes staring frozen in time. The tears not yet dried on her pale cheeks. Voices. Time of death, ten thirty-two. Lights flashing. Pain. He didn't say a word as they moved him out from under the beam. Up onto the stretcher. Out into the ambulance. Time of death, ten thirty-two. Time of death, ten thirty-two. Time of death...

Jasper? Can you hear me?

He blinked his eyes open, confused. He could see, and what he saw was his body tied up with a thick rope, black as night, with a single thread of purple running through it. He couldn't move. People were watching nearby, phones out. His hands shook against his side.

You're stronger than this. Stronger than him. Strong as a tiger. Fast as a cheetah. Sight of an eagle. Hearing of a bat. Smell of an elephant. The kingdom is yours, Jasper Liam Nightingale. You are the Apex Predator. And that little boy can not hold you down. This rope is nothing. Get. Up.

Jasper swallowed, then tapped strength. He stretched his body till the rope snapped. He was on his feet in seconds, holding the rope, what seemed so strong moments before, now limp in his hand. A crowd of people had gathered on the other side of the street now, but Fable was nowhere to be seen.

15
A Really Good Smile

"As you see from the footage, this new guy was *fighting* Fable. And he appears to be the same mysterious person we've seen flying around with Team Silverlight this past week. I think it goes without saying, New York has a new hero. I was so lucky to be on the scene and was able to get his first interview! Here's the clip!"

The video changed to Apex standing there, holding that rope in a tight fist.

"What should we call you?" the woman with the dark curls asked.

"Apex," he answered.

"Can you confirm that you're friends with Kaida and Lycan?"

"Um. Yes?" He seemed so uncertain in the video.

Ren had to hide her smile as she glanced at Jasper beside her in her bed. He groaned and fell backward, then pulled a pillow up over his face and stayed like that.

Ren paused the video. "It's not that bad."

He mumbled something into the pillow.

"Really, do you remember the first time people saw me and Lycan? Our first interview was *terrible*. But people didn't hang onto that, they were just excited the Xyri were back. And they'll be excited by you, too!"

He groaned again and she yanked the pillow off his face.

"If you don't believe me, look at this text Ocean sent me this morning." She pulled it up and shoved the phone in his face.

> |Ocean|
> Did you see the new hero
> Apex? He's so hot!!!

"French girl thinks I'm hot?"

"You are the first new hero since us! The first one in seventeen months! Everyone's gonna love you."

He sighed. "No they won't. No one loves me."

She hit him with the pillow. "I love you. Also literally every girl in our grade is obsessed with you right now. People will love you as Apex, too."

Jasper frowned. "They are not obsessed with me."

Ren raised an eyebrow. "Every other day another girl asks me if you and I are dating. When I say no they ask if you're single and when I say yes they giggle and blush."

Jasper sat up. "I don't believe you but also *who's* asked this?"

"Sabrina, Olivia. Anna, and Amy."

He perked up. "Amy did *not* ask about me."

"She most certainly did. Like three weeks ago!" Ren smiled at him. "You're too hot for your own good. And they're all starting to realize it."

Jasper grinned. The first real smile since she found him after his fight with Fable yesterday.

"No boys asking if I'm single?" he asked.

"No, but you haven't told people you're bi yet. I imagine if they knew they'd also be lining up for you."

His smile widened. "Still don't believe you."

She rolled her eyes and hit him with the pillow again. "I'll prove it when we go back to school after the break."

She was starting to get annoyed by how many girls were asking if she was with him. Her and Jasper dated when they first met for three months, when they were thirteen going on fourteen. But they realized there was no real *spark* and decided to just be friends. Now they were best friends, but people *still* assumed they were together.

She wondered if people would think that about Kaida and Apex, too. There was non-stop speculation about Kaida and Lycan. Even Jasper thought she had feelings for him. The footage from yesterday didn't help. She'd malfunctioned, just stood there hugging him for far too long after they dealt with the gas explosion. And of course people were filming them. It didn't help that it happened to be Valentine's Day. She was probably *never* beating the allegations of secretly dating Lycan.

When school started again it took a few days for a girl to approach Ren. She stood at her locker, suppressing a sigh when Erica approached, her cheeks rosy with embarrassment.

"Hey, Ren."

"Hey."

She couldn't remember the last conversation she actually had with the tall girl. Erica used to make fun of her in middle school. And they only had one class together last year, and none this year.

"You know Jasper, right?"

Ren stared at her blankly. "Yes."

"Do you know if he's seeing anyone?"

Ren released a breath. "He's single."

Erica smiled. "So you two aren't—"

"Nope."

"Cool." Erica nodded then walked away.

Ren rolled her eyes and went to her next class. Jasper didn't believe her when she told him about it.

"You're lying. You're just trying to boost my ego."

"Your ego does *not* need boosting. I'll prove it. Next girl to say something I'm just gonna throw her at you."

Jasper smiled. "Oh *no*, throwing girls at me. How *terrible*."

She rolled her eyes.

The next two classes passed without anyone bothering her about him. Which was annoying now that she wanted to prove it. But then as she tossed her trash at lunch, Harper pulled Ren aside. She had a suspicion Harper was one of the girls who liked Jasper.

"Hey, I was wondering if I could ask you something?"

"About Jasper?"

Harper looked surprised, smiling shyly. "Has he said anything about me?"

"Nope."

"Oh. He isn't with anyone is he?"

Ren smiled. "Hold please."

She turned away and grabbed Jasper from where he was talking to Bellamy and Nico at the table.

"Come."

He let her pull his arm without question as she dragged him straight to Harper.

"Harper wants to know if you're single," Ren said with a wide smile.

Harper blushed, looking panicked.

Jasper blinked. "Uh. Yeah, I'm single."

"Oh." Harper looked like she might faint.

"This is the part where you ask him out," Ren said. "And I go away cause this does *not* involve me."

Jasper stared at her, wide-eyed, like he didn't want her to leave. She smiled as she left. *Not my problem.*

Jasper made it to their next class right before the bell rang, a stupid grin on his face.

"Well?"

"We're going out next weekend."

Ren nodded. "Good. Maybe people will leave me alone now."

Jasper couldn't stop smiling, which made Ren excited for him. Her and Harper weren't super close, but they were friends, and she was nice enough. And pretty. Blonde hair, blue eyes, perfect body. Maybe they'd be a good fit for each other.

At the end of the day while waiting for Jasper, someone slammed a locker behind her and she dropped her chem book in surprise. Then Bradley kicked it. Ren stared as it slid all the way down the hallway, only stopping when it hit someone's feet. She turned a glare on Bradley, who was laughing hysterically, his pale face now red, matching that of the lockers.

With a roll of her eyes she turned to go get it. The boy whose feet it hit picked it up. He wore a black leather jacket and towered over her. Ren didn't recognize him.

"Hi, sorry," she muttered as she held a hand out for the book.

"No worries." He looked down on her with light blue eyes. "Don't think I know you."

"No. I'm Ren."

He smiled and her heart sped up. "I'm Simon." He looked at the book before finally handing it back to her. "Who do you have for chem?"

"Uh, Mr. Carney."

"Carney's a trip."

Ren nodded. He was *so* tall. With black hair that almost fell into his eyes and an intense jawline.

"So, Ren, why don't I know you?"

"I. Uh..." *I'm a sophomore nobody why would you know me?* She swallowed. "Don't know."

He smiled, but didn't respond. She felt so awkward, just standing there, not sure what else to say.

"Ren!"

She spun to see Jasper skipping down the hall toward her.

"Hey, *so* sorry, but I can't walk you home today. *Maybe* your new friend here could walk you?" Jasper turned to Simon, face filled with a mischievous grin.

Simon looked confused. "I could walk you home, sure."

"Oh my *god.*" She glared at Jasper. "You don't have to."

"Listen! After what happened your dads said you can't walk alone and—"

"It's fine. Happy to walk you," Simon said with a smile.

Ren couldn't hide her embarrassment.

"Perfect. Make sure she gets home safe. See ya!" Jasper skipped back down the hall. She was gonna *kill* him.

"After you," Simon said softly.

"You *really* don't have to, I live like seven minutes away."

"Then it's definitely not out of my way." He kept smiling and she couldn't deny it was a *really* good smile.

"Okay."

He didn't say anything as they walked down the hall and outside. She didn't see Jasper anywhere.

"So, why aren't you allowed to walk home alone?"

She blushed again. "Uh, I sort of got mugged last month. So my dads have been extra protective."

"Shit. I'm sorry."

"It's fine. Lycan saved me, actually. So... yeah."

"Right, I heard people talking about that."

Someone she didn't even know heard about it? She sighed. Simon watched her as they walked, but she didn't know what else to say.

"Are you a junior?"

"Sophomore."

"Oh." His smile fell.

"Are you a junior?"

"Senior," he answered. "Almost free."

"Must be nice."

He nodded.

Oh god he's already bored of me. She clenched her hands into fists.

"How old are you?" he asked after a moment.

"Sixteen."

He nodded.

She groaned and he glanced at her, raising an eyebrow. Her cheeks burned. She was absolutely gonna *murder* Jasper.

"You alright?"

"You're bored already," she mumbled, heart racing.

"Oh, no. I just... I'm eighteen."

Ren looked at him with wide eyes. "So?" *oh. I'm young.* She sucked in a breath. "I'll be seventeen in a month!" Her face had to be so red. She shoved her hands in her pockets as the anxiety swirled inside of her.

Simon smiled slowly. "Yeah? I just turned eighteen, three weeks ago."

"So, you're only a year older than me." *That's not weird, is it?* Her heart was pounding. "Happy belated birthday."

He laughed. "Thanks. So, what are you into?"

"Into?"

"Yeah." He laughed. "Like, hobbies, interests? Besides chemistry."

She looked down. "Chemistry is *not* an interest. It is forced upon me. But I like crocheting. And art. And baking." She looked up at him, still surprised by how tall he was. Taller than both of her dads. He had to be at least six foot two.

"What are you into?"

"Music. I play guitar."

"That's cool."

"Yeah, I'm in a band, actually."

"Very cool."

He smiled, more shyly this time. Ren wanted to keep talking now that it felt slightly less awkward, but they were coming up on the bakery.

"This is me," she said as they came to a stop.

He frowned. "You work here?"

She laughed. "No, well, *sometimes*. But my dad owns this bakery, and we live above it."

"Weird."

"Why weird?"

"My friend Kit gets donuts from this place all the time. But I've never actually been."

Her eyes widened. "Do you want free donuts? Or cookies? We have cupcakes and—"

"No, I'm good." His blue eyes were so bright as he smiled down at her. "But it was a pleasure to walk you home, Ren."

She blushed. "Thanks." Feeling awkward, she turned and went inside without another word. Jasper was leaning against the wall, a cupcake in hand. He grinned at her.

"Ay, te voy a matar!" she hissed. "No puedo creer que acabas de hacer eso! Just set me up he was so cute tan vergonzosa!"

"Huh?" Jasper glanced at Marigold and Mateo behind the counter.

"She wants to kill you," Mateo answered.

"I'd pay to see that," Mari muttered.

"Don't be a hater, Mari!" Jasper said with a laugh. Then he turned on Ren. "He was so fine, please tell me you got his number."

"Kill you *dead*." She grabbed his arm and hauled him through the back door.

She dragged him all the way up to her room. He giggled the whole way, annoying her even more.

"Come *on,* tell me that wasn't fun! Cute tall boy walking you home..."

She groaned as she dropped her bag on the floor. "It was embarrassing!"

"He was so into you. I could tell."

"Yeah, *right*. Maybe before he found out I was sixteen." She pouted.

Jasper raised an eyebrow. "How old is he?"

"Eighteen. He's a *senior*."

"Damn. What did you talk about?"

Ren sighed and slumped into her desk chair. "Hobbies and interests?"

Jasper's smile returned. "So into you. If a guy isn't into a girl he's not asking about her interests cause he doesn't give a shit."

"Shut up. Not all guys are like that. You're not."

"No, but I'm special."

"Lycan isn't like that."

Jasper rolled his eyes. "He's a superhero, he doesn't count."

"Ugh. He was... really cute, wasn't he?"

"He really didn't ask for your number?" he asked as he plopped onto her couch.

She shook her head. "That means he wasn't into me, right?"

"The walk was too short. Bet he finds you at school tomorrow."

"Doubt it. He'll forget about me overnight."

"You're not as forgettable as you think," Jasper muttered with a yawn.

Her phone buzzed.

|Starface|
Did you forget about the interview?

"Oh no."

"What?"

"Kaida interview today."

"Oh yeah. Gross."

She sighed and stood up. "I should go. You can wait for me? I probably won't be gone long."

"It's fine. Should head home."

"Stay," she insisted. "You have an hour till you need to be home."

"Alright." He laid back and closed his eyes. "I'll let myself out."

"I'll text you after."

"Oh, Renny." He smiled. "I'll tune in, see it live."

"Ugh." She shook her head and sent a reply to Lycan.

|Bunhead|
Of course I didn't forget.
I just don't wanna go.

|Starface|
So you'll meet me here
In... ten minutes?

|Bunhead|
Five, Starface.

"Good luck!" Jasper called as the suit came over her and she climbed out through the skylight.

16
Team Silverlight

"Did we really agree to this?" Kaida asked as they walked down the street, crowds of people staring at them excitedly.

"We did."

"But I hate it," she said with a groan.

Lycan smiled. "I know. But they've been trying to get an interview since Vendetta fell. It's time. One *quick* interview."

"Fine."

They were filming it live in Times Square. She hadn't been back since the fight with Vendetta, and the memory made her shiver.

"It'll be fine," Lycan whispered.

She sighed and nodded. The area was taped off and there were three different cameras set up, with people bustling about.

"Hello!" A short white man with dark hair approached. "I'm Jason, from Channel Four and I'll be doing your interview today."

Lycan reached out and shook his hand. "Nice to meet you."

Kaida smiled, arms folded across her chest.

She was anxious as they got situated in their chairs across from the cameras. Kaida hated doing these sit down interviews, but it was the best way to appease people when they had questions only Kaida and Lycan could answer.

At least she wasn't alone. Lycan sat beside her, steady as always. He smiled and she released a breath, relaxing a little.

"We go live in two minutes, are you ready?" Jason asked.

Kaida nodded.

It was live, at least. Which meant they couldn't edit and twist her words. That happened once and she hadn't done a pre-recorded interview since.

The camera guy nodded and held up three fingers, counting them down. She took a deep breath, straightening in her chair.

"Hello everyone, Jason here with Channel Four. Today we are live with New York's heroes, Kaida Dragonheart and Lycan Silverstar, also known as Team Silverlight."

116

"Hi," she said awkwardly, putting on her best smile.

"It's been a while since you've agreed to an interview like this. Can we talk about why that is?" Jason asked.

"We've had bad experiences in the past with our words being twisted," Lycan said, taking the lead. "So, we don't generally do this. But people have been asking for a while, so here we are."

"I see. Well, so much has happened since your last interview. You took down Vendetta, stopping one of the worst serial killers we've seen in this city."

Lycan nodded.

"And now, more villains are appearing."

"Not just villains," Kaida said softly. "We have a new hero, Apex."

Jason smiled. "Yes. What can you tell us about Apex? We've seen so little of him."

"He's a great addition to our team. We're lucky to have him. *You're* lucky to have him."

Jason nodded. "Will we be seeing more of him then? Working with Team Silverlight?"

"Absolutely."

"Only one hero in the last year," Jason continued, clicking his tongue. "Three total, since the Xyri returned. Could you shed any light on why that is? What have your Xyri told you?"

"What my Xyri tells me is for me to know," she replied. "If and when he tells me something that concerns the citizens of New York, I'll be sure to inform you."

Zig laughed in her head.

"Fair enough. Now, everyone will come for my head if I don't ask... what's going on between the two of you?"

Kaida sighed as Lycan smiled. "We're just friends. Just like we were the last time we were asked."

"You seemed awfully cozy after the explosion on Valentine's Day..."

"Because we're friends," Lycan repeated.

Ren swallowed, trying not to fidget.

"What's it like to be friends with someone you don't really know? Keeping a secret identity must be hard."

"I know Lycan better than I know most people in my civilian life," she answered. "It doesn't hinder our friendship or our ability to work together to keep this city safe. But there are challenges. It's..."

"Not easy," Lycan took over. "We have to hide things from people we care about. And that can be taxing, but the good we do is worth it."

Kaida nodded.

"I see. Back to the explosion, there's rumors it was caused by Pompeii. Is this true, has she returned?"

Kaida clenched her fists, heart racing. "It was a gas leak. Pompeii had *nothing* to do with it."

Jason didn't look convinced. "What about the strange plants appearing on street poles in Midtown?"

She glanced at Lycan, confused.

"The what?"

"There's been vines grown up out of the ground, wrapped around lamp posts and mailboxes. Weird plants grown over scaffolding. They've been appearing everywhere these last two weeks. Rumors are it's a new Bonded. Do you have any insights on that?"

Kaida met Lycan's eyes again, heart pounding. She was sure he was also thinking about the stuff they found in the park.

"We're looking into it," Lycan finally answered. "That's all we can say for now."

Jason looked annoyed. "Alright. What can you tell us about the new villain, Wonderland?"

"We know about as much as you do," Lycan answered.

"You're the only ones who got close to him in that bubble of hallucinogenic insanity. We don't—"

"Them," Kaida corrected.

Jason paused, frowning. "Excuse me?"

"Wonderland's pronouns are they, them."

He blinked. "Why should I care? He's a villain."

Kaida's blood boiled under her skin. "*They.* You asked what we know about them, that's it."

"Seriously?" Jason laughed. "He literally messed with people's minds. I don't think—"

"We should respect everyone's pronouns." She sensed things changing. Jason's face getting redder as Lycan stiffened in his chair. "While I don't necessarily condone their actions," she continued, mouth going dry. "I wouldn't condemn them a villain at this point."

Jason laughed but there was no humor in it. "Well, *actually,* I'd say playing with people's minds *is* pretty villainous."

She frowned. "No one was hurt by Wonderland. I mean, compared to Vendetta—"

"I just find it interesting that a hero is defending him—"

"No," Lycan cut him off as he stood. He grabbed Kaida's arm and pulled her up. "This interview is over. Thanks for having us."

Kaida didn't argue as he kicked his board up and pulled her onto it. She held him as they flew into the air.

Her anxiety was fully raging by the time they landed on their roof on Spruce Street. She exhaled as she paced away from him, arms wrapped around herself.

"Oh my god. That was awful. I fucked that up *so* bad."

"Hey, hey." Lycan gently grabbed her arms, forcing her to stop moving. She met his eyes. "You upset one idiot. It's not a big deal."

"People aren't gonna like that I said that."

His smile widened. "Fuck those people. You have any idea how many people are gonna love that you said that? Think about them."

She took a deep breath, letting that sink in. Her body started to relax.

"See, you were right to correct him."

"True. But... we ended the interview early. People will be mad. It's been so long since we did one and—"

"There are other ways to talk to people. We don't need Jason from channel whatever. He's a dick. And an idiot."

Kaida closed her eyes and smiled. "Have I mentioned how lucky I am to have you lately?"

"Nope. You're very overdue."

She laughed, looking up at him. "God. That was *live*. I feel sick."

"It's fine. Gives them something to talk about besides us hugging, as if that's not a normal thing for friends to do." He started laughing at her.

"How do you do that?" she asked, realizing he was still holding her arms.

"Do what?"

"Make... everything better."

His smile softened as he looked down at her. "You make it easy." He stepped back then, cheeks flushed as his hands fell to his sides. "So, we gonna talk about it?"

She sighed, shoulders slumping. "You mean how stupid Jason knew about potential Bonded things before us?"

"Plants on lamp posts. Gotta be the same person."

She nodded. "We still don't know for *sure* if it's the same person who destroyed the statue, though."

"And growing plants around town doesn't seem that bad. It's not quite kidnapping, murder, and necromancy levels of villainy. Think we should withhold worry for now."

"But we should still be on guard."

He nodded. "So, how's Apex? I thought you might bring him to the interview."

"Oh, he's still reeling from his accidental interview. I thought it might be a bit much for him."

"Fair. What do you wanna do now?"

"Honestly?" she said in a small voice. "I kind of just wanna nap."

Lycan smiled. "Go home. I got patrol tonight."

"You're the absolute best."

"I know."

She resisted the urge to hug him as she turned and ripped a portal open. "You'll call me if you cross any suspicious plants?"

"Yes ma'am."

She flashed him a smile before stepping inside the portal. She came back out inside her closet and the suit came off. Jasper was gone. Sulking, she went to the couch and pulled out her phone.

|Jasper|
What an interview! 10/10 I fucking love you so much!!!!

She grinned.

|Ren|
Thanks. Your dad home?

|Jasper|
Unfortunately.

|Ren|
Boo. Want me to come over?

|Jasper|
Nah it's fine. He's not drinking.

|Ren|
you sure?

|Jasper|
Yeah. Mom's home, gonna help her make dinner

|Ren|
Kay

With that she changed into some pajamas and crawled into bed. Just as she laid on the pillow her phone started buzzing. She sighed as she sat up and answered the video call from Ocean.

"Hello!"

Ocean stared back at her, her brown skin flawless as always, her heart-shaped face tilted to the side. Her smile turned to a frown immediately, brown eyes narrowing. "Are you in *bed*?"

"Yes."

"You forgot we were gonna video? After rescheduling like *five* times..."

Ren scrunched up her face.

"It's *my* bedtime, not yours."

"Yes, *sorry*. Just a long day. But I'm here!" She took a deep breath and smiled as she crossed her legs. "What is up?"

Ocean sighed and pulled on one of her braids. *"So*, I have some news."

"Good news?" Ren asked, resisting the urge to yawn.

"Are you *sure* it's a good time?" Ocean asked.

"Yes!" She shoved her guilt down. She'd been blowing Ocean off for weeks now. Every time they were supposed to chat something came up that Kaida was dealing with. "You have my full undivided attention and also I love you and you're so pretty," Ren said with a big smile.

Ocean laughed. "Fine. Okay. Are you ready?"

"Seated. Should I be taking notes?"

Ocean looked genuinely nervous. "So... I'm... moving back to New York."

Ren blinked. "I'm sorry. It sounded like you just said..." Her mouth fell open.

Ocean smiled slightly. "Surprise!"

"Oh my god. Seriously? Don't fucking lie to me Oce. You're coming *back*?"

"Yep. For good, too. Like, not just a visit. We are *moving* back."

"Why do you look so worried? This is amazing news!" Ren hadn't seen her in person in three years, and there were only two visits before that, after Ocean moved away when they were eleven.

"I wasn't sure if... you'd be happy?"

Ren's eyes watered. *Oh I'm a shitty shitty friend.* "Ocean, this is literally the best news I've ever heard. I'm *so* sorry I kept pushing back our call."

"Really?"

"Yes!"

Ocean nodded. "I uh, won't really know anyone, when I come back. You were my *only* friend before I left."

"And I'm still here," Ren said, smiling wide. "Oh god. I can't fucking wait! When do you arrive?"

"Not till summer. I kinda wish we could just... come *now*. But Dad says I should finish this semester, deal with the move over the summer, then I can be settled for school *next* year."

Ren nodded. "Best news ever. Ahhhh!"

Ocean laughed. "Okay. Cool."

"You finally get to meet Jasper!"

"Oh boy."

"It'll be great."

Ocean shook her head, but she was smiling, her nerves seemed to have faded. "Okay, I'll let you go now."

"Keep me updated on the move! Love you!"

"Je t'aime!"

Ren released a breath as she hung up, her heart racing. Ocean was coming back, after five long years. She fell back into her pillows, feeling giddy.

17
Never Met Calm

Friday after school Simon was waiting by Ren's locker. She tensed as she walked up to him.

"Hi." He smiled down at her. "I wanted to offer my walking services, in case they're needed again."

She blushed as she opened her locker and switched some books from her bag. "Sure."

Jasper tried to tell her that Simon was into her, but she didn't believe it. How could a guy like her after only five minutes? But now, walking with Simon again, she thought *maybe*. He walked slow, like he wanted it to last.

"So, what else are you into?"

She smiled. "Uh." *Fighting crime. Saving the world. Normal girly things.* She sighed. "I like movies. And cats. I have a cat! His name is Breadcrumb."

"Cute." His smile made her heart absolutely race.

"What kind of music do you play?"

"Uh, like, punk pop rock." He blushed.

"What's your band called?"

He glanced at her. "You don't wanna listen to us."

"What if I do?"

He smiled, eyes softening. "Look at that, we're here."

She sighed as she looked at the bakery doors, then back at Simon.

"See you Monday," he said before turning away.

Monday?

I believe Jasper is right. The boy likes you, Zig said.

She swallowed. *You and Jasper are wrong. There's literally no way a senior boy with a jawline that sharp likes me.*

Then why did he walk you home again?

Just being nice?

She was proven wrong when she was back at school on Monday. Simon was once again waiting by her locker at the end of the day. He offered to walk her home, and she had to admit she *really* liked walking with him.

This continued throughout the week. Every day they chatted while he walked her home, and then that was it. She expected him to be there again on Friday, but now that she was admitting how much she liked it, he'd probably stop showing up.

But there he was, in his leather jacket, with a grin on his pretty face. Heart racing, she approached him with a smile.

"Can I walk you home today?" he asked.

"Sure."

He looked pleased as they moved outside.

"What would you have done if I said no?" she asked after a moment.

"Hm? If you said no to me walking you?"

"Yeah."

He looked up at the sky, hands in his pockets. "I'd have played it so cool. Just walked away, completely unbothered."

"Really?" Her smile fell.

He looked down at her and laughed. "Yeah but I would have been *so* disappointed."

"Oh." She smiled.

"God, you really are *so* short."

Ren opened her mouth, offended. "I'll have you know I *like* my height."

Simon laughed. "What are you like, four feet?"

"Five foot two! You're the one who's freakishly tall! Okay, *no one* is that tall!"

"I assure you, other people are six four. It's not that freakish."

She blushed. "You're *not* a freak. Just freakishly tall."

"I like your height, too," he said softly as he leaned down a bit. "Not that hard to get on your level."

Heart racing. Blood rushing. She swallowed. "Have I mentioned that I have two dads?" she blurted, coming to a stop.

Simon frowned as he straightened.

"Cause sometimes people get weird about that and—"

"My best friend is gay," he interrupted.

"Oh. Okay." She started walking again. "Have I also mentioned," she said, spinning around. "That I'm Mexican? Cause I'm kinda white passing and I mean—I'm also white I'm both—but I'm *more* Mexican and—"

Simon laughed.

Ren froze, face heating. "Is that funny?"

He shook his head. "My best friend, the *gay* one? Also Mexican."

"Oh." Ren nodded.

"Anything else on Ren's checklist?" Simon asked.

"I..."

"Kinda feels like you're trying to scare me away. But I'm not homophobic, or racist, so you'll have to find something else."

"What? No!" She looked up, meeting his eyes. "I just..."

"Would you have been disappointed, if I hadn't asked to walk you home today?" he asked, serious.

"Yes."

He smiled slowly. Ren swallowed and turned away, continuing their walk. Her heart was absolutely pounding. *He likes me? I think he likes me.*

Yes, Ren. That is obvious.

She tried to calm herself as they stopped outside the bakery.

"God, I hate that it's Friday."

"You don't like weekends?" she asked.

"Well, I won't see you."

Oh lord. "Does that mean you wanna see me?"

He didn't answer immediately, stepping closer as he looked down into her eyes. "It does."

Her cheeks burned. "Okay."

"Okay?"

She grinned. "See you Monday."

It wasn't until she was recounting this conversation to Jasper that she realized she fucked up. She laid in her bed, face smooshed into the pillows while Jasper cackled beside her.

"Seriously. You just said okay and left?"

"Mhm," she mumbled.

"Renny baby, that's *so* stupid. I love you so much."

"Ughhh."

"Okay okay. Here's the plan. On Monday you find this tall snack of a man and you go up to him and say 'Simon please—'"

Ren slammed her pillow into his face, knocking him back into the wall. He started laughing again.

"If by some miracle he still wants to see me on Monday then... I'll deal with it then."

"Sure you will."

She groaned again, clutching her pillow. "Enough about me. Your date with Harper, what's the plan?"

"We were supposed to go out tomorrow, but something came up with her mom. We're rescheduling for next Sunday."

"Booo."

"But I think our plan is the same if weather is decent. Gonna go for a walk in Washington Square, get to know each other better and stuff. Then grab lunch after."

"Park date is cute."

He grinned. "I'm pretty excited."

"Well, don't worry about anything during date. Lycan and I will take care of anything that comes up."

"Could take care of each other instead," he said with a raised eyebrow.

"Stop. You know we can't do that. Besides—"

"You're about to have a tall snack named Simon Sims?"

She blushed. "Ugh. I don't know." She hugged the pillow against her stomach.

"Oh come *on,* you're so into him."

She looked down. "But I like Bellamy."

"Yeah, and how's that going for you? Is Bellamy walking you home from school every day while flirting with you the entire time?"

She sighed. "No."

"He probably *would* if you told him how you felt."

"Absolutely not."

"Well. Simon *is* and he's super hot."

"No more boy talk please." She laid back on her pillows. "Too tired for boys."

"I'm a boy."

"You don't count."

Later that evening Kaida sat on the roof of the skyscraper on Spruce Street, suited up and waiting for Lycan. He hadn't actually said he was coming, but she couldn't remember the last time she asked and he hadn't shown up. In the meantime, she mentally studied for the history test.

"You could just tell me the answers," she mused. "You've been alive forever. You know all the history."

I did suggest this to you last year and you were so appalled by the idea you did not talk to me for the rest of the day.

"Oh."

You've changed a lot since then.

"Have I?"

The Ren I met back then would never want to cheat on a test.

"I was not suggesting cheating! I was just saying you could tell me the answers *now.* For *studying!*"

Zig laughed. *You are silly.*

"Yes, but you love me."

"I'm not supposed to do that," Lycan said as he sat beside her.

She laughed. "I was talking to *Zig*."

He blushed. "Oh. Me too."

Ren frowned.

"Uh so where's bird boy?"

"His name is Apex."

"Is he joining us?"

"Nope. Just you and me."

"Nice, let's go." He leaned forward and dropped off the roof.

Kaida sighed as she stood up, pushed her wings out then dove after him. They didn't have a real plan on patrol nights. They flew around, looking for trouble. Most nights they crossed average criminals. Other nights they crossed proper villains. But sometimes they weren't needed much, and they just hung out. This was one of those nights. They simply walked and talked.

"So, you know how I told you about the Xyri books my mom had?" Lycan said.

"Yeah." She stared at him. "Did something happen?"

"No. I just found another one. About Xyri powers."

Kaida stopped. "You think she knows you've Bonded?"

"I've been careful, I *swear*. But it's stressing..." Lycan trailed off, eyes moving across the street.

Kaida followed his gaze, stiffening when she saw Fable, his sleek black suit shining with a purple glow. He glanced at them, then kept walking. She frowned as Fable turned the corner and left their sight.

Sighing, she turned back to Lycan. "Did she have interest in the Xyri before this at all?"

He paused, meeting her eyes. "Maybe? She's sort of a historian so..."

Kaida nodded and they started walking again. "If she found out you Bonded, do you think she'd say something?"

"Definitely."

Kaida kicked a rock. "What's Zeli think?"

"That I'm overthinking it." He smiled. "She's probably right."

"As long as you're safe," she replied. "You better keep it that way."

"Promise."

Her phone buzzed in her pocket and her heart sped up. Had her dads noticed she wasn't in her room? She came to a stop and had Zig pull the suit back enough to get her phone out. Lycan watched curiously as she opened a text from her cousin.

|Marigold|
There's a boy named Simon here to
see you. Should I tell him I don't know
you or you wanna come down? I just
closed up and he cornered me. Kinda
sketch but he's cute.

"Oh."

"Something wrong?"

She looked up, heart racing. "Would you hate me if I left patrol early?"

"I'd never hate you," Lycan replied softly. "Is... everything okay?"

"Yeah, just... my parents need something and if I don't get home fast they might notice I'm *not* home." She laughed nervously. "Sorry."

"It's cool." He shook his head. "See you tomorrow maybe?"

"Tomorrow maybe!"

She pulled on the air, forcing her portal to appear. Rippling pink light burned in front of them. She waved to Lycan as she stepped through, wasting no time as she walked right back out into her rooftop garden. The portal disappeared and the suit came off.

She quickly texted Mari back to say she was coming out as she quietly ran down the stairs. By the time she got to the front door she was out of breath and realized she hadn't even checked herself in a mirror. She pulled her front camera open and brushed her hair out of her face frantically while taking a few deep breaths. Then she opened the door.

Simon stood there, tall and gorgeous in his black leather jacket. Ren swallowed as she stepped outside and closed the door behind her.

"Hi."

"Hi." His smile was wide as he stepped closer. "I realize it's a bit late, but I've been thinking about you all day and... I started going a little insane thinking about waiting till Monday to see you again."

"So, you came here... at nine o'clock?"

He actually blushed. "Yes? See, I would have just texted you. But I don't have your number. My first mistake. So, my thought process was I should come by to get your number. So I could text you and ask you out." He paused. "But now I'm saying it I hear how dumb that is. Cause who's asking girls out over texts? I'd ask you in person."

Ren's heart beat frantically in her chest. "You... wanna ask me out?"

"Yes. That is in fact what I'm doing now. Ren, would you like to go out with me? On a date, to be clear."

She couldn't hide her smile. "When?"

He raised an eyebrow. "Uh, will I sound desperate if I say tomorrow?"

Her stomach turned and twisted, making her giddy. "No. And yes. I... I..." The giddiness turned to panic. "I..."

Stop overthinking. If you want to say yes, do it. It is okay, Ren.

It is? She stood there, frozen, stuttering.

You are allowed to have a life outside of the powers. I want you to be happy, Ren. Safe, whole. Could this boy do that for you?

Happy.

Safe.

Whole.

"What?" She blushed, realizing she spoke out loud.

Simon stared at her, confused. "You can say no," he muttered softly. "It's fine."

Is it? "No." Her eyes widened. "I mean, no I *don't* wanna say no! I... yes. I want to go on a date with you. Tomorrow? If you still want to after my brain just malfunctioned."

He smiled. "You're so cute, you know that?"

What? Her wires were all crossed.

"Here." He pulled his phone out and handed it to her.

She took it in a shaking hand and entered her number, feeling strangely disconnected from herself. Bellamy. *He'd* asked for her number recently. Had put his in her phone...

"Simon, I wanna go on this date with you," she said, stomach twisting with nausea. "But I wanna be honest with you. I sorta kinda have feelings for another boy. And it doesn't feel right to agree to a date with you when that's a thing."

Simon was very still, his blue eyes analyzing her carefully. Her hands wouldn't stop shaking as she handed his phone back.

"Is this other boy your boyfriend?"

"No. Just a friend. He has no idea I like him."

Simon nodded slowly. "And... do you think it's possible you could develop feelings for me?"

Such a forward question.

You need to calm down, Zig said.

Yes but I don't know calm I've never met calm in my life!

She balled her hands into fists, trying to get a grip on herself. "Yes? Maybe. I mean, I don't know. But... yes, that's... very possible."

Simon smiled. "Then I wanna take you out tomorrow."

"Really?"

"Literally all I can think about." His smile widened. "I'm gonna text you, okay? And we can figure out what time you wanna go."

She nodded, head bobbing up and down like a damn doll. "Okay."

He bit his lip. "Goodnight, Ren. I'll see you tomorrow."

Her head continued its silly bob as he walked away. She wasn't sure if it stopped when she went inside. She only made it up two flights of stairs before her phone vibrated. Dad was by the landing, frowning as she passed.

"Thought you went to bed?"

She stopped. "A boy just asked me out." She grinned. "On a *date*."

His frown deepened. "What boy?"

"His name is Simon."

Dare appeared behind Dad, wearing a matching frown. "You're going on a date?"

"Tomorrow."

"What *boy?*" Dad asked again. "We haven't met anyone named Simon."

"No, you haven't."

"You're not going out with a boy we don't know. We have to meet him first!"

"Okay. You can meet him tomorrow. Before our date." She couldn't stop smiling as she started up the stairs again. She didn't take her phone out till she was back in her room, sitting in her bed.

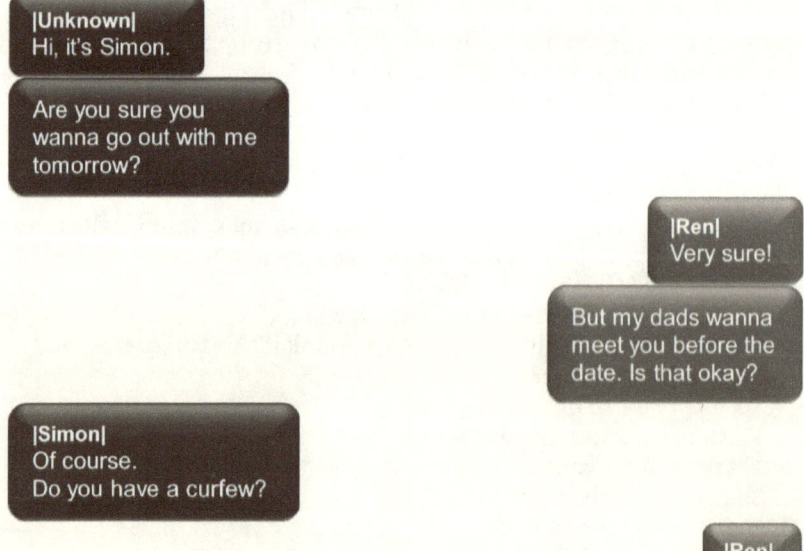

|Unknown|
Hi, it's Simon.

Are you sure you wanna go out with me tomorrow?

|Ren|
Very sure!

But my dads wanna meet you before the date. Is that okay?

|Simon|
Of course.
Do you have a curfew?

|Ren|
Ten.

|Simon|
Alright, how about I pick you up around four? Or should I come earlier to meet dads?

|Ren|
Three forty-five?

|Simon|
Perfect. You strike me as the type who doesn't like surprises…

Should I detail my plans for you?

|Ren|
I would like to know the plans, please.
So I know what to wear.

|Simon|
Very casual. Wanted to take you to a museum, then out to dinner.

Somewhere nice but not too fancy so it doesn't seem like I'm trying too hard. That okay?

|Ren|
Sounds perfect.
Just anywhere but the Met.

|Simon|
Done.
I can't wait to see you.

After this she frantically texted Jasper.

|Ren|
SIMON SIMS JUTS
SHOWED UPAND ASKED
ME ON A DATE!!!!!!!

|Jasper|
Oh mg od what the fuck
Ddis you say yssss???

|Ren|
YES! Date tomorow please
come pick my outfit!!!!

AHHHHHHH!!!!!!

|Jasper|
I can sneak out in like
20 calm dawn

Ahhh!HHH

18
Just a Trick

Ren paced back and forth anxiously as she waited for Simon. She'd been so stressed about what to wear, overthinking until Jasper saved her. He didn't try to convince her to dress up, instead suggesting something comfortable, more *her*. They'd settled on straight fit light wash jeans, and a yellow knit sweater with black boots. She thought it looked good but sent pictures to Ocean for a second opinion.

|Ocean|
You look amazing! I wanna hear about the date after!!!!!

|Ren|
Thanks!!

Finally the door buzzed and she sprinted across the hall to open it. Simon stood there, a bouquet of red roses in hand. He held them out to her.

"Thanks. I apologize in advance for whatever my dads are gonna say," she said as she took the flowers and smelled them.

"I can handle it."

Ren grinned as she led him upstairs and into the kitchen. He was wearing a dark blue button up with a black tie under his leather jacket. It was a *very* good look.

Both her dads stood by the couch, waiting, arms crossed. She rolled her eyes at them as she brought Simon closer.

"Simon, these are my dads, Cas and Arrow. Dads, this is Simon. My date." She tried not to blush as she busied herself looking for a vase for the flowers.

"Hi, it's nice to meet you both," Simon said. "You must be real dad. I see the resemblance. So, you're stepdad then?"

"Oh boy," Dare laughed as Ren spun around.

"He's *not* my stepdad he's just my dad!"

Simon froze, eyes widening. "I'm sorry."

Ren's face burned and she closed her eyes as Dare put his hand on her shoulder. "Oh god."

"You really got that automated response just embedded in there, huh?"

She groaned. "Simon I'm so sorry I—"

"No, it's fine," Simon said, smiling slightly. "It was my bad."

Dad stepped forward, his brown eyes intense as he analyzed Simon. "How old are you?"

"Eighteen, sir."

Dad turned to her. "No."

"Dad!" Her heart was racing.

"He looks twenty-five."

"He's *barely* a year older than me! It's fine! Porfis porfis porfis actúa normal sobre esto!"

"Si actuaría normal sobre esto, yo no te hubiera dejado ir a la cita," Dad grumbled back.

"Where are you taking her tonight?" Dare asked. Ren appreciated that he looked a *little* less murdery than Dad.

"Museum of Natural History, then dinner at Bellini."

Dad made a noise.

"Por favor cálmense," she said, embarrassed. "I'll be home by ten."

"Nine," Dad replied. "Curfew is nine tonight."

"Yes, sir," Simon replied with a nod. "I'll have her home by nine on the dot."

"Okay," Ren said. "This was very fun, but we're gonna go now." She grabbed Simon's arm and pulled him back to the stairs.

"Ren Rivers, you text me every hour on the hour till you're home. ¿Estamos claras, pequeña dragón?"

"Yes got it love you bye!"

Her dads were usually chill, but to be fair, Ren had only ever dated one boy before. And that was Jasper. They hadn't liked Jasper then either, but they weren't *this* weird about it.

"I am so sorry," she mumbled as they made it downstairs and back outside.

"Everything's fine," Simon said as he brought her to a motorcycle parked on the side of the road.

She shook her head immediately. "No. Nope."

"No?" He grinned as he held a helmet out to her.

"No, seriously. My dads would kill me *and* you if I get on that thing. My dad Arrow used to have a bike and Dad made him get rid of it after he got in a bad accident. It was so serious I think they almost broke up over it. It's been drilled into my head that I am never ever allowed on one at all. Ever."

"I see."

She blushed. "Could we just take the subway or... I... do you just... wanna cancel?"

Simon laughed. "Cancel our date? *Please*. Come on." He grabbed her hand and they started walking down the sidewalk. "I guess I thought the bike would be cool. Girls are always impressed by it."

"Oh."

He looked down at her. "I swear it's fine. Subway is perfect, cause we can *talk*."

Ren smiled.

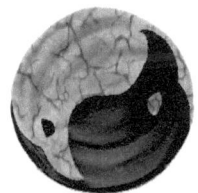

Jasper stood in front of his closet, staring at the cork board he'd hung up behind his clothes. He didn't want his parents seeing it, and there wasn't really a better place to put it. His room was too small. He'd been looking up all the sightings of Fable since he first appeared a year ago, trying to find a pattern. If he kept track of these maybe he could hone in on his actual location.

He'd dreamed of seeing that asshole taken care of for months. But now he had powers. *He* could take care of it. And that's exactly what he intended to do. It took him two hours to pin all the things on his board to see the radius better.

Most of the locations did sort of make a circle, only a few of them were farther out. He grinned as he hung his clothes back up.

We going out? Pozi asked.

Yep.

He climbed up on his bunk and fixed his pillows to make it look like he was asleep in the bed. Both his parents were working late, but Mom might check on him when she got in. And he didn't know when he'd be getting back. He reached down to the laptop on the desk under his bunk and closed it. Then he glanced around the room, noting the dirty clothes spilling out of his hamper in the corner... he'd get to that later.

The window squeaked as he slid it open and climbed onto the fire escape. Then he put the suit on.

Are we gonna stalk Ren on her date?

Jasper smiled. *No, Poz. That was a joke. We're gonna find Fable.*
Oh.
Jasper frowned. *You don't want me to go after him?*
You know how you feel about Ren? Pozi asked.
"Yeah?"
That's sorta how all Xyri feel about Nellithi.
"Well, if Fable's Xyri is so cool why'd she let him kill that girl and break my leg?"
Pozi sighed. *You think we have more control over you humans than we do. I told you Nellithi has never Bonded before. She's one of the oldest, and the only one from the first generation to never Bond.*
"What does that even mean?" Jasper asked, hands on his hips. "First generation? You told me you're third?"
Pozi said nothing.
"Hello. Do Xyri like... reproduce? Are generation one like, the parents of generation two or? How does it work? Are there Xyri babies?"
Pozi said nothing. Jasper rolled his eyes. He hated when he got like this.
"Fine. Be silent. But we're going to fight Fable, whether you like it or not."
Hmph. Be careful, kid. I have a feeling Fable is more powerful than anyone realizes.
Yeah, well. So am I.

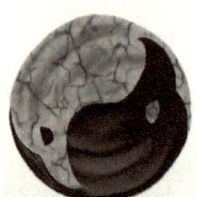

Simon held Ren's hand as they walked through the museum. Every time she looked up at him he was smiling down at her, and those blue eyes watched her with interest. But *why* was he interested in her?
You're neat.
Ren smiled. *Your opinion doesn't count, Zig.*
How could it not count? I chose you out of billions of people. You are very choosable.
Thanks.
"What are you thinking about?" Simon asked.
She blushed and looked down. "Why you're interested in me?"
"You want me to tell you?" His smile was *so* pretty.
She nodded.

"You're honest. Everything you say is so honest." He held her eyes as he spoke and they slowly came to a stop. "Not that other girls aren't honest. It just... feels like everything's a game sometimes. Everyone's playing a part and talking to you felt so real and genuine. And I just wanted to keep talking to you. Those five minute walks to your place were way too short."

She smiled. "Really?"

"I asked you out and you told me you liked someone else. You're probably the most honest person I've ever met."

And yet there's one thing I can never ever tell you, she thought sadly. "That's sweet."

He grinned and grabbed her other hand. "Don't suppose you're finding yourself more interested in me yet?"

"If the uh, butterflies in my stomach are any indicator..." She swallowed. "I think maybe yes, I am."

He gently swung their joined hands, and the crowds of people had to part to get around them. She didn't care.

"That's good."

They started walking again, her heart pounding uncontrollably in her chest every time he looked at her.

"So, I clearly said something wrong about your dads back at the house. I really am sorry about that."

Her cheeks burned. "No, I'm sorry for snapping. It's just..." She sighed. "When I was little everyone acted like Dare didn't matter as much as Dad, since he wasn't biologically related to me, which is *stupid.* And I hated it. Teachers did it all the time, even when I called him my dad they'd say stepdad or like, the *other* one. But he's been in my life since I was two." She let out a breath. "I didn't realize I was still so touchy about it."

"It says a lot about you, how much you care about him."

She smiled. "He's always been there for me. Dare even legally adopted me when they got married, and Dad and I took his last name. Before it was Martinez, from Dad obviously. Not my mom. But, Rivers suits me best."

"Why do you call him Dare?"

Her smile widened as they turned a corner. "When I was little I'd call him Daddy Arrow, or I'd try to. I wasn't very good at pronunciations, so we shortened it to Darrow, which evolved into Dare."

"That's adorable," he said, smiling. "So, no mom in the picture then?"

Ren shook her head. "She ditched Dad and I two weeks after I was born. I've seen her maybe, three times? In my whole life. She's irrelevant."

Simon nodded.

"What about you? You told me about your mom but not..."

"Dad died when I was ten."

"Oh, I'm sorry!"

"It's fine. I mean, it *sucks*. But I'm fine now. And, my mom's the best."

Ren smiled. "No siblings?"

"Nope. Only child, just like you."

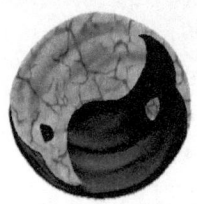

Jasper moved on from his fourth location with no sign of Fable. Or anyone doing any crime, which was honestly very rude of them. He hadn't had a chance to prove himself to the public yet. Ren was right that people wouldn't stay hung up on his terrible fight with Fable three weeks back, but they were only talking about him as a sidekick to Team Silverlight. He wanted to make his own mark. It would be perfect if his first victory was against Fable.

Southeast, Pozi muttered.

Jasper turned and spotted someone with stupid ass fucking bunny ears walking down the street. He tensed, his blood boiling as he landed on a roof and hunched down. Fable had some kind of bag slung over his shoulder. Jasper watched, body burning with adrenaline.

Are you ready for—

Jasper jumped, swooping down low.

—you weren't ready last time!

I'm so ready.

Jasper fell to the ground in front of Fable, straightening as his wings folded in.

Fable stopped in his tracks, eyes narrowing. "You again."

"Did ya miss me?"

"Not really."

Jasper's eyes moved over the boy, noting the bag over his shoulder was definitely a pillowcase, stuffed full of money. "Been busy tonight, have you?"

"Yeah." Fable licked his lips. "And I'm still busy, so scram."

"Not a chance."

"What do you want?"

"To kick your ass."

Fable sighed heavily and dropped his bag on the ground.

"A pillowcase, *really?* You look like you're fucking trick or treating."

Fable's lips curved a little. Then candy rained from the sky. Jasper flinched as it hit. *It's not real.* It felt real for a moment, but once his brain acknowledged the illusion he couldn't feel anything. The fake candy fell faster than rain, piling up on the pavement around them.

"Nice trick," he hissed. Then he rushed him.

Ren sat across from Simon at dinner, unable to stop smiling. She'd been afraid the date would be awkward, they wouldn't know what to talk about, but things had been so easy. They talked nonstop through the museum, and she was feeling more comfortable by the minute. Her heart was finally somewhat steady, even with him smiling at her like that.

"Yeah," he continued. "We haven't played anywhere cool recently. But next time we do... I could bring you. If you wanted to come?"

"That would be so fun."

"Yeah? So, you like concerts?"

Ren raised an eyebrow. "Who doesn't like concerts? I'll admit I haven't been to one recently but..."

"What was your last one?" he asked.

"August Rain." She narrowed her eyes. *"Don't* make fun, she's the biggest star for a *reason."*

Simon laughed. "I am so happy to hear this."

"You are?"

He nodded. "I can play *several* August songs. Can't wait to impress you with that later."

Ren smiled.

Conversation slowed when their food arrived and they started eating, but she liked hearing him talk about music. He seemed to perk up when talking about something he was really interested in, which made her wanna ask more questions about it.

Her phone buzzed and she sighed. Her dad had *not* been joking about texting every hour.

|Dad|
Still alive?

|Ren|
Yes! We're at dinner.
It's romantic and
amazing.

Thanks for asking!

|Dad|
Glad you're having fun

Be home by nine!

|Dare|
We really are glad it's going
well, but we love you and we
worry.

And Cas is pretty much
having a heart attack over
this right now so please
remember to text

|Dad|
I am not I am totally fine!

Love you nine on the dot!!!

|Ren|
Love you too. But it's
fine! Text ya soon.

She rolled her eyes but then her heart stopped as she saw her notifications. Alerts for Apex and Fable. Dread filled her as she scanned through them. They were fighting in the streets of Lower Manhattan. She sucked in a breath then looked up at Simon.

"My dads," she said, shaking her phone. Then she sent a text to Lycan.

|Bunhead|
Hey I'm busy but Apex is fighting Fable in lower Manhattan can you PLEASE go make sure he doesn't get himself killed I'll buy you a cookie!!!

|Starface|
I want two cookies!

Relief. Lycan would handle it. But... with a sigh she looked up at Simon. "I uh... my dads want me to come home early," she mumbled.

"Oh. Okay."

"I'm so sorry."

"It's fine, Ren." He didn't complain as he paid for their meal and walked her out.

When they got to her house he paused a few feet from the door, pulling her hands closer. Her heart raced as she looked up into his eyes.

"I had a great time," he whispered.

"Me too."

"I'd love to take you out again."

"Me too."

He smiled and leaned a little closer. Panic rose up inside of her. She hadn't kissed someone in two years. What if she forgot how or was bad at it or—

He cupped her cheek as he searched her eyes, then he leaned in, lips pressing gently against hers.

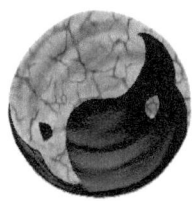

A fist slammed into his mouth and Jasper fell back with a groan.

"How's that for a trick?" Fable asked, standing over him.

"I'm gonna k-kill you," Jasper hissed.

"You'll have to catch me first."

Jasper pushed himself upright as Fable split into fifty different people, each one staring back at him. His heart pounded with fear. He'd done the same thing that night in the shop. Many Fables...

"You think you're funny? I know what you really are."

"Just a trick." The words echoed around him. *"Just a trick. Just a trick."*

"A murderer," Jasper growled.

Every Fable head turned to the side. "What are you talking about?"

"I'm talking about you, murdering a little girl in a shop on 8th Avenue. On September sixteenth. At 10:32 PM."

Fable blinked, purple eyes surprised.

"Yeah," Jasper muttered as he stepped forward. "Some fucking *trick.*"

Fable shook his head. "I haven't killed anyone."

"A liar *and* a coward. You don't wanna face me?"

"I am facing you." There was so little emotion in his voice. "Are you?"

The illusions evaporated, leaving only one Fable remaining.

"You don't want to fight me," he said.

"I've never wanted anything more," Jasper replied.

Fable sighed. "Fine."

He moved toward Jasper, but he sidestepped, way too fast for Fable. Then he blocked the next punch, hand catching Fable's wrist. Fable tried to grab his arm, but Jasper yanked him back then shoved him forward. Fable stumbled but recovered quickly, throwing himself at Jasper.

He grabbed the back of Jasper's hood, yanking it off as they tumbled to the ground and rolled. Fable landed on top and punched Jasper in the jaw again. He groaned, blinking spots out of his eyes as Fable jumped up and started walking away.

"You think you w-win cause you knocked m-me down?" Jasper spit blood out of his mouth as he pushed himself up. "That's not how you *win.*"

Fable just stood there, staring at him. So Jasper tackled him. Or so he thought, but he hit the ground alone and grunted in frustration, turning to see another Fable behind him. He got to his feet and sharp pain exploded in his side. Pozi *screamed.* Jasper looked down at the black knife sticking out of his body.

Jasper? Jasper!

"It's just... just a trick," he whispered, feeling faint.

"No," Fable's breath was hot against his neck. "A *treat.*"

PART TWO

LETTING GO

Some would argue that humanity only thrived because
of the Xyri. That we benefited from their gifts.
As if they didn't cause most of the deaths in the war.
As if there wouldn't have been a war without them.
We never needed them.
Now that they're gone, we can finally prosper.

- A World Without Xyri

19
Another Roof, Another Injury

Ren was nauseated as she paced back and forth in the top of the sky, waiting. Lycan texted that Apex was hurt, and that he was bringing him, but that was all he said. Worry gnawed at her. She'd been so excited to go home and tell Jasper about her date. About her *kiss*. Now her hands shook as she wondered if he was even alive.

"Special delivery," Lycan called from above.

She jumped as he descended on his board, Apex in his arms.

"Is he—"

"Totally fine! A little bloody, but he's okay. I *promise*." Lycan set him down and Ren fell to her knees beside him, holding back a sob. She could see blood muddying the lines of glowing green at his waist.

"Apex?" She gently brushed his hair back, heart thundering a rhythm of terror in her chest.

"Hi," he mumbled, eyes still closed.

She released a breath, afraid she might vomit. Lycan knelt beside her and she leaned her head on his shoulder.

"What happened?"

"Found him like this. Well, found him with *this* in his side, actually." He held up a knife, black as oil, with a line of purple, like amethyst, running through it.

"Fable stabbed him?"

"Yes. He was gone when I got there. But Apex is fine. Already healing. Just needs to stay in the suit."

"Did he need to... fuse, or whatever?" She gripped Jasper's hand in hers, remembering another roof, another injury, Lycan nearly dead in her lap.

"Zeli says it wasn't that bad. He's gonna be okay, Kai. I swear." He sighed. "I don't know why Fable attacked him though, seems... unlike Fable."

Ren swallowed. "Apex... probably attacked *him*. Like last time. Cause he hates Fable."

"Why?"

She shook her head, unable to explain.

Lycan nodded. "He's gonna be okay."

"Thank you for going. Thank you."

Lycan put his arm around her shoulders. "Of course."

They didn't stay long. Kaida formed a portal and carried Apex through it, out into her bedroom, where she laid him on her bed. Then she stood over him as his eyes fluttered. Her suit came off and she slowly tiptoed downstairs. Her dads weren't in the living room, which meant they were probably in their room. She got her phone out and texted them to let them know Jasper came over to talk about her date and was staying the night. A minute later she got a response saying they had to be asleep by eleven.

She exhaled as she went back to Jasper, asleep in her bed. Her hands shook as she sat beside him and sent a text to his mom to let her know he was staying over.

"Why him?" she whispered as she put the phone down.

What do you mean? Zig asked.

"Why did Pozi Bond *him*?" Her eyes burned with tears as she stared down at him. "My best friend in the whole world." She glanced at Zig. "It's bad enough I have to live with the threat of losing Lycan every fucking day. Now Jasper?" A tear slid down her cheek.

Ren, he is alright.

She wiped her eyes. *This time.*

Ren, I understand you're hurting but—

Stop. Please. She sucked in a breath as her phone vibrated. "I just wanna be mad," she muttered, not meeting Zig's eyes as she grabbed her phone.

> |Simon|
> That might be the best date I've ever been on.

She stared at the text, heart racing. Then she closed her eyes and put her head on her knees. Jasper almost died. While she was out on a date getting a kiss that was almost perfect...

The phone buzzed again. She sighed, lifting her head.

> |Simon|
> You sure you want a second date?

Ren breathed out slowly.

|Ren|
I do.

|Simon|
What do you think about
next saturday?

She closed the texts without responding. Her suit came back over her as she hit the call button beside the contact Starface. Her heart raced as Lycan's soft voice answered.

"Is he okay?"

She sniffed. "Yeah. But I'm not."

"What can I do?"

She let out a breath. "Talk to me?"

"About what?"

"Anything at all."

She wasn't sure how much time passed, with Lycan talking and her listening, as Jasper slept beside her. He switched topics at least seven times before he started running out of things to say. That's when he began to read to her, straight from a book off his shelf. Ren relaxed, leaning against the wall, eyes closed as she listened. It was Howl's Moving Castle. She'd only ever seen the movie.

Something about Lycan sitting in his bed in his bedroom reading to her over the phone felt oddly... intimate. But it was the only thing she could hold onto. It wasn't until the sun came up and Jasper was no longer in the suit that she was able to fully relax.

"You have a good voice," she mumbled with a yawn.

"I do?"

"Mhm. Should read to me more often." She thought she could hear him smiling. "Thank you, for staying up with me."

"Always."

"Normal people start waking up soon," she continued, yawning again.

Lycan laughed. "Who needs normal when I got you?"

Ren smiled. "I should let you go."

"Okay. See you later, maybe?"

"Later maybe."

Once they hung up, she glanced over to see Jasper staring at her with a frown on his face. "What..."

She glared. "You almost died and Lycan read me a story." Her shoulders slumped. "I am *so* sleepy."

Jasper smiled softly.

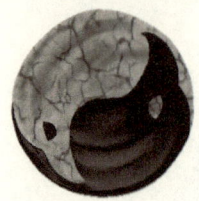

Jasper decided getting stabbed super sucked. He'd spent that first night at Ren's completely out of it. When he went home the next morning he was still unwell and had to cancel his date with Harper. His mom thought he was sick, so he also missed school on Monday. Thankfully Dad was gone when they had that conversation. If he knew Jasper skipped school, he'd probably stab him too.

Ren brought his homework after school. She sat at the end of his bunk by his feet, talking at him while he was stretched out on his back.

"Jas?"

He sighed. "I'm fine."

Her brown eyes were intense as she glared at him. "Are you?"

"Physically, totally fine."

"Did it scar?"

"No idea." He hadn't looked.

He still couldn't believe how badly the fight had gone. Fable didn't have any weapons on him when he stabbed Jasper. But then suddenly a knife, a *real* non-illusion knife was just buried inside him. It never disappeared. Jasper still had it, in the top drawer of his dresser, next to that damn rope.

"Do you want me to do the homework for you?"

He blinked. "What?"

"I know that's cheating but—"

"Ren, I'm not *dying*." He sighed and sat up. "You were really scared?"

"Yes!" She put her notebook down. "Lycan didn't say what happened, you know. Just said you were hurt. I couldn't fucking breathe. Not until you were in front of me. Not till the suit was off." She paused, meeting his eyes. "I'm not sure I'm breathing now. You seem *so* out of it."

"I just feel stupid. I really thought I had him."

"I'm sorry."

He nodded and leaned against the wall. "It's fine. At least there weren't any clear videos this time. No proof of my failure."

Ren didn't respond, still watching him with worry as she shook her pencil back and forth.

"I swear I'm okay! Just annoyed. I was supposed to go out with Harper yesterday."

148

Ren sighed. "I know, she asked about you at lunch."

"She did?" He smiled slightly.

"Told her you had a cold. You guys still going out or?"

"Yeah, now it's this Saturday."

"That's good!"

"Enough about me. You haven't told me about your date yet. Distract me from my sorrows."

That got her to smile, barely. But the pencil kept swinging, showing her anxiety. "It was good."

"He kissed you?"

Her cheeks turned pink. "Yes."

"And?"

"And it was good."

"But, not better than me?"

Ren laughed. "I don't know. I kissed you a lot. I've only kissed Simon once." She shook her head. "I was *so* nervous. Like full panic as it happened. But then... it was happening." She bit her lip.

"You going out again?"

Ren sighed and picked her notebook back up. "He asked after the date, and again at school, but I haven't responded about when yet."

"Why not?"

She raised an eyebrow. "Oh, I don't know? Maybe cause my best friend almost *died* and has been depressed since almost dying!"

He rolled his eyes. "I did not almost die. Pozi said it wasn't even close."

"Pozi told *me* it scared the daylights out of him."

"Yeah, cause a normal knife couldn't pierce my suit. But it wasn't a normal knife!" He sat up straighter. "It was a fucking imaginary knife made with the powers of fucking trickery. Did you know that Fable's Xyri has *never* Bonded before? That's what Pozi said. She's first generation, whatever *that* means. But never Bonded! None of the Xyri even knew what her powers would *be!* How insane is that? Fable is so fucking powerful, Ren."

She let out a slow breath. "Do you think maybe... it might be better for like, your mental and physical health if you let go of this grudge against Fable?"

He blinked. "You're fucking kidding right?"

"Jasper, I know how you feel—"

"No you don't! You weren't there!"

"I was!" she yelled back, her eyes watering suddenly. "I watched them wheel you into that ambulance."

Jasper fell still. "What?"

Ren blinked and wiped her eyes. "I didn't even know it was you when I got there."

He didn't know what to say, his brain frantically trying to process those words. Ren was there?

Not Ren, kid.

He closed his eyes. "Kaida."

"I wanted to kill him," she whispered.

Jasper looked at her, surprised to hear the anger in her voice.

"You almost died. And it was Fable's fault. So I went *after him*."

"I..." He knew that, didn't he? There was footage of Kaida fighting him, but that was before he knew...

"I wanted to end him I was so so angry and I couldn't..." She paused, looking down at the notebook in her lap. "It's hard to win a fight against Fable. He's not stronger, or faster, maybe not even smarter. His real weapon is confusion. He sneaks away while you're still trying to catch up." She sighed. "Lycan talked me down. I had to let it go. I was on a vengeance quest when we had bigger problems."

"Bigger problems?"

Vendetta, Pozi whispered.

Jasper swallowed.

Ren looked over, meeting his eyes. "I think it was an accident."

"What was?"

"The explosion, with Fable. He's *never* hurt someone before or after that."

"Okay, even *if* that's true, he's still a criminal. A thief. I mean he steals *all* the time! You don't care about that?"

She looked away.

"Ren, seriously?"

"I assume he steals so much cause he... has nothing."

"You can't know that."

Ren took a deep breath then looked back at him. "He's homeless, Jasper. Or, he was a few months ago."

He paused. "How do you know?"

"Found him sleeping in an alley one day."

He raised an eyebrow. "In his suit?"

"You can't freeze to death in the suit. And it was November. A cold night." Her shoulders slumped. "He's just a kid, like us. All I'm saying is... you don't know his story. And... this anger you have for him it's... I don't want you to get hurt."

"I won't."

She laughed. "You already *did*."

He ran his hands over his face. "Okay, I'm sorry. I'll be smarter next time. I... I'm sorry."

She wasn't looking at him. Jasper sighed.

"Ren, I'm sorry, okay? Can we talk about something else *please*? I'm so moody and I don't wanna fight."

"I just need you to understand that fighting another Bonded isn't like fighting a normal person. Someone tries to stab you, and it's not gonna do anything. A Bonded tries *anything* and you could *die*, just like that."

"Right yeah. Got it. New topic, *please.*"

She sighed.

"So, your date was good. Your kiss was good. Text Simon, tell him you'll go out again."

"Maybe."

"What are you afraid of?"

"Don't know."

"What does Ocean think? You told her about the date?"

Ren nodded.

"And? She's still moving back here, right. You were *so* hyped about that last week..."

Ren nodded again.

Jasper sighed. "You're afraid cause you were on the first date when I got hurt?"

She looked at him with sad eyes.

He sucked in a breath. "Make a date for Saturday. I'll be out with Harper, okay? No chance of me getting hurt. At least, not like that."

She leaned her head back into the wall. "Maybe."

20
Better Together

Bellamy walked alongside his mom through the farmer's market. She'd been waiting for him outside of school, and they walked down together. It wasn't planned, but he didn't mind.

"After this we could go to the bookstore," she suggested.

Bellamy smiled. "Really?"

"And was thinking I could cook tonight," she continued.

He frowned. "Is something wrong?"

She didn't meet his eyes as they moved to the next booth, each one covered in a white canopy. The smell of coffee was strong on the air. "Nothing's wrong."

"*Mom.*"

She stopped and looked up at him with sad eyes. "I guess I just miss this. I've been so busy lately, and..." She sighed.

"Mom, it's fine."

It was true she'd been busier than normal, but it worked out for him. He had way more time to do Lycan things when she was caught up in her work.

"You probably don't miss it," she mumbled, turning away. "All that time I spent hovering over you. But now it feels like I'm not involved at all."

"I do miss it," he replied, pulling her to the side so they wouldn't be in anyone's way. "I guess maybe I don't miss the *hovering*. You were... really overprotective when I was little. But, I do miss hanging out with you. *Obviously* I do."

She smiled, but it didn't reach her eyes. "Even after seventeen years, I feel like I've never quite figured out this mom thing."

"What are you talking about? You're a *great* mom."

She shook her head, looking past him. "I never had an example. Of how to do it. It's easier now, but I still worry."

"About me? Cause, I'm fine. Really."

"Are you, Belly?"

He swallowed. "Yes?"

She sighed and started walking again. He followed, gut twisting. *She doesn't know. She can't know.*

"Are you... worried cause I haven't been telling you stuff lately?" he asked, cautious.

She met his eyes. "I suppose, that's part of it. And I get it, you're growing up. You've got friends to talk to. You don't wanna rant to me about every little thing like you used to. It's *okay.*"

"Mom. I... I mean, I..." he stumbled over the words, mind racing. She didn't know he Bonded, but she could sense he was hiding things. "I guess I've just been stressing... about... a girl. A friend."

Mom's green eyes widened. "The one from your party, Ren? She was the brown hair, big sweater?"

Bellamy smiled. "Yes. Definitely Ren."

"Did something happen with her?" she asked softly.

"Uh." His mind blanked. Could he tell her what happened with Kaida? Pretend it was Ren? Maybe she'd have good advice. Mom *was* a girl after all.

"I, so..." He licked his lips as he started walking again, unable to be still. Mom followed at his side.

"I told her I liked her and..." *She jumped off a roof and didn't speak to me for two weeks and I thought I was gonna die about it.* "And she very gently told me she didn't feel the same. Said she liked someone else. We're still friends, *great* friends."

Mom nodded.

"But I guess. It's kind of hard, to be friends with someone when I feel this way... I mean, I don't wanna *not* be her friend. It just... hurts, I guess? Does that make sense?"

"Yes," she whispered, staring at the clouds. "I once... fell in love with a man I wasn't supposed to. And, he gave me the just friends talk."

"And?" Bellamy stared at her, heart racing. "How did it end?"

She released a breath, eyes far away. "*Oh,* that's not important." She brushed some hair off his forehead before continuing. "It's going to be hard, no matter what you do. Staying friends, or putting distance between you. You're going to hurt." She smiled sadly. "It's not the kind of hurt a mom can protect her baby from."

"Mom..."

"You can try moving on. Perhaps that works for some people."

Bellamy blinked. "Move on? How do I do that?"

"I suppose, you find someone else? Try letting go." She shook her head. "I wish I was better equipped to help with this."

"No, you're doing great. I could... move on. I can do that. Thanks, Mom." He forced a smile. "So, what are you gonna make for dinner?"

"Not sure. What sounds good?"

"Anything."

She smiled as they continued browsing the stalls. Mom picked out several jars of jam and some fresh asparagus. They were about to leave for the bookstore when screeching tires and screams of alarm erupted around them.

Mom grabbed his arm, shoving him behind her as a car came through the square. Before he could react Kaida fell from the sky, landing in front of the car. She flung her arms out, and light exploded behind her in a wave, solidifying into a wall at her back right as the car slammed into it. The entire square seemed to be collectively holding their breath as police cars came crashing in.

Kaida straightened and turned, her wall melting to mist. She yelled as one of the cars rammed right into a vendor's booth.

"Can you not!" She jumped onto the hood of the first car, peeking in through the windshield as cops ran toward her.

"This isn't your business," one of the cops hissed as he got closer.

"You almost ran these people over!" she yelled back.

"This isn't a villain," another cop said as they opened the door of the car she stood on and pulled the man out of the driver's seat. "Normal crimes don't require *you*."

"Pues si no fueran tan pésimos a hacer su puto trabajo yo no tendría que intervenir cada puta ves!"

Bellamy smiled. He didn't understand a word, but he loved when Kaida ranted in Spanish.

With a sigh Kaida hopped off the car and turned to face the crowd in the square. "Is everyone okay?" she asked, her tone softer now.

Her eyes moved over them, then stopped on Bellamy. His heart raced. *Does she recognize me? No. That's impossible.* But she stared at him, blue eyes wide. He realized that Mom was still clinging to his arm and he blushed.

"Everyone's okay," someone else answered. "Just the booth got toppled."

Kaida nodded slowly and went to help them. Bellamy pulled Mom with him as several people started assisting with the fallen goods. Bellamy's hands shook as he got closer to Kaida and knelt down. She looked up, meeting his eyes.

"Hi," she said.

"Hello." He swallowed. "That uh... was very cool. With the wall."

She smiled and his heart pounded a mile a minute. She was so close and so gorgeous and he wasn't Lycan. He wasn't Lycan, but she *still* smiled at him like he mattered.

"Thanks. I was trying to catch the car before it crashed in here. So... kinda failed."

"Everyone's okay though. So not a failure."

Her smile widened. They continued picking things up, making piles of what was ruined and what was salvageable. Other people seemed just as impressed by Kaida, several of them trying to get her attention. She spoke to each of them in turn, a smile on her face. Bellamy glanced over his shoulder to see Mom watching him with a curious expression. He looked back at Kaida. She was taking a picture with the booth owners now. She met his eyes and he blushed.

"So, what's your name?" she asked as she stepped up to him.

"Uh, Bellamy."

"It was nice to meet you."

"Yeah, you too."

She looked like she was going to say something else, but no words came out. His heart wouldn't stop racing as her eyes moved down, landing on his wrist.

"Nice bracelet," she finally said.

His face heated. "My friend made it for me." It was starting to fray a little. He met Kaida's eyes. She wasn't making fun of him, was she? No... "She crochets, my friend. And so she—she made it for me cause I was I was um I uh—"

"Kaida!"

Kaida spun around and Bellamy fell silent.

"What's wrong?"

The person who screamed held up their phone. "Something just happened in Irving Square Park. Something about the ground collapsing and—"

"On it!" Kaida's wings erupted out as she gave a quick wave to the crowd. Then she took off running and leaped into the air, flying away.

Bellamy watched her with wide eyes. Something happened. Lycan was needed but... He glanced back at Mom. She was still watching him with a small smile. *Kaida will call if she needs me. It's fine.*

He forced down his panic and walked back to Mom.

"Do you still wanna go to the bookstore?" she asked.

"Huh? Oh um. Yes?"

She laughed. "You're so flustered."

"What?"

"Kaida. You have a crush on her?"

He swallowed, throat dry. "Oh. I mean. Doesn't everyone?"

Mom's eyes were so bright, her smile wide. "I'm sure. Come on, Belly. We'll get you some books. I'll cook dinner. Maybe we could watch a movie?"

"Really?"

"If you want to."

"Yeah, I'd like that."

If Kaida needed him she'd call. And he'd find a way to get away. For now, he decided to enjoy the day with his mom.

Did you see him?
Yes, Ren.
He was so cute! Out with his mom. Did you hear him talk about me? Ren me!
I thought you liked the new boy, Simon?
Ren blushed. *I barely know him. I do like him though.* She just... still liked Bellamy, apparently. The shock she felt at stumbling into him at the market was still running through her.
Could you focus on the giant hole in the ground down there instead?
She gasped as she saw it and descended from the sky. It looked about a hundred feet across, spanning from the corner of the park out into the street. She couldn't guess how deep it was. People were screaming and crying in a panic around the rim. She dove right past them into the hole. Four cars had tumbled inside along with several people, most of which were still moving. She landed among them in the bottom of the pit as light streamed out of her feet, forming solid ground around her for them to walk on.
"On the platform if you're able!" she yelled as she moved through them.
Several of them stepped up onto the crystalline floor. But a few ignored her, one of whom was absolutely wailing on her knees in the shifting dirt.
Kaida sucked in a breath, steadying herself as she got close, light spinning around her fingers.
"Her son is buried!"
"We can't get him out!"
The mother continued to scream, digging with her hands frantically.
How do I get the kid out?
Relax. Let me guide the light.
She nodded and the light moved, free of her thought. Hundreds of thin little wisps worked their way into the dirt, slithering inside like diamond snakes.

The woman fell silent, tears streaming down her face as she watched. Everyone held their breath, including Kaida. She could feel the light, moving slowly. It was wrapping around something, encasing it, becoming solid.

Now.

She pulled on the light, stepping back. A body burst forth from the dirt, tangled in her shimmering webs. The small boy was coughing as his mother sobbed harder. She pulled him into her arms, rocking back and forth while everyone around them cheered.

Kaida couldn't cheer. One of the cars was upside down, the doors still closed. Nobody had climbed out of that one.

"On the platform now, please," she said before she went to the car.

Kaida braced herself as she ripped one of the doors off it and tossed it behind her. Her eyes burned before she even placed her fingers on the neck of the girl in the passenger seat. Blood was dripping from her forehead.

Ren...

She's dead.

She trembled as she reached for the man in the driver's seat. His eyes stared blankly. No pulse.

There's nothing you could have done for them, Zig said.

She didn't respond, brain shutting down as she pulled the girl's body out and gently laid her on the floor of light. Her hands were shaking so much as she got the man out.

"Is... is everyone else..." She squeezed her eyes shut. *Where is Lycan?*

"Everyone's okay," a man answered. "My arm might be broken but... I'm alive. The boy, he's alive. Because of you."

Kaida opened her watering eyes and nodded. Then she pulled on the air, ripping a portal open. Some of them gasped as it formed.

"Everyone in," she said as she stepped halfway into the portal.

Kaida gently placed a hand on each person's shoulder, guiding them through until all of them were in. Then she carried the bodies of the dead through. Everyone was crowded together, staring up at the brilliant sky full of golden stars with wonder in their eyes.

"Where *are* we?"

"Another time, another place," she mumbled as she moved to the other side. "Everyone out now."

They came out on the street a short ways from the pit. Kaida wasn't really present as she spoke to police and paramedics on the scene, making sure the injured were seen to.

"This wasn't natural, was it?" one of the cops asked.

Was it?

No. More and more I'm convinced this is Voltius.

She sighed. "My Xyri believes it was the work of a Bonded."

The officer nodded, her brown eyes worried. "What can we do? To prevent this?"

Kaida's heart twisted. "I don't know, yet. It's possible it was an accident, the Bonded working with their powers without knowing their capabilities. It's happened before. Or, it could have been malicious intent. I assure you, either way, I will find who is responsible and make sure it doesn't happen again."

The woman nodded. "Thank you, Kaida."

Kaida forced a smile and looked up at the sky, wondering where Lycan was. The crisis was over. Handled. But she still wished he was there.

An hour later Ren finally made her way home, up up up the stairs, to find Dad and Dare sitting on the couch in the living room. She stopped in her tracks. They were watching the news.

"Thirty feet deep. Jesus," Dad muttered. "You ever think this city's getting incredibly dangerous to live in?"

"Sometimes," Dare agreed softly.

"You know Miss Gardner wants to end her lease early so she can move out of the city?"

"Shit. You gonna let her?"

Dad sighed. "Yeah. Can't make her stay when I agree with her on why she should leave."

Dare nodded.

"Things were better before the Xyri came back."

"Yep."

Ren stood there, frozen. Dad kissed Dare on the cheek then turned the TV off with a sigh. He stood with a stretch before he noticed her behind the couch.

"There you are. You didn't text back, where were you?"

She blinked. "I... at Jasper's." She swallowed as she pulled her phone out, only now seeing two missed texts from Dad. "I didn't realize, it's on silent. Sorry."

He nodded. "Was thinking pizza tonight. Sound good?"

"Yeah, sure. Let me know when it's here." With that she turned and went to her room.

Bellamy closed his bedroom door with a sigh. Movie night with Mom had been fun, but he felt so tense the whole time, sneaking glances at his phone to see that a sinkhole caused by a Bonded killed two people and injured over a dozen. Kaida handled it. He wasn't needed, but he still felt shitty for not being there to help.

As if reading his mind, a text from Kaida came through.

|Bunhead|
Missed you today.

|Starface|
I'm so so sorry I wasn't there. Was busy, family stuff. I couldn't get away.

|Bunhead|
It's okay.

|Starface|
Are you okay??

|Bunhead|
Yeah.

|Starface|
Are you lying?

|Bunhead|
Yeah.

|Starface|
Sorry.
Anything I can do?

|Bunhead|
You're already doing it.

Zig is sure it was a Bonded. I'm worried

|Starface|
Me too. We'll figure it out.

You and me.

|Bunhead|
You and me.

Bellamy stayed up late into the night, patrolling while Zeli told him about the Xyri, Nagalix and Voltius, and what to expect from their potential Bonded. He barely slept and was still stressing about it when he got to school the next morning.

He smiled at Ren as he sat down beside her in geometry, glad for a distraction. "Guess what?"

"What?" she asked.

"I met Kaida yesterday."

Her eyes widened. "Really?"

"Yeah. I mean, I guess it's not as exciting as Lycan saving you, but... she's way cooler than Lycan."

Ren frowned. "She is not."

"Of course she is."

Ren shook her head. "Absolutely not."

"What are you guys talking about?" Nicholas asked as he dropped his bag on the floor and sat at the table beside them.

"Uh, who's the cooler superhero, I guess?"

Ren seemed embarrassed.

"Oh, it's for sure Lycan."

"No," Freddie mumbled as he sat beside Nicholas. "Kaida all the way."

"What about Apex though? I know he's new but, he seems cool," Destin chimed in.

Lola shook her head. "It's Kaida, a thousand percent."

Bellamy met Ren's eyes as the others continued arguing about it. "Do you not like Kaida?" he asked in a whisper.

She sighed, leaning back in her chair. "No. I just... she never stops things from happening. She never saves *everyone.*"

Bellamy shook his head. "Are you kidding? Ren, she's *perfect.* At least she knows what she's doing, you know? She always has a plan and she's *so* smart. Lycan is just out there fumbling his way around, has no idea what's going on. He just gets lucky sometimes."

Ren smiled slightly. "He's sweet."

Bellamy stilled, heart beating fast. "He is?"

She nodded, cheeks turning pink. "Yeah. I mean, when he... saved me that night? He walked me home and was so sweet. I don't think the world needs more Kaidas but, it could *really* benefit from more Lycans."

His eyes burned and he blinked, pulling back a little. Why was he so emotional? "I... you really think that?" *Ren thinks I'm sweet.*

"But, they're better together," Ren continued. "Kaida and Lycan, as a *team*, is the coolest."

Bellamy grinned. "I could not agree more."

21
Pebble

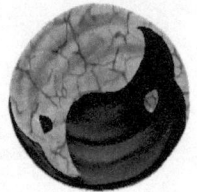

Jasper was actually nervous for his date with Harper. He'd only ever been on dates with Ren, but they'd dated for three months, so he clearly did something right. He was older now. Wiser. Hotter. He could do this.

Sure ya can.

He sighed as he looked around his room for the Xyri. But there wasn't really anywhere for him to hide. His room only had the desk under his bunk bed and a dresser across from that, beside the closet. No Xyri.

"Are you planning to say nonsense shit in my head during my whole date?" he asked as he continued inspecting his clothes.

Maybe not.

"I'd appreciate it if you didn't," he replied as he texted Ren, asking her what he should wear. "Where are you, anyways?"

Watching ducks.

Jasper frowned. "Ducks?"

On the water, yes.

He shook his head as Ren responded, telling him to wear his red plaid flannel over a white tee, paired with his nicest jeans. It was funny how often she asked him to pick her outfits. He'd never asked her for the same before.

He sent her a picture after he dressed and she responded with fire emojis. She was probably stressing about her second date with Simon, which was happening at the same time as his date with Harper. He hoped he'd have good things to report back.

How are your ducks? he asked Pozi as he walked to the park where he was meeting Harper.

Wet.

Harper was already there, waiting for him by the fountain. Her blonde hair was curled, and she wore a tight gray sweater with a red skirt over black tights. He grinned.

"Hey, you look nice."

She blushed. "Thanks. We kinda match!"

He mentally thanked Ren for picking the red shirt. "Yeah, we do. Uh, should we walk?"

She nodded and they started walking, both quiet. He wondered if she was nervous, too. She really was very pretty. Bright blue eyes, light blonde hair, rosy complexion. She was shorter than him, which he liked. When he dated Ren they'd been almost the same height. It wasn't till after they broke up that he'd grown taller.

"So," Harper said softly, looking at anything but him.

"So, how long have you liked me?" he asked.

Her cheeks reddened. "Um. Well I guess... it's weird. I don't wanna say."

"Come *on*. I swear I won't make fun of you."

She kicked a rock, scaring some pigeons. "When you were on your crutches."

He laughed. "I see. So you like them completely defeated and handicapped."

"No! I just... I remember you coming to class with those knit octopus things on your crutches? It was so cute. And then I realized... *you* were cute."

"They were squids," he said with a smile. "Ren made them to cheer me up."

She nodded. "I um... did you... ever think I was cute?"

"Obviously. Have you seen yourself?"

Harper smiled.

"I probably never would have asked you out though. I am not that confident. I'm lucky you talked to Ren about me."

"So many girls are into you. I didn't think I had a chance."

"See, Ren said the same thing. But, I don't get it. Like, no one's ever said anything to me. No one's flirting with me."

"Well, some of us are shy! But you're genuinely like, the cutest boy in our grade."

He couldn't stop smiling as her hair lifted in the breeze. "No way. Absolutely not."

"Really. You're the most talked about boy among the girls I know. You, Bellamy, and Freddie. But everyone's too intimidated by Freddie, since he's so quiet. No one knows what his deal is so they won't tell him. And Bellamy, he's nice and all but he's... well he's kinda awkward sometimes, you know? But you..." She looked away. "You're nice and funny and extremely cute."

Jasper reached out and grabbed her hand. She turned, eyes wide, cheeks pink.

"This okay?" he asked, swinging her hand a little.

"Yes, very okay."

"Cool."

They continued walking, hand in hand, as they talked. The plan was to walk around for an hour then grab lunch at a pizza place around the corner, but they hadn't made plans for after. He kinda hoped the date wouldn't end there. It felt like things were going well so far.

Harper opened up more, telling him how she liked to make jewelry and wanted to have her own jewelry shop one day. He let her talk, listening as she showed off the necklace she was wearing, which was a thin white shell in the shape of a heart hanging over her sternum.

"You made that?"

"Yeah. I get a lot of stuff from craft stores, and just collect weird things I find that I can turn into something unique. It's fun. I got this shell from a beach and sanded it down to this shape, then drilled a hole in it and now it's a necklace."

"That's so cool."

"It's not that impressive. Anyone could do it."

"I couldn't. And even if I could, that doesn't take away from the fact that that's a skill you have. A talent you should be proud of."

"Thanks."

He bit his lip. "You can turn anything into jewelry?"

"Maybe not anything but... most things?"

"What about... a pebble?"

"Yeah, I could do something with a pebble."

Jasper dropped her hand and knelt down, scooping up a small round white rock the size of his pinky nail. He placed it in her hand.

"A pebble."

She laughed and tucked it into her purse. "I'll see what I can do with it."

Jasper pulled his phone out to check the time. They'd been walking for almost an hour now, so they could grab food soon. He paused, staring at his various notifications. Something was happening in Central Park... a new Bonded making people sick? He looked up at Harper, stomach turning. Ren was on her date with Simon, at the movies. Kaida wouldn't be checking on that situation. Lycan might, maybe?

"Everything okay?" Harper asked.

"Uh..." He didn't know what to do. Leave it, and hope Lycan showed up? *What kind of hero am I if I don't go?*

"Jasper?"

He sucked in a deep breath and met her eyes. "Would you absolutely hate me if I had to leave?" He felt sick at the way her smile faded.

"Leave? I thought... we were gonna get pizza?"

He swallowed. "I um, I just... I have a text, from my mom. And she has an issue, so. I have to go home. I'm really sorry."

"Oh. Okay. I could wait, if it won't take long?" she asked, hopeful.

"I don't know how long it'll take." He took a step back, heart beating frantically as he made his choice. "I'll text you, okay?" He turned away, leaving her standing there alone.

22
You're Not a Werewolf, You're a Bird

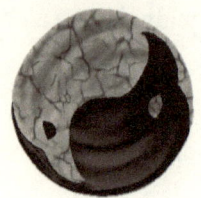

It took Jasper an embarrassingly long time to get somewhere he could transform without being seen, but the flight from Washington Square to Central Park was quick. He arced low, scanning for the problem. It wasn't hard to locate, people running and screaming in a panic gave it away.

He landed in a field of grass that was no longer green. From the center it was black, bleeding out into gray and brown, like it had died. In the center of the blackened circle stood a girl in a skintight suit, black, with twisted lines of lime green running through it. Scattered across the suit were patches of gray-white blobs. She was taller than Jasper, with warm brown skin and golden hair falling to one side of her face, shaved on the other side. Her mask puffed out around her eyes in the shape of a butterfly. It was black and green, matching the suit.

"Hey, whatcha doing there?" he asked as his wings folded in.

She smiled, a wicked look in her eyes. "Making friends."

I don't think she's making friends, he thought at Pozi.

No, she made the ground sick.

And the people who were on it? He could see some of them still, not far away, groaning on their knees. The sound of retching reached his ears, and he grimaced.

"Always down to make new friends," he replied.

You don't wanna be her friend. I know her Xyri. Do not let her touch you.

The girl took a step towards him. Jasper stepped back.

What happens if she touches me?

Well...

"I can be very friendly," the girl said.

Well what?

"Yeah, I can see that. All your friends ran away. What did you do to them?"

She can poison you in multiple ways. Some would make you sick or crazy, but she can kill with it. Be fucking careful.
Her smile widened as she moved towards him.
Great. If she poisoned him he'd never hear the end of it from Ren. Jasper held his ground. *How do I fight her without touching her?*
Mmm, that seems like a you problem.
Oh, very helpful. Maybe you should give me my weapon now?
No, you're not there yet.
Jasper rolled his eyes, bracing himself as the girl approached. She stopped and knelt right in front of him, placing her palm on the ground. The brown grass blackened.
Uh, Jasper...
He ignored Pozi, not wanting to attack the girl unprovoked. It wasn't like fighting Fable. He needed her to attack first or it wouldn't feel right.
Now is not the time to be chivalrous! She's trying to poison you, dumbass.
That's when the nausea hit, like a punch to the gut. He blinked in surprise.
Poison, dumbass, Pozi repeated, annoyed.
"Ugh."
The girl smirked. "You're kinda cute. Too bad."
"Too—"
She punched him in the face.
He stumbled back, sure he was gonna vomit. "Okay, that wasn't friendly at *all!*"
"But I said you were cute first." Her smile widened.
Jasper laughed, straightening himself. "Okay, listen here lady—"
Her fist slammed into his jaw again. She cackled as he hit the ground.
"Call me Elixir," she said as she gave a little bow above him.
Jasper growled, tapping strength. It helped him ignore the pain and nausea as he forced himself up. She danced back from him, her black eyes glittering. Then she dodged as he came at her, but when he turned, she leaned into him, hands grabbing his face as she got within his grasp. For a moment he thought she was gonna kiss him as she gripped his cheeks.
Uh oh.
A tingle ran through his skin, moving from his face down into his neck.
What did I say about touching her?
Not helping!
She let go, laughing loudly as she jumped back. The combination of the tingling with his nausea overwhelmed his senses.

"You're not very good at this, are you?" Elixir asked, amused.

"What did you *do* to me?" He stumbled, dizzy, as she walked backwards.

"Nothing deadly, *yet*. You know, maybe you're not bad at this. Maybe I'm just *really* good at it?"

Jasper stopped and let his wings fold out, focusing on the feel of that to ignore the sickness. He was hot, like he had a fever, and the tingling was turning itchy.

"Gonna fly away, tail between your legs?" she asked.

"I don't have a tail," he mumbled.

I do.

"Well, there's your mistake!" The gray-white blobs on her suit started to float off her into the air, dispersing into thin smoke around them.

"What i-is that?"

God dammit Jasper.

"You'll see."

Lycan arrived at the park to find Apex lying on his back in blackened grass, moving his arms as if to make snow angels, while a Bonded girl stood near him, cackling. Her laughter died out the moment Lycan landed. She took a nervous step back.

"Ariel *can* be a cowboy!" Apex yelled, his eyes shut.

"What did you do to him?" Lycan asked, moving toward the girl, who took another step back.

"Just a little bit of fun. He'll be fine. Eventually."

Anger burned inside of him. *Is she lying?*

I am uncertain.

He sighed. "Did you hurt anyone else?"

"Wouldn't admit it if I did, fluffy ears."

He frowned, touching one of his wolf ears. "Not fluffy," he mumbled.

"You just take care of your friend there, I'll see myself out." With that she turned and sprinted away.

Lycan could easily catch her but Apex's babbling on the ground pulled his attention.

"Oh no I'm becoming a fox aga—" Apex shifted, turning into a small black animal with glowing green eyes.

"Uh, Apex?"

You know he can't answer you now, Zeli said.

"Right. He's gonna detransform. I can't see that."

Box him up. Wait.

He sighed and made a silver box around the fox, which was now rolling on its back resuming whatever Apex had been doing before.

"You think we can fix him before Kaida finds out?"

You think she'll think you broke him?

No, but still. If she sees him in this state she won't be happy.

Whatever the girl did is likely to wear off soon.

"Define soon?"

Anywhere between five minutes and an hour, Zeli replied.

Great.

He stood there as people slowly approached from the outskirts of the blackened grass. He still wasn't entirely sure what went down there.

A loud crack split the air, and he heard a groan from inside the box.

"Apex, you good?"

"Just chokin' myself, bro. Don't worry about it."

"Uh, I'm kinda worried about it."

Apex started coughing.

"Put the suit back on so I can let you out."

"I don't like your neck teeth."

Lycan blinked. "*What?*"

"Not you, Poziiiiii!" Apex called from inside the box. He started coughing again. "Oh god are we dead?"

"No. Put the suit back on, okay? Transform."

"But it's hard to have a brain and be a werewolf."

Lycan tried not to laugh. "You're not a werewolf, you're a bird. Get your suit on so I can drop the box!"

"Drop drop drop oh *damn.*"

Kaida is gonna kill me.

Maybe.

He knocked on the side of the box as the people edged closer, holding up their phones. Why were they filming? He wasn't doing anything exciting.

"Lycan?"

"Yeah?"

"Please stop talking. I have to quack at you."

Lycan lost it, laughter bursting out of him. He waited, expecting Apex to start quacking, but he went silent.

"Are you in the suit yet?"

169

"Uh? Am I? Pozi, am I wearing you?" He devolved into giggles. "Pozi suit is on!"

"Finally." Lycan dropped the box to find Apex sitting cross-legged, a dazed smile on his face.

"Come on," he said as he pulled him to his feet.

"Are we dancing?" Apex asked.

"No, bud. We're leaving." He kicked up his board and pulled Apex onto it.

Apex laughed as they zipped into the air. Lycan was sure if he didn't hold onto him he'd simply fall to his death.

When they landed on the roof at Spruce Street Apex immediately laid on his back.

"Oh *god*." He looked at the sky with horror. "The trees are talking. Lycan? They *aren't* very nice, Lycan."

Lycan smiled and pulled out his phone to call Kaida.

23
Kissed and Confused

Ren sat across from Jasper on her roof. He was flat on his back in his suit, eyes closed. Her mind still raced from her date with Simon, and that second kiss. But her heart still pounded from the panic of getting the call from Lycan and having to end the date early. She'd found Jasper high out of his mind and covered in hives, while Lycan reassured her that he was *okay*.

"What happened to 'no chances I'll get hurt on my date?'" she asked.

Jasper groaned in response.

"Still itchy?"

"Yes, but the crazy wore off so I should be grateful."

"Hm."

"You're mad," he muttered.

She sighed. "Not mad at you."

"But still mad." He let out a breath and sat up, looking at her with sad golden eyes. "I'm sorry."

"You should have just let Lycan handle it."

Jasper's eyes widened. "How was I to know he'd show up?"

Cause he always does, she thought.

"It's not like I could text him."

"Oh. Right." She frowned. "We need to fix that."

"Obviously."

"What happened? With Harper, I mean." Lycan already told her what happened with the new Bonded, called Elixir, and Apex.

"It was good. Like, really good? Until I bailed mid-date to go fight a villain."

She gave him a sympathetic smile. "Sucks, doesn't it?"

"How have you been doing this for so long? The first time I have to leave a normal situation to be a hero, and it's on my first date with a girl?"

"What did you tell her?" Ren asked as she cracked her knuckles.

"I don't even know. I babbled something about my mom needing me? She's not gonna go out with me again."

"I'm sure it's fine. She really likes you."

He sighed and leaned back on his hands. "What about Simon? You left early again. Cause of me. *Again.*"

"Yeah, but he was fine with it. We were planning to grab food after the movie, but that was it cause he's got band practice tonight. He asked if he was getting a third date and I said yes. And then he kissed me," she said wistfully, blushing. "It was *very* nice." Her mind kept replaying the moment, over and over. Simon leaning in slowly, the world going quiet around them...

She kept expecting Simon to get bored, change his mind, anything but the consistent interest he was showing. And her interest in him was growing by the day.

Jasper grinned. "So, you're gonna keep seeing him?"

She nodded. "He's sweet. I like talking to him."

"And he's hot."

Ren laughed and rolled her eyes. "Yes, that too. He's like, *so* pretty. But that is just a bonus. He listens when I talk, he remembers what I say. He's fun."

Jasper sighed and closed his eyes.

"You should text Harper. Apologize again and ask her for a second date."

"Ugh." He opened his eyes. "Alright. I'll try."

"Just gotta stop trying to get yourself killed by Fable and Elixir and whoever else in the meantime," she replied.

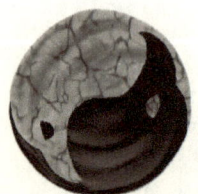

Jasper was hopeful after texting Harper. She said she was down to go out next weekend. But then on Monday morning she avoided his gaze in homeroom. She rushed out so fast when the bell rang, he didn't get a chance to talk to her.

Maybe she doesn't like me anymore.

Maybe.

You know, he started, *when Ren is depressed, I'm pretty sure Zig tries to cheer her up.*

Lucky Ren.

He rolled his eyes as he made his way to chemistry. He tried getting Harper's attention when he walked in, but she had her head down, staring at her notebook. He sighed and sat by Kevin in the corner, then texted Harper.

|Jasper|
You look nice today

She blushed as she read it then her eyes darted to him before she started typing.

|Harper|
Thanks

|Jasper|
You wanna sit with me at lunch? could figure out next date plans.

She glanced up again.

|Harper|
You really wanna go out again?

|Jasper|
Yes... do you not want to?

|Harper|
It seemed like you didn't like me...with the whole leaving mid date thing...

|Jasper|
I'm SO sorry! I didn't wanna ruin the date, I was having a great time before that. I get it if you don't wanna go out again but I'd like to. if you do

|Harper|
I do. So... we'll talk at
lunch?

|Jasper|
Yes!!

When lunch rolled around Jasper stood by his table, waiting. Harper approached nervously, tray in hand.

"Hey," she said as she sat.

"Hey you." Jasper gave her his best smile.

"You sure it's okay if I sit with you?"

"Of course you can sit with us," Ren answered for him as she sat on Jasper's other side.

Harper seemed to relax at that. But she already knew everyone at his table. He didn't understand why she'd think it wasn't okay.

"So," Ren said as she passed Jasper a sandwich from her bag. "Jasper's excited for your date this weekend."

Harper's face split into a smile. "You've been talking about me?"

"Yeah, cause I like you," he replied.

Harper's face turned red, and she stared down at her pizza, trying to hide her smile. "I like you, too."

"Good. It would be awkward if you didn't, since we're going out again."

"Will you guys *please* help me convince Bellamy to let me have a costume party at his house," Nico said as he sat across from them with Bellamy.

Bellamy sighed. "You know I hate parties."

"Yeah, but you don't have to do anything! I'll do all the work, and you know your mom will say yes!"

"It's March," Bellamy continued. "Why would we have a costume party?"

"Cause it's fun? Why do you hate *fun*, Bellamy?" Nico pouted.

Bellamy rolled his eyes and looked across the table for help.

"A party sounds fun," Harper replied.

"I'm down for a party," Ashley muttered, as she ran her fingers through her long red hair.

"Yes to party!" Kevin added, head bobbing up and down as he stared at Ashley.

"Nari?"

Nari looked up and frowned. "I don't care."

Jasper glanced at Ren. Her eyes were locked on Bellamy's.

"If you don't want to have a party you say *no*," she said, voice low.

"Oh, Ren, don't be like that!" Nico said.

Bellamy smiled at her. Jasper watched them, wondering what silent conversation was passing between their eyes.

"I'm just saying, everyone loves a party. And you got the *best* place to throw one!" Nico paused and looked at Ren. "*Or,* we could have it at your place! Your house is huge."

"Absolutely not," Ren said, then she grinned at Bellamy. "See how *easy* that was."

Bellamy's smile widened.

Jasper was convinced if Ren just told him how she felt they'd start dating immediately. He couldn't be sure if Bellamy was romantically interested in Ren or not, but there were times when she was the only one who could hold Bellamy's attention in a room full of people. He seemed to light up when she spoke. If Bellamy knew how she felt there was no way he wouldn't wanna be with her. But Ren would never tell him. He couldn't understand why she was so afraid to admit her feelings.

The topic changed from parties to the history test and Ren took out her notes to study. Jasper and Harper talked about their upcoming date while Ren and Nari quizzed each other.

"Why can't I remember this?" Nari asked, putting her face in her hands, messing up her bangs.

"You totally know it," Ren said as she flapped the note card back and forth.

Nari groaned. Jasper always thought she was so pretty, with her olive skin and shiny black hair. She had the cutest smile, but he hadn't seen it in a while.

"You got this Nar," Kevin said. "You're the smartest one at this table."

"Probably true," Nico added.

Nari sighed. "I give up."

"It's—" Ren jumped, falling silent. Simon stood behind her. She looked panicked for a moment, then her face split into a smile as she looked up at him. "What are you doing here?" she asked. "You're not in our lunch."

"Dipped out of class to come see you."

Ren blushed. The entire table went quiet as they stared between Ren and Simon.

"You shouldn't ditch class for me," Ren said, cheeks burning. But she was still smiling.

"You're way better than class, though," Simon said, smooth as butter. "Come here."

Ren looked surprised as he grabbed her hand and pulled her up off the bench. Then Simon led her a few steps away from the table before taking her face in both of his hands as he kissed her.

Jasper looked around the table, noting Harper's wide smile and Nico's wide eyes. Most noteworthy was Bellamy's frown. He looked away from the passionate kiss quickly, but that frown was plastered to his face. He almost looked *mad*. Jasper tried not to smile as he glanced back at Ren and Simon, now no longer kissing, just staring intensely into each other's eyes.

"See you later," he whispered, before giving her one more quick kiss.

"Uh huh," Ren mumbled, face beet red as she slowly turned and sat down.

"Ren!" Harper giggled. "I didn't know you had a boyfriend?"

"When did *that* happen?" Nari asked.

Ren didn't answer as she sat back down and pressed her face into Jasper's shoulder, clearly embarrassed. He didn't think it was the kiss itself, he and Ren used to make out in the halls all the time. But she'd only been on two dates with Simon, and still seemed nervous about going all in. But that was a declaration. Simon could have pulled her farther away or waited to see her. He wanted to kiss her in front of her friends to send a message. She was *his* now.

Jasper looked back at Bellamy. He was still watching Ren, still frowning. *Interesting.*

When the bell rang Bellamy pulled Jasper aside as Harper and Ashley giggled at Ren in front of them, asking about Simon.

"How long has Ren been with that guy?" Bellamy whispered.

"Like, five minutes," Jasper answered, giving the oblivious boy a look of implication. Trying to convey '*hey, you still have a shot!*' but Bellamy just nodded.

"Why does it bother you so much?" Jasper asked.

"I'm... not bothered," Bellamy replied, sounding completely bothered.

He does like her, doesn't he? He almost said something but... Ren would kill him.

When he sat beside her in history she was face down on her desk. He sent her a text.

> |Jasper|
> That was one hell of a kiss.
> are you guys official now?

She slowly lifted her head and pulled her phone out, audibly sighing before responding.

|Ren|
I think so? Maybe? I don't know! How do I know??? Do I ask him????

|Jasper|
If you're not sure, yeah

|Ren|
Ughhhhhhh

Jasper caught Bellamy watching Ren as he put his phone away. He wondered if being kissed and confused by Simon was enough to make Ren do badly on the test. Maybe seeing Ren kiss someone else would make Bellamy do badly on it?

You're probably gonna do bad, for no reason!

Don't be rude, Jasper replied as Mr. Spritz started handing out the tests.

Ren typed as fast as she could then panic hit send.

|Ren|
Hey so I have a question are we together now? like are you... my boyfriend??

"Ren, phone down," Mr. Spritz called.

She groaned and put her phone away. Her mind was still reeling from Simon's kiss. It was the first time he'd kissed her at school, and everyone was just *staring*. She tried to push the thought away, focusing on the test.

When class ended she checked her phone. Simon hadn't replied.

"That's fine. Totally fine."

"What's fine?" Jasper asked.

"I asked Simon if he was my boyfriend now and he didn't respond and I'm gonna throw up oh my *god*. Why did I *ask?*"

Jasper put a hand on her shoulder, steering her down the correct hall.

"I'm so stupid. He's not gonna wanna see me again I ruined it I—"

"Calm *down*. He was also just in class? Give the guy a minute."

"Ugh. Okay."

"Breathe. Bet he texts by the time we're in art."

She tried to calm herself, but once they were seated, she pulled the phone back out to no texts.

"I absolutely fucked up," she mumbled, putting her face down on the table.

"Ren, he just kissed you like he was *dying* and your lips were the cure. You didn't ruin anything."

She didn't agree.

Are you alright, Ren?

She sighed. *Yes. Just did a dumb thing cause I'm stupid.*

So, you are not alright?

For some reason, that made her smile. *I'm mostly alright, promise.*

She could sense Zig didn't believe her, but she didn't believe her either.

Class went so slow as she continued to check her phone over and over. She was absolutely spiraling by the time she got to chemistry with Bellamy. She felt so awkward. He kept glancing at her, not saying anything conversational outside of their current assignment, which was unusual.

Part of her wondered what he thought about seeing her kiss Simon, but he probably didn't think about it at all. Bellamy had two years to like Ren and... he didn't. And he never would. She was finally coming to terms with that.

Now she actually liked someone new and attainable and... and maybe it was over before it even began.

"Are you alright?" Bellamy asked in a whisper.

"Huh?"

"You seem... distracted."

"Oh." She blushed. "Guess I am. Sorry."

"What's wrong?"

"Nothing. I'm fine." She forced a smile.

He tilted his head a little, reminding her of Lycan. She blinked, heart racing as she looked away.

"You don't seem fine."

She swallowed, glancing back at him, searching his face. *No.* "Uh, just overthinking some things. But I'm okay. Promise."

His eyes narrowed. "Okay."

By the time class was over Ren's anxiety about Simon was at its peak as she walked down to her locker. Simon wasn't waiting for her like usual. Her eyes burned as she opened her locker and swapped books from her bag.

"Pssst."

Ren jumped, dropping her bag as she spun to see Simon smiling down at her.

"Why so jumpy?" he asked.

She made a noise and covered her face with her hands.

"Ren?" He grabbed her upper arms, gently pulling her closer to him. "Ren, look at me."

"No," she mumbled.

"Why are you hiding?"

"You didn't answer," she continued as her hands fell to her side, but she kept her eyes closed.

"Ren, please look at me?"

"No."

"I'm not answering till you look at me."

She let out a breath, bracing herself as she opened her eyes. He was smiling as he gently cupped her chin.

"I wanna be your boyfriend," he whispered. "I didn't *answer* cause I'm not asking you to be my girlfriend over *text*."

Ren swallowed.

"Do you wanna be my girlfriend?" he continued, blue eyes looking uncertain now.

She nodded, heart racing.

"Yeah?"

She grinned. "Yes."

He smiled and kissed her. Somehow her heart beat faster.

"Does this mean... the other boy you like isn't a problem anymore?" he asked in a whisper.

"Not a problem," she replied.

His smile faltered, eyes softening. "Do you promise?" He looked so vulnerable, so unsure.

Ren wrapped her hands around his neck as she pulled him closer and kissed him. It was the first time she'd initiated a kiss, but it felt *right*.

He was grinning when she pulled back. "So, was it one of the boys at your table?"

"Does it matter?" she asked as she closed her locker.

"Just curious."

She sighed. "Yes."

"Can I know which one?"

"The blond one. His name is Bellamy."

"Oh, of *course* it's the blond one." He shook his head.

"Why's it matter if he's blond?"

"Makes me feel like I'm not exactly your type," he replied.

Ren rolled her eyes. "I do not *have* a type. Besides, I like your dark hair and your blue eyes. Have I told you you're really pretty?"

Simon's smile widened. "Am I taller than him?"

She snorted. "You're taller than everyone. *Freakishly so.*"

He laughed and pulled her into his arms, hugging her tightly. "Wanna hang out today, shorty?"

"Don't you have band practice?"

"Shit. Right." He let out a breath. "I could ditch it..."

"No. I want your friends to like me, so don't cancel things because of me."

Simon pouted at her. "But I'd rather spend the day with my *girlfriend.*" The way he said that word made her stomach flutter.

"Not today. Besides, I have stuff to do."

He rolled his eyes. "Fine. But I'll be thinking about you the *entire* time," he said as he grabbed her bag.

"Really?"

"Yes." He kissed her one, two, three more times. "Can I call you later tonight?"

She nodded and he kissed her again.

"Alright, let's get you home before your dads kill me." He put his arm around her shoulders and led her down the hall and outside.

24
Down To Clown

"You're absolutely sure you don't wanna do anything special for your birthday?" Dad asked as he wiped down the counter.

"Very sure," Ren answered. "Just wanna stay in and watch movies with you guys. And Jasper."

Dad smiled. "But we always go out."

"She's growing up too fast," Dare said as he pulled a soda out of the fridge. "Going out with your dads isn't cool when you're seventeen."

"It's not *that*," Ren said with a laugh. "You're the coolest dads *ever*. I just... I'm tired. So, we stay in? Movies, and order food?"

"If you're sure?" Dad looked disappointed.

She nodded, feeling bad.

Ren really was breaking tradition. She couldn't remember the last time she had a birthday where they didn't do something. Well, her fifteenth, but she was sick, so it didn't count. They canceled her quinceañera. They'd done her quince on her sixteenth instead, so that one had been a *whole* party. But before that it was karaoke and museums and fancy dinners. Something simple just seemed better these days.

"Do you... want to invite the boy?" Dad asked.

"Absolutely not." She couldn't imagine having Simon over for her birthday. They'd technically been dating for three weeks now, but only just became *official*. If she invited him he'd have to skip school. It was a miracle Jasper was actually allowed to skip for her birthday every year.

"Just Jasper, and us." She wished Ocean could be there. She was missing Ren's birthday by only two months.

"Okay, kiddo. Figure out what movies you wanna watch," Dad said as he kissed the top of her head, making her smile.

The next day Ren climbed out of bed to the sight of at least fifty purple and silver balloons scattered through her room. She giggled as she kicked her way through them to get to her bathroom. Once she was dressed for the day, she opened her trap door and laughed as more balloons flew up through it.

"Too many balloons!" she yelled as she carefully walked through even more balloons on the stairs.

"Too many? *What?*" Dad slid into view at the bottom of the stairs, a stupid grin on his face and a bouquet of sunflowers in hand. "I was thinking I didn't get enough."

She giggled as she hugged him.

"Happy birthday, little dragon," he whispered, lifting her off the ground.

"Thanks, Daddy." She took the flowers, certain there were exactly seventeen of them. He got her sunflowers every birthday, one for each year she was alive.

"Made your favorite," he said as he pulled her into the kitchen.

"Chocolate chip pancakes!" She rushed to the island where large stacks of pancakes awaited on plates.

"Straight to the food, no hug for me?" Dare pouted.

"Sorry sorry." She put the flowers down and threw her arms around him.

"Happy birthday, kiddo," he said as he swayed her back and forth.

"Thanks, Darey. Love you."

She pulled back and frowned at the stupidly big shiny purple box that was beside Dare. It was as tall as Ren's waist and two feet wide, with a large silver bow on top.

"Jasper is inside that, isn't he?"

A giggle came from the box and Ren smiled as she ripped the top off. Jasper jumped up, laughter pouring out of him.

"How did you know?"

"There's no way you weren't already here and you're *stupid*." She hugged him while he still stood in the box.

"Is it pancake time?" he asked.

"No you have to suffer hug longer."

"Oh okay."

Jasper tripped trying to get out of the box. A chorus of laughter followed as Dad took the box away and Ren and Jasper sat at the table to eat.

After breakfast they settled on the couch, Ren and Jasper covering up under the orange throw blanket she'd made last year. Dad closed the curtains and turned the lights off before they started the movies. They were watching all the Jurassic Parks, since they were her favorite. Her dads spaced out her presents, having her open them between the movies.

The first was expected. A little purple porcelain dragon, about three inches tall. Dad got her something dragon related every single year since she was a baby. It was a tradition she loved. After the second movie they ordered some lunch and Dare gave her a framed painting of her and Jasper that he'd done himself. It was *beautiful*.

"Getting a lot of texts from Simon?" Jasper asked as he leaned over, looking at her buzzing phone.

"No, but group chat is going off."

"Has Simon not texted?"

"No."

"You told him it was your birthday, right?"

"Yeah. I mean, I told him like... a while ago?" She shrugged.

Jasper made a sound.

"We just started dating okay, he doesn't need to know it's my birthday. I don't care."

Jasper smiled suddenly. "But do you care about Bellamy wishing you happy birthday in the group chat? Look at that heart emoji!"

She rolled her eyes and took a picture of the painting Dare made and sent it to the chat.

After the third movie she got a set of fancy yarn and new crochet hooks. Then Dad unveiled the cake he made. Purple, two tiers, and piped with sunflowers. The inside was chocolate with strawberries. Jasper managed to eat three slices.

That's when Simon finally texted, asking where she was. So she explained she always skipped school on her birthday.

|Simon|
Why didn't you tell me?

|Ren|
It doesn't matter.

|Simon|
It does to me. You're my girlfriend.

Can I see you later?

|Ren|
No, busy all day with dads. Sorry.

|Simon|
Tomorrow?
I can take you out for dinner after school?

They ordered dinner after the fourth movie, and she got a new jacket. After the final movie she got a set of four Broadway tickets to see Hadestown in a few weeks. Then Jasper finally gave her his gift. A set of seven different coloring books of Kaida, Lycan, and Apex. He grinned excitedly when she opened them. He always got her something they could do together, which she loved, but she suspected part of him was just excited that Apex was *in* the coloring books now.

Bellamy laid in bed, feeling shitty for forgetting Ren's birthday. He would have given her something. Something *nice*. He wasn't creative, so he couldn't make her something like Rufard the bear, as she'd done for him. But he had money, he could find something.

Why are you so mopey?

"I'm not mopey."

Hmph.

He sighed. "I forgot Ren's birthday." He'd missed her birthday last year, too, only showing up after it had ended.

Zeli didn't respond.

He started shopping around on Valkyrie for something. He wasn't sure if Ren liked jewelry, but she did wear a necklace every day, though he'd never seen it. She always kept it tucked under her shirt. But it felt fitting, since she'd given him the yarn bracelet, which he still wore. He ordered a bracelet, putting her name and address down for delivery.

Now you're anxious.

I'm fine.

He sighed and opened his texts from Kaida and Apex. They'd started a group chat, which Kaida was thrilled about.

|Bird Boy|
Who's ready to party tonighttt

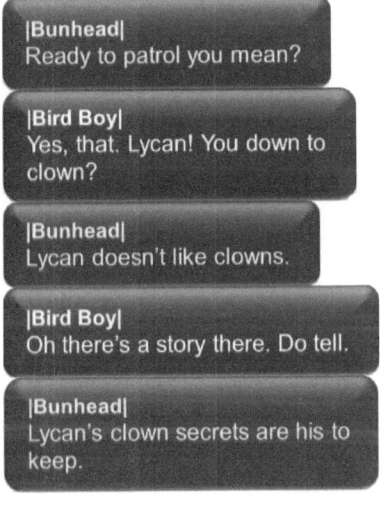

|Bunhead|
Ready to patrol you mean?

|Bird Boy|
Yes, that. Lycan! You down to clown?

|Bunhead|
Lycan doesn't like clowns.

|Bird Boy|
Oh there's a story there. Do tell.

|Bunhead|
Lycan's clown secrets are his to keep.

|Starface|
No clowns please.

But I'm down for patrol. Can probably meet around eleven?

|Bird Boy|

|Bunhead|
Won't be free till after midnight.

|Starface|
Can do.

|Bunhead|
See ya then, wolf boy.

He smiled and pulled some books out of his bag. He only had homework for English, but wanted to finish it before he left. Zeli hopped on the bed while he worked. She really did look like a normal dog to him now, even though she looked like the night sky, with silver sparkling in her fur and wisps of silver mist rising from the tips of her ears and tail.

Are we going out tonight? she asked, eyes closed.

"Yeah, just gotta finish this then we'll grab food, make sure Mom's eaten, and go."

Okay.

He stretched as he finished the homework, then he pet Zeli's head before leaving the room. She didn't get annoyed when he did that anymore.

All the lights were off, so he assumed Mom hadn't left her office for a while. He rummaged through the fridge and found some leftover pasta. He heated up two plates then took one to the office.

Mom smiled as he entered.

He sighed as he flicked on the light. "You know that switch works, right?" he asked as he set the plate in front of her.

"I was distracted," she answered as she glanced out the darkened window. "Didn't notice the time passing." She released a breath. "You didn't have to bring me dinner."

"I know, but I wanted to."

She smiled. "Thanks, Belly Bear."

He nodded then went to his room to eat with Zeli. She was asleep when he got in bed and checked his phone again. Nico was still trying to convince him to host a costume party, talking about it non-stop in the group chat. He sighed, thinking of Ren. She was the only one who hadn't tried to get him to do it. Cause she knew him better than they did. He hoped she'd like the bracelet.

When he put his plate in the sink he heard Mom talking and slowly tiptoed to the office, listening outside the door.

"I can't just leave on a whim," she said.

Bellamy peeked in to see she was on the phone, her face lit by her laptop screen. At least the pasta was gone, her empty plate pushed to the side of the desk.

"I know," she continued. "But things are different now. Well, how sure are you? Last time you said you were sure and we didn't find anything." After a pause she laughed. "Very funny. But this is *hard* for me. I don't wanna keep getting my hopes up, Eric."

Bellamy frowned. Was this a work call?

"No, *of course* I want to find him. More than anything. But you said it was unlikely at this point without the Xyri."

Bellamy sucked in a breath, heart racing. *The Xyri?*

"But we didn't find that one." A pause. "Really? This weekend? No, I can't. Because I have a kid, Eric. And a job, which I actually have to do. I'll send you my schedule. Pick a time I'm available and we can go. *Yes.* Alright. Bye."

He panicked when she hung up and sprinted back to his room.

Zel, did you hear that?

She lifted her head, yawning heavily as he closed the door.
Something about... no. I did not catch it.

*My mom was talking about the Xyri! Something about needing
Xyri to... find something?*

Zeli perked up at that. *To find what?*

Missed that part. That's weird, right?

Zeli seemed to consider. *It's probably nothing. Don't stress
yourself.*

Too late, he thought. "Let's go."

Lycan arrived just as Kaida and Apex descended from the sky, both
laughing loudly. He sighed. *Not a third wheel.* Kaida smiled as she
crossed the roof, Apex on her heels.

"You still haven't answered me," Apex said.

"And I'm not gonna!"

"I'm just saying, from my point of view it looks like *I'm* the better
boyfriend!"

Kaida rolled her eyes. "Make him shut up please."

Lycan stared between them. "What are you talking about?"

"How I'm the best boyfriend she's ever had," Apex answered
smugly, "cause I wouldn't—"

Kaida slammed her hand over his mouth.

"You... you guys are dating?" His heart constricted in his chest.

"No!" She dropped her hand. "We did, once. Forever ago. So, don't
get all jealous on me, okay?" Her voice softened as she stepped closer.
"Seriously. Apex and I dated for like, five minutes, *years* ago. Not
relevant now."

He nodded, but thought maybe he should jump off the roof instead.

"And *you,*" she said, glaring at Apex, "shouldn't have said that!"

"Right. Sorry."

Lycan tried to smile but he wasn't sure if it was working because
Kaida looked at him with more concern.

"You okay?"

"Yeah. No, I'm fine. Just, learning Apex isn't just your friend but
your... ex-boyfriend... wasn't information I was prepared to receive.
Doesn't help with the whole third wheel thing."

"You're *so* wrong about the wheels," Apex said. "*I'm* the third wheel
when it's the three of us."

Lycan frowned. "How so?"

"Cause you two are like..." Apex made a face. "Two halves of a
whole little hero unit. And I'm just the new kid who can't keep his
mouth shut."

"You got part of that right," Kaida mumbled.

Lycan's throat was so dry. "I um... if you guys are together you can tell me. I swear I'm okay."

Kaida blinked. "I am *not* dating Apex. We are *just* best friends. But I am... dating someone else."

His throat tightened as he looked into her blue eyes. "You're seeing someone?"

She nodded slowly. "I'm sorry."

He shook head. "No it's fine. Uh, so." He forced a smile. "You finally told that boy how you felt then?" he asked, feeling like he was floating away from his body.

"Uh, no. I... I'm dating someone else, actually."

Lycan laughed. He didn't mean to, it just burst out. He turned away from her, fully understanding her impulse to jump now.

"Lycan?"

"I'm fine," he replied, voice higher than usual.

"Ly?"

He shook his head, trying to get his emotions under control as he looked back at her. "I swear I'm fine. You and I can't be together and I am going to get over my f-feelings for you and not make things weird. I promise. Can we go punch someone now?"

Apex nodded. "Yeah, let's go buddy." He put his arm around Lycan and walked them away from Kaida. "If it makes you feel better," he whispered, "I don't think this guy is her endgame."

Lycan shook his head. "Don't tell me that. I can't be hoping for *anything* with her."

Apex sighed and nodded. Lycan almost asked what the look on his face meant, but he held his tongue. He didn't need to know. *Couldn't* know. He had to get over Kaida, sooner rather than later.

You can try moving on. His mom's words. *You find someone else.*

Back at school, in the cafeteria, he'd almost thought... but no.

25
Collapsed Crypt

"So should we check out that cemetery thing?" Apex asked, his wings shaking a little.

"Cemetery thing?" Lycan blinked, trying to come back to the moment. "What cemetery thing?"

Apex grinned. "Finally, I know something before you guys. So, headstones were disintegrated into little piles of rubble."

"Like the statue?" Kaida asked, stepping closer.

Apex nodded.

"Lead the way, then."

Apex jumped off the roof. Lycan moved to follow but Kaida grabbed his arm, pulling him back.

"Hey, I'm sorry."

He shook his head. "You have nothing to be sorry for."

She stared up at him, her blue eyes glistening. "I'm hurting you. And I *hate* that." Her voice cracked.

"Hey." He pulled her into his arms, hugging her. "I want you to be happy, Kai. And I don't want you feeling guilty about it."

She buried her face against his chest, arms wrapped around him. She didn't say anything as he held her, his heart racing.

"I swear I'm gonna get over you, alright?" he whispered after a moment. "And everything will be okay."

She sniffed as she pulled back.

"Not that you're gonna be... easy to..." He swallowed. "But I promise I can. I can do that for you."

"I'm sorry you have to," she whispered. "I wish we..." Her eyes watered even more.

"Shh, it's okay." He brushed his thumb against her cheek. "You and me. Friends. Partners. That's perfect, Kai. It's enough for me."

She smiled and nodded.

"Third. Fucking. Wheel."

Lycan jumped, turning to see Apex standing on the edge of the roof, arms folded across his chest as his wings gently drifted.

"I flew all the way to the cemetery and back, you know." He continued. "And here you are... cuddling."

Kaida rolled her eyes. "Shut *up*. Let's go."

Apex raised an eyebrow at Lycan. "You see what I *mean*? It's you two. And then also me. Third wheel." He smiled. "I'm happy to be your third wheel though."

Lycan grinned as he kicked up his board.

Be careful, Zeli said as he flew.

About what? Kaida?

It's too late for your heart. I meant the Bonded. Kirzigith is certain it's Voltius and I have to agree.

He took a deep breath. *And that's bad?*

It is not good. Please, be careful.

Yes ma'am.

They landed in the middle of Greenwood Cemetery. Kaida sighed, lifting a ball of light in her hand as she looked around. He smiled, not needing the light. They were in the center of a half circle of gravestones.

"Here, see," Apex called.

Where the line of tombs ended there were piles of crumbled rock every few feet.

"The rest of the circle?" Lycan asked.

"I think these went all the way around," Apex continued. "Someone disintegrated them. Not just these, apparently there were more headstones missing elsewhere in the cemetery. This was just the most noticeable."

"So, definitely the same person who did the statue. *Why* would they do this?" Kaida asked, scanning the area.

"Maybe they're just practicing with the powers in a way that won't hurt anyone?" Lycan suggested.

"That sinkhole killed two people." Kaida looked tense. "But I guess it *could* have been an accident."

Apex knelt, picking up a piece of the rubble. "What if they're still here? In the graveyard?"

"Listen," Kaida said.

"Huh?"

She sighed heavily. "Listen with your *powers*. See if you hear anything. If they're still here I'd like a fucking word with them."

"Oh, right." Apex nodded and closed his eyes.

Lycan put a gentle hand on Kaida's shoulder and she relaxed into it. He wanted to tell her everything would be okay, that they'd find the Bonded and figure it out. But he kept his mouth shut, not wanting to disrupt Apex. She seemed to understand anyways, smiling softly. He loved how easy it was to be around her, for her to understand him.

Words weren't always needed. How could there possibly be anyone else for him?

Bellamy...

I'm fine.

"Shit." Apex jumped up and took off running. Lycan and Kaida stared for a moment.

"Uh..."

"Let's go." She took off after him.

Careful, remember.

Always careful, Zel, he answered as he ran.

They didn't go far. Apex came to a stop, looking confused as he spun in circles. "Shit shit. They're underground?"

"Who is? What's happening?" Kaida asked, breathless.

"There's people crying. Hurt, I think? They need us... I think they're... here." He stopped and looked down. "Under us."

"Here?" Kaida knelt down, placing a hand on the dirt. "Oh, there's tombs... underground..." She closed her eyes.

"How do we get them out?"

"Kaida," Lycan answered. "She can portal them out, right?"

She nodded slowly, hand still pressed to the grass. Then she moved a few steps and placed her hand back on the ground. Little threads of light started seeping out of her into the dirt. Kaida crouched, eyes closed, silent.

After a moment her eyes snapped open. *"There."*

She stood and the air split, forming a portal ringed in burning pink light. A small buzzing sound emanated from it, very noticeable in the silence of the cemetery. Kaida stepped through, leaving the boys alone in the dark.

"How did they get stuck?" Lycan asked.

"I think... ground collapsed on them?" Apex shrugged. "Pozi says that Bonded could do that. Make the ground cave in, like with that sinkhole?"

Lycan nodded, apprehensive. One could be an accident. Two *could* be a coincidence. But he wasn't convinced.

Kaida stepped out into a tight dark space filled with bodies. She tried not to gag at the smell of sweat and urine as she threw a ball of light into the air. Over a dozen people were huddled in the corner, staring at her in shock.

"Kaida!"

"You found us!"

"Oh, thank God."

She released a breath. "Is anyone hurt?"

"Yes, Johnathon's unconscious, his pulse is weak and..."

"Others, were on that side when it caved in. We... we think they're dead."

Kaida glanced at the wall of rubble and exhaled. "Everyone who can walk, up and in, now." She pointed at her portal.

Several of them started shuffling about, slow at first. She guided them in the portal, one by one, until only three remained. The unconscious man, his brother who refused to leave him, and a woman whose ankle was maybe broken. Kaida helped the woman through then came back to carry the man out, his brother at her side.

"There's dead inside," she mumbled to Lycan and Apex as she ducked back into the portal.

She detransformed inside the collapsed crypt, letting darkness surround her for a minute before she was able to put the suit back on and flood the small hall with lights.

She stared at the rubble, thinking. "If I dig out the bodies, this will all collapse, won't it?"

Maybe.

"So how do I do it? I can't just leave them."

Lights, Ren. You know how to do this now.

She nodded slowly as light poured out of her in those thin tendrils. She didn't need Zig to guide them, she knew how to see through the light. To feel her way through the rocks, even as more light poured out behind her, moving up into the air, forming a ceiling above in case the rest of the structure tried to cave in. Rocks pulled free with her lines of light, slowly but surely, while other threads worked to find the bodies, slowly wrapping them, encasing them protectively.

They are dead, Zig said softly.

She nodded, but it hurt to know she couldn't still help them.

You're getting better at this.

"At what?" she grunted.

The power. Using it in multiple ways at once. I've had many Bonds who never got the hang of such things.

Really?

You are stronger than you know, Ren.

She couldn't feel pride in that now, straining under the weight of the power as the first body pulled out of the rocks. She wasted no time, her light moving from them and back into the rubble to find the next body.

Can you see how many are in here?

Two more.

She continued working to get them out. She wasn't sure how long it took, but she wouldn't leave them buried. Once she had the bodies free, she encased them in light again, then opened a new portal and carried them through.

When she stepped out the other side there were two ambulances on the scene, with paramedics tending to the injured. Lycan rushed forward, helping her with the bodies.

"You alright?" he asked in a whisper, guiding her away from the others.

She shook her head.

He pulled her into his arms, holding her tight.

"I can't help thinking this wasn't an accident," she mumbled into him.

"I was thinking the same thing." He rested his chin on her head. "We'll find them, and stop them."

"Five people dead already..."

"Shh, it'll be okay."

She sighed as she pulled back. "What if this is like Vendetta all over again?"

"It won't be, okay? I swear it won't be. We're gonna handle it."

She wiped her eyes and glanced over at Apex. He was talking to the people, trying to cheer them up. She smiled as he let one of the women pet his wings.

"They were doing a tour of the catacombs when it caved in," Lycan said. "They were trapped for hours."

She nodded. "Box me up please?"

He smiled and waved his hands, silver pouring out of them as he made a silver box just tall enough for her. She stepped inside and he closed it. The suit came off. She closed her eyes, taking in a deep breath. How were they supposed to find the Bonded when they kept disappearing after each incident?

They continued patrolling after the cemetery, though Lycan knew Kaida wasn't in the mood to keep going.

"Hey." He pulled her aside. "You should go home."

"Can I go home?" Apex asked, yawning loudly. "Very tired."

"Yeah, I can handle things. Both of you go rest."

Kaida bit her lip.

"Seriously, I'm not even tired."

"What if they do something else tonight? What if they—"

"I'll call you."

"Come *on*, it's late. I wanna sleep before school," Apex mumbled.

Kaida sighed once more and pulled her phone out. "I guess it is late..." Then her face changed, frown turning into a slight smile.

"Oh, is the *boyfriend* texting?" Apex teased.

"Yes. Shut up." She blushed as she met Lycan's eyes. "Sorry. You should rest too, ya know."

He nodded, throat tight. "I'll patrol for another hour, then home to sleep. Promise."

"Okay." She gave him a smile as she tore a portal open and pulled Apex through it.

Lycan was left standing there alone in the street, feeling defeated. Kaida was happy, with someone else. He *needed* to find that.

The next day at school Bellamy decided he was getting over Kaida, one way or another. But he had no idea where to start, so he asked Nico for help.

"And who exactly are you trying to get over?" Nico asked, eyebrows raised as they walked out of history. People were crowded in the halls, their voices all overlapping. Lola waved to them as she filled up her water by the bathrooms. "Is it R—"

"She doesn't go here you don't know her. It doesn't matter. What *does* matter is that I need to move on. So..." He felt so stupid asking. "Do you know any girls who might like me? Figure asking out someone already into me might be easier."

Nico smiled. "You're kidding, right?"

"No? Does no one like me? I guess that makes—"

"*Ren.*"

Bellamy blinked. "Ren? Ren doesn't..." His heart sped up. "Ren doesn't like me?"

Nico laughed, throwing his head back, his dark curls bouncing all over the place. "Pretty sure she's had a thing for you since last year."

Bellamy smiled as they turned the corner. Ren was down the hall at her locker, talking to Jasper, her face scrunched up like Jasper said something stupid.

"Ren? *Really?*" He watched her, heart thumping out of control as he got closer, weaving through the moving bodies.

"Yes. She's not subtle either. You're just *really* stupid," Nico replied. "I was kind of suspecting that you... already..."

Ren was one of his best friends. One of his favorite people. And she... liked him? He felt *giddy* as he got closer. *I could ask Ren out. Ren...* he looked at the yarn bracelet on his wrist. *Ren knows me. Ren...*

He stopped in his tracks as that senior boy with the black hair appeared behind Ren. He pulled her around to face him and kissed her. Bellamy clenched his fists, feeling like he'd just been punched in the gut.

"Nico, you stupid bitch," he hissed, coming to a stop by the vending machines. "Ren has a *boyfriend.*"

"Right." Nico laughed, but Bellamy didn't get the joke.

"Does... does anyone else like me?" he asked as he continued to stare at Ren.

"Uh, Jules Han."

Bellamy considered that, forcing himself to look back at Nico. "Jules?"

"Think so. She seemed into you at your birthday party at least."

Bellamy nodded. Jules was nice. Smart, pretty. He glanced back at Ren as they passed. Her freckles stood out against her extra red cheeks, nearly the same shade of red as the lockers behind her. *Ren.* She caught his eye and smiled at him. *Damn.*

What's happening? Zeli asked.

What? Nothing.

You just got so sad.

He swallowed. *I'm fine.*

Bellamy you are swimming in disappointment. What happened?

Nothing. Just... He looked over his shoulder to see Ren still standing there, that boy's arm slung over her shoulders. They didn't look right together. *Nothing.*

He made his way to English and sat in the very back. He caught himself looking at Jules throughout the class, trying to build up the courage to ask her out. When the bell rang he followed her into the hall, pulling her aside.

"Hey, Jules, can I talk to you for a second?"

"Sure."

"I was... wondering... um. Could you. If I..." He blinked. *Shit. This would have been way easier with Ren.*

Jules stared at him, frowning.

"What I'm trying to say is..." He thought of Kaida, how much he loved her. How much it hurt. *I'm letting go.* "That I... would you..."

"Are you asking me out?"

"Yes! That is what I'm trying to do," he answered, blushing.

Her honey eyes lit up, face filling with a bright smile. "I'd love to go out with you."

"Really?"

Jules really was pretty, with that flawless golden skin, and her blonde hair, pulled up in a high ponytail. It suited her well, maybe even better than the black hair she used to have.

"Yeah, let me give you my number," she said, handing him her phone.

He felt like he was in a daze as he typed it in.

Her smile grew as she met his eyes. "I'll text you."

"Cool."

You sure you're okay? Your heart is racing like you're in a fight for your life.

Totally fine, he answered, feeling totally unfine.

26
No Hero In Sight

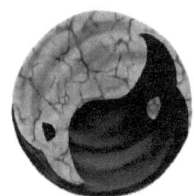

Jasper was halfway to The Grey Dog when he realized he left his phone at home. He didn't turn back for it. If he was late to his second date with Harper she'd *really* think he didn't care.

"Hey! I was just texting to see when you'd get here," she said when he arrived.

He laughed. "Forgot my phone."

"Oh, You wanna go get it?"

"Nah, it works out."

"It does?"

"Yeah." He smiled. "This way I can't get distracted. You have my undivided attention all day."

Harper grinned. "I guess that's not so bad. But we can still get it if you want. We're gonna be out a while, aren't we?"

"Don't need it. And yes," he continued as he grabbed her hand and led her inside the restaurant. "We're gonna be out all day."

"Oh, we match again!" she said, excitedly pointing at his shoes. They were both wearing blue jeans and black converse, but his were high tops and hers weren't.

"Look at us, so in sync."

They got settled in for lunch, where they ordered a grilled cheese, a burger, and some sweet potato fries while he asked about her home life.

"Yeah, it's just my mom. I usually go see my dad two weekends every month though."

Jasper nodded. "I live with both my parents but... kinda wish I didn't."

"Oh?"

He shook his head. "So, what do they do?"

"Mom's a lawyer. Dad has a fancy corporate job. Not really sure what he does though."

"Only child?" he asked.

She nodded. "You?"

"Yeah."

He took a sip of his soda, not sure what else to say. Jasper was usually good in a conversation, but he felt the pressure, trying to get this girl to like him after fumbling the first date. She also seemed hesitant now, which didn't help. He hoped things would be easier when they went to Coney Island later.

"Do I look okay?" Bellamy asked Zeli. She was curled up in a ball on the bed.

She slowly lifted her wolfish head and stared at him. *How should I know?*

"If you were a human girl would you think I look good?"

She made a disgusted sound. *Ask a human girl.*

He smiled. "I am not asking my date if she thinks I look good on the date."

Ask a different human girl.

He paused, thinking of Ren. The idea of sending her a picture of his outfit to see if it was good enough for him to go out with a different girl was too much. Bellamy *thought* he looked okay, but it was pretty basic, gray jeans, with a white tee under a black jacket. He sighed and left to go to Jules' apartment. He was nervous, overthinking it. He'd never been on a date before. It didn't help that they were going to the Met. He was fairly certain most people didn't take their dates to their mother's workplace.

When Jules walked out to meet him her face lit up. She looked good, her honey blonde hair up in a tight bun.

"You look nice." He wondered if her high heeled boots would be good for walking around the museum. They went well with her short black skirt and tights.

She grinned. "You look nice, too."

"Thanks."

"So," Jules said as they started walking. "Have you done the assignment for creative writing yet?"

"No, I'll probably do it tomorrow."

She raised an eyebrow. "It's due on Monday."

He smiled. "I know. I just can't pick what characters to use." He met her eyes as they walked into the subway. "Who did you pick?"

"Elizabeth Bennet and Frankenstein's Monster," she answered.

"Oh, that's good. What's their argument?"

"Prejudice, obviously."

"I'm never gonna come up with something as good as that."

"I'm sure you will." She had a nice smile.

They fell silent as they got settled on the subway.

"Is your mom gonna be there?" she asked after a minute.

"Yeah, she's there till five. Then she's leaving on a business trip."

"We should say hi to her while we're there."

Bellamy frowned. "You wanna say hi to my mom on our date?"

"Well, I've met her once but... not as your date."

"Uh. Okay, sure. She actually oversaw the Indian art exhibit you wanted to see."

"That's so cool."

He nodded, resisting the urge to play with his yarn bracelet. "So, what do your parents do?"

"Mom's a doctor, and Dad... he's into sculpting." She paused. "You... you just have your mom, right?"

He nodded. "Never met my dad. She pretends she doesn't know who he is, but I know it's a lie. She gets so weird anytime I've brought it up."

"Maybe he wasn't a good guy?"

He shrugged. "Maybe. I don't really care. Mom's great. I'm not like, out here wishing I had a dad. She's enough."

"That's sweet."

They talked more about their homework. They had three classes together, and Jules was already done with the homework for all of them. She probably thought he was lazy, but he couldn't exactly explain he procrastinated so he could go out and fight crime every night. But he always managed to get it done on time, and he got good grades.

When they got to the Met a feeling of dread rushed into him. He hadn't been back since...

"Have you been here, since it happened?" Jules whispered softly as they started up the steps.

"No."

"Me either." She glanced at him. "Are you gonna be okay?"

"Yeah. I'm fine. You?"

She nodded. "Almost a year now, since Clea died. It's so weird to think about."

"Yeah." He swallowed.

Bellamy spent weeks blaming himself for that loss. Not being able to save her as Lycan... After that disaster he and Kaida trained every night, getting good with the powers. But it still hurt, failing Clea then, no matter how improved they were now.

"What's with the bracelet?" Jules asked as they went inside.

"Uh." He looked down, realizing he'd been fidgeting with it. "Ren made it for me."

"Ren..." Jules nodded slowly.

He changed the subject, asking more about her family. She talked about her older sister, who was in college and working as a comic book artist.

"What do you wanna do with your life?" she asked as they moved through an exhibit.

"Uh..."

She smiled. "No plans for the future?"

"Not really." He felt stupid. Jules seemed so organized, so on top of things. "I guess I haven't given it a lot of thought. For the longest time I was moving around with my mom. Was home-schooled till freshman year, and Mom never pushed me in any one direction."

"That's fair."

"I assume you know *exactly* what you wanna do?" he asked with a smile.

"Doctor," she replied. "Like my mom."

"Impressive choice."

"It's a lot of work, but I like having a goal to reach towards."

He nodded.

"I think it's okay though," she said, face softening. "That you don't have one. I mean, you could always be a stay-at-home dad... or something. If you want kids..." She blushed, looking away.

"Uh, maybe."

She changed the subject to extracurriculars, and told him about all the things she was doing to look good for college.

He felt like he had nothing impressive to tell her. She liked that he was a reader, but it was his only hobby. Sometimes he hated not being able to tell people what he really did. Being Lycan was a job, but he also *loved* it. He loved flying through the night and helping people. He loved hanging out with Kaida and Apex. He liked making a difference. But no one could know that. He just seemed lazy and unmotivated. Jules probably thought he was so boring.

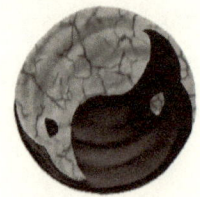

Harper started opening up more on the long subway ride, telling him about her life, and how her mom was always bringing different men home every week. She admitted she'd rather live with her dad, but she didn't wanna leave the city.

When they arrived at Coney Island Jasper noticed Harper wrapping her arms around herself as the chill air hit them. He pulled his jean jacket off and handed it to her.

She held it, staring at him in surprise.

"You're cold," he said. "Put it on."

She smiled. "Thanks."

"Looks good on you."

Harper blushed. He liked seeing the color in her cheeks.

"So, where do you wanna start? Rides, games? Walk by the water?"

"Uh. Rides."

He slid his hand in hers and pulled her along. They talked more while waiting in lines as they worked their way through some of the rides before walking the boardwalk.

"This date doesn't feel real," Harper whispered.

"What do you mean?"

She looked up at him. "My last boyfriend like, never listened to me? He didn't really talk much either. He really only cared about the physical stuff. So it's just weird that you keep asking me stuff, and... listening when I talk."

Jasper smiled. "I like listening to you. And, only caring about the physical would be so boring."

She raised an eyebrow. "Are you saying sex with me would be boring?"

He laughed. "No! That's not what I meant. I just, like... if you're gonna date someone, spend time with them, you should like *all* the aspects of the relationship, right? If you're only there for one thing what's the point?"

She stared up at him, blue eyes shining. "I like you so much."

"I like you." He leaned in, feeling brave. "Can I kiss you?"

Her eyes widened. "Yes."

He closed the distance, pressing his lips gently against hers. She seemed to melt into him, and he had to force himself to pull away after a moment. Harper was grinning, her face flushed. He took her hand in his and started walking again.

"So, who is your ex-boyfriend who's *definitely* not better than me?" he asked.

She laughed. "He's a junior. Gabe Phillips."

Jasper paused. "Gabe... from the basketball team?"

Harper's eyes widened. "Oh, you knew him. I forgot." She frowned. "You... didn't like him?"

"You could say that."

"Why?"

He shook his head. "Doesn't matter."

"You can tell me. It's not like I'm still with him."

Jasper sighed. "When I was on the team Ren would do her homework in the gym during practice. And Gabe always made gross comments about her. Kept trying to get me to hook him up with her."

Harper blinked. "When was this?"

"Uh, like a year ago?" He paused. "When did you guys go out?"

"All of freshman year," she said softly. "So, he was trying to get with her while he was with me?"

"Knew he was a prick," Jasper hissed. "When did you break up?"

"September."

"Damn. I'm sorry."

"It's fine. This single date is better than that entire relationship," she muttered.

"And it's not over yet," he whispered, pulling her closer. Then he stopped and scanned the ground till he spotted a small white rock. He grinned as he picked it up. "For you."

She blushed. "Just like the one from our first date."

Jasper nodded as she slipped it into her bag. He leaned in and kissed her cheek. "We should play games. I could win you something."

"You don't have to."

"But I want to. So, is there anything here you'd want, if I could hypothetically win it for you?"

She bit her lip, looking around the booths they passed. Then she stopped at one. "Pink sloth."

He followed her gaze to the stuffed animal with the long arms. "One pink sloth, coming up."

Bellamy and Jules finished their walk through a second exhibit, then made their way to his mom's office. He'd specifically asked her not to try and find him on his date. He hadn't planned on Jules *wanting* to meet his mom.

Her office was in an employees only area, but he'd been allowed back there plenty of times. He flagged down an employee he recognized, and she led them back to her office. Bellamy took a deep breath before knocking. A moment passed before his mom opened the door and frowned at him.

"Hey, sweetie."

"Hi, my date wanted to meet you."

Her green eyes lit up. "Oh, okay." She turned behind her. "We can continue this later."

"Sure thing, Lucy Goosey." A man appeared beside his mom in the doorway, brushing past them.

Bellamy frowned as he watched the man. That voice... he seemed familiar. Short dark hair, long black coat. *He was there on my birthday.* The hair had been different then, longer. But the silhouette and voice were the same.

"Come on in, Belly," Mom said as she stepped back into the office. He sighed and walked in with Jules.

"Hi, Miss Grey," Jules said softly. "It's nice to meet you."

Mom stared at Jules as she leaned back on her desk. "Nice to meet you..."

"Jules Han."

"You were at Bellamy's birthday, weren't you?"

"Yes, Miss Grey."

"Mom, who was that man?" Bellamy blurted.

Her eyes moved to him. "Just a coworker. So, how *is* your date going?" She smiled. "I was told I wasn't allowed to—"

"*Mom.*"

Her smile softened.

"Date is going very well," Jules answered. "Bellamy is an absolute gentleman. We really enjoyed the new Indian Summers exhibit. Bellamy said you worked on that?"

"Yes, I'm glad it turned out so well," Mom answered.

Bellamy sighed as Jules continued talking about the exhibit. It was clear she was trying to make a good impression on his mom, which must mean she liked him enough for that to matter. He realized they were kind of dressed similarly, both in white sweaters of different styles, and black skirts. Only Mom's skirt was way longer than Jules, but they both had on tall black boots, and both had their blonde hair pulled up in tight buns.

"Belly, you're gonna be okay, right?" Mom asked as she turned back to him.

"Huh?"

"With me going out of town?"

"Oh, yeah. I'll be fine."

"You'll call me if you need anything?"

He nodded. "Yes, Mom. Have a safe trip." He kissed her on the cheek, before walking Jules out.

"You and your mom are so sweet."

He smiled.

"So, where should we go for food?" Jules asked.

"Let's see what's nearby..." He pulled his phone out to check their options and his heart sank. Alerts about a Bonded growing trees on 10th and West 48th were blowing up his phone. Reports of injuries, with no hero in sight.

He took a deep breath, closing his eyes for a moment.

Zeli, get ready we're about to go.

Always ready.

He opened his eyes. Jules was watching him. "I... I feel kinda sick," he said, embarrassed. It wasn't a full lie. He *did* feel sick, at lying to her.

"Oh. Do you need the bathroom?"

"I... god, I'm *so* sorry."

"It's okay. It's fine."

"I think... I think I might just go sit in my mom's office for a bit. You should head home."

"Oh, so... no food then."

"I'm so sorry."

She shook her head, smiling. "It's okay. You can make it up to me... on our next date?"

He forced a smile. "Yes, let's do that."

"I hope you feel better. Text me later? We can plan that date."

"Sounds good."

He turned back like he was going toward his mom's office, but once Jules was out of sight he rushed to the nearest bathroom, then transformed inside one of the stalls. He waited a moment so no one who saw him walk in would see Lycan walk out.

Then he ran toward the exit, people gasped and shouted as he passed. Once outside he formed his board and kicked up into the air, flying toward Hell's Kitchen.

27
So Far Still To Go

Kaida watched the scene unfold. Pavement cracking, people screaming. Rumbles like thunder as trees burst to life in the middle of a street corner, springing up through apartment buildings. She stared, transfixed. *I got you now,* she thought as she took a deep breath and rushed inside one of the buildings.

Don't engage! Wait for the others! Zig yelled.

What? Why?

She forced her way through debris as she formed beams of light, placing them to hold up a section of the ceiling. Screaming rang out from above and she worked her way toward the voices till she found two people trying to pull another out from under a collapsed wall.

"Step back!" she yelled, placing two more beams before lifting the wall with her hands. She put more beams under it before letting go and pulling the person out.

"Are you alright?" she asked, kneeling beside them.

"Legs..." they mumbled, eyes shut, tears leaking out of them. "It hurts."

"Anyone else in here?"

One of the others shook their head. Kaida sucked in a breath and opened a portal in the tiny destroyed living room. Then she hoisted the injured guy into her arms.

"Hands on my shoulders please."

They complied, each placing a hand on her as she walked them through. They gasped at the golden stars above in her portal before they came out on the street a ways away from the growing destruction on the corner.

She gently laid the injured person on the sidewalk. "When the medics get here make sure he gets looked at!"

"Thank you!"

She stepped back in her portal and out into the apartment building. Pausing, she took a deep breath and let the suit come off. *Only four more apartments above this. And the building next to it.*

Deep breaths, Ren. You're doing great.

She nodded, anxious, as the suit came back on. She worked her way through the entire building, portaling people out, detransforming several times, but she'd been too late to save two of them.

You're barely winded. You've come so far.

So far still to go, she replied as she found herself back out on the street.

The fire department arrived and was helping civilians nearby as more trees formed, making the street look like a mini forest.

"I need to find the Bonded and stop this, before more people get hurt." Her wings unfurled from the suit and she took off in a run, taking to the air. She rose higher and higher, landing on top of a building on the other side of the street.

Wait for Lycan.

"There's no time!"

Call Apex!

She frowned as she scanned the scene. *Why are you so worried?*

It's Voltius. They can kill you.

Kaida paused. *All the more reason not to call him. I can handle it.*

Ren, please be careful.

I will, Zig. Promise. She took a deep breath. "Time to end this."

She felt a crack in Zig's confidence, but he held steady as she jumped off the roof, air slipping past. Once, this is what terrified her. Jumping. Leaping. Letting go. Now it came as natural as breathing. What wasn't natural was the speed at which the plants in the street below were growing.

Kill me how? she asked.

Their second power. A destructive touch.

Will I know when they're gonna use it?

Maybe? Zig replied. *It'll depend on their suit. Watch their hands.*

And it'll straight up kill me?

No. But it could. It might.

The fear in his voice scared her more than his words.

"I've got this," she whispered.

Kaida moved slow and careful among the growing trees as light trailed on her fingertips. A thought crossed her mind and she ran as she spotted a new crack forming in the concrete. Before the tree could rip free she poured her light into the crack, filling and covering it. A force pushed against her light, and she pushed right back.

Smart.

Thanks.

Kaida waited, knowing this would draw the Bonded out. Sure enough, a girl finally appeared behind a tree just across from Kaida. Her hair was a long vibrant blue-green, the ends getting lost in the green leaves coming off her suit. The main part of her suit looked like a dress, falling to mid-thigh, while her legs were covered in a darker green legging with light glowing green lines running through them. Her mask was like two green crescent moons going from her temple to her cheek, meeting in the middle between her eyes. Even those eyes were green. Only the flower crown wrapped around her head wasn't green, instead it was a bright pink.

"Hey," Kaida called. "Tell me, what the fuck is the point of this?"

The girl slowly stepped out from behind the tree, slinking closer. She looked a bit older than Ren in the face, but she was thinner, and shorter by several inches.

"Chaos," she finally said.

"Chaos is the point?"

"Why not?"

"So, before... the sinkhole, the cemetery, those weren't accidents?"

The girl's head tilted a little. "What I caused wasn't my intent. But I don't regret it."

"I see."

"Do you?" she asked, eyes narrowing.

"I'm not a fan of hurting people. Intentionally or not. Wild idea, I know."

"I create life," the girl whispered. "Nature is alive. And I help it flourish. How is that bad?"

"If you wanna flourish nature, restore a rainforest. Don't ruin cities. Especially *my* city."

"Maybe they deserve to be ruined."

Kaida rolled her eyes. "I'm so done with you."

"No, you're not." The girl's eyes looked wild as she tilted her head back.

Kaida's light cracked like glass, shattering to mist as the tree burst out of the ground. She fell back, watching as it went up up up into the sky. *That is a problem.*

"Can't beat me, dragon."

Kaida fumed as she got up and turned to the girl. "Who do you think you are?"

"Gaia."

Kaida snorted. "Mother earth? *Please.*"

Light streamed out of her, forming into a spear. She chucked it at Gaia. Fear crossed her face as she dropped to the ground, barely avoiding the weapon. More roots poured out of the concrete, wrapping around her and raising her up into the air.

Kaida leaped, wings stretching behind her as she flew after Gaia. She circled the trees, some of which were as tall as small skyscrapers.

At least the area below was clear of civilians now. She didn't have to worry about them while she was up here.

Something wrapped around her ankle, yanking her back. She gasped as her body slammed into the trunk of a tree. The vine had a tight grip on her, slithering its way up her leg. She hung there, upside down, confused for a moment. Then a light knife pooled out of her palm and she reached up, slicing through the vine quick and easy.

Air rushed past as she plummeted. Panic threatened to take over as she spun in the air, a rope of light appearing in her hands. She swung hard and it caught on a branch, pausing her fall. She took a deep breath as she pulled herself up to the branch. Gaia was perched above, grinning at her, entangled in the vines.

"It's *my* city now," Gaia hissed as she reached out and brushed her fingers against Kaida's hand. "Bye!" Her hand turned black and Kaida screamed.

Air whistled past.

Pain. So much *pain*. Moving through her wrist, up into her arm.

Zig was screaming.

She couldn't think.

Her body slammed into the ground, air rushing out of her lungs. She saw a spark of silver, like a shooting star, speeding toward her before everything went dark.

PART THREE

WEATHER THE STORM

It's unclear what the Bond did to humans,
as the Xyri were never forthcoming on those details.
But it was clear it changed them in many ways. They were stronger,
and healthier. Even in documented cases where the Bond was ended
prematurely, the humans still exhibited incredible strength and lived
lives longer than that of the average human.

- Xyri Bonds: Life and Death

28
Burning Gold

Lycan flew through the trees, searching for the enemy. The entire street was overgrown with wild greenery, looking like a proper forest.

Voltius, Zeli hissed. *Be very careful, Bellamy. This Bonded is more dangerous than you know.*

He took a deep breath as he maneuvered through the trees, but he didn't see the Bonded anywhere. They were too thick, grown too closely together. Laughter echoed through the branches above. *Gotcha.*

He sped up through the canopies and finally spotted her sitting in the branches. A girl with blue hair and fair skin, stark against the brown of the bark in her white shirt and blue jeans. Something was off. She wasn't in a suit...

Is that the Bonded?

"You're too late, little wolf!" the girl called when she saw him.

Oh no.

"I'm obviously not." He got closer, silver seeping out of his hands, ready to cage her as he hopped off his board and onto a branch.

"Your girl already swung by." She stood and stepped back. "She's dying as we speak."

Find Kaida, now!

Lycan's heart lurched as he turned, scanning the trees. The smallest spot of bright red caught his eye from below. He dove, jumping out of the tree before he could reform his board. He fell fast, barely righting himself with it moments before he landed on the ground beside her.

"Kaida?"

The right hand of her suit was no longer glowing, the flames on her black sleeve had gone out. He brushed a strand of hair off her sweaty face. She was burning up.

"What's wrong with her?"

I'm sorry. I'm so so sorry.

"No. No. She's still breathing. She isn't dead!"

But, Zeli's voice cracked. *She is dying.*

"No!" Lycan pulled on the fabric of time, yanking himself back five minutes.

He found himself midair, disoriented. He flew as fast as he could, this time ignoring the Bonded entirely, going straight for Kaida. Her body was already on the ground. He was still too late.

"How do I fix it?"

Zeli didn't answer.

"Help me!" he screamed, terror overwhelming him. He couldn't lose her. He wouldn't. "*Please!*"

It's too soon. Oh, it is too soon. Kirzigith... She sounded like she was in pain. *Check her eyes.*

Scared and confused, Lycan gently lifted one of Kaida's eyelids. Her eye was burning gold, glowing softly.

He will not let this child die without trying. Of course he won't. Get her out of here, now.

He scooped Kaida into his arms as his eyes watered. He kicked up his board and flew them away. Kaida was dying, and he didn't know where to go or what to do. His first thought was that he needed to take her home, but he didn't know where her home *was.* No one in her life knew she was Kaida. Besides Apex.

Lycan took her to his home, instead. Mom was going straight to the airport after work, and she wouldn't be back till Tuesday. Kaida would be safe there.

He walked through his balcony doors then laid her body in his bed.

"Kaida? Can you hear me?"

He gently pulled his comforter out from under her legs and tucked her in. Then he grabbed her hand, ignoring the tremors running through him.

"Talk to me, Zeli. What's happening?"

The power of Voltius touched her. The power of destruction. If she were a normal human, she would have died instantly.

"She's not normal! She's Bonded."

Yes. And... Zeli was practically shaking with fear inside of him.

He let out a choked sob as tears fell from his eyes. "She isn't gonna make it, is she?"

I'm sorry, Bellamy. Kirzigith is fusing with her.

"That's supposed to save her, right?"

The fuse so rarely works. More often than not, fusing will kill our humans. You can not understand such pain. We only ever risk it if there is no other option. If our human would die, otherwise.

Bellamy didn't know what to say.

Kirzigith loves her so much. We will lose him, if he loses her. Xenos isn't here...

"No. No, she's *not* gonna die. You hear me, Kaida?" He leaned closer, and brushed his thumb against her cheek. "You're not gonna leave me. I will *never* forgive you."

Bellamy's whole body shook as he detransformed. Zeli appeared beside him. She hopped up on the bed and laid her chin down on Kaida's stomach. Her silver eyes looked hopeless.

"How rare is it?"

Zeli was quiet for a moment before answering. *Kirzigith has only ever had two successful fuses. He's tried to fuse over a dozen times.* She paused, slowly lifting her head to look at him. *I have never had a successful fuse.*

He nodded and texted Apex, then the suit came back over him. He grabbed Kaida's hand again.

"Kaida..." he whispered, staring down at her face. "I love you. I love you so much. And I don't mean in the way I'm not supposed to. Just. I love you. As my best friend and my partner. And I *need* you. Please don't leave me. *Please?*"

His tears fell.

Kaida didn't wake up.

Hours passed. He barely moved.

Mom called to check on him. He didn't answer.

He forced himself to text her a while later so she wouldn't worry, then he went back to his silent vigil.

The sun went away and they were left in darkness. He couldn't bother getting up to turn on a light.

Kaida finally moved. A small sound left her mouth as she turned her head to the side. His heart pounded.

"Kaida?"

"Hm?" She didn't open her eyes.

Air rushed out of his lungs as he gripped her hand tightly. "Hey, Bunhead. It's me, Lycan."

She made another noise, a small smile forming on her face. Then the smile twisted and fell, her face scrunching up.

"What... *ow.*"

What's happening?

This is good, Zeli said. And finally, he could hear a spark of hope in her voice. *She's made it this long, now she is talking. This is very good.*

So she's gonna make it?

Zeli hesitated. *Maybe.*

He sucked in a breath. "You almost died," he whispered. "Are you... how do you feel?"

"I don't like it. *Ow.*" Her eyes snapped open. They still shone pure gold. "What... the fuck..."

"You're fusing with Zig."

She squeezed her eyes shut, turning her head to the side again. "Oh that's not nice. Ow ow ow." Her eyelids fluttered, light seeping out every time they opened just a fraction. "Is... that a storm outside? Is it *in* me?"

"What?"

"I can hear the stars. Oh *god.*" Her whole body spasmed, hand tightening around his as she *screamed.*

He stared, wide eyed, unsure what to do. She continued to scream her lament of light, wisps of gold shining out of her mouth.

After a moment she stilled and went silent.

"Kaida?" He watched her chest rise, and fall, slower than it should have.

"Lycan?"

His heart pounded. "Yeah?"

She exhaled. "Starface. I *missed* you."

"I'm here. Right here. Not going anywhere."

She smiled again and rolled onto her side, pulling his hand with her, clutching it tighter. He shifted his position, moving closer so she could keep hold of him.

Is she gonna be okay?

I can not be sure, Bellamy. But the fuse is working, so far.

A fresh tear slid down his cheek. *How long is she gonna be like this?*

A while. Kirzigith is trying to keep her unconscious. She will be in extreme pain, so the sleep is good. She'll sleep a lot, even when it's finished. She will also need a lot of food when it's over. Fusing takes so much out of both human and Xyri.

He nodded. She said when, not if. He clung to that hope as he checked his phone again. No reply from Apex yet.

Another hour passed before Kaida moved again. Her leg jerked in a small spasm and she gasped, eyes fluttering. After a moment she seemed to relax.

"Lycan?"

"I'm here."

Her grip on his hand tightened. "Where are we?"

"Uh, you're at my house. In my room."

She frowned. "Not smart."

"I had to take you somewhere safe," he whispered. "It's just me here today. No one will see you."

"Is this your bed?" she asked, shifting slightly.

"Yes."

A smile. "Comfy."

He grinned. "Glad you like it. Do you need anything? Zel said you should eat."

She frowned again. "I..." Her eyes snapped open, still golden. She blinked a few times then squeezed them shut, groaning. "How long have I been here?"

He glanced at the clock on his desk. "About seven hours. It's a little after nine."

"Oh *god*. I need my phone. Zig, my phone..."

"I texted Apex, but he isn't answering..."

She groaned. "I can't... can't move my arm."

Lycan pulled her hand up. "Injury is in your right hand. This one seems to be working though."

She wriggled her fingers in her left hand as he let go of it, then slid her hand under the blanket. She pulled out her phone a moment later. It was camouflaged to look like her suit, the case covered in red scales. Her eyes opened and she winced. The golden eyes slowly faded, then her eyes turned brown. Bellamy felt his breath catch at seeing those eyes again. He'd only ever seen her real eyes once, when they first met, before she changed them to blue.

She lifted the phone up, squinting as she tried to text with one hand. After a moment the phone slipped from her fingers and fell on her chest as her eyes turned gold again.

"You said... Apex—"

"Not answering."

"Tell him he needs to—to cover for me. Tell him..."

"Yeah, okay. Are you ready to eat anything?" he asked as he grabbed his phone and sent the text.

She mumbled what sounded like a no, then shifted again, her face pressing into the pillow. "Cold," she whispered.

He stood and stretched then grabbed another blanket from the closet in the hall. He gently laid it on her, tucking her in even more. When he sat beside her again, she was sound asleep.

She's going to be okay, right?

I believe she will be. At this point... she's a strong kid, Bellamy.

I can't lose her.

I know.

Bellamy settled back, then tried Apex again, letting him know she seemed to be healing but things were still uncertain. Part of him worried Apex got himself in trouble again. Bellamy couldn't worry about that, though. Apex would have to handle himself. He wouldn't leave Kaida.

Somewhere in the back of his mind he realized he never dealt with the Bonded. He left her there to do as she pleased. But Kaida was more important.

Another hour passed before she woke again, her eyes no longer golden as she blinked up at him.

"Am I still alive?" she asked in a small voice.

"Yeah. Good thing too, cause otherwise I was gonna go insane."

She smiled. "Wouldn't want that."

He shook his head. "Hungry?"

"Yes. I think if I don't consume food in the next five minutes I might actually die."

"In the mood for anything specific?"

"Food."

He grinned. "I'll see what I can do. Don't move, okay? Stay in bed. Eyes closed."

"Promise," she whispered, eyes already shut.

He slid out of the bed and walked down to the kitchen, nervous about leaving her alone. *Zeli, go watch her.*

I can't unless you—

He detransformed, cutting her off. Zeli appeared on the floor in front of him.

Oh. She stretched. *Make her a lot of food, she will need it.*

He watched her turn the corner, then started pulling things out of the fridge. He ended up making some grilled cheeses. When he entered the bedroom Kaida was asleep, Zeli lying with her face on Kaida's stomach again.

She is recovering well, Bellamy. She is going to make it. I am sure now.

He released a breath, then transformed again. Zeli disappeared from the bed and he took her spot, gently nudging Kaida awake.

"Food for the lady," he whispered.

"Oh. Yay."

He helped her sit up, then set the plate in front of her. She grabbed one of the sandwiches, biting into it with a smile. She was halfway through it before he grabbed one for himself.

"Did I tell you that?" she asked through a mouthful.

He frowned. "Tell me what?"

"Grilled cheese. My favorite comfort food."

Bellamy smiled. "No, I don't think so."

She leaned back into the pillows, eyes closed, as she finished the sandwich. Kaida ate four of them, while he ate two. Sleep took her again when the food was done.

His phone buzzed with a call from Apex.

"Fucking finally," he answered, slowly getting off the bed and walking out of the room.

"Is she okay?" Apex's panicked voice replied.

"So far, yes. She's been in and out of consciousness for a while. I've been going *insane*."

Apex was quiet for a moment. "Where is she?"

"At my house."

"Your house?"

"Yeah, it's safe. We're alone. And, she's not seen anything to give away my identity."

Apex released a breath. "She's gonna be okay?"

"I think so. I can bring her to you. Wanna meet somewhere?"

"Yes. I... fuck. Okay I'll text you a location."

"Kay."

He hung up and waited, pacing through the room. Three minutes later the text came.

"Kaida?"

"Hm?"

"Apex called. I can take you to him."

"Okay."

"Can you stand?"

She didn't say anything, her face scrunching up. "I don't know where my legs are."

He tried not to laugh. "I can carry you, if you're okay with that?"

"Carry on... my wayward..." She giggled and nodded.

It's like she's on drugs, he said to Zeli as he pulled the blankets back and slid her into his arms.

She kind of is. The fuse is... a strange experience.

Lycan stepped onto the balcony, making sure he had a good hold on her before speeding through the air on his board. It only took two minutes to get to the place Apex suggested. He found him standing by the fountain in the center of the park, looking worried as Lycan approached with Kaida in his arms.

"Kai, we're here," he whispered in her ear.

"Okay," she mumbled as he tried to set her on her feet. She seemed unsteady and kept her arms around his neck.

Apex smiled. "Is she high?"

"Little bit. Not as bad as you were last week," Lycan replied. "Whatever Zig did made her a bit loopy though."

"As long as she's alive." Apex stepped closer and put a hand on her shoulder. "Kaida?"

"Hm?" She had her face pressed against Lycan's chest, still holding onto him. He wondered if she noticed how his heart raced against her.

"You gotta let go of the nice wolf boy now," Apex said, slowly pulling one of her hands away from Lycan.

"Oh. Okay." She didn't resist as Apex pulled her toward him. She pressed her face into his chest as he put his arms around her.

"She's really gonna be okay?"

"Zeli is sure. She's gonna be in and out for a while, though. Needs lots of sleep and also a lot of food. I fed her like thirty minutes ago, but she'll need more."

"Thank you."

Lycan nodded. Even if he and Apex never got close, there was one thing they would always have in common. They both loved this girl more than anything.

29
Xyri Juice

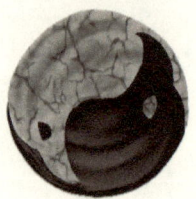

Jasper got Ren tucked safely in her bed before sneaking downstairs to see if her dads were awake. All was quiet so he snuck back up then sent her dads a text saying Ren didn't feel well and they were coming back. He'd hoped they wouldn't see it till morning, but ten minutes later Daddy Cas came in through the trapdoor and gently knocked on the wall by her bed.

Jasper peeked out over the stairs and grinned. "She's asleep."

"What happened?" Cas asked.

"She started her period early. Didn't have pads at my house so had to get some anyway, and she just wanted to come back. My mom drove us," he lied, hoping he wouldn't check with his mom.

Cas nodded. "Does she need anything?"

"She was super hungry before she dozed off."

"I can make something. You hungry too?"

"Yeah."

"I'll be back up in a bit."

"Best Daddy ever."

When Cas left, he settled back in beside Ren, who was still in her suit. Her dad could *not* see that.

"Renegade?" he whispered. She let out a soft sigh. "Renny? Gotta wake up and take the suit off before your dad comes back."

She mumbled, rolling over.

He sighed. "Zig? Can you hear me? She can *not* be suited up when Cas comes back!"

Silence. Then Ren groaned as the suit disappeared. Now he could see the bags under her eyes, how pale her face really was. She blinked up at him, eyes flickering gold then brown, gold then brown. Zig appeared beside him.

She will recover. But she is not yet done recovering, the Xyri said, voice strained.

"You saved her?"

I am saving her. Do not let her dads see her hand.

218

Jasper's eyes widened. Ren's right hand was a dark ashen gray, like it was dead. "Is her hand gonna be okay?"

I am still reversing the process. Stopped it from reaching her heart first. Now, I push it back.

Jasper nodded and pulled the blanket up over her hand to hide it.

When her dad came back in a few minutes later he climbed out of the bed to meet him on the steps. Cas had a tray in hand, with two plates of grilled cheeses, a bowl of tomato soup, and two sodas.

"Best Dad ever," Jasper said as he took the tray from him and walked back up. Cas followed.

"Ren, baby, you need anything else?"

"Nooo," Ren muttered. "Do I smell food?"

"Here." Jasper set the tray beside her.

"Food." Ren groaned as she tried to sit up then tipped over into the wall.

Cas frowned and came in closer. Jasper watched, heart racing. Ren's hand was still under the blanket, but if Cas saw it Jasper had no idea how to explain.

"Ren?" Cas placed a hand on her face. "Baby, you're burning up."

"Burnin up... burnin up..." Ren mumbled.

"Is that normal?" Jasper asked. "Fever with the period?"

Cas sighed. "Sometimes, but... not this hot. I'll get her some medicine."

Jasper nodded.

Once Cas was gone, Zig disappeared and the suit returned over Ren's body. She took a deep breath, blinking rapidly as her eyes flickered back to gold.

"Bleh," she mumbled as she grabbed a sandwich. "Weird."

"You're weird," Jasper replied. "Also, you ever die on me again I'll kill myself and then annoy the hell out of you in the afterlife."

Ren frowned. "Didn't die."

"You almost died."

"Hmm..."

"I'm serious. Don't *ever* do that to me again."

She nodded. "Where were you? Lycan said..."

"Accidentally left my phone at home while I was out with Harper. Didn't get back till late." The one fucking time he didn't have his phone and Ren almost *died*.

"Good date?"

"My best friend almost died, so no."

She rolled her eyes as she pushed the tray toward him. "Cheese."

He sighed and grabbed a sandwich. "The date was good," he mumbled before taking a bite.

"Good."

"I'm sorry I wasn't there. I should have been there."

Ren shook her head. "I'm *fiiiine*."

"Your hand looks dead and you're high on Xyri juice, so you're not fine."

Her face scrunched up in confusion. "No juice in a cheese."

She said it *so* seriously, Jasper burst out laughing. "You're so high."

"You're high," she spat back. "Gonna eat that one?"

He pushed his plate back, giving her his second sandwich. "You're still hungry?"

"Zig ate all my food," she mumbled.

Jasper laughed. "I don't think he did."

When they finished eating, Ren detransformed again as he helped her to the bathroom. That's when Cas came back up with medicine. Ren chugged it back with a groan.

"Can I stay up here with her?" Jasper asked. "Since she's sick."

Cas sighed. "*Couch.* If she needs me call me, okay? I have to work soon but I can come right back up. And you can wake Arrow too, if you need to."

"Yes sir."

Cas kissed Ren's forehead then left. Jasper got her back in bed, where she fell asleep immediately, back in the suit. He checked his phone, finding texts from Harper and Lycan.

|The Wolf|
How's Kaida? Any better?

|The Bird|
Better. She ate and is sleeping again. Still high as shit though

|The Wolf|
Good. Keep me updated?

I know she's gonna be okay but I can't stop worrying

|The Bird|
Absolutely. Also have I mentioned lately how much I fucking love you?

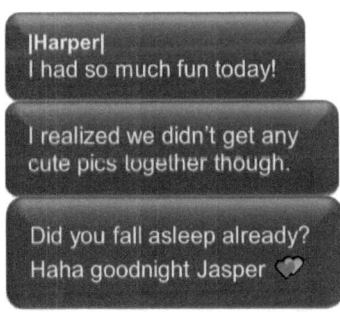

|The Wolf|
No I don't believe so.

|The Bird|
Well I do. Thanks for saving her. I'm so glad she has you watching her back

|The Wolf|
Always.

He switched to Harper's texts.

|Harper|
I had so much fun today!

I realized we didn't get any cute pics together though.

Did you fall asleep already? Haha goodnight Jasper 🤍

|Jasper|
We can get pictures on the next date. and I had fun too! 🤍

It was five in the morning at that point, and he was tired as hell, but couldn't bring himself to sleep. He stayed there, playing games on his phone as Ren slept beside him. She tossed and turned constantly, but the suit stayed on. Every now and then she groaned, eyes blinking open, shining golden.

Why do her eyes do that?

It's Kirzigith, Pozi answered. The little Xyri was resting on the floor beside the bed, his wings tucked into his sides. *Fusing is complicated. His cells are literally tangling with hers. Those are his eyes. It's quite traumatizing for both of them. He's trying to keep her unconscious to help her weather the storm.*

Storm?

Pain, kid. She's hurting. But she probably won't remember much of it.

How long till the fuse is complete?

Few more hours. Pozi paused. *Don't mean to scare you, but... she is extremely lucky. Most humans do not survive the fuse.*

He swallowed. Jasper joked, but the thought of losing Ren scared him more than anything.

You must be very careful facing Voltius's human, Pozi continued. *I don't wanna be the one to kill you.*

Jasper turned to look at Pozi. "What do you mean?"

Pozi sighed, his wings shaking a little before he tucked them back in. *We do not fuse unless you're already dying, with no hope of recovery. But the fuse can kill too. It's not logical. We know you were already dying, sure. But... it's different, when your heart stops during the fuse. That's on us. And we live with it forever.*

Jasper blinked.

Do not put me through that.

"I'll try not to."

Eventually he must have dozed off, because he snapped awake to hear Ren talking to Zig. The little Xyri was nestled against Ren's side, under her arm.

"Zig, you're shaking..."

"Ren?"

She turned, looking over at him, confused. "What the fuck happened?"

"You don't remember?" he asked as he sat up, noting her eyes were back to brown.

"I..." She closed her eyes. "I was sick. Really sick? Was Lycan here?"

He smiled. "No, but you were in Lycan's house though. In his bed. *Very* intimate."

Her eyes opened but the frown remained. "I'm better now?"

"Are you?" he asked, serious.

She nodded as she looked down at Zig, tucked against her. "It was bad?"

"Very bad."

She slid over a little and laid her head on his shoulder. "Sorry."

He put his arm around her. "I'll forgive you in about five years, cause that's how much you took off my life."

She nodded again, head rubbing against him.

Jasper stared at her hand. It looked less gray now, but still kinda pale.

They went downstairs to get breakfast, though it was actually lunch time. Both her dads started fussing over her. She still had a fever and Cas mentioned taking her to a doctor, so Ren faked cramps and went back upstairs to rest. Jasper went with her to get his phone, but part of him was afraid to leave her.

"Zig isn't well," she mumbled, rubbing her eyes as she sat on her couch.

Jasper looked down at the little red-scaled Xyri, who was curled up beside her.

"He did so much to heal me. He says I shouldn't transform for a few days."

Jasper nodded. "Pozi said it was hard, on both of you. But don't worry, Lycan and I can handle things while you guys recover. Promise."

"You're going home now?" she asked, looking exhausted.

"Want me to stay? I can stay."

Ren smiled softly. "Yes please."

"Let me just tell my mom."

He grabbed his phone from Ren's bed, finding missed texts from Harper.

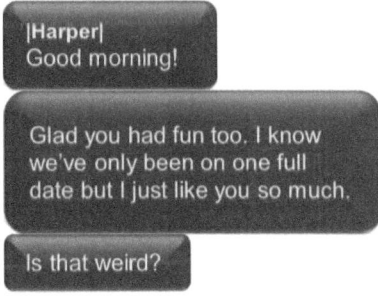

|Harper|
Good morning!

Glad you had fun too. I know we've only been on one full date but I just like you so much.

Is that weird?

|Jasper|
Not weird I like you too

|Harper|
It feels like you're already my boyfriend haha

Jasper grinned as he sat on the couch beside Ren.

|Jasper|
I mean, I can be. If you want?

|Harper|
Yes!!! ♡
Do you wanna get together today? We could take pictures!!

|Jasper|
Can't today, Ren needs me but I'm down for tomorrow after school?

|Harper|
Ren needs you? For what??

|Jasper|
She's having a bad day. I swear you get me tomorrow.
We can have a whole photoshot if you want

|Harper|
Okay. Tomorrow sounds good. ♡

Jasper really liked her. Despite how badly his night ended, the date with Harper had been awesome. She was pretty and fun and he really liked kissing her.

She texted sporadically throughout the day, like she worried he'd forget she existed if he didn't hear from her often. But he didn't mind.

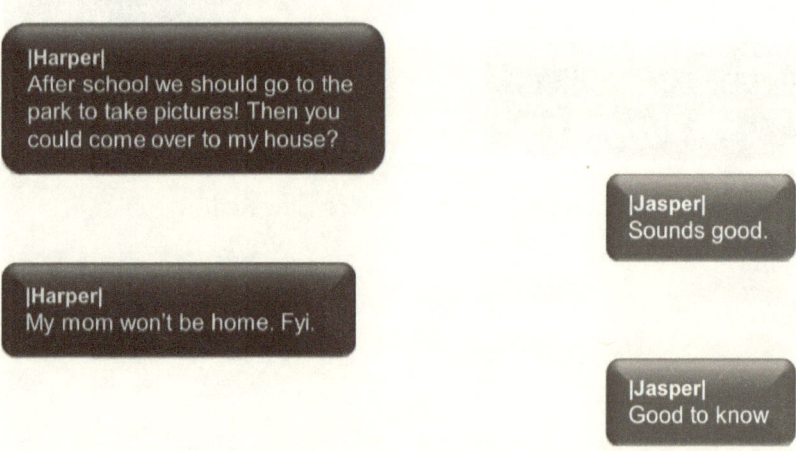

|Harper|
After school we should go to the park to take pictures! Then you could come over to my house?

|Jasper|
Sounds good.

|Harper|
My mom won't be home. Fyi.

|Jasper|
Good to know

|Harper|
Is Ren feeling better?
What are you guys up to?

|Jasper|
Video games.
She says hi!

|Harper|
Tell her I said hi too!
Are you winning the games?

|Jasper|
Yes. I definitely win every game

|Harper|
Haha

Ren smiled as he put the controller down to respond again. "Harper still?"

"Yeah."

"So, things are good then?"

"Yep. We're official now." He looked up at her and frowned. "Your phone is awfully quiet. What's Simon up to?"

"Band practice," she replied. "He sent me a picture of him with his guitar."

"Hot."

She nodded, cheeks turning red.

"You know what else is hot?" Jasper asked. "Sleeping in Lycan's fucking *bed*."

Ren rolled her eyes. "I barely remember that."

"You said he held your hand the whole time."

Her cheeks got redder. "Yeah."

"That's hot."

Another eye roll. "It's not hot. It's *sweet*. And, I was dying. And Lycan and I can't be more than friends so it doesn't matter and I don't like him like that." She let out a breath. "I have a boyfriend now."

Jasper didn't respond. The more time he spent around both Simon and Lycan, he knew who he preferred. Not that there was anything wrong with Simon, the guy seemed fine. But he did feel a *tad* possessive of Ren, like he wanted everyone to see him kiss her. On the other hand, Lycan confessed his love to her, then acted completely cool after she rejected him. One of those things felt more mature. And Lycan simply seemed to *fit* her in a way that Simon didn't.

Ren dozed off on the couch. He didn't wake her till her dad said dinner was ready. Arrow ordered Chinese and they ate in the living room together while watching an episode of Law & Order. Cas continued fussing over Ren. Her fever was still raging and she couldn't stay awake, but she convinced him it was just her period. When the episode ended they went back to her room. Zig was sound asleep in Ren's bed, while Pozi lounged on her desk chair.

His phone lit up with a video call from Harper. He was surprised as he answered it, flopping down on Ren's couch.

"Hey!"

"Hi!" She was blushing, face bright with a smile. "I just wanted to—" Her smile fell. "Are you still at Ren's?"

"Yeah. Ren say hi." He turned the camera so Harper could see Ren as she moved things on her desk. Ren waved awkwardly but didn't say anything.

"Why... are you still at Ren's?" Harper asked, her voice changing.

Jasper paused, realizing his girlfriend might not like that he stayed the night at Ren's house regularly. He wasn't going to lie, so he took a deep breath before responding. "I'm staying over. Did I not mention that?"

Harper blinked, mouth open. "You're... staying at Ren's tonight?"

"Yeah. I stay over all the time. Cause... well she's my best friend and... things kinda suck at home, so I like being anywhere else when I can and..." He swallowed at the look of hurt in her eyes. "I'm sorry, I should have told you earlier."

"You're staying at Ren's," Harper repeated slowly.

Ren appeared behind Jasper's shoulder and grabbed the phone out of his hand.

"Harper, I am *so* sorry, he's *such* an idiot," she said.

Jasper turned around to watch Ren move through the room, Jasper's phone held tightly in her hand.

"He doesn't stay over like that. I have a guest room that's literally two floors below mine, he sleeps there when he stays over. My dads are pretty strict about that. And I assure you nothing weird happens between us. Just friends! *Also* he was talking about you *all* day. Telling me about your date and how he can't wait to see you again," Ren finished with a smile.

Jasper wished he could see Harper's reaction to that, but Ren was facing the wrong way for him to see.

"Oh." Harper laughed nervously. "I guess that makes me feel better."

"I know it seems weird. People always think that cause he's a boy, but it's literally no different than you staying over at Lola's. Promise."

Silence. "I'm not allowed to stay at Lola's on a school night."

Ren smiled. "My dads are very chill. Anyways, Jasper's *really* into you," she whispered.

Jasper jumped up. "Ren gimme the phone!"

Ren danced back as he approached and the phone fell out of her hand. "Oops." She went to her knees and picked it up before he could grab it. "He thinks you're so hot and he told me you're a really good kisser and—"

"Give me!" He snatched it out of Ren's hands, heart racing as he looked at Harper. She was smiling now. "Okay so all of that is true but can we pretend you didn't hear it?"

Harper shook her head. "Absolutely not. I'm gonna be thinking about that all night."

Jasper grinned. "Yeah, well. Maybe I'll be thinking about you all night."

Harper giggled, cheeks turning pink. "We are for sure getting together after school?"

"Promise."

She nodded, looking relieved. "Okay. See you tomorrow."

"Goodnight."

He turned a glare on Ren once the call ended. She was on the edge of laughing, still on her knees. He softened, taking in her smile and the color in her face resembling something more normal than the corpse she'd looked like last night. She was *okay*.

30
Useless

Kaida crossed the roof and threw herself into Lycan's arms. He grunted in surprise as he slowly slid his arms around her. She buried her face in his chest, ignoring the exhaustion as he held her.

"What's this for?" he whispered, chin resting on her head.

"You know what it's for." She pulled back a bit and looked up at him. Four days since she almost died. Four days since she'd seen him. She'd slept through most of that time, missing three days of school so far. "You saved me."

He tilted his head a little. "Zig saved you."

Kaida shook her head. "I was helpless. Gaia could have finished the job. You got me out of there. You took care of me." She swallowed. "You saved me."

He released a breath. "Of course I did."

She tightened her hold on him, staring up into his yellow eyes. "I love you. Not... not how I'm not supposed to but as my best friend," Ren whispered, heart racing like wild in her chest.

Lycan blushed. "You... you heard that?"

She smiled. "Thought I might have dreamt it." Her heart continued to flutter. "But I do love you, and I need you too. You know that?"

He nodded. "You and me."

"You and me, Starface."

He swallowed, looking away, the blush still stark in his cheeks. "You need to rest. Why are you here?"

"I needed to see you."

"You can barely stand, Kai. I can feel how unsteady you are."

She shook her head. "But I needed this. It was important to me."

He smiled softly. "You could have called."

"It was very important."

"Noted. Go home and rest, *please*. I promise Apex and I have things under control. All you need to do is recover."

She sighed. "I trust you both just... *please* be careful. If Gaia shows up again... she's now killed thirteen people. And injured over fifty."

"We got this. I *promise*."

She nodded and hugged him again, pressing her face into his chest for a moment. When she pulled back she ripped open a portal and glanced back at him.

"Oh, Zig wanted me to tell you to tell Zeli that he's *fine* and she *shouldn't* worry."

Lycan smiled. "Zeli says she knows he's lying."

Kaida nodded. "He is. But we *will* be fine."

With that she stepped through the portal and crossed it swiftly. She came back out in her closet. The portal collapsed and so did she, falling to her knees as the suit came off.

Guilt filled her when Zig appeared beside her, panting.

Sorry.

It is fine, he answered as she scooped him into her arms and forced herself up. She carried him up to her bed and put him on the corner where he liked to sleep. Then she laid down beside him.

Ren had slept so much since her fight with Gaia, but still didn't feel healed, though Zig assured her she was well now. Her right hand was still numb, but she didn't tell him. She needed him to get better, too.

A knock sounded in the floor, then she heard the trapdoor lift.

"Ren?" Dare called.

She crawled to the end of the bed and peeked around the wall at him.

"Your boyfriend is here to see you," he said, forcing a smile.

Ren's heart fluttered. "What, really?"

"I can have him leave."

"No! No. I'll be down in two minutes, please don't kill him in that time."

"I'll do my best."

She watched the trapdoor close then sighed, sparing a glance for Zig. He was sound asleep. She gently ran a finger down his forehead before climbing out of the bed. She went to the bathroom and groaned at her reflection. Her hair hadn't been properly brushed through in days and the bags under her eyes were so prominent no makeup could hide them.

It took her five minutes to brush her teeth and fight her hair before she went downstairs to find Simon awkwardly standing in the kitchen, both her dads watching him with glares. Simon hadn't been in her house since their very first date, any time she invited him in he declined.

"Hi," she said, nervous.

"Hey. Feeling any better today?" Simon asked as he crossed the room to her and gently pulled her into his arms.

"A little," she lied. She hadn't seen him since before her injury. Everyone thought she just had a cold on top of her period, which she finally started last night.

"So, I wanted to ask you something," he whispered in her ear.

She looked up. "What is it?"

"I was wondering if..." He looked nervous. "If you wanted to go to prom with me?"

Ren blinked, surprised. "Prom?"

Simon nodded. "I know that's probably not really your thing but, I figured, could be fun. Getting dressed up, dancing." He leaned closer. "Kinda romantic."

Ren couldn't stop smiling as she tried to process that. She completely forgot Simon was a senior. She wouldn't have thought he'd wanna go to his prom. It didn't seem very *him*.

"What do you say?" His blue eyes searched her face.

"I'd love to."

"Really?"

She nodded, sliding her arms around him again.

"I know I shouldn't kiss you while you're sick, but..."

Ren pulled back, looking up at him.

"It's worth the risk," he continued.

His lips met hers, soft and warm. Her heart pounded. The kiss was brief, and once he pulled away she became overly aware of her dads still in the room. She glanced over her shoulder to see them both pretending to clean the counter, which was very much already clean. Dare didn't even have a cloth and was wiping it with his hand. She grinned as she turned back to Simon.

"You should ask my dads," she whispered.

"Hm?"

"Ask them if I can go with you." She nodded at the look of confusion on his face. "Trust me, they'll say yes but they'll like that you asked."

Simon sighed. "Alright." He took a deep breath and turned toward her dads.

"Uh, Mr. Rivers..."

Her dads stopped feigning cleaning.

"Yes?" Dad asked.

"Um. I was wondering if it would be alright if I took Ren to my prom?"

Dad blinked, then met her eyes. She gave him a hopeful smile. He seemed to assess her a moment before looking at Dare, who made a face that Dad seemed to understand. He sighed.

"When is this prom?"

"About a month from now. First weekend of May."

Ren bit her lip anxiously.

"Alright," Dad said. "Ren can go but there's gonna be *rules* that night."

"Understood, sir. Thank you." Simon paused, still seeming nervous. "I uh, like your tattoos," he continued, nodding at Dare.

Dare grinned and held his arms out to show them off better. He had full sleeves on both sides, all of them in black ink except for the red dragon wrapped around his right arm, the head of it hidden under his shirt on his chest.

"That dragon is *so* cool," Simon added.

"Got that for Ren," Dare replied, proud.

"She's our little dragon," Dad said, showing off his own dragon tattoo on his right inner forearm, much smaller than Dare's. He only had four tattoos, a lotus flower under the dragon inside of his wrist. And a sunflower with the stem spelling out the name *Robin*, with an arrow band above it around his bicep on the left arm.

"I drew all the stars," Ren said softly. "On Dare's arms."

Dare grinned as he flipped his arm around so Simon could see them. There were so many little stars, some quite sloppy, and some very neat, filling the gaps around his other random pieces. He had her draw one on him every year on the anniversary of him becoming her dad, then he'd go straight to the shop and have Olivia tattoo them.

"That's so cute," Simon said. "They all look so cool."

"Simon wants tattoos," Ren added.

Dare sighed. "Yeah? Well, if Ren still likes you when you're ready to get one, maybe I'll give you a discount."

"Seriously?" Simon's eyes widened.

"I think I will," Ren said.

Simon grinned at her. She got lost staring up at him and her dads stepped away after a moment.

"Maybe one day I'll get a dragon tattoo for you, too."

Ren giggled.

"And I get to take you to prom. I'm having a great day."

Ren's smile fell as she realized. "I'm gonna need a dress."

Simon leaned closer. "Can't wait to see *that*."

She blushed.

"Maybe we could go out this weekend?" he asked as he tucked her hair behind her ear. "If you're feeling better? I've missed you."

"If I'm better, yeah." She took a deep breath. "Miss you too."

He kissed her forehead. Then he kissed her cheek. Then her lips, lingering there a moment before pulling away. "I'll text you later?"

She nodded.

"I'll let myself out," he called to her dads as he went downstairs. Dare rolled his eyes and followed Simon down.

Ren sighed as Dad came up to her.

"How are we feeling?"

She wanted to lie. To say she was better. That she was good. But she could barely stand. Now that Simon was gone, whatever facade of strength she'd had disappeared. "Icky," she muttered.

Dad nodded, putting an arm around her shoulders. "How about you rest on the couch while I make you some soup?"

"Okay," she replied, trying not to cry.

She hated feeling like this. *Useless*. She couldn't do things as Kaida, she could barely be Ren. Missing school, missing her boyfriend, missing Jasper. It felt like everything was falling apart, not just inside of her but outside, too.

"So, prom?" Dad said as he pulled a blanket up over her and tucked her in. "Didn't think I'd have to worry about that for two years."

Ren smiled. "You don't have to *worry* about it. It's just a dance. Maybe when I'm better we could go dress shopping?"

Dad's face softened. "We?"

"Yeah. I know it's not my prom. But I always pictured you and Dare helping me pick my dress. Should for this one, too."

Dad blinked, eyes full of emotion. "I'd love that."

Ren grinned up at him. "Remind me to text Ocean about it later. She's gonna freak."

He smiled. "What kind of soup do you want?" He brushed her hair back and she knew he was trying to assess how bad her fever was.

"Uh, that one Abuela makes? Spicy. With the chicken."

"I can do that. It'll take a few hours though."

"That's fine. I'm sleepy."

Dad nodded and kissed her forehead before walking into the kitchen. Ren closed her eyes, smiling despite the pain.

31
Stasis

Lycan hovered in the air, confused. Several cars were stopped as a dense fog grew across the street. But what drew his eyes were the four identical girls fighting what looked like wolfhounds made of mist or smoke. Their suits were black with pink lines going down it in a V shape, and little specks of pink light, like stars, all over it. There was a swirl of pink in the center of their chests, like a black hole. And their long hair was varying shades of pinks, blues, and purples.

He couldn't even begin to guess what was going on as he slowly lowered himself to the sidewalk, watching curiously. A guy standing nearby was filming the scene. Lycan sighed and approached him.

"What's going on?"

"Yo, Lycan! Wassup man!"

"Hi hello, what's happening?" he repeated.

"Oh right. That creepy fog rolled out and everyone stopped. Then that blue haired lady just ripped the back of the car off like it was nothing, then this pink lady showed up and turned into multiple ladies and now she's fighting the fog creatures..."

Lycan blinked, confused. He didn't see a blue haired lady before. He walked toward the fight and finally saw the other girl, sitting in the back of the van where the door had once been, her legs dangling, a carefree smile on her face.

Her suit was striking, with various shades of pink, blue, purple, and green in scaled diagonal strips across it, the colors shifting ever so slightly, as they bled into each other. Her shoulder length hair was in fact blue, but only on one side, the other was deep purple. Her mask wasn't like any he'd seen before. Like very thick eyeliner around her eyes, continuing from the inner corner on both sides to meet at the bottom of the Xyri-esque purple crystal on her forehead. Her eyes were the same shade of purple, with no pupils.

Those eyes turned to meet his and her smile fell as she sat up straighter. The other girl in pink was fully wrestling the mist hounds as they attacked her. They seemed solid but then a moment later were mist again, evaporating around the girls, then reforming. Lycan put two and two together. The color-shifting scaled girl was controlling them and clearly had been trying to rob the armored car. The logo of the winged horse inside a V on the side made it clear it was a Valkyrie car.

Lycan moved toward her, since the other Bonded seemed to be handling the creatures okay.

"I don't think that belongs to you," he said as he approached, nodding to the brown leather bag she clutched in her lap.

The girl's purple eyes looked angry for a moment, then something hit him from behind. He wasn't prepared and barely caught himself with his hands on the pavement as one of the mist hounds tried to bite his leg. Lycan rolled, getting to his feet just as the hound jumped at him. He caught the dog's head in his hands, holding it back as its jaw snapped. He chanced a glance over his shoulder as the girl got out of the car, grabbing two more of the bags before she approached. The mist hound evaporated and he stumbled. As he straightened, ready to face her, everything stilled.

He couldn't move. He couldn't even blink. *What's happening?*

The two girls in pink that he could still see were also frozen, one stuck with her arm up in front of her defensively, the other hunched over. Nothing moved. No cars, no civilians.

You're in stasis, Zeli replied. *It's her second power. You will be free in five minutes.*

Great.

He tried to move, attempting to clench his fists or make silver come out of them. Nothing happened.

"Big bad wolf not so scary now, huh?" The girl with the blue and purple hair stepped in front of him, the only moving thing in sight.

She smiled sadly as she met his eyes, only a few inches shorter than him. "The name's Vapor," she said. "This has been fun. But stay out of my business from now on, kay?"

He couldn't respond as she collected three more bags from the back of the van and walked away, unbothered, as the world was still around her.

At least she didn't hurt anyone, Zeli offered. *Unless we are counting your pride,* she chuckled.

He tried to roll his eyes, but of course he couldn't. *Why is five minutes so long?*

Do not complain to me about the movement of time.

Time... can I rewind? Even as he said it he knew he couldn't. He never thought being unable to move would make him unable to use his powers.

Patience, Bellamy. The other girl was fighting her.

He tried to nod, frustration growing. *Right. Another new Bonded, one who maybe isn't terrible. That's something.*

Put your rage away. You don't want to scare her when this wears off.

Right.

After a moment someone walked into Lycan's view. A short woman with dark curly hair and bright hazel eyes. She looked at Lycan with concern.

"Are you okay?"

Lycan tried to calm his anger, unable to answer.

"They're like, frozen? But awake? I think he can hear me."

"It'll probably wear off," another voice said, though Lycan couldn't see the speaker.

"This one." The woman smiled as she looked past Lycan at the Bonded in pink. "A new hero? Oh, this is *so* exciting!" The girl turned to look at the person she'd been talking to, her expression darkening. "What are you doing?"

"No one is guarding this money, like..."

"You can't just steal that! Lycan is right here."

"And he's stuck."

The girl looked upset as her eyes turned back to Lycan. "I don't know what to do."

His anger finally softened, wishing he could tell her it was fine. More people approached, more than he could see by the sound of their voices. One of them pulled out their phone and took a selfie with Lycan.

This is kind of humiliating.

It's almost over.

"Leave them alone!" the girl said, defensive as she tried to get the others to stop taking pictures.

When at last it faded Lycan stumbled forward, surprised to find his limbs working. "Ugh." He stretched.

Most of the civilians backed away now that he was moving, and a few more who'd been pillaging the armored car took off running. He let out a breath as the girl with the dark hair stepped closer.

"Hi," he said, smiling at her. "Thanks, for trying to help."

She nodded. "Of course. I... um..." She bit her lip.

"Give me just a second, okay?"

She nodded, curls bouncing around her face.

He turned to the Bonded in pink. All four bodies seemed to blur for a moment before three of them disappeared, and only one stood in front of him. She looked a bit older than him, maybe in her twenties, with chestnut skin and bright pink eyes. Her mask was shaped in a star around each eye, mostly black, but outlined in glowing pink.

"Nice trick," he said, smiling. Then he noticed red blood marring one of the pink strips on her arms. "You're hurt?"

She looked up at him, terrified. "I gotta go!"

"Oh—" Before he could say another word she took off running down the street. "Okay." He sighed, turning back to the other girl. "Did you wanna ask me something?"

She swallowed. "I um. Was wondering if I could get a quick interview? I know you don't normally do them so it's fine if you don't want to I just thought—"

"Sure. Quick, though."

"Oh god. Okay, awesome." She pulled something out of her purse while smiling so wide it looked like it hurt. Then she unfolded a small handheld tripod, connecting it to her phone. She stood beside him while holding the phone in front of them and hit record.

"I'm here with Lycan, after an encounter with *two* new Bonded here on 3rd and 79th. What can you tell us about what just happened?"

He sucked in breath. "There was a girl, calling herself Vapor, who was stealing from a Valkyrie armored car in mid-transport. She put me and everyone else in the vicinity under some kind of stasis where we— we couldn't move. Don't know much about her yet, but I suggest people keep their distance if she appears again."

"And what about the other girl?"

"Didn't catch her name, but she appeared to be trying to stop Vapor before I arrived. Hope I see her again."

"Can I ask one more question?"

"Sure."

"What happened to Kaida? There's footage of her falling from the trees during the fight in Hell's Kitchen, and ... you, carrying her body away. Is she..." The girl swallowed, unable to finish the question.

"Kaida is alive and well. She sustained an injury during the fight, and is taking time to recover, that is all. If that Bonded, calling herself Gaia, should appear again I urge *everyone* to get as far away from her as possible. No one but myself or Apex should approach her."

She nodded. "Let Kaida know we wish her a speedy recovery. And thank you for giving us some of your time."

"Of course." He smiled as she stopped recording. She released a slow breath. "Are you alright?"

"Yeah that was just, very exciting. I can't thank you enough!"

"You're very welcome... what's your name?"

"Tess."

"It was nice to meet you, Tess. But I gotta go. Thanks again."

"Thank y—"

He was in the air before she finished the sentence, eager to get somewhere he could be alone and text Apex.

They had a deal not to involve Kaida in these things. She still seemed so exhausted when he'd seen her earlier. He didn't want to stress her anymore. So once Lycan landed on the roof on Spruce Street he sent Apex a text and waited.

Ten minutes later Apex landed beside him, dark wings outstretched.

"What do you *mean* there's two new Bonded? I'm too tired for that."

Lycan smiled. "I was frozen in place by this girl, like, *completely* helpless. It was kinda scary."

"And the other one?"

"I think she's on our side? She ran before I could talk to her. She was hurt in the fight with Vapor's mist creatures."

"Damn." He folded his wings in and rolled his neck. "Are we telling Kaida about this?"

"Absolutely not."

"She might hear about it anyways."

"When she does she can get mad at us for not telling her."

Apex grinned. "You know her so well."

"So do you."

"Do we have a plan for Gaia? I mean... Kaida almost died and we both know she's better than us at this."

Lycan nodded. "We both need to be prepared if she shows up again. We go together. Maybe with two of us we can take her down without her—"

"Killing us with a touch?" Apex sighed. "What if one of us is busy?"

"We can't *be* busy. Keep alerts on. And drop everything the moment she resurfaces. But don't go in alone. We go together, that's a rule."

"Alright. I got your back. Kaida would kill me if I let anything happen to her precious wolf."

Lycan's heart raced. "Yeah, and she'd kill me if I let anything happen to her stupid best friend."

Apex's smile widened. "Yeah, she would." He held out his fist to Lycan.

He grinned, bumping it with his. "Okay. See you later then?"

Apex nodded. "Later." His wings unfurled, spreading wide across the roof as he turned and jumped, gliding through the air.

Everything is gonna be fine as long as you two are careful.

We will be.

32
Proof of Life

Lycan stood on a roof in Times Square, feeling a sense of deja vu. Apex crouched beside him, staring at the taped off area below.

"What if we don't do it?"

He shrugged. "Think we shouldn't?"

"Dunno. Just seems stupid," Apex said as he straightened.

"What's stupid is how many people think Kaida is dead after I *specifically* said she was okay."

"That was your mistake. Not talking was better. Now you've said she's fine but they haven't seen her, they're assuming the worst."

Lycan shook his head. "They're all idiots."

It had been a week since he did that interview after his encounter with Vapor. Two weeks since Kaida was injured. And still so many questions were being asked. So many that someone decided to set up a whole press conference for Lycan to answer them. They built a little platform for him and had the area taped off, with around twenty reporters standing in front of it, waiting to see if he'd show up.

It was always a gamble when they pulled stuff like this, putting out a plea for Lycan and Kaida to come to something. They didn't *have* to. No one could force them. But not doing it this time would probably send a bad message, like he had something to hide.

"We should just get it over with," he finally said.

"So, we tell them she's fine and that's it? We can go?"

"They'll have more questions. They always do. But we don't have to answer and..." Lycan met Apex's eyes. "Maybe I should do the talking?"

Apex smiled. "Smart."

Lycan let out a breath then kicked up his board just as Apex's wings unfurled from his back. They jumped together, gliding and swooping down onto the platform to gasps of surprise as every camera turned on them.

Apex waved awkwardly.

"Do you have an update on Kaida's condition? Are we gonna see her returning soon?" a woman asked.

Lycan stepped up to the microphone. "Kaida is doing well, recovering from her injury. But I can't say how long it'll be till she's back with us."

"How do we know she's still alive? All we have is your word," another reporter said.

"Is my word not enough?" Lycan asked with a frown.

Apex grinned.

"We don't even know who you are under that mask."

"Yeah, for all we know you're hiding her dead body in your closet." Apex laughed. Lycan glared at him. It's what Kaida would do.

"I assure you Kaida is alive. She's simply recovering."

"Can you prove it?" another man asked.

Lycan sighed in frustration.

"I got this," Apex said, stepping back.

He pulled out his phone, presumably to call Kaida. The phone was neon green, to match the glow in his suit. Lycan shook his head. Kaida didn't need to come down here, transforming wasn't good for her right now.

"Proof of life is on the way," Apex said when he stepped back up.

Within seconds a portal appeared behind them, pink light burned bright against his eyes as he stared into the darkness at the center. Kaida stepped out of it a moment later. He gave her a sad smile as she met his eyes, then she stepped up to the mic.

"Hi, I'm alive."

"What can you tell us about your injury? Aren't you supposed to be indestructible?"

Kaida's eyes narrowed and Apex grinned.

"None of us are indestructible. The Bonded, Gaia, has a lethal power, and she touched me with it. It almost killed me, but Lycan and my Xyri saved my life," she answered.

"You look fine, are you recovered now? Should we expect—"

"Expect *nothing* from her," Lycan interrupted. How could they think she looked fine? He was sure she was barely keeping herself on her feet. "She still needs to rest."

Kaida put her hand on his arm and smiled at him.

"Kaida's gonna go now, but Apex and I can answer any further questions you have."

He turned, guiding Kaida back to her portal. "You shouldn't have come," he whispered.

"It's fine." She looked so tired. "Are you guys—"

"We're good. We got this." He leaned closer, looking into her eyes. "Just get better, please?"

"Promise?" she asked, holding out her pinky.

He smiled and wrapped his pinky around hers. "Promise."

She let out a breath and nodded. Then she disappeared through her portal. It collapsed a moment later. Lycan sighed, realizing he'd left Apex to answer questions without him. He stepped up, trying to figure out what they were discussing now.

"I think as long as no one approaches her it'll be fine..."

"But you aren't safe from her either, so how are *we* supposed to feel safe with her out there?"

"We're gonna deal with it. Lycan and I have a plan, and it's—"

Lycan put a hand on Apex's shoulder, staring at the faces in the crowd. "What are we talking about?"

"Gaia."

"What is this plan you two have for dealing with her?" one of the reporters asked.

"We're not airing our plan on national TV for her to see. Just know we *have* a plan. If she reappears everyone should clear the vicinity as quickly as possible and let us handle it. And no matter what, do *not* let her touch you."

"And what about—"

"Wait!" someone interrupted. "That new girl with the mist is robbing a bank, up on 3rd and East 56th right now!" they shouted as they held up their phone.

"That's our cue to go," Apex said.

"Thank you for your time." Lycan's board formed under his foot and he and Apex took off into the sky.

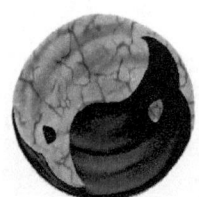

Jasper landed beside Lycan in the street outside the bank just as an explosion sounded inside. The ground shook under their feet.

"Plan?" he asked.

"Maybe I should go in alone? In case she freezes us, one of us will be free."

"Right, and if she freezes you in there how am I gonna know you need help?" Apex asked.

Lycan made a face. "Intuition?" With that he ran inside, leaving Jasper alone on the street.

He pulled out his phone and texted Ren.

|Jasper|
Lycan thinks I have intuition lol

He put the phone away, wondering exactly how long he was supposed to wait to go in after Lycan. Just as he was considering going in, glass shattered as Lycan's body was thrown out the window. He landed on his back right in front of Jasper.

"How's it going?" he asked, staring down at him.

"Peachy," Lycan growled.

"You want some help now?"

"Tiger!"

Jasper blinked in confusion. Then a tiger made of smoke jumped through the broken window.

Ohhh, Valaries Bonded.

Jasper ignored Pozi and jumped forward, tapping strength as he dove in front of Lycan, intercepting the tiger with his wings spread out.

He expected to be knocked down but his own strength matched that of the misty cat. He grabbed the side of its head, holding it back from straight up eating him.

It can't eat you. Can bite you though.

Good to know.

Lycan was back up, weaving silver like a spider with a web around the tiger while Apex held it in place. Within seconds it was contained. He grinned as Lycan stepped back.

"Here she comes. Take to the sky," Lycan muttered as a girl stepped out of the bank, her feet crunching on the shattered glass.

Jasper's wings moved to lift him up as the girl approached Lycan. She looked Asian, and she was absolutely stunning. With long hair that was deep blue on one side, and purple on the other. A mask didn't cover her eyes, instead there was a purple diamond in the center of her forehead, like a Xyri, connected with dark lines that rounded her eyes.

She spared him a glance, smiling slightly, before turning her attention back to Lycan. Her suit was one of the coolest he'd seen. Blues, greens, pinks, and purples, all shifting, like a fiber optic lamp across her scales. It was mesmerizing and he wondered if she made it shift like that simply to help distract her enemies.

"I told you to stay out of my business," she said, voice low and sultry.

"You blew up half the room in there! Could have hurt someone. That *is* my business."

"No one died. And I have my money. That concludes this delightful meeting."

Lycan scoffed. "I'm gonna *oh so* politely ask you maybe don't bring explosives... literally *anywhere* and then act like it isn't a problem because it didn't end lives this one time!"

I feel like I should film this and send it to Kaida.

Why?

Cause Lycan is so hot and she's missing it.

Humans are fucking weird.

Heh, yeah.

Something hit Jasper from behind and he fell from the sky. A giant mist eagle hovered above him. Then it shifted, growing as it lowered to the ground and turned into a bear.

He rolled before it could attack, jumping to his feet then he punched it in the face. It dissolved to mist just as another larger one formed, going for Lycan.

"Elephant," he yelled as the giant creature charged at Lycan.

Lycan dodged just in time, silver seeping out of him, forming small lines that solidified into ropes, slithering up the elephant's legs.

Damn he's good at this, Jasper thought as Lycan pulled the ropes and the elephant burst apart. The mass of mist shifted, changing into hundreds of bats. They swarmed around them. He gasped, arms flailing around his head wildly to knock them away.

Pozi started laughing. *Yeah, he's way better than you.*

Hush.

After a moment the bats started evaporating. Jasper stood there, panting as he realized Lycan already handled his and was now getting Jasper's. He had a small silver baseball bat in one hand, and a large silver net in the other.

"You good?"

"The goodest," Jasper replied as he readied himself for the next attack.

She was backing away from them now, a look of fear in her eyes at how easily they were dealing with her creatures.

How easily Lycan's dealing with them...

Jasper rolled his eyes.

The ground split in front of him, opening into a whole ass hell mouth. His heart pounded as a tree burst forth, brown and green, moving scary fast before his eyes.

"Apex back!" Lycan called from somewhere across the crack.

He jumped, looking for Gaia.

Do not engage with her!

Jasper's hands shook, anger filling him. *She almost killed Ren.*

She could kill you too!

"Why's she here?" he yelled, having lost sight of both Lycan and Vapor.

Lycan descended from the sky on his board, breathless. "Don't know. Helping Vapor?"

"Since when do villains team up?"

Lycan shook his head. So far just one tree had spawned in the street.

"Two against one ain't so nice, boys," a voice called.

There she was. A tiny thing, shorter than Ren, with green leaves draping off her shoulders. She smiled as she stepped around the trunk of the tree, staring at them.

"What's not fair is *you*—"

Lycan gripped his shoulder, pulling him back. "No," he hissed.

Jasper could barely contain his rage. He wanted nothing more than to fight the tiny bitch for what she did. That scared him, so he didn't resist Lycan's touch.

"Still wanna fight?" Gaia asked as Vapor slowly walked up beside her.

"I didn't ask for your help," Vapor muttered. "I don't even know you."

"Don't gotta ask. Sometimes a girl needs help. And I'm nothing if not a girl's girl," Gaia answered, not taking her eyes off Apex and Lycan.

Don't fight her, Pozi pleaded.

What? Why not?

I've only had you for four months, I am not *losing another one so soon!*

Jasper tried to process those words as Lycan flicked his hand out and his fancy whip appeared, striking against Gaia. The end wrapped around her arm and pulled her to the pavement.

Gaia growled, and the ground cracked under their feet.

Apex grabbed Lycan, yanking him up just as the tree burst free where they'd been standing.

"Thanks," Lycan muttered as they fell back to the ground.

"What do we do?"

"Stop her."

Jasper nodded just as more misty creatures, long and writhing like snakes, came flying through the air toward them.

"We got this."

"We better."

Jasper found himself against more mist creatures, Vapor creating them faster each time he overpowered one. He could barely see Lycan, flying up through the trees, facing off with Gaia. Silver flashed here and there in the corner of Jasper's eyes, but he couldn't get through the mist creatures fast enough to help him. Lycan seemed to be holding his own fine, but no progress was being made in the fight.

Jasper's frustration grew as a whole damn mist gorilla tackled him, the weight of it suffocating him as it roared in his face.

Scream back at it! That'll show him!

Jasper growled, body aching, not even sure where Lycan was. But silver caught his eyes and the gorilla was knocked back off him.

He released a breath as he forced himself up, looking for Lycan. But standing in front of him was not the wolf boy. Instead, a girl stood there. Slightly taller than him, she had light pink hair, up in a high ponytail, with black and pink cat-like ears sticking out of her hair. Her mask was split magenta and blue, going up and out toward her temples, and down toward her jaw. The color split continued in her suit with a wavy line, like a backwards S down her torso. There was a pink star over the blue side on her chest, and a blue star over the pink side on her stomach. Pink butterfly-like wings fluttered on her back.

She flashed him a beautiful smile as she held a giant shiny silver hammer in her hand. It was so big it was comical.

"Who the fuck..."

"Hi! Here to help!" she called as the hammer disappeared. She looked down at her hands and frowned. "Never used the powers before this is so weird."

"What are your—"

She reached out and touched his arm for a moment then looked at her hands again. "Huh. What is this? *Oh.* Stronger? Faster. Not as fun as silver."

"What?"

She's borrowed your powers.

Borrowed my...

"Oh, gorilla."

Jasper spun. The gorilla returned, somehow even bigger as it charged at them.

"Where'd your hammer go?"

"I switched to you! You don't have a hammer!"

"What?"

She didn't respond as the gorilla's assault landed. Jasper dodged and the new girl took the full force of it. She gasped, hitting the ground hard, but she was back up in a second, moving faster than before. She drew the gorilla away from him. Jasper grinned as his eyes landed on Vapor. Take her out, and the creatures stopped. Just as he moved toward the girl, Gaia appeared in front of her protectively.

Jasper stopped, staring her down.

Do not!

"Let's get out of here," Gaia muttered over her shoulder.

Vapor nodded and a mist horse formed at her side. She climbed on it with ease, then pulled Gaia up behind her. Lycan fell from the sky just as they rode off down the street. The new girl slowly walked up to them, frowning.

"That was... a lot," Lycan muttered as the three of them stood there, taking in the damage.

Cars turned over, glass everywhere. And of course, the trees. Sirens sounded in the distance.

"Was I helpful? I wanted to be helpful but I'm not sure I think maybe, was I just in the way? That was so stressful but—"

Jasper put a hand on her shoulder. "You were *literally* perfect. Thank you for helping."

"What do we call you?" Lycan asked, a grin taking over his face.

She tucked some hair behind her ear. "I was thinking... Parody."

33
Unresponsive

Lycan smiled at the girl. He'd been surprised when she showed up and grabbed his arm, then started making things out of silver. Zeli explained she didn't have his power, but copied it. In the moment he hadn't really processed what that meant.

"Parody." Apex nodded. "Nice. So, you parody our powers?"

"Yep. That was the first time I've ever done it. Obviously." She smiled nervously, flipping her ponytail.

"How long have you been Bonded?" Lycan asked.

"Like four days. I've been waiting for something to come up I could help with. So I could meet you guys."

So many are coming now, Zeli said, excited. *I wish Xenos was here to see it.*

Lycan grinned. "We're happy to have you."

"We should set up a time for you to meet Kaida when she's better," Apex said. "She's gonna be so excited about you."

"Really?" Parody's smile was so bright. "I'd love to meet her. When she's well, of course."

"So, you can't use your powers without having someone else with powers to pull from? Is that how it works?" Lycan asked.

"Not *quite*. I can pull any kind of attribute from anyone. Like, I could touch a person and get their... good balance or their good memory. Things like that. But those sorts of skills aren't as helpful in a fight. And I have to be intentional with what I want, like one of your powers. Or I'll just get something super random."

"You could train with us," Lycan offered. "Get familiar with our powers at least."

"Really?" Her pink eyes were wide with excitement. "That would be great!"

"You free on Saturday?" Lycan asked. "We could get together then, start training you."

"Definitely free. Just busy on Mondays, Wednesdays, and Thursdays," Parody replied. "I'll be in class, but outside of that I'm super free!"

"High school?" Apex asked curiously.

Parody laughed, her wings flittering. "God *no*. College." Her eyes narrowed. "You're *really* that young? I'm twenty-*four*."

Apex opened his mouth but Lycan put his arm around his shoulder and slammed his hand over his mouth before he could speak.

"Superhero 101, don't say things about your civilian life that could give away your identity, like your *age*."

Apex rolled his eyes.

"He made that mistake on day one, too," Lycan continued, hand still covering Apex's mouth.

"There's a *billion* sixteen year olds in this city," Apex grumbled.

Parody smiled. "Where am I meeting you children?"

Lycan smiled as he let Apex go. "Prospect Park, by the baseball fields, around midnight?"

"Sounds good."

"Kaida *might* be able to join us then but... maybe not," Apex said.

Parody nodded. "She should focus on getting better first but I can't wait to meet her."

They fell quiet as fire trucks arrived on the scene. Lycan sighed at the looks on their faces while they took in the mess. If Gaia kept this up she'd ruin the whole city. Almost two weeks since she'd made her debut in Hell's Kitchen. Some streets and subway lines were still closed off, as workers tirelessly worked to clear out the trees.

One of the firefighters approached them, a sadness in her eyes. "She got away again?"

Lycan nodded. "We tried, but there were two of them this time, working together."

"We'll get her eventually," Apex added.

The woman nodded as others approached in silence. The street was eerily quiet, no civilians in sight. Lycan was glad they'd taken their warnings to heart and cleared out when Gaia arrived. People liked to stick around to watch and film a fight sometimes, with no care for their safety. Seeing Kaida fall must have really scared them.

"Should we... help?" Parody whispered.

"I don't think there's much we can do, unfortunately."

She nodded. "So, now what?"

"I actually... have somewhere to be, you know, unless another emergency arises," Apex said through a yawn.

"Alright, we call it a day? Pending emergencies." Lycan met Parody's eyes. "Do not under *any* circumstances try to go after Gaia on your own, okay?"

"You got it, boss. So, see you boys Saturday?"

"Saturday."

Parody took off in a run before taking to the air, her pink translucent wings shining in the sunlight.

"She seems cool," Apex said.

"Yeah. You think Kaida's okay? I feel bad we made her come out earlier."

"She's..." Apex sighed. "Been sleeping a lot. Like, a *lot*. Barely there. Zig says she's healing fine. It just took a huge toll on her. The injury and the fuse. But, I think she'll be back soon?"

Lycan nodded. He didn't wanna admit how much he missed her. How he hated not seeing her. Hated doing any of this without her. He was genuinely glad to have Apex at his side though. He hadn't seen any of his friends recently, since it was Spring Break and they were out of school. Nico and Jules were out of town, and Ren was sick with the flu last he heard. And of course, Kaida was out of commission.

She'll be back soon.

I know I know. Have you seen Zig at all?

No, he won't leave her. We both must be patient.

"Alright. Be smart, make good decisions. See ya next time things implode."

"Ah yes, imploding hour. See ya then," Apex replied.

He's not so bad, is he? Zeli asked as Apex flew away.

No, not bad at all.

Ren was in a daze, in and out of consciousness as time slipped by like water through her fingers. She'd had two decent days where she'd felt better, recovering from the initial injury. There'd been some amount of clarity in her head, some amount of energy in her body. But now she felt like she was falling backwards, never stopping. Never resting. Never still. Yet she wasn't moving at all.

Zig said it was because of the fuse. Though he also said it never went on this long. Ren was the youngest he'd ever Bonded, the youngest he'd ever fused with. And he'd never fused so early in the Bond, either. He seemed to think the complications were due to the fact that her body wasn't done developing yet.

But what does that mean?

It means you must weather the storm. When it passes, you will be stronger for it.

What if it doesn't pass?

I promise it will.

The exhaustion weighed heavy on her. She barely remembered getting a call from Jasper and forcing her body up, forcing the suit on, forcing the portal open in the bathroom, worried if she was gone too long Dad would come check on her.

But she'd only been gone a minute. It felt like hours when she stumbled her way back into the living room after proving she was still alive to the public. Dad watched her with worry as she collapsed on the couch again. She'd been sleeping there for days now, since it was easier than going up and down the stairs.

"Ren, are you hungry?" Dad asked softly as he looked down at her from behind the couch.

"No," she mumbled, closing her eyes.

She didn't hear his response, slowly falling back into a dazed sleep.

When Ren opened her eyes, Dad was sitting on the floor, his back against one of the love seats.

"Dad?"

He turned, eyes lighting up. "Hey, baby. How you feeling?"

"What time is it?"

"Uh, about three in the morning."

"Why are you awake?" she asked, confused.

"Just working on some stuff," he said, nodding to his laptop on the coffee table.

"You have an office."

He smiled. "I wanted to stay close, in case you needed me."

Emotion crashed into her.

"You alright, you want food now?"

"Yeah, I guess."

He moved closer, putting a hand on her forehead, then he sighed. "Your fever is back."

Ren closed her eyes.

"I think it's past time to take you to a doctor, kid."

Her eyes snapped open. "No!"

"*Why* are you so against it?"

"I..." She swallowed, unsure. Her thoughts felt slow, like she was thinking through a puddle of sludge. "I just don't want to. *Please.*"

Dad sighed, but didn't argue. "I've got leftover meatloaf and potatoes. And there's some soup still. Or I could make you something else."

"Meaty potats."

He smiled. "I'll be right back."

Ren tried not to fall asleep while he bustled through the kitchen. When food was ready she forced herself to stay sitting up. Dad watched her with narrowed eyes.

"What's wrong with your hand?"

Ren froze, fork gripped awkwardly in her left hand, halfway to her mouth. "Huh?"

"You're not left-handed."

She swallowed. "Slept on it weird, it's just a little cramped."

Dad frowned.

"It's *fine*, promise." She'd have to hide that better.

Sometime after eating Ren did fall back asleep, though she thought maybe Dad was talking to her. She heard voices but couldn't quite understand. They floated above her, in and out as she drifted.

"She can be here in twenty minutes."

"Alright. I'm just... do you think something's *happened* to make her so unwilling to go? Something we don't know about?"

"I don't know. You think she'd tell us?"

"She used to tell us everything."

None of those words registered to Ren. Only when Zig spoke did she understand, but it still took a few nudges.

Ren. Someone's here. You need to wake up. Ren? Ren, wake up.

"What?" she snapped, eyes opening. She squeezed them shut again, unprepared for the sun streaming through the windows.

Ren, there's a woman here, to examine you.

What?

"Ren?"

She forced her eyes open again to see both her dads, Grandma Daisy, and a woman she didn't know standing in front of the couch. She yawned, pushing herself to a sitting position.

"What's happening?"

"You said you wouldn't go to a doctor, so... we brought one to you," Dare said, voice soft. "She works with my mom at the hospital."

Ren stared between him and the unknown woman. She had blonde hair pulled back in a tight bun and smiled at Ren with kind brown eyes.

"Hello, Ren. I'm Kathy. I hear you've not been feeling well? Wanna tell me what's wrong?"

Ren frowned, unable to find any words, too groggy to think. After a moment Dad stepped up with a sigh.

"She's been fatigued, sleeping a lot. Fevers off and on. Not much of an appetite. It's been going for two weeks now."

"I see."

Ren closed her eyes, tuning them out. *Is there anything weird in me?*

Weird? Zig asked.

If she does tests on me will it look weird, like not human? Cause of the fuse.

Oh. I... do not... know.

She sucked in a breath, anxiety churning. *What?*

This is new for me, too, Ren. My last Bond was two hundred years ago. My last fused Bond was four centuries back. They could not test things like they can now.

Ughhh. She opened her eyes, trying to comply with the woman as she took her blood pressure. Then she checked her temperature and listened to her heart and lungs.

I think you will be fine. She isn't taking your blood or anything.

Would it not be fine if she did?

I really don't know.

Ughhhh.

Ren barely paid attention as the woman talked. She didn't mean to be unresponsive but it was taking all of her concentration to communicate with Zig. Her dad seemed fine to speak for her. She wondered if he'd be mad at her for being so stubborn and childish, but it was hard to tell. It was hard to do anything at all.

Eventually the woman left and Ren laid back down, not entirely sure what conclusion she'd come to. She was asleep before Dad could say.

Some time later she woke to Dad and Dare kneeling in front of the couch. She rubbed her eyes, noticing it was much darker now, the sun long gone.

"Hey, kiddo. We got you some medicine," Dare said as he held out a bottle with pills in it.

"From the doctor?" she asked as Dad helped her sit up.

"Yes. It might help."

She nodded. Dad gave her a bottle of water and Dare dropped one of the pills in her hand. She swigged it back, already wishing she could lie back down. It was like she was on another planet, and the gravity was all wrong, pulling against her.

"Are you upset with me?" Dad asked, voice soft as he brushed her hair back.

"Upset?"

"For bringing a doctor?"

She shook her head. "No. Just tired."

"I know, baby. I made a pot of vegetable soup, and some homemade bread... if you're hungry?"

She nodded and he smiled.

"Are you mad at me?" she asked.

"Of course not. I just... if there's a reason why you didn't want to go to the doctor, I need to know."

Ren stared at him, unsure what to say.

"I always got your back, kid. You tell me something makes you uncomfortable, you're not okay with it, we figure something else out. But if I don't know what's going on I can't *help*. You understand?"

She nodded slowly.

He kissed her forehead. "I'll get you some food."

Ren sighed as he walked away, then she turned to Dare, who was watching her carefully.

"Was Grandma here?"

"Yeah, she left you a present."

"A present?"

He smiled. "We added it to your pile."

"Pile of what?"

"You've got some mail while you've been sick. It's on the counter, by the fridge. Want me to bring it over?"

"No, I'll get it later."

"You're gonna have to take this medicine twice a day, okay?"

She nodded.

"Love you, little one." He stood and kissed the top of her head.

She smiled, then grabbed her phone off the table. There were many missed texts. She opened Simon's first.

Her smile stayed in place as she texted him back.

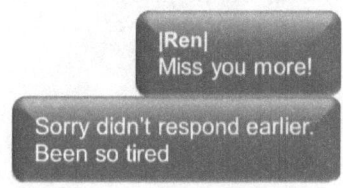

But I have medicine now.

After that she opened the group chat.

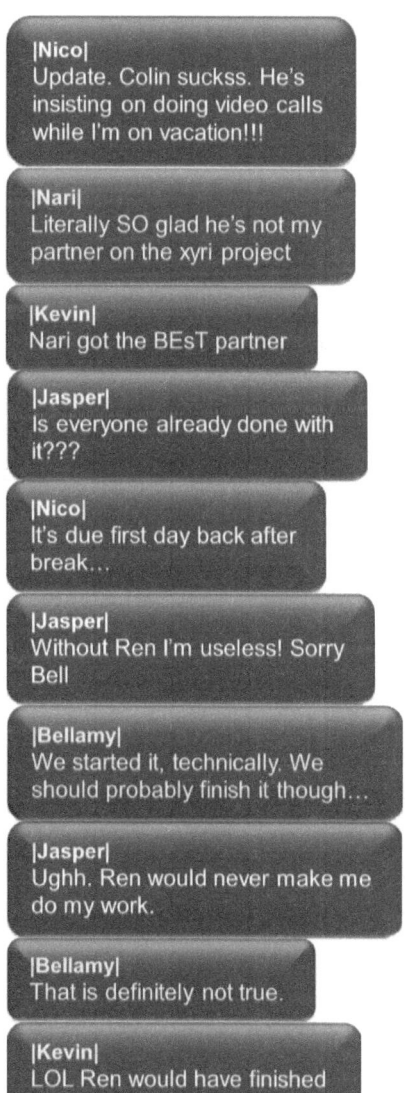

|Nico|
Update. Colin suckss. He's insisting on doing video calls while I'm on vacation!!!

|Nari|
Literally SO glad he's not my partner on the xyri project

|Kevin|
Nari got the BEsT partner

|Jasper|
Is everyone already done with it???

|Nico|
It's due first day back after break...

|Jasper|
Without Ren I'm useless! Sorry Bell

|Bellamy|
We started it, technically. We should probably finish it though...

|Jasper|
Ughh. Ren would never make me do my work.

|Bellamy|
That is definitely not true.

|Kevin|
LOL Ren would have finished it the day it was assigned

|Bellamy|
Also how is Ren? Is she better
yet??

|Jasper|
Nope poor Renegade been sick all of
spring break and it's the worst thing
to ever happen to me, personally

|Bellamy|
Damn that sucks.

Miss you Ren! Hope you feel
better soon!!!!

She smiled and sent a heart emoji in response, then checked her
texts with Jasper.

|Jasper|
Lycan thinks I have intuition lol

|Ren|
Silly wolf.

How did rest of interview go?

|Jasper|
Oh babe. You haven't seen
the news?

|Ren|
No? Afraid to ask

|Jasper|
Here's what you missed:
New villain Vapor robbed a bank
and Lycan and I were being
awesome but then Gaia showed up
out of nowhere? Teamed upp with
Vapor and that got wild but THEN a
new HERO showed up!! She's
called Parody. Super hot. We're
gonna train her on saturday

Also I met up with Harper after and we made out for like an hour and that was awesome

|Ren|
I can't process any of that.

|Jasper|
You better or worse? I could come over!!!

|Ren|
I don't know. Tired.

Dad's making food and I've got fancy meds now

|Jasper|
Fancy!

|Ren|
Come see me tomorrow?

|Jasper|
Sure thing boo

Later that night after eating and watching some TV with her dads she was left alone on the couch. Dare was in the shower while Dad did the laundry. So she forced her legs to move and found the small pile of mail Dare mentioned. There were two small packages and two envelopes.

She opened the one from Grandma Daisy first. It was a fifty-dollar gift card. She made a mental note to send her a thank you text, then opened the next envelope. It was a birthday card from a woman she'd never met, her grandma on her mom's side. Ren smiled as she read it. Her own mother never bothered to send one, but a grandmother she didn't even know never missed her birthday and always sent Christmas cards.

She yawned as she set those aside and opened one of the packages. It was addressed from Ocean. There was a little porcelain cat about two inches tall inside. It looked an awful lot like Breadcrumb, only it was wearing a beret. She giggled, taking a picture of it and texting Ocean.

|Ren|
This is so stupidly cute I love it!! And I love you!!!

|Ocean|
Love you more!

Can't wait till I'm there!!!

|Ren|
Me too!!!!!!

She set it aside and opened the last package. It was from Valkyrie but she didn't remember ordering anything.

There was a note with a small silver box inside. She read the note, taking a moment to process it.

Hey Ren, happy birthday! I know this will be late, but I really wanted to get you something. I hope you like it. Totally fine if you don't though!
-Bellamy

Bellamy... Bellamy sent her a birthday present. She stared at the little box, almost afraid to open it. Her heart thumped as she slowly pulled the lid off. A golden bracelet was nestled inside. It had a little bedazzled bear face charm hanging from it. Her face hurt from smiling so hard. *A bear.*

"What's that?" Dare asked as he looked over her shoulder.

"A bracelet. From my friend Bellamy. For my birthday."

"Bellamy. That's the one you like, right?"

Her cheeks burned. "No I mean, not anymore. He's just a friend." She looked up at Dare. "I have a boyfriend."

"Right, of course." He smiled. "Do you need anything before I head to bed?"

"No. Love you."

"Love you."

She watched him leave, glancing at Dad over by the laundry. She knew he'd stay up here again. Ren was fairly certain he hadn't left her alone for more than twenty minutes. He hadn't even gone to work in days, getting Naomi to cover for him all week. She loved him for it.

34
Venom

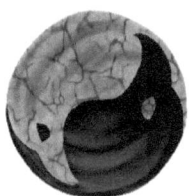

Jasper sat on Bellamy's giant couch, books spread out between them as they tried to find more information on their Xyri for the history project. They'd been assigned a specific pair of Xyri who the historians described as siblings because they always Bonded together, similar to how Zig and Zeli always did. Jasper knew that was extremely rare, but he wasn't sure if the books knew it was rare. He had to be careful not to seem like he knew too much about the Xyri.

Haha. How could you possibly know too much? You don't even know enough about humans.

Jasper held in a laugh as he looked around Bellamy's living room. He tried not to feel insecure every time he went to a friend's house and saw how much more they had than him. But the place was just *so* fancy, with those giant windows and open kitchen. Jasper could fully lie down on that island and there'd still be room to spare. The light wood floor was *real* wood, and there were several sculptures behind the couch that belonged in museums. The fridge and stove were tucked into their own nook that was the size of his whole kitchen.

"Oh, I found another passage, this one had a drawing." Bellamy passed his book to Jasper.

"Interesting. They kind of look like dogs. Or wolves."

"Yeah."

"I'll take a picture for the presentation."

One of the Xyri, known as Aetheria, looked like she was made of crystals. There were feathers, or maybe scales, along the face and legs. The other Xyri, called Galaxias, looked darker in the black and white picture, more wolf-like in the face, but with the same feather-scales, and spikes sticking out of its back.

"Did we find any pictures of their Bonded?" he asked.

"A few, they're in... this one I think?" Bellamy shuffled through the pile of books. He smiled as he handed it over. "Sorry you're stuck with me on this. I know you'd prefer Ren. She's more organized."

"Eh. You're not so bad, Bell."

"Is she gonna be back at school on Monday?"

"Yeah. She's better now." Jasper studied Bellamy's face. "You miss her?"

Bellamy grinned, his green eyes lighting up. Jasper couldn't blame Ren for her crush, he was too goddamn pretty. "Chem is *so* boring without her. Sucks she was sick during spring break."

"Yeah," Jasper said. "She's been sad she couldn't hang out with her boyfriend."

Bellamy's smile fell as he looked back down at his notes. "She's still with that guy then?"

"For now."

He nodded. "This book says Galaxias could mind walk, but it doesn't *really* explain what that means. You think it's like, possession? Or just telepathy?"

"Uh."

It means he can speak in the minds of others.

So, telepathy then?

Sorta, Pozi answered. *I'm surprised they've not yet Bonded.*

Are they good? Like, you're friends with them?

They're more prone to letting their humans decide their course, but they have limits.

"Jasper?"

He blinked and looked up. "Uh, right. I think telepathy, probably?"

Bellamy nodded, writing it down.

"I wish we could have gotten a cooler Xyri," Jasper said with a sigh. "Like Stardust, or Lifelight."

Bellamy paused. "Stardust... that's..."

"Lycan's Xyri's last human? Yep!" He leaned forward excitedly. "She's *so* badass in the comics. Though I am starting to wonder how accurate the comics are."

Heh. Azazelith hates those comics.

"You've read them?" Bellamy asked.

Jasper nodded. "Yeah. I used to collect them when I was younger. I could lend them to you, if you want?"

Bellamy swallowed. "Uh, thanks. Maybe?"

"Never actually thought the Xyri would come back during our time," he continued.

"Me either."

Jasper sat up straighter. "What did you know about them, before they came back?"

Bellamy stared down at his notes. "Uh... I don't know. Some things, I guess. Mostly cause of my mom, since she's a historian."

"Right right. I remember this kid I used to know thought they were abducted by aliens, and that's why they disappeared."

Bellamy laughed. "I bet there were so many weird theories."

"I'm gonna look it up," Jasper said, opening a new tab on his laptop. Then he started laughing as he found a list. "Okay, top conspiracies online are that 'God called them back.'"

"Back *where*?"

"Heaven, I guess? There's theories they were actually angels? Or something. Uh, another one says they *were* aliens, and returned home. Then the abducted by aliens one is here, too."

Bellamy shook his head.

"Some people thought they never existed, like it was all a lie."

"Weird."

"Oh, this one's fun. Theory says that we're in a simulation and they were just deleted from it."

He laughed. "What do you think is the truth?"

Jasper looked up, meeting Bellamy's eyes. *Any chance you'll tell me?*

Absolutely not. But none of those are even close to correct.

Jasper sighed. "No idea. They're back, so they probably didn't *leave* leave, ya know?"

"Agreed."

Bellamy started compiling his notes into something more coherent while Jasper worked on the slides for the presentation on his laptop.

"I think we might be good?" Bellamy said as he read back through what they had.

"I think so?" Jasper replied. "I'll send you the slides and you can make sure I didn't fuck up."

Bellamy laughed. "I'll also send you the essay and you can tell me if it's good."

"Kay. I guess I'll head out? I have a date with Harper in a bit."

"Nice, have fun."

Jasper nodded. "See ya Monday."

Later that night, Jasper laid in bed with Harper at her house. This was the second time they'd slept together. He'd tried talking her out of it, making sure she knew there was no rush, but Harper was persistent. Jasper wasn't complaining. She wore his shirt, her head nestled against his bare chest as she scrolled on her phone. He was careful to keep his out of sight as he texted Ren and Lycan in their group chat. He had fake names for them, Ren had been adamant about that. He couldn't be texting 'Kaida' so he changed her name in the group to Small and Lycan to Tall.

|Small|
I'm not coming out tonight, sorry.

|Tall|
Are you sick? Or is it Zig? I thought you were better??

|Small|
Uhhh

|Goldilocks|
What the fuck aren't you telling us?

|Small|
So, I'm fine. I feel better. Zig is better. But...

My hand is numb? I keep dropping things. I'm worried I'll be a liability on patrol. And don't wanna meet the new hero like this

|Tall|
Did you tell Zig about your hand? Zel says there's something he can try

|Small|
He just started getting better I don't wanna stress him out!

|Tall|
You are stressing me out!!!

|Goldilocks|
Me too. Tell Zig or I will.

|Small|
Ugh okay. I'll figure it out. Still missing patrol though. You boys can handle it without me?

|Goldilocks|
Yeah we're a dream team babyy. All the criminals fear us.

Wait what time is patrol? I'm with my girlfriend now

|Tall|
Bird boy has a girlfriend?

|Goldilocks|
Yeah babu you missed your shott

|Tall|
Sorry but I also have a girlfriend.

Or well, I've got a girl I'm seeing? I don't think she's my girlfriend yet.

|Goldilocks|
Wait I thought you were in love with our Kaida?

|Tall|
I was but I moved on. Anyways.

I'll be out for patrol after ten. And we're meeting Parody at 12.

|Goldilocks|
Good for you! Can meet around 11

Jasper waited, noticing Ren was seeing the messages but not responding. Perhaps she wasn't pleased to learn Lycan had a girlfriend? She pretended to be fine when she heard about Bellamy and Jules last week.

He sighed and looked down at Harper as she continued her scroll. His heart stopped when he saw what she was looking at. A picture of Fable with some random person on the street.

Harper shifted, looking up at him. "Why so tense?"

"Not tense. What are you looking at?"

She sighed, looking back to her phone. "Oh, that's Fable. Isn't it weird seeing him take pictures with people? He's such a mystery."

Jasper clenched his jaw.

"What, you don't like Fable?" she asked. "I think he's kinda cute. Not as cute as *you*, obviously. Just... the ears."

Jasper forced a smile.

"So." Harper eyed his phone. "Who were you texting?"

"Ren."

"Oh." She frowned. "I was thinking..."

"Yeah?"

"Maybe you could... spend a little less time with Ren? Now that you and I are dating..."

"Huh?"

Harper blushed, looking away. "I just mean, everyone still thinks you two are like, an item. And *I* know you're not, but not everyone does. It kinda sucks being your girlfriend while people think *she's* your girlfriend."

Jasper rolled his eyes. "People probably think that cause they remember when we did date."

Harper stilled. "When you what now?"

"Uh... when I..." He suddenly realized Harper didn't know that fact. "Dated Ren..."

"Ren. You dated. Ren." She sat up, eyes wide. "When the fuck was this?"

"In eighth grade." He laughed. "For three months. We were like thirteen, okay? It was when we first met. And didn't last long."

Harper's eyes grew sad.

"Oh, come *on*. It's not a big deal."

"We've only been together like three weeks, I can't compare with that!"

Jasper laughed again. "You dated Gabe for a *year*. Come on, Ren's with Simon. And I'm with you. Anyone who's confused by that is stupid."

Harper smiled but it didn't meet her eyes. "Well, maybe you could spend more time with me, and less with her. Like, *way* less..."

Jasper frowned. He'd barely seen Ren in weeks, what the fuck was she—

You keep telling her you're with Ren though. When you're being Apex.

Shit.

He had lied about that a few times. But even so... he sighed, trying to gather his thoughts. "Sorry I haven't been spending as much time with you," he said. "Just been worried about Ren, since she's sick. But you don't gotta worry about it. I'm *not* interested in her like that. At all. And she's not into me, I swear."

Harper nodded.

He gently lifted her chin, forcing her to look up. "I swear," he repeated. Then he kissed her.

She relaxed against him as he wrapped his arms around her. He didn't like her being jealous of Ren, but didn't know how to fix it.

Maybe don't use Ren as your excuse so much, Pozi suggested.

Maybe don't talk while I'm kissing my girlfriend.

When they broke apart Harper was smiling.

"I should go, it's getting late."

"Right." She looked disappointed as she sat up and stretched. "Am I getting my shirt back?"

"Nope," she answered with a mischievous grin. "This belongs to me, just like you."

He smiled and kissed her again before pulling his hoodie on and heading out.

He walked a bit before finding a corner to transform, then went to meet Lycan.

"Where we starting tonight?" he asked when he landed.

"You're starting at Kaida's house," Lycan replied.

"Huh?"

"You and I both know she's not gonna tell Zig about her hand. Go, make sure she fixes it."

Jasper smiled. "Can do."

"If she's okay, meet us at the park. But stay with her, if she needs you. Just, help her."

Jasper saluted before turning and jumping off the roof into the air, flying all the way back to Ren's.

He gently tapped on her skylight door before pulling it open. Ren looked up at him from her bed with surprise. He detransformed as he dropped into the room.

"What are you doing here?"

"Show me your hand," he said, sitting on the bed beside her.

She sighed and held it out. It didn't look quite right, pale and clammy instead of her usual tan.

"You said it's numb?"

She nodded. "I can't... I can't feel you at all."

Jasper frowned, heart twisting at the fear in her eyes. "Where's Zig?"

"Couch."

"Call him."

Ren sighed. A moment later Zig was up, stretching his back in an arch before unfolding his wings and flying up to her bed. He settled beside Ren, looking between the two of them.

"Ren's hand isn't working."

The Xyri turned his little head to look at Ren, golden eyes analyzing her. *She did not tell me of this.*

"Cause you're still recovering too," Ren said softly.

Zig growled and Jasper actually saw a fang, sharp and golden. *Hand, now.*

Ren sighed as she placed her hand in front of Zig.

You're gonna wanna get her a bucket, Pozi said.

A bucket?

She's gonna vomit after this.

Uh...

Jasper hopped off her bed and down to the main floor, grabbing the trash can beside her desk before going back up.

Ren frowned but didn't question it as he sat beside her.

This is going to hurt, Zig said as he opened his mouth. Ren nodded. Then Zig *bit* her hand.

Ren screamed. Jasper covered her mouth to silence her, pulling her against his chest. Her eyes watered as blood pooled over the side of her hand. The skin grew more pale and the Xyri didn't let go, his fangs fully inside her.

"What's happening? What's he doing to her?"

Injecting her with Xyri venom, Pozi answered as he hopped up onto the bed beside them.

"Since when do Xyri have venom?"

Since forever. Their Bond is strong. She survived the fuse. This should strengthen her.

"Should? What happens if it doesn't?"

A normal human would die from the venom. But not Ren. She's fused with Kirzigith now.

Ren whined, eyes squeezed shut, tears pouring down her cheeks.

Jasper swallowed, trying not to let his own worry show as he held her. Blood continued to drip down the sides of her hand, staining her pink blankets.

It works, Zig said into Jasper's head, voice strained as he slowly unlatched his jaw from Ren's hand.

Ren trembled, liquid gold seeping out of the punctures for a moment before the holes started to close. Then she groaned, eyes widening.

Bucket! Pozi yelled.

Jasper lifted the trash can up to Ren. She grabbed it with both hands and hurled. Jasper winced as she emptied her stomach.

"Oh god. Sorry sorry," she mumbled as she pulled back.

She will sleep now, Zig said.

Jasper nodded. "Shh, Renny. It's okay." He set the trash can aside and handed her the bottle of water from her nightstand. She downed half of it, eyes still watering.

"Rest, okay? I'll be here if you need me," Jasper whispered as he pulled her comforter up and tucked her into it.

Ren nodded, eyes already closing.

35
The Wrong Someones

Bellamy passed Jules as they walked into geometry. She handed him a note with a shy smile before they went to their seats. It was written in a sparkly green ink. She had really nice handwriting.

How was your break? Did you do anything fun?

He glanced at her, wondering why she didn't just text. As he pulled out a pencil to respond, he realized he had nothing he could say. *Oh I flew around the city racing Apex and fought a girl who creates mist creatures and I taught a girl how to use my powers and I stopped criminals and it was so spectacular and awesome...* He sighed.

Nothing exciting. Finished a few books. What about you?

He folded up the note as the bell rang and Mrs. Moore called attention.

"Alright, class, I've got your tests from before the brea—"

The door opened, interrupting her as Ren walked in, breathless. She was flushed, eyes wide as she closed the door behind her.

"Ren, welcome back," Mrs. Moore said. "Perhaps you should try being on time?"

"Yes, Mrs. Moore. Sorry." Ren rushed to her seat beside Bellamy, embarrassed.

He smiled at her. "Hey, glad you're back."

Her blush deepened. "Thanks."

"As I was *saying*," Mrs. Moore continued, walking forward, a stack of papers in hand. "Here's your tests from before the break."

"Tests?" Ren mumbled. "I missed a test?"

"Yeah," Bellamy answered. She looked so tired. "Sorry."

Mrs. Moore handed him his test. He let out a relieved sigh at his score of 93.

"Mrs. Moore, will I be able to make up the test?" Ren asked.

"I'll give you some extra assignments to make up the grade. See me after class and I'll get you what you need."

"Thank you."

Bellamy gave her a reassuring smile as Ren rolled up her sleeves and pulled out her notebook. His heart raced when he saw the bracelet on her wrist. Shining gold, a little bear charm hanging from it. *She got it. She's wearing it.* He completely forgot about it since he hadn't seen her recently and her birthday was a few weeks ago.

When class was over Bellamy slipped his note to Jules and she flashed him a smile before walking out.

"You get these back to me by the end of the week and you'll be all caught up, alright?" Mrs. Moore said as she handed Ren a folder.

"Yes ma'am, thank you." Ren turned and smiled at Bellamy, walking out with him. "Hey, I never got a chance to thank you for this," she said, shaking her wrist to show off the bracelet.

"You like it?"

"I love it. Better than yarn."

"Hey, I *love* my yarn bracelet."

Her cheeks reddened.

"So, how are you?" he continued. "Better now?"

"Yeah, much better!"

"That's go—"

He cut off as Ren's boyfriend walked up and put his arm around her, pulling her against him.

"Oh, hi!" Ren glanced at Bellamy, then back at the taller boy. "This is my friend, Bellamy. Bellamy, this is Simon. My boyfriend."

Bellamy nodded. Of course he knew that, but they'd never been formally introduced. He wasn't sure what it was about the guy, but Bellamy didn't like him.

"Bellamy... I'm gonna *steal her* now," Simon said in a low voice as he turned Ren around and started walking her away. He heard her giggling as they moved down the hall.

You okay? Zeli asked.

Fine.

He sighed and went to his next class, wishing he was Lycan instead.

When he got to creative writing Jules passed him the note back and sat at the desk beside him. She didn't usually sit there. He smiled as he unfolded the note, surprised to see her new addition in a sparkly blue ink.

Spent time with my sister. We went shopping, saw some shows, had fancy food. It was nice cause we don't hang out as much now that she's in college. Do you wanna sit with me at lunch today?

He glanced at her. She was watching him.

Yeah, sure!

He folded the note up and handed it to her just as the bell rang. He tried to pay attention to Miss Higgins, but halfway through class he sent a text to Kaida instead.

|Starface|
Are you still dying?

|Bunhead|
Nope!

He grinned.

|Starface|
Coming out tonight? You could meet Parody!

|Bunhead|
Yeah, I'll come.

I've missed you.

|Starface|
Miss you too.

|Bunhead|
But you've had so much Apex time!

From what I hear you're besties now.

|Starface|
Oh yeah, we're SO close.

Like, glued at the hip close. Cause if you're not that close to Apex he'll fucking die.

|Bunhead|
Toddler on a leash.

Oh he's offended by that. Says he for sure saved your ass three times while I've been away.

|Starface|
And how many times did I save his?

|Bunhead|
He says 2 but I'm guessing at least 12

"Bellamy, phone down," Miss Higgins called.

Bellamy's head snapped up. "Sorry." He tried to pay attention after that.

At the end of class Jules passed him a new note. He read it as he walked to gym.

So, you wanna make plans for another date? I'm free on Saturday.

He didn't have time to answer so decided they could talk at lunch.

When he walked into the cafeteria he started looking for Jules. Her table wasn't far from his normal spot, and she was already there, sitting with Lola, Sophie, Eira, and Imani. He felt awkward as he sat beside her. She gave him a reassuring smile and he tried to relax.

"Hi."

"Hey. So, uh, we can definitely go out Saturday."

"Yeah?" Her smile widened. "I was thinking we could go to some bookstores, maybe get dinner?"

"Sounds good."

"Cool."

He fell quiet as the other girls pulled Jules into their conversation. It felt weird to sit there, he knew all the girls at her table, but he wasn't particularly close with any of them. He glanced back at his normal spot to see Jasper had his arm around Harper while she was laughing, her pale cheeks now rosy. Harper used to sit with Jules before. And now Bellamy was there. He wondered if Jules would be down to alternate, sitting at his table sometimes, with his friends. But with Harper at his table now it could get cramped if he brought Jules over too.

"You're quiet," Jules whispered.

"Oh, sorry."

Toward the end of lunch, Bellamy looked to his table just as Simon came in for his ritual kiss with Ren. He looked back at Jules and forced a smile. Everyone had someone now. But it felt like they were all with the wrong someones.

Ren pressed her face into Simon's chest as he held her. He didn't usually see her this often throughout school. She'd normally see him in the mornings, sometimes, then he'd come see her at lunch for a minute, then again at the end of the day to walk her home. But today he'd met her between every class, spending every minute with her till the bell rang, making him late for all of his classes.

"Can we hang out after school?" he asked.

She pulled back a little, looking up at him. His blue eyes were so pretty. "I... oh I wanna say yes."

"Then say yes," he whispered with a grin.

She laughed and he leaned in to kiss her again, lips warm against hers.

When they broke apart she shook her head. "I have so much homework from the days I missed."

"But you missed me, too," he said, mouth still close to hers.

"I did but—"

"But but but," he teased and kissed her again. "Kissing me is better than homework."

She let out a soft sigh. "Very true but—" Another kiss. She laughed. "Simon!"

"Sorry sorry. Okay." He took a deep breath, pulling back.

"Homework tonight. Does that mean you'll be free tomorrow?"

Ren grinned. "I dunno? I'm supposed to video chat with my friend Ocean tomorrow. But maybe after that?"

The bell rang, bringing her back to her surroundings, standing in the cafeteria by the wall. She glanced at her table to see Jasper taking her trash and adding it to Harper's tray, before putting it away for her. Ren's eyes moved to Bellamy, sitting with Jules. He'd never not sat with Ren before. Since the second day of freshman year, Bellamy always sat with her. She sighed as she turned back to Simon.

"Ready to go?"

"You're walking me to class again?" she asked as they went to grab her bag.

"Gotta take all the time I can get," he said, keeping his arm around her.

"You *really* missed me, huh?"

"So much. We've been seeing each other for over a month now, but two weeks of that was mostly just texting, and rarely at the same time."

She swallowed. "I'm sorry."

He laughed. "For getting sick? Not your fault babe. Just happy to have time with you now."

Ren couldn't hide her smile as they moved down the hall, stopping outside of her world history class. Simon pulled her closer and kissed her again. Someone whistled and laughter followed.

"Damn, Ren, are you *breathing* in there?" Kevin asked.

She pulled away from Simon, eyes wide.

"Shut the fuck up guys," Jasper muttered as he gently pushed Kevin and Nico into the classroom.

Ren groaned.

"Ignore them," Simon whispered as he grabbed her face in his hands. Her heart raced as she met his eyes. He smiled before leaning in and kissing her again. She let herself melt into it, but only for a moment.

When she pulled back, Bellamy was walking by, actively staring at the floor as he passed to get into class. Her heart sped up.

"I gotta go," she mumbled.

"See you after class." Simon gave her one more quick kiss before she turned into the room, face burning as she found her seat by Jasper in the corner.

"You guys are pretty inseparable today," Jasper whispered.

She nodded. "He missed me. It's *cute*."

"He's not the only one," he said. "Being here without you sucks."

She smiled. "I'll try not to do it again."

"That's all I ask."

They fell silent as Mr. Spritz started writing on the board.

Simon continued to meet her outside of each class, walking her to the next one, but at the end of the day she decided to meet him at his locker instead of waiting for him at hers.

He wasn't hard to find, tall as he was. He was facing the other way, talking to some people, so Ren approached slowly.

"Can't believe you're dating a sophomore," one of the guys said.

"She's supposed to be a junior, alright," Simon said. "She's seventeen."

"Oh," the guy continued. "So she's young *and* stupid."

"Fuck you, Sora," Simon hissed. The guy just walked away, laughing loudly.

Ren stood there, frozen. Simon turned around, then his eyes widened when he saw her.

"Ren... I can tell by your face," he said softly as he reached for her, "that you overheard that."

She didn't know what to say.

"That was just Sora, he's like the *biggest* jerk ever."

She nodded. "I shouldn't have come up here I should have just waited for you I—"

"*Ren,* it's fine." He looked past her. "Hey, look here's Cam, a *normal* friend of mine. Cam come meet Ren."

Ren sucked in a breath as a Hispanic boy with curly black hair walked up. He was a few inches taller than her, about Jasper's height.

"Hi. Why am I normal?" he asked Simon.

"She met Sora. Well, *no,* she walked up while Sora was being Sora. Which is maybe better, but still."

"Ah." Cam nodded. "Sora is our worst friend."

"We use the term friend *very* lightly."

"Yeah, we kinda just tolerate him, cause we like his brother, Riku." Simon smiled.

Ren nodded, feeling awkward.

Simon put his arm around her. "Cam's in the band with me and he's my best friend."

Cam grinned. He'd seemed sullen before, but that smile lit up his whole face. "Telling Kit and Allie you said that."

Simon made a face and Ren relaxed a little.

"Well, would you look at *that,*" a girl's voice said.

Simon froze, his smile vanishing.

"Finally replaced me, did you?" she continued, raising an eyebrow at them. She was tall and gorgeous, with bright green eyes, shiny black hair, and a perfectly sculpted figure.

"Oh my *god*," Cam said. "Vicky, go *away*."

Ren looked up at Simon. His carefree demeanor was gone.

"Quite the height difference, huh?" She laughed. "How does that even *work?*"

"Go away," Simon said, voice cold. His arm around Ren's shoulders tightened.

She just smiled, meeting Ren's eyes. "Has he made you listen to his shitty music yet? It sucks," she continued. "But he's great in bed."

Simon winced at the words, as if she'd hit him.

"Fuck *you*, Vicky," Cam said, stepping forward defensively. "You got five seconds till I forget you're a girl and fight—"

"It's *Victoria*," she hissed. "Good luck, new girl."

Simon closed his eyes.

"Well, now she's been subjected to Sora and the *devil*," Cam said with a sigh. He smiled at Ren. "Promise the rest of us are very nice normal people."

Ren tried to smile, then looked up at Simon. His eyes were still closed. "Simon?"

He slowly released a breath. "Sorry," he mumbled. "So you've met my ex now."

"She... looked like a supermodel," Ren said. How could she ever compare to that?

"Yeah, well Lucifer was the prettiest angel, and *yet...*" Cam said.

Ren snorted.

"You are a thousand percent more beautiful than... literally *everyone* I know," Simon said, looking into her eyes. He seemed so... sad, after that encounter.

"Oh gee, thanks," Cam said.

"Sorry Cameron you're so pretty," Simon said, not taking his eyes off Ren. "But no one's as pretty as *her*."

Ren blushed.

"Can I ditch band practice?" Simon asked, glancing at Cam.

Cam stared at him.

"I have homework, remember," Ren said.

"Right. Ugh." He sighed. "Can I be slightly *late* for band practice?"

"Fine." Cam rolled his eyes. "Was nice to meet you, Ren."

"You too!"

Simon relaxed more when they were alone. "We could take a little walk in the park before you do your homework?"

She nodded. "I'd like that."

He kissed her cheek and took her backpack, leading her outside.

They managed to kill a good thirty minutes before he took her home.

When she made it upstairs she found Dad in the kitchen making a pot of coffee.

"Hey, how was school? Feeling okay?"

"I'm fine. And school was good. Got to see Simon, and that was great! Except. Extra homework." She shook her head. "But Jasper got me out of having to do *three* different projects. I just have single assignments to make up instead."

Dad grinned. "That's good. You hungry?"

She shook her head. "Maybe in a bit. Wanna get through some of this homework."

"Alright. Let me know if you need anything."

She flashed him a smile before darting up to her room.

36
Best Ears

The next three hours passed in a daze of concentration while she sat at her desk working on the assignments. She got through more than she expected, but the rest weren't due till the end of the week, so she had time to finish them later.

After dinner she lied, telling her dads she was going to bed early so they wouldn't check on her while she was out.

Ren, can we talk before we go?

She froze in place as she walked out of her bathroom. Zig stood on the floor in front of her.

Talk about what?

Sit.

Her anxiety spiked as she walked to her couch. Zig followed, then jumped up and sat beside her.

"What's going on?" she asked, scared.

There are some things you should... know. Now that you have survived the fuse.

"Okay..."

Remember when we first Bonded, and we had that conversation about how... you would live longer than the average human.

"Yes." That idea still freaked her out. She tried not to think about it.

Well... He paused for a minute, like he was afraid to continue.

Ren pulled her legs up against her chest.

Your lifespan is even longer, now.

She stared at him, shaking a little.

Quite a bit longer, actually. Because we fused. And now... the venom as well. It is in your system. Part of you.

"What does that even mean?"

You will be stronger. Faster. Better reflexes.

"But... wait." She licked her lips. "How much longer?"

Zig sighed. *Perhaps another hundred or so... give or take.*

"Another hundred? *Years?* In addition to the original fiftyish?"

Give or take.

"I'm gonna be sick." She felt the panic swirling up, her stomach cramping in response.

I know you don't like this. I thought about keeping it from you. But Azazelith insisted I tell you. Said it would not be right to withhold this information.

Ren nodded, head spinning as she rocked back and forth a little. The average human lifespan for a woman was around a hundred years. So she... she could live to be two hundred and fifty?

"I hate it."

I know. But it is... not all bad.

How was it not all bad? Everyone she knew and loved would be *extremely* dead and gone long before her. Even Jasper and Lycan. Their lives were extended through the Bond, too, but now... now hers was even more and she'd lose them she'd lose them she'd lose them and be alone and—

You will have me, Zig whispered sadly.

The racing stopped. She took in a deep breath. Of course. Zig only had so much time with his humans. Her life being longer was a blessing for him.

She nodded slowly. *I'll have you.*

I am sorry, Ren.

No, it's... well it is your fault but I'd be dead without you.

You will weather it, like everything else. You will be okay.

Right yeah. It's fine totally fine. Let's go and stop thinking about it now please.

Okay.

She transformed into Kaida, eager to not be Ren anymore.

When she got to the park, Lycan and the new girl were already there in the center of the field, laughing loudly. She landed at a distance, approaching slowly as Lycan waved around a silver sword. The girl was trying to copy his moves with her own silver sword. It took a minute before either of them noticed her. Lycan's eyes lit up and the girl's sword puffed to mist.

"You're here!"

He ran to her, taking her by surprise as he lifted her off her feet and spun her around in a hug. Her heart raced as she held onto him.

"Oh, you *really* missed me," she mumbled into his neck.

"Like you wouldn't believe," he said, the joy clear in his voice as he slowly put her down.

She laughed as she met his eyes.

His smile fell. "What's wrong?"

"What? Nothing."

"You're a terrible liar," he whispered, leaning low. "You okay? Are you still not well?"

"I'm fine I just..." She looked away. "It's not important. Can I meet her now?"

"Liar." He stepped back and grabbed her hand, pulling her over to the new Bonded.

"Kaida, meet Parody. Parody, this is the one and only, Kaida Dragonheart."

Parody's smile was wide. "Hi! It's absolutely amazing to meet you!"

She was taller than Kaida, with bubblegum pink hair pulled up into a high ponytail. Her suit was annoyingly cool. But Kaida's eyes lingered on the wolf-like ears in her hair. Ears like Lycan's. She swallowed, forcing a smile.

"It's nice to meet you, too." She didn't know what else to say. All she knew about the girl was that Jasper thought she was hot and she could copy their powers.

Do you know her Xyri?

I could guess, but not entirely certain.

Would it be weird if I asked?

...I suppose not.

"My Xyri wants to know who you're Bonded to?"

Zig made a sound almost like a snort.

"Oh, her name's Zephyreas. But I've been calling her Zephy. She's *so* cute. Like a weird cat."

Ah.

Good ah or bad ah?

Zephyreas is one I trust.

Okay.

She smiled. "So, you've been practicing with Lycan's powers a lot?"

"Tonight's only the third night, but he's a really good teacher."

Her chest tightened as she looked at Lycan, who was still watching her with a frown.

"Parody, give us a sec?" he said.

"Oh, sure thing. I'll just keep working on those stances."

Lycan nodded and grabbed Kaida's hand, towing her away.

"Don't lie to me," he said when they stopped.

She just stared at him.

"Kai, it's *me*. What's wrong?"

She released a breath. "Zig told me I'm gonna live for a billion years."

"Huh?"

"Slight exaggeration but that's how it *feels*."

"Ohhh." He closed his eyes. "The fuse..."

She waited, assuming Zeli was explaining it to him. After a moment his eyes opened and he pulled her into his arms, hugging her as he rested his chin on her head.

"Sorry," he whispered.

She just sighed, holding onto him.

"Is that why you're being weird with Parody?"

She groaned.

"Or is it something else?"

She groaned louder.

Lycan laughed as he pulled back to look at her. "You're jealous?" He shook his head, smiling. "Now you know how I felt when you brought Apex in."

"Oh, that's *different.*"

"How so?"

"Apex was already my best friend. You've known her like five minutes and you're already *such a good teacher,*" she grumbled.

"First of all," he said, eyes softening. "No one could ever replace you for me. Literally ever. Okay?"

Ren sighed. "Okay."

"I'm serious. You and me?"

"You and me." She smiled.

"Now, will you come back and be nice to our new friend? She's way more excited about you than me, by the way."

"You have matching ears," Kaida mumbled.

He laughed. "She's twenty-four, and *yes*, I told her she shouldn't have told us that," he whispered. "Besides, *my* ears have stars in them and *hers* are pink and fuzzy." He frowned. "And mine are better, right?"

Kaida smiled. "Best ears I *ever* saw."

Lycan grinned. "So, can we go be normal with her now? She just wants to learn to use her powers to help people..."

She sighed. "Okay okay. I'm good. I'm fine."

"I'm glad you're back."

"Me too."

Parody stood alone in the middle of the field, swinging her silvery sword as they walked back.

"Is our dear Apex joining us tonight?"

"Should be..." She frowned, worry settling in, but before she could pull out her phone to call him the flapping of wings signaled his arrival.

Apex landed in front of them, a wild grin on his face. "Tricycle!"

Kaida laughed. "Wait, with Parody that's more like..."

"A four wheeler? Oh god that's cool."

"Cool, but not as cool as our tricycle," Lycan whispered.

"Damn right." Apex said as he fist bumped Lycan.

Kaida shook her head.

Are you okay?

She watched as Apex ran up to Parody and high-fived her. Then they both took off running, laughing loudly as they moved at an intense speed, neck and neck with each other. She glanced at Lycan. He was watching her, a small smile on his face.

Yeah, I'm okay.

37
Reading People

Ren felt weird as Simon dragged her through the Ice Cream Museum. It didn't seem like his sort of thing, and he was awfully quiet as they walked through the different installations. But he *was* smiling, insisting on taking pictures together, which they'd never really done before. She decided she liked having the pictures when they left, though.

"So..." She glanced up at him as they walked to Johns for pizza. "What are you working on at band practice tonight?"

Simon shrugged.

Normally if she brought up his music he'd talk her ear off. Her anxiety doubled by the time they were seated in a booth waiting for their food.

What's wrong?

She sighed, running a finger over the carvings in the wall. *Simon's acting weird. Dunno why.*

You could ask him why, Zig offered.

It's like you don't understand humans at all.

Just ask him, Ren.

She ignored Zig and looked at the photos she took with Simon instead, then posted one on her Instagram.

"You're so pretty," Simon said softly.

Ren's head snapped up. "What?"

He laughed. "What do you mean what?"

"Are you breaking up with me?" she blurted, face burning.

Simon blinked. "Excuse me?"

Her heart was absolutely pounding as she looked down at her hands. "You're being so quiet you've barely spoken at all and you took me to the Ice Cream Museum which is so weird and you—"

She cut off as Simon appeared beside her and pulled her into his arms.

"Why the *fuck*," he whispered, breath warm against her neck, "would I take you to the goddamn Ice Cream Museum if I was gonna break up with you?"

"I don't know."

"You're so silly. I'm not breaking up with you, Ren."

She slowly looked up and met his eyes. "You're not?"

"Hell no. Why would I break up with you?" He smiled. "You're *perfect*."

She swallowed, eyes burning with the threat of crying. "Oh. Why are you being weird then?"

"Hang on. What's wrong with me taking you to the—"

"It's not *you*. You don't even *like* ice cream and the pictures! We've never done that before and—"

He laughed. "But you do. I thought you'd like it?"

"I did."

"Okay. So, how did we get here again?"

She released a breath. "You, being weird and quiet all day?"

He nodded, pulling back a little.

"Something *is* wrong, isn't it?"

Simon sighed. "I wanted to give you a really nice date before..."

"Before what?"

He met her eyes. "Before I told you that... my band has a gig."

"Why... is that bad?"

"It's on prom night."

"Oh."

"I tried to convince my friends that I can't do it, but none of them care about prom. They don't have dates, you know, they're not seeing anyone so they don't get it. And I don't wanna do that to you. I mean, *I* asked *you* to go and you seemed so excited and—"

Ren grabbed his face and kissed him. He melted into her as one of his hands slid up into her hair.

When she pulled back he still looked upset. "It's okay," she whispered.

"Ren, I'm so sorry. I really wanted to take you, I—"

"It's okay," she repeated. "I was excited but..." She blushed. "I was nervous too. Like, *really* nervous about it."

"Why?"

"Uh, cause its senior prom? And you're the only senior I know. I'd feel awkward around all your friends and stuff and just, out of place, and god a *dress?* I was somewhat excited about the dress but also you know, like, being *seen* in a fancy dress stresses me out..." She swallowed.

"Did you already buy the dress?" he asked, eyes sad.

She shook her head. "I was looking online but never actually went to try any on. So it's not a big deal."

He was quiet for a moment, searching her face. "Why didn't you tell me you were nervous about it?"

She shrugged.

"I wouldn't have let you feel awkward," he continued. "You would have been dancing with me in your fancy dress and no one else in that room would have even existed. And the whole time I'd be thinking, '*damn*, look at Ren in that dress... most beautiful girl in the whole world.'"

Ren blushed, heart racing. "You make it sound so romantic."

"It would have been so romantic." He sighed and gently brushed his thumb against her cheek. "I'm gonna make it up to you, okay? We'll do something so fucking romantic that prom wouldn't even compare."

She laughed. "Okay."

"Sorry I stressed you out. I was just... worried about letting you down."

"It's fine, I promise." She bit her lip and grabbed her phone. "Wanna see me in a fancy dress?"

"Obviously."

She pulled up a picture. "Here."

Simon's mouth opened. "Oh my god. You look like a princess. When was this?"

Ren blushed. "It was my sixteenth birthday. Technically we do the big quinceañera party as the fifteenth, but I was sick. So dad convinced me to combine the quince with my sweet sixteen."

"You look gorgeous." He grinned and scrolled up, looking through her other posts. Most of them were of Breadcrumb, but there were a few of her with her dads or Jasper.

Simon paused. "Wait. That's us. We took that today." His smile was so wide, blue eyes shining.

"Is it okay that I posted that?"

"Are you kidding? Why didn't you tag me in it?"

"Wasn't sure it was allowed."

"Allowed?"

"You're a rockstar. You got *fangirls*. Didn't know if it was like... bad for your image or something."

He laughed. "I don't have an image. What I have," he said, pulling out his own phone. "Is an amazing girlfriend that I'm beyond proud to be with. And I don't care who knows it."

Ren beamed at him as she leaned her head on his shoulder and watched as he posted his own picture of the two of them together, then reposted hers, and commented on it. Ren couldn't stop smiling.

Bellamy followed Jules through the shelves of the bookstore. She kept glancing at him, smiling. She was dressed more casual today, black jeans and a light blue sweater, with white sneakers. Her shiny blonde hair was down, falling loose past her shoulders. He wasn't sure he'd ever seen her with it down before.

"So, what's your favorite book?" she asked.

"Favorite book..."

"You can't tell me you don't have one."

Bellamy smiled, thinking of Ren, and the bear.

"No favorites?"

"Uh..." He thought about another favorite book, staying up all night on the phone, reading it to Kaida. *No.* "I really like... Long Way To A Small Angry Planet," he finally said.

Jules frowned. "Never heard of it."

Bellamy released a breath. "Then I'm gonna buy it for you."

Jules smiled. "Oh? Well, then I should buy a book for you, too."

"What's your favorite?" he asked as they continued through the store.

"Probably Pride and Prejudice." She raised an eyebrow at him. "You've read it, right?"

"Of course."

"Hm. What about other Austen's?"

He shook his head. "That's the only one. So far."

Jules grinned and moved away from him. He watched her go, then went looking for the book for her.

When she found him again she had a book in hand. "This is Persuasion."

"This," he said, holding up his book. "Is probably very different from that."

She smiled. "Just gonna look through the records then we can go to the next bookstore."

"Take your time."

He watched her sift through them, like she was looking for something specific. She caught him watching her and smiled as she walked over with a record in hand.

"Just gonna buy this and we can go."

He pulled the record out of her hands and walked to the counter. "What are you doing?"

"Buying it for you."

"You don't have to do that."

"I know." He met her eyes as he put it on the counter. "Will you let me buy it for you?"

She sighed and nodded. "But I'm buying your book," she said, defensively holding Persuasion in her hands.

"Fair enough."

Bellamy carried the bag as they walked to the next bookstore. Jules was quiet and he didn't know what to say. Three dates in and he was still so bad at this. Was she just being nice or did she actually like him? He couldn't tell. He thought maybe he was getting better at reading people, something he absolutely couldn't do before freshman year. But now he wasn't so sure.

As they walked he spotted Ren with her boyfriend on the other side of the street. Simon had his arm around her shoulders, annoyingly tall next to her. Ren looked happy at least.

Once they got to the next bookstore they split up again, looking for any good finds through the stacks. By the time they were done, Jules picked out three books, and Bellamy had two more. He grabbed the stack from her hands with a smile.

"Bellamy!"

"What?"

"You can't buy all the books."

"I really can," he replied as he turned away.

"No, it's too much. You have to let me pay for stuff."

He ignored her as he put the books down on the counter. "Tell you what, you let me buy all the books and you can pay for our food later."

Her shoulders slumped and she sighed. "Fine. But this is gonna add up, it's gonna cost more than the food."

"It's fine, promise."

By the time they went to the diner for dinner they had three different bags of books and Jules seemed happy.

"When are you gonna read Persuasion?" she asked as they ate.

"Depends. When you reading Angry Planet?"

She raised an eyebrow. "I can be done by Monday."

"So can I."

"Okay... whoever finishes their book first gets to pay for the next date!"

He laughed. "Deal."

At least there was gonna *be* another date.

After dinner he walked her back to her apartment, which was just around the corner. She stopped in front of him, a frown on her face.

"Everything okay?" he asked.

She let out an exasperated sigh. "Do you even *like* me?"

Bellamy blinked. "What?"

"Three dates. *Three*. And you haven't kissed me once. You haven't even held my hand, like... what is *wrong* with me?"

Bellamy stood there, heart pounding. "I... uh. You... you wanted me to kiss you?"

Her amber eyes widened. "That's what people *do* on dates! The first date ended early, so you know, that's fine. Whatever. But the second date, I was *sure*. Then nothing! And now... here we stand and you're not making *any* moves and I wanna know if I'm wasting my time with you or not."

He stared at her, heart racing. "I... I know you're supposed to kiss at the end of a date okay, I'm not stupid. But I've never *been* on a date before I've never kissed a girl! And how am I supposed to know if you want that? I'm so bad at reading people and if you *didn't* want me to kiss you and then I *did* that would be so bad and I thought taking it slow was ni—"

Jules kissed him. He stood there, stiff, panicking before she pulled back, face flushed.

"Was that... good?" she asked.

"I... um... yes?"

Her blush deepened and she smiled. "So... you do like me? And you were just too nervous to try anything?"

"...yes?" He felt so awkward, so out of place. Like he was somewhere else, but locked in this moment of staring at her, that smile on his face. It didn't match how he felt. He pulled at the bracelet on his wrist.

"So... should we make things official?"

"Official?"

She laughed softly. "Like, me being your girlfriend? That kind of official... unless, I mean if you don't want to..."

"No, I do!" he blurted, trying to overcome the anxiety boiling inside of him. "I'd... I'd like that."

Her smile widened and she leaned in again. He felt more ready for it this time. The kiss lasted longer, and felt even weirder, but it wasn't *bad*. Just... new. Weird.

"I'll let you know when I finish the book, which will definitely be before you."

He smiled. "Good luck with that."

"Goodnight."

"Goodnight."

He stood there a moment after she went inside, then finally turned to walk home.

Are you alright?

He sighed. *Just had my first kiss.*

That is not an answer.

He took a deep breath. *I'm fine. How was your day?*

Been with Kirzigith and Poziarne.

So, none of us are patrolling?

It's a quiet night, she responded.

I'll patrol after I check on Mom.

Okay.

He checked his phone, expecting texts from Kaida, but all he had was a notification that Ren posted a new photo. He opened it to see a picture of Ren with her boyfriend. Simon had his arm around Ren, and her head was on his shoulder. He stared at her face, wondering if she was nervous the first time she kissed Simon, if it was awkward for her.

I'll get used to it eventually, he thought with a sigh.

38
The Fourth Wheel

"They're really competitive, huh?" Parody asked as her and Kaida sat in the grass, watching the boys fly by.

"You have no idea," she replied, smiling. "But they're surprisingly good sports when losing."

"How often do they lose to you?"

Kaida turned to her. "I wish I could say often, but they're both faster than me, I rarely win raccs. But I have my strengths."

Parody smiled. "You definitely do."

Kaida leaned back, looking up at the black sky. "I love them to death, but I gotta be honest..." She met Parody's pink eyes again. "It's *really* nice having another girl around. Even in my civilian life I'm kinda... surrounded by boys. So, I'm very glad you're here."

Having Parody around, and knowing Ocean would be back soon, was making Ren feel like a weight was lifting off of her. One she hadn't known she'd been carrying.

"I bet. I *was* worried you guys might not like me much. It's like... I'm a fourth wheel, I guess?"

Kaida threw her head back with a laugh.

"Is that funny?"

"No. Well, yes. You see, *both* Apex and Lycan think *they're* the third wheel when it's the three of us. And now there's four. And everyone expects me to drive our weird little vehicle. And I don't even know how to drive."

"I do," Parody said with a smile. "But it gives me anxiety. Who wants to drive in this city anyways?"

"Exactly! My dad hates it."

"Good thing we can fly," Parody said as she leaned back and released a breath.

Kaida was obsessed with her suit, and the color split going down the middle, blue and magenta, with the mismatched stars on her stomach and chest. It was so cool and creative. She wore a hot pink cape now, which was new.

"Won't the cape be weird with your wings?" Kaida asked.

"Don't need the wings to fly," she replied. "And I think the cape is cooler."

Kaida smiled. "I think it fits you better than the wings."

Parody grinned as the boys flew past again. "Can I ask you a weird question?"

"Sure."

"Why'd you call yourself Kaida? It seems most Bonded name themselves something related to their powers, but not you."

She smiled. "Kaida means little dragon in Japanese. And..." She hesitated, but Lycan already knew this. "It's something my dad called me since I was a baby. Little dragon... and then when I met Lycan, my suit was covered in scales and *he* called me little dragon, and... my Xyri kinda *looks* like a little dragon so. It seemed fitting."

"I love that."

The boys zoomed past again and Kaida grinned.

"Can I ask another question?"

"Shoot."

"What's up with Apex and Fable? The other day we were talking about who had the coolest suits, you won by a *landslide,* by the way. But when I mentioned liking Fable's, Apex got so upset I don't think he spoke to me the rest of the night."

Kaida sighed. "He has a personal grudge against him."

"Really? Fable doesn't seem... that bad? Or did I miss something?"

"He steals a lot. But doesn't really hurt anyone. Except once. And, let's just say Apex doesn't believe that was an accident, even though I do."

Parody frowned. "Did Apex get hurt by him?"

Kaida didn't respond.

Parody nodded slowly, looking away. "I won't say anything."

"Thanks."

"It's so weird," Parody continued. "Being Bonded. I used to think the Xyri had like, a mass extinction event or something."

"Really?"

She nodded, her pink ponytail swishing behind her. "I thought maybe they caught a virus, that only affected them? Since they disappeared so quickly. And they ended their Bonds..."

"Has Zephy told you what actually happened?" Kaida asked, curious. Though she suspected she knew the answer. Zig, Zeli, and now Pozi, refused to tell them anything about the war and why they left.

Parody sighed. "No. But I think we must have betrayed them, somehow."

"We?"

"Humans. We must have done something *so* awful, so *atrocious*, they couldn't forgive it. The way Zephy talks about it, or well, the things she leaves unsaid leads me to believe it had to be *really* bad. I mean, all the Xyri agreed to stop Bonding at the same time, out of nowhere, when right before that they were *fighting* each other on different sides of the war?" She let out a breath. "We lost their trust. And I don't quite think we've earned it back yet, even with them Bonding again."

Kaida nodded slowly. Human history was littered with atrocities, but they were, as far as she knew, all *documented* events. So why wasn't that one? She sensed Zig's annoyance at the thought and sighed.

The boys landed in the clearing in front of them, breathless and grinning.

"I won!"

"One out of three," Lycan replied.

"Still." Apex approached them. "Ladies, care to partake in some actual training?"

"Yes please!" Parody took the hand Apex offered, rising to her feet.

Kaida sighed as Lycan stared down at her.

"Not in the mood, Bunhead?"

"Just tired." She pushed herself up, stifling a yawn.

"Should we do two v two?" he asked.

"Wait, can we do three v one?" Apex asked.

Kaida raised an eyebrow. "You think you can take on *all* of us?"

"For sure."

She tried not to laugh. "Kay. Parody, who you taking?"

The taller girl stared at the three of them, then held her hand out to Lycan. He tapped her. That was all it took, a single touch from Parody to copy one of their powers. They wanted her to get familiar with all of them so she could easily switch between them during a fight. But she seemed to favor Lycan's silver the most. She'd described it like water, dense but fluid in its motion. Whereas she'd described Kaida's light as wispy, like air, more abstract and harder to shape.

After a moment a giant silver hammer formed in Parody's hands. It looked comical, but she held it with confidence. Lycan's whip appeared in his hand. Every time Kaida saw the whip it reminded her she didn't have a real weapon yet.

Patience.

She stuck her tongue out in response, unsure if Zig even noticed the gesture. Then a sword of light coalesced in her fist as they all stared at Apex. His smile faltered a little.

"Let's remember you're not actually trying to kill me, this is *training*."

"Sure." Lycan grinned.

Apex cracked his knuckles. "Poz, now would be a great time to give me a weapon." He scrunched up his face. "Oh, *fuck you.*"

Parody lunged, swinging her hammer at Apex. He barely jumped back in time, wings fanning out dramatically behind him.

"Jesus woman!"

"You asked for this," Parody replied, steadying her hammer on her shoulder. "Also, if you want a weapon, why don't you just have the creation kids make you one?"

Apex blinked. "What?"

Lycan met Kaida's eyes. "I never even considered that."

She shook her head.

"You guys... could make me a fucking weapon?"

"I mean, it would disappear eventually, so you couldn't trust it in a fight but..."

"But you could make me a *fucking weapon?*"

Kaida grimaced. "Yes? Would you like a sword?" She felt stupid for never considering it.

"Yes!"

Lycan giggled.

Kaida rolled her eyes as she formed another sword, making it slightly longer and heavier than hers, then she flipped it in her hand and held it out hilt first.

"I cannot fucking believe..." Apex grumbled as he took it. "I don't know how to use a sword," he continued with a pout.

"Alright, new plan. Drop the hammer."

Parody nodded as Lycan's whip disappeared and he made a sword. Parody studied his for a moment before making a perfect copy.

Kaida let out a little laugh. "We must look so silly. If anyone walked by now..."

Apex's pout turned into a smile. "Four losers in costumes with glowing swords in a park in the middle of the night... that's totally normal."

"I honestly wouldn't question it," Parody added with a nod.

"Alright. Watch us." Lycan turned to Kaida.

She couldn't hide her smile. It had been a while since they sparred with swords. She'd never forget the weeks they spent training after Clea died. Every night, just the two of them, learning to be better. Stronger. Faster. Learning not to fail.

"You miss this, Kai?" he asked as he held his sword out.

"Miss kicking your ass? Always." She lunged. He parried the attack, a smug smile on his face.

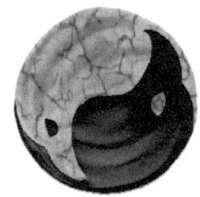

Jasper watched them, swinging back and forth, almost like a dance. They seemed so evenly matched, he had no idea who would win.

They work so well together. Two halves of a whole. How it's supposed to be.

Jasper rolled his eyes. *Yeah, I know. I'm the third wheel.*

No, I mean... it's been a while since Kirzigith and Azazelith got it right.

He frowned. *What do you mean?*

Hm. I probably shouldn't elaborate.

So? Do it anyway.

Watch the shiny swords, kid.

Jasper rolled his eyes again.

Kaida and Lycan moved fast, both smiling as they swung their blades. He held up the sword Kaida gave him. It was smooth and cool, like crystal and felt nice in his hands.

"Are you learning anything from watching them?" Jasper asked.

"Uh," Parody said. "I'm learning they've maybe been holding back on training me. How'd they get that good?"

"Been doing it longer than us." Jasper grinned. "Wanna play swords with me?"

Parody's smile was beautiful as she nodded, holding her blade out, trying to copy the stance the other two had done. Jasper wondered how long it would take Kaida to notice them whacking their swords at each other. She seemed lost in her own little world with Lycan.

"At least I'm not alone now, when they get like this," he said as he swung at Parody.

She blocked it awkwardly. "They get like this often?"

He smiled. "Only every time they're together."

"Oh, *well*, that's not so bad then," she replied.

Jasper felt like a kid with a stick compared to the other two, but Parody seemed to grow more confident with every passing minute.

"This is kind of fun!"

"Wanna try in the sky?"

"Okay!"

He took off running, wings flapping as he rose into the air. Parody followed, her cape billowing out around her, sword gripped tightly in her hand.

"Feels weird."

"You did it with the hammer before."

"I like my hammer."

"Let's stick to swords, till mine melts at least."

He glanced down. Lycan had his sword to Kaida's neck as she was pulled against him. She was laughing, loud and joyous. They hadn't even noticed Apex and Parody weren't there anymore. He shook his head, then swung at Parody. She blocked it, then swung at him.

"This is so not easy."

"Probably why they're doing it on the ground."

He swung again. She tried to dodge instead of parry and Jasper's sword slammed against her shoulder. Parody dropped with a scream.

He let go of the sword, heart racing as he dove to the ground after her. "I'm sorry I'm sorry I'm sorry I'm—"

"What the hell are you guys doing?" Lycan yelled, rushing over.

"I'm fine! It's fine," Parody said as she held her arm. "It was an accident."

"I'm so sorry." He fell to his knees beside her, guilt overwhelming him.

"It's okay. I swear I'm totally okay. Already healing." Parody smiled, her pink eyes bright. "Zephy says this is great practice for all the injuries I'm gonna get later."

Jasper couldn't smile, couldn't relax. It was taking everything in him not to cry. Kaida put her hand on his shoulder.

"Hey," she whispered. "It's okay."

He nodded as she pulled him closer.

"Lycan and I have cut each other while training like, fifty times," she continued. "And he still loves me."

"Didn't cut him deep enough," Jasper whispered.

Kaida giggled and Lycan flashed him a smile.

"We can keep training, I swear I'm all good," Parody said. "Totally perfectly fine, Apex."

He nodded but his stomach still squirmed.

"We should probably actually train you instead of showing off, huh?" Lycan asked.

"You were *very* impressive, but that might be for the best," Parody said with a smile.

I like her, Pozi said.

Me too. And he hurt her...

This training continued every night that week and Jasper was exhausted. Between school, hanging out with Harper after, then spending his nights in the park with the team, he had no time to even think.

You don't think much anyway.

Ha ha.

He laid there in the cool grass, close to falling asleep while Kaida and Parody laughed somewhere nearby.

"You sleepy, little bird?" Lycan asked as he sat beside him.

"How do you do this?" Jasper groaned. "I'm so fucking tired."

"You get used to it."

Jasper shook his head. "Maybe you're an alien because what do you *mean* get used to not sleeping ever? Kaida isn't used to it, she's just better at hiding it when she's tired. Sometimes."

Lycan smiled.

"Guys! Off your butts!" Kaida called.

"Ugh."

"Stop whining," Lycan said as he stood.

Jasper followed him slowly.

"Why are you ruining my grass nap?"

"Zephy finally told me my second power. It's a big moment!" Parody said excitedly.

Jasper smiled. "Congrats. What is it?"

"I can absorb energy, I guess? It's not the same as my copying power. If I touch you and take your energy, it makes me stronger and you weaker. The boost only lasts five minutes for me, though."

"Oh god please don't take my energy, I got none to spare."

Lycan rolled his eyes. "Test it on me."

"You're sure?

Lycan nodded and Parody reached a hand out, touching the silver star on Lycan's chest. After a moment Lycan winced.

"Oh."

"Oh!" Parody grinned. "Interesting!"

"How do you feel?" Kaida asked.

"Feel like I could run a mile in seconds. Or fly for hours. Or fight a bear! This is neat!"

"That'll be super handy in a fight."

Parody nodded then she frowned at Lycan. His eyes were closed, his face stuck in that wince.

"Are you okay?"

"Think... I'm gonna sit down," Lycan mumbled, though he didn't move.

Jasper laughed. "That's what you get, little alien."

"Alien?" Kaida asked.

Parody shrugged. "Boys are sad. Girl race?"

"Gotta be quick," Kaida said. "Before you transform back."

Parody nodded and they took off running through the dark.

"Grass nap?" Jasper asked.

Lycan nodded slowly and they both laid back down in the grass, oblivious to whatever the girls were doing.

39
Allergic To Bowling

Ren sought out Harper on Friday after school. She found her at her locker, talking with Lola and Sophie. Ren waved awkwardly as she approached the group and the girls fell silent.

"Hey, Harper. Can we talk for a second?"

"Sure."

"See ya," Lola said as she pulled Sophie away.

"What's up?" Harper asked.

"I was thinking, maybe we could try to do a double date, with you and Jasper and me and Simon?" She'd been wanting to get Simon and Jasper to hang out. It bothered her that her best friend and her boyfriend barely knew each other.

Harper frowned. "Why would we do that?"

Ren blinked. "Um... I just thought... it would be fun?"

Harper made a disgusted face. "I don't know. Oh, there's Jasper!" She brushed past Ren to throw herself into Jasper's arms.

Ren sighed and went down to her locker, where Simon was waiting for her. He pulled her out into the sunlight, talking about a new guitar he got.

"Ren?" He paused as they came to a stop outside the bakery. "Are you okay?"

"Oh. Sorry." She blushed. "I was listening I swear."

He smiled. "What's going on in that head of yours?"

She leaned back against the wall. "I was thinking it might be fun if we did a double date with Jasper and his girlfriend."

"Oh. Okay."

"Harper didn't seem interested," she said with a sigh.

"You seem... pretty upset about this." Simon frowned, stepping closer.

"Jasper's my best friend," she mumbled. "You guys have spoken to each other like, four times? I just thought it would be a good way for you guys to get to know each other. Harper's my friend but Jasper isn't yours and that bothers me. A lot."

His face softened. "I'm sorry. I've been busy with the band, I didn't even think about this. But I'm so down to double with your friends."

She smiled. "It's fine. Harper didn't want to so... it doesn't matter."

Simon hugged her tightly, cradling her head in his hands. "Sorry, babe."

She sighed as he pulled back.

"Text you later." He gave her a quick kiss then left.

While working on her homework she received a text from him.

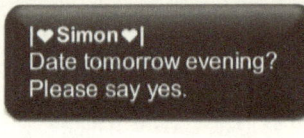

|♥Simon♥|
Date tomorrow evening?
Please say yes.

|Ren|
Sure! What are we doing?

|♥Simon♥|
It's a surprise. But I promise it'll be good!

|Ren|
Hmm. I'll accept a surprise. But only cause I like you.

|♥Simon♥|
♥ ♥ ♥

The next night Ren was actually excited for Simon's surprise, even though she hated not knowing what they were doing. She decided to get fancy for it. Well, fancy for *Ren* at least. She wore a black long sleeve shirt under a red corduroy overall dress, black tights under that, and black boots with red socks to match the dress. She even did her makeup, going all out, covering her freckles with foundation and doing a smoky eye. The final touch was curling her hair. Simon had *never* seen her like this, which made her self conscious as she went downstairs and opened the door.

Simon took a step back, blue eyes lighting up. "Fucking hell, Ren. You look *so* good."

"I do?" she asked, stepping out.

"So beautiful." He grabbed her hand, pulling her into him. "Like, so pretty I just wanna take you right back *inside* instead of going out," he whispered into her hair.

Ren blushed, heart racing. "My dads are home," she blurted.

Simon laughed. "Come on."

She tried to calm her nerves as they walked hand in hand to the subway. "Any hints to where we're going?"

"It's kinda goofy, but it felt like the right sorta thing for what you wanted."

Ren frowned. "What I wanted?"

"You'll see."

Just like that the nerves were back. She had to resist texting Jasper. Instead she talked to Zig.

How are you feeling today?

It's been weeks, Ren. I'm fine. Stop fussing.

I wanna fuss! Fussing makes me happy! Are you lying?

I'm immortal. I literally can not die.

But... you were sick. Sort of.

Zig audibly sighed in her head. *A Xyri can hurt. We can feel pain, through you. It is not a natural thing for us, but we always recover. You are the fragile one, little human.*

"Are you alright?"

Ren blinked, coming back to her surroundings. "Fine."

Simon was smiling. "You're so gorgeous. I really love the makeup."

"You do?"

"Yeah. It looks really good."

For some reason this made her stomach drop, anxiety swirling inside. She forced a smile.

When they got to their stop Simon had to nudge her. She swallowed and got to her feet.

"Sorry."

"Are you sure you're alright?"

"Mhm."

She tried to be present in the moment after that, focusing on the feeling of Simon's hand in hers as they walked up the steps onto the street. They walked for a bit, coming up on Chelsea Piers. She paused in her tracks when she spotted Jasper and Harper, arms looped, waiting for them.

"Hey," Jasper said with a grin.

"What are you guys doing here?"

"Simon set this up. Double date," Jasper replied. "We're going *bowling*," he continued with a malicious grin.

Ren blinked, ignoring the look of pure disgust on Harper's face as she turned to Simon. "What did you do?"

"What you wanted," he replied with a smile. Then he kissed her. "I know bowling is kinda silly. But we'll get to know each other this way. Friendly competition. It'll be fun!"

Ren smiled at how sincere Simon was, but then she caught Harper's eyes and her anxiety tripled. She wished she could fake an emergency. Instead, she followed everyone inside.

"Oh my god," the boy at the counter said. "She's *real.*"

Simon sighed heavily. "This is my friend Kit."

Ren blushed. She hadn't been prepared to meet a friend of his.

He was tall, but not as tall as Simon. Pale, with green eyes, and black hair that was shaved on one side, with a streak of bleached blond coming down around the other side of his face. A dusting of freckles covered his cheeks.

"Did he *pay you* to pretend to be his girlfriend," the boy continued. "Cause he's been talking about this perfect girl for *weeks* but I don't think she exists!"

Simon rolled his eyes.

"Hi," Ren said, awkward. "I'm Ren... pretty sure I'm real."

"Not a paid actor," Jasper said with a smile.

"This is her friend Jasper, and his girlfriend Harper. Now that's out of the way," Simon said, leaning forward. "We'd like to bowl."

"Uh huh uh huh. She's *cute*," Kit replied.

Simon sucked in a breath.

Kit grinned. "What sizes?"

Simon looked down at Ren.

"Uh, seven."

"Six," Harper said, arms folded across her chest. She looked annoyed.

"Eight," Jasper said.

Kit nodded. "And an eleven for the giant."

Ren giggled as Simon rolled his eyes and took out his wallet.

Kit frowned. "You don't have to pay. You know that."

"I'm on a *date,*" Simon replied. "I'm paying."

Kit rolled his eyes. "Not very rock and roll of you, but *okay.*"

Jasper pulled her away while Simon paid. "You alright?"

"Harper doesn't wanna be here," she whispered.

"Huh?"

"I *asked* her if we could double date and she said hell no. How did Simon get you to do this?"

Jasper blinked. "Uh, saw him right after he left you at the bakery yesterday. Said you really wanted a double date so I said sure."

"Did you tell Harper about it?" she asked, bouncing on her toes.

"No, we were gonna do something else but..." He looked over at Harper. She was glaring at them. "I don't get why she'd be mad?"

"I'm so anxious." She let out a breath. "I didn't know I'd be meeting Simon's friend tonight."

"Well, he seemed chill." Jasper put a hand on her shoulder. "It'll be alright. We're gonna have fun, okay?"

She nodded.

Simon and Harper walked over, handing them their shoes then they moved to their lane.

"Thinking we should do teams?" Simon said. "Couple against couple?"

"Sounds good, man," Jasper replied.

Ren just nodded, trying not to spiral. She could feel anger pouring out of Harper, and it was directed at her. Was the concept of a double date that bad? Maybe she was allergic to bowling.

After she got her shoes tied, completely ruining the look of her cute outfit, she texted Lycan.

> |Bunhead|
> Any emergencies I'm
> needed for you?

> Please say yes.

> |Starface|
> No emergencies.

> But you're welcome to
> come hang out with me
> regardless.

> |Bunhead|
> Can't.

> |Starface|
> What's wrong???

> |Bunhead|
> Nothing yet. Just feel
> like I'm about to have
> a bad night.

> |Starface|
> Then bail on it. Come see
> me. I'm already patrolling.

|Bunhead|
No it's fine. Apex is with me.
I'll be alright.

|Starface|
I'm here if you need me. Okay?

|Bunhead|

"Who you texting?" Simon asked as he sat beside her.

"My friend Ocean," she lied. "So, *bowling.*"

"You know how?" he asked.

"Yes, but I haven't been since I was like, ten?"

He smiled. "You'll be fine."

"Have you played any games with Ren yet?" Jasper asked.

"I have not," Simon answered. "Should I be worried?"

"She's pretty competitive."

"Of course you know that," Harper mumbled.

Jasper turned to her. "You alright?"

"Bowling isn't exactly a cute date," she replied.

"Sure it is. It'll be fun." Jasper brushed his thumb across Harper's cheek and her anger seemed to dissolve, some pink blooming into her face. "We're a team," he continued, pulling her closer. "And I'm more competitive than her. So we're gonna win."

"Being competitive doesn't grant you skills," Ren said, trying to feel normal. To act normal. But all she wanted was to text Lycan again. "You're probably really good?" Ren asked Simon.

He nodded. "We play for free a lot since Kit works here. So, I'm not half bad."

Ren smiled but she couldn't fully shake her anxiety with Harper glaring daggers at her.

Why are you so stressed?

I'm fine.

You feel like you're cornered by six villains with nowhere to run. Where are you?

On a date. Bowling.

Hm...

Ren relaxed more once they started the game. Simon *was* good. And Ren didn't suck. She was strong and had great aim. She'd never really been athletic or coordinated before Bonding, but now she was in excellent shape, even without the suit on.

"Damn, Ren," Simon said after she got a strike. "You're so hot when you're winning."

Ren blushed, unable to respond.

"Who's hungry?" Jasper asked, standing up. "Ren, come grab food with me?"

She nodded, following him away from the lanes. He pulled her aside before they even got to the food counter.

"How we doing?"

She laughed nervously. "I do not know."

"Well. You're hot when you're winning, apparently." He smiled. "Interesting compliment."

She groaned, putting her face in her hands.

"Harper keeps getting quiet, too," he continued.

"It's cause of me," Ren said, dropping her hands.

"Why?"

"Cause I'm your friend."

Jasper stared at her blankly.

"Because I'm a girl! And she's your *girlfriend*. She doesn't like it."

Jasper closed his eyes and leaned his head back. "I already talked to her about this. *Twice.*" He shook his head. "It's fine. I'll talk to her when we leave. Let's grab food and go back."

"Want me to pay?" Ren asked as they walked to the counter.

Jasper sighed.

"Shh, it's fine."

When they stepped up to the counter, Simon's friend Kit appeared beside them.

"Put their food on my tab," he said to the girl. Then he flashed Ren a smile.

"You don't have to do that," she said.

"Yeah, but I can. Simon's stupid, thinks he still needs to impress you by paying for things. *Anything* you want, free on me."

"That's real cool of you," Jasper said.

"Thanks. Kit, right?" Ren said.

He nodded.

"You're in the band?"

"Yep. Bass." He raised an eyebrow. "Simon keeps saying he's gonna bring you to a show."

"He does? He hasn't... invited me yet."

"We haven't had one recently. But... hope to see you there when we do." He smiled again then dashed back to the front counter.

"Look at that," Jasper said after they ordered. "His friend likes you. Nothing to be nervous about."

"What about Harper?"

"I'll fix that. Don't worry."

They walked back with a sampler plate of fries, chicken, and pretzels plus some sodas. Simon grinned at her and took the food, setting it on the table. Then he pulled her into his arms. Her heart fluttered and she let herself relax into him as he kissed her.

When he pulled back she glanced at Jasper and Harper to see them embracing as well. Jasper whispered something she couldn't hear, and Harper nodded.

"What did Kit say?" Simon asked, keeping his arm around her.

"He said, uh, that he plays bass in your band. And that you're stupid."

Simon laughed. "Both true I guess."

"He seems nice."

"He is."

They continued the game, going slower as they ate.

"Oh, nice shot, Harps!" Jasper cheered as she walked back, a smile on her face. He lifted her up and spun her around. Harper giggled.

Ren relaxed a little.

"Pretty close now, babe." Simon said, checking the scores.

She smiled over her drink. "We can totally beat them."

"Not going down easy," Jasper said.

"You literally *always* go down," Ren replied. "I beat you nine times out of ten!"

"Listen that's with video games and board games. This is different, this is *physical*. And I'm gonna—" Jasper paused at the look on Harper's face. "Hey, you alright?"

"No. I am not. In fact, we're not gonna win cause I'm leaving."

Jasper blinked. "What?"

Harper started untying her shoes.

"Harper?"

She threw the shoes aside and pulled her converse over.

"Harper, what's wrong?"

Once she finished tying her shoes she looked up at him with a glare. "What's wrong is you bringing Ren on our date."

"It's... it's a double date. Harp's, listen—"

"I don't think Ren should be anywhere near our dates," she continued under her breath.

Ren watched, frozen still, heart pounding wildly.

"Harper..."

She ignored him, storming off.

Jasper looked stunned. "I... uh, I gotta go fix that."

Ren nodded, shrinking down in her seat. Simon pulled her closer.

"Ren? I'm sorry."

"For what?"

"You really wanted this and it just exploded."

She sighed as she leaned her head back to look up at him. "Not your fault Harper hates me now."

"I thought you guys were friends?" Simon said softly.

"We were. Before she was dating Jasper."

"I'm sorry. I shouldn't have set this up. I just wanted to make you happy and—"

"No!" Ren pulled away so she could face him properly. "No, Simon, this was so fucking sweet." The way he looked at her, she thought she might melt. "I love that you did this for me."

"You do? Cause... you looked like you were gonna cry thirty seconds ago."

She laughed. "I maybe was. Maybe still am? But, you doing this for me... it's so sweet. Shows how much you care."

"I do care about you. A lot." His lips quirked up in a smile and he leaned in, kissing her. "A lot a lot."

Ren couldn't help but smile.

"And this was all cause you want me and Jasper to be friends, right? So, we can try again. Do something just the three of us."

"Really?"

"Of course."

"Maybe, we could do something with your friends, too? I mean, if you want to I—"

"I'd love that. You've met Cam and Kit now. Just need to meet Allie. But, she'll try to steal you from me so... I keep putting it off," he said with a laugh.

"Steal me?"

"Yeah. She doesn't have a lot of girlfriends. She's surrounded by us boys. And she's gonna love you. So she'll wanna go do girly things with you. And *I* don't wanna share you just yet."

Ren smiled. "I don't wanna share you, either."

He grinned and kissed her again.

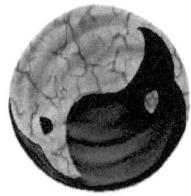

Jasper followed Harper out into the street. "Harper, come *on*."

She stopped, spinning around to face him.

"No. I thought we were going out for *dinner* tonight. *That* was our plan. And then you brought me here. And Ren is just part of our date?" Her eyes widened. "It's bad enough she has to be with us at school. In the halls, in class, at lunch. It's even worse half the time I'm trying to talk to you you're just hanging out with her instead of me. And now she's *here*, on our fucking *date*. And she's all dolled up. I've never seen Ren like that."

"She's my best friend," Jasper spat back. "And the whole *point* of this double date was because Ren wanted me and Simon to get to know each other. Cause we're best friends. And she's dolled up for her fucking boyfriend. Not me. She is with her *boyfriend* on this fucking date. Not *me*!"

"I tried being okay with it," Harper replied, shaking her head. "I really did. But she's everywhere. Surprised she hasn't shown up in my bed while we're fucking."

Jasper let out a breath. "Listen. She's not going anywhere. So, you need to—"

"No!" She threw her hands up. "I can't do it anymore. You have to stop hanging out with her."

Jasper laughed.

"I'm serious! Jasper, listen. She can still sit with us at lunch. But outside of school it's *me*. I'm your girlfriend. You should be at my house, texting me, talking to me. Not her."

Jasper shook his head. "This is what you want?"

"Yes."

"I'm sorry, Harper." He swallowed. "We're done."

She frowned. "What?"

"It's over. I'm breaking up with you."

"No. *No*."

Guilt threatened to overwhelm him for a moment at the look of hurt in her eyes, but he pushed it aside.

"Ren is my best friend. And you know, with time, you could have become as important to me as she is. But right now no one is more important than her. And if you're making me choose, I'm choosing her."

She started crying and he clenched his fists, angry at himself. He didn't want to hurt her. He *liked* her. But he wasn't playing this game. Ren Rivers was his whole world. A girlfriend of one month wasn't changing that.

"Fuck you," Harper hissed. Then she spun on her heels, stomping down the street.

He followed with a sigh.

She glanced over her shoulder, glaring through her tears. "Leave me alone!"

"I'd love to," he called back. "But it's late. I'm not letting you walk home alone."

"Fuck you, Jasper. You don't get to break my heart then act like a fucking gentleman."

"Well... I am," he replied.

He continued to follow her at a distance, trying not to crowd her. But he had to make sure she got home safe. He sent a text to Ren as he walked.

40
Freckles

Ren groaned. "They broke up. I gotta go."

"Oh, okay. We can go."

"No, I gotta make sure he's okay. It's fine."

"He left ten minutes ago," Simon said.

"He's just outside. I'm sorry." She kissed him quickly then started changing back into her boots.

"You sure you don't want me to come? It's kinda my job to make sure you get home safe."

She smiled and kissed him again, taking her time with it. "Jasper can get me back, promise I'll be fine. I'll text you when I'm home, okay?"

He sighed. "Alright."

She took a few steps then paused, turned back and kissed him one more time. "Thank you, for trying tonight."

Simon smiled. "Anything for you."

She finally made her way outside, hoping she could catch up to Jasper. It took her five minutes to realize she was walking to the subway, but Jasper said he was walking Harper home. Ren didn't even know where she lived. She stopped there in the street to call Jasper. He didn't answer. She sighed, spinning around slowly, unsure which way to go.

"Ren Rivers?"

Her heart jumped as Lycan hopped off his silver board onto the street in front of her.

"Lycan? What are you doing here?"

He smiled. "Isn't that *my* line? Are you supposed to be out alone this late?"

Ren glared at him. "Are you supposed to be stalking me?"

"I am not stalking you."

"How can I be sure?"

He laughed. "I'm doing my job. What are you doing?"

"I was on a date."

Lycan stepped closer, yellow eyes shining. "Where's your date?"

She sighed. "I left. Cause my friend had a problem and I was trying to find him and then..." She glanced around. "I got lost."

He raised an eyebrow. "Lost and alone this late. Did we learn nothing from our last meeting?"

Learned you give out your clothes sometimes, she thought. "I wasn't alone."

"And yet..."

Ren sighed as she looked around. "And yet," she agreed.

"Would you like help getting home?"

She smiled. "Are you gonna give me a choice?"

"Well, I'm not gonna kidnap you."

"But you will stalk me."

"To make sure you get home safe, yes." He grinned. "That is my job."

"Yeah, I bet you say that to *all* the girls," she said wistfully as she stepped closer to him. "Chico estúpidas monas con sus estúpidas orejas monas," she grumbled as she checked her phone again, but there was nothing from Jasper. She could just go to his place to check on him later. "Fine, let's go."

"You know, I can understand Spanish in my suit," Lycan whispered, smiling.

Ren froze, cheeks burning. She *did* know that. But she forgot cause she was Ren and Ren was *stupid.* His smile was infuriating.

"I don't know what you think I said but I definitely didn't say that I said something else."

The smile widened. "Sure, sure. So... you wanna ride? Or, are we walking?" He kicked up his foot, silver board forming underneath it.

She was tempted to say yes, but she was Ren, and *Ren* wouldn't do that.

"Walking please."

Lycan nodded, board disappearing. "So," he started. "Are you doing okay?"

"Yes?"

"You... well I mean, that night... when we met. Just, glad to see you're doing okay now."

Ren frowned. "You check up on all the girls you save?"

He glanced at her. "No."

"So, I'm special then?"

"Maybe," he said, looking away.

Her heart swelled. "So, how's hero life?"

"Up and down."

"There's been downs?"

He turned to face her and she noticed the silver glow in his suit had gone out, making him stand out a little less in the dark.

"Well, Kaida almost died recently. That kind of sucked. But, uh... I guess other than that it's going well."

Ren tried not to smile. "Is she better now?"

"Yeah. She's good."

"You worry about her."

"She's my best friend." He said it so matter of factly.

Ren couldn't hide her smile then. *You're mine too, Wolf Boy.* "She's lucky to have you."

"I'm the lucky one."

"Maybe, you're both lucky."

He grinned. "Yeah."

They fell quiet as they walked. She was so used to people gaping at her when she was out as Kaida. But most people they passed didn't even notice Lycan without his suit glowing. To her he was still so obviously *him,* with the ears and the mask and the way he moved. He glanced down at her, smiling. She rolled her eyes.

He stopped suddenly and she looked up to see Fable walking toward them down the sidewalk. Fable also stopped, looking at Lycan. He clearly didn't need to see the glow to know it was him. They stared at each other for a moment, neither moving or speaking.

Ren clenched her fists. She hadn't seen Fable in a while... but he stabbed Jasper. Tried to kill him. If she were Kaida she'd let him know how she felt about that. Instead, she just stood there, silent.

Fable's eyes darted to her before moving back to Lycan. Lycan also looked down at her, then he sighed and stepped aside. Fable continued walking, right past the two of them. She turned, watching him go.

"Should you..."

"No, you're more important."

"Oh." She blushed.

"Come on." He nodded and they started walking again. She realized he was leading them with every step he took.

"You remember where I live?" she asked. They weren't anywhere near the bakery.

"Of course." He raised an eyebrow. "Did *you* forget where you live?"

She laughed. "No, I just... you have a good memory."

"It's not every day you meet a girl who lives in a bakery."

"I live above it. You know that."

"I do." He released a breath, smiling slightly. "I move through this city almost every night. It's my job to know where things are."

"You're good at your job," she replied as she pulled out her phone and sent a text to Jasper.

> **|Ren|**
> Text me backkkk are you okay?

> I'm gonna be home in like 20
> minutes if you wanna come over?

> Or I can come overrrr. Text me backkkk

"So, how was your date?" Lycan asked. He had a look in his eyes that made her defensive.

"It was good!"

"Uh huh. You left alone." He glanced at her. "What kind of date lets a girl walk home alone? At *night?*"

"I told you, I had to find my friend."

"Alone." Lycan shook his head, agitated.

"I might have lied," she admitted. "I told him my friend was still outside, that he'd get me home."

Lycan raised an eyebrow. "Why lie?"

Because Simon probably wouldn't have let me go alone otherwise. She sighed. "Just seemed easier."

"Interesting."

"Me lying to my boyfriend isn't interesting. None of this is interesting."

"More lies." He smiled. "You have a problem."

"Yeah, his name is *Lycan.*"

His smile fell a little. "Are you actually mad I'm walking you home?"

"No," she muttered. "You're very nice. I just wish I found my friend."

"I'm sure your friend is fine."

She nodded. But she had no idea how Jasper was doing. He hadn't been with Harper long but he seemed to really like her. There was no way to guess how the breakup would affect him, considering his only girlfriend before this had been Ren, and they'd had the most mutual breakup ever.

"I get the feeling if you could outrun me you'd simply sprint into the darkness," Lycan smiled as he said it. "If finding your friend is that important, we can go find him together."

"Why are you like this?" she asked, coming to a stop.

He frowned. "Like what?"

"Nice. You're *so* nice."

His smile returned, slow at first. "It's my job to be nice."

"Not true." She shook her head. "It's not even your job to help people. And it's *definitely* not your job to be nice about it when you do. Those are choices you make. Cause you're a *stupidly* good person."

He laughed. "Stupidly good?"

She nodded and started walking again. "Exactly."

"Do you wanna go back? I'll insist on going with you. Fable is that way, after all."

She considered it, then shook her head. "No. I wasn't even sure where I was going. Thanks, though."

They fell silent again. It was oddly comfortable walking and talking with Lycan as Ren. She worried she'd do or say something to give herself away though. She knew too much about him as Kaida. Enough that if she wasn't careful, he'd figure it out. And she couldn't let that happen.

"I don't suppose you're gonna stop wandering the streets alone at night after this?" he said softly as they finally turned onto Seventh. "If I ask very nicely?"

Ren smiled as the bakery came into sight. "I'll consider it."

"Mhm."

"What's your normal life like?" she asked. "I mean, I know you can't tell me who you are but..." She licked her lips. "Do you have a good life, outside of heroing?"

He made a face, not answering immediately. "It's not a bad life."

"You spend so much time as Lycan, though. I mean, I have to *assume*. Due to the stalking."

He grinned. "Sometimes... I feel like I'm more myself in the suit than outside of it. Like I don't... always know what to say, how to be. But... it's easier, with the mask." He blushed.

Ren nodded, understanding. "Thanks, for walking me home."

"Anytime."

"Stalker."

His smile widened as they rounded the bakery and came to a stop. His yellow eyes stared down at her and Ren's heart fluttered. Simon was supposed to be the one standing there at the end of the night... She blushed.

Lycan frowned. "Your freckles..."

"What?"

"Your freckles are gone."

"I... I covered them with makeup."

"Why would you do that?"

She blinked, surprised by the question. "Cause... I was on a date. And I wanted to be pretty." Her blush deepened. "Does it matter?"

"No I just..." He blinked, pulling back a little. "Don't get me wrong, you look lovely." He smiled and reached out, grabbing a lock of her hair, wrapping it around his finger. "The curls are cute." He let go and the curl snapped back against her cheek as her heart raced. "But, you are pretty. *With* the freckles."

She stared up at him, speechless.

His smile started to fall as he searched her eyes. "Was that a weird thing to say?" he asked softly.

"No. Thank you," she mumbled, heart absolutely thundering, so loud he could probably hear it. "I..."

"Oh my god is that Lycan?"

"Lycan!"

A downside of living next to a bar. People were always standing out there, half of them drunk.

"You're about to get mobbed," she whispered.

"Guess I should go." He licked his lips nervously as he held her eyes for a moment. Then he stepped back and addressed the crowd, his nerves vanishing, replaced with a confident demeanor. "Just making sure she got home safe."

"Wanna make sure *I* get home safe?" one of the girls asked. Her friends laughed.

Lycan didn't answer as he smiled at Ren one more time before kicking up his board. Then he was off, into the sky. Ren released a breath and quickly unlocked her door before the girls could say anything to her. She stood there, back against the closed door, trying to calm herself.

Ren?

I'm fine.

Are you?

Yes!

She sighed and pulled her phone out, relief filling her as she opened a text from Jasper.

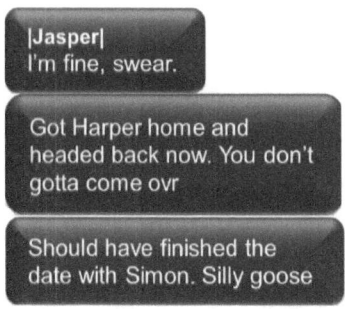

|Jasper|
I'm fine, swear.

Got Harper home and headed back now. You don't gotta come ovr

Should have finished the date with Simon. Silly goose

|Ren|
You're a goose!

Are you sure you're okay?

We can talk about it! if you want.

Am I being annoying?

|Jasper|
You're being a silly goose

I'll come over tomorro

|Ren|
Fine. Love you!!!!!

|Jasper|
Love you too boo

She almost told him about Lycan but decided not to process that as she made her trek upstairs and checked in with her dads. It wasn't until she'd made it to her room, taken off the makeup, and gotten into pajamas that she finally remembered to text Simon.

|Ren|
Made it home. Sorry our date fell apart.

Are you home now?

|♥Simon♥|
Yeah I'm home. I'm sorry too.

Is there anything I can do to make it up to you?

|Ren|
You don't have to do anything ♡

Oh I'm gonna be on best friend duty tomorrow so we can't go out. But maybe after school on Monday we can do something?

|♥Simon♥|
That's so long from now.

I miss you.

|Ren|
You're cheesy. It's been like an hour.

|♥Simon♥|
I can't believe you don't miss me.

|Ren|
I do actually! I got home and was wishing you were here to kiss me goodnight.

|♥Simon♥|
I'll come and kiss you right now.

|Ren|
Ha ha

|♥Simon♥|
I'm so serious. You say the word I'm at your door.

|Ren|
Very sweet in concept, bad in practice. My dads might actually kill you.

Besides gonna sleep soon.

|♥Simon♥|
Alright. Get some sleep. 🤍

|Ren|
You too.

She sighed and put the phone down, flopping on her pillows. *You are pretty. With the freckles.* She felt warm. *Lycan thinks I'm pretty.* She closed her eyes, smiling. She'd never seen him like that with someone before. Not even Kaida. But it... it didn't mean anything. He didn't even know Ren. Not really. And—

Her phone vibrated. She sat back up, expecting another text from Simon, but it was Lycan. For some reason this made her panic, thinking he was texting Ren, not Kaida. But that was *stupid*. It was in the group chat with her, Apex, and Parody.

|Starface|
Got a problem. Serious kind.
On Park Row and Beekman.
Could use backup!

Damn. The suit came over her in a flash and she climbed out of bed and up through the skylight.

41
Little Tricks

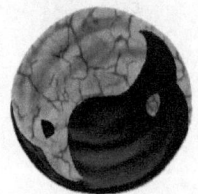

Jasper didn't go straight home after Harper stormed inside. He was frustrated. If Ren were a guy Harper wouldn't care how close they were. Or maybe she would. Harper knew he was bisexual now, he came out to her three days back. Maybe she'd have held any friendship over his head.

He wanted to hit something. That feeling freaked him out, though. He had a lot of rage but it stayed pent up inside, always. If it broke free... he didn't wanna become like his dad. Because his dad hadn't always been an abusive dick. Jasper had vague memories from when he was little where his dad was nice, caring. Sweet with his mom. But these days he'd be lucky to catch her smiling. More likely to find her with tears in her eyes and bruises on her arms. Jasper would have matching bruises more often than not. He couldn't fight back. Every time, he just took it.

You're not like him, Pozi whispered.

How do you know?

I wouldn't have chosen him.

Jasper smiled slightly. *You're just complimenting yourself, aren't you?*

You and me, kid. You would never hit your mother. You cry when she cries. You're hard on the outside, sure. Gotta be to take it. But inside you're soft, and that's the difference.

He didn't know what to say to that.

Your dad is rotten inside and out. Rotting like a corpse buried a hundred years. With stinky rats crawling through his skeleton. But then even the rats decide there's better carrion and they move on.

Jasper laughed. *Interesting metaphor.*

See, you're not a corpse! No rats inside of you.

Just an annoying Xyri.

You can pretend you think I'm annoying all you want, but I'm melding with your soul. I know your insides better than you do. And you love me. Just not enough.

316

Not enough? he asked.

No. If you loved me enough you'd have a fancy weapon you could summon whenever you want. Like Lycan. He really loves Azazelith. Bet he never tells her she's annoying.

Jasper rolled his eyes. *Sorry Pozi. I love you so much. Can I have a weapon now?*

You don't mean it! You gotta mean it! In your soul.

Whatever.

Stop.

Jasper paused. *What?*

Other way. Go the other way.

Jasper stood there, confused. Just as he started to turn around he saw someone skulking by. *Fable.* He'd be easy to miss, his suit wasn't glowing at all now. But those bunny ears were a dead giveaway.

Jasper... don't.

He sucked in a breath as he stepped back into the shadows and transformed into Apex.

Jasper, remember last time...

Yeah yeah. I won't fight him. Just gonna... follow him.

Maybe he could figure out where he was going. Find his hideout. Then he could make a proper plan to deal with him.

Fine. But be sneaky. As Pozi said it, the green glow in his suit went out.

I am.

Are you?

This is why I don't love you enough!

Rude.

Jasper clenched his fists, body vibrating with frustration. After breaking up with Harper and thinking about his dad... he couldn't fight back at home. But here, with Fable, he *could* fight. And he intended to. Just not *yet.*

Maybe we should call Ren, Pozi whispered.

This isn't Ren's fight. It's mine.

You lost it last time. And the time before that. We got stabbed. Do you remember?

I remember getting stabbed.

I didn't like getting stabbed, for the record.

Can you shut up?

I don't think—wait! Jasper!

Something hit him from behind and he fell to the ground.

Kaida landed on a roof beside Lycan, who was overlooking the scene below. A bunch of people with bats and crowbars were breaking into shops on the street. She raised an eyebrow.

"You needed me for petty thieves?"

Lycan turned and smiled. "Nice to see you, too. Look over there. The fox girl." He pointed.

There was a single person standing in the middle of the street watching the chaos with a satisfied smile. She had long wild orange hair and a white and orange fox-like mask over her eyes and nose. It went up into the shape of ears at her forehead, keeping the hair off her face. Those eyes glowed like the embers in a fire. Her suit was pretty. An orange top with the shoulders cut out and sleeves of black, with gold lines pointing down them. Her pants were white up top, but black below her knees, with the same golden lines. Kaida smiled, sensing her own suit inspired part of the design.

"New Bonded?"

"She's controlling them somehow," Lycan replied. "Figured it wouldn't be smart to get too close without backup, in case she got me under her power too."

"Definitely smart. Glad you texted."

He looked up at her, apprehensive. "You sure you're ready for this? You haven't been in a real fight since your injury."

She rolled her eyes. "Yes. Alright, I weathered the storm. Now it can fucking weather me."

He tilted his head a little.

"Besides, Apex and Parody didn't answer. So it's you and me."

He smiled. "You and me."

"What's the plan?" she asked, trying not to think about that smile and how it looked just thirty minutes ago outside the bakery. *You are pretty.*

"I jump in. See what happens? You save my ass if it goes bad?"

"I *am* good at that." She grinned. "Go, I got you."

He nodded, then jumped off the roof. She watched him fall then glide before landing amid the chaos. None of the people ransacking the shops even noticed him. But the fox girl did. She smiled and slowly walked toward him.

"Hey, friend. We haven't met yet. I'm Lycan."

"Call me Rapture," she replied softly. "Would you like to play?"

"I'd like you to call off your goons here, actually."

Rapture moved closer and Kaida noticed a sort of aura around her. How close did she have to be to put Lycan under her spell? Was it about the eyes? The way they glowed, how she wasn't blinking at all as she moved toward him.

"Not gonna happen. But you can join them," Rapture said as she came to a stop in front of him.

Kaida watched carefully, ready. Throwing him in just to get an idea of what this girl's powers were wasn't the smartest idea, but it should work. They'd gone into too many fights without knowing what they were up against. She cracked her knuckles, eager to be back in action.

Any idea what Xyri we're dealing with?

I have a few guesses.

Should I be worried? Like, can she kill him with a touch?

...no.

Kaida released a breath. Rapture was frowning as Lycan just stood there, waiting.

"It's not working." Rapture pouted.

"What isn't? *Oh, are you trying to put your little spell on me?*" He sounded amused.

"You're not attracted to me?" the girl asked. "Lumi says it only works if there's attraction."

Attraction? What's she mean?

Lumi, that would be Lumithi.

You sound worried?

Her first power is not great. Second is worse. Way worse. But she isn't using it here. Attraction, it's more like an affinity. You can resist even if it works on you. But not her second power.

It's not working on him, should I get closer?

Perhaps, but be careful.

Kaida nodded and jumped. Rapture spotted her and immediately stepped back, but it was hard to tell any emotion from her eyes. They were a pure golden-orange, like a Xyri's.

"Am I invited to the party?" she asked as she stepped up beside Lycan.

"Always," Lycan replied. "Apparently her power isn't working on me."

Rapture sighed as her eyes moved between them.

"She doesn't wanna play now?" Kaida asked sadly.

"I don't, but they will," Rapture replied with a smile, stepping back.

Something slammed against Kaida's head. She hit the ground hard.

"Kai!"

Ow.

The people Rapture had been controlling now surrounded her and Lycan, bats and crowbars raised against them.

She pushed herself up, blood boiling as light poured out of her hands, forming into a big shield as she blocked the next blow.

"You good?"

She glanced at Lycan as a rope formed in her other hand. *"Fine."*

The rope slithered out and around two of the men, tying them up tight. Lycan already had three contained, two in cages, one in ropes like hers. They had to be careful. These were normal humans, and they weren't in control of themselves. If Kaida wasn't careful she could hurt them.

"Help! Please help!" someone called from behind them.

"Go, I got this!" Lycan yelled as he weaved silver through the group.

Kaida nodded, slipping out of the fight to find a girl in a pink motorcycle helmet, tears in her eyes.

"What happened?"

"That girl, the fox, she kidnapped my girlfriend!"

"What?"

"Told me to get off the bike and I said no, then she threw me on the ground and told my girlfriend to drive her away and she did. She's... controlling her, or something, I—"

"Which way?"

"That way." The girl pointed. "Up on the bridge. The bike is pink."

"I'm on it."

She took off in a run then jumped into the air, wings spanning out at her sides. She scanned the road below for a pink bike. Orange hair.

What's up with the Bonded?

Any level of attraction and she can force you to do as she wishes. Something as simple as liking the sound of her voice, or the color of her hair would do it. But you can fight it once under it.

Interesting... so, Lycan wasn't attracted to her? Not at all?

It would seem like no.

She couldn't hide her smile as his voice echoed in her head. *You are pretty. You are pretty.*

Ren, focus, Zig said.

She nodded as she finally caught sight of the bike speeding across the Brooklyn Bridge. Kaida arced low, till she landed in front of the bike, forcing it to lean sideways before skidding across the pavement, coming to a stop in front of her. Cars slammed on brakes, swerving around them.

Kaida waited, folding her wings in. Rapture's eyes smoldered as she got to her feet.

"Jump," she whispered, voice low and soft.

Kaida's body halted against her will.

Those orange eyes bore into hers. *Jump off the bridge,* a sweet voice said in her mind.

Her feet moved, not toward Rapture but toward the railing. Fear welled up inside of her as she started to climb up the side. Then with a scream of panic, she jumped.

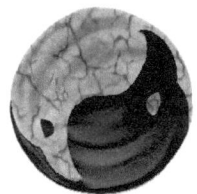

"Why are you following me?" Fable hissed as Jasper blinked up at him.

"You know why," Jasper growled as he pushed himself up.

Fable didn't respond.

"You gonna stand there and pretend like you don't know what I'm talking about?" Jasper shook his head, heart pounding.

Fable didn't respond.

"Such a fucking *coward.*"

"Can't you just leave me alone?" Fable finally muttered.

"Do you deserve that?" Jasper asked coldly. "Do you *deserve* to walk free through this city every fucking night, like you didn't take her life?"

Fable sucked in a breath.

Jasper smiled. "You know I'm right. You *know* you're a piece of shit fucking loser who deserves *nothing.* Maybe that's why you *have* nothing."

Fable's purple eyes darkened.

"Yeah, you wanna fight me now, coward?"

Jasper...

He ignored Pozi. "I can fight back this time." He took a deep breath. "So *fight me.*"

Fable sighed and held up his hands. Two black sticks, about a foot long, appeared in each hand.

What is—

His weapon. Oh, he loves Nellithi!

Jasper rolled his eyes as he tapped strength and took a step back. Fable lunged at him. Jasper blocked the first swing and punched him in the face. Fable stumbled back, but recovered quickly. He swung again, missing with one stick, but the second hit Jasper across the face. He fell to the ground, eyes going dark as blinding pain erupted in his head.

Before he could recover Fable was on him, slamming a fist into his jaw. Jasper groaned.

"I didn't mean to kill her," he growled.

Jasper coughed, blood spraying out of his mouth. "Liar."

Another hit to the face. Jasper's head spun, eyes going dark. He blinked and two or maybe three Fable's hovered above him, purple eyes glowing like demons in the night.

This isn't going well.

Jasper winced.

"Stop haunting me, ghost," he whispered.

With that Fable walked away, leaving Jasper slipping in and out of consciousness on the street.

Lycan's heart stopped when he saw Kaida fall off the bridge. She spun in the air a moment, unable to get her wings out before hitting the water. He dove after her.

The cold water pulled Kaida down into its dark murky depths. He pushed, arms moving fast, following the glow of her suit. It seemed brighter than it had above. Time moved slowly in those seconds it took to reach her. He slipped his arms around her and shot them out of the water as fast as he could.

Kaida was coughing and shaking as he settled them on the roof of number eight Spruce Street.

"You're okay," he whispered.

"I can't—" She coughed again. "I can't swim."

"Shh, you're okay."

She closed her eyes and he thought she might be crying, but it was hard to tell with the water dripping down her face.

"What happened?"

"I don't know. I wasn't in control. She made me jump. I was. I was so scared. I hate water I can't—"

"Shh." He brushed the wet hair back off her face. "You're okay. I *promise.* I got you."

She nodded, pressing her face into his chest.

42
So Good. Very Cat.

"I think I've hit the point in secret life things where going to a party feels weird instead of normal now," Jasper said as they walked to Bellamy's.

"Almost dying two nights before your birthday will have that effect on you," Ren replied.

Jasper sighed but didn't respond.

Ren bit her lip. Jasper had shown up on her roof in the middle of the night after their disastrous double date, his face bloodied. It had been a week since then, but she couldn't let it go.

"I don't like how you keep going after Fable on your own," she continued.

Jasper kicked an empty soda can. "I didn't go after him this time, I told you! He was just... there."

"You're lucky he didn't kill you."

"Oh, so *now* he's not a sad homeless guy but a killer, but *only* when it comes to my safety, and not others?"

Ren took a deep breath, resisting the urge to argue. "You almost didn't make it to seventeen," she said in a small voice. "Maybe you don't care about that but I do. *I* need you."

Jasper sighed. "I care." He put his arm around her when she didn't respond. "I'm fine, okay? And... I'm sorry. I didn't *mean* to get in a fight."

That wasn't what Pozi told her.

"Ren? Please don't be mad at me."

"Not mad," she mumbled. With a deep breath she looked down at her outfit. "Do you think I did enough?"

It was a costume party, and the theme was 'dress as what you wanted to be when you were a kid' though she hadn't wanted to dress up at all. But Jasper said she'd stand out more if she didn't. So she used eyeliner to draw whiskers on her cheeks and a black spot on her nose, with cat ears in her hair to complete the look. It was honest, she did wanna be a cat when she was little.

Jasper's was way better. He stuck a bunch of monopoly money over his clothes, claiming he wanted to be rich.

"You look real cute," he replied.

"You think Harper will be there?"

"Uh. She was invited so, maybe."

"Will you be okay if we see her?"

He gave her an annoyed look. "I told you I'm fine."

She didn't believe him. He seemed off, but that wasn't necessarily because of the breakup. It could have been because of Fable. Or his dad, who forgot his birthday the other day. Whatever the reason, she hated him shutting her out.

When they got to Bellamy's apartment Nico opened the door for them.

"Yo," he yelled as he ushered them inside.

Ren immediately felt overwhelmed at the amount of people crammed inside.

"That costume is sick," Jasper said.

Ren turned to take in Nico's look. He was clearly an astronaut, only he looked kinda dead. "A zombie astronaut?" she guessed.

"Yeah! Zombinaut," he answered excitedly.

"You wanted to be a dead astronaut?" Jasper asked with a grin.

"See," Nico started, "I wanted to go to space, sure, but I also assumed I'd die if I did."

"You look awesome."

"Thanks. Is your boyfriend coming?" Nico asked as they followed him into the living room.

"Nope. He skipped prom to play a show last night and he was up late. Said he was taking it easy today," she replied, resisting the urge to wrap her arms around herself.

She liked wearing looser clothes but Jasper convinced her to wear her old skinny jeans. The shirt wasn't *too* tight but she'd tucked it in, so it felt more form fit than she was comfortable with.

"Wanna find Bell?" Jasper asked.

"He's in the kitchen," Nico replied.

Ren was surprised Bellamy agreed to host the party. He flat out said he didn't want to, more than once. But somehow Nico convinced him to do it.

They shuffled through the costumed bodies, Ren only recognizing half the people. Her eyes landed on Harper and she tensed.

She was wearing the skimpiest cheerleader outfit Ren had ever seen, the skirt so short she might as well have just been in her underwear. Her deep red lips curled into a sneer when she saw Ren.

Jasper sighed and grabbed Ren's arm, pulling her into the kitchen behind Nico. Ren still didn't know what happened. Harper had been her friend before all this, but now she really seemed to hate her.

They found Bellamy leaning against the back counter, arms crossed. He was wearing a red T-shirt with grey jeans and black laced Vans. Not even a hint of a costume. Ren smiled.

"Hey, Bell," Jasper said.

Bellamy straightened. "Hey, love the costume."

"I worked so hard on it," Jasper replied very seriously, making Nico laugh.

"You look really cute," Bellamy said as his eyes moved to her. "Love the ears."

"Thanks." She couldn't help but blush, heart racing. *He just said I was cute. Oh lord.*

"Can you believe Bellamy didn't dress up?" Nico shook his head. "Keep trying to get him to put something on and he refuses."

"You haven't offered me anything interesting," Bellamy replied.

"Oh!" Ren opened her purse. "I have ears. If you wanna cat?"

A smile slowly spread across Bellamy's face, reminding her of Lycan. "You have ears?"

She swallowed. "Uh, yeah. I ordered a pack off Valkyrie and brought extras in case I lose these." She pulled them out and held them up, face burning.

"I could cat with you," he said, taking the ears. He slid them into his blond hair and grinned. "How do I look?"

"So good. Very cat."

"Cute cat?" he asked.

Ren's heart raced. "Yeah yes definitely."

Jasper laughed. "I'll be back, bathroom," he said, smiling wide.

Ren almost grabbed his arm to stop him. She sucked in a breath as she looked back at Bellamy. He was smiling at her.

"So, is Jules coming?"

"Yeah, she's gonna be late though. Was still working on her costume with Eira and Soph last I heard."

She didn't know what else to say. "Cool. Uh. Guess I'm gonna... walk around."

"Thanks for the ears."

Nico was frowning. "That's the first time you've smiled *all* day," he said.

She didn't hear Bellamy's response as she moved through the crowd, looking for Harper. She found her by the windows with Lola, who was dressed in a pilot jumpsuit. Harper glared as Ren approached. Lola forced a smile, looking between the two of them.

"Can we talk?" Ren asked.

"I don't have anything to say to you," Harper replied.

"Please?"

Lola sighed. "Just hear her out. I'll get us new drinks."

Harper rolled her eyes and nodded.

Ren waited till Lola was away before speaking. "Jasper won't tell me what happened with you guys. But, I know it's my fault. I know you didn't wanna do the double date and I guess. I just wanted to say I'm sorry."

"It is your fault," Harper said flatly. "Just admit you want him. We broke up because of you. So you guys should get it over with."

Ren blinked. "I don't want him. I don't know why you think that's a thing."

Harper rolled her eyes. "He broke up with me *for you*. A guy doesn't break up with a girl for another girl if he doesn't wanna *fuck* that other girl."

"Wait." Ren shook her head. "*He* broke up with you?"

"Yes. God, you're so fucking stupid."

Ren flinched. "I... we used to be friends."

"Not anymore. I loved Jasper. But you ruined that. We're not friends. Don't talk to me. Don't look at me. Don't pretend you don't want him. He's all yours now."

Before she could respond, Harper aggressively pushed past her, making her stumble. Ren stood there, frozen, eyes burning.

"Ren, you okay?" Kevin asked, his brown eyes full of concern.

"Fine," she blurted as she turned and went out on the balcony, taking deep breaths.

Her phone started vibrating with a call from Simon.

"Hi," she answered, doing her best to not sound like she was about to cry.

"Hey babe, guess what?"

"What?"

"I got another gig tonight."

"Oh, wow. That's amazing."

"Yeah! Same place as last night. And I can get you in. I want you here *so* bad. Come see me."

"I can't. I'm at a friend's party, remember?"

"So? Ditch it."

"I can't," she laughed. "Besides, my dads would kill me. If it's that same twenty-one plus place I can't go. They already said no to that."

"But they said yes to your party. It's the perfect cover. We can pretend you were there the whole time."

"I'm not lying to my dads."

"You said you wanted to see me play." His voice changed. "Was that a lie?"

"Of course not." She grabbed the railing of the balcony. "But you can't just spring this on me and expect me to ditch my friends *and* lie to my dads."

"Your friends won't care. And your dads don't have to know. You won't do it for me?"

She closed her eyes. "The first thing you said you liked about me was my honesty. Now you're mad I won't lie?"

"I do love your honesty. But I'd also love to have my *girlfriend* at my *fucking show.*"

"You already knew I couldn't go to that place!" She took a deep breath, heart racing. "I *do* wanna see you play, Simon. But not like this. And Harper is here. I'm not leaving Jasper."

He groaned. "Jasper's a big boy, he can handle seeing his ex. If I leave right now I could pick you up."

"No. I can't."

"You're being fucking stupid."

Her eyes burned, throat feeling raw. "You sound so different."

He laughed. "Just come see *me.*"

"Are you drunk?"

"No. Not *really.* Only had a little, I think?"

"I am not coming."

"Ren, don't be like—"

"No sorry bye." She hung up, hands shaking as she shoved her phone back in her pocket.

"Ren, are you alright?"

She spun around, quickly wiping her eyes. Bellamy was standing behind her, watching her with worry. The cat ears in his hair reminded her of Lycan and she forced a smile.

"I'm fine."

"You're lying," he said softly, stepping closer. "I heard Harper, before you came out. And Kevin said you looked upset. I didn't mean to... overhear you on the phone. I just wanted to make sure you were okay."

She closed her eyes.

"Wanna talk about it?"

She sighed, not sure what to say, the urge to cry still so fresh in her eyes. She sniffed and looked up. Bellamy was standing right beside her.

Ren swallowed. "Jasper and Harper broke up and Harper blames me. She basically hates me now, said I should never talk to her again. And Simon called and wanted me to ditch the party to come to his show and he was mad I said no and he was drunk and not himself and I..." She let out a breath, eyes still burning. "I feel overwhelmed. How's your night going?"

"Uh. There's a party in my house." He paused. "But it could clearly be worse. I'm... really sorry about all of that."

"Why did you agree to the party?"

Bellamy shrugged. "Nico kept bringing it up and people seemed excited. Jules said it sounded like fun. I..." He sighed. "Didn't wanna disappoint everyone."

"You *hate* parties."

He smiled, meeting her eyes. "So do you. But you came."

"You invited me."

"Obviously. Like I'd survive a party without you?" His eyes softened. "You're the best person to hide on the balcony with. I'm glad you came."

Ren smiled, remembering that first party last year. She spent the entire night out here with Bellamy, not talking with anyone else. She'd been so in love with him then. It was weird to think about. Her feelings for him weren't *entirely* gone, she knew that. But they were... muted. Was that because of Simon?

"I'm glad I came too."

"Are you? Even after Harper and your boyfriend?"

"Well," she said softly. "I wouldn't have gotten to see you in cat ears. I think it's worth it for that reason alone."

His smile widened and he turned to look out at the view. Ren turned with him, pushing down her anxiety at the height. She used to hate heights, but she'd been forced to overcome that as Kaida.

"Are things good with Jules?" she asked.

"Yeah, I guess. Not what I expected but, good."

"How do you mean?"

He looked down at her, his green eyes intense. "I just... guess I thought maybe..." He shrugged. "It would be someone else? But I like her."

Ren nodded. "That's good."

"Are things... good with Simon?"

"Yeah. I mean, before that phone call it was good. Really good. He was *so* sweet last week."

Bellamy swallowed. "Yeah? What did he do that was *so* sweet?"

Ren looked away. "He tried to do something nice for me. It kinda blew up but... the effort was nice."

"Being mean to you on the phone doesn't seem very nice." He sounded annoyed.

Ren didn't know what to say. "It's fine," she finally muttered.

Bellamy met her eyes. "No one should *ever* be mean to you. Ever."

She nodded, looking away.

He sighed and turned slowly. Then he stilled. "Huh."

"What?"

"Someone's in my mom's office with her." He frowned, leaning over to peek in through the window.

"You don't know him?"

"No, but I've seen him before. Think he works with her at the museum. Something about him just feels... *off*."

"Is he giving her something?" Ren stepped closer, feeling nosy.

They both watched in silence as the tall man in the long coat slid something across the desk. Ren couldn't get a good look at his face, but he was pale, with short dark hair. Bellamy's mom opened the box. Inside was a golden bangle bracelet. The man was grinning like he'd just given her a prize worth a fortune. Bellamy's mom looked surprised as she pulled it out of the box, inspecting it.

"Maybe... they're dating?" Ren whispered, looking up at Bellamy.

His frown deepened. "I don't think my mom's ever been on a date..."

Just then his mom looked up at them, her green eyes narrowing.

Bellamy gently grabbed Ren's arms and pulled her back, his face red with embarrassment.

"Wanna go back inside?" she asked, voice low, as if afraid his mom would hear them as they walked to the other side of the balcony.

"Are you kidding? I'd much rather be out here with you."

Ren smiled, leaning back against the railing beside him.

43
Floaties

"You said you had a surprise?" Kaida said, suspicious as she stood on the roof with Lycan.

It was a few hours after the costume party, and her nerves were still on edge. In truth, she just wanted to curl up in bed and sleep, but Lycan asked her to come out, so out she came.

"I do. Do you trust me?"

"Yes."

"Then come on." He held a hand out as his silver board appeared.

She rolled her eyes, wrapped her arms around his waist, and they took off. He didn't tell her where they were going, but she knew it wasn't hero business. A few minutes later they landed on the street and started walking.

"You know it's two in the morning, right?"

"Yep."

"Where are we going at two in the morning?"

"You'll see." He looked over his shoulder. "Promise you won't get mad?"

"Saying that makes me think I'm gonna be mad?"

He grinned, walking backwards. "I promise it's a good thing. Sort of?"

"Lycan, I swear—"

His smile was infuriating, but somehow it made her relax. He spun back around then turned a corner. He stopped at a door, and broke off the handle.

"Are we breaking and entering?"

"Little bit."

"Ly, where are we?"

He didn't answer, just grabbed her hand and pulled her inside the building. The smell of chlorine hit her in the face as they walked through a dark room. Turning another corner, they came out to an indoor pool. He spun around and smiled with all his teeth.

"Surprise!"

"Explain," she said with narrowed eyes.

"Okay, so. You were pretty upset when you fell in the water last week. I know Rapture made you jump, but you couldn't even orient yourself or get your wings out. You panicked because of your fear. And so I thought... we could face that fear in a controlled way. To help you overcome it."

"You're gonna throw me in a pool?" she asked in a small voice, her exhaustion weighing on her.

"Of course not. I'm gonna teach you how to swim. If you'll let me."

Kaida relaxed. "Teach me?"

He nodded. "I figure, if you have a little training, next time you maybe fall in water, you'll be okay." His smile was so genuine.

She wanted to argue. To say no and walk out. But she couldn't. "Okay. We can try."

"Yeah?" He looked so excited. "Okay, cool. There's floaties in here. Can use those just to get you used to the water. If you feel okay with that then we'll actually try swimming a little."

"And... you're a good swimmer?"

"I saved you, didn't I?"

She smiled. "You always do." Then she frowned. "I'm supposed to swim in my suit?"

"Yeah. I mean, we can't take them off with each other. Can alter them to be more swim friendly though."

"Uh. Okay. How much?"

He made a face. "Hands free, and feet? Could take off sleeves entirely if you want. Might be easier to swim that way. But it's up to you."

She nodded, but her stomach was in knots. Ren was always self-conscious in the Kaida suit, with the way it hugged her entire body, revealing her shape to the world. Pulling the suit back enough to expose skin felt even worse. But this was *Lycan*.

With a sigh she ducked into the changing rooms and instructed Zig to pull the suit back, up to her elbows and ankles. Then she slowly walked back out, bare feet cold against the floor.

Lycan stood there waiting for her. His suit was sleeveless now and her heart sped up at the sight of his arms. He'd also pulled it up to his calves.

Oh lord.

Careful, Ren.

You hush.

Lycan walked over and started putting the floaties on her arms.

"This feels silly."

"It's not silly," he replied.

She groaned but stopped complaining, still distracted by his biceps. He walked down into the pool, the water going up from his calves to his knees, then to his waist. He stopped there and she let out a breath.

"Okay. Okay. Okay. Okay. Okay."

"Does saying okay a lot help?"

"Shut up. Maybe?"

"Okay." That same infuriating smile filled his face.

She let out another breath and walked into the water. It was cool but not freezing. She walked as deep as he was, nervous. "It's so irrational how afraid I am. I *know* I can't sink with these on. I know... you'd never let anything bad happen to me. But I feel like I'm gonna vomit."

"Not irrational." He held a hand out to her and she took it, letting him pull her farther in. "Deep breaths, Kai."

She nodded as the water hit her floaties, making them bob, holding her above the water even though the weight of her underneath wanted to go down. Lycan didn't say anything, so she focused on breathing, trying to get her nerves under control.

Ren had only ever been in a pool once, when she was little. She'd gone with Ocean's family, and she'd had a big donut float around her. She'd had fun floating in the shallow end, splashing with her friend. But then later that day she'd been walking on the edge of the pool, and she tripped over something, falling right into the deep end. She remembered the panic, the thrashing. Ocean's dad pulling her out while she cried and cried. She hadn't been in a pool since.

"You're doing great," he whispered.

"Thanks. Now what?"

"How about we just move through the water a bit?"

"Talk while we do it, please," she muttered, hating how she could hear the fear in her voice.

"So... did you know that wolves are red-green color blind?"

She shook her head.

"Which is sad, right? Cause they couldn't see how you shine in your suit."

She snorted and he grinned, gently pulling her deeper into the water. Her toes barely brushed the bottom now.

"And did you know that the original Lycaon, son of Pelasgus, tried to feed Zeus a human as a sacrifice, and his punishment was to be turned into a wolf?"

Ren smiled. "You're such a nerd."

"Yes."

"That's not a very good fact about your namesake."

"Nope. But it's interesting! Is this helping?"

332

"Very interesting. And yes, thanks." She was a little calmer now, but not enough. Though she wasn't sure how much calmer she could get. "Should we try the hard part now?"

"You're sure?"

She nodded. "I'm... scared."

"I know," he whispered, leaning close. "But I got you."

"I know."

He gently took the floaties off her, then put an arm behind her back. She thought she might be sick as she leaned into the support.

"I want you to get a feel for floating first, so I'm gonna tilt you back into the water, and hold you from below. Okay?"

"Kay."

One hand stayed under her back while the other moved to her legs. She floated on the surface of the water as he held her in place. She had to force herself to look away from his biceps, back to his eyes as he looked down at her. She released a breath.

"This isn't so bad."

"Yeah... wow."

"Wow?"

"Your hair," he said.

It's fallen down.

"Oh." She felt it floating out in the water behind her. It was always up as Kaida, in two buns. Never down.

"It's longer," he mused.

"Huh?"

"Than your real hair I mean."

Ren frowned. "How would you know?"

"I saw it once, remember? First day we met. Your hair was down and brown and..." He sighed. "I haven't forgotten."

She blushed. "It's not longer. I mean, it *is* longer. But my real hair isn't, I don't think. Um. Just Kaida hair. Longer." *God I sound dumb.* "My real hair is about—"

"Here?" he asked, brushing a finger against her arm, making her shiver. "I remember."

"Good memory."

"I also remember your eyes are brown."

Ren blinked. "Stop remembering. That's a secret."

"It's not my fault you kept your real colors on day one."

"I didn't know I could change them!"

He grinned. "Have you... ever wondered what color mine really are?"

All the time. "No. It's a *secret.*"

"I could show you," he said, voice soft.

Her heart was pounding like wild in her chest, and it had nothing to do with the water.

"I think you misunderstand the concept of a secret," she replied, blushing. "New topic please."

He sighed. "How's Apex? Did you talk to him about Fable?"

She swallowed. "I broached the subject but he keeps closing up on me. Which is super annoying cause he rarely ever does that."

"I'm sorry."

"Maybe you should talk to him."

"Me?" Lycan laughed as he pulled her back up. She felt like she was vibrating at the feel of his hands on her. "He's not gonna listen to me."

"No, he might! Cause I'm his best friend, I'm biased and stuff. But if *you* bring it up maybe he'll realize it's *actually* a problem."

"I can try. But I can't promise it'll work."

"Trying is all I ask."

He nodded. "And I ask the same of you now. We're gonna try actual swimming."

She groaned. "Okay."

In the suit she was Kaida. Always. *Almost* always. But Ren was bleeding through so much. He flipped her on her stomach and made her paddle while he held her. The idea of breaking down in front of him was so bad she somehow kept it together out of spite.

They went for a long time, trying different things, across the pool, then back again. In the deep water, and back to shallow. He never let go of her, not once. Even when she suggested trying it on her own, trusting him enough to pull her up the second she went under.

She wondered if maybe he didn't think she could handle it, but that wasn't it. He cared, and he knew how afraid she was. In some ways, Lycan knew her better than anyone. He knew her fears, and how capable she was of facing them. He knew how to help her face them, and when to keep her in check, not letting her go too far, like she wanted to now to prove herself.

Against his arguments, she pulled away from him and tried to swim to the other side by herself. She managed to get halfway before she lost the rhythm and started plummeting.

Before she could begin to panic, Lycan was there, arms around her. He pulled her up onto the steps in the shallow end, holding her as she trembled.

"I'm fine," she whispered.

"You are."

She didn't pull away, instead leaning her head into his shoulder. "Thank you, for this."

"Did it help?"

"I think so?" She sniffed, finding comfort in his embrace. "You're so sweet to do this for me. But I think... that's enough for tonight?"

"Of course." His chin was on her head and she couldn't pretend she didn't love that. "Was this better or worse than the nets?"

She smiled. "Oh, the nets..."

Kaida had been so afraid to fly, in the beginning. He helped her face that fear, too. He'd made giant silver nets, spanning different buildings. And she jumped, over and over, right into his arms, into the nets. Until she wasn't afraid anymore. It took weeks.

"The nets were pretty great," she whispered.

"I agree." He let out a breath. "You wanna go home, or are you up for late night pancakes?"

She grinned. "Always down for pancakes."

"Cool. Let's get dried off." He stood slowly, helping her up with him.

She hated how she shook, but he kept his arm around her till they got to the changing rooms. The moment she was alone she wished she wasn't. With a sigh she detransformed, surprised to find her clothes under the suit weren't wet after so long in the water. She grabbed a towel to dry off what was wet, then put the suit back on before walking back out.

Are you doing alright?

Lycan was waiting for her, leaning against the wall, his blue hair still damp. He grinned and she took a deep breath.

Yeah, I am.

Lycan was her rock. He always had her back, and she was never going to take that for granted.

He pushed himself off the wall. "Pancake time?"

"Yes please."

44
One Drink

Ren ignored Simon's texts the next morning, and left lunch early so she wouldn't see him. He texted again while she was in world history. She ignored it, unable to shake the sound of his voice on the phone. The words *you're being fucking stupid* ringing in her ears.

When she got to her locker at the end of the day she expected they'd have to talk, but he wasn't waiting for her like usual. She tried not to let it bother her as she found Jasper and he walked her home.

Just as she finished her homework she got another text from Simon.

> |♥Simon♥|
> Hey, I'm outside. Can we talk?

With a sigh she got up. She was alone, so she couldn't ask her dads to tell him to go away. She could ignore him, but she didn't have it in her.

I could eat him if you would like, Zig offered as she slowly made her way downstairs.

"You can eat people?"

She could feel his amusement but he didn't respond. For some reason it made her relax, which was helpful, since her nerves were a tangled mess by the time she reached the door.

Simon stood outside, a bouquet of red roses in hand. He looked down at her with soft eyes as she stepped out.

"I was such a dick last night. And I am so so so sorry." He held the flowers out to her.

She took them, unsure what to say.

"I was awful," he continued. "I didn't mean to be. I *swear* I didn't. But... I was drinking and so caught up in the idea of having you at the show, and... I wasn't listening to you and. I'm *so* sorry, Ren."

She looked up from the roses, meeting his eyes.

"I..." He sighed. "I don't entirely remember what I said but I know it was really bad. Cause Allie yelled at me after." He looked on the verge of tears.

"She yelled at you?"

He nodded. "My friends were not happy with me last night."

"You..." Ren swallowed. "You called me stupid," she mumbled into the bouquet.

He blinked, eyes watering. "Ren, I'm sorry. I didn't mean that. I swear I didn't." He stepped closer. "You mean everything to me and I can't bear to lose you. Ren, *please* forgive me."

She thought she might cry as she stared up at his tears. "It's okay," she whispered.

"No, it isn't. Ren, I don't deserve you and no one should talk to you like that, least of all me and—"

"I forgive you," she interrupted.

He released a breath. "Really?"

She nodded slowly. "Will you come in?"

"Okay."

She grabbed his hand and pulled him through the door. He didn't say anything as they walked up the stairs.

"I like the flowers," she whispered.

He nodded.

When they got upstairs she set them on the counter, then pulled Simon over to the couch.

"You're very quiet," she said.

"Yeah. I'm... kinda afraid."

"Of what?"

"Losing you."

She grabbed his hand. "I'm right here."

He shook his head, not meeting her eyes. "I just... can't believe I... jeopardized our relationship like that."

Ren sighed. "Why were you drinking?"

He closed his eyes. "They offered free drinks. I didn't think."

"I... didn't like you like that."

"I didn't like me like that, either." His hand tightened around hers.

"Ren, I'm serious." He met her eyes. "I'm *never* drinking again. That is a promise. I will never treat you like that. Ever again."

Ren smiled. "One drink and you're done forever?"

"Yeah."

"Reminds me of my dad."

"Yeah?"

She nodded, leaning back into the cushions. "When I was a baby, my dad was all I had. He was killing himself taking care of me. Abuela helped, and she told him to go out one night. To have fun with his friends. To be a kid again, while she watched me." Ren paused, taking a breath. "He got drunk. Got in an accident. It was bad. Paramedics said he should have died, that it was a miracle he walked away from it with just a few scrapes."

Simon watched her, listening intently.

"And, Dad swore he'd never drink again. Cause he almost left me all alone. People make fun of him, sometimes. For not drinking. Then he tells that story. It shuts them up."

Simon smiled. "You are worth that sacrifice."

"For the record," she continued. "I really do wanna see you play. And I'm sorry if I made you feel like I didn't."

"That wasn't about you." Simon looked down. "My ex, she never came to shows. And I guess I was just afraid. You'd... be like her." He met her eyes. "But you're nothing like her. And I know that. And I'm sorry."

Ren smiled, leaned forward and kissed him. He melted into her, his hand sliding around her neck and into her hair.

"I forgive you," she whispered against his lips. "And I'll come to the next show, if I'm allowed. I *promise*."

He smiled and wrapped his arms around her, pulling her against his chest. "Thank you."

"You really should let me listen to your music now," she said. "So I can know the words when I do go to a show."

He pulled away from her and put his hand over his eyes.

"Simon?"

He shook his head, sniffling.

"Simon, what's wrong?" She gently pulled his hand down to see him crying. "Simon?"

"You—you really wanna listen to my music?"

Her heart nearly broke as Simon stared at her, blue eyes shining, lip trembling.

"Yes. I *want* to listen to your music and go to your shows. Simon, I'm *so* proud of you and I like you *so* much and any insecurities you're feeling about any of that isn't necessary." She cupped his cheek, brushing her thumb over it. "I wouldn't lie about that. I promise."

He nodded slowly. Ren kissed him.

"I like you so much, too," he whispered. "It's hard to put into words how you make me feel. And believe me, I've been trying."

Ren giggled.

"Are your dads home?" Simon asked, looking over his shoulder.

"No, but Dad should be soon."

"Will they be mad to find me here?"

"Maybe." She sighed and stood up. "Need to put those flowers in a vase."

338

"Should I leave?"

"In a minute," she answered, busying herself filling a vase with water.

As she got the flowers in it Simon snuck up behind her, wrapping his arms around her, then rested his chin on her shoulder.

"You like them?"

"Yes."

He kissed her cheek. Then his lips moved down, kissing behind her ear. Then across her neck, sending shivers down her spine. She felt *warm*. Simon gently turned her around, and his lips found her mouth. She was surprised as his arms pulled her closer, body pressing against hers, the edge of the counter digging into her back.

Panic snuck up on her as his tongue entered her mouth and she pulled back, breathing heavy, heart racing.

"I I I... should find Breadcrumb. My cat. You should meet my cat!"

Simon smiled, stepping back as she moved past him, hands shaking. *Why am I shaking?*

Breadcrumb was asleep in his bed by the TV. She took her time crossing the room and scooping the cat into her arms. He made a little *merp* sound but didn't even open his eyes. Some of her tension eased as she held him against her chest and walked back to Simon.

"So, this is Breadcrumb The Cat. He's six years old and the best boy ever." She grinned, waiting for Simon to say something.

"Isn't he a bit big for a cat?"

"Oh, he's a Maine Coon. They can get real big. Bready is actually kinda small for a coon. Just a *baby,*" she mumbled into his orange fluff. "Do you wanna pet him? He's really friendly."

Simon made a face. "Not much of a cat person."

"Oh."

"You want me to pet him?" He smiled. "I'll pet him for you."

She shook her head. "No. It's fine." *Why am I freaking out?* She put Breadcrumb on the floor, hands still shaking. "You should... probably go."

Simon closed the distance between them. "Are you okay?"

She nodded, forcing a smile.

He leaned in, hands wrapping around her waist, pulling her against him again as his mouth moved with hers.

"How long till your dads are home?" he whispered, barely pulling back.

"Not long," she muttered.

Another kiss.

"How long is not long?"

"Not long enough?" She tried to pull away but his arms held her in place as he kissed her again. Her heart raced and she forced her face down, burying it in his chest.

"Ren?" He stroked her hair. "Sorry. I'm sorry. I'll go."

She shook her head. "It's fine I'm fine."

He kissed her forehead, then slid his hand under her chin, forcing her to look up at him. "Are we okay? We're good?"

Ren nodded. "All good."

"Okay. I'll text you later."

"Okay."

He stepped back and turned toward the stairs. Ren followed him, burning with anxiety. She had to shove her hands in her hoodie pocket to calm the shaking as they walked down together. He stopped at the door, hesitating. Then he kissed her on the cheek, before walking outside.

The second the door closed she turned and sprinted up the stairs, pulling out her phone as she went, checking Jasper's location. Then she shoved the phone away as the suit came over her.

She couldn't be Ren anymore. Not now. She ran, suit on, up to her room and out through the skylight, hands still shaking.

45
Something Feral

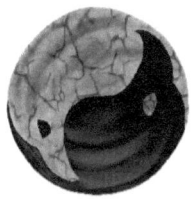

Jasper strolled the streets in his suit, bored and looking for trouble. People only knew him as a sidekick, or that guy who kept getting his ass kicked by Fable. He wanted to do more. To *be* more. People stared as he walked, but they didn't approach him.

Guess I'm not cool enough for that yet.

I think you're pretty cool.

Do you? Jasper sighed. He'd only been chosen to Bond because of Ren. Nothing he did would have been good enough.

You're so dumb, you know that? I chose you because you were right, Pozi said.

You literally told me it was because I was friends with Kaida. He kicked a rock as he walked, ignoring the stares.

I was watching you for four months. I only knew Kaida's identity for two when we Bonded.

Jasper came to a stop. *Really?*

Finding out you were friends with her was never supposed to happen, Pozi muttered. *My choice was already made. I only told ya that cause I'm not sappy and boring and Kirzigith wanted me to anyways. So there.*

Why would you choose me? He started walking again as someone took a picture of him.

The first time I saw you was the night you broke your leg, Pozi said, voice soft.

Jasper turned off the road into an alley to get away from the stares as he processed those words.

What do you mean?

I was already searching for my person. Then that building exploded right in front of me. I saw Fable walk out and I walked in. You made your injury worse, you know? Struggling to get to that girl. You didn't care, didn't even seem to notice your own pain. Because you wanted to help her. To save her. You cried when you couldn't. It still kills you that you couldn't save that child. This is why I chose you, Jasper Liam Nightingale. This is why you are right.

He stopped, back pressed against the wall, eyes closed.

You're worth more than you know.

Stop.

Stop what?

Lying. His eyes burned, emotions crashing into him.

I'm gonna tell Ren you said that, Pozi replied.

Jasper smiled through the pain, eyes squeezed shut. *Stop being nice. Go back to being annoying please, I'm begging.*

Okay I think you got stupid hair and you should open your eyes. We are not alone.

Jasper pushed off the wall, heart racing as he faced the person in the long pink coat.

"Wonderland." How had they snuck up on him like that? They smiled as they got closer. So tall, and striking in that suit. The tie dye-like colors were a nice touch, and the golden boots were so flashy.

"Apex," Wonderland said softly, their voice smooth.

"That's me."

"Top. That's what that means. Is it true?"

"Is what true?"

"Are you a top?" Wonderland asked, smile widening as Jasper blushed.

"I uh, think you gotta get to know me better before we get into that. Buy me dinner first or something."

Wonderland laughed. "Yeah, you like spicy food?"

Jasper laughed nervously. Their pink hair looked so soft.

"What exactly can you do, Apex? The world's been waiting to find out."

"You wanna find out?" Jasper stood straighter. "I can show you, if you're feeling bad."

Wonderland raised an eyebrow. "Now you're speaking my language."

A whooshing sound interrupted them as Kaida fell to the ground between them, burning like a comet. She was breathing heavy as her eyes narrowed on Wonderland.

"What's going on here?"

"A casual chat," Wonderland replied. "Getting to know each other."

"Apex?" She sounded shaken as she glanced over her shoulder at him.

"We're good so far," he replied. Something was *off* with her.

"What are you doing?" she asked Wonderland as she turned back on them.

"Just out for a stroll."

"In your suit? Are you... up to something you shouldn't be?"

"I just like feeling powerful," they replied.

Kaida sighed but she made no move to attack. Apex waited, wondering what she'd do. Before he could ask a bang erupted in the distance, making all three of them jump.

"Is that you?" she hissed.

"Not my party."

"We should go?" Apex asked.

"Why don't you run along," Wonderland said. "I wanna speak with the lady for a moment."

Kaida sighed and nodded. "Go, I'll be right behind you."

He hesitated a moment then turned, wings fanning out behind him.

Kaida stared at Wonderland, not at all in the mood for whatever they were up to. They watched Apex fly away before turning their sparkling pink eyes on her.

"What do you want?"

They smiled. "Just wanted to say thanks."

"For what?"

"Your interview."

She swallowed. *"Right."*

"Respecting pronouns, very hot of you."

She snorted. "Yeah. I should go. Are you gonna behave yourself?"

They bit their lip. "I'll behave for you. Or I won't, if you're into that."

Her eyes widened. "You know I'm only seventeen, right? I have to assume you're a *bit* too old to be flirting with me like that."

Wonderland's mouth opened in surprise. "Uh. I didn't. I'm twenty-five so... forget I said any of that. Sorry." They frowned. "Wait, how old is Apex?"

"Also seventeen."

"Damn. You look older. Maybe it's the masks? Apologies. Will not happen again."

She smiled. "You're making me like you."

"You said it yourself, I didn't hurt anyone. Am I *really* a villain?"

"That's up to you." She paused as another bang echoed in the distance. "I should really go deal with that…"

"Yeah."

"You don't have to be a villain, you know. Come with me, help with whatever that is."

They shook their head. "Nothing in it for me. But you go. Do your little hero thing. You and me, we're good now."

"We are?"

"What you said in that interview was great. Really." Their smile faded, eyes serious. "Thank you, Kaida."

She nodded. "I like the new additions to your suit," she said, eyeing the lapel pins on each side of their collar with *THEY* on one side, and *THEM* on the other.

Wonderland flashed her a smile. With a sigh she turned and ran.

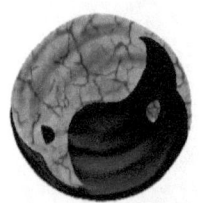

Jasper didn't have time to react as the car flew through the air and hit him. He plummeted to the ground.

"Ow."

You're fine, get up!

Did you feel the ow? He groaned as he forced himself to his hands and knees. The real shock was that his body *was* functional. Nothing broken. "Did he throw a fucking car at me?"

Yep!

He got to his feet as air slowly refilled in his lungs. "That was rude!" he yelled as he moved toward the boy.

His suit and mask were like a white kaleidoscope of fractured glass, with light reflecting off him in a rainbow of colors. His hair was a shock of white with small streaks of black in it. And his mask covered the top half of his face, leaving only his nose and mouth visible. Fair skin, burning blue eyes. He grinned wickedly as another car lifted into the air.

Jasper grinned back, ready this time. The car rocketed toward him and he caught it, holding it up with shaking hands. Then he threw it right back, surprising the boy. He jumped, barely dodging as it hit the parked car he'd been standing on.

"You wanna stop playing games and actually fight me?" Jasper yelled as he stormed towards him.

The boy grinned and dashed down the street. Most of the people had cleared away when cars started being tossed about, but there was still a crowd watching, phones out and filming. The boy ran right toward them.

Jasper tapped speed and air flew past as he ran, catching up to the boy a moment too late. He got his hands on a little girl, yanking her out of reach of her mother. He held a hand around her throat as Jasper skidded to a stop in front of him.

"Be careful now, something *bad* might happen," the boy whispered. "Bad things always happen here."

The girl's mom was screaming. People held her back even as she fought them to get to her daughter. Jasper had to pull his eyes away from her to look at the little girl. Dark tan skin, dark eyes. She wasn't crying or screaming. She didn't even look afraid as she held his gaze, reminding him of a mini-Ren.

She knows.

Knows what?

That you are going to save her.

Jasper nodded, taking a deep breath.

"Only a coward hides behind a child. You wanna fight *me*, not her."

The boy swayed his head back and forth a little. "You have no idea what I want."

"Then tell me and let her go."

The boy shook his head, hands gripping the girl tighter. Jasper lunged and the boy rose in the air with the little girl. He spun as they got higher and the girl finally screamed in terror, waking something feral within Jasper.

You're ready.

Jasper didn't need to ask what that meant as he held out his arm. A long black and green staff appeared in it, cool to the touch, like metal. Without missing a beat he threw it with all his strength. It slammed against the boy's head. He dropped the girl just as Apex took to the sky, swooping low as he caught her in his arms. She clung to him as he spun, orienting himself. The boy slammed to the ground then vanished into thin air. Jasper landed right where he'd been a moment before, but the boy was gone.

Did he just disappear?

Yep.

Great.

With a sigh he gently sat the girl on her feet. She stared up at him with wide brown eyes, a smile on her face.

"You're alright," he whispered.

"Thank you, Apex."

Her mother reached them then, scooping the girl into her arms as tears poured down her face. Jasper released a breath as the woman met his eyes.

"Gracias! Gracias!"

He nodded. "It's what I'm here for."

The woman pulled him into her arms, her daughter now squished between them. His eyes welled up as she let go of him. People were cheering. He smiled slightly, then backed up.

Police were rushing in now that the danger had passed. He looked around, wondering where the hell Kaida was. Then he spotted her walking slowly toward him, a smile on her face.

"What happened with Wonderland?"

"Nothing much."

"So, what took you so long to get here?"

"I was here. You didn't need me. You had it under control."

He smiled. "I did?"

"Yes! Look at them. I told you they'd love you." She nodded toward the crowd, which was growing bigger now. A few of them were trying to get past the line of police who were taping off the area.

"What do I do now?"

"You can stay, talk to them. Help with the cleanup if they want help. Or, you can mysteriously disappear. They kinda love that, too."

He released a breath. "I got my weapon." The staff appeared in his hand, shiny black with little green lines running through it. It was as long as he was tall.

Kaida's smile fell. "Seriously? It's been like four months!"

He grinned. "I'm just as surprised as you."

She pouted, crossing her arms over her chest.

"So what happened with you?" he asked as he met her eyes.

"What do you mean?"

"You were upset, when you found me? Something was wrong."

She shook her head, eyes wide. "Nope I'm totally fine."

He knew she was lying.

Lycan dropped from the sky beside them, his blue hair windswept. "I missed the party?"

"Yep."

Kaida turned to him. "Apex got his weapon."

Lycan's eyes widened. "Really? That's awesome man." He fist bumped Apex.

"Lycan's happy for me," he said, unable to stop smiling.

"I'm happy for you! I'm just also *mad* about it." Kaida sighed, turning to Lycan. "Do you like cats?"

Lycan frowned. "Who doesn't like cats?"

Just like that, a switch flipped inside of Kaida as she stared up at Lycan. Her body lost all the tension and her lips quirked up. Somehow wolf boy fixed whatever was wrong with her with four words and a soft smile. Jasper grinned.

"You alright?" Lycan asked, voice low.

"I'm fine," she answered, staring at him with heart eyes.

"Okay. Guess since I'm here I'll go help them clear that glass. Who did this anyways?"

"New Bonded," Jasper answered. "I think they were moving shit with their mind? Throwing cars and stuff. Then they just disappeared."

Aetheria, probably, Pozi muttered.

Lycan nodded then moved away to speak with the cops.

"Go," Kaida said.

"Go where?"

"To the people, they are desperately trying to get your attention, Apex."

Jasper grinned as he slowly approached the crowd, feeling nervous.

You did so good, kid.

Thanks, Poz.

46
Three Heroes Walk Into a Tree

Lycan's heart twisted as the giant tree grew straight out of the library. Once a beautiful building, now completely destroyed. *I'm always too late. What good is rewinding five minutes if I'm always too late?*

Some things can not be undone. I'm sorry.

He soared in a circle around the tree, looking for Gaia. More trees were bursting to life through the concrete in the surrounding streets. He felt a pang at seeing one of the lion statues in pieces. He'd always loved those.

You are not supposed to engage with Gaia alone! Zeli hissed.

I know. He scanned the sky, urgency weighing on him. It had only been an hour since Apex fought the new Bonded and got his weapon. Surely they saw his text and were on the way...

Like an answer to a prayer Apex fell from the sky, black wings stretched out wide.

"Holy shit!" he yelled as he took in what was happening below.

"Ready for this, Bird Boy?"

"Always, Little Wolf."

"I'm taller than you!"

"Still little. In my heart." Apex cracked his knuckles as he got closer. "Where is she?"

"Not sure yet. Be on guard!"

"Aye aye, captain!"

They descended closer to the madness, each going one way. His whole body itched to run inside the library to help people. But they agreed, next time they saw Gaia, stopping her was the priority. Everything in him rebelled against it, wanting to save first and fight second.

The sooner we stop her the less people we'll need to save from her in the future.

Fair.

He followed the movement in the street. Gaia had to be close to be pulling up those roots. Apex had the same thought, swooping lower, till a vine whipped out and wrapped around his ankle. Apex's body was pulled from flight, slamming directly into the trunk of the tree.

Lycan caught the sound of giggling somewhere in the branches above. His heart raced at the thought of her touching Apex with that power as he angled himself beneath them.

"Fuck you!" Apex yelled as he sliced through the vine then fell.

Lycan caught him, steadying him on his board, wary of the wings. "How'd you do that?"

Apex flexed his hand, the fingertips pointed and sharp.

"Since when do you have claws?"

"Since whenever the fuck I want," he laughed. "Bitch is above us."

Lycan nodded, keeping one hand on Apex's shoulder, the other on his whip, ready.

"Catch me if you can!" the girl called.

"Oh, we will," Apex hissed under his breath. He met Lycan's eyes then nodded, before leaping off the board, wings spreading out as he flew up around the tree.

Lycan rose slower, weaving through the branches till he finally caught sight of the girl's green hair. He grinned as he moved toward her. She watched Apex circling above.

Careful.

He gripped his whip, pulling his arm back then flicking it toward her. It snapped around her wrist and she spun toward him, hissing angrily as her other hand moved up. Something silver flashed in his eyes before a blinding pain took him out.

Bellamy!

He groaned, blinking through the pain as he plummeted. Something crashed into him, air whipping past.

"Did she touch you? Lycan!" Kaida was screaming as everything stilled.

"Kai?"

"Are you okay?"

He blinked several times, trying to force his eyes to work as she came into focus. Her pink buns were frazzled, her mouth open in surprise.

"She hit me with something. Does she already have a weapon?"

No. That was a man-made crowbar.

Lovely. "She didn't touch me," he continued. "I'm fine."

Kaida was holding him in her arms on the sidewalk away from the fight.

"You caught me?"

"Always," she whispered. "Sorry I'm late."

"No, perfect timing."

She released a breath then helped him up as they looked back at the small forest. In a matter of minutes it had grown out of control.

"You good?" she asked.

"Yeah..." He almost asked if she was.

Looking at her face, the fear in him doubled. Having her back here, near Gaia, when she was barely recovered from last time... his instinct was to grab her and run the other way, everyone else be damned.

"Let's go," she said.

He sighed, pulling her onto his board and taking off into the trees.

Kaida held onto Lycan as they rose in the air, preparing to jump off once they were high enough.

Deep breaths, Ren.

She nodded. Showing up just in time to see Lycan falling... she couldn't think. Jasper was still over there with Gaia.

Steady. You are stronger now.

Am I?

Yes. Trust me. And trust yourself.

She wasn't sure she could. Last time she trusted herself she almost died. Almost abandoned all of them. Her dads. Jasper. Lycan... Zig. Her chest tightened as she formed a sword of light, gripping it in an iron fist. She jumped off Lycan's board, wings fanning out behind her as she glided around the big tree in the center.

She caught Apex's eyes. He looked horrified to see her there, his shiny new weapon disappearing mid-swing. Gaia laughed. The sound sent a shiver down Ren's spine. Gaia lunged at Apex with her crowbar. It slammed into Apex's shoulder, but he wasn't fazed, eyes darting between her and Kaida before he summoned the staff again and swung at the girl.

Gaia dodged then lifted the crowbar again and hooked it on his staff, yanking it back out of the tree, then turned her eyes on Kaida, smiling.

"Look who survived," she muttered.

"I'm a real tough bitch," Kaida replied, ignoring her fear. Her wings folded in as she climbed onto a branch and carefully walked closer to where Gaia crouched.

This is how I almost died.

It won't be like last time, Zig said. *You are not alone.*

"You sure about that? One itty bitty touch from me, and *poof.* I saw you fall. Watched your little wolf crying over your body..."

"At least I have someone to cry over me," Kaida hissed back, light dancing on her fingertips. "Is there anyone out there who gives a single shit about you? Cause I'm thinking if so you wouldn't be here, doing this."

Gaia's green eyes darkened, her smile falling. "You don't know what you're talking about." She lifted her crowbar defensively as Kaida inched closer.

"Oh, touchy subject? I must be right then..." She tried not to look past the girl to where Lycan crept up behind her, silver weaving in his hands. "So you come out here to destroy everything cause you weren't hugged enough as a kid? Boo fucking hoo."

Gaia growled as she straightened. Kaida smiled, not bothering to make a move as Lycan's cage was already forming around her and Gaia hadn't noticed.

"Killing people isn't the answer to your problems. It just makes *me* your problem. And you're about to learn why that's the biggest mistake you've *ever* made."

Gaia lunged just as the cage solidified around her, and her face slammed into the bars. She let out a pained scream. Kaida smiled, heart racing.

"You good?" Lycan asked.

"Yeah."

He nodded, but his eyes were still concerned.

"Eyy, we got her!" Apex appeared beside them, wings folding in so he could navigate through the branches. "Three heroes walk into a tree..."

Lycan rolled his eyes at Apex. "What should we do with her?"

Kaida frowned. "I don't know. She's contained for now. We should help the people below."

"You two go. I'll watch her."

Kaida nodded, giving one last look at Gaia before unfurling her wings and jumping out of the tree. With a sigh Apex followed.

Lycan looked back at Gaia. She slowly smiled as her hands gripped the bars.

"Just you and me now," she whispered.

He sat down, leaning against the trunk of the tree. He'd rather go down and help find survivors, but he was afraid of how many bodies they'd find buried in the wreckage. She'd taken out the library and several surrounding buildings with her trees. They feared her second power, but the damage from her first was *horrifying*.

"How did it feel?"

He glanced at her. "How did what feel?"

"Seeing her fall. Seeing her *broken*. Did it hurt?"

Lycan's whole body vibrated, blood boiling.

Easy, Bellamy.

"She should be dead."

He closed his eyes, trying to ignore her, but he couldn't shake the image in his mind. Kaida, body on the ground, barely breathing. In his bed, spasming, eyes burning gold.

"You love her. Everyone knows it. No matter how much you deny it to the cameras. We all *see*. And just like that." She snapped her fingers. "So *easy,* too. One touch. Next time I'll make sure I get her heart."

Lycan growled, his whip forming in his hand as he flicked it straight through the bars. It wrapped around Gaia's neck, pulling her tight against them. He stood slowly as her eyes widened in a panic.

"You ever touch her again," he whispered, "I'll kill you."

Bellamy, relax.

Don't tell me to relax. You don't understand.

Bellamy—

You're immortal! You'll never lose Zig. No one can ever take him from you. This is one thing you won't ever understand.

Are you trying to kill her? Zeli asked, voice calm.

He let out a breath and slowly pulled the whip loose from Gaia's neck. She doubled over, coughing. He felt sick, seeing that red line around her throat. He turned and sat back down.

"Don't fucking talk to me again."

Gaia continued to cough. He closed his eyes.

If you want to kill her, you commit. If you do not...

Right I know. I got it.

Kaida is okay, Zeli continued. *You know that.*

I know.

It didn't matter. He almost lost her. And Gaia was why. His body was so tense with anger and adrenaline. After a moment he just felt guilty for snapping at Zeli though.

It is alright, she whispered.

No, I shouldn't speak to you like that. I'm sorry.

Do not think I can't understand loss, Bellamy Grey. Every Bond before you is dead. Gone.

Bellamy sucked in a breath.

Clara Carter. Stardust. She was my last, before you. That loss still burns inside me. I miss her as I miss them all. As I will miss you one day.

He nodded.

I know this is hard, but you should consider how dangerous Gaia is.

I'm very aware.

Then what do you intend to do with her? Zeli sighed. *Bellamy, she won't stay in your cage forever. A real prison can not contain her. The only solution...*

Bellamy swallowed.

You have to think about these things. I'm sorry.

He sighed, shaking his head. *I'm just a kid. I can't hold the law in my hands like that.*

You already do. You did for Vendetta.

He wanted to say that was different, but, was it?

His cage melted to mist. Lycan jumped up but Gaia was already running, up one branch then leaping to the next before he was on his feet.

Shit shit shit.

Stay focused.

He kept his thoughts and eyes locked on the short girl in green as she ran ahead of him. He closed the distance fast. As he reached out to grab her a thick vine swung around, wrapping tightly around his neck. He didn't falter, a knife of silver forming in his fingers. He cut the vine in seconds. Gaia looked furious as she spun and ran.

Kaida flinched as chunks of concrete flew into the air, a new tree bursting out.

Damn.

She ran, wings spreading out as she jumped into the air. She saw movement through the leaves of a tree and dove, landing on a thick branch and pulled her wings back in. Gaia was running, Lycan right behind her, silver ropes in hand.

Vines reached out, trying to grab Kaida, but her sword sliced through each one. Gaia's angry face got closer with every swing. The girl grabbed one of the vines then jumped out of the tree, swinging down toward the ground.

Kaida's wings fanned out as she jumped after her.

A blur of pink whooshed past.

"Sorry I'm late!" Parody shouted as she landed on the ground beside Gaia. Before the shorter girl could react, Parody touched her chest. Gaia's eyes widened and she fell to her knees in the street.

"She's at half energy!" Parody called as Lycan landed beside her. He made a tall box of silver, and nodded. "Get in."

Parody saluted him as she stepped in the box and he closed it on her so she could detransform discreetly.

Kaida rushed forward, sword steady in her hand as Lycan snuck up behind Gaia once again. His silver ropes snaked out around her wrists, pinning her down. Apex landed beside them, staff in hand as he approached. Gaia looked at the silver around her, then stared up at Kaida.

"You gonna do it?"

Kaida's hands shook.

What do I do?

What do you want to do? Zig asked.

"You're a fucking coward, aren't you?" Gaia spat.

I should... I should...

You don't have to.

She'll keep doing this. Keep killing. It's the only way to stop her, isn't it?

Zig didn't answer.

Isn't it?

What do you want to do, Ren?

Her resolve faltered. *I...*

A girl fell from the sky, landing beside her. Kaida turned to the newcomer as the street filled with a soft gray mist. Everything stilled. She couldn't move.

What.

It's Valaries. Lycan called her Vapor?

Oh no.

The panic at not being able to move, not even blink, was overwhelming. Vapor took in the scene, looking utterly surprised by the wreckage and the trees.

"Jeeze, Gaia, I said *distraction*. Not destruction." She *tsked* as she walked up to Gaia. "Was she about to kill you?"

Vapor's purple eyes moved to Kaida. She reached out a hand, brushing a loose bit of hair away from Kaida's face. Ren wanted to flinch, but she couldn't move. The panic threatened to overload her.

"Damn. You're *way* prettier in person." She let out a sad sigh. "But don't kill my friend here, kay? She's the only one I got."

She walked around behind Gaia, taking in the silver ropes, tying her to Lycan. Then her eyes moved up.

"I guess I can't blame you this time, but I'll be taking her now."

Mist seemed to coalesce around her, before taking the shape of a large cat, like a cheetah. It stood there a moment as Vapor ran a hand over its head. Then it walked forward and bit down on Lycan's ropes. The mist cat chewed through them in seconds. They puffed away before they could hit the ground.

Vapor let out a soft sigh as she awkwardly lifted Gaia's frozen body into her arms. Then the mist cat shifted, changing shape and size until a giant eagle stood beside her instead. The bird knelt for her and Vapor climbed up on its back.

"Till next time!" She called, flashing Kaida a smile.

The giant mist eagle rose into the air, carrying them away.

Kaida waited, expecting the stasis to stop working now that she was away, but it held.

How long are we gonna be like this?

A few minutes. I'm sorry.

Several hours later, Kaida, Lycan, Apex, and Parody stood in the street, surrounded by some of the search and rescue team that arrived after the fight. Night had long since fallen and the final count was in. Over two hundred people were dead. Kaida felt numb. In a single day, a single *hour*, Gaia killed more people than Vendetta had in six months. And Kaida could have ended it. The moment was there, right in front of her...

That is not who you are.

Maybe it should be.

PART FOUR

STILL FALLING

The balance of living two lives took a toll on many of the Bonded, so much so that some retired their Bonds. A process, I'm told, was quite difficult for both human and Xyri. It would seem those who Bonded but rarely used their powers in the spotlight had the easiest time of it.

-Xyri Bonds: Life and Death

47
Echo Fever

"Are you okay?" Simon asked as they walked down the hall, his arm around her shoulders.

"Fine," Ren mumbled. It was a lie and she was in a daze. At least she was aware, but she couldn't pull herself out of it. The dead eyes of every body she carried in the night were imprinted in her mind.

"Ren? What's wrong?" Simon came to a stop, pulling her to the side of the hall.

"I can't stop thinking about what happened yesterday."

Simon's face softened. "I know." He pulled her into his arms, holding her tightly. She'd had about ten missed calls from him by the time she got home last night. Everyone had been in a panic, trying to find their loved ones. She'd lied to her dads, once again. They thought she'd been at Jasper's the whole evening.

"It's gonna be okay," he whispered.

"How do you know?"

He pulled back, meeting her eyes. "The heroes will take care of it."

"They were there and they didn't stop her. Didn't save anyone."

"That's not true, they helped a lot of people last night. It was all over the news. And, I mean, it took time for them to get Vendetta, but they *did*. Trust me, they'll take care of it. They just need time."

She wanted to argue. People were dying, there wasn't time for them to take their time. Instead, she just nodded.

"I got something that will get your mind off it," he continued with a grin as Jasper walked up.

"What?" she asked as she pulled away and forced a smile at Jasper. He forced one right back, his eyes haunted.

"I want it to be a surprise."

Ren frowned as they started walking again. "When do I get this surprise?"

"Friday."

Jasper laughed. "You can't tell her you have a surprise then also tell her she has to wait all week for it. She'll be panicking the entire time."

"Okay okay. So, my band has another gig. It's an all-ages venue this time and... I want to bring you."

Ren stopped in her tracks. "I actually get to see you play? For real?"

Simon started to smile. "For real."

"That's so exciting! Wait, can Jasper come?"

"Yeah, of course." He swallowed. "Actually, invite all your friends. The more people there to hype us up the more likely the venue might bring us back."

"I can't believe I get to see you play!" She seized that emotion, putting all her focus on it and burying her shame and guilt underneath.

Simon's smile widened. "We're just opening for other bands, we only get to play a few songs. Not that impressive."

"Shut up, it's *so* impressive!"

"So, you wanna come?"

Ren gave him a flat stare. "Of course I do. Jasper, you're coming, right?"

"Obviously."

She released a breath, glad she had something to look forward to at least.

"And you..." Simon started, watching her intently. "Still haven't listened to us yet?"

Ren shook her head. "I haven't, but not because I don't want to!" She grabbed his hand. "Just been so busy, but I'm gonna start listening tonight. I wanna know all the words before your show."

Simon smiled, a slight blush in his cheeks. "You're incredible, you know that?"

Ren didn't have to force that smile.

When she sat down at lunch she had several missed texts from Ocean.

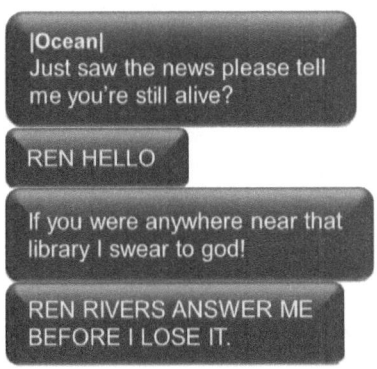

|Ocean|
Just saw the news please tell me you're still alive?

REN HELLO

If you were anywhere near that library I swear to god!

REN RIVERS ANSWER ME BEFORE I LOSE IT.

I'm gonna call your dads and if you DIED me calling to ask is gonna UPSET THEM!!!

|Ren|
Hi I'm alive! Sorry sorry! Been in class. I was with Jasper, nowhere near exploding trees.

And the lies continued.

After school she couldn't even kiss Simon for one minute before Dad came outside the bakery, eyes wide as he stared at them. Simon backed up three steps and smiled nervously.

"See ya later."

"Uh, okay." She turned on Dad, confused. "Hi. Why are you—"

"You're late."

"I'm..." She frowned. "I'm not late."

"You're usually in by three forty and it's three forty-two."

She would have laughed if she had any humor left in her. "Dad, I was kissing my boyfriend. I was right *here*. I am not late. What's wrong?"

He sighed and put a hand on her shoulder, leading her inside. "Listen, I need you home when you're supposed to be home, okay?"

"Why the sudden—"

"Did you know Mari was there?"

Ren stopped, eyes darting between Dad and Marigold, who stood behind the counter.

"Where?"

"At the library," Dad continued, his eyes hard. "Her and Ivy, not ten minutes before everything went to hell."

Her heart raced as she looked at her cousin. "You... were there?"

Mari nodded slowly. "Scary to think, if we hadn't left when we did..." She shrugged.

"You understand?" Dad said softly. She met his eyes and saw the fear in them. "You *can't* be late. You can't be missing. I need to know where you are, okay? The way things are in the city right now I just..."

Ren nodded slowly.

"I'm gonna be scary overprotective dad mode and you just, have to deal with it."

Ren followed him through the back. "I wasn't late. Or missing. *But* I understand."

He released a breath then pulled her into his arms. "Love you, kid."

"Love you more. I'm gonna go do my homework. In my room, very safe."

He rolled his eyes at her.

As she trudged up the stairs she wondered how in the hell she'd convince him to let her go to Simon's concert now.

Later that night after dinner she was alone in her room, trying to sleep. But part of her was afraid to even close her eyes, knowing Gaia could strike again. So she texted Lycan.

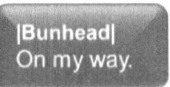

|Bunhead|
You and me?

|Starface|
You and me.

Spruce street?

|Bunhead|
On my way.

She soared through the air above the city lights, tense at every siren she heard. But not every siren was an emergency for Kaida.

When she landed Lycan was already there, stretched out flat on his back. She smiled as she walked over and laid down beside him.

He didn't say anything. Neither did she, but some of her tension eased. Her eyes followed a plane overhead and she idly wondered if she could outfly it.

"We did the best we could," he finally whispered.

"It wasn't good enough."

"I know."

"I should have..." She closed her eyes.

His hand wrapped around hers, holding it gently. "We aren't killers, Kai."

"You killed Vendetta. I killed his zombies..." So why couldn't she do this?

"This is different."

"How?"

"The zombies were already dead. And, Vendetta was already dying when I dealt that blow."

"Two hundred people..."

"I know."

"What are we supposed to *do?*" she asked, rolling her head to the side.

He turned, meeting her eyes. "We stop her. By any means necessary."

She sucked in a breath. "You and me?"

"Always."

"I understood Vendetta, after," she mumbled softly. "I don't understand Gaia."

"Chaos, right? Isn't that what she told you?"

She nodded. "But... I just... so much murder, for *what?*"

"Some people really are just... insane."

"I guess." She squeezed his hand.

They fell silent for a time, just staring at the sky, hands held between them.

"I was supposed to be on a date," he mumbled after a while. "When it happened."

"Oh. So..." She swallowed. "How's that going?"

"I don't know." He sighed. "I like her. But, she doesn't really get me? It's not her fault though. I'm not exactly easy to get."

"Oh shut up."

He turned to her, frowning. "I don't get her either. But that's also my fault. I'm still *so* bad at people."

"Stop. You're *so* easy to get. And you get *me.* Better than most." She smiled. "It just takes some time, ya know?"

A smile slowly formed on his face. "Thanks." He sighed and looked back up at the sky. "Wanna do a sweep then call it a night?"

"Sure."

On Friday Ren was somewhat close to feeling like herself again, so long as she wasn't in the suit or thinking about the hundreds of dead people that she couldn't save. She tried focusing only on Simon when she rushed home with Jasper after school to get ready for his concert.

Ren only started listening to his band a few days back, but she was *obsessed.* They were called Echo Fever, and she had plans to make shirts for the show.

"You're making me one too?" Jasper asked as he sat on the floor across from her while she laid out two black shirts and pulled out some glow paint markers.

"Of course." She glanced up at him. "You don't want to?"

"Nah, it's cool." He smiled then laid on his stomach and held his hand out for a marker. "Am I allowed to help?"

"This one's yours." She handed him a green marker. "Go nuts."

"Is his music actually good?"

"Yes! Have you not listened?" She shook her head and pulled it up on her phone, playing her favorite one so far.

Jasper sat back and listened. "Oh, fuck. That's annoying."

"What is?"

"His voice. It's actually good."

Ren smiled and went back to work with her markers.

"He has thirty-two thousand monthly listeners?"

She looked up. Jasper was staring at his phone, wide eyed.

"They're *very* good," Ren said proudly. "I can't wait to see them live."

"What if he sucks live? A lot of artists can't sing worth shit live."

Ren rolled her eyes.

While her shirts dried, she painted her nails neon green, then did her makeup. Jasper picked some straight cuffed dark gray jeans for her to wear, and she paired them with black boots, but she switched the laces for neon green ones.

"You look great," Jasper said as she stared at herself in the mirror.

"Yeah?" She felt self-conscious as she tucked some hair behind her ear. "Will Simon like it?"

"Why wouldn't he?"

Ren frowned. The shirts looked like a child made them, with the band name written out in big bold letters, and little lines and dots around the shirt. Not to mention she'd completed the look with a glow stick necklace and several glow bracelets. She thought it would look cool, but now she just thought it was silly.

"Ren, you look amazing," Jasper continued. He was wearing the bracelets, too. So maybe it wasn't *that* silly. "Be you, and if Simon doesn't like that, then fuck him."

She sighed and let Jasper lead her downstairs.

"You're staying with her the whole time?" Dad asked when they entered the kitchen.

Ren stared up at Dad, half worried he'd change his mind. It took her two days to get him to let her go. He only said yes because Jasper would be with her.

"Glued to her side," Jasper answered.

"We can stay for the whole show, right?" she asked as they started down the stairs.

Dad sighed. "How late is it?"

"Uh..." Ren glanced at Jasper.

"Around eleven probably?" he replied.

"Alright. You can stay. I'll pick you up when it's over."

"Thanks, Dad."

"Yeah, thanks Daddy."

They were quiet on the way to the show and her stomach was twisting into knots. She was meeting Simon's bandmates tonight. She'd technically met two of them already, but only for a minute. The band were his *best* friends. She needed to make a good impression.

"Be safe, okay? No drinking. No drugs. If you need me to pick you up early, let me know. I'm free all night."

"Yes, love you," she said as they got out of the car.

There were already people lined up outside the doors of the venue. She tried to ignore her nausea and texted Simon to let him know they were outside.

A minute later Simon came out, a wide smile on his face. He was dressed in all black, but his usual leather jacket was swapped out for a longer, more rugged jacket that hung to his knees.

"Holy shit, babe! You look so cute!" He pulled her into his arms, holding her tightly.

"Thanks," she mumbled into his chest. He smelled *so* good.

"She's anxious about meeting your friends," Jasper said from behind her.

"Am not!" She pulled away from Simon to glare at Jasper. He grinned.

"You already met Cam and Kit." He smiled. "It'll be fine, come on." He grabbed her hand and led them inside.

"Pretty cool, getting to go in before everyone else," Jasper whispered.

Ren nodded as Simon led them through the main venue space, taking her right up to the stage.

"This is where you'll be when the show starts, if that's cool with you?"

She took in the stage, then looked up at Simon, doing a double take.

"Oh my god."

He frowned. "What?"

"Your... eyeliner..." She swallowed.

"Oh. Is it bad?"

She shook her head. "No no no. No. It is... very very good." She blushed.

"*Really?*" Simon bit his lip. "You like it?"

Ren nodded, unable to speak. His blue eyes were always beautiful, but the black eyeliner made them really *pop*.

"Wow, you made her malfunction," Jasper said. "She's right though, looks good."

Simon's smile widened. "Damn. I usually only wear it for shows but maybe I should wear it more often if this is how you're gonna react."

Ren put a hand over her face, heart racing.

Simon laughed. "Come on, gotta meet Allie. She's more excited to meet you than to play today."

He pulled her through a door and down a hall, then into another room.

"Guys, this is my girlfriend, Ren. And her friend, Jasper."

"Ren!" A girl with long brown hair jumped up off the couch in the corner. "It's so nice to meet you!" She had a round rosy face, wide curves, and was almost as tall as Simon. "I'm Allie."

"Nice to meet you," Ren said softly.

She was wearing a thin black hoodie under a denim vest that was *covered* in colorful pins, paired with tight black leggings.

"Simon talks about you *all* the time, but he wouldn't let us meet you—"

"Cause he's embarrassed of us," Cam said.

"Damn right," Simon replied.

Cam squinted at her. He looked so chill in his striped sweater and grey cargo pants compared to Simon, with his dramatic coat, and Allie's fancy makeup. Ren couldn't get over how beautiful it was, oranges and pinks blended together on her eyelids, like a sunset, with a white eyeliner in the shape of flower petals coming out of the corner of her eyes.

"But I already met her and she thinks I'm *awesome,*" Cam continued. "¿bien?"

Ren giggled. "Definitivamente asombroso."

"Well, I've been *begging,*" Allie said, rolling her eyes. "He's making us play a song abo—"

"Stop, no, shut it." Simon glared at her. "Allie is a liar don't listen to anything she says. Ever."

"Rude."

Simon shook his head. "And you remember Kit."

Ren turned. Kit wore a black and purple plaid vest over a black tee, with black skinny jeans tucked into his purple high tops. He jingled as he moved, wearing more jewelry than the other three combined.

He saluted Ren. "Pretty girl, who's probably too good for you."

"Don't ever talk to him, actually," Simon continued.

Ren laughed. "It's nice to see you boys again. And very nice to meet you, Allie."

"She's gonna like me most," Allie said with a wide grin as she grabbed Ren's arm, pulling her away from Simon.

"I know," Simon said, resigned.

"He seems really happy now," Allie whispered once they were on the other side of the room. "I've been dying to meet you. He's just been nervous."

Ren nodded.

"I promise we're so chill."

"So, what do you do in the band?" Ren asked as she looked around the room. Jasper was chatting with Simon and Cam across from them, too quiet for her to hear.

"Drums. Cam's guitar, Kit is bass and vocals. And of course Simon is guitar, lead vocals. Sometimes keys."

"You sing, don't you?" Ren asked. She was sure she heard a girl's voice in some of the songs.

"Just backing vocals, sometimes." Allie smiled. "Also I *love* the shirts, that's so sick. I don't think I've ever seen someone make a shirt for us before."

Ren beamed. "Cool." She looked back at Simon. He had his elbow on Cameron's shoulder as he watched her with a smile.

"You done hogging my girl?" he called.

"Nope," Allie replied cheerfully.

Simon rolled his eyes and Cam laughed.

Kit walked over, a sly smile on his face. "You know," he said in a low voice. "At our last two shows there were all these girls, *older* girls, like in their twenties, just trying to throw themselves at Simon."

Ren's stomach dropped.

"But he didn't even *notice*," Kit continued, voice lowering. "All he talked about all damn night was *you*. Even to the girls trying to get his number."

"Really?"

"He's head over heels," Allie whispered.

"He's *obsessed*," Kit added.

"You'll see."

"See what?"

"What are you assholes whispering about?" Simon asked, crossing the room. He grabbed Ren's hand and pulled her back against him.

"They're talking about how much you like me," Ren replied.

Simon looked down at her and her heart raced. She was sure he'd never looked better than he did right then.

"Well, that's true." He kissed her softly.

"Alright, stop being cute. We go on soon," Cam said.

Simon sighed. "Alright, I'll take them back out."

He grabbed her hand and nodded to Jasper then they went back into the main space. They stopped in front of the stage again.

"I'll be standing right *there* when we come on," he said.

"So, I get the best spot in the place," she replied with a smile.

"You are the best spot in the place." He kissed her again. "I can't believe you're here," he whispered. "I'm so happy."

"Me too." She couldn't stop smiling. Something about seeing Simon in this setting, he seemed so *himself*. So genuine.

He gave her another kiss. "Stay with her," he said to Jasper.
"Of course."

Ren watched him go then she leaned over, putting her head on
Jasper's shoulder as people started to make their way inside. Soon
enough there was a crowd of people standing around them.

"I got you," Jasper whispered.

She nodded, releasing a breath as the smell of alcohol reached her
from somewhere nearby.

Finally, the lights went out and Echo Fever came on stage.
Somehow, Simon was even more attractive as he stood there in his
long black coat, blue guitar in hand. He walked up to the mic and
grinned right at her.

"We're Echo Fever," he said softly. Then they launched right into
the first song.

Ren's mouth fell open. She was sure he'd be good, but she thought
maybe he sounded even *better* than the recorded songs.

48
Heart Eyes

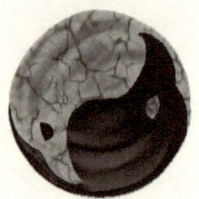

Jasper watched Ren watch Simon. She seemed in awe. But even he couldn't deny how good Simon sounded. He had an incredible voice, and the music was good, even if some of the lyrics seemed depressing. Ren was absolutely enraptured, staring up at him with heart eyes while Simon sang right at her.

She seemed to forget all her anxieties. The way Simon looked at her, as if she was the only one in the room. At least she was happy. That was all Jasper cared about.

Though he was sure he still preferred her with Lycan, there was nothing to be done about that. She wouldn't admit her feelings, or break the rules. And, she had Simon now.

They went straight into the second song while Jasper's eyes moved across each member of the band, annoyed by how hot they all were. The big girl on drums was especially pretty. Her drums were a neon pink with the band logo on the front. The words ECHO FEVER on a black background in a mix of blues, greens, purples, and pinks that bled into each other, on top of a colorful lightning bolt.

The boys looked so good, too. He idly wondered if they were straight as the song faded out. The Mexican boy seemed quiet and moody, but he had pretty eyes, and held his green guitar with confidence. The other one *had* to be some kind of queer, with his split hair, black with a streak of bleach, and that purple guitar.

Simon stared at the crowd for a moment. "This one's a cover, so if you know it, sing along."

Ren gasped after the first word and grabbed Jasper's arm. "This is August Rain!"

"It is?"

"Love story!" Her smile was wide, face red, as she looked back up at Simon. His eyes were glued to Ren.

Jasper realized he did know the song as it continued, and sang along.

When it got to the bridge Simon swung his guitar behind his back, grabbed the mic, then knelt down in front of Ren. He sang directly at her. For a moment all the music stopped as he continued singing, showcasing just how good his vocals were. He reached out, lifting Ren's chin, going silent right before the word *ring*, then he kissed her quickly before jumping up as the music came back in.

Ren's cheeks were as red as Zig's scales. Everyone in the crowd seemed shocked, staring at Ren in confusion.

"She's his girlfriend!" Jasper yelled.

They went into the next song like nothing happened. Jasper had to admit it was so ballsy. Ren was never gonna recover from that. *I wouldn't either, if a guy did that to me.*

Simon paused before the next song, somehow looking hotter now that he was sweatier.

"This is a brand new song, not out yet. But I have to play it, since my girl is here tonight." He locked eyes with Ren, smiling at her before they started.

It was very clearly a love song *about* Ren. Her blush deepened as she listened, starry eyed. Jasper had to admit it was cute, but he hadn't realized things with her and Simon were serious enough for him to be writing things like that about her.

They finished with a faster song, then reminded everyone to check them out. When the lights came back on, they started moving their equipment as the next band, Residual Bear, started setting up. When they disappeared into the back, Ren let out a breath.

"Wow."

"Yeah."

Simon came back out on stage a moment later then jumped right down into the crowd, grabbing Ren and pulling her into an intense kiss. People around them cheered. Simon was grinning when he pulled back. "If you wanna meet us we'll be back by the merch tables!" he yelled.

Then he started pulling Ren through the crowd. She grabbed Jasper's hand in a panic, pulling him along. He didn't mind crowds, but Ren did, so he let her drag him away.

Simon took them to the side of the room where his friends were waiting and they started talking about the energy of the crowd. Ren looked nervous as Simon kept his arm around her shoulders. After a few minutes she excused herself to go to the bathroom, so Jasper took his chance and pulled Simon aside.

"What's up?"

"Ren's not gonna tell you this, but she doesn't like being in crowds," Jasper said. "She's super anxious right now. So, if you don't have to stay, maybe you could get her out of here?"

"Oh." He nodded. "Yeah, yeah I can do that. Thanks for telling me."

"No problem."

He didn't really think Simon was right for Ren, but Ren was his whole world, and right now, she liked Simon. So Jasper needed to try. If he suggested she leave early, Ren would definitely refuse. But if Simon suggested it... he grinned when Ren came back and Simon pulled her aside.

Ren smiled up at Simon, assuming he was going to kiss her when he leaned down, but instead he whispered in her ear.

"Wanna get out of here?"

"What?"

"I know it's a lot. The crowd, the noise. We can go, if you want."

"It's fine. Don't you have to stay?"

He shook his head. "Come on, we can get some ice cream, then I'll take you home."

"You're sure?"

He didn't respond, already telling his friends they were heading out. She grabbed Jasper's arm.

"Simon wants to leave, wanna come with?"

"I might stay."

"Really?"

"The next band is called Optimism Bagel. I gotta see what that's about."

Ren giggled. "Okay. Be smart. No weird decisions."

"Yes, mom."

She glared. "Text me when you go home."

"Will do."

"You *will* go home after this and not... out?"

"Promise."

Ren hugged him then let Simon pull her through the crowd toward the exit. Once outside she relaxed, breathing in deep as Simon walked her down to where his car was parked.

"We didn't have to leave."

He gave her a look. "I could tell you were uncomfortable. It's totally fine."

She smiled.

"So... did you like our set?"

"Are you kidding? It was amazing."

"Yeah?" He smiled. "Even the very forward song I wrote about you?"

Ren blushed. "*Especially* that."

Simon didn't say anything as they got in the car, but his smile stayed in place as he grabbed her hand, holding it while he drove.

"Where are we going?"

"I promised you ice cream."

"Oh. Okay." She couldn't stop smiling as she texted her dads that she left early with Simon and would be home soon.

Simon's smile was stuck in place. He almost felt like a different person. "I'm so happy you came tonight. Getting to play for you..."

"It was amazing. Like, actually *so* incredible. I loved every second. And I think... maybe that's the most romantic thing that's ever happened to me."

Simon was actually blushing.

"I can't wait to see you play again," she continued.

Simon let out a breath as he parked. "Fuck, Ren. You're killing me right now."

"What?"

He was shaking his head as he got out of the car and walked around to her side. He pulled her into his arms, hugging her and swaying back and forth. She giggled as she slid her arms around him.

"This has been the best night," he whispered, then kissed the top of her head.

"I hope you know I wanna come to every show from here on out."

"Front and center, baby," he muttered as he led her down to the shop.

He bought her a double scoop of mint chip and a cup of rocky road for himself, then they went back out and ate in his car.

"Play some music," she said, sitting back with her cone.

"What kind of music?"

"*Your* music, obviously."

Simon was grinning ear to ear as he pulled it up. He put on her favorite one, Anxiety.

Simon's voice filled the car and she was still so surprised by how *good* he sounded. She had to force herself to stop staring at him while she listened and ate her ice cream.

By the time he was driving her home they'd listened to every song he played at the show, aside from the cover and the new one.

"I hate this part," he said as he parked down the street from the bakery and turned the music down.

"The part where you drop me off?"

"The part where I have to say goodbye."

She checked the time. *"Technically*, I was gonna be allowed to stay out till eleven tonight and it's only nine forty-five. We could just... sit and talk for a bit before I have to go in?"

"God yes. Wanna sit outside?"

She nodded and they got out, walking toward the bakery, then they sat on the curb. Simon put his arm around her and she leaned into him.

"This was literally the best night," he whispered, mouth close to her forehead.

"I love seeing you like this," she said as she tilted her head up to meet his eyes.

"Like what?"

"Happy."

He was so cute, smiling at her like that. She leaned up and kissed him, melting into the feeling of him as he put his hand behind her neck.

"I've never felt this way before," he whispered. "You're so special, Ren."

She blushed. How did a girl respond to that? "You seem so surprised, that I like the music. That I liked the show."

He sighed. "I was so scared you wouldn't."

"Why? Cause of your ex?"

He nodded.

"She really didn't like it?" Ren didn't understand. Even if Simon's genre of music wasn't her thing, why wouldn't she go to the shows to support him? He sounded amazing and looked even better.

Simon stared down at his boots. "She didn't take it seriously. Music is like, all that I am? And she thought it was just a silly hobby. Thought I spent too much time on it, not enough on her, even though *she* blew me off all the time. She said it wouldn't lead anywhere, never came to shows. Just hated all of it."

Ren frowned. "Not a single show?"

He smiled sadly. "She came to one show. And she left during the second song."

Ren opened her mouth, horrified. "You're kidding?"

He shook his head. "I was afraid to share this with you because of her. But... Ren, you're literally *so* incredible. I mean, look at your shirt. I can't believe you did that."

"It's not dumb?" She looked down, glow sticks still shining against her wrists. "I worried maybe your friends would think it was silly or something."

"You showed up a hundred percent. And you look *so* fucking cute." He kissed her again. "I'm so happy I'm with you."

"Me too." Blush burning in her cheeks, she pulled off one of the glow stick bracelets and slid it onto his wrist. She wasn't sure why she did it, but he grinned.

"Can I ask you a question?" he asked softly.

"Yeah."

"Am I your first boyfriend?"

"Second."

He nodded.

"Funny story actually..."

"Yeah?"

"Jasper was my first boyfriend."

Simon pulled back, frowning. "You dated Jasper?"

"We were thirteen going on fourteen," she replied. "And we like, immediately had crushes on each other and just started going out. It took us three months to figure out there wasn't really a *spark*. Like, we had fun, we liked each other. But there was no romance to it. So we broke up, stayed friends. Became best friends. It like, *barely* counts as having a boyfriend. Dating you is very different. But maybe that's just cause I'm older now?" She let out a breath. "Simon?"

He nodded slowly. "Didn't know Jasper was your ex."

She tilted her head. "Were you even listening? We were kids who made out for a few weeks. It wasn't serious. He's not my ex. He's my best friend. And *you*," she said, grinning, "are my boyfriend."

Simon smiled again. "I love being your boyfriend."

"You do?"

His answer was another kiss.

"When do I get to see you play again?" she asked when he pulled back.

"Don't know. No shows lined up yet."

"But you'll tell me about the next one? And I can come?"

He smiled. "I want you at every show."

Her phone buzzed with a call from her dad and she sighed. "Hello."

"I thought you said you'd be home soon," Dad said.

"Oh, I am home! I'm still outside, but I'm here."

"You are?"

"Yeah. Simon and I are just sitting here, talking. Can I stay out a little longer? I swear I'm right here. You can probably see us from a window."

Dad sighed. "Ten minutes, then you come in."

"Thanks."

"Dads mad?" Simon asked as she hung up.

"Nope, I can stay out ten more minutes."

He smiled, putting his arm around her again. She leaned into him.

"So, exactly how many girlfriends have you had before me?" She tried not to feel self-conscious asking that question.

"Two."

She released a breath. "Only two?"

He laughed. "What were you expecting?"

"I don't know. You're older. Hot *senior* boy. I assumed at least like five."

His laugh continued. "I've dated two girls before you, so you're number three. Though there was one or two I really liked, but never dated, if that matters."

Ren nodded.

"Why?"

She shrugged. "I told you about my past relationship, if you could call it that."

"Speaking of..." He was staring at her intently, smile gone. "How are you doing on the whole Bellamy thing? You liked him a lot before you met me."

Ren leaned back, looking up at the sky. "I haven't really thought of him like that in a long time."

"So, you like me more now?" His lips curved a little and she got lost in his eyes.

"So much more." She kissed him.

"That's good, considering I confessed my feelings in front of a crowd of like a hundred and fifty people tonight."

Ren blushed. "You haven't recorded that song yet?"

He shook his head.

"But you will?"

"Eventually."

"I wanna hear it when you do."

"Yeah?" His smile was back, the one that went all the way to his eyes and made her feel dizzy.

"*Yeah.*"

He laughed then kissed her again.

Ren's face hurt from smiling so much. "You know... I sorta felt... trapped, I guess? In feelings I... had for other people."

"Bellamy?" he asked.

"I felt like I could never tell him, it'd make things weird or whatever. I was just, trapped. And scared. And... I'm not with you."

Simon smiled.

"I feel so free with you. I didn't know..." She blushed, eyes burning a little. "Didn't know it could be like this. I can just tell you I like you. I can want to kiss you and *actually* kiss you and not... have a panic attack about it."

He frowned at that.

"I just... I love feeling like this. With you."

He cupped her cheek. "The day I met you I was having the shittiest day."

"You were?"

"Yeah. Like, everything that could go wrong *did* go wrong. I was in the worst mood, couldn't *wait* to be done with that fucking day." He let out a breath. "And then that book hit my foot. And," he laughed, "it annoyed me."

Ren held his gaze, transfixed.

"But I grabbed it. And when I looked up... there you were. And suddenly, my day wasn't so bad anymore. In fact, it was perfect." His smile widened. "The best day. Walking you home, over and over... Ren, I fell every step of the way. Still falling now."

Ren pulled him close. "Please don't stop."

"Never."

Her heart raced as she stared into his blue eyes. "I still can't believe you wrote that song for me. And how talented you are. Like... it's *unfair*, honestly."

Simon looked down, a blush stark in his pale cheeks.

"I mean it."

"I know you do." He met her eyes. "You still haven't told me what you wanna do," he said.

"Do about what?"

He laughed. "With your life? Like, what you're passionate about. Last time I asked you didn't answer. But you know how much I care about my music now, I wanna know yours."

"I... don't know," she answered, honest. That's what she told him last time, too.

"How can you not know?" He shook his head. "I think you're just too embarrassed to tell me. But you don't have to be!"

Ren sighed. She really didn't know. She'd never had a consistent dream of what her future might look like. And she was kinda grateful for that, considering any dreams she had would have died the moment Zig Bonded her. Her future was Kaida. For as long as she lived, she would be Kaida. Using her powers for good, helping people... she closed her eyes, thinking about all those who died last week. All she wanted to do was help people. But no one would ever know that Kaida was Ren. Except for Jasper.

"I really don't know," she finally replied. "I've never had a thing like you with your music."

Simon sighed. "Come on, you can tell me. I *swear* I won't make fun of you. I just wanna be a supportive boyfriend."

She smiled. "I don't have any secret dreams I'm hiding from you. But if I come across one, I promise to tell you," she said.

"*Ren.*"

She jumped, turning to see both her dads in the doorway, staring down at them.

"I said ten minutes, it's been twenty."

"Oh. Sorry." She looked from them to Simon, then back. "Five more minutes? Please?"

Dad sighed but Dare nodded. "Five minutes, no more."

She nodded as they closed the door.

"They really hate me, huh?" Simon asked, leaning back.

"They don't know you. Not yet."

"That glare is intense."

"Forget about it. Hey, stop frowning. I want your smile back."

He laughed, the smile spreading across his face. "This smile?"

"That's the one." She leaned in, kissing him again, getting lost in the moment.

"You should probably go in," Simon whispered against her lips. "Before they kill me."

"Yeah, okay."

He stood with a sigh and helped her up. She slid her arms around him and he held her, swaying a bit.

"Literally the best night ever, Ren. Thank you."

She pulled back, smiling up at him. "I had so much fun."

"Miss you already."

She giggled as she opened the door, waving awkwardly as it closed.

You're really happy tonight.

Yeah. Tonight was good.

I'm glad. It's nice to see you like this again.

49
Hoax

Ren made her way upstairs, finding Dad and Dare in the kitchen.
"How was your night?" Dare asked.

"*Really* good." She frowned. "Are you mad I left the show early?"

"No. Jasper texted and told us about fifteen minutes before you did, though."

"Oh." She grinned.

Dad shook his head, but he was smiling. "Remember what we talked about? I have to know where you are."

"I'm sorry."

"Did you eat?" he asked, tone softening.

"Uh, ice cream. No real food."

"Lucky for you we made a roast with mashed potatoes," Dare said.

"Oh, potats! I'm gonna change, be back for food."

"Kay."

She sent a text to Ocean as she made her way upstairs.

> **|Ren|**
> My boyfriend wrote a song for me!!!

> **|Ocean|**
> Omg! Me WHEN

Ren couldn't stop smiling through dinner as she told her dads about the show. Simon texted her to let her know he was home and that he still missed her. When she went to bed, she sent him a goodnight text that resulted in a phone call.

"I thought you already went to sleep."

"Can't sleep. Thinking about you," Simon replied.

"Would probably be easier to sleep if you weren't calling girls while trying to sleep."

"Not girls. *My girl*."

"I guess that's okay then."

"Yeah?" She could *hear* his smile and it just made her more giddy.

"Why'd you call?" she asked, trying to calm her fluttering heart.

"Just wanted to say goodnight. Hear your voice."

"Oh."

"Is that okay?"

"Mhm."

"You're amazing, Ren."

"Shut up."

"No."

"We need to sleep," she giggled.

"Do we?"

"Yes!"

He laughed. "Okay, goodnight, babe."

"Goodnight."

She laid there in the dark, smiling like an idiot for a while before she was able to doze off.

She woke an hour later to her phone buzzing with alerts about something happening up in Harlem with that same telekinetic boy Jasper fought last week. They were calling him Prism. With a sigh she crawled out of bed and put on the suit.

Bellamy locked the door behind him and kicked off his shoes. His date with Jules had gone well, but he kept overthinking things, and he could sense her getting frustrated with him for not picking up whatever signals she was sending. And he learned just *asking* wasn't romantic.

He sighed as he moved into the kitchen, then stopped in his tracks and turned to the living room. Muffled crying was coming from Mom's office. He walked slowly, tension building inside him as he pushed the door open.

Mom was on her knees, her back toward the door. He stood there a moment, shocked, then the sound of her cries kicked him into gear and he crossed the room.

"Mom?"

Her head jerked up as she looked over her shoulder. "Belly? What are you doing here?" She scooped what looked like pictures into her hands then got up and shoved them into her desk.

"It's almost midnight?"

"Is it?" She blinked and wiped her eyes.

"What's wrong?"

"Nothing."

"Mom, you're literally crying. What the hell happened?" He put his hand on her shoulder.

She stared up at him, then smiled sadly. "You used to be so small. Just the littlest thing. Now you're taller than me."

"Mom... what is it?"

She shook her head. "Nothing, baby. I was just... remembering."

"Remembering *what*?"

Another tear slid down her cheek and he pulled her into his arms. "Doesn't matter," she mumbled into him. "You're such a good kid."

"What is wrong?"

She pulled back, forcing a smile. "It's nothing. Really." She gently pat his cheek. "Think I'm gonna go to bed. Don't stay up too late, okay?"

He nodded, unsatisfied as he left the room. She closed the door behind him and he heard the lock turn.

What's wrong? Zeli asked.

I don't know.

He sighed and went to his room, head spinning. She'd been looking at pictures of... something. Maybe after she went to sleep he could see what it was.

What happened? Zeli asked, more insistently this time.

Mom. She was crying. I don't know why.

She's human. Humans have a variety of emotions. Some of which cause them to cry.

He sighed. *Something's wrong.*

I'm sure she's fine.

No. She's been different lately...

He considered the possibility that she *was* dating the strange man he kept seeing. That's what Ren thought when they saw him give her a bracelet at the costume party last week. He had seen her wearing the bracelet. Maybe they'd been dating and he broke it off? It could explain the crying but... as far as he was aware his mom hadn't gone on a single date in his entire life.

"I'm gonna be stressing about this all night," he muttered as he sat on the bed and pulled out his phone. "...or not."

What is it?

Time to go, he replied as he stood up.

His phone had twelve different notifications for something happening in Harlem. He sighed as the suit came over him and he walked out to the balcony.

When he arrived on the scene he spotted Kaida standing on a rooftop, arms crossed as she stared down at the street. He landed beside her.

"Why are we up here and not down there?"

"Someone else has it covered," she said softly.

He followed her gaze. "A lot of someones..."

"It's that same girl you met before, who can split herself."

"Right. Why aren't we helping?"

"I tried. She told me she had it *handled.*"

"Really?"

"She wants to prove herself I guess? Or she thinks I suck so much after the fight with Gaia..."

Lycan didn't know what to say to that. They stood there, watching, as the girl did in fact handle it. The boy she was fighting was the one called Prism that Apex fought last week. And just like last time, he gave up and disappeared in the middle of the fight.

"Should we go formally meet our new hero now?"

Kaida sighed. "I guess."

He grinned. Something about grumpy Kaida...

She climbed onto his board and he took them down to the street. The new hero reformed into just one person, a wide grin on her face. They walked up to her and he nudged Kaida. She forced a smile.

"What do we call you, then?" Kaida asked.

"Hoax," the girl answered.

"Nice to meet you. I'm Lycan, this is Kaida."

"Yeah, I know." The girl shook her head and ran her fingers back through her long multicolored hair. "I'm not really looking to join your little team so, we don't gotta do this."

Kaida's eyes widened.

"Uh, that's fine," Lycan replied before Kaida could say anything. "You don't gotta team up with us or um..."

"Why don't you like us?" Kaida asked bluntly.

Hoax blinked. "Nothing against you. You guys are great. You do a great job! But, I wanna make a name for myself. And besides, there's a lot of people in New York you can't represent. But I can. And I will."

"What? What's that supposed to—"

"Alright nice meeting you bye!" Lycan interrupted as he pulled Kaida away. He could feel the annoyance radiating out of her. "Come on, Bunhead." He forced her onto his board before she could say anything else and took them to the sky.

When they landed on their roof at Spruce Street Kaida stomped away from him, grumbling.

"Alright, talk to me."

She turned, blue eyes shining with frustration. "There's *so* many people we can't represent." She rolled her eyes. "A lo mejor sí nada más hablo en español la gente se darían cuenta que no soy una puta chica blanca."

He raised an eyebrow. "You think that's what she meant?"

"Claro que sí. ¿Cuántas veces tengo que repetir me para que me crean? Nada más porque mi mamá era blanca no significa que puedan borrar la otra mitad de quien soy. Esa mitad que importa... ella nunca estaba *ahí*."

He didn't know how to respond to that.

"This is Apex's fault," she grumbled.

"It is?"

"I stole his eyes. It's the eyes, right?"

Lycan laughed.

She glared at him. "It's not funny!"

"No, but I was so stressed like ten minutes ago. And I'm way less stressed now."

Her face softened. "You're welcome why were you stressed?"

He shrugged. "Doesn't matter. Where's Apex?"

"Sleeping, probably."

He nodded. "Wanna call it a night? Seems like our new not-friend has things under control right now."

Her frown returned.

"Are you just annoyed that she didn't immediately wanna be friends, or is it really the race thing?"

She sighed. "She thinks she's the first person of color hero now."

"So? If it bothers you so much we can make a declaration. 'Kaida is half Mexican' in big letters in the sky."

She was trying not to smile, and failing miserably. "It's not a big deal."

"Okay. So... wanna go get pancakes?"

"You know I can't say no to pancakes," she replied, still annoyed.

"That *is* why I offered. Come on."

She rolled her eyes but didn't argue, climbing onto his board.

When they landed outside of the diner he thought she was maybe in a better mood, but then Kaida frowned, and walked right past the doors.

He stared after her, confused. Then he saw the tall black ears as Fable walked past.

Kaida went right up to the guy and slammed him back into the wall. Fable's purple eyes widened in shock as Kaida held a shimmering blade of light against his throat.

"You *ever* hurt Apex again and I'm gonna *eviscerate* you. Are we fucking clear?"

Fable blinked. "He attacked *me*. Every time."

"I'm aware. Are we clear?" She pressed the knife harder against his throat.

Lycan watched, unsure if he should pull her back or not.

"Tell him to find me on a day I wanna die," Fable hissed back at her, leaning into the knife a little. "Shouldn't be too hard, they happen frequently. *Otherwise*, I'm gonna fucking defend myself when someone attacks me." Red blood bubbled against her blade as he spoke.

Kaida stared into his eyes a moment, pouring all her anger into the glare before the knife misted away and she pulled back. Lycan put a hand on her shoulder as Fable stalked past.

"What was that?" he whispered.

"He tried to kill my best friend," she mumbled as he guided her inside the diner. "Now he's been warned."

Lycan smiled. "You need to calm down or you'll scare the waitress."

Kaida released a breath, nodding.

50
Twins From The Dawn of Time

"You didn't get any sleep?" Jasper asked when he found Ren after first period.

"Nope," she answered. The exhaustion went deeper than her bones. "There was a whole lot going on last night. A fire in the Bronx, a robbery in Brooklyn where a kid got hurt. I was gonna go home after that, but then—" She paused, lowering her voice. "That Rapture girl was causing chaos again. I missed her but the *mess* she left." She shook her head. "And it was just me."

"You could have woken me! And where the hell was you know who?"

She sighed. "Probably sleeping? It was like five in the morning."

"Doesn't he patrol literally every night?"

"Most nights, but he deserves a night off. I'm not mad about it. Just so sleepy." She yawned for dramatic effect. "Anyways, think I'm gonna nap after school?"

"No worries. I'll patrol tonight. You take it easy," Jasper replied as he pat her on the head.

She smiled.

"Would you look at that," Harper's voice called from behind them. Ren stopped in her tracks and turned to face her.

"Cutest couple in the whole school," Harper continued, her mouth twisting in a sneer as the ice in her coffee clinked.

"Give it a rest," Ren said, shaking her head. She was way too tired to deal with her.

"Sure, sure," Harper said. Then she pulled the lid off her coffee and splashed it at Ren.

She gasped as the cold liquid soaked into her shirt, dripping down into a puddle around her on the floor.

"Harper!" Jasper yelled but Ren grabbed his arm to silence him. "Hoodie?"

Jasper understood and dropped his bag. Then he pulled off his hoodie as Ren pulled her shirt off over her head before the coffee could fully soak into her jeans. Only a moment passed with her standing there in her bra before she was able to get Jasper's hoodie on, hands shaking with embarrassment and rage.

"You good?" Jasper asked, standing defensively in front of her, hands on her arms.

"Yes. No. Yes?"

She pressed her forehead into Jasper's chest and he put his arms around her. The bell rang. She didn't move.

"Is Ren okay?" That was Bellamy's voice.

"We saw what Harper did." That was Nico.

Ren groaned into Jasper.

"She's a little upset," Jasper answered.

She slowly pulled back, on the verge of tears. "I'm fine. I—I should clean this. So no one slips. I..."

The hall was empty now, just the four of them, and coffee all over the floor.

"I got it," Bellamy said softly. "I'll clean it. You go to class."

Ren nodded and Jasper guided her away. The disconnect between her mind and her body was disorienting. She still stood in the puddle, but Jasper had her halfway down the hall already.

"We can skip," he whispered. "Your dads won't care."

No, she thought. *But your dad will.* "I'm fine. Let's just get to class."

"Bathroom first. You're gonna be *sticky*," he replied as they walked.

Ren zoned out during class, unable to pay attention. By the time she walked to lunch she felt a *little* better. She didn't partake in conversation, just waiting for the end when Simon showed up.

His routine was always to ditch the last five minutes of his class to come see her. His teacher was fine with it, so he did it every day now. Sometimes he'd just sit at the table, arm around her while he tried to engage with her friends. And sometimes he'd pull her away and they'd kiss a bit before the bell rang.

Today he sat beside her, casually kissing her cheek. She smiled at him.

Simon frowned. "You weren't wearing that this morning," he muttered. "Who's hoodie is that?"

"Jasper's."

"Why the fuck are you wearing Jasper's hoodie?"

Everyone at the table fell silent, turning to look at Simon.

"If you were cold you could have had *my* jacket," he continued.

"Harper threw her fucking coffee at me," Ren replied, trying not to cry.

"Her shirt was soaking wet, dude," Jasper said, voice laced with anger.

Simon took a slow deep breath, but didn't say anything. He just put his arm around her, pulling her closer to him.

"Are you alright?" he asked.

She nodded.

He didn't say anything else after that. Just kissed her cheek then got up to leave when the bell rang. She was so surprised that she didn't move.

"Renny?"

She blinked. Jasper, Bellamy, Jules, Nico, Kevin, Ashley, and Nari were *all* staring at her.

"I'm fine," she mumbled.

"Uh huh. Come on," Jasper said as he gently grabbed her arm and helped her up.

World history was next, but they had a sub and were told to just read quietly. Instead she pulled out a notebook and doodled with pen on paper, trying to calm down. She noticed Zig sitting on the floor beside her leg after a while.

How long have you been here? she asked. He rarely came to school.

I came the moment that drink hit you.

She stared at him. *Really?*

You were upset. Scared. So I came.

Her eyes watered. *Thanks.*

At the end of the day Simon met her at her locker like usual.

"Are you mad at me?" she asked in a small voice as he hugged her.

"Of course not." He smiled, but it seemed forced. "Are you okay?"

She nodded slowly and he kissed her cheek.

"Is it okay if I skip the walk today, got band stuff."

"Oh. Okay."

Simon almost always walked her home after school.

"Jasper can walk you, right?" he continued.

"Uh. Yeah."

Simon nodded and left. She stood there, confused as Jasper came up.

"Everything good?" he asked.

"He isn't walking me today."

Jasper made a face but didn't say anything. "Come on." He put his arm around her.

The weekend with Simon, his concert, everything had been *perfect*. Now it felt weird. And she didn't understand why.

Zig walked beside her and she smiled. It was freaky how he could phase through things, and even people. To her he was solid, always. But that was because of the Bond. Something green caught her eyes and she realized Pozi was also with them, walking on Jasper's other side. She wondered when he showed up and why he was letting her see him.

Ren!

She stopped in her tracks. "What?"

There's a man. Across the street, turning left. The one in the black coat.

Ren started walking that way, confused.

"What are we... oh, we're following someone?" Jasper asked. "Pozi sees him too."

She nodded. "Why am I following this man?"

Don't worry about it.

Zig I am always worried about it. Who is he?

It might not be who I think. Just follow him, discreetly. I'll explain later.

"Do we need to follow? Why can't they do it?" Jasper muttered. "It's not like he'll see them."

Zig made a noise like a groan. *If it is who I think I need you to know what he looks like.*

Jasper shrugged.

If you're not careful he will know he's being followed. If it is him, Zig continued.

And who do we think it is? she asked as she slowed, staying about twenty paces behind the man. He was easy to follow, about six feet tall, with short red hair. His long leather coat billowed dramatically as he moved. Was he not burning up in that thing?

Zig was silent a moment before hissing the name *Xereth* in her head.

The name meant nothing to her.

"What are we supposed to do if this is the guy?" Jasper whispered.

Nothing.

Ren sighed. "He's *very* stressed."

"So is Poz."

She nodded. The man stopped, turning slowly, his long coat swishing at his ankles. Ren didn't think, just turned and shoved Jasper into the brick wall then buried her face in his chest. Jasper slid his arms under her backpack, and put his cheek to her head.

Good job, Zig muttered.

Is he still looking?

No. He's suspicious, but didn't see your faces. That was smart. Thanks.

She pulled away from Jasper, staring down the sidewalk. The man was gone.

"Did we confirm if it's who you think?" Jasper asked.

Unfortunately. Go home.

She nodded, pulling Jasper's arm and turning them around.

They sat on her bedroom floor, their two Xyri sitting in front of them, anxious and concerned. It was strange to see that in Zig's face, when his eyes were solid gold. When they first Bonded she thought he lacked emotions simply because she couldn't see them expressed in those eyes. But even without feeling his emotions through the Bond, she could see the stress in his face, the way he held himself. She knew this creature so well now.

"Tell us who that was," she said softly.

Xereth, Zig answered.

He's immortal, like us, Pozi added. *One of the Timeless.*

"Wait, I thought that was Xenos?" Ren asked.

There is more than one, Ren.

Fifteen more, to be exact, Pozi said.

She narrowed her eyes. "You only told me about one."

Xenos is the most important to us. The one who's been missing for seventeen years.

It's not normal, Pozi added. *He wouldn't abandon us. And our inability to find him is concerning.*

"Okay, what's the deal with the dude we followed?" Jasper asked.

Xereth. He has... been off the rails for a long time, Zig answered. *We didn't Bond for over two hundred years, because of what happened in the war. Xenos and Xereth were on opposite sides of that war. For the first time in human history. It was the most split the Xyri have ever been. So much was lost. So we made the pact. No Bonding for a very long time.*

"And you broke the pact."

I did. Because things are changing. Azazelith and I are convinced Xereth is to blame for Xenos going missing. He's putting plans into motion. Plans he's been making for over two centuries. Maybe longer. Enough Xyri would choose him, do whatever he asked. Just as many of us would do the same for Xenos. We are still split. And with Xenos out of the way... the others won't get involved.

They might! Pozi's tail wagged for a second. *If we went to them with the right argument, the right evidence. I know Xatie would listen. Or maybe Xaran.*

Zig sighed. *I don't know. Everything is so different now. They all moved on.*

"Hold on. You said... all because of what happened in the war," Jasper said as he pulled at a thread in Ren's rug. "So... *what* happened in the war?"

Zig and Pozi fell silent, blinking up at them.

"See, cause, the history books don't *say* what ended the war, right? Like, it just stopped. And you all disappeared. No one knows why."

We're gonna keep it that way, kid.

Ren smiled at Jasper's frown. She'd tried getting this information out of Zig when they first Bonded, but he refused to tell her. Whatever happened in that war was wiped from the histories for a reason. He wouldn't budge.

"And like, Lifelight and Stardust... they killed each other but that doesn't make *sense*," Jasper continued.

Zig tensed.

Ren shook her head. Zig did *not* like talking about Lifelight.

Jasper rolled his eyes. "Who's... Xatie and..."

Other Timeless.

"More immortals?" Jasper smiled. "Cool."

They stopped Bonding with us long ago. Before the war.

"But Xenos and Xereth didn't?"

No. They've remained with us, always.

Always there to help, when the Bond breaks, Pozi added.

"But you stopped Bonding, so, you didn't need them?" Jasper asked.

No one was brave enough to break the pact, Pozi muttered. *Until Kirzigith Bonded you.*

"It set things in motion," Ren said softly. "You told me that choice would be a catalyst event."

And the dominoes are falling now, Ren.

We gotta be ready for what's coming.

"What's coming?" Jasper looked between them. "You're not making that very clear."

We don't know what he plans. All we know is Xenos isn't here to stop it. To balance it.

"Balance," Ren whispered. "There isn't a balance."

No.

Xenos and Xereth are brothers. Twins from the dawn of time. Always two, for balance. There are sixteen total, but the others all drifted. Xereth and Xenos were the only ones left, holding the balance, Zig said.

Balance in humanity. Balance among the Xyri. Balance among the Bonded, Pozi continued.

Only there is no balance without Xenos, and there's no balance now.

Ren nodded. "No balance in the Bonded. It was just me and Lycan for so long. But so many others now. Villains." She looked at Pozi. "Till you chose him."

More are *coming,* Pozi said. *Zephyreas is here now. We're all afraid. But it's working. You are working, Ren Rivers. Lycan is working. More will come. We can return the balance.*

She swallowed and met Jasper's eyes.

"We can handle it," he said softly. "Whatever comes. We got this."

She wasn't so sure. They couldn't even handle Gaia. What were they gonna do about an immortal threat?

"How do we stop this guy?" she asked. "If he's immortal, as in can't die... that's a big ask."

We can not stop him before he makes his move.

"I'd prefer preventing things before they begin, actually."

"Me too," Jasper said.

We must speak with Azazelith. She needs to know he's back. Then we can make a plan for you little humans, yeah?

Jasper smiled and Ren sighed.

"Okay. Go. Tell Zeli. But I don't want any secrets, Zig. No more I'll tell you what you need to know when you need to know it. This Bond isn't new anymore. We're a *team*, you and I. You tell me everything when you get back, got it?"

She felt Zig's smile as he met her eyes.

You and I, Ren. Promise.

51
Context

Anxiety thrummed through Ren. She couldn't even distract herself with homework cause she didn't have any. With a sigh they went downstairs. Dare was sitting on the couch with Breadcrumb asleep in his lap, tablet in hand as he worked on a new tattoo concept. They sat beside him.

"Where's Dad?" she asked as she looked at the design.

"He's downstairs, interviewing a new hire. Said he'll grab dinner when he's done."

Ren nodded then leaned on his shoulder. Dare put the tablet down and put his arm around her.

"Everything okay, kiddo?"

"Long day."

"My ex-girlfriend threw coffee at her," Jasper said coldly.

"She did *what?*" Dare tensed.

"It's not a big deal," Ren said softly. "Was cold coffee. She blames me for their breakup but she'll get over it."

"Why does she blame you?"

Ren sat up and looked at Jasper. "Don't know. *You* still won't tell me what really happened between you guys."

"Doesn't matter."

"It matters to *me*."

Jasper leaned back. "She wanted me to stop being friends with you so I broke up with her. That's it."

Ren blinked. "She asked you—"

"It wasn't a choice, Ren." He met her eyes. "She was insecure. I can't be with someone who can't accept that you're gonna be in my life. Always."

Her eyes watered, lip trembling. Words failed her so she just threw her arms around him. "I'm sorry," she mumbled into his chest.

"For what?" He laughed. "We were together like a month. I literally don't care. You're way more important." He paused. "I hope someday I have a romantic someone who's as important to me as you, but it wasn't gonna be her. And that's okay."

Ren kept her face in his chest, overwhelmed. "I love you."

"Love you too."

It took a minute to compose herself, slowly pulling away from him and wiping her eyes. She hadn't even noticed that Dare went to the kitchen to give them some space.

Her phone buzzed and she pulled it out to see a text from Simon.

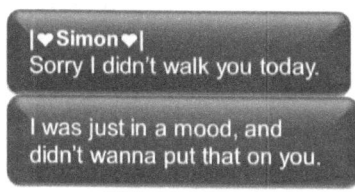

|♥Simon♥|
Sorry I didn't walk you today.

I was just in a mood, and didn't wanna put that on you.

|Ren|
Were you in a mood because of me?

|♥Simon♥|
Absolutely not. You only ever put me in a good mood.

I'm sorry 🤍

|Ren|
♡

She relaxed a little after that. "God it's been such a day. You wanna stay over tonight? We could play games and—"

"Ren!"

She turned at the sound of Dad's voice calling from the stairs. "Up here!"

"Got a big surprise!"

A moment later he entered the room, but he wasn't alone. A tall girl with dark brown skin and long black braids was with him. Ren's jaw dropped, heart racing.

"Ocean?"

"Ren!"

She jumped over the back of the couch to intercept the incoming hug.

"How are you *here*?" she asked as they clung to each other, swaying back and forth.

"We moved back early. Surprise!"

Ren laughed. "Oh my god oh my god."

Ocean pulled back, absolutely beaming. "Look at you! Ahhh!"

"Ahhhhh!" Ren screamed and hugged her again.

Ocean wasn't supposed to be moving back to New York for another month. Ren couldn't believe she was *here*.

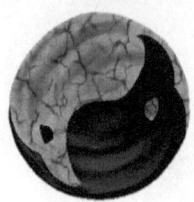

Jasper sat on the couch, watching the reunion, feeling suddenly invisible.

Something wrong? Pozi asked.

No I'm fine.

He was annoyed with himself for being jealous, and tried to push it away as Cas came over and put bags of takeout on the coffee table.

"Staying for dinner?"

"Uh..." Jasper blinked.

"I got your favorite," Cas continued, nodding to the bags.

Jasper grinned. "You didn't even know I'd be here."

"You're always here, kid."

"Sure. I'll stay."

Breadcrumb jumped on the table, investigating the bags. Jasper scooped the cat up and cuddled him to his chest while Ren and Ocean laughed and giggled. It seemed like minutes passed before Ren dragged the girl over to him.

"This is Jasper, my best friend in the entire world."

"New York, maybe," Ocean said with a smile. "But *I'm* the best in the world."

"Jasper, this is Ocean!" Ren was so excited as she looked between them.

Jasper took a deep breath then forced a smile. "Nice to finally meet you. Ren talks about you all the time."

"Ren pretty much *only* talks about you," Ocean said.

Jasper had seen pictures of her before, but she was annoyingly attractive in person, with bright brown eyes and flawless brown skin. Her black braids were intertwined with golden thread, and she wore a long sleeve blue crop top with tight black skinny jeans that fit her figure well.

"You'd think she doesn't have any other friends," Ocean continued.

"She does, I'm just the best one."

"You are," Ren said softly.

She looked happy, her eyes bright. It was nice to see that smile back on her face after the day she had.

"Ocean, you wanna stay for dinner? Dad, do we have enough?"

"We got enough," Cas said with a smile.

"Wait, did you know Ocean was coming today?" Ren asked, frowning.

"We got the text from her dad last night."

"Can't believe you didn't tell me!"

"Worth it for the look on your face," Arrow said.

"Ocean, you staying?"

"Yes!"

Ren started pulling containers out of the bags, passing one to Jasper then offering two options to Ocean. Her dads took their food to the kitchen table.

"So, how's Wade?" Ren asked.

Ocean grinned. "He came out last year. And he's not here yet, he's visiting his *boyfriend* now."

"Damn."

"Wade's my brother," Ocean said to Jasper. "Ren used to have a *huge* crush on him when we were kids."

"Oh, yeah? Is he a douchebag in a leather jacket?" Jasper asked. "Cause that's her type lately."

"Jasper!" Ren glared at him.

"Oh, do tell?" Ocean said, eyes wide.

"First of all, I do not have a type," Ren said defensively.

Not true, he thought. But she'd never admit her type was *actually* a guy in a skintight suit with wolf ears and blue hair.

"Second of all, Simon isn't—"

"The boyfriend's a douchebag?" Ocean interrupted, looking at Jasper.

"He is not!"

Jasper just smiled. "Ignore me. I embellish."

Ocean held his eyes for a moment then nodded.

"He's not! Okay, Simon's great," Ren continued.

Jasper leaned back, eating his food in silence as Ren started talking about just how great Simon was, starting with how they met and ending with his concert. She left out the part where he got pissed at her for wearing Jasper's hoodie that afternoon. Jasper was starting to think maybe Simon was too possessive. He didn't like it.

As the girls talked he tried to put his jealousy aside. Ocean seemed nice enough. He just hadn't been prepared for her yet. He knew she was coming, knew he'd feel this way when she did. He wondered if Ren was secretly panicking, since this early arrival wasn't *planned*.

Breadcrumb jumped on the couch again and he pulled the cat into his lap as the girls laughed. He'd stopped following the conversation.

"Ren, I think I'm gonna go," he said after a while when the cat abandoned him.

She paused in her chatting, looking at him with sad eyes. "What, why?"

"You're busy catching up. It's fine. It's getting late anyways."

"But, you were gonna stay?"

"Actually, I should go," Ocean said. "We just got in this morning. There's still *so much* to unpack. And time difference got me all *wonky.*"

"Oh. Okay. Do you need a ride?"

Ocean grinned. "Nope."

"You sure?"

"Let's just say I live within walking distance now," Ocean continued as she stood.

Ren grinned. "Oh my god. How close? I can walk you downstairs at least."

"It was nice to finally meet you, Jasper."

"You too," he replied.

"Nice to see you guys again!" Ocean called to Ren's dads.

"Of course. You're welcome over any time."

Jasper watched them leave then flopped over on the couch and groaned.

"You okay?" Arrow asked as he leaned over the back of the couch to look down at him. "Feeling left out?"

"No."

Arrow smiled. "Trust me, you're her favorite."

Jasper sighed. "I *know.*"

"What was that you were saying," Cas started as he appeared over the couch beside his husband. "About a leather jacket wearing douchebag?"

Jasper smiled.

"Ren's been raving about him," Cas continued. "But if there's something she isn't telling us..."

"Eh, it wasn't a big deal. Just annoyed me." He forced a smile.

"You called him a douchebag," Arrow said flatly.

"And we trust your opinion."

"Aw." Jasper's smile turned real. "Listen, he's not bad or anything. He's just not right for her. But she'll figure it out. She's smart."

"I don't want her getting hurt," Cas said softly.

"Smart people can still make bad decisions. You've got her back though, right?" Arrow asked.

"Literally always."

"Why can't you guys just date instead?" Cas asked with a sigh.

"Excuse me?" Ren's surprised voice answered from behind them.

Jasper sat up, frowning. "Yeah, *what*?"

"You two would be so good together," Cas continued.

Ren's mouth was wide open. "I can't believe this. You *hated* Jasper when we dated!"

"Listen," Arrow started. "It was your first boyfriend..."

"We weren't ready for that."

"But now—"

"We can handle it."

"And we love Jasper."

"Aww." Jasper grinned. "Thanks daddy squared."

"I'm just saying—" Cas continued.

"No, stop saying." Ren shook her head. "Jasper and I are just friends. We tried dating. There wasn't a spark."

"Is there a spark with Simon?" Arrow asked, seeming genuinely curious.

Ren hesitated. "Maybe. I'm..." She smiled slightly. "Still figuring it out."

Jasper was trying not to laugh and Ren glared at him.

"I like Simon," she continued. "A lot. *Anyways*... video games?"

"Sure." He hopped off the couch then started walking backwards as he smiled at her dads. "Sorry you'll never have me as a son in law, but you could just adopt me if ya want!"

Cas shook his head. "Wait, do you guys know a kid named Freddie Reeves?"

Ren froze, slowly turning around. "Yes. Why?"

"Interviewed at the bakery today. Mentioned he went to your school."

Jasper grinned at the blush in Ren's cheeks.

"You're gonna hire Freddie?"

Cas watched her intently. "Should I not? He seems like a good kid but..." He sighed. "I don't really hire guys anymore. Not after..." He didn't finish the sentence but Jasper nodded, remembering.

Ren just stared at him. "Huh? Freddie's fine."

"Then why do you look like that?"

Jasper's smile widened. "She had a crush on Freddie in seventh grade. I killed it though."

Ren's blush deepened. *"Ugh."*

"What? I did! You didn't give a shit about Freddie after you met me."

Ren rolled her eyes. "Shut up." She continued toward her stairs.

Jasper glanced at Cas. "Freddie's fine, I think."

Cas nodded.

Bellamy sat next to Jules on his couch, working on homework, but his mind kept wandering back to Ren. She seemed so out of it after what Harper did. Then with Simon, at lunch...

"You're awfully quiet," Jules muttered.

He looked up at her. "Sorry. Just worried about Ren."

"Oh."

"That was weird at lunch, right? Simon getting mad about her wearing Jasper's hoodie?"

Jules put her pen down, seeming thoughtful. "I mean, I can kinda see where he's coming from. Not within this context though, that's dumb."

"What do you mean, see where he's coming from?"

She sighed. "I mean, if some other guy gave me his jacket and I wore it you wouldn't get jealous?"

Bellamy blinked. "No?"

Jules laughed. "I don't believe you. Anyone would get jealous over that. Not like, an extreme amount, but a little."

Anyone normal maybe. He sighed. "But it was Jasper. Ren's best friend."

"Well, yes. Context matters. And also the whole coffee thing." She frowned, amber eyes sad. "I still can't believe Harper did that. She's been so off since the breakup."

"Maybe you could talk to her about it? Tell her to fucking ease up on Ren. She didn't do anything."

Jules nodded, her shiny blonde ponytail swishing behind her. "You really wouldn't get jealous?"

Bellamy leaned back. "Would you be mad? If I'd been the one to give Ren my hoodie. Would you see that and get pissed about it, like Simon did?"

"Not in this context."

"So, without the context you *would* get mad?" Bellamy was so confused.

"I wouldn't say *mad*. Not like Ren's boyfriend. That jealousy was palpable." She shook her head. "But I might be a little upset."

"So, if Ren was just... cold. Didn't have a jacket, and I lent her mine, cause, she's my friend and I'm nice, would that be a problem for you?"

Jules smiled. "You're taking this hypothetical *way* too seriously."

He sighed, still confused.

Jules stared at him a moment, then her eyes softened. "I'll talk to Harper about it. That stunt was uncalled for."

"Thanks."

They fell silent and started working on their homework again, but his mind was drifting further and further from the English assignment. He felt like he soured the mood with that conversation. *I do that with every conversation.*

Every time they hung out, every date, he said something wrong, or didn't say the right thing. Or do the right thing. Even now, he never really knew when he was supposed to kiss her. He knew she wanted him to, in a general sense, but being the one to initiate the physical intimacy freaked him out. He tried explaining to her that he wasn't always good at reading cues and was way better with written words. Which was why he liked passing notes with her at school or texting when they weren't together. But when they were together he felt awkward, out of place, overthinking everything. If he asked if she wanted him to hold her hand, or to kiss her, she got a look on her face that made him realize he was not supposed to *ask*. He should just *know*. But he never did.

"Bell?"

He blinked, looking up at her. "Yeah?"

"You're quiet again."

Right. "Sorry." He smiled. "So... did you know that the US Apollo Space Program was named for the Greek God, simply because the guy naming it liked the imagery of Apollo riding his chariot across the sun?"

Jules frowned. "That's... very random."

"Oh. Uh. Sorry. It's what I'm writing about for the history assignment. I thought it was interesting. Did you not get the same one? About myths influencing historical things?"

"Oh. Well yeah."

He waited. "...what's yours on?"

"Yin-Yang, and the cultural influences of it throughout Chinese history."

"That's really cool."

She nodded, looking back down at her notebook.

Bellamy sighed. He would have liked talking about that, but she seemed uninterested. He picked up his pencil, falling silent again, eager for the end of the night when he could go out and be someone else.

52
The Same Page

Ren's heart raced as she knocked on the door of Simon's apartment. He'd invited her over for dinner with his mom, who she'd only met once for about two minutes a few weeks ago. He seemed so excited, so *she* should be excited but instead she was anxious.

Part of that was definitely Zig's fault. He'd been off most of the week with Zeli and Pozi since the day they'd seen the man, Xcreth. She'd summoned him only once for the Valkyrie warehouse Gaia destroyed on Wednesday night. But Hoax arrived well before Kaida, along with *another* new Bonded. They chased Gaia off before Kaida even arrived.

Stop being annoyed there's new heroes. This is what we wanted.

She rolled her eyes. *I am not annoyed! I just... Hoax brushed us off, like we haven't been doing this for almost two years now. It was rude!* She paused. Hoax *had* stopped Elixir from making people sick at a protest earlier that week though. It *was* good, and she needed to stop being annoyed. *Are you still looking into Xereth?*

Yes.

She sighed.

Are you gonna knock on the door?

Ren groaned. *Yes.* Then she did knock, trying to ignore the twisting in her stomach.

"Hey, baby. Come on in." Simon held the door open for her. "You look nice."

Ren smiled as she walked in. "Thanks."

Simon's mom was in the small kitchen, cooking something that smelled delicious. Her black hair was in a tight braid, her green eyes shining as she smiled at them.

"Hello, Ren!"

"Hi, Mrs. Sims. How are you?"

"Oh, just fine, honey. You guys go hang out. I'll let you know when dinner's ready."

"Do you need any help?" Ren asked, eyeing the pots on the stove.

"Oh no, you kids go. I got this."

"Come on." Simon pulled her farther into the apartment.

"Your mom is so nice."

"Yeah, she's the best." He took her down the hall.

Ren paused, looking at the pictures on the wall. Then she frowned. "Who are all these kids?"

"The band," Simon answered with a smile.

"Oh, you've *really* known each other forever," Ren said.

"Literally. Our moms were all best friends, before they had us. And they had us close together. My mom basically has four kids."

"Cute."

Simon nodded as he pulled her into his bedroom.

"Many guitars," she said as she took in the space.

Four guitars hung on the wall above his bed, two acoustic, two electric, with a fifth acoustic one in a stand on the floor by his desk.

"This one's my dad's," he said, pointing to one of the acoustic ones on the wall. "He used to play it for me when I was little, so it's my actual favorite. But this one's my favorite to play," he continued, pointing to the blue electric one. "I use it at most of our shows."

"I thought you usually left that one at Kit's."

Simon blushed a little. "I brought it back so my room would look cooler."

Ren giggled as she looked around the room. Black comforter on the bed, black rug on the floor. There were records hung on the wall, which was painted a soft grey. She noticed the glow bracelet she'd given him resting on his desk and her heart swelled. Then she saw the pair of black glasses beside it. She grabbed them and turned to Simon with a frown.

"You wear glasses?"

His eyes widened. "No, no. I don't." He reached for them but she backed up.

"You never told me you wear glasses."

"Cause I don't."

"Contacts?"

He sighed. "Yes."

"Are those blue eyes of yours fake?"

He laughed. "No. All natural."

"Okay, but, I gotta see them on you."

His blush deepened. "Nope. I look terrible in them."

"Please?" She pouted.

He stared at her. "Fine."

She held the glasses out, smiling wide as he slowly slid them on his face then sighed at her.

"See, terrible."

Ren shook her head. "You're kidding, right? You look so cute." And he did. The glasses suited him in a way she hadn't expected. "Who told you you look terrible in them?"

"Everyone. Literally."

Ren frowned. "Bet your mom didn't. Can't imagine Allie would."

He rolled his eyes. "Allie most certainly did. In the fourth grade."

Ren laughed. "Oh my *god*. Fourth grade? You didn't look like *this* in fourth grade!"

He still looked embarrassed. "Victoria hated them," he mumbled after a minute.

"Victoria," Ren said, stepping up to him. "Is the devil, according to Cameron," she continued, then pulled him down and kissed him. He melted into her. "You look amazing, with or without them," she whispered against his lips.

He groaned against her, and pulled back. "You are killing me."

"What?"

He shook his head and put the glasses back on his desk. "I have something for you," he said, swallowing. She was sure she'd never seen him blush so much.

"Really?"

"Yeah." He grabbed a small box off his desk and handed it to her.

She took it, heart racing. Inside was a red guitar pick attached to a shiny silver chain.

"Simon..." She pulled it out of the box, unable to hide her smile.

"This is the pick I used when I... wrote that song for you. And I used it at the show, too," he said softly.

"Will you put it on me?"

"Of course."

A shiver crawled up her spine as his fingers brushed against her neck, moving her hair out of the way. Then he slid his fingers under the chain for a second before spinning her around, a wide grin on his face.

"Kinda clashes with your other necklace."

Ren's hand moved to where her Xyrial now rested on her chest. She quickly tucked it back under her shirt. "Oh that. Um, was my Aunt Robin's. She passed away right before I was born. I always wear it, but under my shirt."

He nodded. "New necklace looks great on you."

"Thank you. I *love* it."

She grabbed him, pulling him closer so she could slide her arms up around his neck and kiss him again. Warmth spread through her as she got lost in it.

"You look so good tonight," he whispered as she pulled away.

"Shut up." She pushed him back. "Your mom is out there."

He kissed her again, as if to make the point that he didn't care.

"Simon!" She pushed him back again and he laughed.

"Alright, alright. Come on." He grabbed her hand, pulling her back down the hall and into the living room. The couches were a soft green with dark wood accents, matching the dining table by the wall.

They talked on the couch while his mom worked in the kitchen. When dinner was ready they sat at the table together, and his mom asked her about herself, so she talked about the bakery and her dads.

"I can't believe Simon's graduating so soon," his mom said, shaking her head. "Feels like just yesterday you were in diapers."

"*Mom.*"

She smiled, a twinkle in her eyes.

"It'll be weird," Ren said. "You not being at school."

"I only graduate two weeks before you finish school. Then we'll have the summer together."

Ren grinned, idly playing with the guitar pick necklace.

"Well, time for me to go," his mom said as she stood and started cleaning up the table.

"Go?" Ren asked.

"To work." His mom smiled. "You two behave, alright?"

Simon rolled his eyes. "Yes, Mom."

"We should do this again, with all the kids," his mom said as she mussed Simon's hair, then waved to Ren before grabbing her purse and walking out the door.

Ren turned to Simon. "I thought she was gonna be here the whole time? She was gonna watch the movie with us."

"Uh, yeah. She was. Must have been called in..." He shrugged. "Come on, movie time."

Ren didn't say anything as he went to the couch. She got up slowly, her anxiety bubbling as she settled beside him.

He frowned at the TV.

"What?"

"It won't let me log in." He sighed. "It's fine. We can watch in my room." He stood, holding a hand out for her.

Ren felt disconnected from her body as she took his hand and let him pull her off the couch, back down to his room. He dropped her hand as he laid back on the bed and turned his TV on. Ren stood there awkwardly. He smiled and pat the spot beside him.

"Come on."

With a deep breath she got on the bed, trying to calm her nerves.

He got the movie on and put his arm around her, pulling her closer.

Are you okay? Zig asked.

Debatable.

I'm coming.

No, I'm fine. I'm just being dramatic.
What's wrong?
Nothing I'm fine.
She could tell he didn't believe her, but he didn't argue.
"You okay?" Simon asked in a whisper.
"Yeah."
"You're so tense."
"Am I?"
"A little." He smiled and planted a small kiss on her cheek.
After a minute he leaned over and turned off the light on his nightstand. This just heightened her anxiety. Alone, in his bed, lights off...
"I have to go to the bathroom," she blurted, pulling away from him.
"Oh, okay. It's the door across from the kitchen," he replied as she left the room.
Once inside she sat on the floor, back to the door, hands shaking as she pulled her phone out and texted her dads.

|Ren|
Text me and tell me you need me to come home early please then come pick me up from Simon's please.

She deleted the text after sending it, then waited. Not a minute passed before they texted her back.

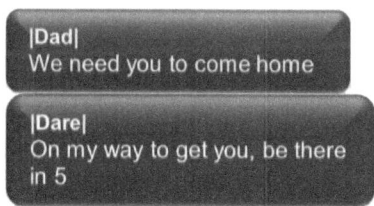

|Dad|
We need you to come home

|Dare|
On my way to get you, be there in 5

Ren released a breath then waited another minute before she stood, flushing the toilet and washing her hands as if she'd actually used the bathroom. When she went back out, Simon was waiting in the bed where she left him, movie paused.
"My dads just texted, they want me to come home," she muttered.
"What? Why?" He looked at the clock. "It's barely eight. Your curfew is ten."

"Don't know. They didn't say." She turned her phone around to show him the texts. "I'm sorry. Maybe we can do the movie another day?"

"Yeah. Sure."

"I'm sorry," she repeated as she walked over to kiss him quickly, then pulled away before he could say anything. "I'll text you later."

"Okay."

She didn't look back as she grabbed her bag and walked out.

Ren?

I'm fine. Going home.

You are not fine.

It's okay. My dad's about to be here.

Fresh air enveloped her as she stepped outside. Dare was already there, standing by the car in front of the building. She crossed to him and he pulled her into his arms.

"Are you okay? Did he hurt you?"

"No. Nothing happened. I just wanted to leave."

He held her so tightly. "Let's get you home."

She nodded and he kissed her forehead before helping her into the passenger seat.

He didn't say anything and neither did she. By the time they were home and walking upstairs she wondered if she was overreacting. She couldn't be sure that's what Simon wanted. But the panic won and she just ran.

Dad was waiting in the kitchen when they walked in and he pulled her into his arms. "What happened?"

"Nothing."

"I don't believe you."

She sighed as she pulled back. "Literally nothing. I just... freaked out."

"About what?" Dare asked.

"I thought..." She closed her eyes, embarrassed to say it out loud. "I thought Simon maybe wanted to have sex so I panicked and left."

"What—what uh... what did he—"

"His mom was supposed to be there, but she left right after dinner. And Simon wasn't surprised, like he knew. And the movie wouldn't work in the living room so we had to watch it in his bed and I I I panicked."

Dad pulled her into his arms again. "I'm so proud of you."

"For what?"

"For getting yourself out of a situation that made you uncomfortable. And for telling us."

"Thanks for getting me," she said as she pulled away from Dad and hugged Dare.

"Always, kiddo. You say the word, we come running."

She nodded, eyes closed as he held her.

After that she went to her room to get ready for bed. She felt silly now, like she probably overreacted, panicking for nothing. But she couldn't help it. She was only seventeen and she'd never been with someone like that. The thought of it made her absolutely wanna hide in a closet never to be found again. Which was stupid.

Once in bed her phone started buzzing with texts from Simon.

|♥Simon♥|
Is everything okay?

Did I do something wrong?

Ren?

Please talk to me

She ignored Simon's texts and opened her chat with Lycan.

|Starface|
Zeli's been with your Xyri all day so I can't patrol which means I'm very bored.

|Bunhead|
Worse things to be than bored.

|Starface|
True.

How's your night going?

|Bunhead|
Not bad but I'd still prefer to forget it happened.

|Starface|
Sorry to hear that. I'd say come see me and we'll get your mind off it, but Xyri meeting is still underway.

|Bunhead|
It's okay. Their stuff is important. Did Zeli tell you anything about this Xereth guy?

|Starface|
Not much.
One of sixteen immortals.
We don't trust him. That's about it. I've been promised more eventually.

|Bunhead|
Same.

|Starface|
So, you had a bad day and I can't distract you with a nighttime stroll. What can I distract you with?

|Bunhead|
Words.

|Starface|
I'm not very good with words.

|Bunhead|
Liar.

|Starface|
Tell me something good.
Let's forget the bad day.

|Bunhead|
I recently saw a friend I haven't seen in a long time. That was good.

|Starface|
Heck yeah.

|Bunhead|
Now you tell me something good.

|Starface|
Hm...
I guess things are okay
with my girlfriend?

|Bunhead|
You guess?

|Starface|
I'm not good at things!
I'm figuring it out as I go.

|Bunhead|
I'm happy for you but if
she hurts you I'll lock her
in a portal for all eternity.

|Starface|
Thanks Bunhead.

If your boyfriend hurts you I'll
pour molten silver down his
throat till he drowns.

|Bunhead|
Dark

|Starface|
Silver is pretty bright, actually.

Ren couldn't help but smile as they talked. She eventually dozed off with the lights still on.

The next morning Ren had more texts from Simon asking if he could come over to talk. She ignored them for a while, putting it off till later in the afternoon before asking Dare if Simon could come by. Once she had permission, she procrastinated actually telling Simon to come over. The day slipped away and it was almost dark by the time she sent the text.

Dare agreed to give them some space to talk when Simon showed up thirty minutes later. He gave her a look on his way out and she knew he'd be randomly checking on them.

"So," she said awkwardly as she led Simon to the couch. Simon sat beside her, watching her intently. "What did you wanna talk about?"

"Last night?" He smiled softly. "You left so fast, and didn't text me so... something's wrong."

"Nothing's wrong."

"Ren, it's okay. You can tell me. I wanna fix whatever I did."

"There's nothing to fix."

Simon sighed. *"Please?"*

Her heart raced and she just knew her cheeks were burning. He grabbed her hand, holding it gently. That made her heart beat faster. She sighed, staring down at their hands.

"I guess... it seemed like you were maybe... setting things up for us to have sex and I panicked," she blurted the words quickly, as if that would make it better.

"Oh."

"I just... I haven't... *you know*. Not with anyone. And I'm not ready to and so when you—"

"Ren, it's okay. Hey, look at me."

She took a deep breath and looked up. He was smiling.

"I'm so sorry. I didn't necessarily think we'd have *sex* but, I guess I thought, maybe something would happen? But there's absolutely no rush for us to do that. You know that, right?"

How could she know? They'd never talked about it. She didn't know what to say, her insides were so squirmy.

"I'm so sorry. It's totally fine that you're not ready. I promise." He squeezed her hand. "I'm not in any hurry."

"It... doesn't bother you? That I don't want to?"

"Of course not." He paused and released a breath. "I... with my ex, after we broke up she still... would come around, for that. And I just let it happen. Cause I thought it meant that... she actually loved me." He shook his head. "But she was just using me. And... it hurt like hell."

Ren squeezed his hand.

"It's not *meaningless* to me," he continued, voice soft. "I'm happy to wait, as long as you want."

"Okay."

He smiled as he let go of her hand and put his arm around her, pulling her closer to him. She exhaled, feeling a little better.

"I'm so sorry I scared you. I swear I'd never force you into something you don't want."

She shook her head. "I wasn't scared of you. Just... scared. I don't even know why."

He smiled. "Everyone's scared their first time, even if they don't admit it. I was."

"Really?"

He nodded. "You know, we could just stick to dates out for now? Nowhere near a bed. No temptation for me. No anxiety for you. Would that make you more comfortable?"

She nodded slowly, her body finally relaxing. "I guess."

He smiled and kissed her cheek. "Do you wanna do anything tonight?"

"Sure."

He pulled back, grinning. She really did love that smile of his.

"We could go out to a movie?"

"Perfect. Let me just go ask my dad."

He nodded as she got up and made her way to the stairs just as Dare turned the corner, coming up them.

"All good, kiddo?"

"Yeah. Is it okay if I go to a movie with Simon?"

"Do you actually wanna go?" he asked in a whisper. "Am I supposed to say no?"

She smiled. "I wanna go. We talked about things and it's all good now."

He raised an eyebrow.

"I overreacted," she mumbled. "And... we're on the same page now, with waiting." She blushed as she said it.

Dare sighed. "Alright. Movie, then straight back home, okay?"

"Thanks." She hugged him then went back to Simon.

By the time they were seated in the theater most of her tension was gone.

"You're sure you're okay now?" Simon whispered as the lights went out.

"Yes." She was confident it wasn't a lie.

He grinned and put his arm around her. She released a breath and leaned her head into him, feeling content.

53
Normal Happy

Ren sat on Ocean's colorful bed, unable to stop smiling as Ocean talked at her from across the room. She was setting up her walk-in closet, which was almost as big as Ren's. All of her furniture was black, and already put together, contrasting nicely with the lilac walls. The TV stand sat across from the bed, blocking a section of the floor to ceiling windows. Her desk was on the wall by her closet, and she had bookshelves on each side of it, both still empty.

Ocean was focused on the small details, like organizing her closet and hanging up art.

Ren still couldn't believe she was back full-time. She'd struggled so much to make friends as a kid, till she met Ocean. And then Ocean left. And then she lost Clea... Ren loved Jasper more than *anything* but it was nice to be close with girls, too.

"So excited to have American food again. I mean, you can get it in France but it's not the *same*."

Ren frowned. "Don't you miss France though? And your friends? This is the second time you've had to up and leave everything."

Ocean paused, glancing back at Ren. Then she forced a smile. "Yeah, but, I've been missing you for *years!* And now I live on your street. So everything is *great*."

"Did something happen?" Ren asked as she grabbed the yellow stuffed bunny beside her. Ocean had that for as long as she could remember. She hugged it to her stomach.

Ocean fell silent again, then slowly walked over and sat on the end of the bed.

"I maybe had a falling out with my friends." She sighed. "At first, when Dad said an opportunity to move back here came up I wasn't sure but... things got worse. And worse. And *really very* worse. It's why we came back earlier than planned."

"Wanna talk about it?"

Ocean swallowed. Ren passed her the bunny and Ocean held it to her chest as she tucked her legs underneath her and sighed again.

"Okay so, you know my friend Eloise?"

Ren nodded.

"Well I sorta maybe kinda had feelings for her? Surprise, I'm bi! Anyways, I eventually confessed how I felt and she was great about it at first, thanked me for being honest, promised things wouldn't be weird and all that. But *then* she told her boyfriend, Jean, and *he* got mad and told her to stop being friends with me." She paused, releasing a breath. "And then she told *everyone* that I was gay, so Juliette and Genevieve stopped talking to me too. I was getting bullied and it was kinda awful. So, when Dad said we could move now I was like get me *out* of here. I made him promise to get me into your school, and try and pick a house near you cause..." She paused, smiling. "You're like, my *only* friend now."

Ren crawled across the bed and hugged her. Ocean let out a deep breath, leaning her head into Ren's shoulder.

"That sucks so much. I'm sorry. I promise you're never ever gonna lose me. Especially over something so stupid."

Ocean didn't say anything at first, just leaned her head against Ren's.

"Why didn't you tell me about any of this before?" Ren asked after a moment, pulling back to look at her.

Ocean didn't meet her eyes. "I... was gonna but, you kept... pushing back our calls." She shrugged.

Oh god. Guilt filled her up. "I'm so sorry, Oce. I didn't mean to not be around."

Ocean nodded. "It's fine. I know it's hard to get together when I was there but..." She smiled nervously. "I'm here now."

"Yeah! And I got you, okay. You need me, I am *here*." Ren hugged her again. "I know what it's like to have no one, remember?"

Ocean laughed. "But then I came along."

"You certainly did. Changed my life. And now you're back here, you're not alone anymore."

Ocean nodded, her brown eyes glistening. "It was really bad."

Ren sat up straight, holding her gaze. "I won't let anyone *ever* treat you like that again."

She wiped her eyes. "You've gotten fiercer with age."

Ren smiled proudly, trying not to think about *why* that was. Ocean couldn't know about Kaida. It dawned on her that all the pain of lying and hiding and disappointing she'd gone through with Jasper was bound to repeat now, with Ocean. The weight of it all felt so heavy in that moment as she stared at her friend. A girl she'd known since the age of eight. The first friend she'd ever really made. *I cannot ruin this.*

Ocean sighed. "Are you still friends with the boy that fell in love with you?"

Ren's eyes widened. She only told Ocean about that because Ocean wasn't *here*. She forced a smile. "Yes. But, he left. Doesn't go to our school anymore."

"Oh. Boo. Anyways, thanks for understanding. Coming out to people is weird, but, I knew you'd get it."

Ren grinned. "Well, I do have a bisexual dad, a gay dad, and now, *two* bisexual best friends, so..."

Ocean squinted at her. "You *sure* you're straight?"

Ren laughed. "So far."

"Are there any kids out at the school?"

"Uh, well Jasper isn't really out at school yet, so keep that to yourself. There's a few that are though. Lola, she's a lesbian. We love her. I think Destin is bisexual maybe? Oh and one of my boyfriend's bandmates, Cameron, he's gay. And there's Jackson. *Very* gay."

"And... everyone else is cool with them?"

"Oh, yeah! I haven't seen anyone getting like, outwardly bullied for it or anything. So, if you wanna be out at school I think you'll be fine."

Ocean nodded slowly, seeming uncertain. Exactly how bad had things been for her? Ren's guilt swirled. She should have noticed. Should have been there for her when Ocean needed her.

"You think your friends will like me?"

Ren smiled. "They're gonna love you. I think you're especially gonna get along with Nico. He's just, a very extroverted people person. Kevin's really funny, always puts a smile on everyone's face. There's Nari, she's the sweetest. Ashley's super easy to talk to. And, Bellamy likes everyone."

Ocean raised an eyebrow. "Oh my god I get to meet *Bellamy.*"

Ren paled. "Oh. God. Please don't say anything to him about—"

"I would *never*! I'm just excited to meet the boy you've been in love with for two years." Ocean smiled. "Are you still?"

"No. Absolutely not. I'm..." She paused. "With Simon."

"Simon is *so* hot. Do I get to meet him on Tuesday too?"

Ren smiled. "Yes. Simon and I talked about doing a big movie night, with his friends, and you and Jasper. Think it could be really fun."

"I'm so down." Ocean exhaled. "I just want... normal happy friends. No more stressing about what people think of me. Not being myself around them."

Ren grabbed her hand. "It's gonna be great. I *promise*."

Ocean smiled then she sighed as she glanced at the clock on her wall. "You gotta go soon, right?"

"Oh, yeah. Simon invited me to his band practice."

"You're just gonna sit there and watch him play his guitar and sing?"

"I guess so?" She shrugged. "He said I could work on my homework while they practice."

Ocean sighed dramatically. "I want a hot musician boyfriend."

"His bandmates are *all* single."

Ocean grinned.

54
Chemistry

Ren was nervous as Dad dropped her off outside of a white townhouse. Simon stood outside waiting for her, a smile splitting his face as she walked up. He pulled her into his arms.

"I'm so excited you're here."

"I'm nervous."

He backed up and looked down at her with a frown. "You already met the band. They think you're great."

"I met them for like five minutes."

"Five minutes with you is enough," he replied. "But... we could have a code, if you get overwhelmed?"

"Code?"

He nodded. "Yeah like... if you grab your ear, I'll know you wanna leave. I can make an excuse." His smile was lovely. "Yeah?"

She giggled. "Okay."

He grabbed her hand and pulled her in through a door into Kit's house. He guided her past the stairs and through another door. It opened into a huge studio space with red brick floors and white brick walls. Their band stuff was all set up on the left side of the room, across from a big black couch, with green accents in it. There were so many posters on the wall above the couch, and two mini fridges beside it.

"This is where the magic happens," he said, pointing to the set up. The instruments were on a circular black and white rug. "Back through that door," he pointed toward the back wall, also covered in art and photos. "That's where we record the music. Uh, that door is a bathroom." He smiled as he looked down at her. "And this couch is where you sit while we play."

She nodded as voices echoed from behind them. They turned to see the rest of the band walking in.

"Ren!" Allie's face lit up when she saw her. She didn't have any fun makeup on today, but was still so pretty, her brown hair pulled up into a messy bun on top of her head.

"Oh good, you're here," Cam said. "Maybe you can tell Simon to stop trying to cancel the damn tour."

Ren frowned. "What?"

"Dude, shut the fuck up," Simon hissed.

"What's he talking about?" she asked, looking up at Simon.

"She doesn't even know? You wanna cancel it for her and she doesn't even know." Cameron rolled his eyes.

"That's not what I said!"

"Guys, give it a rest. *Now,*" Allie said.

"I'm just saying—"

"Can we not do this right now?" Simon glared at Cam before looking at Ren, embarrassed.

"Uh, can I have a moment alone with Simon, please?" Ren asked, heart racing.

"You got him in *trouble,*" Kit said with a laugh as Allie turned both boys around and shoved them back toward the door by the stairs.

Ren waited till she couldn't hear them anymore before meeting Simon's eyes. "Okay, what's going on?"

"Nothing."

She gave him a flat stare.

He rolled his eyes. "Cam's mad cause I said we should hold off on adding *more* shows to the tour we're planning. I never said I wanted to cancel it."

"You never told me about a tour. That's exciting... but, you're not excited?"

He stared at his boots. "I'm graduating in two weeks. Done with school, so I won't see you there. Summer is the only time I'm gonna get with you. When that's over, you still got two years of school and you're probably gonna go to college cause you're so smart. And I'll be doing shows, hopefully. Traveling maybe. I just feel like after this summer I'll see you a lot less, and I can handle that I just... don't wanna lose the time we have now."

Ren's heart raced. *He sees all that with me?* She swallowed. "Simon, I'm not going anywhere. If you guys can do a tour, you should do it. And I mean, if some of the shows aren't too far, maybe I could come? It'll be summer, so my dads might say yes to that."

He stared at her. "You wanna... come on tour with me?"

"Well, I don't think I'd be allowed to go *with* you. My dads would probably drive me. Staying in a hotel and stuff. But—"

"I'll take it," he said, face slowly softening. "You'd seriously come to some of the shows?"

She laughed. *"Simon,* I've already been to one and I loved it. Why wouldn't I wanna go?"

His eyes were so sad.

"I *hate* your ex-girlfriend," she mumbled.

"What?"

"For making you look at me like that. Like I wouldn't care. Like I wouldn't still be here, if you left." She grabbed his face with both hands. "I love your music. And I'm not gonna disappear if you're gone for the summer."

His eyes watered. "Ren..."

"I promise," she whispered, holding his gaze.

He nodded, blue eyes shining. "I think you're the best thing that's ever happened to me."

Ren smiled, heart pounding. She pulled him closer, lips crashing into his. He wrapped his arms around her, holding her tight. She felt so *warm*. When he pulled back he rested his forehead against hers.

"I wasn't gonna cancel the tour. I just didn't wanna add more shows. Allie had a whole list of places we could maybe play. She was ready to turn it from six shows into thirty. None of them are in relationships. They don't *get* it. Cam said he was gonna start booking them without even telling me when or where they were."

"Not going anywhere," she whispered.

He kissed her again.

"How far are the shows?"

"Farthest is like, ten hour drive? But the first set of shows is while you're still in school."

"That's so soon." She frowned at him. "You didn't tell me."

"Sorry."

"Well, if you add more shows after school's over for me, I can try to come if they're not too far?"

One moment he was on the verge of tears, now he looked happier than she'd ever seen him. His smile wide and gorgeous. "You're incredible."

She grinned up at him. "Apologize to your friends, okay? And compromise."

"Compromise?"

"Yeah, add more shows, if you want. I mean, this is your career. Your passion. I'm not gonna get mad if you do the thing you love to do, the thing I love seeing you do."

He bit his lip. "Fuck. Okay." He texted his friends and a moment later they came back down.

"Did you convince him to stop being stupid?" Cameron asked.

"Yes. But please don't call him stupid."

Cameron stared at her a moment before smiling.

"Simon agrees not to cancel any shows, but you also have to agree to *discuss* adding more. You *all* have to agree on it. And he's not against adding shows, he just wants *some* of the summer free."

Allie grinned. "That's very reasonable."

"Good plan!" Kit said, raising his can of Coke toward Ren.

Simon and Cameron stared at each other for a moment before Cam finally muttered a single, "Fine."

Ren nudged Simon. "The other thing," she whispered.

He sighed then looked back at Cam. "Sorry."

Ren glared at Cam and he rolled his eyes.

"Sorry."

"Aw, good job boys," Allie said. "Can we play music now?"

"Yes *please*," Simon said. He kissed Ren's cheek then walked over to his guitar.

"Um, wait. I sort of have... presents for you guys," Ren said, anxious.

"For us?" Kit asked.

Ren nodded. "It's super silly and you absolutely don't have to wear them, but..." She unzipped her backpack with shaking hands and pulled out the crocheted beanies she made.

"Oh my god!" Allie dropped her drumsticks as she walked back toward Ren.

"What the fuck." Kit's face was filled with joy as she handed him one.

Even Cameron was smiling as he looked at his. She slowly looked up at Simon, handing him the last one.

His smile was beautiful as he pulled the beanie on. "How do I look?"

Ren bit her lip. "*So* good."

The beanies all matched. Black yarn, with the words Echo Fever on them in different neon colors to match their instruments. Simon's was blue, Allie's pink, Kit's purple, and Cam's was green.

"This is so cool. Oh my god. We're so cute." Allie pulled out her phone and started taking pictures. "I'm gonna die."

"This really is cool, Ren. Thanks," Cam added.

She beamed at them.

"See, I told you guys she's the fucking *best*," Simon said as he pulled her into his arms again.

"Alright alright, she can stay," Kit said. "But we should actually play now. We need to practice The Walk more, if you wanna play it on tour..." Ren's smile widened. That was the song Simon wrote for her.

He kissed her one more time before she sat on the couch while they set up. She leaned into the plush purple pillows, comfortable. As she watched them get ready, she noticed a full-sized skeleton sitting at the keyboard by the back wall. And a stuffed bear in a skeleton shirt sitting on one of the amps. She smiled as she pulled out her homework. It was extremely difficult to focus on anything but the band, though. Simon staring at her while singing *about* her... her heart would not stop fluttering.

"We should practice Colors and Hues, that one is gonna blow up. I can *feel it*," Allie said when they took a break.

"What song is that?" Ren asked.

"A new one, about you," Kit answered.

Ren blinked and turned to Simon, who was blushing, not meeting her eyes. "I thought there was only one song about me?"

Allie laughed.

"There's like six finished ones, and who knows how many works in progress," Cameron answered.

Simon closed his eyes.

"*Stop*, you're embarrassing him," Allie said.

"It's not embarrassing. Most our songs are about Victoria, at least Ren's fucking normal. Did Vicky ever give us gifts? *No*." He smiled at Ren. "*And* I think these are some of our best songs yet."

Kit giggled. "Vicky just gave us a stupider and sadder Simon."

"She was literally the worst. Cheated on him and everything and he *still* kept crawling back to her."

Allie hit Cam with her drumstick.

Ren stared at Simon. He was standing very still, his eyes closed.

"Oh come on, don't be like that," Cam said. "We *like* Ren. We're being nice!"

"Yeah. She's leagues better than Vicky. *And* Hannah, for that matter."

"*Guys*," Allie hissed.

"Yes, great. Make it very clear how fucking stupid I was in my last relationship," Simon said coldly. "You're making me look *so* good in front of Ren."

Ren pushed her books aside and got off the couch. They were all silent as she grabbed Simon's face, forcing him to look down at her.

"You look very good from where I'm standing," she whispered.

Kit snorted.

"Alright alright," Allie said. "Let's take a break. We'll go up, order some food. Ren, what's good for you?"

"I'll eat anything," she said, glancing at the girl as she pushed both boys toward the stairs.

"Pizza?"

"Yeah."

Simon held her eyes while they disappeared from the room, then he slowly exhaled.

"Hey," she said, smiling. "You okay?"

He nodded. "Sorry about them."

"Nothing to be sorry about." She leaned up and kissed him. He seemed to relax a little. "You look so good in the beanie."

He smiled. "Really?"

Ren nodded and wrapped her arms around herself as she stepped back, looking around the room. She just noticed another skeleton stuffed animal, this one a bunny, tucked behind the cookie jars on top of the mini fridge.

"You're cold? Kit keeps it like an icebox in here." Simon took off his jacket and handed it to her.

Ren took it in her hands, confused.

Simon stared at her, frowning. "Put it on."

Ren slowly slid her arms into the soft black sleeves, trying to calm her racing heart as her mind drifted back back back to an alleyway with Lycan. She still had that jacket, tucked away safely in her closet. Lycan hadn't been wearing a tight black tank top though. Her face heated as she stared at Simon's arms. He didn't seem to notice, grabbing her hand and pulling her back to the couch.

"You alright?" he asked, frowning. "You wanna leave now?"

"I... you..." She licked her lips as she sat beside him.

"Did I do something wrong?"

She shook her head fervently. "You look good," she blurted.

Simon smiled slowly.

"I... haven't seen you in a... tank top..." Her face was absolutely burning.

"*That's* why you're flustered." He laughed. "Okay. Tank tops are hot. Good to know."

"You're always hot."

He tilted his head, eyes narrowed. "Am I?"

"Yes. *Obviously.*"

"Well, you don't normally say things like that. Girls never do."

"Oh. I'm sorry? I can say it more."

He bit his lip, staring at her with those bright eyes.

Ren grinned, trying to shove down her embarrassment. "You, Simon Sims, are *so* pretty. Genuinely beautiful. With those eyes and that smile. And your arms, my *god*. Who gave you the *right*?"

He laughed again.

"And your voice, don't get me started on that. And—"

He kissed her. Ren melted into it, his hand sliding up into her hair. She was breathless when he pulled back. She couldn't stop blushing, so she looked around, avoiding his gaze.

On the table beside the couch was a bottle of black nail polish. Ren picked it up, needing something to fiddle with.

"Is this Allie's?" she asked.

"It's mine."

Ren paused, looking back at him. "Yours?"

He nodded.

"Never seen you wear nail polish."

"Yeah, well. Some people don't like that. I stopped wearing it when we met. Didn't wanna scare you away."

Ren giggled. "You're silly." She opened the bottle and started painting one of her nails. "It's kinda hot. Like the eyeliner."

"You are *very* attracted to me today," he mumbled, taking the bottle from her hands.

She stared as he took her hand in his and started painting the nails for her. Something about that felt very intimate, as she looked up into his eyes.

"Do you only wear black?" she asked, heart thumping loudly in her chest.

"Usually." He smiled. "Not against other colors though."

"Would you... wear blue? Would match your eyes. Or something shiny."

His smile widened. "I'll wear whatever you want."

"Really? Pink?"

He nodded. "I'm used to people judging me for it. I don't give a shit. Bring pink polish next time you're here. Or purple. Since that's your favorite color. We could match."

Ren beamed at him as he switched hands.

"You know," he said softly. "You keep really showing up for me. And I love it, Ren. And I just..." He paused, sighing. "I want you to know I see you."

"See me?"

Simon nodded. "How creative you are. How *talented* you are. I see that, and I see you."

Ren blinked. "Well now I really wanna hug you. But I can't, cause my nails are wet."

Simon grinned as he closed the bottle of polish. Then he gently lifted her chin and kissed her. "Does that help?"

"Definitely."

"This... feels kinda perfect," he whispered, lips close to hers.

"Definitely kinda perfect," she agreed.

The others came back down a few minutes later and they ate pizza together, all of them pointedly avoiding the subject of Simon's ex and songs he'd written about various girls, including her.

They practiced a bit more after food, but then Ren had to leave.

She stood outside with Simon while waiting for Dad to pick her up. He kept his arms around her, his smile unfaltering.

"How'd I get so lucky to get you?" he whispered.

"I think someone kicked my book down the hall."

"*Chemistry,* wasn't it?" His smile widened.

She nodded and he leaned in, kissing her. She got lost in it for a moment, not noticing when the car pulled up behind them.

"Ren!"

She jumped, glancing over to see Dad staring at her through the rolled down window. She blushed.

Simon laughed. "Guess you gotta go."

She pushed her head into his chest. He held her a moment, seeming to not care that her dad was watching.

"You think he'll like, get out of the car if we just stay like this?" he asked.

Ren giggled. "Maybe."

"Alright. I don't wanna die. You should go."

"I was thinking..." She paused, looking up at him. "Maybe you could come over for dinner sometime, at my house. With my dads."

Simon made a face. "I don't know."

"What? Why not?"

He shrugged. "They're never gonna like me, Ren."

"Well, they don't know you. *Hence* the dinner." She grinned but he just shook his head. "I had dinner with your mom. You can do one dinner with my dads."

"Yeah, but that's different."

"How so?"

"My mom likes you?" He laughed. "Listen, dads never like me. And you have two of them. I'm never gonna win that fight. I'm a musician with a motorcycle." He shook his head again. "Sorry." He kissed her on the cheek then pulled back.

She sighed as he turned away. "Wait, your jacket?"

Simon looked back at her and smiled. "That's yours now, my dear."

Ren softened at the look in his eyes. "I can keep it?"

He nodded. "Should have given you one ages ago. For the record, *all* my jackets are yours. If you want them."

She smiled and he waved before going inside. She wanted to press him about dinner, but that would have to wait. With a sigh she got in the car.

55
Bigger Problems

Lycan sat on the roof, feet hanging over the edge as he waited for Kaida and Apex to arrive. Their Xyri were finally ready to tell them more about this Xereth guy, so he had to make up a lame excuse to Jules about why he couldn't study with her. He kept overthinking that conversation as he idly shifted the fidget toy he'd made in his hand.

A few minutes passed before they landed behind him. He stood with a sigh, his toy puffing to mist as he crossed the roof. Kaida rolled her shoulders as her wings went in.

"How do we do this?" Apex asked, his wings slower to fold away.

"Zig says we gotta touch if we wanna be able to hear each other's Xyri."

"Touch?" Apex raised an eyebrow.

"Our hands, dummy," Kaida said with a roll of her eyes.

Lycan grinned, feeling a little lighter in their company. He nodded and they sat in a circle in the middle of the roof, then Kaida held both her hands out to them. Lycan took one, Apex took the other.

"Kumbaya, kumbaya..." Apex sang.

Kaida glared at him but Lycan could tell she was trying not to laugh.

All of their suits pulled back, exposing their bare hands. He tried not to notice how soft Kaida's hand was. After a moment their suits moved back, going over each other's hands and sealing tight. They couldn't let go without undoing it.

Hello kiddies, a voice said in his head.

"That's Pozi," Apex muttered.

Lycan smiled.

Hope the rat is treating you well, Zeli replied.

"Oh, she sounds nice."

I'm not a rat!

"She is."

Debatable.

424

Enough, a new voice spoke. *We need to talk about Xereth.* Zig's voice wasn't as erratic and gritty as Pozi, but also nowhere near as calm and distinguished as Zeli. There was depth to it.

"Okay, what do we know about this man and what he's doing?" Lycan asked.

We know he's responsible for Xenos going missing, Zeli answered.

"And there's no way to find him?" Kaida asked. "I mean, if we found Xenos, then he could deal with the other one, right?"

We should be able to find him, and Xereth.

But we can't now. He's gone. Poof!

"Are other Xyri looking for him?" Lycan asked.

Yes. Many of us have been searching. But not all of those believe he is missing. Some think he is hiding intentionally.

"Would he do that?" Apex asked. "Hide on purpose?"

No. Zeli sounded certain.

If he was, Dorixi would have lured him out last year. We believe that was his plan in the first place, Zig replied.

"Who's... Dory?"

The Xyri who Bonded with Vendetta.

"That Xyri was willing to let him kill hundreds of people just to lure this one guy out of hiding?" Kaida asked.

I believe so, yes.

Dorixi does not normally Bond. He isn't an evil careless creature, despite what he let that boy do with the powers. We assumed he was trying to get Xenos's attention, Zeli said.

And it didn't work, Pozi added. *Which just confirms it. Xenos can't get to us. And Xereth is responsible.*

"And he's in New York now. For what?"

We... do not yet know.

Lycan frowned, sensing the hesitation in Zeli's words. She had a theory, perhaps? And she didn't wanna share it.

"If we don't know what he's gonna do or when, do we really need to be worried about this?" Apex asked with a frown.

"Yeah, we have bigger problems right now," Kaida added. "Like Gaia."

Trust me. Xereth is a big problem. You are not ready for what he is capable of. Zeli's voice was filled with hatred, and her darker emotions about Xereth surprised him.

"What should we be expecting here?" Kaida asked. "Like, can we even anticipate what he'll do?"

"Could we even stop it? You said he's immortal."

Xereth started the French Revolution.

The Great Fire of London.

The Titanic, Pozi added.

Lycan frowned at that last one. "He sank the Titanic? Why?"

We could not say, Zeli answered. *Suffice it to say, he will go to great lengths, ignoring the cost of lives, to benefit himself and his wishes.*

"What did he do in the war?"

The Xyri didn't respond. Lycan felt tension in both of their hands as they all met each other's eyes.

"You said Xereth and Xenos were on opposite sides of the war," Apex continued. "Who was on which side, what were they trying to accomplish then?"

"They're not gonna tell us," Kaida grumbled.

Some things you don't need to know, Zig answered.

"What if we do need to know?" Apex shook his head. "What if it's relevant?"

Xereth was on the side of the Bonded, Pozi said with a sigh. *Xenos was not.*

Kaida frowned at that.

"Xenos wasn't on the side of the Bonded? But..."

It wasn't as simple as Xyri versus humans. Or Bonded versus non Bonded. There were some of each on each side of the conflict, Zeli explained. *And that is all I will say on the subject.*

"But—"

No. Moving on, Zeli continued.

"But wait. What side were *you* on?" Apex said. "All three of you fought in the war, right?"

Zeli sighed.

Kirzigith and I were on the side of the Bonded, Pozi answered, sounding resigned. *Azazelith was not.*

Apex looked surprised to hear that, but Lycan already knew it. He'd done some research on Stardust when he first Bonded Zeli. She fought and died for those without power.

"I still think this isn't something we need to worry about now," Kaida said, voice low. "There's nothing we can do about it."

Lycan sighed. Their Xyri were on one page, while the three of them were on another. There *was* nothing they could do about Xereth. They needed to focus on Gaia before she hurt more people. But that rage he felt inside of Zeli made him want to do *something*.

"What about the other immortals? You said there were more. Can any of them help?" Lycan asked.

The Xyri stayed quiet a moment.

Most of them haven't been around in a long time. They stopped getting involved long before the war, even. Xenos and Xereth were the last to still Bond with us when needed.

But... I think some might help if we found them. If we asked, Pozi replied.

I'm not so sure. But Xarax is in New York. We could consider approaching her, Zig said.

Xystos is also here, Zeli added.

Pozi groaned. *He's not gonna help us.*

Probably not.

Xinav would help... Pozi muttered.

Yes, but she's busy with... you know what. We can not involve her.

Not under any circumstances, Zig added.

Pozi grumbled but didn't argue.

Lycan raised an eyebrow at that. The Xyri had so many secrets. There was so much they didn't know.

"Okay... so, there's other immortals we can approach," Kaida said.

Timeless, yes.

"So, we make a plan to ask the Timeless for help. But, in the meantime I still think Gaia is the bigger problem. She's killed a lot of people in a short amount of time, and now she's working with Vapor... it's more important. We gotta focus on stopping her. *Then* we can worry about Xereth."

"I agree," Lycan said. "Get Gaia out of the way, then put all our focus into the Timeless."

Fine, Pozi muttered. *But be wary. If any of you see Xereth again we need to be prepared.*

"Always prepared," Apex replied. "It's a good plan."

Kaida nodded. Lycan let out a breath as he looked down at their intertwined hands and smiled. He knew his feelings for her were still there, just under the surface. Perhaps he'd never be rid of them, but over time he could push them down, more and more, until they didn't sting.

"Meeting adjourned then?" Apex asked.

For now.

All three suits pulled back, exposing and releasing their hands. Kaida dropped his then stood and stretched. He watched her walk across the roof, looking tense. He sighed as he glanced at Apex, who was still holding his hand, a sad smile on his face as he also watched Kaida. Lycan grinned then wiggled their hands.

"Oh, sorry." Apex dropped his hand then proceeded to lie down on his back.

Lycan shook his head as he got up and moved toward Kaida.

"Hey," he muttered as he gently grabbed her arm, the suit covering his hands again. "You good?"

She nodded. "Just, worried about Gaia. It's one thing for me to confidently say 'we gotta stop her' and another to... do it."

"Listen, we'll manage. Okay?"

"Did I tell you that my cousin was there?"

He frowned. "Where?"

"At the library. Not ten minutes before Gaia attacked. Ten minutes is all that separates it from a thing I can *say* or a thing that would have truly *ruined me*," she said, eyes watering.

He didn't know what to say. "When the time comes, I'll take care of it. You don't need to worry about it."

Her blue eyes were so sad as she stared at him. "Ly…"

"I can handle it," he whispered. "You distract her. And I'll end it."

She nodded slowly. "You and me."

He smiled. "Always. Remember, we don't approach her alone. You went to that warehouse without me…"

Kaida frowned. "I was too late so it didn't matter."

"Yes, but you didn't *call*. We had a deal."

She sighed. "Promise." Her shoulders slumped then she reached out and pulled him closer, wrapping her arms around him. He relaxed at her touch, resting his chin on her head.

"Told you I'm the third wheel!" Apex called.

Lycan glanced at him as Kaida pulled back. She was smiling now but it didn't reach her eyes.

56
Flatline

After their meeting Bellamy went home to have dinner with his mom.

"How was Jules?" she asked as she set out the containers of Mexican they ordered on the counter.

"Huh?"

She raised an eyebrow. "Your girlfriend? I assumed you were with her after school."

"Oh, yeah. I was." He forced a smile. "She's fine."

"So, did it work? Are you over Ren?"

"I don't know." He grabbed his food and moved to the table. "I like Jules though."

"That's good. How's school?"

"Good," he answered. "How was work?"

"Good," she replied. Then she smiled. "What about *books*? What have you been reading lately?"

Bellamy laughed. "Well..."

He spent the entire dinner talking about books. It was one of the things he and his mom had in common, she loved reading as much as he did, though she didn't get to do it for fun as often anymore. Though, neither did he.

After dinner he showered then retired to his room, preparing to do some homework before patrolling. His phone started beeping with alerts before he could even pull out his books.

Here we go, he thought as he grabbed the phone and put on the suit.

Three minutes later Lycan stared in horror at what once was The Brooklyn Bridge, sinking into the East River. He tugged on time, and ended up back in his bedroom. It did no good. By the time he returned to the scene the bridge was already gone.

Kaida arrived a moment later, followed by Apex.

"Holy shit!" Apex yelled as his wings slowed.

"There's a lot of people in that water, get to work," Lycan replied.

Apex nodded, and dove downward. He turned to Kaida. Her blue eyes were glistening.

"We got this, stay here."

"But—"

"Medics will be here any second. Help them, okay? We'll bring up the survivors."

"But—"

"You're better suited for that," he continued. "Go by the banks, wait for the medics!"

He didn't wait for her answer as he turned and dove in the water. Apex was already splashing back out, a body in his arms. The water was cold and murky. A good portion of the bridge was sinking slowly, cars all around it. He ignored the bodies floating around him, hoping they could swim as he went for the cars instead. He was more worried about people drowning, trapped inside them, trapped under the debris of the bridge.

He reached the closest car and pressed his hands against the glass. A woman and her small child were inside, the car nearly full of water as the woman held her little girl against her chest, tears in her eyes. He tried to mimic holding his breath to her before he grabbed the door and *pulled*, ripping it clean off. Water rushed in around the woman as she shoved her kid toward him. He grabbed the little girl, holding her against him with one arm while he pulled the mom out with the other. Thankfully the mom could swim, so he focused on getting back up with the little girl.

When he broke the surface, he turned to see the mom appearing beside him.

"You're good, you're good," he said as they swam to the rocks where Kaida waited.

Once they were safe on solid ground he dove back in, crossing Apex. The second time he brought someone up, Parody was there. She reached out to Apex, taking his power before diving in the water with them.

He spotted someone else in a suit in the water, a Bonded he'd never seen before. But there'd been reports of a new hero at the warehouse last week. This had to be him. Lycan saw the guy disappear right in front of him, replaced with a civilian floating in the water. A moment later the guy broke out of the car he'd been beside. Lycan didn't stop to wonder how the power worked, he was just grateful they had more heroes now as they moved, back and forth, pulling people out.

Lycan's lungs burned as he moved through the water, forcing his body down toward a car, slowly sinking toward the bottom. His heart stopped as he saw the boy in the back seat. Big curly hair, frantic amber eyes. *Nico.* The car was almost entirely full of water now and

Nico wasn't alone. Someone was in the driver's seat, banging on the window, while Nico held someone else, seemingly unconscious, up in the back seat. The green glow of Apex swam past him. Lycan turned, throwing out a silver rope in his panic. It wrapped around Apex's arm and pulled him close. Apex's eyes widened as he looked into the car. Three bodies, nearly submerged. Lycan couldn't save them all. Together they ripped the doors free.

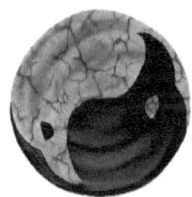

Jasper was grateful he could barely feel the cold water as he dove in and out, pulling bodies free. He felt so fast, so energized, getting two people out for everyone one Lycan did. When Parody showed up she tapped his arm and dove right in, moving just as quickly. *This* is what his powers were for. Saving people in need, being the hero in that final moment where they thought they wouldn't make it. But then he pulled them out, took them to shore, saved their lives.

Something grabbed his arm. He turned in surprise as a silver rope pulled him to Lycan. Then he saw Nico's face pressed against the glass, Kevin's limp body held above him. He nodded to Lycan and they pulled the doors off together. He took Kevin immediately, heart pounding frantically in his chest.

Lycan had *no idea* they were saving his friends. *Please let us save them. Please.* He couldn't tell if Kevin was even breathing as he swam up to the surface. At least Nico and his mom were still awake, still alive. Lycan followed with both of them in his arms.

Come on, Kevin. Don't you dare fucking die on me. He ran up the bank toward Kaida. Her blue eyes widened in terror as she recognized Kevin's face.

She took his lifeless body from Jasper and turned, disappearing inside her burning pink portal. Jasper stood there a moment as Lycan came up, Nico and his mom collapsing to their knees in the dirt.

"I..." He couldn't move. Was Kevin...

"Back... back in the water, Apex," Lycan breathed.

He sounded as terrible as Jasper felt. He glanced at Nico, before he turned and ran back toward the water. He wanted to scream, to cry, to be *sure* his friends were okay. But others needed him. He had to be a hero.

He is not breathing, Zig said as she stepped into the portal.

Kaida fell to her knees, dropping Kevin on the floor. *No no no.* She began chest compressions, feeling so disconnected from herself as she counted.

It felt like hours passed, in that singular moment, hovering above Kevin, his face pale and clammy, his chest still. *Please no.* She could almost hear the flatline. Could almost hear the words... *no.*

He seemed so small, even though he was taller than her by several inches. He hadn't been, when she met him. Kevin always had the biggest smile, he was *so* full of life. Where was that now?

She continued compressions, arms aching, eyes burning.

Finally he moved. A cough burst forth, water spilling out of his mouth. Beat. Beat. Beat.

Ren started sobbing over his body, clinging to him as he slowly breathed against her.

You should take him to the hospital now.

She nodded, but it took a moment for her to rise, to pick him up, to continue onwards.

The ache in her chest didn't calm when she returned, finding Nico and his mother sitting with the other survivors where the medics had set up. She had to wonder, who else. Who else. Who else. *Just like Vendetta,* she thought as Lycan brought another body forward.

For the next three hours, Kaida stood there, portaling the injured across three different hospitals as they were brought up from the water. She only had five minutes for each portal, then had to detransform before she could make a new one. One of the firemen was letting her use his truck to hide each time.

When things started to calm down she'd already made ten portals, taking around fifty people to the hospitals. She was sure she'd need to stop soon, sure she shouldn't be able to make this many portals this quickly back to back, but in truth she felt okay, physically. It was her emotions weighing her down, making her want to crawl in bed forever, to hide from it all.

"You alright, Kaida?" one of the medics asked, her once perfectly slicked back hair now frazzled.

"How many dead?" she asked softly.

The woman shook her head slowly. "We don't know yet, but... a lot."

Kaida nodded, numb.

You couldn't have stopped this, Zig whispered.

Ren didn't respond. She knew he was right, in a technical sense. Gaia used her second power on the bridge, the same one that almost killed her. It was astonishing to know something that really only wrecked her hand took down this entire structure. It happened so fast, even if Kaida *had* been there, she couldn't have stopped Gaia from doing it.

But she could have stopped this, by stopping Gaia before today. Before last week. Hundreds of people dead. *Again.* Because of one crazy girl. For what?

I'm sorry.

She sighed as she watched Lycan walk toward her, dripping wet. He looked exhausted.

"Did we get everyone?" she asked.

"Hard to say. Search and rescue is still going, but I think we've found everyone."

She nodded as he hung his head. There was nothing else to say.

"You can close the portal," he muttered as he made a silver box for her.

She didn't respond as she walked inside the box and he closed it over her. The suit came off and she released a breath. Only seconds passed before the suit was back on.

I can do that faster now.

You're stronger.

I don't feel stronger.

Zig didn't respond. He knew it wasn't true. She *did* feel stronger, physically. But that didn't seem to count for much right now. So many dead. Her friends among the injured. Kaida felt like a failure. With a sigh she gently knocked on the box and the silver puffed to mist around her.

The rest of the heroes slowly trudged up on the banks. Every one of them looked depleted. All seven versions of Hoax went right past her toward the medics. Kaida watched as each one knelt beside one of the injured and touched them, her heads bowed.

"What's she doing?" Apex asked as he moved up beside Kaida and put his arm around her. She leaned into him.

"She's healing them. It's her second power."

Everyone turned to look at the tall guy who spoke. A new hero. She tried to focus on that.

Pink light shone from his dark blue suit, rimmed around the eyes of the mask that covered the top half of his face. His sparkling white teeth stood out against his dark brown skin, and he had tight curly hair coming up over the top of the mask. The same pink lines spread out from the blue diamond on the center of his chest, running down the entire suit. Draped across his shoulders was what looked like a ragged shawl of purples and blues, but she knew they were wings. He'd flown out of the water with them spread wide several times.

"She can heal?" Apex asked. "Why wasn't she doing that before?"

"I reckon she was more help getting people out," Lycan replied.

Even as he said it Hoax stumbled, falling to her knees as her copies fuzzed then faded away, leaving her back to one body. She let out a low sigh as she looked up at the rest of them.

"Are you alright?" The new hero walked over and pulled Hoax to her feet. She nodded, seeming too tired to speak as she leaned against him.

"New guy, what do we call you?" Parody asked as she wrung water out of her ponytail.

"Tag." He bowed his head. "Was really hoping to meet you guys under better circumstances, but..."

"Sometimes these are the only circumstances," Kaida muttered as she held a hand out to him. "It's nice to meet you."

Tag smiled as he shook her hand. "You too."

"Thanks, for showing up. You helped a lot with getting people out of the cars," Parody said. "Very cool."

He nodded. "Glad I made it in time." He stared around them. "What do we do now?"

"Hoax will detransform soon. Five minutes, every time," Lycan said softly.

Hoax nodded, fully leaning into Tag, looking like she was gonna collapse.

"I can get her out of here." Tag smiled again. "We're a team now, her and me."

Hoax frowned. "I never agreed to that."

"Eh, you will." He saluted Kaida. "Till next time, friends." With that he and Hoax disappeared in a flash of light.

Kaida was terrified of what next time would bring.

57
Tired of Being a Teenager

Ren tried to force a smile as she walked to school with Jasper and Ocean. But last night's events weighed on her. Two hundred and ninety-seven people died from the bridge collapse.

You saved over a hundred, though.

She wished she could focus on that part, but the eyes of the dead flashed in her mind, over and over. She'd stayed awake for hours, waiting for news when Nico finally updated the group chat. Kevin was still in the hospital, in stable condition, but not entirely out of the woods yet.

Sometimes she wished she was just a kid. Not a hero. Not a savior or a fighter. Just a normal girl with a normal life.

With a sigh she pushed the door open, not following the forced conversation between Jasper and Ocean. Whispers followed Ren as she moved toward her locker. Jasper and Ocean fell silent. Then she saw why.

"Fucking hell," Jasper hissed as she took in the pictures taped up every few feet across the lockers.

Pictures of Ren in her bra. She stopped, still, as she stared at one of them, unable to process.

"Ren?" Jasper put his arm around her shoulders.

She didn't move.

"Who the *fuck* did this?" Ocean asked.

Ren didn't answer.

The sound of tearing paper snapped her out of it, and she turned to see Bellamy ripping them off the lockers. One by one, his green eyes fuming as he crumpled them in his hands.

She swallowed. The bell rang.

"Let's go," Jasper whispered, guiding her toward class.

She didn't argue, letting him sweep her away as she fell deeper within herself.

First period was a blur. Time passed slowly and all at once. She was surprised when the bell rang. She walked back to her locker in a daze.

Jasper found her quickly and put his arm around her. The pictures were all gone from this hall now, but she'd heard the whispers. Everyone probably saw them.

Laughter echoed behind her as she stopped at her locker and turned to see Harper across the hall, giggling. Something feral filled Ren and she moved. The giggles stopped, surprise flashing in Harper's eyes just before Ren grabbed her by her jacket and slammed her into the lockers. People around them fell silent. Ren held Harper's gaze.

"What the fuck is your problem?" she growled.

"You stole my boyfriend," Harper replied defensively.

"I didn't steal anything." She tilted her head a little. "And he was my best friend before he was your boyfriend. And guess what? He's *still* my best friend. He broke up with you because you're an insecure little girl who can't understand the concept of friendship cause you're too fucking stupid. And none of that is *my* fault!"

The hall was dead quiet. Harper's jacket was balled tightly in her fists. She slammed her into the lockers again and the girl winced, closing her eyes.

"You do *not* wanna fuck with me."

Ren didn't look very strong. She was small and kept to herself. A quiet girl who rarely argued with anyone. But Ren was also Kaida and had been training and fighting for almost two years now. She *was* strong. Very strong. And now Harper knew it.

"Do you understand?" she whispered, face close to Harper's.

"Yes," Harper mumbled, terrified.

Ren nodded and let go, only then realizing she'd actually been holding the girl off the ground.

"Harper Miller to the principal's office," a voice called over the intercom.

Hushed whispers followed Harper as she stalked off, cheeks flushed with embarrassment. Ren stood there, looking around the hall at the thirty some kids who stared at her. She shoved her shaking hands in her pockets as she spotted Simon rushing toward her.

Don't shrink down, Ren. You're so tall right now.

She blinked, surprised to find she had been deflating, the adrenaline evaporating as quickly as it came.

Simon pulled her into his arms and she released a breath, leaning into him. "Are you okay?" he whispered into her hair.

"No."

He pulled back a little, looking down into her eyes. "I didn't see them, didn't even know till Kit told me."

She swallowed. That meant they weren't near his locker, at least.

"Is there anything I can do?"

She shook her head and he pulled her back into his arms. She was overly aware of the crowd still staring.

"Ren!"

She pulled away from Simon to see Bellamy coming their way, a trash bag in his hand.

"I pulled them all down. They're all gone. And I reported Harper." He swallowed. "Are you okay? Do you... need anything?"

"She doesn't need you at all, she has *me*," Simon hissed.

"Simon!" Ren stepped back.

He looked down at her. "Sorry, I just meant—"

"No." She shook her head, on the verge of tears as everyone stared. "No. I—I have to go. I need to go. Jasper?"

He appeared beside her, gently grabbing her arm. "I got you."

"Ren?" Simon called after her.

"No!" she yelled without turning around. "*Don't.*"

"Shh, it's okay, Renny. I got you." Jasper kept a tight arm around her as they walked outside. She noticed him texting one handed as they moved.

"Who are you—"

"Your dads."

She nodded. "I've changed my mind."

"About what?"

"I'm tired of being a teenager."

"Oh, yeah?" He tucked his phone away and looked at her.

"Yeah. I think I'm gonna quit being a kid. Go full time hero."

He smiled. "Am I invited to the full time hero party?"

"Literally always."

"Sweet."

Dad was waiting for her in the kitchen when they arrived.

"What happened?" he asked as he pulled her into his arms.

She sighed, resting her head against his chest. "Jasper can tell you."

"So, my ex-girlfriend is an uber bitch, actually. And a week back she threw her coffee at Ren, Ren took her shirt off and put my hoodie on. And in the like, three seconds she was shirtless Harper apparently took pictures." He paused for a breath. "So when we walked in today there were pictures of Ren in her bra posted in the school. Hundreds of them, around the sophomore lockers. And Ren, very rightfully upset by this, slammed Harper into the lockers and told her to back the fuck off and I think that set the message in. It was amazing, by the way. Little Renny can be *super* scary. You should be proud."

Dad's arms tightened around her.

"And then Simon was an ass because he's Simon and he fucking sucks—"

Ren groaned.

"—So Ren said fuck you! And we walked out and came home. The end."

"Is that accurate?" Dad asked.

"Yes."

Dad rubbed her back.

"I should add," Jasper said, voice softening. "This was after we found out two of our friends were hurt in the bridge collapse last night."

Ren sniffed.

"Shit. Are they okay?"

"Kevin's still in the hospital, but Nico made it out okay," Jasper said, sullenly.

"Okay. Okay. You kids go relax. I'm gonna call the school, sort things out. You won't get in trouble for leaving."

"I will," Jasper said with a sigh.

Ren pulled away from Dad to look at him, feeling guilty.

"No, you won't. I'll make sure your dad knows you weren't skipping and you were simply helping Ren get home when she was distressed."

Jasper nodded but didn't look hopeful. That might not be enough for his dad, but it was better than just hearing Jasper walked out after first period.

"Arrow will be home in about two hours, we can order some food. Whatever you want. *Anything* you want."

Ren nodded slowly. "Can we do board games?"

Dad smiled. "Absolutely. Whatever you want. Go relax while I make these calls."

She scooped Breadcrumb from under the kitchen table then let Jasper guide her upstairs.

He was quiet as they settled in, him on the floor with Bready in front of her couch while she was draped across it, eyes closed.

"So..." He broke the silence.

"How bad was that?"

"Which part?"

She groaned. "All of it?"

"Okay, so, the picture wasn't bad. Like, it wasn't a clear hi-def picture. But also, you're hot so no one who's seen it is thinking like 'ew, Ren Rivers in her bra' like, you look *good*."

She groaned louder.

"So, Harper. Insane. Like, absolutely wild. They're gonna forget the pictures by tomorrow and be talking about *that* for three months."

"Is that bad?"

"Every single person who saw you slam her into the lockers probably got so turned on. I'm dead serious. Expect the amount of people hitting on you at school to go up."

She snorted. "Up from zero."

"How'd you end up with Simon? Guy hitting on you at school. Never a zero."

"Speaking of..." Her phone was buzzing with texts from him.

|♥Simon♥|
I'm so sorry.

I just wanted to help, I
didn't mean to upset you.

She sighed and sat up.

|Ren|
Not really upset with you.

|♥Simon♥|
No?

|Ren|
Two of my friends were on
the bridge. They're okay, so
far. But I was already a mess
before the pictures

|♥Simon♥|
Fuck. I'm so sorry. Anything
I can do?

I can leave school, come
see you. Get you food,
anything, everything.

Whatever you want.

She smiled.

|Ren|
You're sweet.
I just wanna nap.

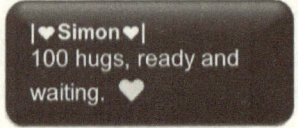

But I'd like to request
extra hugs tomorrow

|❤Simon❤|
100 hugs, ready and
waiting. ❤

Ren put her phone down. "Three months?"

"Hm?"

"You said they'll be talking about me pushing Harper for three months?"

"Yeah, probably. Are we gonna talk about Bellamy? I think he literally skipped class to tear those pictures down."

Her eyes widened. "Oh god. You're right. He wasn't in first period. And I didn't even say thank you! I was so..." She shook her head.

Bellamy wasn't the type to hate someone without reason, but Harper was really testing him. After she threw her coffee at Ren, he knew he didn't like her anymore. But this was a whole new level of hatred he felt as he pulled down picture after picture. He'd be pissed anyways, but the hurt in Ren's eyes when she saw them... it made him wanna burn the entire school down.

He crossed people laughing, or simply ignoring the photos. But then there was Bradley, cackling as he took a picture of one of them.

Bellamy grabbed him by the shoulder and slammed him against the lockers. "Delete it."

"Oh come on, Bell," Bradley said. "You're telling me you don't—"

"Delete it or I'm gonna break your fucking nose," Bellamy hissed, almost eager to swing at him.

Bradley rolled his eyes as he deleted the picture. Bellamy shoved him aside, and continued to rip the pictures down. He liked having something to focus on, other than Nico and Kevin.

He replayed it over and over, seeing their faces in the car, pulling them out, up through those murky depths. Kaida took Kevin to a hospital and he didn't *know*. For hours, he had to keep going. Saving who he could. Even now, they weren't sure if Kevin was going to be alright. He had to be grateful that Nico was, but every few minutes he felt a weight in his chest as he pictured Kevin, laughing, then remembered him, unconscious, limp in Apex's arms.

He saw a girl he didn't know also ripping the pictures up. She eyed him suspiciously.

"You collecting those, *perv*?" she asked.

"No, I'm throwing them away."

She didn't seem to believe him, her eyebrow raised.

"Ren's my friend," he continued. "Who are you?"

"I'm also Ren's friend. Name's Ocean."

"*Oh.*" He smiled. "Ren was talking about you last week."

Ocean's face softened. "And who might you be?"

"Bellamy."

Her eyes widened and she grinned. "Bellamy. Oh, she's told me a *lot* about you."

"Good things, I hope?"

"Ren only says the *best* things about you."

Some of his anger eased. "Wait... is this your first day?"

She nodded, making the gold beads in her black braids jingle. "I am missing my first class right now."

Bellamy shook his head. "You can't do that. I got this. You get to class."

"I don't even know where my first class is. Ren was *gonna* show me around but..." She sighed. "Her day kinda got extra fucked."

"What class?"

She pulled a paper out of her pocket. "Chemistry? With Mr. Carney. The room number is supposed to be printed here but the ink is smudged."

"I can take you, we got all the pics in this hall anyways. Come on."

"So, you really are just the *nicest* guy, like she says, huh?" Ocean asked. She was only a few inches shorter than him and walked with confidence.

"Ren says that?" His heart sped up.

"Nicest boy in the *whole* school. Likes *everyone.*"

"I don't know about all that."

"You like Ren?"

"Of course. She's the best."

Ocean nodded.

Bellamy made an excuse for her to Carney so she wouldn't get in trouble, and also got a trash bag from him before he continued tearing down the pictures. He moved through the entire school, searching, but it seemed they were only posted in three sections of lockers, not close to most of the classrooms.

His trash bag was still full by the time he finished and went to report Harper to the principal. The bell rang while he was still in the office.

"Don't miss your next class, I'll take care of this," Principal Mathews replied with a tired sigh.

He went looking for Ren after that. He found her in the hall by her locker, surrounded by people, Simon holding her in his arms.

"Ren!" he called as he got closer. "I pulled them all down. They're all gone. And I reported Harper." He felt embarrassed suddenly. "Are you okay? Do you... need anything?"

Simon turned, and yelled at him.

Bellamy stood there, surprised, as Ren pulled away from Simon. She looked like she was going to cry and their voices all drowned out as Bellamy stared at her, suddenly wishing he was the one holding her instead of Jasper. He didn't hear a word as Jasper turned her around and walked her away. All he wanted to do was follow her, comfort her.

Instead he stood there, still, as Simon glared at him before walking the other way.

Finally a teacher came and yelled at everyone to get to class.

He was late to French but was excited to see Ocean was in the class with him. He smiled and took the seat beside her.

When class was almost over he received a text from Ren.

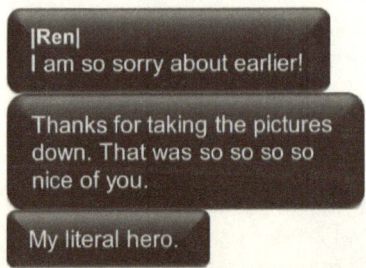

|Ren|
I am so sorry about earlier!

Thanks for taking the pictures down. That was so so so so nice of you.

My literal hero.

He waited till he was in his next class to type a response, but then he deleted it before hitting send and shoved his phone away. He tried again at lunch, but was distracted by everyone jumping between talking about how Harper was definitely getting expelled or how Kevin might not wake up. He tried texting Ren again after sixth period, but deleted that one too. Finally, when he was home and lying in his bed, he pulled the phone out and started typing a response again, settling on something simple.

|Bellamy|
Are you okay?

He ordered tacos and tried not to stare at his phone, waiting for her response. His food arrived thirty minutes later, and he turned a movie on, eating in his bed when she responded.

|Ren|
I'm trying to be okay. Playing monopoly with my dads and Jasper.

A moment later a picture came through of Jasper with a stack of monopoly money in his hands. Bellamy smiled and took a picture of his tacos.

|Bellamy|
More fun than my solo dinner.

|Ren|
Tacos!

He had a silly idea and pulled Rufard the bear off his desk, then took a picture with him and sent it to her.

|Ren|
Tacos with Rufard!
A delightful evening!

|Bellamy|
I'm glad you're feeling
better.

She responded with a selfie, her face bright with a smile, doing a peace sign, her fluffy orange cat behind her on the couch.

All the tension left him then.

|Ren|
Ocean told me you helped
her today. I can't thank you
enough.

I kinda failed on best friend
duty for her first day.

|Bellamy|
Of course. Happy to help!

She sent a picture of just her cat. This continued through the evening, both of them sending silly pictures back and forth, with less and less conversation to accompany them. Part of him wanted to talk about Kevin and Nico, but he couldn't tell her the worst part. *I was there. Pulled them out of the water.* He received another picture from her and smiled.

You really like that girl, huh? Zeli asked.

He glanced to where Zel was curled up in the chair in the corner. Her wolfish head rested on the arm, her silver eyes shining as she stared at him.

"Of course I like Ren. She's one of my best friends."

You seem to like her more than the girl you're dating. Her ear twitched, silver mist curling up into the air from the tip.

Bellamy blinked. "What."

Zeli didn't respond as she shifted in her chair, the little sparkles in her black fur shining as she moved.

"I don't like Ren like that..."

You don't sound very sure.

"I am. I'm... dating Jules. So, I like Jules."

And what about Kaida?

He sat back, thinking on that. He loved Kaida, more than anyone. But... he thought maybe he *was* getting over her. It helped, knowing she was with someone else, that he never had a chance. And being with Jules, that probably helped too.

"Think I'm in the process of getting over her."

Falling out of love?

Bellamy sighed. "I think... part of me will always love her. I don't think I'll shake it fully. But I can get to a point where it isn't crippling me, or interfering with our friendship, and that's good enough."

Interesting.

He ran his hand over his face. "Any more sightings of Xereth?"

Not yet. I think he knew he was being followed that day they spotted him. He's being careful now. We should be able to find him, but he does not wish to be found. Not by us, at least. I wonder if Poziarne was right.

"About what?"

Reaching out to the others. Xarax is nearby.

He felt so much anger in her as she thought about Xereth. That hatred made him anxious. He wanted to find the guy and be done with it, for her sake. But all he could think about was Gaia, and the bridge, and his friends.

"Xarax, that's another Timeless?"

Yes. I will consider approaching her.

He nodded as his phone buzzed. He expected another picture from Ren, but it was an alert about Vapor in upper Manhattan.

58
Could Have Been a Hero

Bellamy sent a text to the Hero Chat before flying off. They'd decided approaching Vapor alone was just as dangerous as approaching Gaia, maybe even more so, with her being able to freeze them. And since her and Gaia seemed to be working together now... fighting them solo was not ideal.

You should get the numbers of the other new heroes.
Not a bad idea. More of us should make this easier.

He slowed down as he got closer to the destination and pulled his phone back out.

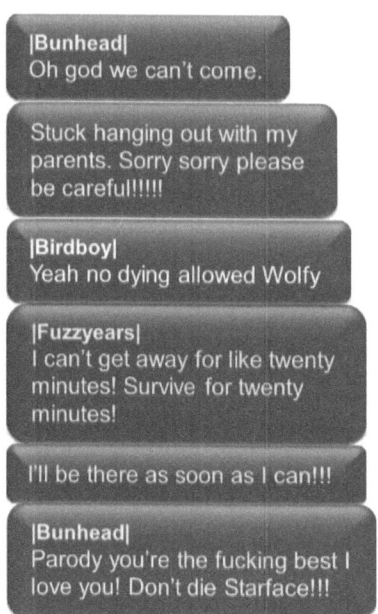

|Bunhead|
Oh god we can't come.

Stuck hanging out with my parents. Sorry sorry please be careful!!!!!

|Birdboy|
Yeah no dying allowed Wolfy

|Fuzzyears|
I can't get away for like twenty minutes! Survive for twenty minutes!

I'll be there as soon as I can!!!

|Bunhead|
Parody you're the fucking best I love you! Don't die Starface!!!

He smiled. *Just gotta keep things in check till Parody arrives.*

He flew closer to see what Vapor was even doing, and realized it was another Valkyrie warehouse. The first time he met her she'd been robbing one of their cars. Then recently Gaia destroyed one of their warehouses. And he'd heard the CEO was murdered recently.

She's got it out for them I guess? He landed on the ground by two parked cop cars and slowly walked around the building. He couldn't say he blamed Vapor, but murder and destruction weren't exactly how he'd go about it.

How would you go about it? Zeli asked. *A strongly worded letter?*

He laughed. *You're making fun of me.*

Only a little.

He shook his head as he kept moving, looking for the cops but there was no sign of them or Vapor. They had to be inside.

I should go in.

You need to wait for backup.

The cops went in. Vapor could kill them.

Has she killed anyone yet?

I'm starting to think she probably killed the CEO of Valkyrie. He checked the time. Ten more minutes till Parody was coming. *I'll be sneaky.*

Bellamy...

I'll be fine. The sneakiest.

If you get yourself killed, so help me...

He grinned as he slipped through a door on the side. He immediately found the cops, standing frozen with their guns out, next to an employee of the warehouse.

"Sorry," he mumbled as he walked past. There was nothing he could do for them, they simply had to wait for the stasis to wear off.

That meant she'd already used her second power. He wasn't sure if enough time passed for her to destransform and transform back, or if she was still running on those five minutes. If she was, she couldn't freeze him.

Bellamy...

I'm being careful, Zel. Calm down.

She growled.

He passed a few more frozen bodies, their eyes wide and scared. He kept moving, following the only sound in the building until he found Vapor. She was in her suit, her back to him as she poured a tank of gasoline over the floor.

"Just gonna burn the place down with these people inside?"

She dropped the can in surprise as she spun to face him. "Lycan."

He smiled. "Hi. I believe we talked about blowing things up..."

"We also talked about you staying out of my business," she replied, glaring.

448

"*Well*, can't say I care much for the building. But the people inside, *that's* my business."

"I wasn't gonna kill them." She rolled her eyes and picked the can up without a care. "They'll unfreeze soon and can run off before I light my matches."

"You're gonna stand there and act like you're a saint for not murdering people you trapped in the building you're burning down?"

"If you had *any* idea what Valkyrie has done to me. To my family..." she hissed.

"I'm all ears."

She continued to pour gasoline out as she walked across the room. "My brother worked in one of their factories. And he died mysteriously on the job. He wasn't the only one. They just couldn't cover it up as well because my dad worked high up in the company. When he started looking into what happened he found more and more shitty things they've covered up. And then *he* mysteriously died. Everything I ever loved was taken from me in the span of a month."

Lycan sucked in a breath. "I see."

"Do you? Because it wasn't just my family. By taking them down I'm getting justice for everyone they've killed. Saving even more from them in the future. The world was better off before they took over fucking everything anyways."

He nodded slowly.

She held his gaze. "No arguments?"

"How many have you killed?"

She blinked, stepping back. "Seven."

"Seven people. In the company?"

"Yes."

"So," he started with a sigh. "You're not one for reckless murder. You're very intentional with your crimes."

"So?"

"So, tell me why the *fuck* you've been letting Gaia kill hundreds of people every week."

Her face changed, guilt and shame flashing in those purple eyes.

"I know you're working together. I heard you that day at the library. Distraction, not destruction, was it? *You* set her loose to create diversions so you could get away with something small. Petty. But over two hundred people died that day. And another three hundred last night on the bridge! My *friends* were hurt. *You* told her to do that?"

"No. I wasn't specific, I just—"

"She does what you ask? So why haven't *you* stopped her? She's not even helping with your little grudge against Valkyrie!" His heart pounded as his anger grew. "She's killing innocent people for *no* reason! The same people who work in these warehouses and factories. The ones you *claim* you wanna spare."

Her lip trembled.

"Well?"

She stood there, silent.

"You're better than this," he hissed, anger burning. "You didn't need to choose this path, Vapor. You could have shed light on what Valkyrie was doing. We could have helped you! You could have been a hero. Instead you chose murder? *Really?* Did you even think—" He cut off and spun, grabbing Gaia's wrist just before she could place her blackened hand against him. Her eyes darkened as Zeli screamed. He yanked the girl down, forcing her to her knees and pressing her palm against the floor.

For a single moment black cracks spread out from where she touched it. Then the entire floor buckled and they fell. Vapor screamed. Before they even hit the floor below something was tangling over his body, green and slithering. Vines.

That was close, Zeli sounded near to tears.

Don't you worry, Zel, he thought back as he struggled against the leafy ropes sprouting up from underneath them. *You're not gonna lose me.*

He formed a small knife of silver and started slicing through the vines as Vapor crawled out from under some rubble beside him, without her suit on. Her natural hair was longer, shiny black. Her brown eyes were terrified as she looked up at him.

"Eden?" Gaia called from somewhere Lycan couldn't see.

More vines tightened around him as he kept cutting through them.

Vapor coughed through the dust as she glanced at him. She held his gaze a moment before she moved past, struggling through the debris.

"I'm fine!" she yelled as Gaia appeared. "We have to get out of here!"

Gaia grabbed the taller girl with shaking hands. "Let me finish it," she whispered, eyes moving past to look at Lycan.

"Fucking try it," he hissed, anger burning inside of him.

"We should go. His friends will come. We can't take them all."

"Sure we can."

Vapor shook her head. "Let's go. *Please.*"

Gaia sighed as she reached up and brushed her thumb across Vapor's cheek. "He's gonna keep getting in the way."

"I sure fucking am," Lycan growled. It was hard to maintain the awkward position he was in, making it seem like he was still caught in her vines when he'd already cut through them. He just needed one lucky strike, and it would be over.

Gaia grinned, moving toward him. Lycan smiled right back. Once she was close enough he swung his arm, silver sword forming in his fist. Vapor screamed, jumping in front of Gaia, taking the hit on the shoulder. Her eyes widened and she fell to her knees just as her suit came back over her.

He'd been prepared to swing again, but he wasn't here to kill Vapor. Only Gaia. His sword puffed away as something slammed into him. He tumbled under the weight of the mist creature. Something sharp sunk into his arm and Zeli growled.

I told you to wait!

He wrestled with what he now realized was a wolf made of mist. *That's insulting.* He punched it in the face, knocking it back as his silver sword formed again and he rose to his feet.

Parody fell into the room, pink cape flapping wildly around her shoulders as she landed behind Gaia and Vapor. She pressed her hand against Gaia's back and Gaia gasped, her head flinging back.

"Sorry I'm late!" Parody called as she spun past the girls as Vapor only just realized she was there. She slid across the room and held a hand out to Lycan. He tapped it and she formed a giant silver hammer, standing steady beside him.

"I got the civilians out," she whispered, breathless.

"You're the best."

Vapor eyed them as mist coalesced around her, turning into two more wolves. They just stood there, on guard, growling as she knelt beside Gaia, who seemed to have passed out.

"Took her energy?" he asked.

Parody nodded. "You okay? Your arm…"

"Fine."

Two of the mist wolves merged, turning into a giant eagle like she'd done before. Vapor lifted Gaia up onto the back of the bird before meeting Lycan's eyes. She pulled out a match, blood dripping down her arm as she struck it. It fell from her hands as she climbed onto the eagle.

Fire erupted around them as the girls soared away. Lycan's sword dissipated as he pulled Parody into his arms, board forming under their feet. When they cleared the building Vapor and Gaia were already out of sight. He stared at the flames as they grew, feeling like a failure.

"So close," he whispered.

"Next time," Parody said, her voice cold. "We'll get them next time."

59
Spinning. Floating. Flying.

Ren detransformed behind a dumpster, breathless. Five days had passed since the bridge collapsed. Five days of wondering if Kevin would be okay. Five days of throwing herself into *doing* things as Kaida, trying to make up for that failure.

But she failed. Again. And again.

Ren?

She was silent, head bowed, trying to compose herself.

Sometimes I hate this.

I know.

I'm supposed to be stressed about math tests and boys and zits. Not this. Not...

I know.

She closed her eyes, but all she could see was the dead boy in the street. She'd been too late to stop it. With a shaky breath she pushed herself off the wall and walked out onto the sidewalk, the afternoon sun burning bright in her eyes.

It didn't happen to me. It happened to Kaida. Not me.

Ren?

She swallowed, ignoring Zig as she moved.

"Ren?"

She stopped, realizing that one wasn't in her head.

"Ren, hey. What are you doing here?"

She forced a smile as she finally noticed Nico approaching. He'd been pretending to be okay, when he came back to school. But no one was more worried about Kevin than him.

"Oh I was just..." She glanced around, not even sure where she was. "Shopping. What are you doing?"

Nico nodded. "Was hanging at my uncles. Headed home now."

"Me too."

"Wanna share a car?" he asked as he pulled out his phone.

"I was just gonna walk," Ren replied.

Nico frowned at her. "That's like an hour walk?" He shook his head. "Come on. I already got one. It'll be here in two minutes."

She didn't have it in her to argue. In truth she could have flown home. Or portaled. But she didn't want to be Kaida right now. She was Ren. And *Ren* wasn't supposed to be walking anywhere alone, so she forced her smile back in place and got in the car with Nico when it arrived.

"Have you seen him?" she asked after a moment.

Nico sighed. "Yeah. He's awake, but his breathing is still bad. They're still doing tests and stuff."

"But he *is* okay, right?"

Nico nodded, his curls bouncing. "So far." He swallowed. "So... how's things with your boyfriend?"

"Pretty good."

"So... you're not still into Bellamy then?"

Ren's face flushed. "What? What are you what do you mean? Bellamy what?"

Nico smiled. "I notice these things. Like, I know Lola's been in love with Eira for the last year. I know about the various girls obsessed with Jasper. I know about Kevin's crush on Ashley. And..."

Ren groaned. "Well it doesn't matter anyway. I was mostly over him after freshman year."

"Right. Sure."

She shoved her hands in her pockets, feeling like she should be more embarrassed. But her mind just replayed the scene in the street, the boy shot down. Blood on the pavement. Kevin's heart, still under her shaking hands... Ren sighed. "Does Bellamy know?"

Nico shook his head. "He's clueless, promise. Most people kinda are when it comes to these things. And I wouldn't tell him unless..."

"Unless what?"

"Unless he was into you too."

Ren swallowed. "Which he isn't and never has been. Cause... you'd know?"

Nico nodded slowly.

She released a breath, feeling stupid. It didn't matter. She knew Bellamy never liked her like that. And she had Simon. And he had Jules. So it didn't matter.

Sorry, she thought at Zig. She could feel his worry tangling with her disappointment.

Are you alright? I know that... was rough.

I... She paused, unable to lie. *I will be alright. Don't wanna think about it anymore.*

"You're definitely a better match for him, though," Nico mumbled.

Ren frowned. "What's that?"

"Better for him. Than Jules." He raised an eyebrow at her, waiting.

Ren almost laughed. How could *she* be better than *Jules?* Jules was lovely and tall and smart and driven and—

REN!

Her head banged against something and everything blurred.

REN!

Glass shattered. She was spinning. Floating. Flying. Everything went black.

REN?

Nico groaned beside her and she heard the driver grunting as he tried to get the front door open.

REN!

"Ren? Ren! Are you okay?"

She blinked, eyes unfocused. "I have to go," she mumbled as she struggled with her seat belt. A Bonded was just outside in the street. That's what hit the car. She had to stop them. She had to—

"Ren?" Nico sounded scared.

She tried to focus her eyes. Where *was* she? Everything was so blurry. Was she moving?

"Can you hear me?" She didn't recognize that voice.

"Yes." The word was hard to get out.

"Do you know your name?"

"Ren. I'm..." *Kaida.* "Ren Rivers."

"Is she alright?"

"Hit her head pretty hard."

"Oh god. This can't be happening again."

Ren? Can you hear me? Ren?

Zig? Where—

You're hurt. I'm here.

The Bonded. I have to help I have to—

Hoax and Tag are here. They're fighting Prism. It's okay.

But—

It isn't your problem! Please, relax. Breathe. I need you.

She tried to nod, but everything was so fuzzy. "I... feel dizzy," she muttered.

"You're gonna be okay," someone said as they touched her face.

Bellamy put his book down with a sigh and started getting ready for his date with Jules. As he pulled on his hoodie his phone buzzed with a call from Nico.

"Hello?"

"I am freaking out!" Nico hissed.

"What's wrong?"

"Was sharing a car with Ren and we drove right into a fucking *villain* attack. Something hit the car and we flew like thirty feet down the street."

Bellamy's heart raced. "Are you guys okay?"

"I'm fine. Just a few scrapes. But Ren... I don't know. She passed out and there was blood in her hair. They took us to the hospital and I'm panicking man. I can't stop shaking. How is this happening *again?* Am I cursed I—"

"What hospital?"

"Presbyterian in lower Manhattan."

"On my way," Bellamy said, feeling detached from himself as he put the phone down and went looking for his keys. But he didn't need those. He opened the balcony doors as the suit came over him then he jumped over the railing.

Risky, Zeli hissed in his head as his silver board barely appeared in time for him to glide smoothly through the air instead of crashing to the ground.

Ren's hurt.

You probably shouldn't storm into the hospital as Lycan.

Good point. He was careful, finding a spot to detransform before going inside. It took a few minutes to get to Nico in the waiting room, where he was pacing back and forth in front of a row of chairs. He had a cut on his cheek but otherwise looked alright.

"I'm here."

"I feel like I can't breathe," Nico whispered. "I said we could share the car. She was gonna walk but I insisted and it's my fault and—"

Bellamy pulled Nico into his arms. "It's absolutely not your fault. Ren's gonna be okay. Did you call Jasper?"

"No. I—I—" He pulled his phone out with a shaking hand.

"I got it." Bellamy took the phone from him.

"Hello," Jasper answered.

"It's Bellamy. I'm at the hospital with Nico. Ren was in an accident with him and we don't know how bad it is yet, but you need to call her dads and get down here."

A beat of silence. "Text me where." He hung up before Bellamy could say anything else.

I'll go check on her, Zeli said softly as he sent the text.

She phased through the doors back to where they were keeping Ren. He waited, anxious.

A concussion, Zeli said after a few minutes. *She should be fine.*

His hands were shaking. *She's okay?*

Yes, I believe so. They are still doing tests though.

Bellamy released a breath, so much weight leaving his shoulders. *Thank you.*

It hadn't even been a week since Kevin's injury, and now, Ren... he glanced at Nico. The boy looked numb.

"Not your fault," Bellamy whispered again.

Nico didn't respond.

Twenty minutes later Jasper came bustling in with Ren's dads, all of them frazzled.

"She's in the back," Bellamy said. Her dads nodded, rushing past to the counter.

"What the hell happened?" Jasper asked.

"Our Uber got tossed in the air," Nico said softly.

"Did they say if she's—"

"She'll be fine," Bellamy said, hoping he was right.

Jasper nodded but didn't look convinced.

"Jasper, come on," one of Ren's dads called.

Jasper looked surprised as he went back with them, leaving Bellamy and Nico alone to wait.

The waiting was dreadful. He felt sick and took over Nico's pacing as the boy finally sat in a chair. Eventually Jasper came out and said they could see her, that she was okay. But Bellamy couldn't relax until he walked in and saw Ren lying in the bed. She frowned at him.

"Bellamy? What are you doing here?"

"He came the second I called," Nico said. "Bell estaba muy preocupado de ti. Nunca lo he visto tan estresado..."

Bellamy frowned, not sure what Nico said. "How are you feeling?"

"Fine," Ren answered. "Still kinda fuzzy. Confused, but okay."

"Concussion," Jasper said. "Hit her little head."

Ren stuck her tongue out at him.

Bellamy finally relaxed a little. "You scared us," he whispered.

Ren stared up at him, smiling slightly. Her normally tan skin was paler than usual, and she had a bandage around her head. "Didn't mean to. Also, um. Does anyone know how things went with the Bonded attack?"

"No idea," Bellamy replied, feeling guilty he hadn't even thought to stop and check. But surely Kaida and Apex were on it.

Nico looked it up on his phone. "Seems like the new heroes were there. Hoax and Tag? And Parody. They handled it fine."

Not fine, Bellamy thought. *Ren was hurt.*

Ren bit her lip. "Lycan wasn't there?"
Nico shook his head. "No. None of the others."
"They must have been busy..." Jasper offered.
Bellamy nodded.

Ren was tired from whatever the doctors dosed her with, her mind still fuzzy. Her dads left to find her some food. She was absolutely starving. Nico finally left as well, after she assured him it wasn't his fault. After what happened with Kevin, she could see that guilt floating in his eyes. She'd have to text him later, reassure him.

She was just glad he was okay, and so was their driver. It could have been worse. Like what happened to Kevin...

Ren was left alone with Jasper and Bellamy, one on each side of her on the edge of her bed.

"Jasper, where's my stuff?" she asked, anxiety growing with each passing moment.

"Stuff?"

"Stuff I had on when I was brought in... like my necklace?"

Jasper's eyes widened. "Uh, hold on." He crossed the room and grabbed a bag, peeking in it before handing it to her. She pulled her Xyrial out, gripping it in her fist, the metal cool against her skin.

Zig?

I'm here.

She didn't see him, but hearing his voice made her relax. When she'd woken up her Xyrial was gone. Without it her connection to Zig was weaker. She couldn't transform, could barely hear him with her head so blurry.

Where are you?

Above you.

She turned her head and smiled. Zig was curled up on the top of the bed behind her. He gently touched her forehead with his nose.

Always here.

Thank you.

"Are you gonna miss more school?" Bellamy asked.

She looked back at him. "God I hope not."

Jasper shook his head. "Only girl who doesn't wanna miss school."

"Well, I hope you're there on Monday," Bellamy continued. "If I have to suffer one more chem class without you..."

Ren laughed, then she fell quiet as the door opened and Simon walked in. He stopped in his tracks as Jasper hopped up to make room for him.

"What the fuck is *he* doing here?" Simon growled, eyes on Bellamy.

Before Ren could even process those words Jasper stepped up to Simon, putting a hand against his chest.

"Speak to her like that again and we're gonna have a *problem.*"

"Jasper, stop, it's fine."

"It's not fine. You were in a fucking accident and the first thing he does is *yell* at you, instead of asking if you're okay?"

She could see the fury in Simon's eyes as he glared down at Jasper.

"He wasn't yelling it's fine," Ren groaned as she pushed the blankets back, trying to get out of the bed. But Bellamy put a gentle hand on her shoulder, shaking his head.

"You stay. We'll step out, give you two a minute." He tucked her back in then crossed the room and grabbed Jasper's arm. "Come on."

Jasper growled but let Bellamy guide him out. The door closed behind them, leaving her alone with Simon.

He slowly sat on the edge of the bed. "I'm sorry," he whispered. "Are you okay?"

She nodded. "Just a concussion."

He let out a breath and put his arm around her, pulling her against him. Then he kissed her forehead. "Why didn't you call me? You called *Bellamy*, but not me?"

Ren blinked. "I didn't call him. I didn't call anyone." She paused. "How did you even know I was here?"

"Jasper messaged me. At least he thought your boyfriend should know you were in the hospital."

She swallowed. "I was a little bit unable to call, due to being in an accident."

Simon sighed. "I know. I just... *god*. Coming in here and seeing you with that fucking kid you liked before me... knowing I was the last one notified hurts. Him, sitting in your bed, like..."

Ren leaned away from him into her pillows and closed her eyes. "You can't do this. You can't be like this. They're my friends and if you're gonna get upset every time I'm with them... I can't *do that*, Simon. It won't work. I can't I—"

"I'm sorry. I'm sorry, hey. Hey, look at me? Ren?"

She sniffed, keeping her face away from him. She was just *so* tired.

"Ren, baby, I'm sorry. Okay, I'm sorry." He grabbed her face, gently pulling her around to face him.

"You can't do this," she whispered.

"I'm sorry. I'm *so* sorry."

She stared up into his eyes. He was on the verge of tears.

"You didn't act like this before. What changed?"

He swallowed. "I guess... I didn't realize how close you were to him. I thought he was just a kid you had a crush on. That he sat at your lunch table and that was it. I didn't realize—"

"Why does it *matter*?"

He looked away. "I know this isn't a good excuse, but... my ex cheated with the guy she told me not to worry about. I trusted her. I *believed her* and it was all a lie. The whole time. So I guess I've just been... overthinking it."

Ren frowned. "I really hate her."

He turned, meeting her eyes. "I'm sorry for being a jerk. I know you aren't her. I know that. I'm just... I don't wanna lose you."

She reached up, brushing his cheek. "You won't if you stop being like this. Promise."

He nodded, then leaned in and kissed her softly. Some of the tension left her as he pulled back, smiling.

"I'm so sorry. I'll try to be better."

"I'm not with him, okay? Bellamy is just my friend, and he has a girlfriend. And I have you. Youuuu. Dummy."

"I do trust you, Ren. I'm sorry I—"

"Shhh. Cute sad boy. I'm gonna *fight* her. I mean it. It's on *sight* with Vicky the Devil. Tell Cam! I bet he'd love to fight her. We'll team up."

He laughed. "Are you on drugs?"

"Maybe?" She scrunched up her face. "I'm so sleepy."

"Should I go? Let you rest?"

"I guess." She leaned up and kissed him again. Then she smiled as she looked into his eyes. "Thanks for coming."

"Of course." He brushed his thumb against her cheek. "I'm sorry."

"Shh. Cute boy." She kissed him again. "I'm falling."

"Asleep?"

"For you. *Still* falling."

He laughed as he pulled back. "Sleep, my dear."

"Kay. Please don't fight with Jasper on the way out."

"Promise." He kissed her forehead. "I'll text you later, okay?"

She nodded and closed her eyes, her hand resting on the Xyrial on her chest.

You're okay, Ren, Zig whispered.

A moment later her dads were back with bags of food. She wanted to just sleep, but forced herself to sit up and eat the burger and fries they brought. No one spoke while they ate, and in the back of her mind she could sense something wasn't right, but she couldn't pinpoint what or why.

Once the food was finished, Dad met her eyes. "Ren, what were you doing today?" he asked.

She blinked. "What?"

"You weren't with Ocean, where you were supposed to be. You weren't with Jasper. You weren't with Simon. You weren't *home*. What were you doing?"

"Um." *Ocean.* She forgot about their plans completely.

"Do you have any *idea* what it's like to get that call?" Dad continued, his eyes welling up. "Jasper telling us you were in an accident but he didn't know how bad it was, he didn't even know what happened."

"I'm sorry," she mumbled.

"I didn't even know if you were alive, Ren."

"I..."

"You're supposed to tell us where you're going, who you're with," Dare said. "Ocean had no idea where you were, she called us to see if you were home."

She looked between them, eyes burning. What could she say?

Repeat after me, Zig said.

What?

I was with my friend Nico. He wanted to visit his uncle, to get his mind off Kevin, and I wanted to go shopping for a gift for Simon's graduation before going to Ocean's...

Ren blinked, repeating the words without processing them. "...so we went together and I went to the shops while he was there and I just lost track of time. We left together, sharing a car."

Good lie, she thought to Zig when she finished.

"You didn't tell me you were going *anywhere*," Dad said. His brown eyes were so sad. "Here I thought my kid was safe, just a few houses down the street."

"I'm sorry," Ren mumbled, tears burning in her eyes. "I wasn't... trying to..." She sniffed.

"Maybe we shouldn't do this now." Dare put a hand on Dad's shoulder and he nodded.

"Shh," Dad whispered, brushing his thumb across her cheek. "You just rest, okay? We can talk about it later."

She nodded, but her insides still squirmed with guilt.

60
The Other Option

Bellamy could barely contain his rage as he waited with Jasper. "Is he always like that with her?" he finally asked in a whisper.

Jasper met his eyes and sighed. "I don't know. I kinda don't like him if I'm being honest? He keeps getting pissy over small shit, like that time she wore my hoodie. And yelling at you the other day, when you took the pictures down."

"He was mad at her during the costume party, too. Because she wouldn't go see him. He called and almost made her cry."

Jasper's eyes darkened. "She didn't tell me about that."

"Why is she *with* him?"

"I... honestly think it's just a distraction? He's hot and supposedly nice, when they're alone at least."

"Distraction from *what*?" Bellamy asked.

Jasper sighed. "Just... stuff she's been stressed about."

"Dating an asshole isn't a good distraction."

Jasper smiled. "Why does it bother you so much?"

"She deserves better. Ren's the nicest person in the world. I just..." He swallowed. "I hate seeing her with someone like that."

Jasper raised an eyebrow. "When are you gonna stand the fuck up and tell her you *like her*?"

Bellamy stared at him. "What."

Jasper rolled his eyes. "I used to wonder, you know. The way you are with her... it's different, than everyone else. She chalks it up to you just being *nice*. But it's more, isn't it? You *do* have feelings for her."

Bellamy blinked, heart racing. "I... I'm with Jules."

Jasper stared at him. "All the more reason to figure your shit out, for her sake too."

"Ren is with Simon. Even if I... I don't. I..." *Did he?*

"Well one day, Ren's gonna figure out Simon isn't the one for her. And I'm not sure it's you, either. But she won't accept the other option. So *figure it out*."

Bellamy didn't know what to say. Fortunately, he didn't have to respond. Simon walked out, passing without a word to either of them. Before they could go back in, Ren's dads returned with food for her, so Bellamy and Jasper left. Ren would be staying overnight so they could monitor things, but they said she should be clear to go home tomorrow.

He walked home instead of flying, needing the time to process his conversation with Jasper. He'd liked Ren, once. But then... Kaida. And now, he was with Jules. Was he really different with Ren? Sure, she was easy to talk to and she always seemed to understand him even when he wasn't making sense but... he sighed as he walked into his apartment. Then he froze. Jules was sitting on his couch.

"What are you doing here?"

She blinked up at him. "Are you serious?"

"Uh..."

His mom burst out of her office, green eyes wide and watery. "Bellamy Owen Grey, where the *hell* have you been?" She pulled him into her arms as he stood there, stunned.

"What?"

"We had plans, four hours ago?" Jules said from behind his mom.

"You weren't answering your phone," Mom mumbled into his shoulder, hugging him tightly.

"I... I'm sorry. I. Uh." He felt at his pockets, realizing his phone wasn't in them. "I think I left my phone here?"

Mom finally pulled back, her teary eyes turning angry. "You *can't* do this. You can't just disappear. I *have* to know where you are!" The tears slipped down her cheeks.

"Mom, I'm sorry. My friends got in an accident and I went to see them. I wasn't trying to—"

She shook her head, grabbing his face with both her hands. "I was this close to calling the police. I *can't* lose you."

His eyes watered as he watched her cry. She hadn't been like this in *years*. "I'm so sorry. I didn't mean to scare you. I'm sorry. I'm okay, see? I'm all good." He met Jules' eyes again. "Can I talk to Jules alone for a minute, please?"

Mom sniffed then wiped her eyes. "Fine." She went back to her office.

Bellamy tried to calm down as Jules stepped closer to him.

"What the hell happened? Did you forget about our date? Here I was thinking there must be some great reason you stood me up. Because Bellamy is so nice, he'd *never* do that. Then I came here looking for you and your mom didn't even know where you were and she was so worried, I started to think something might have happened..."

"Ren was in an accident. I went to the hospital to see her."

Jules looked surprised. "Is she okay?"

He nodded. "Yeah. She has a concussion, but she'll be okay."

"And... you couldn't text or call me to tell me that?"

"I didn't have my phone..." He glanced at Mom's office. The door was open. He sighed. "Can we talk in my room?"

Jules nodded and followed him down the hall. He closed the door behind them then turned to face her.

"I am *so* sorry I missed our date. I swear I didn't mean to. I was just so worried about Ren I completely forgot."

"I understand." Her eyes looked hurt. "I would have gone with you to the hospital to check on her. I don't care about the date, okay? I'm glad Ren's okay. But... you couldn't bother to let me know, because of another girl?"

"I didn't have my phone," he repeated. "Look, see, it's right here." He picked it up off the desk, noting the many missed calls from Mom and Jules.

"They have phones in hospitals," Jules muttered. "Ren has a phone."

"I didn't think about it. I'm sorry."

"I was waiting there for hours, Bell. I was so sure you'd show up. Call, text, *something*."

"I'm so sorry. I really really am." He felt like absolute shit. "What can I do to make it up to you?"

"Be honest."

He nodded. "I can do that."

She swallowed. "Do you like Ren? Does she mean more to you than your other friends?"

Jasper's voice echoed in his ears. *When are you gonna stand the fuck up and tell her you like her?* He swallowed. "She's just a friend."

Jules' brown eyes were unconvinced. "And you're telling me if one of your male friends was in an accident you'd be *so* worried you'd forget about your girlfriend entirely and rush to go see them?"

"Yes? And Nico was in the accident with Ren! He's the one who called me."

She blinked. "You didn't even *mention* him."

"Cause he was fine. Ren wasn't. At least, not at first."

"Bellamy..."

"I promise I don't have feelings for Ren, okay?" He took her hands gently in his, praying that wasn't a lie. "And I feel so bad about standing you up. *Please* let me make it up to you?"

She sighed and nodded. He grinned and leaned in to kiss her, hoping that's what she wanted. She was smiling when he pulled back.

"Never been in here before," she said as she glanced around his room.

"You haven't? You've been in my house several times now."

"Yeah, but never in your room."

He felt self-conscious as she took in the space, running a hand over his dark blue comforter, then turning to look at his desk. She picked up the framed picture of him with his mom from his thirteenth birthday and smiled.

"Cute." She stopped on the knit bear on the corner and picked it up, grinning. "This is adorable. How long have you had this little guy?"

"Uh, since my birthday."

She frowned. "This past birthday?"

"Yeah. It was a gift," he answered, waiting for the inevitable question.

"From who?"

He released a breath. "Ren."

Her smile fell and she put the bear back on the desk. "Oh."

"She's just a friend."

"Right. Yeah, okay." Her smile came back as he grabbed her hand. "I haven't given you any cute homemade gifts... I should get on that."

"You don't have to."

"No, but, I'm your girlfriend. If Ren is giving you things like that I definitely should be doing more."

"You don't have to," he repeated, feeling weird.

"Well, I'm gonna. Cause I want to," she mumbled.

He nodded, unsure what else to say.

61
Apexable

Kaida hunched over on the roof, staring down at Rapture in the street below. The fox girl was leaning against a brick wall while the ten or so people under her control ransacked the shops lining the street. She still hated how cool her mask was, with the ears holding her fiery hair back from her face. Kaida sighed.

You know you can take a day off, Zig said.

I took three days off. I'm fine, okay? Head is all better.

She noticed someone else creeping up the street, their tall pointy bunny ears unmistakable even in the dark. Kaida watched as he got closer to Rapture. It took a moment for Rapture to see him. She pushed herself off the wall and approached Fable with a wicked smile.

"Fable, a pleasure to meet you," Rapture said in a sultry voice. "I could put your talents to good use."

Fable was silent, standing very still.

"What is *wrong* with you Bonded boys?" Rapture growled.

Fable said something too low for Kaida to hear. She sighed, leaning forward, as if that would help.

"You're seriously gonna stand there and *not* be attracted to me?"

"Sorry?"

Kaida gave up on eavesdropping and jumped off the roof.

Ren, don't!

She landed in a crouch then slowly walked up behind Fable.

Don't what?

"Maybe if I didn't look so feminine, perhaps?" Rapture continued.

She made you jump last time.

Fable didn't respond, slowly turning around then stopping when he saw Kaida standing in front of him.

So?

"I'm not really in the mood for a villain team up tonight," she grumbled at him.

"I'm not with her," Fable replied.

Kaida narrowed her eyes. Fable moved so he could keep an eye on both girls.

So, once you've been under her power you can not fight her.

"It's true, he's not falling for my charms. *Bad* bunny." Rapture grinned. "But I seem to recall it working on *you...*"

What do you mean? "Only cause I liked your outfit! But then you threw me off a bridge, so fuck your fashion sense!"

Rapture growled. "You're lucky I'm not supposed to fight you yet."

I mean you can not harm her in any way. You should leave. Now.

Fable stepped back just as Apex finally arrived, landing directly in front of him.

Fable sighed. "Do we have to do this right now?"

Apex's smile widened. "Aw, got somewhere to be, Trick?"

Fable glanced at Kaida. "You see, I don't start this."

"Won't finish it, either," Apex growled. "Come on, let's *play.*"

Fable's eyes darkened as he stepped forward, two small sticks appearing in his hands. "I'll fucking finish it."

Apex swung his staff at him. Fable dodged and Apex's smile fell as his eyes moved past Fable toward Rapture. His mouth opened, eyes glazing over as he stilled.

"Oh, good boy."

Kaida groaned.

This isn't good.

"Apex, fight Kaida till I'm gone," Rapture continued. "But don't hurt her too much."

Apex stiffened then moved toward her.

Kaida sighed. "You could fucking help," she hissed at Fable as he backed up.

"This is not my circus, and that is definitely not my monkey," he replied. "Have fun."

Apex slammed into her, knocking her to the ground as Fable continued walking away.

"Next time I see you, Ghost... you're dead."

Kaida growled in response as she wrestled with Apex. She couldn't go after Rapture or Fable, stuck there as Apex punched her in the face. She fell back, then rolled sideways and blocked his next hit. Apex's yellow eyes were frantic.

Put him in a portal, Zig said.

She ripped the air around her, the portal forming just as she turned and grabbed Apex while he tried to hit her again. She dragged him inside the portal then let go. He fell to the floor, his eyes clearing.

"Fuck." He groaned, squeezing his eyes shut. "I'm sorry I'm sorry I'm sorry."

"It's okay. Stay, I'll be right back."

She hopped out of the portal to find Parody standing in front of it.
"Sorry I'm late," she said, glancing around. "I don't see the fox girl."
Kaida sighed. "She snuck off while Apex was attacking me. I put
him in time out," she added with a nod toward the portal.

"Poor baby." Parody smiled. "Should we try to go after her?"

No.

"Uh..." Kaida shook her head. "I'm gonna detransform soon.
Fable's around, too. And he *pissed me off*. You keep patrolling, and if
you see them, text me. I'll come back."

Parody saluted. "You got it, boss."

Kaida waved, then went back inside the portal. Jasper sat on the
floor, out of the suit, Pozi beside him.

"You alright?" she asked as she knelt in front of him.

"She got me so easily. Told me to fight you and I just... did it." He
was on the verge of tears.

"I'm fine. And falling to her power doesn't make you weak. She got
me to jump off a bridge, remember?" Apparently falling to her power
did make her weaker to her in the future though... *I really can't hurt
her now?*

No. Neither can Apex.

Great.

Jasper nodded but she could tell he didn't feel better. Pozi was
staring up at the golden stars in the distance. His black and green fur
stood out against the crystalline floor. She idly reached out and pet his
head. He didn't seem to mind.

"Come on, let's go."

She dragged Jasper by the hand, out onto her roof and down into
her bedroom. He sat on her bed, sulking.

"Jasper?"

She leaned her head on his shoulder and he sighed.

"I feel so shitty."

"You weren't in control. I know you'd never hurt me. Never ever.
Jasper, look at meee."

He sighed again as he looked down at her. She grinned, holding his
gaze. He finally broke, a small smile cracking through.

"I love you," she whispered.

"Love you, too."

She convinced him to play video games after that, which helped
fully pull him out of his head. He was back to his regular self, laughing
and joking.

"We should sleep soon," she mumbled after a while.

"Yeah, probably." He sighed as he put the controller down and
pulled his phone out, starting to scroll.

She rolled her eyes and checked her texts.

|♥Simon♥|
We still down for movie
night after school?

|Ren|
Yes! I miss you.

|♥Simon♥|
Miss you more, beautiful.

|Ren|

"Fucking hell," Jasper groaned.

"What?"

"Did you see Harper's post?"

Ren tensed as she looked. It was a cute picture of Harper with Jasper, but she put some kind of shattered glass effect over it. The caption read *"The real reason Jasper and I broke up is cause he's actually gay!"*

"Oh my god."

"I genuinely hate her now," Jasper muttered, but he smiled as he said it.

"What are you doing?"

"Commenting."

Ren refreshed the page then Jasper's comment loaded in.

"I'm bisexual actually, hope that helps!"

"Wow."

Jasper giggled under his breath. "God. She really sucks."

"She got expelled, right?" Ren asked as she continued scrolling on her phone.

"Yeah. Heard her mom sent her to stay with her dad for now. But she loves her dad. It'll probably be good for her."

Ren nodded, trying not to feel guilty. She hated Harper after everything she'd done. But somehow it all still felt like it was *her* fault. Which was stupid.

"Ugh."

"What?" Jasper asked.

"Look at this poll someone made, shipping the heroes."

Jasper raised an eyebrow as he looked at it.

What are the BEST Bonded ships?	
Silverlight	56%
Apexable	29%
Lypex	10%
Parodyland	3%
Kapex	1%
Kaidaland	1%
16,242 votes · Final results	

"They're right. You should be with *Lycan.*" His nose scrunched up. "Wait, what's Apexable?"

Ren tried not to laugh. "Pretty sure that's you and Fable."

His eyes widened. *"Why?"*

She couldn't keep her laugh in then. "See, it's *silly.* People shipping us. Parody hasn't even *met* Wonderland. It's weird."

Jasper sighed. "So many votes..." He shook his head as he looked at the comments. A lot of people shipped him with Elixir as well, but he'd only met her the one time. "Whatever. Bedtime. Not setting an alarm, just drag my corpse out of bed when it's time to go."

She nodded as he left to go downstairs to his room.

The next day at school Ren walked out of chem class with Bellamy at her side.

"You're still wearing it?"

"Hm?" She followed his eyes to see him looking at the bracelet on her wrist. "Oh, yeah. I told you I loved it!"

His smile widened. "Yeah, but you could have been lying."

"I'd never lie to you."

His eyes softened. "That could be a lie."

Ren laughed.

"I'm glad you're back," he continued.

"You said that already."

"Did I?"

She nodded. "In geometry this morning. And again at lunch."

His face flushed. "Sorry. Just like it better when you're here."

Ren blushed. "Me too. You think Kevin will be back soon?"

Bellamy shrugged. "Nico said he's out of the hospital, but still taking it easy."

Ren nodded as they walked.

"Did uh... Did Jasper talk to you, about me?" he asked, not meeting her eyes.

"About you? What about you?"

He shook his head. "Nothing just. Something we talked about in the hospital."

"No, he didn't. You can tell me." She paused, waiting.

Bellamy's eyes widened. "No no. It was, uh... personal. Embarrassing."

She nodded slowly. "Well, he didn't say anything."

"Good."

She watched him go to his locker, curious about what weird personal thing he and Jasper talked about. Part of her wanted to ask Jasper, but he would have told her if it was something she should know. Ren waited at hers as Jasper and Ocean walked up.

"It just makes sense! It's confusing if—"

"It's not confusing to people who have eyes!"

Ren sighed. "What are you guys arguing about now?"

Jasper and Ocean fell quiet then Jasper sheepishly muttered "Oxford commas."

Ren tried not to smile. "Okay. Well, can you maybe keep the bickering limited tonight?"

Ocean frowned and glanced at Jasper then back at Ren.

"What?" She paused, heart sinking. "Oh god, you're still mad. About missing our plans the other day. I said I was sorry and I—"

"Not mad," Ocean cut her off. "You were in the hospital. I'm *legally* bound to let you off the hook."

"Okay then... why the weird?" Ren met Jasper's eyes, waiting for him to explain.

"Uh..."

Ocean sighed. "Jasper said Simon was a *dick* at the hospital."

Ren rolled her eyes. "Oh my *god*, it wasn't a big deal! He was a *little* jealous of," she paused, lowering her voice, "Bellamy. Cause he knew I liked him before we were dating. But, we talked about it. Twice! Cause I was drugged the first time. And he's working on it and it's *fine.*"

Ren hated that Jasper didn't seem to like Simon anymore. Two of the most important people in her life not getting along was stressing her out. And she was stressed *enough*. She hoped it wouldn't be an issue with Ocean at least. On the one hand, they seemed united on this, which was nice, considering how much they'd been arguing over silly stuff since Ocean arrived. She knew they were both just getting used to each other, and used to sharing her. But uniting on hating her boyfriend was *not* what she wanted. Couldn't Jasper see how important Simon was to her?

"I'm just saying," Jasper started, "Simon is—"

"Right there," Ocean hissed.

Jasper's mouth closed and he faked a smile as Simon came up and put his arms around Ren from behind.

"Is he wearing... purple nail polish?" Ocean whispered, not quiet enough.

Simon kissed Ren's cheek then grinned at Ocean. "It's Ren's favorite color." He wiggled his sparkling fingers in front of her.

Ren giggled, remembering him coming into the hospital the morning after her accident with four different shades of purple polish. He painted their nails to match while her dads had fetched her breakfast.

"You guys need a ride to Kit's tonight?" Simon asked.

"My dad is gonna drop us off, and pick us up," Ren said, leaning back to look up at him.

"Alright." He kissed her cheek again, then spun her around and kissed her on the mouth. "So." He let out a breath as he pulled back. "Did you... wanna invite any other friends?"

Ren raised an eyebrow.

"Cause I'm so chill and normal. About your other friends."

She laughed. "No one else. Maybe, one day. But just them for now."

"Okay. But I'm so chill and normal," he said seriously, nodding.

"I see." She leaned up and kissed him again. "See you in an hour."

She watched him walk away then turned back to Ocean and Jasper. Ocean made a face. "Okay, he seems sweet."

"He is sweet!" Ren said, defensively. "Jasper doesn't know what he's talking about because Jasper doesn't know Simon yet. Not really. But you both can get to know him tonight." She met Ocean's eyes as they started walking. "Also never let Jasper form your opinions."

"Hey! I have mostly good opinions!" he replied.

Ocean shrugged. "We'll see."

62

Forcing Smiles

Ren anxiously watched Dad bustling around the kitchen, pulling things out of cupboards.

"What are you gonna make?"

He stopped and stared at her. "Oh, pues se me vino a la mente hacer costillas de puerco con chile. Derretirle la cabecita de tu pequeño chico blanco."

"Dad! Por favor actúa normal sobre esto!"

Dad smiled. "I'm gonna make some fucking *spaghetti*. Calm down."

She pouted. "Spaghetti is good."

"And salad. And garlic bread."

Her pout turned to a smile.

"It's gonna be fine, I promise."

"You'll be nice to him?" she asked as she leaned onto the island. She was worried about Simon coming over, but things had been *so* good with him lately. Movie night had gone perfectly, and he was getting along with her friends. Now she just needed him to get along with her dads.

Dad sighed as Dare walked in.

"I promise to make sure Cas is nice to him," Dare said as he put a hand on Dad's shoulder.

Dad rolled his eyes. "I'm so nice. I'm the nicest."

Dare met her eyes and they both laughed.

"Oh come on I'm *so* nice," Dad continued. "Ask Jasper. He thinks I'm the nicest."

"Took you a year to be nice to him."

"Not true." Dad pulled away from Dare and started rummaging in drawers. "I was nice to Jasper within three months."

"That's true," Dare said.

She rolled her eyes.

"Listen, we've been wanting you to bring Simon over," Dad continued. "You're getting serious, so we wanna know him better."

"You never told me that."

"We been letting you take the reins," Dare replied. "Didn't wanna push."

Ren smiled.

"What kind of dessert should I make?"

Ren bit her lip and Dad frowned at her.

"Oh no." Dare laughed. "Boyfriend doesn't like sweets?"

"I've offered him stuff from the bakery and he never says yes."

"Kinda offended," Dad mumbled.

"Well don't say that if he doesn't wanna eat your cookies."

"So I'm making cookies?"

"Chocolate chip? Safest bet. He *did* have a bite of chocolate cake on movie night and liked it. There's hope for him."

Dad nodded. "I got this, kid. *Relax.*"

She sighed and moved to the living room, scooping Breadcrumb up as she made her way to the couch. Exhaustion from her period was really starting to hit her now, and part of her just wanted to nap. But Simon was supposed to pick her up for a dinner date in a few hours. She changed the plans and hadn't told him yet, but if dinner was already made, he couldn't say no. Then her dads could finally get to know him, and maybe Simon wouldn't be afraid to step inside her house.

She busied herself with crocheting for a while. Simon's graduation was tomorrow and she'd only finished the small gift. As she worked on the big one she worried he wouldn't even like it.

Why wouldn't he like it? Zig asked.

She sighed. *I don't know.*

Lycan loved the keychain you made him. And Bellamy loved the bear. Jasper's loved everything you've made him. Not to mention the hats. Simon liked those. And that turtle thing you made him.

I know. I'm just... anxious for no reason. He'll like it. I still worry though.

That is silly.

She smiled. *Sometimes I'm silly.*

Most times.

A little while later Simon texted and her heart raced.

| ❤ Simon ❤ |
Be on my way to get ya soon.

| Ren |
Change of plans!

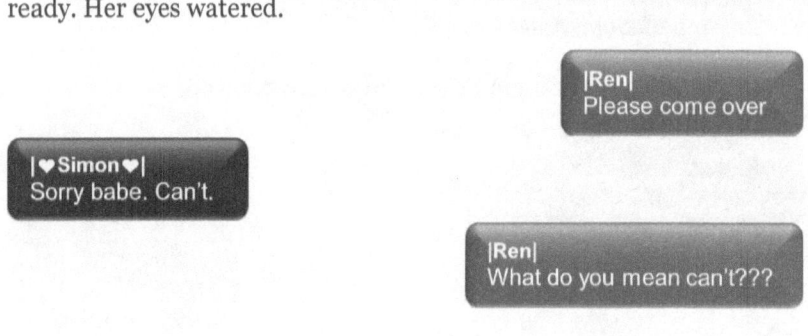

|♥Simon♥|
You can't come out??

|Ren|
Instead of going out I was
thinking...

|♥Simon♥|
Yes?

|Ren|
You could come over and we
could have dinner with my dads?

|♥Simon♥|
I told you I didn't wanna
do that.

|Ren|
My dad's been cooking for
a while. And it smells so
good! And I can't wait to
see you!!!

|♥Simon♥|
Then see me outside.

|Ren|
Simon, please have dinner
with us?

She waited, stomach twisting. He didn't respond. She glanced over her shoulder to see Dad setting the table. Everything was done and ready. Her eyes watered.

|Ren|
Please come over

|♥Simon♥|
Sorry babe. Can't.

|Ren|
What do you mean can't???

> You were gonna come get me a
> minute ago.

> Simon?

She tried to call but he didn't answer.

Dad walked over and put a hand on her shoulder. "Everything's ready. When's he getting here?"

She didn't respond.

"Ren?"

She shook her head, a tear slipping down her cheek.

Dad sat beside her. "Baby girl, what's wrong?"

"He doesn't wanna come."

He sighed and put his arm around her. "Why not?"

She shook her head again, closing her eyes. Dad kissed her forehead.

"Why don't you text some friends to come over? Made a lot of food, be a shame to let it go to waste."

She opened her eyes and sniffed.

"It's alright." He rubbed her back. "Text Jasper, Ocean, anyone you want. Invite em all, we got enough. It'll be fun, alright?"

She exhaled slowly then nodded as she wiped her eyes and started typing out a text to the group chat.

> |Ren|
> My dads made too much food
> if anyone wants to come over
> for dinerrrr

> |Nico|
> For real? Cause I'm not
> busy...

She smiled.

> |Ren|
> For real. Come overrr

> |Jasper|
> Shit party at Rens!

|Ocean|
Oh oh okay I'm on my way!!!

She leaned back and closed her eyes, trying to get her emotions under control before they showed up.

Ocean arrived first and it was easier to pretend then, forcing smiles as Ocean eyed the mountain of pasta dad made.

"Oh my god this is the *best*."

"Happy to have you," Dad said as he made her a plate.

Jasper and Nico arrived together. That made forcing smiles even easier, but she knew Jasper saw through it. He didn't say anything, but in those moments she was quiet he watched her like a hawk.

"This is so good," Nico moaned through a mouthful of garlic bread.

Between the six of them they made quick work of the meal, then Jasper and Nico moved on to the cookies.

Her phone vibrated and her heart raced as she grabbed it, hoping it was Simon. But it was Bellamy in the group chat.

|Bellamy|
Can't believe I missed dinner at Ren's.

This is devastating.

Nico responded with a picture of the cookies.

|Bellamy|
I'm missing cookies too? 😩

|Nico|
Ya snooze ya lose

Ren sighed.

Jasper eyed her. "Too bad *Bellamy* couldn't come. Seems like he wanted to. Maybe should invite him over more often..." he teased.

Ren didn't respond.

Jasper frowned. "What's wrong?"

She shook her head and moved to the window, lifting it up and climbing out onto the fire escape. Fresh air washed over her face. A minute later Jasper climbed out and sat beside her.

"What's wrong?"

"I like him so much," she whispered. *Maybe more than like him...*

"Bellamy?"

She closed her eyes.

"We're not talking about Bellamy..." Jasper sighed. "You mean Simon?"

"*Yes*," she snapped. "I mean my fucking *boyfriend*. Who I invited over for this special dinner with my dads and he said *no*. He won't even text me back."

Jasper put his arm around her. "Sorry. I was being a dick."

She shook her head. "Not mad at you."

He nodded, leaning his head against hers. "Still a dick. Still sorry."

She couldn't hold it in then, tears slipping out. She was embarrassed to be crying about it.

"I'm sorry," Jasper whispered again. "I love you."

She wiped her eyes. "Love you, too."

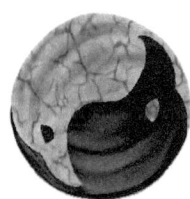

Jasper watched those tears fall and wanted to die. No. He wanted to *kill* Simon. This whole time he hadn't really thought it was that serious. He thought it was more like him and Harper. He liked her, things had been fun, but when it ended he wasn't surprised or that upset about it. But he should have known better, after the other night, watching movies at Kit's. Seeing them together like that...

It dawned on him now that Ren might actually be in love with Simon. He hadn't considered that before.

Cause you're convinced she's in love with Lycan.

She definitely is.

People can love more than one person at a time.

I suppose.

"So," he muttered. "Simon was supposed to come. Where is he now?"

She shrugged. "I don't know. At Kit's? That's where he was before... doesn't matter. He isn't here."

Jasper started swaying her, his arm around her shoulders.

She sniffed. "We should go back in."

"Soon."

"They're gonna know I was crying."

"No they won't."

"But—"

"It's Ocean and Nico. They're not gonna say anything."

She sighed. "I feel stupid. He told me he didn't wanna do dinner with my dads. I just thought, if I set it up anyway..."

"He'd come?"

"Don't say it," she whispered.

"Say what?"

"Whatever it is you're thinking about him."

"Not thinking nothing."

She sighed and took a deep breath. "Okay. We can go back in. I can act normal."

"Yeah, just needed some air. It's so stuffy in there." He grinned and helped her up.

When they went back inside Nico and Ocean acted like nothing happened and Ren forced herself into the conversation.

When Jasper left Ren's he went straight to Kit's house. He knew it was weird to just show up and ask if Simon was there. But his rage propelled him forward now that he was out of Ren's sight.

She rarely ever cried. Even over the worst things she'd been through, yet this punk ass bitch made her cry over a goddamn dinner.

Remember not to actually kill him maybe, Pozi said.

Sure sure.

He stopped in front of the white town house feeling possessed as he knocked on the door. A moment later hot boy Kit opened it, a frown on his face.

"Is Simon here?"

"Uh, yeah. Hold on."

Jasper waited until Simon walked out, looking confused. He closed the door behind him, staring at Jasper.

"What are you doing here?"

Jasper shoved Simon back against the white bricks. "You made her *fucking cry,*" he growled.

"What?" Simon's eyes darkened. "What are you—"

"Ren! That girl you claim to fucking care about. All she wanted was for you to show up to a nice dinner with her family. And you couldn't fucking do it? Ren never cries. *Ever.* But she cried tonight because of you."

Simon blinked, looking ashamed. Jasper dropped his hand from his chest, panting.

"She cried?"

"You didn't hear it from me."

He sighed, leaning his head back. "Fuck."

"Yeah. You better have one *hell* of an apology for this one. Or better yet, end it, if you're gonna keep disappointing her."

Simon shook his head. "I love her."

Jasper laughed. "Fucking funny way of showing it. Do you even *know* her?"

"Of course I do."

"You didn't know how important this dinner was, or you might have shown up. Do you know she sings in the kitchen when she's cooking? She even dances sometimes. And she'll spend hours and hours with a pile of yarn, not noticing the time passing. She used to love drawing, but only does it when she's anxious now. You'd know this shit if you bothered to spend any time with her at her fucking house."

Simon blinked. "I'll fix it."

"You really love her?"

"More than anything."

Jasper couldn't be sure if Ren felt the same, but she sure felt something for this boy beyond *hot* and *in a band*. Jasper really did want them to just end it. He was sure that was for the best, that Ren was *meant* to be with Lycan. But right now, she couldn't see that. All she saw was *him*. So Jasper reigned in his rage.

"You ever make her cry like that again and I swear to god I'm gonna kick your ass."

He expected Simon to get defensive. Instead he simply nodded. "If I do I'll deserve it."

Jasper rolled his eyes. "Don't tell her I was here. And *don't* fuck up again!" He didn't wait for a response as he turned and walked away.

63
Little Ren Flowers

The next morning Ren's anxiety bubbled as she got to Simon's graduation. He never texted her back, and she worried. But she couldn't *not* go. It was a big day for him. So there she was, walking around looking for a place to sit when someone called her name. She blushed as Simon's mom waved at her. Ren recognized Kit's mom, sitting on her other side.

"Hey, honey."

"Hi, Mrs. Sims, Miss Greenberg." Ren sat beside them, feeling awkward.

"Oh, you can call me Rachel," his mom replied. "Simon's been so nervous today, he's gonna be glad you're here."

"He's nervous?"

"He was up all night. Don't think he slept a wink. Poor thing."

Ren nodded, feeling sick. He was up all night? But he never texted or called her...

"Meanwhile, it took me *three* tries to get Kit up this morning," Miss Greenberg said.

Ren fidgeted with the strap of her bag as the ceremony started. She spotted Kit early on as she eagerly searched for Simon, but they weren't close to the S names yet. She finally saw him in line, waiting to walk on the stage. Ren tried to smile but thought she might vomit. As he crossed the stage he caught her eyes. He looked surprised, then his face lit up.

Once he had his diploma in hand he made a beeline for her. She stood awkwardly as he approached. Then he wrapped his arms around her and lifted her right off the ground, spinning her around.

"I can't believe you're here," he whispered into her hair. "Did you like the flowers?" He set her back down and she stared up at him, confused and breathless.

"Flowers?"

His smile fell. "I sent so many flowers this morning. To apologize. I... I assumed you wouldn't come today."

Air left her lungs. "Of course I came."

His eyes watered and he glanced past her at his mom, flashed her a smile, then pulled Ren away from the chairs.

"I was such a jerk," he said as they came to a stop. "I'm so sorry."

She didn't know what to say.

"I know I fucked up," he continued, eyes shining. "That dinner was important to you and I was a complete piece of shit. I just... I wasn't thinking about it like that, you know?"

"Like what?"

"Like it mattered. To you. I just brushed it off."

"But, you know it matters now?"

"Yes. I'm so so sorry. I should never have bailed on you. I should have been there." His lip trembled. "I—I understand if you... don't wanna forgive me for that. But I *swear* I'll make it up to you if you give me another chance."

She blinked, trying not to cry as his eyes welled up. "You will?"

He nodded. "We can do dinner. The whole thing. I'll even wear a suit. Go all out to impress your dads. *Anything* you want."

"Really?" Her heart raced.

"Really." He smiled slowly. "You mean the world to me, Ren. You know that?" He held her eyes a moment before leaning in, kissing her soft and gentle. "I'm sorry," he whispered against her lips. "I keep fucking up and I... I don't deserve you and—"

"You'll really do dinner with my dads?"

"Yes. I promise." His smile fell as he pulled back a little. "But, could we maybe wait a bit to do it?"

"Why?"

He laughed nervously. "I sort of just made the *worst* impression possible by not showing up last night. Um. So, if we could give them some time to maybe *forget* about that... but I swear I'll do it. I'll do ten dinners. Dinner every night."

"Why didn't you wanna come?"

He grabbed her hands and looked down. "I think... I'm kind of terrified of them hating me."

"And that makes you not wanna try?"

He winced. "The thing is, in my head, I thought... if they don't know me they can't *really* hate me. Even you said that. But once they do know me, I got one shot. And then it's over."

She frowned. "Over?"

Simon shook his head. "I know how close you are. If they don't approve of me..."

Ren deflated. "I don't really think they'd forbid me from seeing you. But even if they tried, I wouldn't listen."

He gave her a look, like he didn't believe that.

"You're not just... some boy I got a crush on. Simon, you mean the world to me, too."

He softened at that.

"Besides, my dad *married* an artist with a motorcycle. Dark hair, blue eyes. He can't say *shit* about you." She bit her lip. "And they're perfect together." She smiled slowly.

"There she is." He kissed her again. "Can't believe you came after I was such an ass."

"I wouldn't miss it."

"I really am sorry. After movie night, everything was *so* perfect. Seemed like your friends maybe didn't even hate by the end of that and now..." He sighed. "Jasper's *never* gonna like me again."

Ren wanted to argue with that, but she didn't know how. "Jasper doesn't know you. He doesn't, just like my dads don't. One day they will. And they'll see you how I see you. Then it'll all make sense."

He shook his head, but he was smiling. "I don't deserve you."

"Shut up. I don't wanna hear any talk like that."

"Okay."

She took a deep breath. "So, I have presents for you."

"*What?* You didn't have to get me anything."

She blushed as she pulled out a small black gift bag and handed it to him. "It's not that great..."

He opened the bag with a raised eyebrow and slowly pulled out the keychain she'd made. It was a tiny crocheted guitar that looked just like his blue one.

"Oh my god. This is adorable."

"There's more."

He grinned as he pulled out the other one and held it out. Then his mouth fell open. "Is this a fucking guitar strap?"

"I don't know if it'll work very well. It *should,* theoretically. Um. Yeah."

"You made these?" He shook his head and kissed her again. "I love them, so much."

"Really?" She blushed. "Even the flowers?"

The guitar strap was made out of black yarn, but she'd worked a handful of little blue lotus flowers into it. He ran his hand over one of them.

"It's beautiful, Ren."

"Um. They're lotus flowers. And my name, Ren... it means lotus and—"

He made the cutest face she'd ever seen. "These are little Ren flowers?" He was on the verge of tears again as he pulled her into his arms and held her tightly. "I love it."

She closed her eyes, breathing him in.

"I have to go soon," he mumbled. "But I kinda wanna ditch my friends and just hold you forever."

She laughed. "No, go with your friends."

He kissed her and her heart fluttered. "Are you sure cause I'll ditch em right now."

She shook her head. "Go, it's fine. Besides, you got dinner with your families after. We're good. Promise."

He sighed. "Alright alright."

"Oh, your mom told me to call her *Rachel*, by the way." Ren said, smiling slightly.

His mouth opened in surprise. "She's never let one of my girlfriends call her that. Even the band don't call her that. She *really* likes you."

Ren blushed.

"I hope you enjoy the insane amount of flowers when you get home, and I'll see you tomorrow for the big group date?"

"Yes, you will." She leaned up and kissed him again.

"You're the best. And I love this, I'm gonna wear it to every fucking show."

Ren giggled. "Shut *up*. Go."

He rolled his eyes and kissed her one more time before he jogged off to where his friends were waiting.

When Ren got home she found a frazzled Dad in the kitchen surrounded by what looked like twenty different bouquets of all different kinds of flowers.

He smiled at her. "Did you see him?"

She nodded, blushing.

"And?"

"And... things are good. He sent all these for me?"

"Yeah... please get them out of my kitchen before dinner, okay?"

Ren laughed. "Okay."

The next morning Ren lay on her couch, arms wrapped around her stomach. Jasper was frowning at her from the floor.

"You okay?"

"Cramps," she mumbled.

He nodded. "Should stay in tonight."

"Got plans with Simon. Then patrolling with Parody."

He shook his head. "Bail on Simon. And I can handle patrol with her." He rolled his eyes at her. "I'm serious. Stay home, he'll survive without you."

She considered it, but Simon and his friends made these plans weeks back. They were supposed to go to Coney Island with some of his friends and their partners. A celebration of the senior graduation. But the thought of it nauseated her as sharp pain radiated through her abdomen.

Jasper sighed. "Cancel the date boo." He stood up and patted her head as he passed.

"Leaving already?"

"Dad," he mumbled.

"Sorry."

He gave her a smile. "It's fine. I'll sneak out for patrol tonight."

"Kay. Don't die!"

"I'll try." He scrunched up his nose as he walked away. "Get rid of some of these flowers, it's so rosy in here."

Ren smiled. "I like the flowers!" They were literally *everywhere*. On her desk, her shelves, her table. Her room smelled like a flower shop, but she loved it. He hadn't known what her favorite flower was, so he sent one of every type he could. And every bouquet Simon sent had come with a note, each one different little poetic lines, detailing what he liked about her. Apparently that's why he'd been up all night before his graduation. He'd been writing them all out by hand. She hoped to press some of the petals into a book later, when she wasn't dying from cramps. She groaned against the pain.

Are you dying?

She opened her eyes and looked around. "Where are you?"

With Azazelith. Are you dying?

"Just period cramps."

Ah.

"Why can't you cure me of them? You give me literal superpowers, but I still have to *bleed?*"

Zig didn't respond.

"No cure for the blood?"

Sorry, no. Do you want me to come back?

She smiled. "No. You can't help with this. Unless your scary venom would fix it."

...no.

"I'll be fine. Enjoy your time with Zeli."

She leaned back and closed her eyes again, feeling fatigued.

Ren was woken sometime later by her phone vibrating with a call from Simon. Her heart raced in a panic as she fumbled to answer.

"Hello!"

"Hey, I'm here. You ready?"

"Oh god."

"What?"

"Uh. Give me a minute." She hung up then forced herself to move off the couch.

She didn't even bother rushing to get ready, and just went downstairs in her sweats. Simon frowned at her when she opened the door.

"You do not look ready."

She groaned.

"I mean, you look cute. *Obviously.*" He smiled. "Do you need more time?"

"I was... thinking maybe we could reschedule?"

Simon stilled. "You're not serious?"

She swallowed, feeling icky.

"Ren, we can't reschedule. Allie and the guys just left. Riku and Kelly are already there. If we don't leave soon we'll be late."

"I just... I feel really shitty and don't wanna do all that tonight."

"Ren, baby, what's wrong?" He stepped closer and grabbed her hands.

"It's my period," she mumbled. "I literally feel like I'm dying."

He made a face. "You get your period every month. You're telling me you can't power through for one night? You don't miss a week of school every month. You can handle it, right?"

Her heart raced and her hands shook even as he held them. "I feel so gross. Everything hurts. I really don't wanna—"

"So you're just gonna cancel our date when I've barely seen you all week?" He dropped her hands and turned around. "Seriously, Ren?" He ran his hand back through his hair. "Is this cause you're still mad about me bailing on dinner?"

"That's not it! I..." She closed her eyes, groaning in frustration. "I don't wanna cancel the date, I just don't wanna go to Coney Island with a bunch of people I don't know while I feel like I'm being stabbed in the vagina!" She blushed, realizing they still stood in the open door and people were staring. "Will you *please* come inside to talk about this?"

She didn't wait for a response, grabbing his arm and pulling him back through the door. She exhaled slowly once it was closed.

Simon stared down at her. "You don't wanna cancel?"

"No. Could we please just do something else? Just you and me? We can do a big fun group thing another time. *Please?*"

His face softened as he pulled her into his arms. "I don't give a shit about Coney Island. I just wanna be with you," he mumbled into her hair. "Something just us?"

"Yes, please," she muttered, sniffling.

"Okay. Go get ready. I'll let the others know we aren't coming."

She nodded, feeling guilty as she made her way back upstairs. She wished she could just stay in her sweats and crawl into bed. But that wasn't cute, so she pulled on her comfiest jeans and a loose shirt, then threw her hair up into a bun.

When she got back downstairs Simon looked sad.

"Ren, I'm sorry."

"What?"

He closed his eyes. "You said you felt shitty. I wasn't even... listening. I'm sorry."

"It's okay," she whispered, grabbing his hand.

He smiled sadly as he met her eyes. "No, it isn't. I can't treat you like that. Don't *let me* treat you like that."

She nodded slowly.

"You wanna stay home, you can."

She gripped his hand tighter. "I'm fine doing something just us."

"You're sure?"

"Yeah."

He released a breath and pulled her into his arms. "We could grab some food, maybe go eat in the park? Stay close, in case you feel worse so I can bring you home quicker."

"That sounds perfect."

They walked outside, his arm around her.

"Were they mad? That we canceled?"

"Little bit. But, they'll get over it. All I care about is you." He kissed her cheek. "Do you need anything before we go?"

She shook her head, wincing against the pain in her abdomen.

"I feel insane," Simon mumbled after a minute.

"Why?"

"I literally carried pads in my backpack the last four years, for Allie. I remember when she started, us boys just tripping over ourselves to accommodate her. It's like, I was possessed, speaking to you like that." He sighed. "I *know* how bad they can be. Please don't ever let me say something so stupid to you, ever again."

Ren smiled softly and squeezed his hand. "Promise."

They grabbed some burgers then went to sit in Washington Square together under some trees. She tried to relax as they ate, but she felt guilty for canceling with his friends.

Simon frowned at her over his drink. "You wanna go back?"

"No, I'm fine. Just feel bad, about your friends."

Simon sighed. *"You* don't feel bad, okay. I feel bad, for being a jerk. Besides this is *so much* better than that would have been."

She smiled. "You really think so?"

He nodded. "How are you feeling, physically? We can go back."

Ren shook her head and scooted closer to him. He moved their trash to the side and put his arm around her. After a minute he laid down on his back. Ren giggled and laid beside him.

"If I was smart," he said softly, "I would have brought a blanket. Pillows. Made a whole picnic."

She leaned her head to the side to look at him. "Picnic is nice. We should do this more often."

He grinned and kissed her, lips soft against hers. "Ren…"

"Yeah?"

Simon stared into her eyes. "I'm all in, with you. I mean it. Dinners with your dads. Picnics, just us. You at my shows. I want it *all.*"

Her heart fluttered as she cupped his cheek, pulling him in for a kiss. "That sounds kinda *perfect,*" she whispered against his lips.

64
Impulsive Thoughts

"I can't believe I'm being forced to go to another party," Ren groaned as they walked. "Finals start tomorrow."

Jasper stared at her. "You're forcing *me* to go to this one."

She rolled her eyes. "We have to go. It's Ocean's birthday and this is her last chance to make more friends. And *maybe* the two of you can stop fighting over me like I'm the shiniest toy on the playground while we're there."

"But you *are* so shiny," Jasper said in a small voice.

Ren smiled. This last week she'd managed to get the two of them to hang out without bickering, a small step. She could tell Jasper and Ocean didn't actually dislike each other, they just both wanted to be Ren's *best* friend, neither of them liked the idea of her having more than one. She had to remind Jasper she already had more than one, with Lycan. But Jasper seemed to think that didn't count.

"At least my period is over," she mumbled as she knocked on Ocean's door. It had been a very long week, going out with Simon almost every evening, then patrolling all night while bleeding and cramping.

"You're here! Yay!" Ocean said as she opened the door. Her black braids were twisted up into two buns on top of her head. She grabbed Ren's arm and pulled her inside, leaving Jasper to follow with a dramatic sigh. "What's in the boxes?"

Ren smiled as she moved through the living room into Ocean's kitchen. "Cookies."

"So many cookies," Jasper added as he heaved his stack of boxes onto her counter.

"Oh, cookies from your hot dad?" Ocean grinned. "Happy Birthday to *me*."

"Please no," Ren mumbled. "There's like two hundred rainbow macaroons in here."

"Tell daddy thank you from me," Ocean replied.

Ren sighed as Jasper grinned.

"One thing we can agree on," he said. "Ren's dads are *so—*"

"Please no!" Ren repeated.

Ocean just laughed.

"Nice hair," Jasper said. "Very Kaida-like."

"Kaida is *iconic,*" Ocean replied. "Anyways, need outfit opinions."

"Jasper's gonna be better at that," Ren replied as they went upstairs and down the hall to Ocean's room.

"It's true. I'm a fashion icon," he said, dead serious.

Ocean looked back at him, taking in his green hoodie and faded jeans. "Fine, you can help."

Ren noted the new stuff on Ocean's walls as they entered. Little fairy lights hung by the bed with pictures clipped to them, and little pink butterflies to the sides. She had a cool floor lamp, and a new black rug under the bed. Ren smiled at the large bisexual flag over the desk.

"Should I go all out?" Ocean asked as she slid open the door to her closet and walked in.

"I don't know."

Ocean's eyes narrowed as she took in Ren's outfit.

"Maybe we should both dress up."

"What's wrong with my clothes?" Ren asked, though she knew the answer. It was too casual. Boring.

"Nothing's wrong with it, it just doesn't scream Best Party of the Year! And that *is* what we're aiming for."

"So you can dress for party of the year and I can dress like Ren."

"Please dress up with me? It'll be fun!"

Ren groaned.

"Nothing too fancy. Just a *small* upgrade? I only turn sixteen *once* ya know."

Ren sighed. "Jasper, help."

Jasper poked his head in the closet. "What?"

"She wants me to wear something else. An upgrade."

He raised an eyebrow.

"You pick something for me," she muttered. "I'm going to the bathroom."

When Ren came back Jasper had an outfit for her. Light blue skinny jeans and a black long sleeve top. It wasn't too bad, considering some of the stuff Ocean had. She grabbed the clothes and went back to the bathroom to change. The top was off the shoulders, showing way more skin than she liked, and there was a hint of cleavage with it. But it wasn't *too* bad. At least her bra was black so the straps matched. She stared at herself in the mirror. The jeans were too tight, making her feel less like Ren and more like Kaida.

With a sigh she went back to Ocean's room to find Ocean in a stunning green sequined mini dress, with a cut out on one side and one long sleeve. It was off the shoulder on the opposite side.

"What do you think?" She spun around.

"I think I'm still severely under dressed. You look amazing!"

"You look amazing, too." Ocean grabbed her hands. "Simon is gonna lose his *mind*. Has he ever seen you like this?"

"Uh. He saw me in a dress once but it wasn't a dress like that."

"He *is* coming tonight, right?" She turned to Jasper before Ren could answer. "Also I made sure everyone knows not to invite your ex-bitch."

"Appreciate it."

"Simon's coming, but he'll be late. The band is prepping for their shows this week."

Ocean nodded. "Awesome. Is the band coming?"

Ren shook her head. "Allie said she's *very* sorry to miss the party but they got so much to do."

"Fair. Nico should be here soon. He's coming early to *help*."

"That's very Nico."

Ocean smiled and skipped out of the room as the bell rang. Ren sighed as she looked at Jasper.

"You hate the outfit, don't you?"

"No." She folded her arms across her chest. "It's not very me but I don't hate it."

"You look good."

"Thanks."

"So, Simon's coming?"

"Yeah."

"And, things are good with you two?"

"*Yes.*"

"Cause he sent you a billion flowers?"

Ren glared at him.

Jasper forced a smile. "I feel like he only gives you flowers when he needs to apologize for something. Which is... often."

"That isn't true. He got me flowers twice this week."

Jasper frowned. "What'd he do?"

"*Nothing*. He was just being sweet. Trying to make up for... before. And he left me a voicemail of him singing which was *so* cute and—"

Jasper rolled his eyes.

She sighed. "Can we not talk about this right now?"

"Fine."

Ren left the room and walked into Wade, Ocean's older brother. She blushed as she looked up at him. He was so much taller than she remembered. And his hair was different, shaved on the sides. But his eyes were the same lovely brown from her memories.

"Ren! Look at you. All grown up," he said with a laugh.

"I didn't know you'd be here!"

"I'm the adult supervision," he replied. "Mom will be here later, but till then I'm in charge."

"Good luck."

He grinned. "Thanks. I'll probably need it."

Ren nodded, then moved past him to find Ocean, Nico, and Kevin in the living room downstairs. They were trying to connect Nico's phone to the sound system.

"Hey, Ren!" Nico smiled. "How you doing?"

"I'm good."

"Bellamy's coming," he replied, watching her closely.

"He is? He hates parties. ¿Crees que Jules lo está haciendo venir?"

"Ni idea. Pero el pregunto si tú vendrías antes de confirmar que él iba a venir," he answered with a raised eyebrow.

"Oh, this is a *great* playlist," Ocean said as she scrolled through Nico's phone.

"Thanks."

Ren ignored Nico and looked at Kevin. He looked thinner, and there were bags under his eyes. He smiled at her, but it wasn't the smile she was used to seeing from him. She'd tried ignoring the guilt, which was easier when he was missing school. But seeing him again, it rushed back in.

His body, light in her arms. His heart, so still under her shaking hands. Gaia was still out there, and Ren was at a *party*.

With a sigh she went into the kitchen and busied herself with setting up snacks. She opened all the cookie boxes and lined them up on the counter, then filled a bunch of chip bowls for the table.

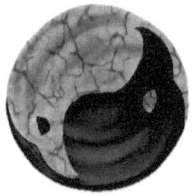

Jasper moved through the crowd of people, a bag of trash in hand. He and Ren volunteered to help keep the snack bowls full, and to keep things clean, so they wouldn't have to socialize too much. He didn't mind a party, but he wasn't in the mood. He yawned as he dropped the trash outside then went back to the kitchen. He hated how nice Ocean's house was. A spacious four-story brownstone. The back of the kitchen was open, looking down on the room below and he could see people in the back garden through the giant windows. He glanced back at the kitchen table, where Kevin was sitting with Ashley. He swallowed. Kevin was alive, but he wasn't *okay*. There'd been complications, from almost drowning, and he had trouble breathing now. Jasper sighed and pulled out his phone.

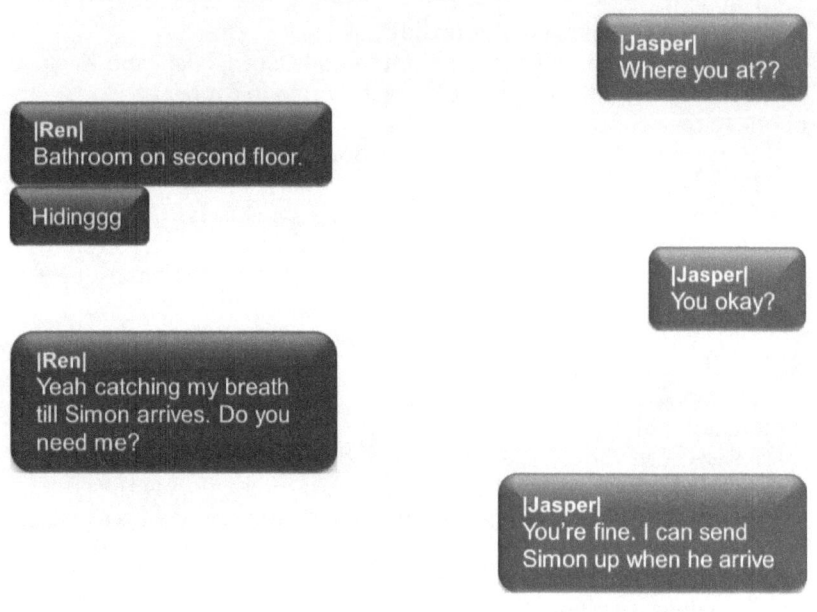

"Jasper, sup."

He turned to see Colin walking over. He was taller than Jasper, with brown curls that fell into his blue eyes. He leaned against the wall beside him, staring out at the kids, laughing and drinking and dancing.

"Hey," Jasper replied, confused.

Colin never talked to him. They weren't friends. They were barely acquaintances, having had only three classes together the last two years.

"You try this?" he asked, holding a blue solo cup in his hand, swirling it around. "I don't drink so no idea how strong it is, but tastes kinda good."

"Nah, I don't drink either."

"Try it."

Jasper hesitated then grabbed the cup and took a swig. It was fruity going down but had a strong aftertaste.

"Good, right?"

Jasper nodded and tried to hand it back, but Colin shook his head. "I'll get a new one."

He pushed himself off the wall and disappeared through the crowd again. Jasper sipped the drink, surprised by how it burned in his chest.

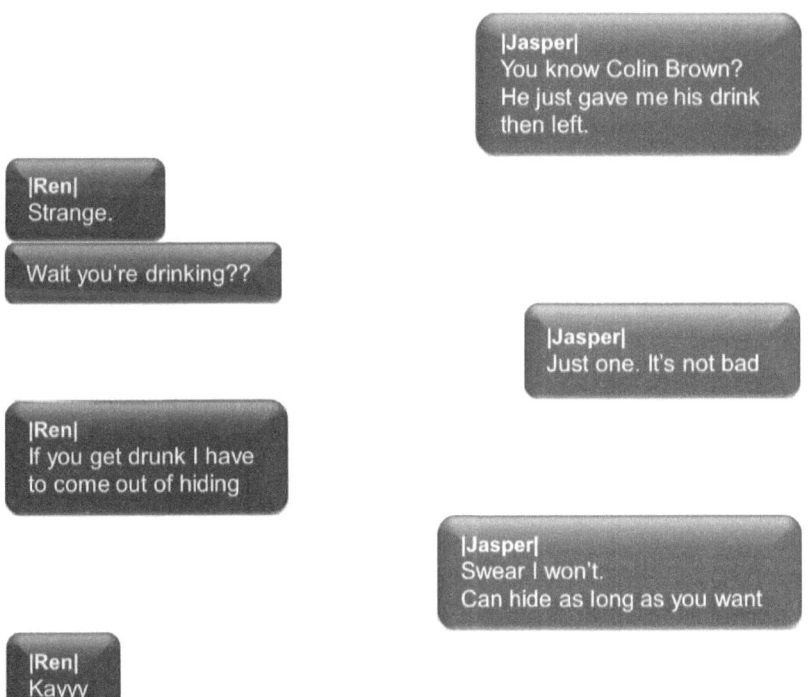

|Jasper|
You know Colin Brown?
He just gave me his drink
then left.

|Ren|
Strange.

Wait you're drinking??

|Jasper|
Just one. It's not bad

|Ren|
If you get drunk I have
to come out of hiding

|Jasper|
Swear I won't.
Can hide as long as you want

|Ren|
Kayyy

He tossed the cup and checked the snack bowls. Most of the cookies they brought were gone. He spotted Ocean laughing with Nico and Lola in the living room. He smiled. At least she was having fun. He really didn't mind her, but for some reason when they were both with Ren, they could *not* have a normal conversation without arguing about something.

After a while Colin found him again, a new drink in hand. He was grinning as he stumbled over.

"Yoooo, Jasper."

"How many of those have you had?"

"I do not know." He laughed. "You want some?"

"Nah, I'm good."

Colin nodded, then his head fell forward a little and he closed his eyes.

"You okay?"

"I think I might vomit."

Jasper sighed. "Let's get you to a bathroom."

Colin nodded again as Jasper put an arm around him. There was a line outside the bathroom on this floor, which he should have expected since Ren was hiding in the one upstairs. He took Colin to the third floor, but the only doors he saw were Ocean's parents' bedroom and her dads office, which had a sign taped to it saying DO NOT ENTER. Jasper ignored the sign and pushed the office open.

"Okay," he said as he closed it behind them. "Trash can here. Puke in that. Need anything else? Should I go?"

Colin straightened and came closer, suddenly seeming less drunk.

"I just wanted to get you alone," he whispered.

Jasper blinked. "Why?"

"Saw your comment on Harper's post."

Jasper took a deep breath as Colin stepped even closer, leaving barely any space between them.

"And I thought, damn. He's hot *and* into guys..."

Jasper raised an eyebrow. "I didn't realize you—"

"I'm not!" Colin hissed. "As far as you or anyone knows. And what we do in here *dies* in here, understand?"

Jasper's heart raced. "What we do?"

"If you want to," Colin whispered. "We could do a lot."

He leaned in and Jasper's back pressed against the door. Colin reached past and locked it. Jasper could smell the alcohol on his breath as his lips pressed against his, slow at first, then faster, like he was desperate. Jasper's body reacted before his mind could catch up, his hands moving down Colin's back.

Colin groaned against his mouth. As his lips went to Jasper's neck it was his turn to groan. Colin kissed his way down his throat, then his hands fumbled at the hem of Jasper's hoodie. He reached down and pulled it off himself, suddenly heated. Colin was grinning.

Jasper never really thought of Colin Brown as hot before. He was a preppy know-it-all who all the girls fawned over. But now Jasper saw the appeal as Colin slid his hands up under Jasper's shirt and pulled that off too. Then he went back to work with his mouth, kissing down his neck, his chest, his stomach. He dropped to his knees and grinned up at Jasper as he unzipped his pants, slow and seductive. Jasper couldn't think as all his blood rushed to one place.

Bellamy sighed as Jules texted, saying she'd be late to the party. He arrived alone, anxiety swirling in his stomach as he stepped through the door. It was louder and more chaotic than the costume party by far. He texted Ren before the panic could settle in.

|Bellamy|
Are you at this party?

|Ren|
Yes, but I'm hiding.

|Bellamy|
Wanna share your hiding spot?

|Ren|
Bathroom on second floor!

It's the first door on the left.
I'll unlock it for you.

He grinned as he found the stairs and forced his way through everyone. It was dark, very few lights on, but everyone was wearing glow in the dark jewelry, which was jarring to his eyes, the music so loud he could barely think. He knocked on the door Ren indicated. It opened and Ren was there, smiling at him.

"Welcome to my hideout." She closed the door and locked it again. "I was gonna just hide in Ocean's room, cause assumed she wouldn't want people in there, but she's got almost the whole house open to party-goers. So, naturally, people are making out in her bed."

"Naturally," he said with a nod.

"Where's Jules?" she asked as she sat on the blue rug in the middle of the floor by the bathtub, crossing her legs.

"Gonna be late." He frowned as he took in her outfit. It wasn't very *her*. "No Simon?"

"Also gonna be late."

"Ah. We can wait together then."

She grinned. "This does seem to be our way of attending parties."

"Hiding with you is the only way I enjoy them." He sat across from her, heart racing a little as he met her eyes. He'd been thinking about that conversation with Jasper over and over the last two weeks. And he felt confident he didn't have feelings for Ren, until he was *with* her. Then, he wasn't so sure.

"So, what's new with you?" Ren asked, pulling a bowl of pretzels over and putting it between them. "Did you finish that book?"

"Oh, yeah. Finished it last night. The twist completely fell flat."

"No, really?" She shook her head and popped a pretzel in her mouth. "That sucks."

"Yeah, so, *don't* read that one."

"Noted."

He grabbed a pretzel. "I'll find a good one for you, I swear."

"I'm sure you will."

She pulled her phone out, scrolling through it with one hand as she ate pretzels with the other.

His phone vibrated in his pocket.

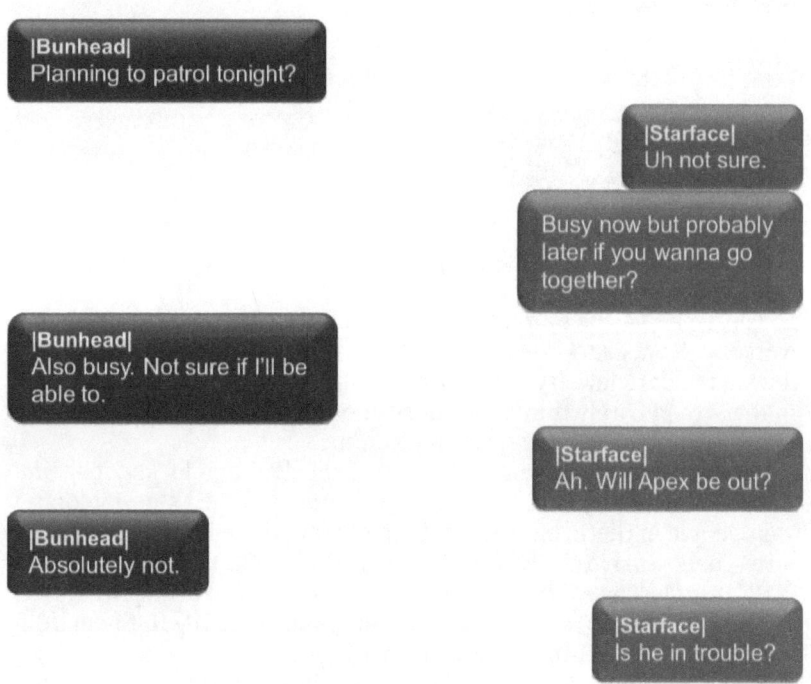

|Bunhead|
Planning to patrol tonight?

|Starface|
Uh not sure.

Busy now but probably later if you wanna go together?

|Bunhead|
Also busy. Not sure if I'll be able to.

|Starface|
Ah. Will Apex be out?

|Bunhead|
Absolutely not.

|Starface|
Is he in trouble?

|Bunhead|
Undetermined. But definitely
not patrolling, unless
emergency.

|Starface|
Got it.

He looked up, feeling rude for texting Kaida while he was with Ren, but she was also texting someone. Probably Simon. She glanced up and smiled. Then she threw a pretzel, hitting him in the forehead. He opened his mouth in shock and she laughed.

"What was that for?"

"Impulsive thoughts." She threw another one, and this time he was ready, catching it in his mouth.

She burst out laughing and threw another.

"Give me those."

"No!"

"It's only fair if I can throw them at you too!"

She giggled as she clutched the bowl to her chest. "My pretzels."

"So you're allowed to throw them and I'm not?" He pouted.

Her smile softened and she held the bowl out to him. He took it then dumped the pretzels out over her head. Ren's mouth opened in surprise.

"Sorry." He couldn't help but laugh.

"Whyyyy?"

"Pretzels in your hair is a *very* good look on you," he replied. "I simply had to." He pulled one out of her hair, heart racing. "Sorry."

"I'll forgive you. One day."

"Hm..." *Definitely not sure...*

Someone knocked on the door. "Ren?" Simon's voice called from the other side. Ren's laughter died out as she hopped up, pretzels tumbling to the floor around her as she opened the door.

Simon stood there, frowning as he noticed Bellamy.

"Whatcha doing?"

"Hiding," Ren said. "Party is loud."

Simon released a breath. "Wanna come out?"

Ren glanced back at Bellamy and the pretzels on the floor.

"I got this, my mess. Go."

She nodded, giving him a small smile before following Simon out of the room. He sighed as he started picking up the pretzels and putting them back in the bowl.

"Bell?"

He turned. Jules stood in the doorway, a frown on her face.

"Hey, you're here."

"Were you... in the bathroom with Ren?"

"We were just hiding from the crowd." He picked up the bowl. "And eating pretzels."

"Oh."

"Are you okay?"

"Yeah." She nodded. "Totally fine. You wanna keep hiding?"

"No, we can... we can go out." He forced a smile and went back downstairs with her, trying not to think about Ren's smile, and the pretzels in her hair.

"We can leave," Simon whispered, arm tight around her shoulders.

"What?"

"You said it was too loud. We don't have to stay. If you're just gonna hide the whole time we might as well go."

"Oh." She paused, looking through the bodies dancing and laughing around them. "Okay let me find Jasper. He was drinking earlier and I don't wanna leave him if he's a mess."

"Alright."

She couldn't find Jasper so sent a text and waited.

|Jasper|
Uh. So. I just hooked up with Colin.

|Ren|
WHAT?!

|Jasper|
Yeah. It wassudden

|Ren|
Are you still with him?

|Jasper|
No he left and I'm
processing. In the office

|Ren|
Are you okay??
You wanna leave?

|Jasper|
Yes to both

|Ren|
Coming

She grabbed Simon's hand, dragging him up the stairs to the third floor. She pushed the door open a fraction to find Jasper standing there, looking flushed. Her stomach twisted as she grabbed his hand and dragged both boys with her back down to the front door. Cool air swept over her as they walked outside.

"Can we give him a ride?" Ren asked, looking up at Simon.

"Of course."

Jasper didn't protest. Something was off, but she couldn't ask in front of Simon, so sent him a text when they were in the car.

|Ren|
Sneak over later??

|Jasper|
Yeah

Then she sent a text to Ocean, feeling bad for leaving without saying goodbye.

|Ren|
Jasper's not feeling well so we left, but I love you so much and hope you had fun!!! Best party ever!!!

They dropped Jasper off at his apartment. He muttered a quiet thanks as he hopped out of the car and rushed inside. Ren sighed as Simon started driving again.

"Where we going now?"

"Taking you home?"

"Oh." They hadn't spent any time together and he was leaving tomorrow. "You don't wanna hang out for a bit?"

"I'd love to, but I should just call it an early night. Allie wants us to get up at the crack ass of dawn to head out."

"Oh."

He glanced at her. "Sorry I was late."

"It's okay. I knew you would be."

"I should have been there." He sighed.

"Are you... mad at me?" she asked softly. He was surprisingly calm, which made her think maybe he wasn't calm at all.

"No, babe. Of course not. You are allowed to hang out with friends you previously had crushes on." He smiled. "I am so okay with it."

"Just friends," she said softly.

"I know. I'm not mad." His smile softened as he glanced at her. "I'm gonna miss you so much."

She relaxed as he pulled up outside of the bakery. "I'll miss you too. But it's only a week, right?"

"One week." He leaned over, grabbing her face and kissing her. "Then I'm back for a week and a half before we leave again. And was thinking, when I get back... dinner with the dads?"

She smiled. "Yes! And I asked my dads about those shows."

He raised an eyebrow. "And?"

"It's a maybe, right now." She grinned. "He was making excuses about not having the time, *but* my Aunt Aza said *she'd* take me if he can't. So, I think he's just gonna give in."

Simon's eyes were bright and he kissed her again. "God. You look *so* good tonight, by the way. Really wish I had more time with you."

She blushed, realizing she left her clothes at Ocean's. "It's okay. Text me before you leave? And when you get to your hotel?"

"I will." Another kiss. She melted into it before he pulled back.

Then she sighed and got out of the car. She gave her dads a quick update on how the party went before rushing to her room to wait for Jasper to arrive.

65
Always Pretty

Jasper climbed down through the roof and settled on Ren's bed. She handed him a cup of cocoa as he leaned back against the wall and closed his eyes.

"What happened tonight?"

"I don't even know. He saw Harper's post and I guess he's so fucking deep in the closet he's never known another guy into guys? So there *I* was, easy pickings."

Ren frowned, but didn't say anything.

"We hooked up and... it was hot, honestly."

"But?"

He sighed and sipped the cocoa. "But when we were done he got angry."

"About what?"

"Being gay? I don't know. He threatened to kill me if I ever told anyone about it. I thought he was joking, cause like obviously I wouldn't out him? So I laughed but he was serious. And he wanted me to know it."

"What did he do?" she asked, heart racing.

Jasper sighed again and lifted his hair to show her the swollen red cut on his temple.

"He did this to you?" Her hands were shaking.

"Grabbed my head and slammed it into the corner of the desk to get his point across."

Ren stood up on the bed and reached for the skylight. Jasper grabbed her ankle.

"What are you doing?"

"Gonna go kill—"

He pulled her back down and she gasped in surprise as she landed on her butt.

"No. Leave it. It's fine."

She couldn't accept that, but bit her tongue and put her arm around his shoulders, pulling him closer. He leaned into her and closed his eyes.

When Ren stepped outside in the morning Simon was standing there waiting for her.

"Simon! I thought you left already?" she said as he pulled her into his arms.

"I made them wait so I could see you again," he said. Her heart raced as she clung to him. "*And* I got you this." He pulled back and handed her a cup, clinking with ice.

"What's this?" she asked as she took it.

"Tea, from that place we went to last week. You said you really liked it."

She beamed up at him. "You didn't have to do that."

"I know." He leaned in and kissed her.

"You're *so* sweet."

He bit his lip as he looked down at her. "Fuck. I'm gonna miss you so much."

"I'll miss you too."

"Yeah?" His smile faded a little and worry flashed in his eyes.

She cupped his face with her hand. "I'll be here when you get home and I'm gonna text you every day and you can call me after each show and I'm gonna miss you the *entire* time."

His smile returned and he kissed her.

"I put the little guitar you made on the mirror in our van, so I'll be seeing it and thinking of you on the long drive."

Ren giggled.

He sighed. "Okay, don't wanna make you late. Good luck on finals. I'll call you when we get there."

"Okay."

Another kiss, this one lasting longer, then he hugged her again before walking away.

"Simon! Wait!" she called, heart thumping as he turned back around. She closed the distance and looked up into his eyes. "I am all in, too. With you."

His face lit up and he pulled her back into his arms, lifting her off the ground for a moment. "I can't believe I'm not gonna see you for a week," he said, smiling wide as he leaned in and kissed her again. "Get to school. I'll text you later, beautiful girl."

She couldn't stop smiling, that was until Jasper showed up to walk with her. Then she remembered last night.

When they got to school Ren was determined to make Colin pay, stalking him through the halls between classes, trying to plan something. She spotted Ocean and pulled her aside.

"Wanna help me get revenge on someone?" she asked in a whisper.

Ocean sighed, her brown eyes disappointed. "Really? You're not even gonna apologize?"

Ren's heart sank. "Apologize?"

Ocean laughed, a humorless sound. "For disappearing during my birthday party."

"I—Jasper, he—"

Ocean shook her head. "He didn't feel good, right. So you take him home then come *back*." She blinked, her anger melting into something sadder. "It was my birthday and you just *left*."

Ren's eyes burned. "I'm sorry. I didn't..." She couldn't even blame this one on Kaida. It was all Ren, being the worst friend ever. "I'm sorry. I thought, you seemed fine, with Nico and the others and—"

"I barely know them!" Ocean spat back. "I get you don't like parties, and I was fine with you coming and going throughout, I get it's overwhelming for you. But just leaving... you didn't even say bye to my face."

She grabbed Ocean's hands. "I am so so sorry. It's *not* a good excuse but, something happened. With Jasper," she said, lowering her voice. "He wasn't sick. He was fucking assaulted."

Ocean blinked. "What do you mean?"

"I *mean*," she hissed under her breath, "Jasper hooked up with a boy in your dad's office during the party. And when they were done he *hit* Jasper. Slammed his head into the desk. Threatening him."

Her eyes widened. "What the *fuck*."

Ren nodded. "I should have just told you the truth, I was just trying to help him, I did *not* mean to abandon you on your birthday."

Ocean's face softened and she gripped Ren's hands. "Okay, I'm still a little upset but I assume this is the revenge you spoke of? Count me the fuck *in*."

Ren grinned.

After fifth period she had Ocean call Colin over, getting him to stand in the right spot.

"Colin, right?" Ocean said, her voice awfully flirtatious. "How'd you like my party last night?"

"It was an unforgettable experience," Colin replied with a smirk.

Ren stood at her locker, not looking at either of them. Colin was turned slightly, almost facing her direction.

"Oh, Ren, hey!" Ocean said, making Colin move to look at her.

Ren slammed her locker open. Colin screamed as it hit him in the face. Blood dripped down his chin.

"Oh my god," Ren muttered. "I'm *so* sorry!"

"My nose," he mumbled through his hands, tears streaming down his face.

"Yikes." It was hard not to smile in satisfaction. "You should go to the nurse, get that checked out."

"That looks *bad,*" Ocean said. "Come on, I'll walk with you."

"Ren, what was that?" Jasper asked as he passed them.

"An accident," she whispered gleefully.

He smiled then pulled her into his arms, burying his face in her shoulder. "Thank you."

When Ren went to her locker after sixth period Bradley was standing in front of it, blocking her way.

"Hey, Ren," he said, eyeing her.

"What?"

"Why do you hide all that?"

She stared at him. "What?"

His eyes roved down her body. "I saw you at the party. You looked so hot. Should show us more of that."

Ren was too stunned to speak.

He licked his lips. "You're really fuckable under all those clothes, huh?"

"Fuck off, Brad."

She turned to see Bellamy standing behind her, glaring at Bradley.

"I was just giving her a *compliment,*" Bradley continued with a laugh.

Bellamy shoved him against the lockers. Ren stared, wide eyed, heart racing.

"How about you don't talk to her like that, *ever again.* Or at all."

Bradley rolled his eyes and pushed past Bellamy. Ren released a breath as Bellamy turned to her, fuming.

"Did I really look that different at the party?" she asked, feeling self-conscious.

"You looked pretty. But, you're always pretty."

"I'm... *what*?"

"I think I prefer you like this, though," he continued.

"This?" Her throat was so dry.

He nodded. "Yeah, those clothes."

"You do? Why?"

"You're happier in them. You seem... uncomfortable when you dress differently." He shrugged. "But always pretty. Ignore Bradley, he's an ass."

She nodded, confused. He just said... pretty. *Always pretty*. A few months ago that would have sent her spiraling. Total malfunction. Now it just... *slightly* made her brain glitch.

"Bell?"

They turned to see Jules waiting for him. He went to her and Ren shut her locker, walking away in a daze. She had to find a way to make things up to Ocean.

Bellamy walked with Jules back to his apartment after school. She seemed extra quiet, but perhaps she was just worried about their finals. She didn't say anything till they were all the way in his bedroom.

"We need to talk," she finally said as she sat on the edge of his bed.

He sat beside her. "What's up?"

"I think we should break up." She said it so calmly, he wasn't sure he heard her right.

"Break up?"

"You like Ren. I know you said you didn't and I don't think you were lying to me. I just think you're kinda lying to yourself."

He frowned. "What?"

"You told her she was pretty. Like, three times. Said she's always pretty. Is there literally any other girl you'd say that to?"

"You."

She rolled her eyes. *"Besides* me. And if you want to get technical, you've only told me I look pretty when we're going out and I'm dressed up. You said it *so* casually to her today."

"So... you're breaking up with me because I said she was pretty?"

Jules smiled. "I'm breaking up with you because you don't like me. You like *her*. You think she's pretty and you nearly killed Bradley after his gross comment. You rushed to the hospital to see her, forgetting everything the moment she was hurt. She made you that bear... Bellamy, you were hiding in the bathroom with her at the party. You're the one who suggested we go to that party and I *know* you don't like parties."

Bellamy swallowed, heart racing.

"You went to the party knowing you'd see her." She let out a breath. "You still look confused but just think about it for a second. You tell me you're bad at reading people, but not *her*. The second Ren walks in a room you're reading her like she's a book you've read a hundred times. Like you have her memorized. And I think maybe she reads you too... you *like* her. And listen, that's fine. Ren's great, I get it. I just wish you'd figured that out *before* we tried this."

"I... I'm sorry, Jules. I don't—"

"I like you," she interrupted. "And I wanted to see where this could go, cause I think we're a good fit for each other." She shook her head. "But you and her are better. Maybe that scares you? So you asked me out instead? I don't know. But you need to sort that out. I don't wanna waste my time. Best we break up now before it's too late. Cause I don't wanna fall in love with you, Bellamy Grey. It'll hurt more later, when you figure out it's not me. It's her."

His heart pounded as he stared at her. "Okay."

"I'm sorry. But trust me, it's better this way. For both of us."

"Do you... hate me now?"

Jules' eyes softened. "No. And I think we can probably still be friends? I just... want some time away from you. For now."

"Okay."

She smiled. "So... see you around."

He walked her out then went back to his room and flopped down on his bed, mind racing.

You're taking that rather well, Zeli said softly.

Do I like Ren?

Yes.

He groaned, squeezing his eyes shut. He couldn't like Ren. *Ren* was with Simon. Simon, who was a possessive piece of shit. Ren... who was beautiful and smart and kind and *knew him*. He screamed into the pillow.

PART FIVE

THE BOND BROKEN

While I have documented many accounts from the war,
from soldiers, civilians, and Bonded, on both sides...
There is one account I never got. That of the Xyri.
We are left with so many questions.
Did they agree with the choices their humans made?
Were they aligned in their beliefs?
What, truthfully, caused them to abandon humankind?
There was so much bloodshed in the battles. So many dead.
They let that happen, they fought for it.
So why, then, did they leave us at the end?
I'm afraid we may never know the answer.

- Secrets of War

66
Harmless Fun

Ren usually tried to avoid looking up what people were saying about Kaida online, but Jasper insisted she look at what he sent her, which made her assume they weren't saying *bad things* at least. There were hundreds, maybe thousands of posts under the hashtag #KaidaIsMyHero.

I'm trans and I've been afraid to tell anyone, but knowing Kaida would support me makes me feel like I'll be able to do it someday. **#KaidaIsMyHero**

Kaida saved my life. Carried my broken body through a portal and got me help. I would have died without her. She should intervene more often, if you ask me! **#KaidaIsMyHero**

I love that Kaida stood up for Wonderland! When everyone was ready to condemn them a villain she made it clear they'd done nothing wrong AND insisted everyone respect their pronouns. Not to mention she did the same thing for Pompeii last year. Everyone wanted a witch hunt for that girl, and we all know it's cause Pompeii is Black. But Kaida insisted what happened was an accident, and she'd know better than us. Kaida really is the hero we need. **#KaidaIsMyHero**

I don't care what anyone says. Kaida saved me. Not against some mysterious villains, but against those who abuse their power and the people they're supposed to protect. Maybe it's time we put our trust in her and the other heroes instead. No one else is looking out for us like them. **#KaidaIsMyHero**

Ren realized as she read through them it must have been in response to something *not* so nice about Kaida. For her own peace of mind she didn't go looking for it. She wiped her eyes as she continued reading. Seeing posts from actual people she'd helped was making her warm and fuzzy. One sentence in an interview months ago *had* resonated with people. Because of that there was an overwhelming amount of posts asking her to come to Pride, which was tomorrow.

|Ren|
This is insane I'm crying!

|Jasper|
They love you!!!

|Ren|
I wish I wasn't straight.

I guess they don't know that, which explains why they're asking me to come to pride.

|Jasper|
The gays love to project

We should still go! I was planning to go anyways

|Ren|
As yourself though. Not Apex. It'll be weird if I go, won't it?

|Jasper|
No boo. You've been invited by like a thousand queers. It'll be fine. and fun!

|Ren|
You sure?

|Jasper|
Yeah!!!

|Ren|
Okaaaay. We can go.

The next day Kaida and Apex stood on a roof overlooking the Pride Parade. Her heart caught in her throat when she saw the float they'd made for her. A big square platform covered in shiny red scales to match her suit, with her name in giant rainbow letters on the backdrop.

"Wanna make an entrance? We could just land on it," Apex said.

She smiled, nervous. Showing up here felt like a lie. Kaida was an ally, but that was all. It wasn't a space she needed to take up. She looked at Jasper. It was *his* space.

"Let's go."

Kaida jumped, flying straight to the float, while Apex did a few swoops to show off before landing dramatically behind her. She rolled her eyes at him, but couldn't hide her smile. People cheered and she blushed.

The attention made her squirm, so after a few minutes she hopped off the float and walked toward a crowd of people on the side of the street holding signs with **Kaida Is My Hero** on them.

"Hi," she said, feeling awkward.

"I can't believe you came!" A girl with frizzy brown hair said. Her eyeshadow made a full rainbow across her face.

"Does this mean what we think it means?" another girl asked. She had pink hair the same shade as Kaida's.

"Probably not," Kaida said softly as Apex stepped up beside her. "Uh, any of you wanna film me for a minute so I can make a point?"

Every single one of them lifted their phones, staring at her in disbelief.

"What are we doing?" Apex whispered.

"Something important." She took a deep breath. "So, I know a lot of people wanted me to come here today and I know there's a lot of speculation about... me. Um. But I wanna be honest. I absolutely support everyone in the LGBTQA community, but I am not *part* of it. And I don't wanna take up space when there are other people who belong in that space, and it's their voices who should be heard. Not mine." She paused, glancing at Apex, giving him a look.

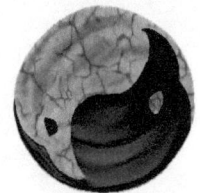

Kaida raised an eyebrow at Jasper, waiting.

"Are we doing this now?" he asked, voice low.

"Only if you want to," she replied.

"I guess."

She grinned, stepping back so those filming could focus on him instead.

"Uh, hi," he said, trying not to laugh. "I'm Apex. And uh. So, Kaida might not be part of the community, but I am."

People started screaming and cheering. Jasper's laugh escaped as he looked at Kaida, who was grinning like an idiot, blue eyes shining with pride.

"I uh, I've never really come out before. This is a weird way to do it."

That wasn't true of course, he came out to her. And her dads. And they'd reacted nicely, but in the back of his mind he knew how it could go. How it *would* go if he told his dad.

Kaida hugged him.

"Are you willing to tell us—"

"I'm bisexual," Apex interrupted as he pulled back from Kaida.

"You just got so much hotter," the same guy continued. He had glitter all over his face.

"Thank you."

"Wait, are you two together?" one of the girls asked, looking between him and Kaida, eyes wide.

Jasper laughed again. "We're just friends. In fact, I am *very* single."

"Are you out to anyone in your real life?" the girl with pink hair asked.

"A small handful of friends, yeah."

"When did you know you were bi?"

"Uh, first time I saw Star Wars. Was never Han *or* Leia for me," Jasper answered with a nod.

Kaida laughed.

"I'm gonna go... enjoy the festivities," he continued. "But it was great talking to you guys."

He grabbed Kaida by the hand and pulled her away.

"Where we going now?" she asked.

"Wings out, boo."

She shook her head as her wings unfolded. People moved out of the way as they started running, before they jumped, flying high above the crowd. He led her to a roof overlooking the parade. She was grinning when they landed.

"How are you feeling?" she asked.

"That was fucking awesome."

"Proud of you."

"Aw, shucks." He laughed. "You good?"

"Of course."

He gave her a look. "You hate crowds. And that was a lot of people filming us. I thought maybe you'd want a break."

Her face softened as she reached out, hugging him.

"We don't have to stay. I mean, not like this. I'm supposed to meet up with Ocean later, as myself. But you don't have to stay."

She pulled back, eyes wide. "You're hanging out with Ocean? Without me?"

He frowned. "Is that not allowed?"

"No it's *great!*" She was smiling so wide. "You guys doing friend things together, like *friends.* I could cry."

"Yeah, well. We're trying."

"Thank you."

"Do you wanna leave?" he asked.

"I'm fine. Swear."

"Yo!" Someone yelled from above them.

They looked up just as Tag descended from the sky, a rainbow pride flag tied around his neck like a cape, waving in the air between his silky wings.

Jasper grinned. "Hey, Tag."

"That was some speech, guys. Also, *welcome.*" He bowed his head to Apex.

"Are you..."

"Very gay," Tag replied, his smile wide. "And too old for you."

"I'm *seventeen*," Jasper said defensively.

"I'm twenty-three. Sorry, kid." He grinned. "So, what are we doing on this fine day?"

"Hopefully just this," Kaida replied. "Normal fun."

"I do love fun," Tag said as he untied his pride flag. "No tragedies today." He draped the flag across Jasper's shoulders and tied it. "Let's go."

Jasper met Kaida's eyes and she nodded.

Things were a bit chaotic after that, but in a good way. Walking through the crowds, taking pictures with people, answering more questions. Everyone they met was thrilled to learn both Apex and Tag were queer. He could tell Kaida felt out of place, but she stayed with them, trudging through the parade, a smile on her face.

After a while Hoax and Parody found them and it was a whole little hero party. He noted Kaida texting Lycan, asking him to come. The boy showed up within ten minutes.

Jasper did a double take as they walked through the street. Someone was dressed up as Apex. He grinned, thinking of asking them for a picture, but then the person started making out with someone in a costume with black bunny ears.

His smile was replaced with a glare. "Don't they know we're *enemies?*"

Parody laughed as she put a hand on his shoulder. "Think that's part of the fun, Apex."

He grumbled in response.

Kaida pulled him and Lycan aside, distracting him. "Zig wants us to tell them about Xereth," she whispered. "Warn their Xyri."

"Oh, fair."

Lycan nodded and gathered the other three. They settled on a roof again.

"What's up?" Parody asked, her cheery demeanor making Jasper smile.

"So, there's this guy," Kaida started.

"An immortal," Apex added.

"Technically called a Timeless," Lycan continued. "Named Xereth."

"Your Xyri should know him."

"And he's here, in New York."

Tag frowned. "Zichii isn't happy to hear that."

"Wait wait," Parody interrupted. "What about Xenos? Do any of your Xyri know where he is? Zephy talks about him a lot."

Kaida shook her head. "He's still missing. And they blame Xereth."

"And he's here," Jasper repeated. "Which they think is a big deal but—"

It is a big deal.

Jasper sighed. "But we do have bigger problems."

"Like Gaia," Hoax muttered.

Jasper was sure that was the only the third time he'd heard her speak. She was *so* quiet.

Kaida nodded. "She's the biggest problem we have right now. But, my Xyri was insistent I warn you about Xereth."

Tag nodded. "It's good to know, but I agree. We need to deal with Gaia."

"I was also thinking..." Kaida said. "We should exchange numbers. The four of us have, but we should with you two as well." She nodded at Tag and Hoax.

"No one's supposed to know our identity," Hoax said, pink eyes wide.

"Yeah, but we don't use our real numbers."

"It's really clever actually," Parody said, her ponytail swishing as she turned her head. "There's this app that generates a fake number but still comes through in your texts."

"So, none of us know each other's real numbers but we can still communicate."

"That's a good idea," Tag replied. "What do ya say, partner?" He looked down at Hoax.

She rolled her eyes. "I never agreed to be your partner."

Tag just smiled. "They got each other," he said, nodding at Kaida and Lycan. "Don't you think we should have someone watching our backs, too? We should be a team."

Hoax just glared.

Tag's smile widened. "I think she's coming around on the idea."

"I don't think we need to trade numbers. If something big is happening, we'll figure it out. We'll show up. Like we did with the bridge."

She turned away from them, stalking to the other side of the roof, her long multi-colored hair blowing in the breeze.

"I think she's maybe been through some shit. Slow to trust," Tag whispered. "She'll come around eventually."

Kaida nodded, eyes distant. "I'll... be right back. You guys keep having fun and stuff."

Jasper watched her go, worried as she jumped off the roof and flew away.

Glitter rained from the sky. Kaida landed underneath it, spinning in a circle, looking for Wonderland. It looked so real, she could almost feel it. *Almost.*

It took only a moment to find them, leaning against a wall behind the crowd, their pink coat a bright spot against the bricks. She walked over and they smiled at her.

"You're going viral," they said.

"Huh?"

"Your little ally declaration. Your friend coming out." They held up their phone. "Sixteen million views and counting, on just this one video. There were about twenty videos posted already."

She blushed. "What's with the glitter?"

"It's fun. Ain't hurting nobody."

She sighed and leaned on the wall beside them. "I suppose. No plans to do anything that could hurt people?"

"These are my people. I'm here to protect them."

She raised an eyebrow. "It would be so easy for you to be a hero."

"And yet... the people still think I'm a villain."

"I don't."

Wonderland smiled as they looked down at her. "You're a bit unreal, you know?"

"What do you mean?"

They shrugged. "You're just... rare in all the right ways. I don't need to be a hero. They have you. That's enough."

She nodded slowly. "You said you're here to protect them. Do you think something bad is gonna happen?"

"You know how often these people are targeted on a normal day? Things have been batshit in this city lately. Figured I'd stay close. Just in case." They met her eyes. "That why you're here?"

"Just in case."

Something flew across the sky and for a moment she thought it was Apex. It wasn't. It was a unicorn.

She laughed. "You're having fun, aren't you?"

"So much. What else should I do?"

"Not enough rainbows. I mean, the glitter is fun. But like... we should probably have at *least* ten rainbows."

"Ten rainbows coming up."

"You know, the first time I saw a real rainbow I was just a kid." She smiled as she leaned on the wall beside them. "I was in the car with my dad, and I got *so* excited. I kept asking if we could get closer to it. Dad just dropped everything. We must have driven for over an hour, chasing that rainbow."

Wonderland grinned at her. "Sounds like a good dad."

"He is."

Ren was increasingly sure Wonderland was someone she could trust. So what if they didn't use their powers to save people or stop crimes. They were having harmless fun and that was okay.

She pulled her phone out to check the time then realized she'd missed two calls from Simon. Her heart raced as she glanced back at Wonderland.

"Gotta make a personal call."

They nodded as she ripped open a portal right there and ducked inside.

67

Doomed From The Start

Lycan sat on the roof next to Parody while the others went back down to join in the fun. There were so many couples in the crowd, kissing, holding hands, laughing. He thought coming here would take his mind off Ren.

All week during finals he caught himself staring at her, feeling shy every time she smiled at him. He barely slept last night, thoughts of her coursing through his mind. Several times he got out his phone to text her then changed his mind. Ren had a boyfriend. Even if he was brave enough to... what? Ask her out?

You wanted to ask her out a long time ago. After you met her.

Zeli you are not helping.

She was right though. He'd almost asked Ren to the homecoming dance last year. *We did dance that night...* he smiled at the memory. He told her he didn't know how to dance and she told him no one knew how to dance. But then she grabbed his hands and they swayed, alone in the courtyard, no music to accompany them but their laughter. But later that night he'd seen her with Jasper, and assumed they were dating. *That's why I didn't ask her out.* By the time he found out they were just friends he'd fallen so far for Kaida. But then... just a few months ago he wanted to get over Kaida.

"Do you know any girls who might like me? Figure asking out someone already into me might be easier."

"You're kidding, right?"

"No? Does no one like me? I guess that makes—"

"Ren," Nico said.

"Ren? Ren doesn't... like me?"

"Pretty sure she's had a thing for you since last year."

He blushed, thinking back on that day. He'd been excited at the idea of asking Ren out. But then Simon was there. Stupid Simon with his stupid face.

You've been in denial about this girl for a while now.

Not helping.

"You're awfully quiet," Parody said as she looked at him. Her pink cape lifted with the breeze behind her. "Wanna go join the others?"

He sighed. "No. I just... in my head about something."

"Wanna talk about it?"

He met her eyes. "Have you ever... had feelings for someone you're friends with?"

She smiled. "Is this about Kaida?"

He laughed and leaned his head back, looking up at the clouds. "No, although you're not wrong about that. I was... so in love with her. For the longest time. But now I... I maybe have feelings for a friend from school? And I don't know what to do about it."

"You could tell her how you feel?"

"Can't."

"Why not?"

"Cause last time I did that she jumped off the roof."

Parody blinked, her pink eyes confused. "Are we... still talking about Kaida?"

He put his face in his hands. "*Yes.* I told her I loved her and. She just left in a panic." He sighed as his hands fell. "Please don't tell her I told you that. And we're good now. She was so kind about rejecting me after we talked."

"But now you're afraid to tell someone *else* how you feel because it didn't go so well last time you did that?"

He nodded.

Parody smiled. "Lycan, you just said it. Kaida was kind. And you're good now. Can't you put your trust in that? If this person you like is a real friend, trust they'll be kind too. And that's assuming they'll reject you. What if they feel the same way?"

He swallowed. "She would be kind. She's... the nicest person in the whole world. But another problem is... she can't feel the same. She's seeing someone else."

"Ah," Parody said as she leaned back. "That does make things more complicated. Tell me this, how did you feel before telling Kaida the truth?"

"Like I was dying. Drowning. Suffocating."

"And after? Not immediately, but once you talked it out. How did you feel then?"

He sighed. "Better."

She nodded. "Sometimes you gotta get your feelings out, one way or another. What do you think will happen, if you tell this friend you like her?"

He considered it. "She'd listen. Those brown eyes would be staring into mine as she took in my words, which I would fumble over. For sure. Um. She'd blush, probably. And she'd apologize to me. Probably ten times. Tell me she's sorry, cause of him. She has him. Wants him. Not me." He sighed, heart aching in his chest. "She wouldn't be mean. She wouldn't even be weird. She'd be gentle and lovely and she'd still be my friend."

Parody smiled. "I think you have your answer, then."

He nodded, smiling at her. "Thanks, for talking with me. It's nice. Like, having a big sister or something."

"Aw." Parody's eyes watered. "I always wanted a little brother."

He laughed. "Well, you got one now."

She put her arm around his shoulders, laughing. "I'm so glad I met you guys."

"Me too."

Soon after that Lycan headed home. He detransformed, walking the whole way, his thoughts circling Ren. Now that school was over he wasn't even sure when he'd see her again. He could text her. Ask her to hang out... *no.*

Why no?

He sighed.

Bellamy?

It doesn't matter.

And it didn't matter. Ren was his friend and that was good enough. Just like being friends with Kaida was good enough. Maybe he was destined to be alone. Always loving people from a distance, never getting close. His relationship with Jules blew up. His first attempt and it ended so quickly.

It was kind of doomed from the start, wasn't it?

Why do you say that?

Because of Ren? You liked her before you asked out Jules. It's no wonder Jules figured it out, too.

Figured it out before I did?

Yes, well...

He grinned. *You saying I'm an idiot, Zels?*

No, I would never. There was humor in her voice.

Maybe I don't really like Ren that much? You know, like, Jasper said it and Jules said it, and you said it... so I'm thinking about it a lot but maybe it's not that serious?

No? Then why are we here?

Bellamy stopped in his tracks, looking up. Over The Grainbow Bakery was directly in front of him. He walked straight to Ren's without even thinking about it. The urge to text her nearly overwhelmed him. *Hey Ren, I'm outside. Come see me.* But he didn't move.

Ren. The first person at school to talk to him. Also the first to yell at him. And the first to befriend him. The girl he'd hide with at parties... because he didn't like parties. But he still threw them or went to them... *cause I know she'll be there.* Ren, with her soft words and sweet smile and lovely eyes.

Do you remember the night you got your weapon? Zeli asked.

Of course. It was the night Ren was assaulted.

Do you remember how you felt?

I was angry. So angry. Someone was hurting her and it killed me. All I wanted... He swallowed. *I see what you're doing.*

But it didn't matter if he liked Ren. Because Ren... was walking down the street towards him.

His stomach fluttered, anxiety rushing in. He spun around, looking for somewhere to hide. There was a line of people wrapped outside of the bakery for the pride cupcakes. In his panic he grabbed the street pole and pressed his face against it. Maybe she wouldn't see him, wouldn't notice him standing there, wouldn't—

"Bellamy?"

Oh god. He lifted his head then laughed nervously. "Ren! Hey. What are you doing here?"

She smiled, her eyes bright. "I live here. What are you doing here?"

"I'm not here." *Fuck.*

"What?"

"What?"

Her smile faded, a frown taking its place. "Are you okay?"

"Totally. Bye." He turned but she grabbed his arm, forcing him to a stop. A shiver ran through him at her touch.

"Bellamy, what's wrong?" Her voice was so soft as she stared into his eyes. Her long brown hair lifted in the breeze and for a moment he wondered what it would be like to touch it.

"Nothing. I uh... I just didn't sleep much last night."

"Do you wanna come inside? I can get you some cookies." She let go of his arm, nodding toward the bakery. "I can bypass the line, obviously."

"Hahaha no I'm fine." *I like her I definitely like her I am. So fucked.*

She looked disappointed, like she knew he was lying. **I think maybe she reads you, too.** Jules' words. Ren searched his face and saw right through him. He smiled, knowing she hated lies. He thought she was so pretty that first day he met her, but the memory didn't compare to how gorgeous she was now, looking up at him with those beautiful brown eyes.

"I like your freckles," he whispered.

Ren's eyes widened and he blushed, realizing he said that out loud.

"My... freckles?"

"Uh yeah. I gotta go."

"Oh. Are you... sure you're alright?"

"Yeah." He turned away before he could say anything else. It was hard to think straight, heart pounding in his chest. After a few steps he turned and looked back at her. She was still watching him.

"We should hangout over the summer," he said. "Cause we're friends and it would be stupid not to see you for two months."

Ren smiled. "I'd love to. Just text me whenever."

"Kay. Bye." *Oh my god.*

Zeli laughed. He ignored her as he made his way home, feeling absolutely insane. Mom was out when he got there, so he went to his room and flopped onto his bed.

As interesting as it is to watch you discover you like a girl, I'm gonna go see if Kirzigith is around yet. I'll be back if you need me though.

He grunted in response, pulling out his phone and looking at Ren's Instagram. She didn't post very often, and most were of her cat or little crocheted animals she made, like his bear Rufard.

His heart twisted as he looked through the most recent pictures. Her with Simon, his arm around her while she leaned her head on his shoulder. It looked wrong to him. Another of her holding a guitar with Simon behind her, his hands on hers, showing her how to hold it.

Riversrenegade Always lost looking at you @echofeversimon ♥
Thanks for trying to teach me to play, but I think I should leave the
music to you. ♪

She looked so happy, so in love. He scrolled fast, trying to breathe
normally till he found one without Simon. Her and Jasper on Jasper's
birthday, both of them wearing silly party hats. Her smile was
gorgeous.

Riversrenegade Happy 17th to my favorite person, @disasterjasper!!!
Love you more than life. Sorry the hats were broken, but think it was
better that way. 🖤

A knock at the door brought him out of staring at the picture. He
sighed as he made his way down the hall and opened the door. That
same man who was always around his mom stood there. Once again
his hair was different, short and red now. But he recognized that face.

"Oh," the man said, surprised to see Bellamy.

"Hi…" Bellamy sighed. "Are you looking for my mom?"

"Yes, is she here?"

"No." Bellamy frowned. The longer he stared the more convinced
he was that his mom was *not* dating this man. Something about him
felt… *off*. "Who are you?"

"No one," he replied hastily. "A friend."

"What's your name? I can tell her you stopped by."

"Eric. Tell her to call me. It's important."

"Kay." Bellamy didn't like his vibe and wasn't sure he'd pass along
the message. The man didn't say anything else as he turned away, his
long black coat swishing around dramatically. Bellamy shut the door
then went back to his very important task of moping about Ren.

68
Kinda Perfect

Ren's bones were filled to the brim with exhaustion. She was sure she hadn't had more than three hours of sleep a single night recently. Even with school finally over and Simon out of town she was still *busy*. Busier even, with making time with her dads, Ocean, and Simon over the phone. She'd watched two of his shows live, his poor friend Riku having to hold the phone up the entire time. They also video chatted every night *after* his shows, before he went to sleep. Then she'd patrol through the night.

She worried about Gaia and what she'd do next. Over five hundred people were dead. Because Kaida hadn't stopped her. Her own friends hurt in the crossfire. The people were scared, waiting for Kaida to end the threat. So she exerted herself in the hopes she'd be ready next time Gaia struck.

Her phone vibrated against her thigh as she flew through the air. She slowed, landing on a random roof, worried it was her dad. He'd been so overprotective lately. She lied about being at Jasper's every other day. But it wasn't Dad calling, it was Simon. She smiled as she sat down and detransformed.

"Hello!"

"Hey beautiful. I have a surprise for you," Simon said.

"A surprise?"

"Are you home?"

She hesitated. "Uh, yeah. Why?"

"Come outside."

"Outside?"

"Yeah."

"For a surprise?"

"Yes," he laughed.

"You're... you're not there— *here*, are you? You're not supposed to be home till tomorrow night!"

"Please come down I'm dying to see you."

"Ahh! Give me two—no five minutes!" She hung up as her adrenaline built with excitement.

The suit came back over her and she pulled on the air, a portal forming in front of her. She rushed through, out the other side into her bathroom. She detransformed then stared at herself in the mirror, frowning. No time to fix those bags under her eyes, but she ran a brush through her hair a few times then brushed her teeth before running downstairs.

When she opened the front door Simon was there, smiling down at her. She threw herself into his arms, elated as he lifted her off the ground, arms tight around her.

"How are you here?" she asked as he released her.

He didn't answer. Sliding a hand around her neck he pulled her closer and kissed her passionately, his fingers getting lost in her hair. She was breathless by the time he stopped.

"I convinced the others that we should drive home today. Drove all night. They kinda hate me for it but I don't even care."

"Did you just get back?"

"Yeah. Well, like, thirty minutes ago? I showered before coming here."

She bit her lip then pulled him closer, hugging him again. "I missed you so much."

"Missed you more." He kissed the top of her head as he held her. "I know you weren't expecting me, so if you're busy I get it. But if not... maybe we could do something? Go to a movie or out to eat or just, walk around or—"

"Oh." She pulled back, staring up at him.

"You have plans?" he asked.

She shook her head. "No plans. I'm just... *so* tired. Could we just watch a movie here? Or at your place?"

He frowned.

"No? I mean we can go out if you really—"

"You wanna stay in? Go to my place?"

"Yeah, if that's okay?"

He smiled. "Yeah. Yeah no that's—that's perfect. I actually have something for you at my place." He pulled her into his arms, hugging her again. "Need anything before we go?"

She shook her head. "Just gonna text my dads and let them know," she replied as she pulled out her phone.

He put his arm around her and they started walking back to his apartment.

"Why you so sleepy?" he asked after she yawned.

"No sleep," she mumbled.

"Silly girl."

She looked up at him. "Have you slept? You drove through the night you said?"

"Who needs sleep?" He laughed. "Worth it, for you."

She beamed at him, and he kissed her cheek. She yawned again.

You're pushing yourself too hard, Zig muttered.

I know. But, things will calm down after we get Gaia. I promise I'll take better care of myself then.

Or you could take better care of yourself now! I don't know that you're in the best shape to take on Gaia.

Ren frowned, annoyed. *I'm fine.*

When they got to Simon's, he immediately took her to his room, blushing as he handed her a small purple box.

"You didn't have to get me anything," she whispered as she slowly lifted the lid.

"I saw it and thought of you. Couldn't leave without it."

Ren's mouth opened as she pulled out the gold bracelet. The links were made of little cat heads.

"This is so cute."

"You like it?"

She smiled at him. He was biting his lip, blue eyes bright. "I love it so much." She leaned up and kissed him. "Put it on me?"

"Yes ma'am."

Once the bracelet was on, he grabbed her hand and led her into the living room. She took her boots off and settled on the couch.

"Where's your mom?" Ren asked, just now noticing she didn't appear to be in the apartment.

"She's out with Mom Squad. You want some soda?"

She nodded as he went to the kitchen. Alone in the apartment, and she wasn't even nervous. Ren grinned at him when he sat beside her and handed her a Coke. She leaned her head on his shoulder as he got the movie on.

"You gonna fall asleep on me?" he asked after a while.

"No."

"You didn't have to come over, if you're so tired."

"But I want to be with you."

He grinned and kissed her. "You know, I've kinda been a shitty boyfriend lately."

"You have not!"

He stared at her, smiling.

"Okay, there were a *few* instances..."

"Where I was shitty. But, this week away from you... all I could think was, 'damn, I wish I went to that dinner.' I just... I wanna give you everything, you know? I wanna be someone who deserves you."

She blushed. "You are."

"Maybe, now I am. Or, I'm trying to be."

"I should have explained," she mumbled.

"Hm?"

"About the dinner. I asked once, you said you didn't want to. And then I changed the plans on you. I didn't tell you it was important. I feel like, if we'd had a real conversation about it you *would* have been there."

Simon nodded slowly. "Regardless, doesn't excuse how I acted."

"I know. But..." She smiled. "You've been kinda perfect since then."

"Kinda perfect, huh?"

She giggled. "Yeah. Hush now, we're missing the movie."

"Right, sorry." He kissed her cheek. "I just... I'm not gonna disappoint you again. I promise."

She squeezed his hand.

"Wanna order pizza after movie?" he asked after a few minutes.

She nodded, yawning again.

Once the movie ended, he kissed her cheek again and she grinned.

"Wanna cuddle while we wait for food?" he whispered, mouth against her ear. "Since you're so sleepy."

"Yes."

He stood up, surprising her. Then he gently grabbed her hands and pulled her off the couch, down the hall toward his room. Her body came alert as he pulled her to his bed.

She stood there, staring.

His eyes widened as he looked up at her. "Oh, bed bad. Right, sorry."

"No—no it's fine." She tried to relax as she got on the bed with him.

"I'm not putting the moves on you, promise." He laid back and pulled her into his arms. She giggled as she laid her head on his chest. "Just wanna hold you."

His nose brushed against her forehead.

"This is nice," she whispered, the sound of his heartbeat thumping in her ear.

"Yeah?"

"Yeah. Kinda... perfect."

"Very kinda perfect," he replied. "You look so beautiful tonight."

She moved her face up to look at him and he kissed her before she could speak. Lips moving against hers, soft and warm.

When he pulled back, he was smiling, blue eyes glittering in the dim light.

"Simon... I don't think you're a shitty boyfriend."

"No?"

She smiled, shaking her head a little.

He brushed his thumb against her cheek. "Ren... I love you."

69
Those Three Words

Ren's heart raced, fast. Unsteady.

"You don't have to say it back," Simon continued, voice low. "I've just been... holding that in for a while now and don't think I can anymore. I needed you to know."

Her lip trembled as she stared at him. *I needed you to know.* "Simon..." *Kaida... I love you. I needed you to know,* Lycan's voice echoed in her mind.

"Shh, it's alright. Don't gotta say it back. *Promise.*"

Her eyes burned and she grabbed his face, pulling it to hers, kissing him intensely. She got lost in the kiss, only focusing on that and not the words stuck in her throat.

When he pulled back for air he was smiling. She didn't let him breathe for long. He seemed surprised by how passionately she was kissing him, but she wasn't in control. Those words reverberated in her mind and she couldn't think straight.

Simon pulled back again, staring at her intently for a moment. Then he kissed her, once. Then again, on her cheek. Then his mouth moved to her neck. "Is this okay?" he asked, breath warm against her skin.

She made a sound that sounded like a yes. Was *supposed* to be a yes. But her hands were shaking and her throat was still choking on the words.

His mouth went back to her neck, moving slowly down then back up, till his mouth found her ear. She felt *so* warm, heat blooming throughout her body.

"Still okay?" he whispered.

She nodded, not trusting herself to speak. Not sure she even could. Somewhere in the back of her mind she wanted to say no, to *scream* it. Because she knew where this was going and fear crawled up her spine, but her brain was still stuck on those three words, torn between this bed and a rooftop far away.

Simon's hand slowly moved up her side. The scream built within her.

"Is this okay?"

"Mhm."

"It's okay if it's not."

She made a sound.

"We don't have to," he continued. "I don't need this."

She tried to latch onto those words, a lifeline in her tempest of emotions, but her brain and body were out of sync. Why was she *so* afraid?

"Ren?"

"It's okay," she forced the words out, shaky and breathless, ignoring the fear. Fighting it. "Keep going."

He didn't argue, putting his mouth back to her neck. "You actually want to?"

She nodded, sure her body was going to sink through the mattress and down through the floor with the weight of her terror. Instead, she simply pulled him closer, desperate to feel something other than the fear.

His hand slowly slid up her chest. She tried to convince herself to stop him. To say never mind. But the words wouldn't come. So she kissed him as he slowly pulled her closer, his body pressed against hers.

The warmth moved through her, like a magnet to his lips, soft against her skin. She closed her eyes, breathing in deep, trying to calm herself. But her heart raced frantically and she thought she might drown in her fear.

"Ren?"

Her eyes snapped open. Simon was watching her, blue eyes sparkling like crystals.

"We don't have to," he whispered, brushing his thumb against her cheek. He sighed and fell back on the bed beside her.

She was still, the absence of him against her extremely noticeable. All she had to do was say *okay. Maybe another time.* But the fear was choking her. Even still, without him touching her.

"Simon?" She struggled to get the word out.

"Yeah?"

"I want to."

"No you don't," he laughed. "It's okay. I promise. Everything is so good. Kinda perfect, right?"

She sucked in a breath and rolled on her side to face him. He was smiling at her, his black hair a little messy. *I can do this. I can do this. It's just me and Simon. It shouldn't be this scary.*

"I want to," she repeated. The only way out was through.

Simon frowned. She didn't give him time to object, grabbing his face and pulling him closer. His mouth crashed into hers, and her heart sped up, somehow faster. Unsteady.

"Ren," he breathed against her.

"Can we just... can we just do it..."

"I don't—"

"Please?" She swallowed, trying to get a hold of herself.

Simon sighed and nodded, then slowly put his mouth back on her neck.

She closed her eyes, trying to focus on the feel of him, the *heat* of it all. There was *not* room in her for it and the fear. One would win.

"You're really sure?" Simon whispered, lips brushing against her nose.

She nodded.

His hands moved to the bottom of her shirt, slowly lifting it up. She started trembling.

"Ren, baby, we don't—"

"It's okay," she blurted as her eyes opened. He was watching her so intently. *Why can't I say it back?* "I'm okay."

He straddled her, frowning as he looked down at her.

"You don't w-want to?"

"I'm not in any hurry. Are you *sure* you want this now?"

She nodded.

Simon hesitated a moment, then slowly lifted her shirt up. She tried to be still, to tame the tremors. Shaking like a leaf while your boyfriend undressed you was probably not that sexy.

She laid back into his pillows, trying not to think about her shirt, now on his nightstand, or her bra, stark white against her tan skin. His eyes stayed on hers. So intense.

After a moment he moved, coming down to kiss her. She let herself get lost in that. Warm, soft, Simon.

"You're so beautiful," he whispered against her lips.

She wanted to say something like "so are you" but getting words out was hard so she stayed silent as his mouth moved to her neck again.

He didn't stop at her neck, gently kissing his way down her chest, down her stomach. She shivered.

"Still sure?" he asked as his chin hovered above the top of her jeans.

She nodded.

He started unbuttoning them. Her shaking wouldn't stop, she felt it down to her toes as he unzipped her jeans and slowly pulled them off. She let it happen. In the back of her mind she wondered why she wasn't saying no. Why she wasn't *begging* him to stop. The way the fear flowed through her, it wanted to take over, to bury her inside of it. She closed her eyes, focusing on the feel of Simon's lips, moving up her thigh.

"That a good sound or a bad sound?" Simon asked.

"Huh?"

He laughed, then she felt his hand on her face. She slowly opened her eyes. "Beautiful girl," he whispered, before kissing her.

She relaxed a little at that. His mouth on hers was familiar. Nice. *Safe.* His mouth... everywhere else was new and foreign and for some bizarre reason the *scariest* thing she'd *ever* experienced.

"Should I stop?" he asked, breath warm on her skin.

She shook her head.

His mouth moved down again, down her neck, her chest. She wondered why he didn't take her bra off. Thinking about *having* the bra off made the fear spike and she was sure if she opened her mouth she'd vomit.

She winced, squeezing her eyes shut as she felt his fingers on her underwear. *This is fine. This is my boyfriend. This is fine!*

She squeaked, sucking in a sharp breath as his mouth moved between her legs.

"Good sound?" he asked.

"Uh. Ah."

He took that as a yes, because he went back down. The warmth she'd felt before was no longer just *warm.* It was the heat of the sun, spreading through her whole body, burning her from the inside out.

Another sound escaped her. She couldn't contain it. *Where are my words?* She leaned her head back into the pillows. Everything he was doing felt so weird but not bad but *so* weird and tingly and maybe kinda good and so very *warm.*

His hands were steady on her thighs, she could feel his calloused fingertips gripping her skin. So many sensations, cascading over each other. Eventually he crawled up over her and kissed her cheek. She opened her eyes, feeling breathless.

"Hi," he whispered. "How you doing?"

"Uh w-warm."

He grinned and brushed her hair back as he searched her eyes. "Is warm good?"

She nodded. It *was.* But *god* the terror was at war with the pleasure. "You're s-still in..." She took a deep breath. "Clothes. Your clothes."

Those blue eyes stared into hers. "You want me to take off my clothes?"

How else were they supposed to—she swallowed and nodded.

Simon just stared at her, so she forced her arms to move, fumbling around his stomach till she found the bottom of his shirt. She pulled it up. He smiled as it came off. Then he kissed her forehead and pulled her up, his hands moving behind her back. Her bra fell loose.

She swallowed as he pulled it off her arms. She felt in a trance, moving on autopilot as she fell back into the pillows. He hovered over her a moment before going on his side. He kissed her neck as his hand moved over her chest. She shivered at the touch.

"Necklace stays on?" he asked.

Ren blinked, her eyes slowly moving down to the Xyrial resting on her bare chest.

Ren...

She swallowed.

You're so scared, maybe you shouldn't—

She gripped the Xyrial and pulled it off over her head, too quick to second guess. She dropped it on Simon's nightstand with shaking fingers.

Simon's hand slowly moved down her stomach, then between her legs.

She whined as she felt his fingers go inside her.

"Still good?" he asked, lips against her ear.

She nodded.

"Ren, baby... if you don't like it, it's okay."

She shook her head.

"You know, some words would be nice here."

She swallowed. "I ch-choked on them."

"On your words?"

She nodded again. His hand disappeared from between her legs, and he kissed her cheek.

"What does that mean?"

"Dunno."

He smiled and kissed her lips. She melted into it as his hand moved over her chest.

She sucked in a breath, pulling back from him. His thumb was gently moving back and forth over her nipple, sending a shock wave of sensation through her.

Simon grinned. Then he put his mouth on the other one. Ren whined, leaning her head back into the pillows. He slowly kissed his way back down her body, then stayed between her legs for a moment.

She fell back into a trance until he stopped. Her eyes opened and she watched as he stood and took off his pants.

He met her eyes. "You're sure?"

"Yes," she whispered.

He hesitated a moment. Then his boxers came off.

Her eyes moved down, she couldn't help it.

He didn't let her look for long, turning around to grab something from the drawer in his nightstand. She watched, confused, as he opened something. A condom. *That makes sense.* She wanted to close her eyes again, but she couldn't, staring aimlessly as she watched him slide it on himself. Then he moved back onto the bed and gently crawled on top of her.

She started shaking again. Maybe she never stopped.

"If you want me to stop, just tell me. Okay?" Why did *he* look as scared as *she* felt?

She nodded.

And then she winced and her eyes shut. Somewhere in the back of her mind she knew it would hurt. That it would feel weird. She'd gotten used to his mouth for a moment, forgetting that was very different. Very very very different.

Sound escaped her.

"Sorry sorry. I'll stop."

"No." She opened her eyes, trying to keep them from watering as she looked up at Simon. "I gotta get through it."

"Ren—"

"Don't stop," she continued. She needed to beat the fear. She wouldn't be afraid when it was done. Then next time, next time would be *better.* That's how it was supposed to go. She just had to get through it *now.*

He moved slowly, and she felt herself *stretching* to fit him inside of her. She didn't even use tampons. Her body was *not* prepared for this.

"You look really unhappy now," he said. "Maybe we should stop. We can try again another time, okay?"

"No. No I can *do* it." She grabbed his arms. That seemed to anchor her as she ran her hands down his biceps and tried to steady her breathing. "Just talk to me. Distract me."

"Talk about what?" he asked, looking baffled.

"Anything. Just... need words. Your voice. Please?"

He blinked a few times, and swallowed. *"Okaaaay."*

She slid her hands up his arms, around his back as his hips moved against her. Finally, he licked his lips.

"My heart skipped a beat..." He didn't *quite* speak it, but wasn't fully singing, either. Something in between. "And now we're... skipping stones on the river."

Ren felt herself relaxing as he stared into her eyes, his words flowing like water over her, sinking into her skin. She felt it more than she felt what was happening lower in the bed.

"A walk down the street," he continued, cheeks red. She wondered if it was from the exertion or the embarrassment she knew he was feeling. "And now I want forever..."

Her heart felt steady and for a moment she thought she beat the fear. How could it exist inside her in that moment? Nothing existed but Simon's eyes and Simon's smile and Simon's voice and Simon's words and *Simon.*

"Looking into your eyes," he cut off, laughing slightly.

Ren felt dizzy. "That was..."

"That was so dumb," he said, but his smile was etched into his face. "Can't believe I just sang during..." He giggled.

"It was perfect," she whispered.

She slid her hand up around his neck, pulling him down to kiss her.

His thrusts got faster for a moment then he stilled abruptly and groaned against her lips. *"Fuck."*

Ren swallowed, eyes wide as he panted above her.

He licked his lips and smiled at her. "I love you so much," he whispered, kissing her again.

Then he pulled out. The absence of him was *jarring.* Her heart raced as he got up.

"Be right back," he whispered.

She blinked, body trembling, suddenly cold. Why was she cold? She'd been warm before... before...

She closed her eyes, overly aware of them burning. When she opened them, she felt sudden shock to see her naked body, shaking in the sheets. She fumbled around, pulling them up over her, breathing heavily. Simon... where was... she blinked rapidly, chest rising and falling fast.

Time seemed still. She thought Zig had been speaking to her but she didn't hear him now. She sat up slowly, looking for her clothes. Simon came back in wearing just his boxers, a soft smile on his face. She awkwardly tried to keep the sheet over her as she forced her legs to work and got up, collecting her clothes from his floor.

She carried them under her arm then grabbed her phone and her Xyrial from his nightstand and stumbled to the bathroom, dragging his sheet the whole way.

Her hands shook as she sent a text to her dads.

|Ren|
Please come get me from Simon's right now.

|Dad|
On my way

She dropped the sheet and tried to get dressed, still shaking. It didn't matter, she wanted to take her time. Once she finally got the clothes on, she washed her hands and face, but it didn't make her feel clean. She slowly walked out of the bathroom and back into Simon's bedroom.

"I gotta go," she mumbled, surprised by the sound of her voice, how unemotional it was.

"Already? We haven't eaten yet," he said as he walked toward her. "Pizza is almost here."

"Dad's coming to get me."

"Oh, okay." He pulled her into his arms and kissed the top of her head. She winced.

"What's wrong?"

She shook her head.

"Ren, baby, you okay?" He searched her eyes, hands holding her arms.

"Fine. I just gotta go." She could tell he didn't believe her.

"Ren..."

"Sorry," she mumbled as she pulled away, feet carrying her out of the apartment, to the elevator, outside.

Dad and Dare were waiting on the sidewalk, matching looks of concern on their faces.

"What happened?"

She shook her head.

Dad hugged her. "I got you, kid. I got you."

"Did he hurt you?" Dare asked.

"No, just wanna go please."

Dad helped her into the back of the car. Her hands were still shaking. She heard them whispering as they drove but none of it registered.

Once home they settled her on the couch. Dad wrapped a blanket around her shoulders and knelt down in front of her.

"Ren, baby, you gotta tell us what's wrong. We can't help if we don't know."

Dare sat beside her, putting a gentle hand on her shoulder.

"We had sex," she said as she stared at her hands, still confused about how that even happened.

Dad blinked. "Did he... force you to—"

"No."

"Was that your first—"

"Yes."

She felt like a machine, running on autopilot. The words came out but her emotions were off. She was hollow. *Why?*

"Did you use protection?" Dad asked.

She nodded. "I—I think so? Yes?"

"Okay. Okay. We should... get you some plan B, just to be safe?"

"I can get it first thing in the morning," Dare said. "Is there... anything else you need right now?"

Ren blinked. "Jasper."

"We'll call him."

Dad got off his knees and sat beside her, pulling her against him. "Are you... sure he didn't hurt you?"

"Yes." She put her face in her hands, trying to come back to herself. If she kept responding like a computer they'd never stop worrying.

"I just... wasn't ready. I didn't wanna do it but I didn't tell him that. I said yes. He didn't do anything wrong. I just feel—" she blurted it all fast, eyes watering. "Weird."

"It's okay." Dad hugged her. "I'm gonna get Jasper over, okay. Have you eaten?"

She shook her head.

"I'll get you food, too. It's okay. You're okay."

You're okay. Those words echoed in her head as Dad walked away. *You're okay.* Whose voice was that? Lycan? She closed her eyes. *Yes. Lycan said those words that night...* why was she thinking of that?

She pulled her knees up to her chest and wrapped her arms around them, putting her face down to hide her tears.

70
No Memory

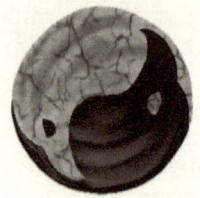

Jasper was startled by the little red Xyri walking through his wall into his bedroom.

"Zig?"

Ren needs you.

"What happened?" he asked as the Xyri turned around. Jasper's suit was on in a second, wings snapping out.

She was with Simon. She's so out of it, took off her Xyrial, falling deeper inside herself by the second...

Jasper felt like he was on fire as he climbed out the window and took to the air. He was going to *kill* Simon. Literally fully properly *murder* him.

She's back home now. With her dads. Zig sounded calmer now.

Jasper planned to come in through her roof but changed his mind, landing on the street outside and detransforming in the shadows before walking up to the door. Ren's dad was calling just as he stepped up to ring the bell.

"Hello?"

"Ren needs you. Could you come over?"

"Already here, daddy-o. Let me in."

"I know you have a key," Cas said. "Use it."

Jasper let out a breath. "Be right up."

Cas intercepted Jasper when he got up, and pulled him to the sink. Ren was bundled in a blanket on the couch.

"She had sex with Simon," he whispered. "She's very... not herself right now. She said he didn't force her, she consented but just wasn't ready. I don't know if I believe her. I *know* my kid, there's something she isn't telling us."

Jasper nodded, his anger growing. "I know when Ren lies."

"You'll tell us what she says?"

"Yes sir. This is ending tonight."

Cas put a hand on his shoulder. "Be gentle with her. Save that fire for another time, alright?"

536

Jasper took a deep breath and nodded.

When he sat beside Ren he saw she'd been crying, eyes red and puffy. Those eyes widened with relief when she saw him, then she tipped over right into his arms.

"I got you," he whispered as he held her, gently rubbing her back.

She sniffed, but didn't say anything.

"Whenever you wanna talk, you let me know."

She pulled back a little, wiping her eyes. Then she took a deep breath and pulled the blanket tighter around her. "I'm fine, really. I... don't know why I freaked out."

"Ren Robin Rivers, don't you lie to me and tell me you're fine when you're not."

She blinked.

"Our mutual friend," he whispered. "With the golden eyes... he came to me because you were so panicked you couldn't even *hear* him."

"Oh."

"Wanna go upstairs and talk?"

"Okay."

He helped her up and they crossed the room, blanket dragging across the floor.

"We're gonna go upstairs, but we'll come back down for food soon."

Cas nodded, brown eyes worried. Jasper tried to give him an encouraging smile. He didn't know what it was like to be loved by a father as much as Ren was loved by hers, but he was glad she had that.

He got her settled in her bed then sat beside her, and waited.

"I don't know what happened," she whispered after a minute. "I think I blacked out."

"During... sex?"

She nodded.

"Ren, are you saying you weren't *conscious* cause that's—"

"No! It wasn't like that I just... zoned out? I didn't wanna do it. But I couldn't tell him."

"Why not?"

She chewed on her lip, and he could tell there was something she didn't wanna say.

"Ren, whatever happened you can tell me. You know that?"

She didn't meet his eyes. "He told me he loved me."

Jasper sighed. "So, you felt like you couldn't say no to sex... cause he said he loved you?"

She closed her eyes.

"I'm gonna kill him."

Her eyes snapped open. "He didn't do anything wrong! I said yes. More than once."

"Yeah well, he doesn't know you well enough to know that your yes was a fucking lie. Ren, you're a *terrible* liar. And if you were so out of it that even *Zig* couldn't get through to you, you clearly weren't being yourself. You can't tell me Simon didn't notice that?"

She didn't say anything, just stared at her hands.

"He ignored your distress so he could get off and that is fucked up."

Jasper couldn't hide his hatred. He knew the truth even if Ren refused to see it. Simon only cared about himself. He couldn't wait to pay the guy a visit later.

"Ren, come *on*. Talk to me."

She sighed and leaned her head back into her pillows, saying nothing.

"Ren?"

"I feel weird," she muttered. "I barely remember it. It's a blur. But I... feel sore? Weird."

Jasper's urge to kill Simon grew. He slid closer and put an arm around her. She leaned into him.

"I don't think I liked it. Is that bad?"

"The sex?"

She nodded.

"No, Renny. Maybe you're asexual. Or demisexual. Or maybe Simon's just *really* bad at sex."

Ren frowned. "What does that mean?"

"Asexual is when someone doesn't feel sexual attraction. Like, they tend to not enjoy sex I think. It's totally normal. And demi is where you only feel sexual attraction with someone you have a deep emotional connection with. But like I said, it could just be... Simon sucks and it was your first time and that's always weird and awkward. But if you don't like sex that's so normal and okay. I promise."

She nodded, pressing her face closer to his chest, eyes closed. "I was so afraid and I don't know why. Like, I was *terrified*. But not of Simon. That isn't normal is it?"

"I mean..." He let out a long breath. "I guess that maybe is normal, considering what happened to you."

She stiffened, then pulled back and met his eyes. "What happened to me? What are you talking about?"

"Uh..." He didn't wanna say it, but she clearly didn't grasp his implication. "The... sexual assault. I imagine it's fairly normal for someone who went through that to be afraid of that kind of intimacy, right?"

Ren was staring at him so intently. "What. Are you talking about?"

"You... Ren, you have to remember that?" He pulled back at the sudden fear in her eyes. "Back when we were dating... that man who worked at the bakery?" His heart raced. "How do you not remember this?"

Her lip trembled. "The bakery..."

He nodded slowly. "It was before school and I was outside, waiting for you... but you didn't come out when you were supposed to..."

She stared aimlessly. "I... don't remember." She shook her head suddenly, eyes squeezed shut. "Broken glass. I... was there glass?"

He nodded again. "I broke the window to get in because I heard you..." His eyes burned at the memory.

"How did I forget this?"

It's a trauma response, Pozi whispered. *She must have suppressed the memory.*

Wish I could suppress it, he thought.

"Was there... blood?" she asked, eyes closed.

"Yes. It was his. He had you..." He paused. "Behind the counter. I think he had your mouth covered but I heard you crying, so I broke the window with a rock. You screamed."

Tears slid down her cheeks. "What did he do to me?"

"He never got what he wanted," Jasper whispered. "When you screamed your dad came out. And he beat the ever loving shit out of the guy. And I held you on the floor."

She nodded. "I remember... glass. And you. Your heart racing against my ear? I..." She put a hand over her mouth.

Fuck. She'd completely forgotten and was now reliving it because of him. "I'm sorry," he whispered, his own eyes watering. "So so sorry."

Jasper.

He paused at the voice in his head. Not Pozi, but Zig. The little red Xyri was sitting on the foot of the bed, his golden eyes staring at Jasper.

This is not the only memory Ren has suppressed, he continued.

Jasper frowned, confused.

When Lycan saved her. She says she was mugged. But the man was assaulting her as well, and she has no memory of it. She blocked it out within minutes, maybe seconds of it happening.

Jasper leaned back, confused. He didn't even know that was a thing a person could do. *Is there anything we can do to help her?*

I will consider. We will discuss it again, Zig replied.

Ren sniffed, oblivious to their conversation. "It makes sense. Why I was so scared. Everything scared me. The words. The pressure."

"The words?"

She shook her head again.

"Ren, I think you should break up with him."

She stared at him and wiped her eyes. But she didn't argue, which was a good sign.

"Do you love him?"

She closed her eyes, more tears slipping out.

"Would you ever tell him you're Kaida?"

"Can't tell anyone I'm Kaida," she mumbled.

"If you can't see yourself even wanting to tell him who you really are then he isn't the person for you. Ren, you're gonna want someone you can share your whole self with. If you can't even *imagine* wanting to tell him? Break it off. Hell, I'll break up with him for you!"

Ren sighed softly. "I..."

"He didn't even *notice* that you were out of it. That, or he didn't fucking care. Listen, we don't have to worry about it tonight, okay? We can do it tomorrow."

She nodded and he was shocked she wasn't arguing. She knew Simon wasn't right for her. Finally.

71
Dangerous Thoughts

Ren sat on the couch while Dad made breakfast. Zig nestled against her leg, his chin on her thigh. Jasper was beside her as well, watching her carefully. She hadn't wanted to be alone, afraid of slipping back in the vague memories, or simply shutting down. Jasper stayed with her all night, even when she stayed in the shower for an hour, he sat outside with the door cracked so he could talk to her.

She still couldn't really remember that day. It was buried too deep, but she got glimpses. Glass. Blood. Heartbeat. Maybe it was for the best she couldn't fully recall it, but the idea of having missing memories scared her more than she was willing to admit.

Dare came over with the pill and a glass of water. "Okay, I did some deep reading on side effects, seems most likely is intense cramping. Similar to period cramps."

Ren nodded as she popped the pill in her mouth and took a swig of water, eager to be done with it. Dad brought over a plate of pancakes and bacon a minute later.

"How are we feeling?" he asked.

She shrugged.

Dad sighed.

"She's breaking up with Simon today," Jasper said. "And she's feeling all weird about it."

"Oh, really?" Dad's relief was obvious.

Ren tried not to cry as she nodded. "He's coming over soon."

"And I'll be here the entire time," Jasper said. "For moral support and any needed ass kicking."

Dad smiled at that. "Good, good."

Ren shoved some bacon in her mouth to keep from screaming.

She didn't wanna break up with Simon. But Jasper's words rattled around in the back of her head on repeat. *If you can't see yourself even wanting to tell him who you really are then he isn't the person for you.* In truth, she'd never thought about telling Simon. He was a huge part of Ren's life, but he was so far from Kaida. That's how it was supposed to be. Wasn't it?

Ren didn't wanna break up with him. She liked him so much, and they were great together. But what was she supposed to *do*? She could *never* tell him she was Kaida. That secret would burn a hole right through her heart one day. Zig told her some Bonded went their whole lives, keeping the truth from their romantic partners. But some didn't. Either way, it didn't always work out. She was starting to think romance just wasn't in the cards for her, with the life she lived.

Twenty minutes later she got the text that Simon was waiting outside. She pulled her jacket on and started down the stairs, hands shaking as Jasper and Zig followed her.

"Do you want me to come out with you?" Jasper asked.

"No."

"I'll be right here then. If you need me."

She nodded, then took a deep breath and opened the door, stepping out into the light. She shivered despite the heat as Simon turned to face her.

"Hey, are you alright? I tried calling and texting and..." He sighed. "Something's wrong."

She shoved her hands in her pockets as she met his eyes. Bright, beautiful blue.

"Ren?"

"Um." *Oh god I can't do it.*

Yes you can.

She shook her head slowly.

Just tell him it's over and go back inside. Simple, Zig said.

"Ren? What is it?"

The idea of her tiny little dragon giving her dating advice was *almost* funny, but her eyes burned and she couldn't find the humor.

I've been alive forever, Ren. I've seen so many relationships start and grow and burn and die. It's time for this one to die. It's run its course.

She winced at the words.

Simon's hands went to her elbows, gently pulling her hands out of her pockets. "Whatever it is, you can tell me," he whispered.

"It's not working," she muttered.

"What isn't?"

"Us." The word broke as it came out and her eyes watered. "I can't..."

"Ren?"

"I can't," she whispered. "Can't do this." Tears slid down her face. "Perdoname, te amo perdón, no puedo no puedo no puedo no es—no hay— nunca podría... con nadie. Dios mío no quiero pero no puedo estar con *nadie*..."

"Ren, I can't understand you."

"I... I wanna break up." The lie *burned*.

"What?"

She shook her head, wishing more than anything she could lean into those arms.

"Ren, what happened? I thought... I mean, last night..." His eyes watered.

She blinked through her tears. "We can't. I can't."

"Is this because I said I loved you? Ren, if I'm moving too fast I'll slow down. We can slow way down, I promise. *Please?*"

"No."

"Please don't do this."

"I wasn't there!" she blurted.

"Wasn't where?"

She squeezed her eyes shut, but the tears still poured out. "With you. In the bed. During... I wasn't *there*."

"Ren, I don't—"

Her eyes snapped open. "I wasn't there. Either you didn't notice or—or you noticed and didn't *care*."

He looked like she'd slapped him in the face.

She pulled her hands away from him, covering her mouth as she cried. She wanted to scream. To run. To fly.

The door opened and Jasper was there, gently pulling Ren back. "Go inside."

"This is between me and Ren," Simon said, voice cracking.

"I'm between you and Ren, actually," Jasper said as he closed the door on Ren.

She sank to her knees, shaking, sobbing, gasping. Zig climbed into her lap, stretching his wings out. He wrapped them around her as she struggled to breathe.

You're okay. It's done. Jasper's handling it and you're okay.

I'm okay, she thought back. The biggest lie.

She leaned down, resting her forehead against Zig's nose.

Time passed, she wasn't sure how much. She didn't move until Jasper came back in and sat beside her.

"How we doing, Renegade?"

She made a sound.

"I see." He put his arm around her. "Simon left. I didn't kill him, even though I wanted to."

She took a few shaky breaths. "What did he s-say?"

"Said he wanted to talk to you. Told him you didn't wanna talk. He tried arguing. I told him to leave. He asked me to ask you to talk to him later, when you've calmed down. I told him I'd tell you, but that's it."

She nodded.

"I think he thinks he can convince you to stay with him."

Ren didn't respond. It was true. He could easily convince her, because she didn't *want this* in the first place.

"Wanna go back upstairs?"

She nodded as Zig backed away, folding his wings in.

He walked her all the way up to her room and got her settled in bed, under her covers, before going back downstairs to get her some water. She dozed off before he returned.

When Ren woke up her head was pounding. She opened her text from Jasper, ignoring the ones from Simon.

> **|Jasper|**
> I love you so much but dad wanted me home dontworry he's not in a mood so it's fine. I can sneak out later if you need me just test melove youu!!!!!!!

> **|Ren|**
> Love you too. it's middle of the night now. I'll probably sleep more

She yawned and crawled out of bed to go shower. The hot water was nice against her skin, and she took her time. When she came out, she went downstairs and found a note on the counter from Dad detailing the three different plates of food that were in the fridge for her. She pulled one out, not bothering to put it in the microwave, just eating it cold as she stood at the kitchen island.

A few minutes later both her dads entered the kitchen, looking sleepy.

"Why are you awake?" she asked as Dad hugged her.

"Gotta start baking soon," he mumbled. "Wanted to check on you first."

She leaned her head into him.

"How are you feeling today?" Dare asked as he started making coffee.

"Gross. Weird. Tired." *Depressed.* She shrugged.

Dad pushed some hair back off her face. "Wanna talk about it?"

She nodded and he led her to the couch where they sat together.

"How old were you?" she asked after a minute.

"When..."

"You had sex for the first time?"

Dad blinked. "I was eighteen."

She nodded. It felt like she was too young, but that was barely older than her.

"Dare?" she asked as he came over and handed a mug of coffee to Dad, then handed her a mug of cocoa. She gripped it tightly, letting the warmth seep into her.

"Sixteen," he replied.

"Did... either of you regret it?" she asked.

Dad smiled. "I got you out of that, so no. I don't regret a single decision that led to you, cause you—" his smile widened, "—are the best thing that has *ever* happened to me. Best thing in my whole world."

Ren's eyes watered.

"I was a bit young to become a single parent, and it was hard. I won't pretend it wasn't. But I don't regret it."

She nodded.

"I did," Dare said softly. "I was pressured into it, was convinced that no one would figure out I was gay if I slept with her, but I didn't want to. And it didn't fix any of my problems."

"Ren, why did you say yes if you didn't wanna do it?" Dad asked. "Were you afraid he'd hurt you?"

She blinked, looking down at the steam swirling out of her mug. "No. I don't think he'd ever hurt me like that. He's never been like that. He's sweet, and gentle. But I was afraid..." She closed her eyes.

"Of what?"

"He told me he loved me," she whispered as the tears formed.

Dad's eyes softened.

"Did you feel like you had to say yes because of that?" Dare asked.

She shook her head. "That's not... what I mean... by afraid."

Dad nodded, like he understood. "Do you love him?"

She started full on crying then. Dad gently rubbed her back.

"Lo amo pero... estoy... muy asustada. Quiero estar con él y no debería..." she muttered.

"El amor puede ser muy aterrador, pero cuando se siente correcto, se soluciona. El miedo que sientes se va ir poco a poco. Te lo prometo," Dad replied.

"I didn't say it back." She wiped her eyes. "I didn't say it *back* but I *wanted* to and then everything happened so fast. I couldn't—I couldn't say it but then I said yes. I said *yes*. He asked again and again and I said *yes* but I was so scared and I didn't want to."

Dad released a breath.

"Are you disappointed in me?" she asked in a small voice as she wiped her eyes again.

"Absolutely not."

"Never, kiddo."

She took a shaky breath, nodding.

Dad kissed the top of her head. "I don't have to go to work, okay. I can stay."

She pulled back, shaking her head. "No no. I'm fine. I think I might just go back to bed."

He sighed. "You sure?"

"I'll be here till ten," Dare added. "If you need me."

She nodded. "Just wanna rest."

"You'll get us if you need anything?" Dad asked. "I'll just be downstairs, I can come right up."

She nodded again and he kissed her forehead.

When she got back to her room, she finally opened the sixteen missed texts from Simon. Her eyes burned as she read them. Against her better judgment she texted back.

> |Ren|
> Sorry, I fell asleep. Didn't mean to worry you.

> I...need space. Please? I promise we can talk later. Just not now. I need to be alone, please.

Her anxiety was out of control so she shoved her phone in her pocket and looked down at Zig.

"We're going out."

You sure that's a good—

Ren transformed, cutting him off. A sense of calm came over her with the suit on, but it wasn't enough. Her body still carried the tension, fear, panic. She pushed the skylight open and climbed out.

Ren...

I'm fine. She jumped off the roof, taking to the skies.

No you are not.

No I am not, but I'm not Ren. I'm Kaida now.

Kaida isn't fine either!

No, but she will be.

She flew straight to Spruce Street. The moment her feet hit the roof she exhaled, some of the tension leaving her. She sent a text to Lycan then sat on the edge of the roof, legs hanging over the side as she looked out at the city lights.

Ten minutes later Lycan appeared, dropping down beside her with a soft sigh.

"Hello."

"Hi."

"What's wrong?"

"Nothing," she mumbled.

"Liar."

Kaida swallowed, but she didn't say anything. Lycan grabbed her shoulder, gently turning her to face him.

"What's wrong?"

She blinked. "I uh... had a bad weekend. Like, really really really bad."

He pulled her into his arms. She closed her eyes, leaning into him.

"I got you, Kai. If you wanna talk, I'm here. And, if not... I can distract you."

She smiled as she pulled back, looking into his yellow eyes. "What kind of distraction?"

He smiled. "Literally anything you want."

She got lost in those eyes and that smile for a moment as Jasper's words came back to her. *You're gonna want someone you can share your whole self with. If you can't even imagine wanting to tell him?*

She realized there *was* someone she imagined telling the truth of who she was to all the time. Someone who, technically, knew both Kaida and Ren already. *Dangerous thoughts.*

"So, what do you say? Distraction or, are we having a deep talk?"

She suddenly wanted to jump off the roof. *I can't have that.* "Distraction, for sure."

Lycan's smile widened. "One distraction, coming up." He stood and held a hand out for her. She took it, heart racing as she climbed onto his board and wrapped her arms around him. She didn't care where they went or what they did, so long as he was there.

72
Stained Red

Bellamy sent a text to the group asking for backup. He had alerts of people getting sick at a rally in the Bronx, suspecting Elixir was the cause.

> |Bunhead|
> Can meet you there!

He grinned, wondering if Kaida got any sleep after their escapades last night. The suit came over him as he flung himself off the balcony, free falling for a moment before forming his board and gliding on the air.

Be careful with Mikkos's human.

She didn't seem that dangerous against Apex, he replied.

She can kill you.

Like Gaia?

Not quite as quickly, but yes. Be wary of her touch.

Noted.

He groaned as he got close to the rally, eyes searching for Elixir's black suit in the crowd. She was surprisingly easy to find amidst the chaos. Police were already rushing through, trying to get to her, but everyone near the girl was falling sick, on their knees and retching. Some of them seemed to have passed out.

Are they dead?

Maybe. Maybe not.

He sighed as he got lower then hovered in the air in front of her.

"Hey, pretty boy." Elixir grinned up at him.

"Whatcha doing?"

"Less than they deserve."

I hate this part.

This part? Zeli asked.

The part where they make me defend shitty people.

"Anyone dead?"

"Not yet."

He let out a breath. "Alright. You've made your point. Wanna call it a day so we don't have to do this?"

She stared at him. "Do you support abortion bans, Lycan Silverstar?"

"No." She seemed surprised by that. "But I *also* don't condone making these people sick as a way to fight that."

"What else is a girl to do?" She sighed, glancing past him at the hoard of cops trying to cut their way through the sick bodies. "You know what they'd do to me, if I wasn't in the suit..."

"Yes."

She nodded. "So why don't you just fly away. And let me make my point."

"Can't do that."

"You like getting in the way, don't you?"

"It's my job. I'm giving you thirty seconds to stop spreading that sickness. Or I'll make you stop."

That fake smile fell off her face as she met his eyes. She knew he meant it. "Let's party."

She jumped on him, knocking him to the ground. He grunted as she landed on him, surprised as she breathed on his face. He blinked, confused.

Oh boy.

Nausea filled his stomach as she laughed. Then her head snapped up, eyes widening as something landed in the blackened grass beside them.

"Shit." She jumped back off him just as smoke erupted over him.

Lycan coughed, disoriented as he tried to sit up. He couldn't see Elixir anywhere. *Where the hell is Kaida?* She said she was coming, but all he saw was smoke.

How are your eyes? Zeli asked.

Fine. Just too smoky. His board formed under his feet and he rose out of the smoke, looking for Elixir, but he didn't see her suit now. She probably detransformed to blend into the crowd.

Bellamy, your eyes...

I'm fine. He looked at the people nearby, hunched over, sick and coughing. There wasn't much he could do for them. Why'd the cops have to throw a smoke bomb? All it did was help Elixir get away and burn his eyes.

It's not the smoke burning your eyes. Go home. Now.

What? Why?

"Lycan!"

He spun in the air, looking for whoever was shouting his name. His blurry eyes locked on a face at the edge of the crowd, waving their arms dramatically while continuing to scream. He flew toward them.

"Are you hurt?" he asked as he lowered to their level.

"Gaia's back."

His heart raced. "Where?"

"People are posting she's in Central Park right now, fighting Kaida!"

"Thanks!"

He sped into the air.

No! You can not go!

What? He blinked, trying to clear his eyes, but his vision seemed even more out of focus.

Bellamy, you are going blind! Do not engage with Gaia!

Blind? What?

She breathed on you! It's one of her poisons!

Panic filled him as he realized she was right, his vision was getting worse as he flew.

No, I have to go. I won't leave Kaida to face her alone.

Bellamy, please! I am begging you. Turn around.

Kaida flew through the air, ignoring her exhaustion. She'd been about to go help Lycan when she got the notification Gaia was back.

Don't go alone, Zig hissed in her head.

She ignored him as she crossed Central Park, descending toward the North Meadow baseball fields. Gaia was seated in a throne made of trees, waiting. Kaida expected destruction and chaos, but the girl just sat there, legs crossed, smiling as Kaida landed on the field in front of her.

Please call for backup.

"We here to play baseball?" Kaida asked, a crystalline bat forming in her hand as she stared up at the girl in green.

"Thought this was a good place for a funeral," Gaia said.

"Whose?"

"*Yours.*" Her green eyes narrowed as she rose from her throne, hopping down onto the lawn. "It's time to end this."

"Couldn't agree more," Kaida replied, wings lifting her in the air just as the ground beneath her started to sink.

Gaia growled in frustration as Kaida flew in a circle, swooping back toward the girl, bat raised. Gaia rose in the air as trees ripped out of the ground around them.

Vines whipped out and her bat shifted to a sharpened blade, slicing through them as they tried to wrap around her. One caught her ankle. She cut it just as another wrapped around her neck. Gasping, she slid a small light knife against it, tearing it free.

Trees were appearing through the whole field and over in the lake, causing water to flood out onto the land. Gaia was running through the branches, from one tree to the next even as they shifted and rose, tearing out of the earth, up through the lake.

Kaida flew after her, diving down into the trees.

Careful. Steady.

Kaida threw the entire force of her body at the girl, knocking her out of the branches. They fell, spinning in the air, before crashing into the water. Cold and dark, she tumbled down, panicked, as she stared through the murky depths.

Behind you.

She spun to see Gaia being carried out of the water by a newly formed tree.

Remember what Lycan taught you.

She tried to move her arms, shoving the panic down as she forced herself up up up. She burst free of the water, gasping for air. Her wings flapped hard, lifting her out and above the trees. Her hands shook as she formed a sword in her fist, searching for Gaia. Trees were growing rapidly as Gaia continued to use them as stepping stones through the park.

Kaida flew after her, breathless.

Lycan saw trees rising in the distance, just as his vision went black.

Oh god.

I told you to go back!

Too late now!

He felt the air moving past him, unsure what to do, heart racing in a panic.

Just land and wait.

Wait for what?

Your vision will come back eventually.

How long? He slowed, coming to a stop in the air, trying to listen. He'd been close to Gaia's trees.

An hour, maybe?

What if I detransform?

You'll fall to your death?

Oh.

What if—

Something hit him, hard. Air rushed out of his lungs as he fell through nothing. Terror threatened to overwhelm him as he spun, frantic, before crashing into what he assumed was the ground.

"I won't let you kill her!"

He blinked, but it did no good. Everything was dark around him and his body ached from the impact.

Who is that?

Vapor.

Dammit.

He forced himself to his feet, hands out defensively as he turned, trying to locate her.

"I'm not here to kill anyone," he replied.

"I don't believe you."

He followed the sound of her voice, turning to his left. Silver seeped out of his hand, forming into a rope. He gripped it tightly, anxious.

"I wanna stop her," he continued. "From hurting anyone else. It doesn't have to end in death."

"She wants to kill you. And the others," Vapor whispered.

He stepped closer.

"That's why she lured you here. I told her not to, I did! I *tried*. But she won't listen, she thinks she has to get rid of you and Kaida—"

He flung the rope out, and felt it make contact against something. Vapor grunted as it slithered around her, tightening.

"She's all I have," Vapor muttered. "I won't lose her, too."

A sword formed in Lycan's other hand as he took a careful step toward her. "If we could just—" Something crashed into him. He tumbled, breathless as something sharp pierced his skin.

Bellamy!

I'm fine! He grunted under the weight of the mist creature, his sword reforming. He shoved it up through the body and it disappeared off him. He released a breath but before he could get up something else slammed into him and his head banged against something hard.

Bellamy?

Ow.

Something heavy pinned him down. Sharp claws raked across his chest, and he screamed against the pain. They dug deeper into his skin, tearing him apart.

Bellamy!

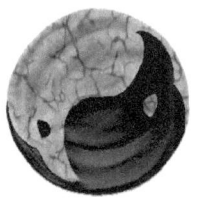

You're gonna be careful?

Yes, Pozi.

Just checking. Sometimes you're stupid!

Jasper rolled his eyes as he flew. He was trying not to think about how pissed his dad would be, when he found out Jasper left on his first shift at the shop. But he didn't wanna work with his dad anyways, and Kaida needed him.

He caught sight of Lycan flying from the opposite direction just as something big and misty tackled Lycan right out of the air.

Shit.

He sped up, diving down to find Lycan standing on the stage of an outdoor theater, facing Vapor. No sign of Gaia. Lycan could handle himself, he needed to find Ren.

He rose up again, then spotted bright red and released a breath. Kaida was alive, moving below the trees just to the left. He swooped in just as a new tree sprouted up. He dodged it, falling to the grass below. Kaida saw him, a look of fear crossing her blue eyes.

"Where is she?" he yelled as he got to his feet.

"In the goddamn trees."

"Lycan's here too," he answered as he moved toward her. "Just over there, fighting Vapor."

Kaida looked overwhelmed as she spun slowly, eyes scanning the trees above. "She blends in so well."

"We got this, okay. We can take her. Together."

She nodded, wings twitching.

"You go up, I'll stay down. We pin her."

"Kay." With that she rose into the air.

He started moving below the trees, wary of the ground as he moved, knowing any moment now the earth could open up and swallow him whole.

Listen.

Oh, right.

Jasper paused, tapping sound. A rush of overlapping echoes overwhelmed his ears at first. Voices in the distance, cascading over each other. Talking, yelling, laughing. Cars driving. Birds chirping. Bugs buzzing. He closed his eyes, trying to reign it in. Wind rushing. Leaves bristling. Groaning. The racing of Ren's heart. Breathing. He grinned as he opened his eyes and moved, knowing exactly which tree Gaia was crouched in.

Kaida fell from the sky, panicked.

"Go help Lycan!"

"What? No I—"

"Something's wrong! Go help him, I got this!" she hissed.

He pointed to the tree, and she nodded. Then he sighed as he jumped up into the air, flying back to where he'd seen Lycan before.

He was on his back on the center of the stage, a misty mountain lion digging its claws deep into his chest. Vapor was on the edge of the stage, struggling to get out of the silver ropes tied around her. They didn't seem to impede her ability to control the creatures.

Jasper's staff appeared in his hand and he slammed it against the head of the animal just as he landed.

"Getting your ass kicked over here?" he asked as he grabbed Lycan's hand, pulling him up.

Stark red blood was running down his chest, marring what little was left of the silver star in his suit. It no longer glowed.

"Apex? That you?"

"Yes?" He frowned. "You're hurt."

"I can't fucking *see*," he said as he reached a hand out aimlessly toward Apex.

He grabbed the hand, pulling Lycan closer. "What do you mean you can't see?" He held his staff with the other hand, ready to whack the next mist creature, an actual lion, now prowling around the edge of the stage.

"Elixir did something to me and now my eyes don't fucking work." He was breathing so heavy, the blood continuing to seep out of him.

"*And* you're fucking hurt. I can see your fucking ribs, dude."

"It'll wear off I'm fine! Where's Kaida, is she—"

"Fighting Gaia still." He glanced at Vapor, who stopped struggling to meet his eyes.

"I won't let you kill her!" she yelled.

"Shut the fuck up," Apex growled back.

"I'm fine, go help Kaida," Lycan said even as he leaned into Apex, unsteady.

"Shut the fuck up," he repeated. "You're not oka—" The lion attacked.

Kaida sliced through another vine, heart racing as Gaia continued to elude her.

"You just wanna play hide and seek now?" she called.

No response. Gaia had been actively trying to fight her till Apex showed up, now she didn't wanna show herself.

You think Lycan's okay?

More worried about you right now.

She rolled her eyes as she formed a second sword in her left hand. *Something was very wrong with him.*

She sliced through another vine, then dropped a sword and started climbing one of the trees, carefully making her way through the branches. She heard rustling ahead of her and smiled. Gaia glanced over her shoulder, panic in her eyes as Kaida slammed her sword against the girl. Gaia screamed and jumped out of the tree.

Dammit.

Kaida leaped after her, but the earth was shifting and moving under her feet. She stumbled, sword puffing away in her hand. She growled in frustration as her wings came back out and she lifted in the air.

Gaia was running fast on the ground, one hand on her bleeding arm. Kaida swooped on her, grabbing her around her middle like an eagle with its prey, and lifted the girl into the air.

"Big mistake," Gaia growled.

Drop her!

Kaida released her, breathing heavy as she realized what almost happened. Gaia fell with a scream, landing in the middle of the stone courtyard below. Kaida dropped in front of her, sword forming again. She stepped closer, ready to swing. Right through the neck, and it would be over. Straight through the chest, and it's done. Her hands shook as she stared into the girl's frightened eyes.

Then Gaia smiled, lunging forward with her blackened hand outstretched. A loud crunch echoed as Gaia was thrown to the side, something wet spraying against Kaida's face.

She stared in horror as someone appeared behind Gaia. Tall. Long pink coat. Wonderland. She slowly looked up, meeting their eyes. They stared at her, aghast. They both looked down at the end of the flail, still stuck in what was left of Gaia's head. Wonderland pulled it back, making a disgusting squishing sound.

"You hesitated," they said as the flail disappeared from their hands. The blood remained. Across the stone. Across her face. Across their coat.

"I..."

"She would have killed you," Wonderland continued, their haunted eyes still locked on the body.

The dead body.

She forced herself to look up, meeting their eyes. "You saved me."

They nodded.

"You killed her."

"I..." Wonderland blinked. "She would have killed you if I—if I hadn't... what's... one death..." They looked sick as they said it. "One life. She took *hundreds*."

Kaida couldn't speak.

"They think I'm a villain anyways."

"You're not," she whispered. "You're a hero."

"They won't think so. Not even after this. Just watch, they'll call it murder."

She noticed their hands shaking as they stared aimlessly. Ren grabbed those hands, gripping them like a lifeline.

"*I* killed her."

Wonderland's eyes came into focus. "What?"

"I killed her. I... *Kaida* killed her. Stopped her. No one needs to know it..."

"You don't have to do that. You don't need that heat."

"I can take it." She shook her head. "I can. I can. I..."

The body detransformed.

They slowly turned to look. The suit was gone. No more green leaves falling off her shoulders. Just a white shirt, now stained red. Green hair now blue. Blue and red and not much hair at all. Ren was gonna be sick.

"Go." She wasn't sure if she was speaking to herself or Wonderland.

Wonderland squeezed her hands. "You're sure?"

She nodded.

"Thank you." They let go and walked across the bloodied stones.

Ren stayed there, staring at the little floating yellow Xyri that appeared above Gaia's body. It was so small, she could have grabbed it with one hand. Its glowing eyes bore into hers, accusatory.

Ignore him.

I...

She couldn't. They stared at each other. Girl and Xyri. Xyri and girl. She felt hatred from the creature. Pain. Loss.

"Kaida!" someone called her name. She wasn't sure who. "Oh my god."

"What? Is she okay? Kaida?"

She didn't move, eyes stuck staring at the Xyri. She could almost feel his pain. His human was gone. Dead. The Bond broken.

Ren... it's okay.

"Gaia's dead."

Someone touched her and she winced.

"Kaida?"

She was forced to turn around by those hands. Jasper. Apex. He stared at her in worry, Lycan beside him.

"Kai?" Lycan whispered her name, holding a hand out toward her. "I can't see, are you okay?"

"Elixir did something to his eyes," Apex muttered.

She nodded, unable to speak. Apex sighed and grabbed her arm, gently lifting it toward Lycan till he grasped her hand, sliding his fingers through hers. A sigh of relief left Lycan.

Relief? Where was the relief?

"I killed her," she muttered. Cold. Detached.

Someone *screamed*. A blood curdling high pitched sound of pain, shocking Ren out of her reverie. Vapor ran up the steps, eyes wide, horror struck.

"Delilah?" She fell to her knees by the body, then leveled that murderous gaze on Ren.

Apex grabbed Ren's hand and jumped. She was pulled into the air, her wings moving effortlessly to lift her up, Lycan dragged with her, his hand still gripped in hers.

Vapor continued to scream below.

73
The Blame. The Victory.

Ren was in a daze as they settled on their roof on Spruce Street. She collapsed to her knees, both boys hands dropping from her fingertips. Apex paced in front of her as Lycan stared blankly.

"I should... clean you up," Apex muttered as he stared down at her.

She nodded, too numb to speak.

"Can you make a portal for me? To your room?"

"I'll detransform."

"Lycan can't fucking see. And you have five minutes."

"What if his sight comes back right when I'm—"

"I'll keep my eyes closed, just in case." Lycan slowly lowered himself down beside her.

She sighed then reached out and yanked on the air, tearing a portal open. Apex stared at her.

"Wait, can I go through without you?"

Can he? She wasn't sure, her thoughts were moving slowly.

By default no one can, but I'll allow it.

"Go."

Apex disappeared inside the portal without another word. She glanced to the side where Lycan sat, eyes firmly closed. She scooted closer, grabbing his arm with both hands, she leaned her head on his shoulder.

"I'm proud of you," he whispered.

No.

"You did what needed to be done. Everyone's better off for it."

No.

"How... are you feeling?"

She squeezed his arm, not trusting herself to speak.

"That bad, huh?" He smiled sadly, leaning his head into her.

She swallowed. "Is it healing?"

"My eyes?"

"The blood, Ly. There's *so* much blood on you."

"Oh." He paused. "Zeli's working on it."

"Does it hurt?"

"Uh. I think it should? It did? At first. I dunno I've been... I'm sorry I wasn't there, to do it for you."

No.

"Kai? Please talk to me."

She closed her eyes. "She almost killed me."

He stiffened.

"And..." *I almost let her.*

A tear slid down her cheek. Lycan turned, pulling his arm out of her hands, then he wrapped both arms around her, pulling her into his bloodied chest.

"It's okay," he whispered.

No.

"I know it doesn't feel like it but, you did a good thing," he continued.

No. "I didn't... I didn't do it."

"What do you mean?"

She sucked in a breath. "Wonderland was there. They did it. They killed Gaia. But it was me." She could sense Lycan's confusion. "Everyone will think it was me. *Should* think it. But it wasn't. I... couldn't."

Lycan gently rubbed her back as she leaned into him.

Apex hopped out of the portal with a basket in hand. He paused mid step. "Am I interrupting?"

Ren sighed as she pulled back from Lycan and wiped her eyes. Apex shook his head as he knelt in front of her.

"Go ahead, detransform."

She glanced at Lycan. His eyes were shut tight, but he gave her a reassuring smile. She swallowed as the suit came off, making her feel more vulnerable, sitting so close to Lycan as Ren.

Jasper pulled a towel and some wet wipes out of the basket, which he'd taken from her bathroom. The wipes turned red as he started cleaning her face. She balled her hands into fists. After a moment Lycan reached out, hand fumbling around till it hit her knee. She grabbed his hand, gripping it tightly. How he knew she needed that when he couldn't even see her...

"How's the chest, buddy?"

"Fine."

"You're still bleeding..."

Lycan just shrugged.

Apex rolled his eyes as he moved in front of Lycan and took a closer look at the tears in his suit where his skin was stained red. Those cuts ran deep.

Apex worked to clean what he could, but they all knew it was pointless. The only thing that would fix Lycan was Zeli. But, she wasn't fusing, so... he was going to be fine...

Zig, is he okay?

Zig didn't respond right away. She could feel him considering.

Place your hand against his chest, where his Xyrial rests.

Why?

I'll see the damage better that way.

She gently laid her hand against his chest and Lycan stiffened, face moving toward her.

"Kai?"

She didn't respond, simply waited with her palm pressed over the small bump of his Xyrial.

Well? Panic stirred inside of her.

He is going to heal.

Why are you surprised?

The damage...

Zig?

"Kai?"

If these wounds were yours I would have fused to heal you. It's remarkable that he doesn't require this now. It is remarkable he is sitting up and breathing...

She swallowed. *He's strong.*

"Kai, what are you doing?" Lycan laid his hand on top of hers against his chest. "Checking for a heartbeat? Swear I'm still here."

She didn't answer, realizing she wasn't in the suit. She was Ren. It wouldn't be Kaida's voice if she spoke. He'd only met Ren twice, would he be able to recognize that voice? Her heart raced as she pulled her now bloody hand away from his chest, then gently cupped his cheek with the other hand.

He shivered under the touch. Skin against skin. "Oh."

"Should I leave?" Jasper asked. "You guys are having some kind of moment."

"She's not... in the suit," Lycan whispered as she dropped her hand. Then he smiled. "Never been near you, not in the suit."

"You guys are weird."

She sucked in a breath as the suit came over her again. "You're weird."

Lycan's smile widened. "*And* she's back."

No.

The next day Ren sat curled up on the couch while the news covered what happened. There were no eyewitnesses to Gaia's death. But apparently some people had crept near at the end. She watched it play back on the TV. Footage of Kaida standing over the body, staring at nothing. Apex and Lycan rushing over, pulling her back when Vapor arrived. The girl screaming and crying over the corpse.

Delilah Pearce. Twenty-four years old. Whatever else they said about Gaia, Ren didn't hear. Dad muted the TV as he leaned down behind her.

"Hey, kid. You alright?"

Ren didn't respond.

He walked around and sat beside her. "Did you talk to Simon?"

She shook her head.

"Ren? I know you're upset, and you're going through it. But..." He sighed as she forced herself to stop staring at nothing and met his eyes. "What can I do?"

She swallowed. "I'm fine."

"Have you talked about it with anyone?"

"Jasper."

Dad's eyes narrowed. "Jasper told me you barely said anything."

Ren frowned at that.

"Why don't you talk to Ocean? Or Marigold? Or your Aunt Aza? Maybe you need... a girl, to talk about this stuff."

She blinked, eyes burning. "I..." Being surrounded by boys wasn't her problem. "I can ask Ocean to come over," she mumbled.

Dad smiled. "Yeah, that sounds good."

She nodded as he left her there. Then she saw the words, scrolling across the bottom of the muted TV.

KAIDA DRAGONHEART, KILLER?

She stared at those words, heart racing.

They should praise you for it.

Some would, probably. But not everyone. Wonderland was right about that.

With a sigh she texted Ocean, asking her to come over for a girl's night. She hadn't told her about Simon yet. *Simon.* Her eyes burned. She couldn't think about him or Gaia without feeling... too much. It was all too much.

Half an hour later Ocean strolled in with a bright smile and a peppy attitude.

"Hey! I am so excited, we haven't had a sleepover in *years.*"

Ren nodded, trying to force a smile as she sat beside her on the couch.

"So, you wanna watch movies or or we could binge a show or..." Her smile fell. "Or we could talk about whatever's bothering you."

Ren let out a breath. "Simon and I broke up."

Ocean's mouth dropped, eyes wide. "Oh my god. *Ren.* I'm so sorry. What happened?" She put an arm around her.

Ren didn't know how to answer.

"I can't believe him. Why the *hell* would he break up with you? I mean, you're perfect, he has no idea how damn lucky he—"

"I broke up with him," she whispered.

Ocean paused. "*Oh.* That's less surprising."

Ren frowned as she met Ocean's amber eyes. "Why?"

"Well, just cause... I mean." She made a face. "He was kinda... *you know?*" She laughed nervously. "I mean I know you liked him but, he was *not* a good fit for you. Good riddance, *right*?"

Ren blinked. "I... I thought you liked Simon?"

Ocean sighed. "*Well*, Jasper and I were talking about it and—"

"About me? And Simon?"

"Not in a *bad* way! Just, think you should be with someone *else*. Like Bellamy. Who we *fully* think likes you too by the way, so now we can make *that* happen!"

I don't want Bellamy.

"A *much* better fit than Simon, right?"

Ren swallowed. "I uh... gotta run to the bathroom. You pick a movie?"

Ocean nodded. "Yeah, sure."

Ren practically ran from the room, upstairs and into her bathroom. Then she sent a text and opened a portal. Every part of her wanted to be out of the suit. Away from the powers. But she needed to be around someone who wouldn't make her wanna *scream* for five whole minutes. Then she'd go back, pretend. Fake it.

She stepped out of the portal onto the roof on Spruce Street. Lycan landed in front of her a moment later. He smiled at her sadly as she crossed to him and pressed her face into his chest.

"You're all better?" she asked.

"Mostly. Just, tired. How are you?"

She groaned.

"I see. You shouldn't listen to what everyone's saying, okay?"

She groaned louder.

"I'm serious, the people who are *actually* mad about what happened with Gaia are—"

"That's not why I'm here," she mumbled into him.

"Oh. What's wrong then?"

She sighed as she pulled back and looked up into his eyes. "I'm just... going through something. Personal. Unrelated to... all of that."

He nodded slowly.

"And every single person in my life..." Her eyes watered as she spoke. "They don't *get it* and they all think one thing and I think another and I don't have a single person on my side with this and it's driving me crazy, like I'm not supposed to be upset because they think it's a good outcome. But I feel so..." The tears tumbled down her face.

Lycan pulled her into his arms. She let herself cry as he held her, chin resting on her head.

"You're the only person who's not got an opinion on this thing. The only person I can be around right now."

"I'm sorry, Kai."

"And I think, if you knew what I was talking about, I think you'd still be on my side. I think... you'd just let me feel my feelings."

"Of course I would."

"I have to go back," she muttered, wiping her eyes. "I'll detransform in a minute."

"Kaida..."

She shook her head. "I'll be fine. I just... needed you, for a moment. Please don't tell Apex about this?"

Lycan nodded. "I'm on your side. Always. You and me?"

She smiled. "You and me." She turned to go back through her portal then paused, glancing back at him. "Is it really bad? What they're saying?"

He sighed.

She released a breath. "Right. Okay."

"It's gonna blow over. Alright?"

She nodded. "Thanks, Starface." She gave him another smile before returning to her bathroom.

After washing her face and going back to the living room, she thought maybe she could make it through the rest of the night. Ocean could tell she wasn't okay, though, and was doing her best to cheer Ren up while Dad made snacks and they watched movies. It just made her feel more guilty. She'd dropped the ball with Ocean again and again this last month, yet here she was, trying to help Ren. She didn't even deserve that.

I will be okay, won't I? she asked Zig.

Yes, you will. She could feel his concern and for a moment she wondered if he didn't believe it either.

Bellamy was furious. No one gave a damn when he killed Vendetta, but the amount of debate on if Kaida was *right* to kill Gaia that he was seeing sent his blood boiling. Part of him wanted the truth out there. Kaida didn't do it, Wonderland did. But it would just make them hate Wonderland for the same reason. And that was wrong, too.

He remembered a time when people liked Kaida more than him. A lifetime ago, when they first Bonded. She was adored by everyone. He wasn't nearly so popular. But now... Kaida couldn't so much as *breathe* without people having opinions on if she was doing it right.

Kaida was going through enough as it was. He wished he could do something, anything to help her. After she came to him, crying her eyes out... He couldn't be there for her, in her personal life. But this... the hero stuff, he *should* be able to help her.

Perhaps you can.

How?

Well, Zeli started. *If they respect you more, even for stupid reasons, you could use that. Tell them how you feel about it. Perhaps then they would listen.*

He thought on that for a moment. Then he went looking for a particular interview he'd done on the street a few months back. He sent an anonymous message to the women who filmed it, and waited.

The next day Lycan sat on a bench in Prospect Park, waiting for Tess to show up. He didn't have to wait long. The girl arrived, her green eyes wide, black hair curled and hanging to her shoulders. She sat down on the bench beside him.

"It's really you."

"You didn't think it would be?"

She laughed. "You get a message from someone claiming to be *the* Lycan asking to meet you on a hidden path in a park and you expect to get murdered."

He smiled. "I'm glad you came."

"Why exactly did you ask me to meet you here?"

"I need to speak my mind on some things and, I trust you."

"You trust me?"

"I only met you the one time, but you were kind. And I've seen the things you post. You're a reporter, not a gossip."

She grinned. "Yes. So. Um, should I be... filming this then?"

"Yeah, sure. Let's dive in."

She pulled some stuff out of her bag, setting up a proper tripod. He grinned as she handed him a small wireless mic as well.

"You're very prepared."

She beamed at him as he pinned it to his suit.

"Whenever you're ready."

He nodded and she hit record.

His throat was dry by the time he stopped talking and she turned the camera off.

"I can't believe I just got that interview. This is insane. No one's *ever* had this kind of exclusive…"

"If you're up for it, maybe we could keep coming to you, with these things?"

Tess's eyes widened. "You're serious?"

"Yeah. You could become the official Team Silverlight and Co reporter or whatever."

Her smile was so wide. "I would *love* that! Any time you need me you just let me know. I can give you my number, or email or—"

"I'll stay in touch."

She opened her mouth, then closed it, blushing.

"What is it?"

She looked down, shaking her head. "I sort of have something I wanna show you? Something I've been working on. For you and the rest of your team."

He raised an eyebrow. "What kind of thing?"

She looked up, eyes alight, as she opened her phone, leaning closer so he could see the screen.

"I made an app. It's not public yet. But basically, it's like a digital 911, specifically for the Bonded heroes."

"Wait, really? How's it work?"

"Anyone can pin their location on the map with a plea for help. They can even write a message explaining what's wrong. I know you guys sometimes make it late to things, because you only see it once it's being reported on by third parties. And you miss so many small things that the cops don't handle or even care about. But I know you do. So, this way you could assess these situations and make a choice to help, faster."

"How would we get these alerts?"

She blushed. "It's not foolproof yet. Basically, I could give the heroes specific profiles, so you'd get the alerts. The biggest flaw though is that anyone can pin anything. So, someone could easily set up a trap or something. Or just, fake an emergency to meet you or—"

"We can handle that," he replied, staring at the app as she moved through different screens. "This is really cool, Tess. We could help people who are too afraid to call the cops. We follow sirens when we can, get there when we can but… there's so many we never get to help. This could change everything."

Tess's eyes shined.

"When can you have it up and running?"

"Uh, soon! Just a few more kinks to work through. I really want it to be free for people to use but..."

"You need funds for it?"

She blushed. "I'm working on it, it's just taking me some time."

"I can help with that," Lycan replied.

Tess blinked. "What—what do you mean?"

"I can fund the whole app for you. Whatever you need, I can cover the costs."

"You're serious?"

"Absolutely. We *will* use it. Tess, you've just made it so we can save so many more lives. This is incredible."

"Oh my god. I love you." Her face was so red, her smile so wide. "Is there... some way I can get in touch with you?"

"Give me your number, I'll text through an app that hides my real number."

"Oh, so smart." She wrote it down and handed it to him.

He tucked it inside the suit so he wouldn't lose it. "When will this interview go live?"

"Give me the weekend? I can post by Monday probably."

"Perfect. Thank you again, for everything."

She stared at him, eyes glistening. "You probably don't remember this, but... you actually saved my life once."

He frowned, searching her face. "I always remember, but I can't place you."

She smiled. "I was probably a bit ashy at the time."

"*Oh*, the fire in Brooklyn? Ocean Avenue. Fifth floor?"

She laughed, a tear sliding down her face as she nodded. "You remember?"

"I always remember." He swallowed, recalling that apartment. That body. She was dead when he found her. But he spun the clock of time, rewrote the story of her life in those five minutes.

And look at her now, Zeli said.

Bellamy smiled.

74
A Plea

Ren lay on the couch, barely paying attention to the TV as Breadcrumb purred against her stomach. She was still exhausted, physically and emotionally. Simon texted again that morning. She ignored him, the guilt biting into her every few minutes.

She hadn't explained *why*. She didn't have a good answer, and the moment she responded to a text of his, she'd fold like paper. He wanted her back and it would be so *easy* to say yes. To run to him, to let him hold her while she hid from her other ghosts.

Despite her frustrations with everyone, she didn't wanna be alone. But Jasper couldn't come over, he'd gotten in trouble with his dad for leaving in the middle of work the other day. He wasn't officially grounded yet, but they didn't wanna press his luck. She considered texting Lycan to see if he was free, but decided against it.

Zig?

Yes?

Where are you?

With Poziarne. Do you need me?

She sighed. *No.*

I'm on my way.

I'm fine, she replied. *You don't have to come.*

Almost there.

Sure enough, a minute later Zig was phasing through the wall. He landed on the couch beside her, shaking his wings.

"You didn't have to come," she mumbled with a smile.

Doesn't matter. Here now.

She did feel more at ease with him at her side. Of course he knew that. He curled up against her leg. With him and Breadcrumb there she felt almost content for the first time in days. Breathing in deep, she closed her eyes and leaned her head back.

"Was Pozi with Jasper?"

Yes.

"How's that going?"

Not well.

She groaned.

It wasn't that bad, just...

"Just his dad is a dick and gonna make him work all summer?"

Jasper's mom was putting up a good argument. They talked about you.

"What about me?"

Said Jasper is young and should be allowed to spend the summer with his girlfriend, he shouldn't have to worry about getting a job till he's done with school. His dad was angry, but it seemed like his mom was winning the argument.

"Really?"

Don't worry. I'm sure it will be fine.

She nodded, but worry still gnawed at her. Spending less time with Jasper would suck but it wasn't the end of the world. The problem was his dad, and Jasper spending more time with him would only result in Jasper getting hurt more often. That made her *burn.*

Ren wished he could just work at the bakery. Her dad offered Jasper a job, but he declined it. She knew it was because of his dad. Mr. Nightingale wouldn't be thrilled about him working in the bakery, considering the theme of the place. He still didn't even know Ren had two dads, and still thought Ren was Jasper's girlfriend. It was safer to lie about those things.

Her phone vibrated. Simon's name appeared and her stomach filled with anxiety. She dismissed the notification without reading the text. If she read it, she'd be tempted to respond, to run to him. She squeezed her eyes shut as she laid back down.

Zig stiffened beside her, his head lifting, ears twitching. *A Xyri is in distress.*

"What?"

Somewhere nearby a Xyri is putting out a call. A plea.

"You can hear them calling to you?"

No, it is like... an alarm. Any Xyri close by will feel it. I... I haven't felt a Xyri distress call in a very long time. Centuries. He sounded worried.

"We should go? See what's wrong."

She could feel the weight of something terrible in Zig's silence. His anxiety bled into her and she took a deep breath.

"I'll kidnap Jasper. We can check it out together, okay?"

Ren... this might be very very bad.

"If a Xyri needs help we have to go. Come on."

She put Breadcrumb on the ground and stretched as the suit came over her body. She ripped open a portal right there in the living room then ducked inside.

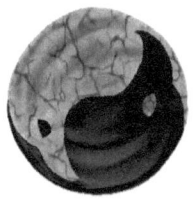

Jasper wanted to scream. Back and forth his mom and dad argued while he stood there, like he didn't exist. Everything in him told him to run from the sound of that voice as it got angrier and angrier, but he couldn't. If he left, his mom would be alone and that anger would only have one place to land. So he stayed, trying to ignore the various suggestions Pozi made in his head as he trembled.

"He ran off in the middle of his shift! This kid has no responsibility, no patience, no fucking—"

"Stop!" Mom cut him off. "Bobby, he's a *kid*. Don't act like you didn't sneak off to see me when we were kids."

"And my dad beat my ass for it every time I got caught! Audrey, he's gotta grow up sometime. You can't keep coddling him."

Jasper? Something's wrong.

Yeah, my whole fucking li—

A Xyri is putting out a distress call, Pozi interrupted.

What's that mean?

They're asking for help. This is very very rare.

Jasper sighed. *How rare?*

It's only been done once in the last two millenniums. Only once... this is very very bad. We have to go. Now.

I can't just leave, Poz. You can go. You don't need me.

Mmm, no I do.

Jasper let out a breath as he tried to tune back into what his parents were saying, but a knock sounded at the door, making him jump and silencing his dad. He released a breath.

"I'll get it," Dad grumbled as he brushed past Mom.

Mom sighed as she pulled Jasper over and hugged him. "It's gonna be fine. I'll get through to him, promise."

He nodded, though he wasn't sure she could.

"Hi, Mr. Nightingale, is Jasper home?"

Jasper spun at the sound of Ren's voice. She stood there in the doorway, a bright smile that was absolutely fake filled her face.

"I know he's... in trouble for coming to see me the other day, but that was totally my fault and I'm very sorry! And I fully understand if he's not allowed to see me right now, but I could *really* use his help on something... if he could come out for just a bit? Please?"

Dad sighed. "Fine. Go."

Jasper didn't waste a second, moving past Dad to go out into the hall with Ren. He didn't even stop to grab his phone or his keys as Ren pulled him down the stairs. The second the door closed behind them she was in her suit and opening a portal.

"What's going on with the Xyri?"

"No idea. We're gonna find out."

He nodded, suiting up as they stepped back out the other side of the portal into a sunlit park.

Be alert, Pozi muttered.

Jasper wasn't sure he'd ever felt Pozi so anxious before.

No worries. We got this.

Bellamy tried to focus on his book but the sound of voices in the living room piqued his curiosity. More than one voice... he put the book down and slowly got out of bed.

"This is big, Lucy," a man's voice said.

Bellamy stayed in the hall, listening. He was sure it was the same man from before, the accent was the same.

"What is?" his mom asked.

"Do you know how many Xyri are Bonded in this city right now?"

"A handful?"

Bellamy's entire body tensed as he slowly peeked around the corner.

"More than that. A lot more."

"You think we can get them to help us?"

The man laughed. "No, not in the way you're thinking. But, their Xyri..."

Zeli? Something's happening.

"Let's see... I'm sure it's started."

"What did you do?"

"All those Bonded are going to the same place. And some of them are, unfortunately, going to die. And when they do..."

"Eric—"

"It's the only way, Lucy. We've been over this, if you want to find Leo, if you want to bring your dead kid back, sacrifices *must* be made."

"They'll Bond with you?"

What the... Zeli where are you?

"Us, Lucy. They'll Bond us, to recover. And with that extra power, I can do more. A *lot* more. I promise, we *will* bring him back."

"But..."

Bellamy's hands shook as he got a good look at the man in the long black coat standing beside his mom, both their backs toward him. He was holding up a tablet, showing her something on the screen.

"Some of them are children, Eric. All of them, really."

"Do you want *your* child back or not?"

Bellamy?

Mom swallowed. "Is there really no other way? After what Vainaira already went through, I don't know if—"

"I've tried everything. This is our *last* shot, Lucy."

Bellamy!

He spun at the yell even though it came from inside his head. *Zeli? What's going on, I—*

It was a trap! And they all went right into it!

What? I don't understand. Bellamy turned back, trying to make sense of everything. A flash of bright red crossed the man's screen. Kaida. Apex. Wonderland. Prism. Tag. This man was showing his mom live footage of them. And they were all fighting each other.

I have to go help.

Bellamy, it is a trap! Do you understand? Zeli walked through the wall, appearing beside him, her silver eyes intense. *If you go they will try to kill you. Every one of them.*

Kaida's there!

Zeli's whole body stiffened, fur standing up like a frightened cat. *Xereth*, she hissed.

Bellamy followed her gaze to the man with his mom, heart racing. *That's... that's Xereth?*

We have to stop him. We have to—

We have to help Kaida, Bellamy cut her off as he turned. The suit came over him before Zeli could argue. He ran to his room, out onto the balcony and jumped into the air.

What happened?

They're trying to kill each other. Compelled. Nothing can stop them till it wears off. You can not get involved.

Rapture?

Yes. They can not resist her second power. It's too late.

Bellamy had never flown so fast in his life. When he got to Prospect Park it was pure chaos. Bodies littered the ground.

75
Kaida Becomes Death

Kaida became death as she lifted a sword of light and sliced through one of Hoax's clones.

How do I stop it?

You can't, Zig answered, voice strained.

Kaida spun, stabbing another Hoax through the chest. She screamed as she did it, horrified. So many were dead already. Innocent people. Civilians.

What if I detransform?

You'll still be compelled to kill, only you would be defenseless.

Ren had never known terror like this. When Rapture spoke the words, it was all she could hear, every other sound muted around them. She couldn't fight it, her body worked against her. She attacked Apex first when it started, but then Hoax was there, splitting into a dozen different people. Three of them rushed Kaida. She was glad for that as she tore her way through the third. It kept her from hurting Apex.

Kill everyone.

The words rang in her ears, guiding her every move. She couldn't fight it, couldn't stop herself. How many were there? She lost track of everyone once Hoax split, but she spotted Wonderland and Parody before the fight began. Bodies were dropping fast around them.

How long?

Five minutes.

How long has it been? She met Prism's eyes and lunged for him.

Thirty-seven seconds.

Oh god.

She swung her sword at him. He dodged. Something hit her back, knocking her down. But it wasn't enough to stop her. It barely slowed her as she pushed herself up, realizing what hit her was a park bench. Prism looked afraid. She bared her teeth as she spun a rope of light and tied it around him. Her sword formed again and she lifted it high, intending to behead the kid. Disgust filled her as she swung but she was thrown back into the air, her sword shattering to mist.

She groaned as she rolled and forced herself up. Fable was across from her, his purple eyes terrified as she threw herself at him, sword forming again. He blocked it just in time with a small metal stick. He had one in each hand as he backed up slowly, then raised the other stick toward her.

How long?

A minute thirteen. The panic in Zig's voice only heightened her own.

A light flashed in her eyes, blinding. Her swing missed.

It's an illusion.

Something slammed against her face, knocking her back. Kaida barely felt it through her rage and terror. She waited a moment then lifted her hand up, catching the stick mid-air before it could hit her again. She yanked it out of Fable's hand, and it puffed into purple smoke in her fingers. He looked annoyed as he held up the other stick, the second one reforming in his fist. Someone was screaming. Ren couldn't look. Couldn't do anything other than try to kill Fable.

She ducked as he swung again and kicked his leg out from under him. Fable crashed to the ground. She pounced, a light knife forming in her fist. She plunged it down just as his body disappeared, her knife sticking in the dirt. Another illusion. Relief filled her even as she jumped back up. Apex was there, fighting Fable now. *No, don't look at him.*

She forced her eyes on Fable instead, her sword reforming. Fable's purple eyes were wild as he parried attacks on both sides from Kaida and Apex. He hit Apex across the face then stumbled back. Kaida took the opening, ramming her sword through Fable's stomach. He grunted, blinking in disbelief. He coughed up blood as she yanked the sword back out, heart pounding. *No no no no.*

Something crashed into her, knocking the air out of her. She grunted in pain as she rolled to see Apex looking down at her. *No. Not Apex. Jasper.* His eyes were terrified.

"*Ren,*" he barely whispered her name.

No no no no no.

But she could not stop herself. Couldn't control the need to kill. Her body worked on its own as she shoved him off her then stood, two small glowing knives forming in her fists.

Please no.

Tears formed, blurring her vision before she moved.

Jasper held his staff in a firm grip as he swung at her.

She dodged.

He turned.

The staff hit her, pain flaring through her arm. She dropped the knife.

He slammed into her, too fast, they both hit the ground.

Please please please.

Her knife pierced his side.

His eyes widened.

Time felt so slow.

Jasper pulled back, then stood and kicked her in the ribs.

She screamed.

He kicked again.

A rope of light formed around his ankle. She pulled.

He fell.

Her hands shook as she forced herself up, rope wrapped around her fist.

Jasper looked up at her, then grabbed the rope, pulling with both hands till it tore in two.

He was on his feet in seconds.

She swung for him.

His wings sprung free and he flew up.

Please stop.

Her wings were out a moment later and she followed him into the sky.

He was stronger. Faster. She couldn't win.

I don't want to win. God please!

He dove toward her, body slamming into hers as they tumbled through the air.

"Ren, I can't—"

"I know." Tears burned her eyes. "I love you. I love you. I love you. I love you. I love you."

"Kill me!" he begged. "Please!"

She shook her head even as she tried to get a hand free so she could form a blade. His fingers dug into her side, flaring up the pain in her ribs.

As they turned through the air she caught a glimpse of the bodies on the ground below. So many were dead already.

This can't be happening. Zig please do something. Please. I can't—

I'm sorry, Ren. His voice trembled.

Ren cried as she let go of Jasper.

She spun, reorienting.

He came at her again. Too fast. Too strong.

The hit made her dizzy and she blinked through the tears, air rushing past. She was sure her ribs were broken, everything hurt. Apex clung to her, golden eyes shining. *Not Apex. Jasper.*

"I love you," she whispered again.

"Love you more," he hissed, angry.

At least Lycan is safe, she thought just before they crashed into the ground.

Ren please. Please please please, Zig sounded like he was crying too. *Please fight. Please. Don't leave me.*

She'd never heard so much pain in his voice.

Never felt so much pain in her body.

If she had any say she wouldn't move. She'd die right there. But her body continued on, forcing her to sit up. To look.

Jasper was on the ground beside her, coughing, eyes closed.

Panic filled her as her hand moved, knife forming.

No no no no no no no NO NO NO NO.

She slammed the knife into his throat.

His eyes snapped open.

Blood bubbled up around the blade. Red.

She didn't move, hand still gripping the knife, eyes wide.

The urge to kill finally wore off.

And Jasper was dead.

76
Webs of Silver

Lycan landed in the middle of a massacre. At least twenty dead bodies on the ground. He scanned them, noting Tag and Parody were dead. His eyes found Kaida, one of the few left. As he got closer he saw the tears in her eyes. Her hand firm around a blade of light jutting out of Apex's throat. The boy detransformed, his hood disappearing to reveal brown hair. Lycan's instinct was to go to her. Instead, he pulled on the fabric of time. *I can undo it.*

Bellamy, be careful.

He was back in his bed, book in hand. He threw it across the room as he ran for the balcony.

Explain to me what I just saw.

Rapture commanded them to kill each other.

How do I stop it?

You can not. It'll last five minutes.

That's too long! Did you see what I saw?

Yes. I... He felt her hesitation.

She knew it was a trap and all of their stupid friends went and fell into it. And then there was Xereth, within her grasp. And Bellamy pulled her away. He couldn't think about that now.

Hurry, you can't stop it from happening. But maybe you can save them from each other.

He felt sick as he flew. The sight of Kaida and Apex... Apex dead. *No, I went back. It hasn't happened yet.*

When he arrived there were civilians dead around the field already. He looked for Kaida, running to her as she slammed a sword in attack against Fable. Apex was beside her, also attacking Fable. He didn't think as he moved, grabbing Kaida from behind and pulling her back.

She yelled as her sword disappeared, then her blue eyes met his. Pleading.

"It's okay, I'm here," he mumbled as she tried to pull away.

She'll try to kill you too, they all will!

Right.

He danced back as she got out of his grasp. Her eyes were wide and horrified as her hands glowed, forming something to use against him. He shoved her back, silver pouring out around him, shaping into a cage.

She banged her hands against it, absolutely feral, but even as she did so she muttered "be careful" with tears in her eyes.

He nodded, turning away. That would contain her for at least a minute. He looked for Apex but caught sight of Tag first. He'd been dead before. Lycan breathed deep as he ran across the field toward him. He was being ganged up on by several versions of Hoax. There was no way to tell which was the real one.

If you can just stop them, contain them, for just two more minutes!

He started forming a cage for Tag but then Tag vanished and suddenly Prism was in his place. The boy growled, confused at being displaced. Lycan was thrown back in the air. He groaned as he hit the ground.

Apex and Fable were closest to him now, Apex staring wildly in confusion at the illusion of ten different Fable's in front of him. The real Fable was behind Apex, swinging one of his sticks toward his head. Apex spun, catching it in his hand at the last second.

"How the hell did you—" Before Fable could finish the sentence Apex kicked him in the stomach.

Lycan ran for them just as Apex slammed his staff through Fable's chest. It looked like it went all the way through and down into the ground below. *Shit.*

Oh no. Nellithi... Zeli was aghast.

Lycan spun, looking for somewhere to go. Then he ran toward the pond.

What are you doing?

Going back.

Bellamy...

It's fine I can handle it!

He could sense her doubt as he dove in the water, sinking low enough to detransform. He held his breath, waiting to re-suit up.

You have to be careful, if you try too many times—

I know I remember! He pulled on time, yanking himself back to his bed, heart racing.

By the time he arrived on the scene again Kaida and Apex were back to fighting Fable. He grabbed Kaida just as he'd done before, quicker to get her encased in a cage of silver before she could fight him. He turned back to Apex and Fable instead of going for Tag, spinning webs of silver, forcing them apart. Fable growled but Apex looked relieved as it caged them.

He scanned the field in a panic, not sure what to do next. There were five other groups fighting each other around him.

Kaida couldn't overcome her panic as Lycan stopped Apex and Fable. She banged on her cage, body eager to get out and fulfill the order to kill. She forced herself to look away from him, so much was happening. Tag fought several Hoax clones. She trembled, eyes moving over the already dead ones on the ground. She'd killed three of them.

She's not dead yet. The clones would disappear if she was dead, Zig whispered.

Ren nodded, but her guilt wouldn't ease. She'd torn through the girl like she was nothing. Lycan spun, looking around in a panic. Just then Wonderland fell with a scream, their entire body engulfed in flames.

Kaida yelled and Lycan turned, his eyes following hers. He saw Wonderland, on the ground and burning. Parody standing over them, crying, her hands on fire just like Pompeii, who was now fighting Prism. Before Lycan could take two steps Tag was down.

The silver around her collapsed. Lycan stood there, taking it all in. Then he ran, not toward Kaida, but away, jumping into the water. Kaida couldn't stop to wonder why that was. Now free, her body forced her forward, toward Parody, Prism, and Pompeii, two long swords of light forming in her hands.

Oh god.

Lycan was beyond overwhelmed by the time he got back to the park. He ignored Zeli's warnings that he stop rewinding. He needed to save them all. But Kaida was his priority, so once again he went to her and caged her in silver.

Then he went for Apex and Fable, moving fast and efficient now that he knew what to do. They were in cages before they even noticed he was there. He went to Wonderland next, as they killed one of the Hoax clones. She fell just as Lycan formed a cage around them before Wonderland could turn that flail on him. He dodged it, dancing back as the cages settled.

He ignored their yells as he moved for Tag but Kaida was out of her cage, already there. She sliced one Hoax clone in half. Lycan blinked, revulsion filling him as he ran for her.

Everything went dark for a second then he was right in front of Kaida instead of behind her. Being displaced by Tag was *extremely* disorienting.

Kaida wept as she lifted her blade, preparing to bring it down on him. Lycan dodged under the sword, then wrapped silver ropes around her waist and yanked her back into his arms. The sight of her tears nearly killed him right then and there.

Something exploded, sending him and Kaida flying through the air. *It's almost over! Hold out just another minute!*

Every Hoax clone disappeared. Lycan gasped till his eyes landed on the one remaining, pinned to the ground under the weight of Elixir, as she poured her sickness directly into the girl. Parody flew through the air, body slamming into a tree. Prism fell to Pompeii at the same time.

Lycan groaned, pushing himself up, looking for Kaida.

She was running her sword through Tag.

Lycan took a deep breath and ran for the water.

77
Devastation

Can I go back sooner?
Technically? Bellamy you are doing too much! You have *to stop.*
Just one more... if he could go back just a minute, before Kaida broke out.

It was harder to pull on time, to move back. It resisted, but he forced his way into the power. *Just a minute.* He found himself standing in the middle of the field with Wonderland, Fable, and Apex still in cages. He ran for Kaida.

He was too late to stop her from killing another Hoax but intercepted her before she got to Tag. Those tears streamed down her face as he wrapped her in silver ropes. Tag switched with him again. He stumbled, confused as he was only displaced by a few feet.

Tag disappeared, appearing inside Fable's cage, leaving Fable free just behind Lycan and Kaida.

Kaida struggled against her ropes. Any second now she'd be free. Lycan knew she was the more dangerous of the two, so he stayed with her. Out of the corner of his eye he saw a Hoax fall to Fable and he growled.

Less than a minute. You can not rewind again!

He grabbed Kaida just as the rope puffed to mist around her. She threw a punch. He took it to the face, stumbling back.

You are too weak for this... you did too much!

He ignored her, reaching for Kaida. He pulled her against him and put her in a choke hold. A sharp pain exploded in his thigh.

She stabbed you!

I'm aware.

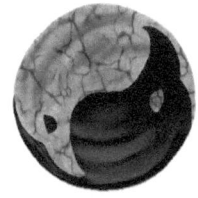

Jasper panicked as the silver finally bent around him. He'd been trying to break out of the cage, but every part of him wanted to stay inside. He'd seen what Kaida did, slicing through Hoax like she was made of butter.

Don't think about that. Think about surviving!

Surviving meant killing. Jasper wasn't in control as he moved toward the girl in the black suit with the sickly green lines running over it. Elixir.

Remember she can kill you! Poisons, Jasper. Do not let her touch you.

Right.

His staff formed in his hand and he swung it against the girl. She jumped back, barely dodging him, grinning, like she was enjoying this. He hit her shoulder, wincing as the staff made contact. She stumbled, golden hair flying over her face. He hovered over her, hands moving, ready to deal the killing blow.

Someone tackled him before it could land. He closed his eyes a moment, relieved, despite the pain in his side. When he opened his eyes, he saw Tag and Wonderland fighting. Wonderland's flail raised, their pink eyes wide as Tag disappeared, Parody taking his place. The flail struck her in the chest. Parody fell with a scream. Then she stilled. Jasper's heart raced as he pushed himself up, every instinct telling him to run to her, to help her. But Fable was across from him, purple eyes angry.

Jasper released a breath as he moved into a crouch. "Well. If it has to be anyone..."

Fable smiled.

Burning pain radiated from his ankle as something touched him. Jasper screamed, falling back. Fable moved fast, kicking Elixir in the face. Then he slammed one of his sticks into the girl's head. She didn't move. Fable turned back to him, panting. Jasper was dizzy, the world spinning around him.

I told you not to let her touch you! Pozi yelled as everything went dark.

Kaida struggled against Lycan, terrified every time she took a swing, grateful every time he blocked it. No one could fight her like him. No one knew her as well.

It's almost over, Ren.

"Don't let me kill you," she hissed through gritted teeth, eyes burning through her tears. *"Please."*

Lycan smiled as they wrestled with each other. "Never, Bunhead."

He pinned her, silver spinning around them. She closed her eyes, breathing deeply as she struggled against him.

Any second now, Ren.

She felt the moment it ended, a physical weight lifting from her body. Every inch of her felt bruised as that tension eased. She blinked up at Lycan.

"It's over."

He nodded, moving back as the silver misted away. He pulled her up into his arms. She held onto him tightly, crying into his shoulder a moment, before pulling back and pushing herself to her feet.

The smell of blood was sharp on the air.

She shook as she saw Apex on the ground and slowly moved toward him. He was still in his suit, so he wasn't dead. Couldn't be dead. She barely breathed as she crossed the field toward him, unable to believe it till he was up and smiling at her.

She heard Lycan cursing behind her, but she didn't dare stop, didn't dare look to see who hadn't made it as she knelt beside Jasper's body. She pressed a gentle hand against his chest. The body puffed away into purple smoke and she screamed.

"What the hell was that?" Lycan asked as he ran over, breathless.

Her heart raced as she stared at the spot where Apex's body had been, hand still hovering in the air. "I... what..."

Someone stepped up beside them. "An illusion. One of Fable's," Tag muttered.

She glanced up at him, tears in her eyes. "Then where is he? Where is Apex?"

"Fable's gone, too," Lycan said.

"Before the command wore off that poison girl got him. Apex fell, screaming, after she touched him," Tag continued, his eyes haunted. "I'm sorry."

Ren blinked. "Got him? What—*where* is Apex?"

"If Fable's gone too, maybe he took him?"

She didn't know what to say. What to do.

"Parody is dead," Lycan whispered.

She turned slowly, heart tight in her chest as she looked up at him. *"No."* Parody dead... Jasper missing. She felt like she couldn't breathe.

"I can fix it. I'll go back again." Lycan looked sick and she realized he said *again*.

Panic filled her as she jumped to her feet just as Lycan's eyes closed and he collapsed to the ground.

"No no no no no...."

Again. Again. How many times did he rewind? She knelt down, holding her fingers against his neck, desperate to feel a pulse. It was slow, barely registering.

She stared up at Tag, helpless.

"I..." Tag swallowed. "I have to find Hoax."

She watched as he moved, kneeling down beside one of the Hoax corpses, checking for a pulse. She watched, some shred of Kaida inside eager to see that the girl was okay. Finally Tag found the right one and let out a breath of relief as he scooped her into his arms, then he disappeared in a flash of light.

Ren was left alone, surrounded by the dead. Her hand still against Lycan's neck, clinging to that pulse.

"You and me," she whispered. "You and me. Please come back. I need you. *Please.*" She buried her face into his chest and let the devastation consume her.

THE END OF BOOK ONE

SNEAK PEEK FROM BOOK TWO
(Disclaimer: This is a rough draft and subject to change!)

Kaida fell to her knees, exhausted, weighed down by her emotions more than the fact she hadn't slept in who knew how long. Any time she stopped to think about that she thought about her dads, wondering where she was. She thought of Jasper's mom, if she'd ever see her son again. And then she'd start heaving, unable to breathe.

Lycan talked her through the panic attack every time it hit. He knelt on the pavement beside her, a hand on her shoulder.

"We can't give up," he whispered.

She shook her head, but all she wanted to do was give in to the pain. To let go. *He's still alive. He's still alive.* She had to repeat the words, or she'd lose herself. What was she without Jasper?

"We should take a break, detransform. Let the Xyri look for a bit."

"No, I'm fine," she muttered, eyes burning.

"They'd cover more ground than we can, Kai..."

She forced herself up, hands shaking.

Lycan sighed, standing beside her. "At this point I'm ready to knock on every door, ask if people have seen them."

She swallowed. "I doubt he's in Fable form now. Or out and about. He has to know I'm c-coming for him. Has to know I'll k-kill him if he... if...."

"Apex is gonna be fine. Pozi would have found us by now if he wasn't. He's likely been in the suit the entire time, healing. Maybe... fusing."

She met Lycan's eyes. Ren nearly died when she fused.

Jasper is strong, Ren. As strong as you.

She nodded. "I... I don't know what to do anymore. I don't know where to go. We walked the whole area. We've flown around. There's n-no trace of them. I..." She squeezed her eyes shut. "I'm so scared."

Lycan's warm embrace enveloped her. He rubbed her back while resting his chin on her head. She breathed out slowly, leaning into his chest.

"I'm scared too," he said, voice low. "But it's not over till Apex is dead in your arms. And he is *not* dead. Not yet. We can still save him."

She savored his warmth a moment before pulling back. "Where should we go now?"

Her exhaustion was mirrored in his eyes. He'd been awake just as long as her, but he almost died. She was sure he was *still* healing from it.

ACKNOWLEDMENTS

There are several people without whom this book would not have happened.

First among those is my partner, Justin Curtis. Thank you for giving me the freedom and space to be creative, for always encouraging me to follow my passion, and accepting that sometimes I will just be locked away to write, with little time for anything else. I love you, forever and ever.

Next, Casey Cassidy. My best friend. My crab crab. You're the Jasper to my Ren. The Jillian to my Rainy. The Stiles to my Scott. The Kelsier to my Vin. You're an essential part of my writing process, and an essential part of my life. I lagoon you.

Special shout out to my brother, Dustin Young, for not only beta reading for me multiple times, but for being part of the reason I learned I was meant to be a writer. I love being on this journey with you.

Of course, thanks to all of my beta readers.

Haley C. and Ashley M. Sousa, you two have my heart.

Josh Goldberg, Elijah Moss, Luna, Kaija Owens, Lauren, Rachel Bloom, Laura A, Helen, Oz Miller, Kay, Taeo Anderson, Kaylee Donovan, Tyler Jenkins, Nicole, and Kevin Coastal.

And a special thanks to Carolina Bartolo, for beta reading and translating all of the Spanish for me! If working retail gave me one good thing, it was you.

And the biggest thank you to Ren Rivers, for choosing *me* to tell her story.

Brianna Young lives in Illinois with her partner, and their seven cats. When she isn't wrangling her creatures, she spends her time drowning out her depression and anxiety by writing about characters with depression and anxiety.

Her debut novel, Lament of Light, fully funded on Kickstarter in under two minutes.

If you'd like to learn more about her books and follow her journey, you can find her everywhere as deviantdrafts.